THE
WAR
OF
TWO
QUEENS

#1 *NEW YORK TIMES* BESTSELLING AUTHOR
JENNIFER L. ARMENTROUT

BLUE
BOX
PRESS

Dedication

Dedicated to you, the reader.

Aegea

EVAEMON

Tadous

Saion's Cove

Mountains of Nyktos

Mists of the Primals

ILISEEUM

DALOS

SEAS OF
SAION

Isles of Bele

WORLD
MAP

To see a full-size version of the map, visit
https://theblueboxpress.com/books/twotqmap/

The War of Two Queens
A Blood and Ash Novel
By Jennifer L. Armentrout

Copyright 2022 Jennifer L. Armentrout
ISBN: 978-1-952457-74-6

Published by Blue Box Press, an imprint of Evil Eye Concepts, Incorporated

Cover design by Hang Le

Additional art used with permission:
Art By Steffani
"Jeleynai" Lea Bichlmaier
Katie Crowley

Acknowledgments

Thank you to the amazing team at Blue Box—Liz Berry, Jillian Stein, MJ Rose, Chelle Olson, Kim Guidroz, and more, who have helped bring the world of Blood and Ash to life. Thank you to my agent Kevan Lyon, Taryn Fagerness, Jenn Watson, and my assistant, Malissa Coy, for your hard work and support. And to Stephanie Brown and Jen Fisher for creating amazing merch. Mega thanks to Hang Le for creating such stunning, beautiful covers. A big thank you to Sarah Maas, Stacey Morgan, Lesa, JR Ward, Laura Kaye, Andrea Joan, Brigid Kemmerer, KA Tucker, Tijan, Vonetta Young, Mona Awad, and many more who have helped keep me sane, laughing, and creative. Thank you to the ARC team for your support and honest reviews, and a big thank you to JLAnders for being the best reader group an author can have, and the Blood and Ash Spoiler Group for making the drafting stage so fun and for being utterly amazing. But none of this would be possible without you, the reader. I can never thank you all enough.

Pronunciation Guide

Characters
Aios – (a-uh-us)
Alastir – (al-as-tir)
Bele – (bell)
Casteel Da'Neer – (ca-steel) (da-near)
Delano – (dee-lay-no)
Eloana Da'Neer – (eee-lah-nah) (da-near)
Ione – (eye-on)
Isbeth – (is-bith)
Jasper Contou – (jas-per) (con-too)
Kieran Contou – (kee-ren) (con-too)
King Jalara – (ja-la-ra)
Kirha Contou – (k-ah-ruh) (con-too)
Kolis – (co-lis)
Malec O'Meer – (ma-leek) (o-mere)
Malik Da'Neer – (ma-lick) (da-near)
Naill – (nuh-ile)
Nektas – (nic-tas)
Nyktos – (nik-toes)
Penellaphe Balfour – (pen-nell-uh-fee) (bal-floor)
Queen Ileana (uh-lee-aaa-nuh)
Rhahar – (ruh-har)
Rhain – (rain)
Saion – (si-on)
Seraphena – (see-ra-fee-na)
     Sera – (see-ra)
Valyn Da'Neer – (va-lynn) (da-near)
Vonetta Contou – (vo-net-ta) (con-too)

Places
Atlantia – (at-lan-tee-ah)
Carsodonia – (car-so-don-uh)
Dalos – (day-los)
Iliseeum – (ah-lee-see-um)

Lasania – (la-sa-nee-uh)
Masadonia – (ma-sa-don-uh)
Massene – (ma-see-nuh)
Niel Valley – (nile valley)
Padonia – (pa-doh-nee-ah)
Pensdurth – (pens-durth)
Solis – (sou-lis)

Terms
eather – (ee-thor)
notam – (no-tom)
Arae – (air-ree)
dakkai – (di-ah-kee)
graeca – (gray-cee)
kiyou- (ki-you)
meeyah Liessa – (mee-yah lee-sa)

I

Casteel

The click and drag of claws drew closer as the weak flame above the lone candle sputtered and then went out, pitching the cell into darkness.

A thicker mass of shadows appeared in the open archway—a misshapen form on its hands and knees. It halted, sniffing as loudly as a godsdamn barrat, scenting blood.

My blood.

The smooth bands of shadowstone tightened around my throat and ankles as I shifted, bracing myself. The damn stone was unbreakable, but it did come in handy.

A low-pitched wail came from the creature.

"Mother—" The thing exploded out of the archway, scurrying forward, its keening moan becoming an ear-piercing screech. "—*fucker.*"

I waited until its stench of decay reached me and then pressed my back against the wall, lifting my legs. The length of the chain between my ankles was only about half a foot, and the shackles wouldn't give an inch, but it was enough. Planting my bare feet into the creature's shoulders, I got a good, most unfortunate look at the thing as its foul breath blasted me in the face.

Man, the Craven was not a fresh one.

Patches of gray flesh clung to its hairless skull, and half of its nose was gone. One entire cheekbone was exposed, eyes burning like hot coals. Lips torn and mangled—

The Craven twisted its head down, sinking its fangs into my calf. Its teeth tore through the breeches and into flesh and muscle. Air hissed between my gritted teeth as fiery pain burned its way up my leg.

Worth it.

The pain was more than worth it.

I would spend an eternity taking these bites if that meant *she* was safe. That it wasn't *her* in this cell. That *she* wasn't the one in pain.

Shaking the Craven free, I dragged the short chain over the thing's neck as I crossed my feet. I twisted at the waist, pulling the dull bone chain tight across its throat, ending the Craven's screams. The shackle clamped down on my throat as I kept turning, cutting off my air as the chain dug into the Craven's neck. Its arms flailed on the floor as I jerked my legs in the opposite direction, snapping the creature's spine. The spasming became more of a twitching as I hauled it within reach of my bound hands. The chain between my wrists, connected to the shackle at my throat, was much shorter—but long enough.

I grasped the Craven's cold, clammy jowls and brought its head down hard, slamming it against the stone floor by my knees. Flesh gave way, spraying rotting blood over my stomach and chest. Bone split open with a wet-sounding crack. The Craven went limp. I knew it wouldn't stay down, but it bought me some time.

Lungs burning, I unwound the chain and kicked the creature away from me. It landed by the archway in a tangled mess of limbs as I relaxed my muscles. The band around my neck was slow to loosen, eventually allowing air into my burning lungs.

I stared at the Craven's body. At any other time, I would've kicked the bastard into the hall like usual, but I was weakening.

I was losing too much blood.

Already.

Not a good sign.

Breathing heavily, I looked down. Just below the shadowstone bands, shallow slices ran up the insides of my arms, past both elbows and over the veins. I counted them. Again. Just to be sure.

Thirteen.

Thirteen days had passed since the first time the Handmaidens swarmed this cell, dressed in black and as quiet as a tomb. They came once a day to cut into my flesh, siphoning my blood as if I were a damn barrel of fine wine.

A tight, savage smile twisted my mouth. I'd managed to take out three of them in the beginning. Ripped their throats out when they got too close, which was why they'd shortened the chain between my wrists. Only one of them actually *stayed* dead, though. The damn throats of the other two had stitched themselves closed within minutes— impressive and also infuriating to witness.

Learned something valuable, though.

Not all of the Blood Queen's Handmaidens were Revenants.

I wasn't sure how I could use that information yet, but I guessed they were using my blood to make brand-spanking-new Revs. Or using it as a dessert for the lucky.

Tipping back my head against the wall, I tried not to breathe too deeply. If the stench of the downed Craven didn't choke me, the damn shadowstone around my throat would.

I closed my eyes. There had been more days before the Handmaidens showed the first time. How many? I wasn't exactly sure. Two days? A week? Or—?

I stopped myself there. *Shut it the fuck down.*

I couldn't go down that road. I wouldn't. I'd done that the last time, trying to clock the days and weeks until there came a point when time simply ceased to move. Hours became days. Weeks became years. And my mind became as rotten as the blood seeping from the Craven's ruined head.

But things were different in the here and now.

The cell was larger, with no barred entrance. Not that there needed to be one with the shadowstone and the chains. They were a mix of iron and deity bone, connected to a hook in the wall and then to a pulley system to lengthen or shorten them. I could sit up and move a little, but that was about it. However, the cell was windowless like before, and the dank, musty smell told me they once again held me underground. The freely roaming Craven were also a new addition.

My eyes opened to thin slits. The fuck by the archway had to be the sixth or seventh one that had found its way into the cell, drawn by the scent of blood. Their appearance made me think there was one hell of a Craven problem aboveground.

I'd heard of Craven attacks inside the Rise surrounding Carsodonia before. Something the Blood Crown blamed on Atlantia and angry gods. I'd always assumed it was due to an Ascended getting greedy and leaving mortals they'd fed on to turn. Now, I was beginning to think the Craven were possibly being kept down here. Wherever *here* was. And if that were the case, and they could get out and get aboveground, so could I.

If only I could get these damn chains to loosen. I'd spent an ungodly amount of time pulling on the hook. In all those attempts, it may have slipped a half-inch from the wall—if that.

But that wasn't the only thing different about this time. Other than the Craven, I'd only seen the Handmaidens. I didn't know what to think about that. I'd figured it'd be like the last time. Too-frequent visits from the Blood Crown and their cronies, where they spent their time taunting and inflicting pain, feeding, and doing whatever they wanted.

Of course, my last go-around with this captivity bullshit hadn't started that way. The Blood Queen had tried to *open my eyes* first, coax me to her side. Turn me against my family and my kingdom. When that hadn't worked, the real fun had begun.

Was that what had happened to Malik? Did he refuse to play along, so they broke him like they had been so very close to doing with me? I swallowed dryly. I didn't know. I hadn't seen my brother, either, but they must have done something to him. They'd had him for far longer, and I knew what they were capable of. I knew what the desperation and hopelessness was like. What it felt like to breathe and taste the knowledge that you had no control. No sense of self. Even if they never laid a hand on him, being kept like this, as a captive and mostly in isolation, preyed on the mind after a while. And *a while* was a shorter span of time than one might believe. Made you think things. *Believe* things.

Drawing my throbbing leg up as far as I could, I looked down at my hands resting in my lap. In the darkness, I almost couldn't see the shimmer of the golden swirl across my left palm.

Poppy.

I closed my fingers over the imprint, squeezing my hand tight as if I could somehow conjure up anything but the sound of her screams. Erase the image of her beautiful face contorted in pain. I didn't want to see that. I wanted to see her as she'd been on the ship, face flushed, and those stunning green eyes with their faint silver glow behind the pupils eager and wanting. I wanted memories of cheeks pink with either lust or annoyance, the latter usually occurring when she was silently—or very loudly—debating whether stabbing me would be considered inappropriate. I wanted to see her lush lips parted, and her skin shining as she touched my flesh and healed me in ways she would never know or understand. My eyes closed once more. And damn it, all I saw was blood seeping from her ears, her nose, as her body writhed in my arms.

Gods, I was going to rip that bitch Queen into pieces when I got free.

And I would.

One way or another, I would get free and make sure she felt everything she had *ever* inflicted upon Poppy. Tenfold.

My eyes snapped open at the faint sound of footsteps. Muscles tensed in my neck as I slowly eased my leg straight. This wasn't normal. Only a few hours could've passed since the last time the Handmaidens had done the whole bloodletting thing. Unless I was already beginning to lose track of time.

An unsteadiness rose in my chest as I concentrated on the sound of the footfalls. There were many, but one was heavier. Boots. My jaw locked as I lifted my gaze to the entryway.

A Handmaiden entered first, nearly blending in with the darkness. She said nothing as her skirts glided past the fallen Craven. With a strike of steel against flint, a flame caught the wick on the candle on the wall, where the other had burned out. Four more Handmaidens entered as the first lit several more candles, the females' features obscured behind winged, black paint.

I wondered the same thing I did every time I saw them. What the fuck was up with the facial paint?

I'd asked a dozen times. Never got an answer.

They stood on either side of the archway, joined by the first, and I knew in my gut who was coming. My stare fixed on the opening between them. The scent of rose and vanilla reached me. Rage, hot and unending, poured into my chest.

Then she walked in, appearing as the utter opposite of her Handmaidens.

White. The monster wore a skintight gown that was a pristine, nearly transparent white and left very little to the imagination. Disgust curled my lip. Other than the reddish-brown hair reaching a cinched, narrow waist, she looked nothing like Poppy.

At least, that's what I kept telling myself.

That there was no hint of familiarity in the set of her features—the shape of her eyes, the straight line of her ruby-pierced nose, or the full, expressive mouth.

It didn't fucking matter.

Poppy was *nothing* like her.

The Blood Queen. Ileana. *Isbeth*. Better known as one soon-to-be-dead bitch.

She drew closer, and I still had no idea how I hadn't realized that she wasn't Ascended. Those eyes were dark and bottomless but not as opaque as a vampry's. Her touch…hell, it had blended with the others over the years. But while it had been cold, it hadn't been icy and bloodless. Then again, why would I or anyone else ever consider the possibility that she was something other than what she claimed?

Anyone but my parents.

They must have known the truth about the Blood Queen—about who she really was. And they hadn't told us. Hadn't warned us.

Biting, stinging anger gnawed. The knowledge might not have changed this outcome, but it would've affected every aspect of how we approached dealing with her. Gods, we would've been better prepared, knowing that centuries-old revenge drove the Blood Queen's special brand of madness. It would've given us pause. We would've realized that she was truly capable of *anything*.

But nothing could be done about any of that right now, not when they had me chained to a damn wall, and Poppy was out there, dealing with the fact that this woman was her mother.

She has Kieran, I reminded myself. *She's not alone.*

The false Queen wasn't alone either. A tall male entered behind her, looking like a walking lit candle. He was one golden motherfucker, from the hair to the winged facial paint across his face. His eyes were a blue so pale they appeared nearly leached of all color. Eyes like some of the Handmaidens. Another Rev, I bet. But one of the Handmaidens whose throat hadn't stayed torn open had had brown eyes. Not all Revs had the light irises.

He lingered by the entryway, his weapons not as hidden as the Handmaidens'. I saw a black dagger strapped across his chest and two swords secured to his back, the curved handles visible above his hips. *Fuck him.* My attention shifted to the Blood Queen.

Candlelight glittered off the diamond spires in the ruby crown as Isbeth glanced down at the Craven.

"I don't know if you realize this or not," I said casually, "but you have a pest problem."

A single dark brow rose as she snapped her red-painted fingers twice. Two Handmaidens moved as a unit, picking up what was left of the Craven. They carried the creature out as Isbeth's gaze flicked to me. "You look like shit."

"Yeah, but I can clean up. You?" I smiled, noting the tightening in the skin around her mouth. "You can't wash off that stench or feed that away. That *shit* is inside you."

Isbeth's laugh sounded like tinkling glass, grating on every single one of my nerves. "Oh, my dear Casteel, I forgot how charming you could be. No wonder my daughter appears to be so taken with you."

"Don't call her that," I snarled.

Both brows rose as she toyed with a ring on her pointer finger. A golden band with a pink diamond. That gold was lustrous, shining even in the dim light—gleaming in a way that only Atlantian gold could. "Please don't tell me that you doubt I'm her mother. I know I'm not a paradigm of honesty, but I spoke nothing but the truth when it came to her."

"I don't give a fuck if you carried her in your womb for nine months and delivered her with your own hands." My hands closed into fists. "You are nothing to her."

Isbeth went unnaturally still and quiet. Seconds ticked by, and then she said, "I was a mother to her. She would have no memory of it as she was just a tiny babe then, perfect and lovely in every way. I slept and woke with her beside me every day until I knew I could no longer take that risk." The edges of her gown dragged through the pool of Craven blood as she stepped forward. "And I was a mother to her when she thought I was only her Queen, tending to her wounds when she was so gravely injured. I would've given anything to have prevented that." Her voice thinned, and I could almost believe she spoke the truth. "I would've done anything to stop her from experiencing even one second of pain. Of having a reminder of that nightmare every time she looked upon herself."

"When she looks upon herself, she sees nothing but beauty and bravery," I snapped.

Her chin lifted. "You really believe that?"

"I *know* that."

"As a child, she often cried when she saw her reflection," she told me, and my chest seized. "She often begged me to fix her."

"She doesn't need fixing," I seethed, hating—absolutely *loathing*— that Poppy had ever felt that way, even as a child.

Isbeth was quiet for a moment. "Still, I would've done anything to prevent what happened to her."

"And you think you played no role in that?" I challenged.

"It was not I who left the safety of the capital and Wayfair. It was not I who stole her away." Her jaw clenched, jutting out in a godsdamn familiar way. "If Coralena hadn't betrayed me—betrayed *her*—Penellaphe never would've known that kind of pain."

Disbelief battled with disgust. "And yet you still betrayed her, sending her to Masadonia? To Duke Teerman, who—"

"Don't." She stiffened once more.

She didn't want to hear this? Too bad. "Teerman routinely abused her. He let others do the same. Made quite a sport of it."

Isbeth flinched.

She actually flinched.

My lips peeled back over my fangs. "That is on you. You don't get to blame anyone else for that and relieve yourself of guilt. Each time he touched her, he hurt her. That's on you."

She drew in a deep breath, straightening. "I didn't know. If I had, I would've cut his stomach open and fed him his own entrails until he choked on them."

Now that, I didn't doubt.

Because I'd seen her do it to a mortal before.

Her tightly sealed lips trembled as she stared down at me. "*You* killed him?"

A savage rush of satisfaction hit me. "Yeah, I did."

"Did you make it hurt?"

"What do you think?"

"You did." She turned away, drifting toward the wall as the two Handmaidens returned, silently taking up their posts by the door. "Good."

A dry laugh left me. "And I'll do the same to you."

She sent me a small smile over her shoulder. "I've always been impressed by your resilience, Casteel. I imagine you got that from your mother."

Acid pooled in my mouth. "You would know, wouldn't you?"

"Just so you know..." she said with a shrug. A moment passed before she continued. "I didn't hate your mother at first. She loved Malec, but he loved me. I didn't envy her. I pitied her."

"I'm sure she'll be glad to hear that."

"Doubtful," she murmured, righting a candle that had tilted. Her fingers drifted through the flame, causing it to ripple wildly. "I do hate her now, though."

I couldn't care less.

"With every fiber of my being." Smoke wafted from the flame she'd touched, turning a dark, thick black that brushed against the damp stone, staining it.

That wasn't even remotely normal. "What in the hell are you?"

"I am nothing more than a myth. A cautionary tale once told to Atlantian children to make sure they didn't steal what they didn't deserve," she said, looking over her shoulder at me.

"Are you a *lamaea?*"

Isbeth laughed. "Cute response, but I thought you were smarter than that." She drifted to another candle, straightening it, as well. "I may be no god by your standards and beliefs, but I am no less powerful than one. So, how am I not just that? A god?"

Something tugged at my memories—something I was sure Kieran's father had once said when we were younger. When the wolven Kieran loved was dying, and he'd prayed to gods he knew were sleeping to save her. When he prayed to anything that could be listening. Jasper had warned him that…something that wasn't a god could answer.

That a false god could reply.

"Demis," I whispered hoarsely, my eyes widening. "You're a demis. A false god."

One side of Isbeth's lips curled up, but it was the golden Rev who spoke. "Well, apparently, he *is* rather clever."

"At times," she said with a shrug.

Holy shit. I'd believed that the demis were as much a myth as the *lamaea*. "Is that what you've always been? A poor imitation of the real thing, hell-bent on destroying the lives of the desperate?"

"That's a rather offensive assumption. But, no. A demis is not born but made when a god commits the forbidden act of Ascending a mortal who was not Chosen."

I had no idea what she meant by a mortal that was Chosen, and I didn't get a chance to question that because she asked, "What do you know about Malec?"

Out of the corner of my eye, I saw the golden Rev's head tilt. "Where is my brother?" I demanded instead.

"Around." Isbeth faced me, clasping her hands together. They were free of jewels except for the Atlantian ring.

"I want to see him."

A faint grin appeared. "I don't think that would be wise."

"Why?"

She inched toward me. "You haven't earned it, Casteel."

The acid spread, hitting my veins. "Hate to disappoint you, but we're not playing that game again."

Isbeth pouted. "But I loved that game. So did Malik. Admittedly, he was much better at it than you ever were."

Fury pounded through every inch of my body. I launched off the floor as the rage was given sound. I didn't make it very far. The bonds at my throat jerked my head back as the shackles on my ankles and wrists clamped down, yanking me against the wall. The Handmaidens stepped forward.

Isbeth held up a hand, waving them back. "Did that make you feel better?"

"Why don't you get close?" I growled, chest rising and falling as the band at my throat slowly loosened. "That will make me feel better."

"I'm sure it would, but you see, I have plans which require me to keep my throat intact and my head still on my shoulders," she replied, smoothing a hand over the chest of her gown.

"Plans can always change."

Isbeth smirked. "But this plan also requires you to remain alive." She watched me. "You don't believe that, do you? If I wanted you dead, you'd already be that."

My eyes narrowed on her as she tipped her chin in a curt nod. The golden Rev stepped out into the hall, returning quickly with a burlap sack. The stench of death and decay immediately hit me. Every part of my being focused on the bag the Rev carried. I didn't know what was in there, but I knew it was something that used to be alive. My heart started pounding.

"It appears that my once amicable and charming daughter has grown quite the…violent streak with a knack for showmanship," Isbeth remarked as the Rev knelt, untying the sack. "Penellaphe sent me a message."

My lips parted as the golden Rev carefully tipped the sack, and a…godsdamn head rolled out. I immediately recognized the blond hair and square jaw.

King Jalara.

Holy fuck.

"As you can see, it was a very interesting message," Isbeth stated blandly.

I couldn't believe I was staring at the Blood King's head. A slow smile spread across my face. I laughed—deep and hard. Gods, Poppy was…damn, she was vicious in the most *magnificent* way, and I could not *wait* to show her just how much I approved of it. "That's…gods, that's my Queen."

Surprise widened the golden Rev's eyes, but I laughed until my empty stomach cramped. Until tears stung my eyes.

"I'm glad you find this entertaining," Isbeth remarked coolly.

Shoulders shaking, I tipped my head back against the wall. "That is the best godsdamn thing I've seen in a long time, to be honest."

"I would suggest you need to get out more, but…" She waved dismissively at the chains. "That was only a part of the message she sent."

"There was more?"

Isbeth nodded. "There were quite a few threats included with it."

"I'm sure." I chuckled, wishing I'd been there to see it. There wasn't a single part of me that doubted it had been Poppy's hand who'd ended Jalara's life.

The Blood Queen's nostrils flared. "But there was one warning in particular that interested me." She knelt in a slow slide that reminded me of the cold-blooded serpents found in the foothills of the Mountains of Nyktos. The orange and red, two-headed snakes were just as venomous as the viper in front of me. "Unlike you and my daughter, Malec and I were never granted the privilege of the marriage imprint—proof that either of us lived or died. And you know that not even the bond shared between heartmates can alert the other of death. I have spent the last several hundred years believing that Malec was dead."

Every ounce of humor vanished.

"But it appears I have been mistaken. Penellaphe claims that not only is Malec alive, but that she knows where he is." The Rev's head cocked again as he focused on her. Isbeth appeared unaware. "She said she would kill him, and the moment Penellaphe starts believing in her power, she very easily could." Her dark eyes fixed on mine. "Is it true? Does he live?"

Damn, Poppy really wasn't messing around.

"It's true," I said softly. "He lives. For now."

Her slender body practically hummed. "Where is he, Casteel?"

"Come on, *Isbitch*," I whispered, leaning forward as far as I could. "You should know there is literally nothing you can do that will make me tell you that. Not even if you brought my brother in here and started cutting off pieces of his skin."

Isbeth eyed me quietly for several long moments. "You speak the truth."

I smiled broadly. I did speak the truth. Isbeth thought she could control Poppy through me, but my stunning, vicious wife had checkmated her ass, and there was no way in hell I would jeopardize that. Not even for Malik.

"I remember a time when you would've done anything for your family," Isbeth said.

"That was a different time."

"Now you will do anything for Penellaphe?"

"Anything," I promised.

"Because of the opportunity of what she represents?" Isbeth suggested. "Is that what truly consumes you? After all, through my daughter, you usurped your brother and your parents. You are now a King. And because of her bloodline, she is *the* Queen. That would make you *the* King."

I shook my head, unsurprised. Of course, she would think that what I felt had everything to do with power.

"You plotted for how long to claim her?" she continued. "Perhaps you never planned to use her to free Malik. Maybe you don't even really love her."

I held her stare. "Whether she ruled over all the lands and seas or was the Queen of nothing but a pile of ashes and bones, she would—*will*—always be *my* Queen. Love is too weak an emotion to describe how she consumes me and what I feel for her. She is my everything."

Isbeth was silent for several long moments. "My daughter deserves to have someone care for her as fiercely as she cares for them." A hint of faint silver glimmered in the center of Isbeth's eyes, though not as vivid as what I saw in Poppy's. Her gaze dipped to the band around my throat. "I never wanted this—this war with my daughter."

"Really?" I laughed dryly. "What did you expect? For her to go along with your plans?"

"And marry your brother?" The light in her eyes intensified as I snarled. "Goodness, the mere idea of that gets to you, doesn't it? If I had killed you when I had you the last time, then he would've aided her Ascension."

It took everything in me not to react—not to attempt to rip her heart from her chest. "You still wouldn't have what you wanted. Poppy would've figured out the truth about you—about the Ascended. She already was, even before I came into her life. She never would've let you take Atlantia."

Isbeth's smile returned, though tight-lipped. "Do you think that all I want is Atlantia? As if that is all my daughter was destined for? Her purpose is far greater. As was Malik's. As is yours now. We are now a part of the greater plan, and all of us, together, will restore the realm to what it was always meant to be. It has already begun."

I stilled. "What in the hell are you talking about?"

"You'll see in time." She rose. "If my daughter truly loves you, this will pain me in ways I doubt you'll ever believe." She turned her head slightly. "Callum?"

The golden Rev stepped around Jalara's head, careful not to brush against it.

My gaze snapped to him. "I don't know you, but I'm going to kill you, too, one way or another. Just thought I should let you know that."

He hesitated, his head cocking to the side. "If you only knew how many times I've heard that," he said, a slight smile forming as he withdrew a slender shadowstone blade from the strap across his chest. "But you're the first I think might actually succeed."

The Rev snapped forward then, and my world exploded in pain.

Poppy

Through the maze of the pines outside the walled city of Massene, I caught sight of a silver and white wolven pacing ahead.

Arden kept low to the thick bushes cluttering the forest floor and soundlessly moved as he neared the edges of the Pinelands. The long and wide region of swampy woods bordered both Massene and Oak Ambler and stretched all the way to the coast of the Kingdom of Solis.

The land was full of insects that smelled of decay and fed from any visible patch of skin with the hunger of a Craven. There were *things* to be found slithering along the mossy ground if one looked long and hard enough. And in the trees, crude circles made of sticks or bones, vaguely resembling the Royal Crest of the Blood Crown, except that the line was at a slant—diagonal—as it pierced the center of the circle.

Massene sat nestled against what was known as the Dead Bones Clan territory.

We hadn't seen any sign of the mysterious group of people who'd once lived where the Blood Forest now stood and apparently preferred to feed on the flesh of anything living—including mortals and wolven—but that didn't mean they weren't there. From the moment we'd entered the Pinelands, it'd felt like a hundred pairs of eyes tracked us.

For all those reasons, I was not a fan of the Pinelands. Although, I wasn't sure if it was the cannibals or the snakes I disliked the most.

But if we were to seize Oak Ambler, the largest port city this far east, we would have to take Massene first. And we'd have to do it with only the wolven and a small battalion. They had arrived ahead of the larger armies led by...*his* father, the former King of Atlantia, Valyn Da'Neer. All but one draken traveled with those armies. But I hadn't summoned the draken, awakening them from their slumber, only for them to burn through cities and people.

General Aylard, who led the newly arrived battalion, had been most displeased to have learned that and our plans for Massene. But I was the Queen, and two things were paramount to all.

Free our King.

And not make war like before, upending lives and leaving cities to become nothing more than mass burial sites. That wasn't what *he* would want. That wasn't what I wanted.

Massene was larger than both New Haven and Whitebridge, but smaller than Oak Ambler—and not as well guarded as the port city. But they weren't helpless.

Still, we couldn't wait any longer for Valyn and the other generals to arrive. The Ascended who lived behind those walls had been leading mortals into the woods, feeding from them, and leaving them to turn. The Craven attacks were becoming more frequent, and each group larger than the one before. Worse yet, according to our scouts, the city had gone quiet during the day. But at night...

There were screams.

Then they had killed three of our wolven patrolling these woods the day before, leaving only their heads on spikes at the Pompay border. I knew their names—would never forget them.

Roald. Krieg. Kyley.

And I could no longer wait.

Twenty-three days had passed since *he'd* given himself over to a monster who'd made him feel like a *thing*. Since I'd last seen him. Saw his golden eyes heat. Witnessed the dimple form first in his right cheek and then his left. Felt the touch of his flesh against mine or heard his voice. *Twenty-three days.*

The armored plates on my chest and shoulders tightened as I leaned forward on Setti, gaining Naill's attention as the Atlantian rode to my left. I kept my grip on the warhorse's reins firm, just as...*he* had taught me. I opened my senses, connecting with Arden.

A tangy, almost bitter taste filled my mouth. *Anguish.* And something acidic—*anger.*

"What is it?"

"I'm not sure." I glanced to my right. Shadows had gathered across Kieran Contou's beige-brown features, the once-bonded wolven and now Advisor to the Crown. "But he's upset."

Arden stopped the restless patrol as we approached, his vibrant blue gaze swinging to me. He whined softly, the sound tearing at my heart. Arden's unique imprint reminded me of the salty sea, but I didn't try to speak to him through the Primal *notam* since the wolven wasn't yet comfortable communicating that way. "What's wrong?"

He nodded his large silver-and-white-streaked head toward the Rise of Massene and then turned, prowling through the trees.

Kieran held up a closed fist, halting those behind us as he and Naill moved ahead, navigating the heavily clustered pines. I waited, reaching for the pouch secured to my hip. The small wooden horse Malik had carved for…*his* sixth birthday pressed against the marriage imprint on my palm.

Malik.

The once-heir to the Atlantian throne. He had been taken captive in the process of freeing his brother. And both of them had been betrayed by the wolven *he'd* once loved.

The sadness I'd felt at learning that Shea had done such a thing was now overshadowed by the grief and anger that Malik had done the same. I tried not to let the anger grow. Malik had been held captive for a century. Only the gods knew what had been done to him or what he'd had to do to survive. That didn't excuse his betrayal, though. Didn't lessen the blow it dealt. But he was also a victim.

Make his death as quick and painless as possible.

What Valyn Da'Neer had asked of me before I left Atlantia sat heavily on my heart. It was a weight I would bear. A father shouldn't have to strike down his own son. I hoped it didn't come to that, but I also couldn't see how it wouldn't.

Kieran stopped, his emotions sudden and intense, slamming into me in bitter waves of…*horror.*

Rattled by his reaction, my stomach knotted with dread. "What is it?" I asked, seeing that Arden had stopped once more.

"Dear gods," Naill uttered, jerking back on his saddle at whatever he saw, his deep brown skin taking on a grayish pallor. His horror was so potent it scratched against my shields like bitter claws.

When there was no answer, trepidation grew, encompassing my

entire being. I eased Setti forward between Kieran and Naill, to where the Massene Rise gates were visible through the pines.

At first, I couldn't make sense of what I saw—the cross-like shapes hanging from the massive gates.

Dozens of them.

My breathing turned ragged. Eather thrummed in my tightening chest. Bile crept up my throat. I jerked back. Before I lost my balance and toppled from the saddle, Naill's arm snapped out, catching my shoulder.

Those shapes were…

Bodies.

Men and women stripped bare, impaled at the wrists and feet to Massene's iron and limestone gates, their bodies displayed for any to look upon—

Their faces…

Dizziness rushed me. Their faces weren't bare. They were all shrouded in the same veil I had been forced to wear, held in place by gold chains gleaming dully in the moonlight.

A storm of rage replaced the disbelief as Setti's reins slipped from my fingers. Eather, the Primal essence of the gods that flowed through all the many different bloodlines, throbbed in my chest. Far stronger in me because what was inside me came from Nyktos, the King of Gods. The essence merged with icy-hot fury as I stared at the bodies, my chest heaving with too-shallow, too-quick breaths. A thin metallic taste coated the inside of my mouth as I looked behind the horror on the gate, to the tops of the distant spiral towers, each a stained ivory against the rapidly darkening sky.

Above, the pines began trembling, showering us with thin needles. And that anger, the *horror* at what I saw, built and built until the corners of my vision turned silver.

My gaze shifted to those who walked the battlements of the Rise, on either side of the gate where the bodies of fellow mortals were so cruelly displayed, and what filled my mouth, clogged my throat, came from within me. It was shadowy and smoky and a little sweet, rolling across my tongue, and it came from a place deep inside me. This cold, aching hollowness that had woken in the last twenty-three days.

It tasted like the promise of retribution.

Of wrath.

And death.

I tasted *death* as I watched the Rise Guards stop mere feet from the bodies to speak to one another, laughing at something that was said. My gaze narrowed on them as the essence pulsed in my chest, and my will rose. A sharp gust of wind, colder than a winter's morning, rolled across the Rise, lifting the hems of the veils and whipping around the guards on the wall, sending several sliding back toward the edge.

They stopped laughing then, and I knew the smiles I couldn't see faded.

"*Poppy.*" Kieran leaned from his saddle, clasping the nape of my neck beneath the thick braid. "Calm. You need to find calm. If you do something now before we know exactly how many are on the Rise, it will alert them to our presence. We must wait."

I wasn't sure I wanted to calm, but Kieran was right. If we wanted to take Massene with minimal loss of life—those innocents who lived inside the walls and were routinely turned into Craven and hung from the gates—I needed to get control of my emotions and abilities.

And I could.

If I wanted to.

In the past weeks, I'd spent a lot of time on the Primal *notam*, working with the wolven to see how much distance we could put between us and still be able to communicate. Other than Kieran, I'd had the most success with Delano, whom I could reach deep within the Wastelands through the *notam*. But I'd also focused on harnessing the eather so that what I pictured in my mind became my will and was carried out by the energy instantaneously.

So I could *fight like a god.*

Fisting my hands, I willed the eather away. It took every part of my being to stop myself from allowing the promise of death to flow out from me.

"You okay?" Kieran asked.

"No." I swallowed. "But I'm in control." I looked at Naill. "Are you okay?"

The Atlantian shook his head. "I can't understand how anyone is capable of doing such a thing."

"Neither can I." Kieran looked past me to Naill as Arden backed away from the tree line. "I think it's good that we can't."

I forced my attention to the battlements along the top of the wall. I couldn't look too long at the bodies. I couldn't allow myself to really think about them. Just like I couldn't allow myself to think about what *he* was going through—what was being done to him.

A featherlight brush against my thoughts came, followed by the springy-fresh imprint of Delano's mind. The wolven was scouting the length of the Rise to gain information on exactly how many were guarding it. *Meyaah Liessa?*

I swallowed a sigh at the old Atlantian phrase that roughly translated to *my Queen.* The wolven knew they didn't have to refer to me as such, but many still did. However, where Delano did it out of what he felt was a show of respect, Kieran often called me that to simply annoy me.

I followed the imprint back to Delano. *Yes?*

There are twenty at the northern gates. A beat of silence passed. *And...*

His grief tainted the bond. I briefly closed my eyes. *Mortals on the gate.*

Yes.

The essence throbbed. *How many?*

Two dozen, he answered, and violent energy pressed against my skin. *Emil is confident he can take them out quickly,* he said, referencing the often-irreverent Elemental Atlantian.

My eyes opened. Massene only had two gates—one to the north, and this one, which faced the east. "Delano says there are twenty on the northern gates," I shared. "Emil believes he can take them."

"He can," Kieran confirmed. "He's as good with a crossbow as you are."

I met his stare. "Then it's time."

Holding my gaze, he nodded. The three of us lifted the hoods on our cloaks, hiding the armor Naill and I wore.

"I really wish you had some sort of armor," I told Kieran.

"Armor would make it more difficult for me if I need to shift," he stated. "And at the end of the day, no armor is a hundred percent effective. There are weak spots—places those men on the Rise know to exploit."

"Thanks for reminding me," Naill muttered as we quietly rode toward the edge of the pines.

Kieran smirked. "That's what I'm here for."

I shook my head as I searched for Delano's imprint, not allowing myself to think of the lives that my order would soon end. *Take them out.*

Delano quickly responded. *Gladly,* meyaah Liessa. *We will soon join you at the east gate.*

"Be ready," I said out loud as I turned my focus to those on the Rise before us.

I lifted my stare to the moonlight-drenched battlement. Three dozen individuals who probably had no choice but to join the Rise Guard stood there. There was little opportunity for most in Solis, especially if they weren't born into families steeped in the power and privilege given by the Ascended. Those who lived so far from the capital. Much like most eastern locales, with the exception of Oak Ambler, Massene wasn't a glittering and wealthy city, mainly consisting of farmers who tended crops that fed most of Solis.

But those who laughed and chatted as if those impaled to that gate did not affect them? That was a whole different breed of apathy and just as cold and empty as an Ascended.

Just like with Delano, I didn't think of the lives about to be cut short by my will.

I couldn't.

Vikter had taught me that ages ago. That you could never consider the life of another when they held a sword pointed at your throat.

There was no sword at my throat now, but there *were* things much worse held to the throats of those inside the Rise.

I summoned the eather, and it responded at once, rushing to the surface of my skin. Silver tinted my vision as Kieran and Naill lifted crossbows, each outfitted with three arrows.

"I'll take those farther down the Rise," Kieran said.

"I'll get those to the left," Naill confirmed.

Which left the dozen by the gates. The eather swirled inside me, pouring into my blood, somehow hot and icy at the same time. It flooded that hollow place inside me as every ounce of my being focused on those by the gate.

By the poor, veiled mortals.

My will left me at the exact moment the image of what I wanted filled my mind. The snap of their necks, one after another in quick succession, joined the snap of released arrows. There was no time for any of them to scream, to alert those who may be near. Kieran and Naill quickly reloaded, taking out the others before the ones whose necks I'd broken even began to fall.

But they joined those struck by arrows, falling forward into the nothingness. I flinched at the sound of their bodies hitting the ground.

We rode out, crossing the clearing as another cloaked figure joined me on horseback, coming from the left of the Rise. A snow-white wolven followed Emil, keeping close to the wall as I quickly dismounted.

"Those sons of bitches," Emil growled, head tilted back as he looked up at the gates. "The utter disrespect."

"I know." Kieran followed me as I went to the chain securing the gate.

Anger brimmed from Emil as I clasped the cool chains.

Arden stirred restlessly near the horses' hooves as Emil quickly dismounted, joining me. Naill pulled them forward as Delano brushed against my legs. I took them in my hand and closed my eyes. I'd discovered that the eather could be used in the same manner as draken fire. While it would not kill a Revenant—or have any effect on them, really—it *could* melt iron. Not in large quantities, but enough.

"We need to hurry," Kieran said quietly. "Dawn is approaching."

I nodded as a silvery aura flared around my hands, rippling over the chain while Emil peered in through the gate, searching for signs of other guards. I frowned as the glow pulsed, and pieces of the metal appeared to darken—thicken almost as if it were tendrils of shadow. Blinking, the wisps disappeared. Or were never there. The light was not the greatest, and even though I was a god, my eyesight and hearing remained annoyingly mortal.

The chain fell apart.

"Nifty talent," Naill remarked.

I sent him a brief smile as he and Emil quickly and quietly moved the gate forward.

The Pinelands came alive as the gate opened, twigs snapping as the wolven prowled forward in a sleek wave of several dozen, led by Kieran's sister.

Vonetta was the same fawn color as Kieran, not nearly as large as him when in wolven form, but no less fierce. Our gazes briefly met as I found her imprint—white oak and vanilla. *Be safe*, I told her.

Always, came the quick reply as someone closed the gates behind us.

Turning from her, I fixed my gaze on the silent, stone, one-story barracks several yards back from the Rise. Beyond them and the fields of crops, the outline of small, squat buildings could be seen against Cauldra Manor and the looming horizon that was already becoming a lighter blue.

Opting for the short sword instead of the wolven dagger, I withdrew it from where it was secured to my back, handle tilted downward, as we raced forward under the darkness of the pines lining the wide, cobblestone road. We halted before the barracks, the wolven crouching low to the ground.

I pressed into the scratchy bark of a pine as I peered into the windows of the gas-lamp-lit barracks. A few people moved about inside. It was only a matter of time before they took note of the fact that no one was on the Rise.

Kieran joined me, his hand landing on the tree above mine. "We probably have around twenty minutes before dawn arrives," he said. "The Ascended should already be retiring for the night."

I nodded. There were no Temples in Massene, or a Radiant Row like in Masadonia, where the wealthy mortals lived side by side with the Ascended. In Massene, all the vamprys lived within Cauldra Manor.

"Remember," I said, tightening my grip on the sword. "We harm no mortal who lowers their weapon. We harm no Ascended who surrenders."

There were murmurs and soft snarls of agreement. Kieran turned to Naill and nodded. The Atlantian slipped forward and then moved with blinding speed, reaching the side of the barracks. He dragged the edge of his sword along the building, creating an ear-aching grinding sound against the stone.

"Well," Emil drawled. "That's one way of doing it."

A door flung open, and a guard stepped out, blade in hand. His head whipped from side to side, but Naill had already disappeared into the pines.

"Who goes there?" the guard demanded as several more spilled out from the barracks. The man squinted into the darkness. "Who's out here?"

I pulled away from the pine.

"Does it really have to be you?" Kieran questioned in a low voice.

"Yes."

"The actual answer is no."

"No, it's not." I eased past him.

Kieran sighed but made no move to stop me. "One of these days, you will realize you're a Queen," he hissed.

"Not likely," Emil remarked.

I walked out of the pines, my senses open. The men turned to me, not having realized yet that no one was on the Rise.

"Who I am is not important," I said, feeling the ripple of surprise that came with their realization that a female stood before them. "What is, is that your city has been breached, and you're surrounded. We are not here to take from you. We're here to end the Blood Crown. Lay down your weapons, and you will not be harmed."

"And if we don't lay down our swords to some Atlantian bitch?" the man demanded, and tart unease and anxiety radiated from a few of the men behind him. "What then?"

My brows rose. These guards were aware that a small portion of the Atlantian armies had been camped out at the edges of Pompay. They weren't, however, aware that a draken was among us.

Or that the Atlantian Queen was also with the encampment and currently the *bitch* they were speaking to.

The words burned to say, but I spoke them. "You die."

"Is that so?" The man laughed, and I stifled the rising disappointment, reminding myself that many mortals had no idea who they served. Who the real enemy was. "Am I or my men supposed to be afraid of a pitiful army that sends overgrown dogs and bitches to fight their battles?" He looked over his shoulder. "Looks like we'll have another head to put on the pike." He faced me. "But first, we'll make real good use of that mouth and whatever is under that cloak, won't we, boys?"

There were a few rough laughs, but that tartness increased from others.

I tilted my head. "This is your last chance. Lay down your swords and surrender."

The silly mortal swaggered forward. "How about you lay down on your back and spread them legs?"

Hot anger pressed against my back as I turned my gaze to him. "No, thank you."

"Wasn't really asking." He took one more step. That was as far as he made it.

Vonetta sprang out of the darkness, landing on the guard. His shout ended with a vicious clamp of her jaws on his throat as she took him down.

Another charged forward, raising his sword at Vonetta as she dragged the foul-mouthed man across the ground. I shot forward, catching his arm as I thrust my blade deep into his belly. Blue eyes set in a far-too-young face widened as I yanked the sword back out.

"Sorry," I murmured, shoving him away.

Several of the guards lurched toward Vonetta and me, only to realize that we were not who they should be worried about—a moment too late.

The wolven came out of the pines, swarming the guards in a

matter of seconds. The crunch of bone and sharp, too-short screams echoed in my head as Kieran drew his blade across a guard's throat.

"When will mortals stop referring to us as overgrown dogs?" he asked, pushing the fallen guard aside. "Do they not know the difference between a dog and a wolf?"

"I'm going to say no." Emil stalked past the one who'd gone at Vonetta, spitting on the dead man. He looked up at me. "What? He was going to knife Netta in the back. I'm not about that."

I couldn't really argue against that as I turned to the soldiers near the back, the ones I'd felt the unease from. Five of them. Their swords lay at their feet. The sickly bitterness of fear coated my skin as Delano stalked forward, blood-streaked teeth bared. The stench of urine hit the air.

"W-we surrender," one chattered, shaking.

"Delano," I called softly, and the wolven halted, growling at the men. "How many Ascended are here?"

"There are t-ten," the man answered, his skin as pale as the waning moonlight.

"Would they be returning to Cauldra Manor?" Kieran asked, coming to stand beside me.

"They should already be there," another said. "They'll be under guard. They have been since the Duke became aware of your encampment."

I glanced at Naill, who led Setti and the other horses forward. "Did all of them take part in what was done to those on the gates?"

The third one—an older man than most on the Rise, in his third or fourth decade of life—said, "None of them resisted Duke Silvan when he gave the orders."

"Who were those they chose to kill?" Kieran asked.

Another wave of disappointment swelled, weighing heavily on my chest. I wanted to—no, I *needed* to—believe that there were other Ascended like...like Ian, my brother, even if we shared no blood. There had to be.

"They did it at will," the first guard, the one who'd spoken his surrender, shared. He looked close to vomiting. "They just picked people out. Young. Old. Didn't matter. Ain't no one who was causing trouble. No one causes trouble."

"The same with the others," another younger guard said. "Those, they led out beyond the Rise."

Kieran focused on the mortal, his jaw clenched. "You know what was done to them?"

"I do," the eldest of them said after the others spoke. "They led them out there. Fed from them. Left them to turn. No one believed me when I said that was what happened." He jerked his chin at the ones beside him. "They said I was crazy, but I know what I saw. I just didn't think…" His gaze went to the gates. "I thought maybe I *was* crazy."

He just hadn't considered what all the Ascended were capable of.

"You were right," Kieran replied. "If it brings you any relief to know that."

Sensing that the knowledge did very little, I turned to Naill, sheathing my sword. "Make sure they remain in the barracks. Unharmed." I gestured at Arden. "Stay with Naill."

Naill nodded as he handed Setti's reins to me. Gripping the straps on the saddle, I hoisted myself up. The others followed suit.

"Did you speak the truth?" the eldest asked, stopping as we guided the horses out from the barracks. "That you're not here to take from us?"

"I did." My grip firmed on Setti's reins. "We're not here to take. We're here to end the Blood Crown."

Dipping under a guard's outstretched arm, the edges of the cloak fluttered around my legs as I spun, thrusting the sword deep into the man's back. I twisted sharply, ducking as someone threw a knife in my general direction. Delano leapt over me, digging into the guard with his claws and teeth as I popped up.

None of the guards outside of Cauldra surrendered.

The pinkish rays of dawn streaked across the sky as I whirled, grunting and kicking out, pushing a guard back. He fell into Vonetta's path. Stalking toward the barred doors, I brought the sword down, clanging off another as Emil came up behind him, dragging his blade across the man's throat. Hot blood sprayed the air. Kieran jabbed out with a dagger up under the chin of another guard, clearing the path before me.

There was so much death here. Bodies scattered about the bare courtyard as blood pooled on the dull ivory steps and splattered the exterior walls of the manor. Summoning the Primal essence as I lifted a hand, bright silvery light funneled down my arm and sparked from my fingers. The eather arced across the space, slamming into the doors. Wood splintered and gave way, exploding into fine shards.

The receiving hall, adorned with crimson banners and bearing the Blood Crown's crest instead of the white-and-gold that hung in Masadonia, was empty.

"Underground," Kieran said, stalking to our right. Blood dotted his cheeks. "They would've gone underground."

"And you know how to get there?" I caught up to him, reaching out with my senses to ensure that he wasn't hurt.

"Cauldra appears like New Haven." He dragged his hand over his face, wiping away the blood that wasn't his. "They'll have chambers underground, near the cells."

It was almost impossible not to think of the cells under New Haven that I'd spent time in. But Kieran was right as he found the entrance along the hall on the right.

He kicked in the door, revealing a narrow, torch-lit stairwell. He sent me a wild grin that caused my breath to catch because it reminded me of…of *him*. "What did I say?"

My brows pinched as Delano and Vonetta streaked past us, joined by a blackish-gray wolven I recognized as Sage. They entered the stairwell before us. "Why do they do that?"

"Because you're the Queen." Kieran entered.

"You keep telling her that." Emil fell into step behind me. "And you keep reminding her…"

I rolled my eyes as we hurried down the musty-scented stairs that stroked a memory that refused to wiggle free. "I may be the Queen, but I'm also a god, and therefore harder to kill than any of you. I should go first," I told him. To be honest, none of us had any idea what *would* kill me, but we did know that I was basically immortal.

I felt a skip in my chest. I would outlive everyone in this manor, some who had become people I cared about. Those I called friends. I would outlive Tawny—who would eventually wake from the injury the shadowstone blade had caused. I couldn't allow myself to believe anything else, even though I knew, deep down, that it couldn't be good for someone to sleep that long.

I would outlive Kieran and…and even *him*.

Gods, why was I even thinking about that right now? *Don't borrow tomorrow's problems.* That was what *he'd* said once.

I really needed to learn how to follow that advice.

"Harder to kill doesn't mean *impossible* to kill," Kieran shot over his shoulder.

"Says the one not in armor," I snapped back.

He let out a rough laugh, but the sound was lost in the sudden, shrill shriek that caused tiny bumps to spread across my skin.

"Craven," I whispered as we rounded the curve in the stairwell, and Kieran stepped into a faintly lit hall. He stopped directly in front of me, and I bounced off him.

Kieran stared.

So did I.

"Good gods," Emil murmured.

The cells were full of Craven. They pressed against the bars, arms outstretched, and lips peeled back, revealing their four jagged fangs. Some were fresh, their skin only now taking on the ghastly shade of death. Others were older, those with sunken cheeks, torn lips, and sagging skin.

"Why in the hell would they have Craven in here?" Emil asked over the pained, hungry howling.

"They probably let them out from time to time to terrorize the people," I said numbly. "The Ascended would blame the Atlantians. Saying *they* turned the Craven. But they'd also blame the people, claiming they angered the gods somehow and this was their punishment. That the gods let the Atlantians do this. Then the Ascended would say they spoke to the gods on their behalf, assuaging their anger."

"People believed that?" Emil eased past several of the bloodstained hands.

"It's all they've ever been allowed to believe," I told him, looking away from the Craven.

The sounds of pawing and scratching led us past the cells— beyond what we'd have to deal with later—and down another hall, through crates of wine and ale. We found the wolven just as they tore through the double wooden doors at the end.

A vampry came flying out of the chamber, a stream of sable hair and fangs bared—

Delano took her down, latching onto the vampry's throat as he dug into her chest with his front paws, tearing through clothing and skin.

I turned away, but there was nowhere to look as the two female wolven did the same with two more that attacked. And then there were only *pieces* left.

"That looks like it would give them an upset stomach," I said.

"I'm trying not to think about that," Emil murmured, fixing his stare on the Ascended who stood within the chamber, frozen with their weapons all but forgotten in their hands. "I bet they're trying not to think of that either."

"Any of you want to meet the same fate?" Kieran asked, extending his sword to the chunks on the floor.

There was no answer from within, but as more wolven filled the hall behind us, the Ascended dropped their weapons.

"We surrender," a male bit out, the last to throw his sword aside.

"Nice of you to do that," Kieran drawled as he kicked the swords out of their reach.

And it was. Nice of them. But it was also too late. There would be no second chances given to any Ascended who'd taken part in what had been done to those on their gates and what was happening in this city.

I did my level best not to step on what remained of the Ascended on the floor as I entered the chamber, flanked closely by Vonetta and Delano. I sheathed the sword and lowered my hood.

"Congratulations," the same male spoke. "You took Massene. But you will not take Solis."

The moment he opened his mouth, I knew this had to be Duke Silvan. It was the air of self-assured superiority. He was an icy blond, tall and well-formed in his fine satin shirt and breeches. He was attractive. After all, very few things in Solis were valued higher than beauty. When he looked upon me, he saw the scars, and that was *all* he saw.

And all I saw was the blood that stained their expensive clothing. It marked each tailored shirt and bodice.

I stopped in front of the Duke, staring into pitch-black eyes that reminded me of her. The Blood Queen. My *mother*. Hers weren't this dark, pitiless, empty, and cold. But she had the same eerie spark of light—though much deeper—that didn't require light to hit their faces at the right angle to see. It wasn't until that very moment that I realized the trace of light in their eyes was a glimmer of *eather*.

It made sense for them to carry a trace. The blood of an Atlantian was used to Ascend them, and all Atlantians carried eather in their blood. It was how the Ascended achieved their near immortality and strength. Their speed and ability to heal.

"Do any Ascended remain?"

Duke Silvan's sneer was a work of art. "Fuck off."

Beside me, Kieran's sigh was so impressive, I would've thought it rattled the walls.

"I'll ask one more time," I said, counting quickly. There were ten. Or parts of ten, anyway, but I wanted to be sure that was all of them. "Are there any more?"

A long moment passed, and then the Duke said, "You will still kill us, no matter how I answer."

"I would've given you a chance."

The Duke's eyes narrowed. "For what?"

"To live without taking from mortals," I said. "To live among Atlantians."

He stared at me for a moment and then laughed. "You really think that's possible?" Another laugh parted his pale lips. "I know who you are. I'd recognize that face anywhere."

Kieran stepped forward.

I held up a hand, stopping him.

The Duke smirked. "You haven't been gone long enough to forget how mortals are, *Maiden*. How they are so damn gullible. How much they fear. What they will do to protect their families. What they will believe to protect themselves. You really think they will simply accept the Atlantians?"

I said nothing.

Emboldened, he stepped closer. "And you think the Ascended will do...what? Trust that you will allow us to live if we do whatever it is you want?"

"You trusted the Blood Queen," I said. "And her name isn't even Ileana. Nor is she an Ascended."

Several sharp inhales sounded, but the Duke showed no sign that what I'd said was news to him.

"So," I continued, "I imagine anything is possible. But as I said, I *would've* given you another chance. You sealed your fate when you ordered those people to be impaled on your gates."

His nostrils flared. "The veils were a lovely touch, weren't they?"

"Very lovely," I replied as Delano emitted a low growl.

"We didn't—" one of the other Ascended started, a male with deep brown hair.

"Shut up," the Duke hissed. "You will die. I will die. All of us will."

"Correct."

His head jerked back to me.

"What matters is *how* you die," I stated. "I don't know if bloodstone is a painful death. I've seen it up close and personal, and it appears to be so. I'm thinking if I sever the spine, there would only be a second of pain."

The Duke swallowed as his smirk faded.

"But what was far more painful was how the ones in pieces died." I paused, watching the corners of his mouth tighten. "Answer my question, and your death will be quick. Don't? I will make sure you feel as if it lasts a lifetime. That's up to you."

He stared, and I practically saw the wheels turning in his mind, searching for a way out of this.

"It's a terrible thing, isn't it?" I stepped closer to him, and the essence pulsed in my chest. "To know that death is finally coming for you. To see it right before you. To be in the same chamber with it, for seconds, minutes, longer, and know that you can do nothing to prevent it." My voice lowered, became softer and colder...and *smoky*. "Not a single thing. It's horrifying, the inevitability of it. The knowledge that if you still have a soul, it is surely bound for only one place. Deep down, you must be so afraid."

A small, visible shudder coursed through him.

"Just like those mortals you led outside the Rise, tore into, fed off, and left to turn. Just like those in the cells and those on the gates." I searched his pale features. "They must have been so terrified to learn that death had come for them at the hands of those they believed protected them."

He swallowed once more. "There are no more Ascended. There never has been. No one wants to rule at the edge of the realm." His chest rose with a deep breath. "I know who you are. I know *what* you are. It's why you're still standing, alive to this day. It's not because you're a god," he said, his lip curling. "It's because of the blood that courses through your veins."

My spine stiffened. "If you say it's because of who my mother is, I will *not* make your death quick."

The Duke laughed, but the sound was as cold and harsh as that space inside me. "You think you're a great liberator, don't you? Come to free the mortals from the Blood Crown. Free your precious *husband*."

Everything in me stilled.

"Kill the Queen—your *mother*—and take these lands in the name of Atlantia?" The spark of eather was in his eyes then. The corner of his lips curved up. "You will do no such thing. You will win no war. All you will accomplish is terror. All you will do is spill so much blood that the streets flood with it, and the kingdoms will drown in rivers of crimson. All you will liberate is death. All that you and those who follow will find here is death. And if your love is lucky enough, he will be dead before he sees what's become of—"

Unsheathing my bloodstone dagger, I thrust it into his chest, piercing his heart and stopping the poisonous words before they could penetrate too deeply. And he felt it—the first splintering of his being, the first tearing of his skin and bone. And I, for one, was grateful for that.

His soulless eyes widened in surprise as fine lines appeared in the pale skin of his cheeks. The cracks deepened into a web of fractures that spread down his throat and under the collar of the tailored satin shirt he wore. I held his stare as the tiny ember of eather went out of his black eyes.

And, only then, for the first time in twenty-three days, did I feel nothing at all.

3

Twenty-eight days.

Nearly a month had passed, and the constant ache throbbed so intensely it hurt. I clamped my jaw shut against the scream birthed from the cavern that had become my heart, one of frustration and ever-present helplessness and guilt. Because if I had controlled myself, if I hadn't lashed out…

There were so many *ifs*. So many ways I could've handled things differently. But I hadn't, and that was one of the reasons he wasn't here.

The fluffy and buttery mound of eggs and strips of fried meat before me lost their appeal as the scream built in my throat, pressing against my sealed lips. A bone-deep sense of desperation rose and swiftly gave way to potent fury. The center of my chest hummed, the ancient power pulsing with barely leashed rage.

The fork I held trembled. Pressure seized my chest, closing off my throat as eather pulsed and swelled, pushing against my skin. If I screamed, if I gave in to all the pain and rage, the sound of desperation and anguish would become wrath and fury. The scream choking me, the power building inside me, tasted of *death*.

And a small part of me wanted to let it out.

Fingers several shades deeper than mine closed over my hand, stilling the tremor. The touch, something that had once been so forbidden, jolted me from the dark path, as did the faint charge of energy that passed between us. Slowly, my left hand was turned so the shimmery golden swirl of the marriage imprint was visible.

Proof that *he* and I were still together, even if separated.

Proof that *he* still lived.

My gaze rose, colliding with the striking winter-blue eyes of a wolven.

Concern was evident in the sharp angles of Kieran's handsome face and the tension bracketing his mouth. He looked tired, and he had to be. He hadn't been sleeping well because *I* had hardly been sleeping.

The fork trembled again—no, it wasn't just the fork or my arm that shook. The dishes vibrated, as did the table. Down the hall, the hanging white-and-gold Atlantian banners that had replaced the ones belonging to the Blood Crown shuddered.

Kieran's gaze flicked past the empty chairs in the Cauldra banquet hall, to where the light-haired Atlantian, General Aylard, stood guard at the pillared opening.

I sensed the same thing now as I had when he first introduced himself. Distrust brimmed beneath his impassive features, tasting of vinegar. It wasn't a surprising emotion. Many of the older Atlantians were cautious of me, either because I had been raised by their enemies, the Ascended, or because I was many things they hadn't expected.

A scarred Maiden.

A hostage.

An unwanted Princess who'd become their Queen.

A god.

I couldn't exactly hold their wariness against any of them, especially when I made the entire manor tremble.

"You're starting to glow," Kieran warned in a whisper that I could barely hear, sliding his hand away.

I looked down at my palm. A faint silver sheen emanated from my skin.

Well, that explained why the general now stared.

Lowering the fork to the plate, I steadied my breathing. I forced my mind past the suffocating burst of pain that always accompanied thoughts of *him* as I slipped my hand under the table to the small pouch secured to my hip and reached for the glass of mulled wine with the other. I washed away the sour taste with spice as Aylard turned slowly, his gloved grip remaining on his sheathed sword. The white mantle draped over his shoulders settled, drawing my gaze to the gold-embossed Atlantian Crest. The same crest now lining the walls of

Cauldra—a sun and its rays, a sword and arrow at the center, crossed diagonally so both lengths were equal. Briefly closing my eyes, I finished off the wine.

"Is that all you're going to eat?" Kieran asked after a few moments.

I placed the empty glass on the table as I glanced at the open window. Broken pieces of a foundation jutted up from bushy yellow wildflowers. Massene was not well kept. "I ate."

"You need to eat more." He rested his elbows on the table.

My eyes narrowed on him. "And you don't need to be concerned about what I'm eating."

"I wouldn't have to be if you didn't leave bacon untouched on your plate—something I never thought I'd see."

I lifted my brows. "It sounds like you're suggesting I ate too much bacon before."

"Nice try at deflecting. But, ultimately, a failure," Kieran replied. "I'm doing what you and Cas asked of me. I'm advising you."

His name.

The breath I took stung. His name hurt. I didn't like to think it, let alone say it. "I'm confident that my daily food intake was not what either of us was thinking when we asked you to be our advisor."

"Neither was I. But here we are." Kieran leaned in so only a handful of inches separated us. "You're barely eating. You're barely sleeping. And what just occurred? The glowing? The making the entire building shake? You seemed completely unaware of it, and it's happening more often, Poppy."

There wasn't an ounce of censure in his tone, only concern, but I still squirmed because it was true. The essence of the gods was coming to the surface when I wasn't using it to take away pain or heal. It happened when I felt something too strongly—when the sorrow and rage made my skin feel too tight, pushing at the fragile seams that held me together.

I needed to keep it together. I needed control. I couldn't lose it. Not when the Kingdoms of Atlantia and Solis were counting on me. Not when *he* needed me. "I'll try harder to control it," I promised.

"This isn't about you controlling your abilities." Kieran's brows knitted. "It's about letting yourself not be okay. You're strong, Poppy. We—"

"I know." I stopped him as memories of nearly the same words whispered through me, spoken from other lips that had blazed a heated path along every inch of my skin.

You don't have to always be strong with me.

I snapped forward, picking up a slice of bacon. I shoved half of it into my mouth, nearly choking myself. "Happy?" I asked, a piece plopping to the plate.

Kieran stared. "Not exactly."

"Sounds like that's your problem." I chewed, barely tasting the crispy meat.

A huff that sounded like a laugh drew my attention to the large, purplish-black draken resting near the pillared entryway of the banquet hall. Smooth, black horns started in the middle of the flattened bridge of his nose and ran up over the center of his diamond-shaped head. The first couple of horns were small so as not to obstruct his vision, but as they traveled up his head, they lengthened into sharpened points that jutted out from thick frills.

Every time I looked at Reaver, it was a shock. I didn't think I'd ever get used to seeing such a magnificent, frightful, and beautiful being.

Twenty-three draken had awakened. The youngest, three in total, remained at Spessa's End to stand guard there, as decided by the draken. Out of the twenty that traveled with the armies, none were as large as Reaver. Instead, they were about the size of Setti, their scales not nearly as thick as Reaver's and more susceptible to the sharp edge of an arrow. But they would still make quick work of any army.

The draken watched us, and I wondered what he was thinking and feeling. Whenever I attempted to get a read on him or any of the others while around them, I felt nothing. It wasn't like the cold hollowness of an Ascended. Either Reaver and the other draken were shielding their emotions from me, or I simply couldn't read them.

"Would you like some?" I offered to Reaver, lifting the plate. I hadn't seen him eat, which drummed up a wee bit of concern over exactly *what* he was eating when he took flight, disappearing from view.

I really hoped it wasn't people...or cute animals.

But I had no way of knowing. Only Aurelia, one of only two female draken who had awakened, had been in her mortal form long enough for me to learn the names of about half of the two-dozen draken who had left Iliseeum. She'd said that my will was theirs before we left Atlantia and parted ways.

The whole, my-will-was-theirs thing hadn't exactly been helpful, but I'd learned that it was somewhat like the Primal *notam*. Reaver seemed to inherently know what I wanted. Like when we left to take Massene, and he'd already hunkered down to sleep for the night. I guessed it was more like the Primal essence in terms of how it responded to what I willed.

Reaver shook his spiked head at my offer of bacon.

"How did he even get in here without bringing the entire building down?" The skin between Kieran's brows creased.

"Carefully," I said as the draken's attention drifted to the wolven. The vertical pupils constricted as his blue eyes narrowed once more. I suspected that the draken would take another swipe at Kieran the next chance he got.

"Shouldn't Vonetta and the others be returning today?" I asked, directing Kieran's attention from the draken.

"Any minute now." Picking up his glass, he added dryly, "As you already know."

I did, but he was no longer engaged in an epic stare-down with Reaver, which would surely escalate. However, anxiety suddenly took flight like a large silver hawk, and it had nothing to do with the probability of Kieran and Reaver maiming or murdering each other.

It had everything to do with the plans regarding Oak Ambler and Solis. Things I would need to convince the Atlantian generals to support, even though I hadn't handled the most intricate part of those plans myself.

"I have this feeling," Kieran began, "that you're still annoyed I advised you against going with Vonetta."

I frowned. "Sometimes, I do wonder if you can read minds."

His full mouth twisted into a smirk as he tapped one finger off his temple. "I just have a knack for knowing things."

"Uh-huh." So did his father, Jasper, but Kieran also frequently seemed to know where my thoughts went. Which, admittedly, was as annoying to me as me reading his emotions was to him. "I wasn't *actively* annoyed by you advising me against going into Oak Ambler, but I am now."

"Great," he muttered.

I sent him a glare. "Why is it when a Prince or a King decides to place themselves in danger or chooses to lead armies into war, it's not an issue? But when a Queen wishes to do the same, it suddenly becomes a *thing* they must be advised against? Sounds a bit…sexist."

Kieran placed his glass down. "It's not a *thing*. I tried to stop Cas from doing idiotic, incredibly dangerous acts so many times, it was practically a full-time responsibility."

A sharp slice of pain cut through my chest. I focused on the unopened bottles of wine the Atlantian Lord who had captained the ship we'd taken to Oak Ambler had shipped in. Perry had ferried in *many* much-needed supplies. Most importantly, the type of wine Kieran had said Valyn favored.

What better way to get someone to agree to what you wanted than to get them liquored up?

"Namely you," Kieran continued, intruding on my thoughts. "I tried to stop him from taking you."

"What?" My head jerked toward him.

He nodded. "When he concocted the plan to masquerade as a guard and take you hostage, I told him, more than once, that it was absolutely insane. That it carried far too many risks."

"Did one of those risks have to do with the fact that it was wrong to kidnap an innocent person and upend her entire life?" I questioned.

His lips pursed. "Can't say that really crossed my mind."

"Nice."

"That was before I knew you."

"That doesn't make it better."

"Probably not, but I don't think you mind how he upended your life."

"Well…" I cleared my throat. "I suppose, in a roundabout, really messed-up way, I'm glad he didn't listen to you."

Kieran smirked. "I'm sure you are."

I rolled my eyes. "*Anyway*, as I was saying, I don't feel that it's right to ask something of someone that I'm not willing to do myself."

"Which is admirable. That will win you the respect of many of your soldiers. Too bad you'll likely be captured or end up dead. Therefore, making what you feel irrelevant."

"That was a bit dramatic," I said. "Vonetta and the others are risking their lives while I sit here, listening to you complain about what I'm eating."

"You're sitting there listening to me complain about what you're *not* eating," Kieran corrected. "And now it's you who's being dramatic."

"I think I've changed my mind about you being the Advisor to the Crown," I muttered.

That was ignored. "It's not like you're doing *nothing*."

There had barely been a moment when I wasn't doing *something*, especially since we'd taken Massene. The Craven in the cells had been dealt with, but I swore I could still smell them if rain came. The manor was in basic disrepair, the second and third floors virtually uninhabitable. The only electricity served a handful of the chambers and the kitchens. The people's homes weren't much better, and we'd done our best to make much-needed repairs to roofs and roads in the last five days, but it would take months, if not longer, to finish it. The crops hadn't fared much better. Especially when so many of those who tended them had been led outside the Rise.

"I just…" Drawing a thumb along the rim of the glass, I leaned back in the chair. I just needed to be occupied. If I weren't, then my mind wandered to places it could not go. Places that had been hollowed out after the failed meeting with the Blood Queen. Cold and angry like a winter storm. And those holes inside me didn't feel like *me* at all.

Or even like a mortal.

They reminded me of Isbeth.

Anger simmered in my gut. I welcomed it because it was far easier to deal with that than sorrow and helplessness. Isbeth was someone I had no problem thinking about. Not at all. She was *all* I could think about at times, especially in those silent, dark minutes of night when sleep evaded me.

No longer did I find it difficult to reconcile the kindness and gentleness she'd showered upon me with who she had been to *him* and countless others. A monster. I had come to terms with who she was. Isbeth may have conceived me through means that were most likely unconscionable, but she was no mother to me. Coralena was. Isbeth was nothing more than the Blood Queen. The enemy.

Feeling Kieran's all-too-knowing stare upon me, I swallowed thickly. "I'm okay," I said, before he could ask the question that often parted his lips.

Kieran said nothing as he watched me. He knew better. Just as he'd known better earlier, when that icy rage had manifested, rattling the table. However, he didn't harp on it this time. He changed the subject. "Valyn and the other generals will be arriving any day now. He will approve of how we took Massene."

I nodded. Valyn didn't necessarily want war. Instead, he had seen it as something inevitable. Neither he nor any of the older Atlantians were willing to give the Ascended any more chances. Once they learned about what the Ascended here had done, it wouldn't help change their minds regarding whether or not the vamprys could or wanted to change their ways or control their bloodlust. And it wouldn't help if the Duke and Duchess Ravarel, those who ruled Oak Ambler, refused our demands.

Shoulders tightening, I stared into the glass of dark wine. *Our demands* had everything to do with going about war differently. It was why we'd taken Massene the way we had. I fully believed there were steps that could prevent unnecessary loss of life on both sides, especially since the mortals who fought for Solis most likely had no choice—unlike those who had picked up their swords and shields to defend Atlantia.

Some in cities like Massene and Oak Ambler would ultimately pay the price of a violent war, either with their livelihoods or their lives. And then there were the Ascended who were like...

I drew in a ragged breath, briefly squeezing my eyes shut before my mind could call forth an image of Ian—of how I'd last seen him. How he died replayed enough at night. I didn't need to see it now.

But I believed there had to be Ascended who weren't evil to their core. Who could be reasoned with.

So that was the basis of our planning. But we knew Oak Ambler wasn't Massene.

Several days ago, we'd sent Duke and Duchess Ravarel an ultimatum: Agree to our demands or face a siege. Our demands were simple, but we weren't counting on them to be reasonable and accept their fate.

And that was where Vonetta came in, along with Naill and Wren, the elder Rise Guard who'd witnessed what the Ascended here had been doing. Wren's extended family—one he believed might be Descenters who supported Atlantia—lived in Oak Ambler. What they were doing, what our plans consisted of, came with huge risks.

However, the impending siege of Oak Ambler and all the ways it could fail in the most spectacular ways possible weren't our only pressing concerns.

My thoughts found their way to another risk we'd undertaken: Our past plans to enter Oak Ambler ahead of when we were to meet with the Blood Queen. Somehow, she had known, either having simply been prepared for the possibility of us attempting to trick them or because someone had betrayed us. Other than those we trusted, only the Council of Elders had known about our plans. Did we have a traitor in our midst? Either someone we trusted or someone who had reached the upper echelons of power in Atlantia? Or was the simplest explanation the answer? That the Blood Crown had simply outsmarted us, and we'd underestimated them?

I didn't know, but there was also the issue of the Unseen—the secretive, all-male organization that had once served the deities. Believing that I was the Harbinger of Death and Destruction that the prophecy warned of, they'd resurfaced once I entered Atlantia. They'd been behind the attack at the Chambers of Nyktos and so, so much more. And the threat the Unseen posed hadn't ended with Alastir's and Jansen's deaths.

I watched Aylard, standing between the pillars. The Unseen were still out there, and there was no way of knowing exactly who belonged to the group and who aided them.

"Do I want to know what you're thinking about?" Kieran asked. "Because you look like you wish to stab someone."

"You always think I look that way."

"Probably because you always want to stab someone."

"I do not." I glanced at him.

He raised his brows.

"Except for right now," I amended. "I'm considering stabbing you."

"Flattered." Kieran raised his glass, eyeing Reaver. The draken slowly rapped his claws on the floor. "You often seem to want to stab those you care about."

"That makes it sound as if I'm…twisted or something."

"Well…" Kieran lowered his glass, narrowing his eyes at the draken. "Would you like me to pose for a painting? Then you can gaze upon me even when I'm not around."

My brows flew up. "Can you not?"

"He started it," Kieran muttered.

"How?"

"He's staring at me." A pause. "*Again.*"

"So?"

"I don't like it." Kieran frowned. "At all."

"You sound like a small child right now," I informed him, and Reaver huffed out another laugh. I turned to him. "And you're not any better."

Reaver reared back his spiked head, blowing out a smoky breath. He looked *affronted*.

"You're both ridiculous." I shook my head.

"Whatever." Kieran's head turned to the entryway at the same moment Reaver's did. "Finally."

I looked over, realizing that both had heard another's approach. How, as a god, I hadn't been blessed with better hearing was beyond me.

Vonetta strode past Aylard, her long legs encased in dusty breeches. She had her tight and narrow, waist-length braids swept up in a knot, highlighting her high, angular cheeks. Except for her deeper skin tone that often reminded me of lush night-blooming roses, in her mortal form, she shared similar features with her brother and looked a lot like their mother, Kirha. While Kieran favored their father, Jasper.

As Vonetta approached us, I wondered who their little sister would take after. The babe had been born only a few weeks ago, and I wished the siblings were with their family now, celebrating the newest addition. But instead, they were here with me, near lands ravaged hundreds of years ago, on the eve of yet another war.

Vonetta wasn't alone. Emil always seemed to be wherever she was of late.

I bit down on the inside of my lip, stopping my grin. At first, I wasn't sure that Vonetta appreciated her Emil-shaped shadow. But that was until I'd seen her coming out of his chamber in the early morning hours on the day she'd left for Oak Ambler. The soft, sated smile on her face made it utterly unnecessary to probe any deeper into her emotions.

Vonetta's steps faltered as she entered the banquet hall, taking note of Reaver. Her brows lifted. "How in the world did you get in here?"

"See?" Kieran lifted a hand. "Valid question."

The draken thumped his heavy tail on the floor as he huffed out a breath. I had no idea what that meant, but he made no move to approach Vonetta or Emil.

Before I could speak, Emil lowered to one knee as he extended an arm wide in an elaborate bow. "Your Highness."

I sighed. Many had taken to using that title instead of *Your Majesty* since it had been used when the gods were awake.

Vonetta stopped, looking behind her. "Are you going to do that every time?"

"Probably." He rose.

"That means *yes* in Emil language," Vonetta remarked as movement beyond the pillars snagged my attention.

Aylard no longer stood there now that Emil and Vonetta were

present. Instead, a hunched figure I'd become familiar with the past five days shuffled past the pillars. Emil had taken to calling her the widow, even though no one knew if she had been married. I wasn't exactly sure what she had done in the manor, as I only ever saw her walking about, sometimes in the ruins in the pines behind Cauldra, which led to Kieran being convinced that she was not flesh and blood but spirit. I'd heard that Aylard had asked her what she was doing here in the manor on the first day, and her answer was only that she was waiting.

Weird. But not important at the moment.

I turned to Vonetta. "Has everyone returned? Wren? Naill—?"

"I'm fine," Vonetta cut in smoothly as she reached over, briefly touching my hand. A soft burst of energy passed between us. "Everyone is fine and back in the camp."

I exhaled slowly, nodding.

"She's been worrying this whole time, hasn't she?" Vonetta asked her brother.

"What do you think?" he replied.

I almost kicked Kieran under the table. "Of course, I was worried."

"Understandable. I would've worried if it was you roaming the streets of Oak Ambler, looking for Descenters and warning others of the impending siege if the Ravarels refused our demands." Vonetta glanced down at the plates. "Are you finished with that? I'm starving."

"Yes. Help yourself." I shot Kieran a look of warning when he opened his mouth. His lips smashed together in a thin, hard line as his sister snatched up a slice of bacon. I glanced at Emil and then looked back at Vonetta. "How did it go?"

"It went good. I think." Vonetta dropped into the chair opposite Kieran, nibbling on the bacon. "We spoke to—gods. Hundreds? Maybe even more. Quite a few of them were…" She frowned slightly. "It was like they were *ready* to hear that someone was doing something about the Ascended. These weren't like the ones who don't question the Rite, believing it an honor or whatever. These were people who didn't want to give their children over to the Rite."

I couldn't think of the Rite and not picture the Tulis family, begging the Teermans to speak to gods who still slumbered on their behalf—pleading to keep their last child.

And no matter what had been done for them, the entire family was now dead.

"You were right, by the way. About telling them about you," she added between bites.

"What I would've paid to see their reactions to that news," Emil mused. "To learn that not only had their Maiden married the dreaded Atlantian Prince but that she was now the Queen of Atlantia and also a god." A faint smile appeared. "I bet many dropped to their knees and started praying."

"Some did," Vonetta reported wryly.

I winced a little. "Really?"

She nodded. "And since they believe the gods are still awake, the news that you joined with Atlantia got a lot of them thinking. Even a few said the gods may no longer support the Ascended."

The curve of my lips matched hers.

"I suppose we should be grateful that they lied about the gods backing Solis instead of speaking the truth—that the gods had nothing to do with the war and are asleep," Kieran noted. "With their lies, they set the expectations of the gods changing their alliances."

I toyed with the ring on my pointer finger. "It wasn't my idea, though. That was...that was *his*. He recognized that the lies the Ascended told would ultimately be their downfall."

"Cas did know that," Emil confirmed. "But that was before he or any of us knew you were a god. It was your idea to reveal that. Give yourself credit."

My neck warmed, and I cleared my throat. "Do you think they'll listen? That they will tell others?"

"I think many will." Vonetta glanced at her brother and then back at me. "We all know that telling the mortals what we planned was a risk—one we believed was worth it, even if the Ravarels learned of our plans."

I nodded. "Giving the mortals a chance to leave the city before we take it so they won't be caught in the middle is worth this dangerous move."

"Agreed," she confirmed. "So, some didn't believe the part about you being a god. They think the evil Atlantians somehow manipulated you," she said, reaching for the other slice of bacon as Emil leaned in and did the same. He was faster. "Hey, that's mine." She shot him a glare. "What are you even doing here?"

"Actually, the bacon is—" Kieran began, and I *did* kick his leg under the table this time. His head jerked in my direction.

"We can share." Emil snapped the bacon in two and handed half over to a less-than-grateful Vonetta. "And I'm here because I missed you that much."

"Whatever," Vonetta muttered. "Seriously, why are you here?"

Emil grinned, his amber eyes warm as he finished off his half of the slice. "I'm here because someone delivered a missive to the Rise," he announced, wiping his hands on a napkin. "It's from the Duke and Duchess Ravarel."

Every part of me tensed. "And you're just now sharing this?"

"You had questions about their time in Oak Ambler. Figured I'd let them get answered," he reasoned. "Plus, Vonetta was hungry, and I know better than to get between a wolven and food."

Vonetta whipped toward Emil, nearly coming out of her chair. "Are you seriously blaming your inability to prioritize on me?"

"I would never do such a thing." Emil pulled a slip of folded parchment from the breast pocket of his tunic as he grinned at Vonetta. "And none of that changes the fact that I did miss you."

Kieran rolled his eyes.

Vonetta opened her mouth and then closed it, sitting back in her chair, and I did what I probably shouldn't. I opened my senses. What I tasted from Vonetta was spicy and smoky. *Attraction.* There was also something sweeter underneath.

"I need wine." She started to lean forward, but Emil was, once again, quicker. As he handed the missive to me, he snagged the bottle of wine and poured her a drink. "Thank you," she said, taking the glass and swallowing an impressive mouthful. She looked at me. "So, what does it say?"

The thin slip of folded parchment felt as if it weighed as much as a sword. I glanced at Kieran, and when he nodded, I opened it. One sentence was written in red ink—a response we all expected but that still came as a blow.

We agree to nothing.

4

"Run, Poppy," Momma wheezed. "Run."

She wanted me to leave her, but I couldn't. I ran. I ran toward her, tears spilling down my cheeks.

"Momma—" Claws caught my hair, scratched my skin, burning me like the time I'd reached for the hot kettle. I screamed, straining for Momma, but I couldn't see her in the mass of monsters.

They were everywhere, skin dull and gray and broken. And then there was the tall man in black. The one with no face. I twisted, screaming—

Papa's friend stood in the doorway. I reached for him. He was supposed to help us—help Momma. But he stared at the man in black as he rose above the twisting, feeding creatures. Papa's friend jerked, stumbling back, his bitter horror filling my mouth, choking me. He backed away, shaking his head and trembling. He was leaving us—

Teeth sank into my skin. Fiery pain ripped through my arm and lit across my face. I fell, trying to shake them off. Red streamed into my eyes. "No. No. No," I screamed, thrashing. "Momma! Papa!"

Fire sliced through my stomach, seizing my lungs and my body.

Then the monsters were falling, and I couldn't breathe. The pain. The weight. I wanted my momma. Nothingness slipped over my eyes, and I was lost for a little bit.

A hand touched my cheek, my neck. I blinked through blood and tears.

The Dark One stood above me, his face nothing but shadows beneath the hooded cloak. It wasn't his hand at my throat but something cold and sharp.

He didn't move. That hand trembled. He shook as he spoke, but his words faded in and out.

I heard Momma say in a voice that sounded strange and wet, "Do you understand what that means? Please. She must…"

"Good gods," the man rasped, and then I was floating and drifting, surrounded by the scent of the flowers the Queen liked to have in her bedchambers.

What a powerful little flower you are.

What a powerful poppy.

Pick it and watch it bleed.

Not so—

I jerked awake, my eyes open wide as I scanned the moonlit chamber. I wasn't there. I wasn't in the inn. I was here.

My heart was slow to calm. I hadn't had such a nightmare in a few nights. Others had found me—ones where pointed nails painted the color of blood dug into *his* skin—hurting *him*.

My closest friend and lover.

My husband and King.

My heartmate.

Those nightmares had joined the old ones, finding me if I managed more than a few hours of sleep—which wasn't often. I averaged maybe three hours a night.

Throat dry, I stared up at the ceiling, careful not to disturb the thick blankets piled on top of the wide bedroll. It was silent.

I hated these moments.

The quiet.

The nothingness of night.

The waiting when nothing could occupy my thoughts enough to prevent me from thinking *his* name—let alone what could be happening to him. From hearing him beg and plead, offering anything, even his kingdom, to her.

Twenty-nine days.

A tremor coursed through me as I fought back the rising tide of panic and anger—

Movement by my hip jarred me from the rapidly spiraling thoughts. A large, furry head rose against the moonlight. The wolven yawned as he stretched long, powerful front legs.

Kieran had made it a habit of sleeping near me in his wolven form, which was why he got very little sleep. I'd told him more than once that it wasn't necessary, but the last time I'd brought it up, he'd said, "This is where I *choose* to be."

And well, that…that nearly made me cry. He chose to be beside me because he was my friend. Not because of some obligation. I wouldn't make the same mistake I had with Tawny, constantly doubting the genuineness of our relationship because of how we had been introduced.

I also thought he chose to be here, needing the closeness, because he too was hurting. Kieran had known *him* his entire life. Their friendship went beyond the bond they'd once shared. There was love between them. And while I kept my senses to myself when there was no need for me to read another's emotions, Kieran sat in silence at times, the sadness swelling out from him and breaking through my shields.

That sorrow also stemmed from the loss of Lyra. He'd been more than just fond of the wolven, even if they hadn't been in a serious relationship. He'd cared for her, and now she was gone—just like the wolven Elashya, the one he had loved and lost to a rare wasting disease.

Kieran's head turned toward me, and he blinked sleepy, winter-blue eyes.

"Sorry," I whispered.

I felt a touch against my mind like a light brush of skin against skin. His imprint reminded me of cedar, rich and woodsy. *You should be asleep,* he said, his words a whisper among my thoughts.

"I know," I replied, rolling onto my side so I faced him.

He lowered his head to the bed. *Another nightmare?*

I nodded.

There was a pause, and then he said, *You know, there are herbs that can help you rest. Help you find the kind of sleep where these nightmares can't reach you.*

"No, thank you." I'd never liked the idea of taking anything that knocked me out, potentially leaving me vulnerable. Plus, I was already taking an herb similar to what *he* had taken for contraception. I'd figured it was wise to see if something was readily available since he wouldn't be able to take anything. Luckily, Vonetta had known just the thing—an herb similar to the one Casteel took, which was ground into a powder and could be mixed with any drink. It tasted like dirt but stomaching that was far better than the potential of carrying a child.

That was the last thing any of us needed.

Though I suddenly imagined Kieran knitting little sweaters and grinned.

What are you thinking about? His curiosity was fresh and lemony.

There was no way I was sharing that. "Nothing."

He eyed me as if he didn't believe me. *You need to rest, Poppy. God or not, you're going to wear yourself out.*

I bit back a sigh as I tugged the soft blanket to my chin, rubbing it. "Do you think this blanket is made of wolven fur?"

Kieran's ears flattened. *That was a poor attempt at changing the subject.*

"I think it was a valid question," I parroted his earlier words.

You think every question is a valid one. He made a very mortal-sounding huff.

"They're not?" Flipping onto my back, I stopped rubbing my chin and let go of the blanket.

Kieran nudged my hand. It was his way of letting me know it was okay to touch him in this form—a way the wolven silently communicated need for affection. I reached down, and like always, it never ceased to amaze me how soft a wolven's fur was. I ran my fingers through the fluff between his ears, thinking Kieran probably believed he enjoyed the touch more than I did. But touch…touch was such a gift. One so very often overlooked and underappreciated.

Several long moments of silence passed. "Do you…do you dream of him?"

I don't. Kieran lowered his head to my hip. His eyes closed. *And I don't know if that's a blessing or not.*

I hadn't been able to fall back asleep like Kieran had, but I waited until the faint traces of light crept through the window and across the ceiling to leave the bed. Kieran always slept the deepest as the sun rose. I wasn't sure why, but I knew that my absence wouldn't stir him for at least an hour or two.

Padding quietly across the stone floor, I secured the wolven dagger to my thigh and then picked up the ruffled, blue dress robe Kieran had found in one of the other chambers. I slipped it on over the slip and tights I'd slept in. It smelled of mothballs, but it was clean and luxuriously soft, made of some sort of cashmere. Tying the sash at my waist, I left the chamber without bothering with shoes. The thick socks were more than enough since I didn't plan to leave the manor *this* early.

The people of Massene would be moving about at this time, meeting at one of the two shops that sat just beyond the interior wall of the manor, getting baked pastries and roasted coffee before leaving to work their crops. I didn't want to disturb what little time they had to talk to one another, repairing their broken community. The people here were only slowly adjusting to our presence—the Atlantian Crests on banners draped in the halls I now walked past and hanging over the Rise. They were still nervous around the Atlantian soldiers and often stared at the wolven, caught between terror and curiosity. And when Reaver took flight...

Chaos ensued.

At least the screams and the running for their lives had abated. But when they caught sight of me, they froze before hastily bowing or lowering themselves to their knees, wide-eyed and filled with the same conflicting emotions they felt when the wolven drew closer.

I had a feeling that Wren had keyed the people of Massene into my whole godhood thing since there was no way anyone from Oak Ambler could've communicated what had been whispered to the people there. While I wasn't upset with him for doing so, I sort of wished he hadn't.

How they stared made things a bit awkward.

The way they hastily bowed as if expecting grave punishment for failing to do so immediately made me sad.

Traveling the empty, winding halls of the main floor, I bypassed the banquet hall where the murmur of either soldiers or wolven drifted out. I continued, passing the lone receiving chamber and moving to the closed doors on the east side of the manor—which appeared to be the oldest part.

Cracking them open, I entered the cold, cavernous chamber. The musty scent of old books and dust greeted me. There was so much dust that neither Kieran nor Vonetta could be in the chamber for long without experiencing a sneezing fit. I stopped, turning on the gas lamp that sat on a tea table beside a worn settee the shade of rich chocolate.

Cauldra Manor was as old as Massene was, likely built when the city was a district of Pompay—much like the still-existing neighborhoods in Carsodonia. I had a feeling that many of the tomes on the shelves here were just as old.

Mainly because three or four had basically fallen apart when I opened them.

It was, admittedly, a creepy chamber with its heavy tapestries blocking any natural sources of light, the faded portraits of who I assumed were either Ascended of the past or perhaps mortals who'd once called Cauldra home, and the array of half-melted candles of various shapes and colors.

But I began to think that what truly kept the wolven and Atlantians away was the *feeling* in here. The distinct sensation of not being alone, even when you were.

I felt it now as I drifted among the rows of tomes and their dusty spines—the press of invisible fingers across the nape of my neck. I suppressed a shiver, withdrawing another ancient book from the shelf as I quickly glanced around the empty chamber. The feeling remained, but I ignored it as I took the book to the settee and sat.

However, I would take the possibility of being stalked by spirits over lying in bed with only my wandering thoughts—worrying about *him,* and Tawny, whether or not I would need to feed, and if we could truly win this war without leaving the realm worse than what it was.

I carefully cracked open the tome. No Atlantians were listed as far as I could tell, though much of the ink had faded. Still, what I could read of the paragraphs narrating the lives of those who'd lived here ages ago was fascinating. The births and deaths had been noted in two columns, grouped together by surname. Mixed in with announcements of marriages were paltry arguments over property lines, accusations of livestock thievery, and much more heinous crimes like assault and murder. Executions were recorded. The manner of death was almost always brutal, and they were held publicly in what had once been a town square.

A part of me realized that what had drawn me to look through these records, long forgotten along the lower shelves of the library, was that they reminded me of when I was in New Haven. When everything I had been learning had been so very confusing to me. But…but *he* had been there, vibrant and teasing as I discovered the different Atlantian bloodlines.

Chest squeezing, I flipped through stiff, yellowed pages chronicling a realm that'd existed long before the Ascended. Long before—

My eyes narrowed on the words before me. What the…? Lifting the book from my lap, I inhaled way too much dust as I read the passage again and then one more time.

PRINCESS KAYLEIGH, FIRST DAUGHTER OF KING SAEGAR AND QUEEN GENEVA OF IRELONE, JOINED QUEEN EZMERIA OF LASANIA AND HER CONSORT, MARISOL, TO CELEBRATE THE RITE AND ASCENSION OF THE CHOSEN, MARKING THE...

The rest of the ink was far too faded for me to read, but three words practically pulsed from the worn page.

Rite. Ascension. Chosen.

Three things that hadn't existed before the Ascended ruled Solis.

But that had to be impossible. *He* had explained that the Ascended had created the Rite as a means to increase their numbers and to make livestock out of mortals. Except they didn't feed from all third sons and daughters. Some carried an unknown trait, which Isbeth had discovered allowed them to be made into those things—a Revenant. Still, it made no sense for a Rite to be mentioned in a time so far in the past where the names of the kingdoms had been nearly forgotten. A time of no Ascended.

My gaze lifted to one of the faded portraits. A time possibly even before the first Atlantian had been created through the heartmate trials? Setting the book aside, the hem of the dressing robe whispered over the floor as I hurried back to the shelves, searching for older records— the tomes which appeared close to disintegrating. Taking one in my hands, I was even more careful as I opened the book and went through the pages, searching for any mention of the Rite—and dates.

I found it—a passage with just enough ink left to make out a reference to the Chosen, but I was even more confused. Because when I cross-checked the births in the other ledger, only the third sons and daughters born of the same family had no death dates—dates only marked by the month, day, and the age. I was positive that wasn't due to faded ink.

"How was the Rite possible, then?" I asked the empty chamber.

The only answer was if the Rite had existed and then had stopped, somehow being forgotten by the time the first Atlantian was born. That was the only explanation, as I knew *he* couldn't have lied about this. Every Atlantian and wolven I'd met believed that the Rite had begun with the Ascended.

As I stared at the ledger, it struck me that these records could be far, far older than I believed. Possibly written during a time when the gods were awake.

My lips parted. "These ledgers have to be—"

"Older than sin and most kin."

I jerked at the raspy voice, my gaze swinging to the half-open doors. A shiver coursed down my spine at the sight of the hunched figure shrouded in black.

It was her. The old woman. The widow…who might not even be a widow.

"But not as old as the first mortal, birthed from the flesh of a Primal and the fire of a draken."

I jolted again. Was that how the first mortal had been created?

The veiled head cocked to the side. "I startled you, I see."

I swallowed. "A little. I didn't hear you enter."

"I'm as quiet as a flea, so most don't hear me," she said, shuffling forward. I tensed. The long sleeves of her robe covered her hands, and as she drew closer, I made out the barest hint of pale, creased skin beneath the lacy veil. "Strange reading for a time when most are sleeping."

Blinking, I glanced down at the ledger. "I suppose it is." I looked back at her, surprised that she had moved so close so quickly. "Do you know exactly how old these ledgers are?"

"Older than the kingdom and most wisdom," she answered in that brittle voice that reminded me of dry branches.

The old woman swayed slightly, and I remembered my manners. Most wouldn't sit before a Queen unless given permission. I imagined mortals would behave the same in the presence of a god. "Would you like to sit?" I asked.

"If I sit, I'm afraid to admit, I'm likely never to get up again."

Based on how the robes barely moved to show whether she was breathing, I was also afraid of that. "I don't know your name."

"I know who you are, with that glow in your eyes as bright as a star," she replied, and I did everything in my power to keep my face blank. "Vessa is what I was once called."

Once called? I resisted the urge to reach out and touch her, to see if she truly was made of flesh and bone. Instead, I opened my senses to her, and what I felt was…strange. It was murky. As if whatever she felt was clouded somehow. But there were faint traces of sugary amusement, which was also odd. I wondered if her age made reading her hazy.

I had a feeling she was likely the oldest mortal I'd ever met— possibly even that existed. But her age meant that she must have seen a lot of what'd occurred in Massene. A lot of what the Ascended had done.

"What did you do here, Vessa?"

The lace in front of her face rippled gently, and I caught the scent of something vaguely familiar. A stale scent I couldn't quite place as she said, "I served," she said. "I serve still."

Figuring that she meant the Ascended, I tamped down the surge of anger that rose. The Royals were all the mortals knew. And living for as long as she had under their rule, the fear of being seen as disloyal—as a Descenter—would be hard to shake.

I forced a smile. "You no longer have to serve the Ascended."

Vessa was so unbelievably still. "I do not serve them while I wait."

"Then who is it you serve?" I asked.

"Who else but the True Crown of the Realms, silly girl?"

"I am neither silly nor a girl," I said coolly, setting the ledger on the tea table, assuming she referenced the Blood Crown.

Vessa gave a shaky bow I feared would topple her. "My apologies, Your Highness. I've lost all sense of coyness with age."

I said nothing for a long moment, letting the insult roll off me. I'd been called far worse and dealt harsher insults. "How is it that you serve the True Crown, Vessa?"

"By waiting."

Between the too-short answers and the longer, rhyming ones, I was quickly losing my patience. "What is it that you wait for?"

She straightened in short, jerky movements. "The one who was Blessed."

I stiffened.

"One born from a grave misdeed, of a great and terrible Primal power, with blood full of ash and ice." Her words rattled her entire body, raising the tiny hairs all over mine. "The Chosen who will usher in the end, remaking the realms. The Harbinger of Death and Destruction."

I sucked in a sharp breath at the all-too-familiar words of the prophecy. She must've heard them from the Duke. It was the only explanation.

"*You.*" The hem of the lacy veil fluttered. "I wait for you. I wait for death."

Icy fingers pressed against the back of my neck once more as if a spirit had touched me there.

The old woman lurched forward, black robes flapping like the wings of a crow as an arm whipped out from the vast folds. A glimpse of silver glinted in the lamplight. I locked up for the briefest second as potent, acute shock swept through me.

I snapped out of it, the dressing robe fluttering around my legs as I shot to my feet. I caught her wrist, my finger sinking through the heavy cloth and around the thin, bony arm.

"Are you serious?" I exclaimed, still caught in shock as I shoved away.

Vessa stumbled back, bumping into the tea table. She went down hard, her head snapping forward. The veil slipped and then fell to the floor. White, wispy hair spilled out from patchy clumps along a wrinkled scalp.

"Did you just try to stab me?" Incredulous, I stared down at her, my heart thumping heavily. "When you know *what* I am?"

"I know what you are." She planted a pale, skeletal hand against the floor and lifted her head.

Good gods, she truly was *old*.

Her face was almost nothing more than skin and skull, her cheeks and eyes sunken in, her flesh heavily lined, creased, and a ghastly, grayish-white. Lips a bloodless, thin line peeled back across stained teeth, and her eyes… They were milky white. I took an involuntary step back. How in the world could she even see me?

But she still clutched the slender dagger, and that was rather impressive considering her extreme, advanced age.

"Harbinger," she crooned softly.

"You should stay down," I warned, really hoping she listened. Something was obviously very wrong with her—perhaps due to hearing that damn prophecy and the fear that festered because of it. Or, this behavior could be a byproduct of her age. Probably both. Either way, I didn't want to harm an old lady.

Vessa heaved herself up to her feet.

"Oh, come on," I muttered.

She lunged at me this time, faster than I expected. Gods, the fact that she'd gotten up at all was, yet again, impressive.

I easily side-stepped her. This time, I grasped both her arms as carefully as I could. Trying not to think of how brittle her bones felt, I pushed her down, this time onto the settee.

"Drop the dagger," I said.

"*Harbinger.*"

"Now."

"Harbinger!" Vessa yelled.

"Godsdamn it." I put the slightest pressure on the bones of her wrist, wincing as she gasped. Her fingers opened, and the dagger fell to the floor with a thud. She started to push up. "Don't even think it."

"Do I even want to know what is happening in here?" Kieran boomed from the doors.

"Nothing." I glanced at him. Clearly, he'd just risen. He wore only breeches. "Except that she just tried to stab me."

Every line of Kieran's body went taut. "That doesn't sound like nothing."

"Harbinger!" Vessa shrieked, and Kieran blinked. "Harbinger!"

"And in case you can't tell, she believes I'm the Harbinger." I looked down at the old woman, half afraid to let her go. "No matter what you've heard or were told, I am not that."

"You were born in the shroud of the Primals," she screamed, and it was *loud*. "Blessed with blood full of ash and ice. Chosen."

"I don't think she heard you," Kieran replied dryly.

I shot him a glare. "Would you like to help, or do you just want to stand there and watch me get yelled at by an old woman?"

"Is there a third option?"

My eyes narrowed.

"Harbinger!" Vessa shouted. "Harbinger of Death and Destruction!"

Kieran twisted at the waist. "Naill! Need your help."

"You could just come and get her," I said. "You didn't need to call him."

"Hell, no. I'm not getting anywhere near her. She's a *laruea*."

"A *what?*"

"A spirit."

"You've got to be kidding me," I muttered as Vessa continued struggling. "Does she seem like a disembodied phantom to you?"

Naill entered, his steps slowing and his brows lifting as Vessa continued screaming. Emil was right behind him, his head tilting to the side. "Oh, hey," he said. "It's the widow."

"Her name is Vessa, and she just tried to stab me," I bit out. "Twice."

"Was not expecting that," Naill murmured.

"I don't want to hurt her," I said. "So, it would be great if you two could take her someplace safe."

"Someplace safe?" Emil questioned as he and Naill came forward, speaking loudly to be heard over the woman's screams. "You just said she tried to stab you."

"You see how old she is?" I leaned back as spittle flew from the woman's mouth as she continued shrieking. "She needs to be put someplace where she can't hurt herself or others."

"Like a cell?" Kieran suggested as the two Atlantians managed to disentangle us. "Or a tomb?"

I ignored that as I bent, picking up the dagger. "Place her in a bedchamber that locks from the outside until you can figure out which of the rooms is hers."

"Will do," Naill said, guiding the now-wailing woman from the library.

"Do you think there's any extra muzzles lying about?" Emil asked as Kieran stepped back, giving them a wide berth.

I turned. "Don't you dare put a muzzle on her." There was no answer, so I twisted to Kieran. "They wouldn't, would they?"

He came forward, his gaze sweeping over me. "She should be in a cell."

"She's too old for that."

"And you shouldn't be roaming around. Obviously."

I tossed the dagger onto the table. "I can take care of myself, Kieran." I dragged my hand over my shoulder, pushing my braid back. "She must've heard the Duke speaking about the prophecy, and it messed with her."

"No one's questioning your ability to handle yourself, but there's no telling how many others have heard about the prophecy."

Maybe that was why the people seemed so afraid around me.

"This is why you should have Crown Guards with you."

"I told you, Hisa, and everyone else who suggested that, that I don't want a guard following me around. It reminds me..." I trailed off, tensing. It reminded me too much of Vikter. Of Rylan. Of *him*. "It reminds me of when I was the Maiden," I lied.

"I can understand that." Kieran stopped beside me, so close his chest brushed my arm as he bent his head. "But sending her to a bedchamber? You are a Queen, and that woman just tried to stab you. Do you know what most Queens would do in response?"

"I would hope that most would do as I did—recognize that she is more of a harm to herself than anyone else," I countered.

His stare hardened. "You should at least exile her."

"If I did that, it would be a death sentence." I flopped down on the settee, surprised it didn't collapse under me. "You saw how old she is. I doubt she'll be an issue for much longer. Leave her be, Kieran. You wouldn't feel this way if she'd gone after someone else."

He didn't acknowledge how right I was, which was annoying. "Is that an order?"

I rolled my eyes. "Yes."

"As your advisor—"

"You will say, '*My, what a kind Queen our people have.*'"

"You are kind. Too kind."

Shaking my head, I looked at the records on the tea table as I shoved thoughts of the old woman aside. "Do you know how the first mortal was created?"

"That's a random, unexpected question." He crossed his arms but didn't sit. "The first mortal was created from the flesh—"

"Of a Primal and the fire of a draken?" I finished for him, surprised that the widow had spoken the truth.

Kieran frowned. "If you know the answer, why did you ask?"

"I didn't know until now." It didn't pass me by that I was called the Queen of Flesh and Fire, but my brain was already too full of confusing things to consider how or if those two items were related. "Did you know that the Rite existed before the Ascended?"

"It didn't."

"It did," I said and then showed him the ledgers.

Kieran's surprise was like a splash of cool water as he dragged a hand over his head. The hair there was growing longer. "I guess it's possible that the gods had some sort of Rite and that the Ascended copied it."

I thought that over. "Malec would've known about it. He could've told Isbeth. But did it stop because the gods went to sleep?"

"That would be a plausible reason." He folded his arms, giving the chamber a not-too-discreet glance.

"It has to be related—why the gods took the third sons and daughters," I said, staring at the ledgers. "And how they can become Revenants."

An hour or so past dawn the following morning, I walked across the vine-smothered remains of one of the buildings situated among the pines that crowded Cauldra Manor. A gust of chilled wind swept through the decaying pillars, ruffling the pure white fur of the wolven prowling the length of the crumbling wall of the structure.

Delano had followed when I left the manor, staying only a few feet behind me as he continuously scanned the ruins that had either been destroyed by time or the last war.

Thirty days.

The shudder rolling through me had nothing to do with the cool temperatures. The sharp swell of pain deep in my chest made it difficult to breathe and blended with the nearly overwhelming need to escape this haunted place and go to Carsodonia. That was where *he* was. That was what the Handmaiden had told me, and I didn't think the Revenant was lying. How could I free him if I were here, trapped amid the skeletons of a once-great city? Held captive by the responsibilities of a Crown I hadn't wanted?

My gloved fingers trailed down the buttons of the woolen sweater coat to where they ended at the waist. I reached between the flared halves and closed my hand over the pouch secured to my hip, clutching the toy horse.

My thoughts calmed.

Near the bushy, yellow wildflowers growing along the foundation,

I sat on the edge, letting my legs dangle off as I eyed the landscape. Waist-high weeds had reclaimed most of the road that had once traveled to this part of the city, leaving only glimpses of the cobbled streets beneath. Thick roots had taken hold among the toppled buildings, and the sweeping pines' heavy limbs climbed through broken windows in the few walls that still stood. Sprigs of lavender poked through abandoned carriage wheels, the sweet, floral scent following the wind whenever it blew.

I had no idea how old Duke Silvan had been, but I was sure he'd lived enough years to clean this part of Massene up. To do something with the land so it no longer resembled a graveyard of what once had been.

The Chosen who will usher in the end, remaking the realms.

A shiver accompanied the memory of Vessa's words. As far as I knew, neither Naill nor Emil had been able to find her chamber, but she was locked away, fed and safe in a room two doors down from the Great Hall.

"You shouldn't be out here," a gruff voice said from above, causing me to jump.

Delano hadn't been the only one to follow. Reaver had, too, taking to the air as he tracked us through the pines. He glided so quietly above us that I'd forgotten he was up there, circling.

The voice could belong to no one but him.

Tilting back my head, I looked up a dozen feet or so to where the draken perched on the flat surface of a pillar. Warmth crept into my cheeks.

Seeing Reaver in his mortal form was already an utterly unexpected experience. But seeing him completely, absolutely naked whilst crouched on a pillar took the oddness of the situation to a whole new level.

Reaver was a…*blond.*

With his somewhat grumpy disposition, I'd conjured up a much darker-haired image of him.

I tried not to stare, but it was hard not to. Luckily, any areas that would've been considered highly inappropriate by most were hidden from view, given how he was positioned. Still, there was a lot of exposed, sinewy, sand-colored flesh. I squinted. Skin that carried the faint but distinct pattern of scales.

"You're in your mortal form," I said dumbly.

A curtain of shoulder-length hair obscured most of Reaver's

features except for the angle of his sharp jawline. "How observant."

My brows rose as I felt Delano brush against my thoughts, his imprint springy and featherlight. Following that unique sensation, I opened the pathway to him, and his response was immediate. *He is an odd one.*

I couldn't really argue against that at the moment. *He probably thinks we're odd.*

He probably wants to eat us, Delano replied as he slid past one of the pillars.

I almost laughed, but then Reaver said, "You are filled with worry. We can all feel it. Even those on their way here."

My attention jerked back to him. *We.* As in the draken. The wolven could sense my emotions when extremely heightened because of the Primal *notam.* "Are the draken bonded to me?" I asked since Nektas hadn't exactly said they were. Just that they were now *mine.*

"You are the *Liessa.* You summoned us. You carry the blood of Nyktos and the Consort in you. You are..." He trailed off. "Yes, we are bonded to you. I am perplexed by the fact that you're only now realizing that."

The corners of my lips turned down. "I'm not just figuring it out. I hadn't really thought that...deeply about it," I finished lamely. "Can I communicate with you like I do with the wolven?"

"No, but as you know," he said, and I blinked slowly, "we will know and answer your *will,* as it has always been that way with the Primals."

"But I'm not a Primal."

"What you are is not wise," he responded, and now I really frowned. "You shouldn't be this far from the manor."

"I'm not far." I could still smell the wood smoke mingling with the lavender.

"These mortals are afraid of you, as you already know," he continued, and my stomach twisted. "Fear tends to lead to poor choices."

"I won't let anyone get close enough to do me any harm," I said. "Neither will Delano."

"One does not need to be near you to harm you," he pointed out. "As you were told before, you may be hard to kill, but it's not impossible. That woman may not have succeeded, but others could inflict damage."

My fingers stopped their ceaseless toying with the sweater's buttons as wind tossed strands of hair back from Reaver's face. I finally got my first true look at him.

There was a strange asymmetric quality to him as if his features had been plucked from random traits. His eyes were wideset and tilted down at the inner corners, giving him a somewhat mischievous impression that didn't match the somberness of his vivid sapphire stare. Nor did the full, distinctively bow-shaped lips seem to belong to the strong, chiseled jaw and light brown brows that arched in a sardonic, almost taunting way. His cheekbones were high and sharp, creating shadows below them. Somehow, the hodgepodge of features worked. He wasn't classically handsome but so interesting to look upon that he was thoroughly striking. He had a hint of gauntness to his face that made me wonder if he was still recovering physically from such a long sleep.

I pulled myself out of those thoughts with a shake of my head. "Exactly what *does* kill a god?"

"A god can kill another," Reaver said. "Shadowstone can also kill a god."

The same material had been used to construct many of the Temples and the palace in Evaemon. I'd never thought of it as a weapon until those skeletal guards we'd seen after entering Iliseeum had wielded shadowstone weapons.

It was what had punctured Tawny's skin in the chaos after everything had gone so terribly wrong.

"Through the heart or head," he elaborated.

Immediately, I saw the arrow the Revenant had pointed in my direction, but the Revenant had spoken as if she hadn't believed the shadowstone would kill me. I supposed it was a good thing she'd obviously thought wrong.

"What happens if a mortal is stabbed with shadowstone?"

"It would kill them," he said, and air fled my lungs. "But your friend lives. There has to be a reason for that."

Reaver had definitely been listening whenever I spoke of Tawny. "What kind of reason could there be?"

"I wouldn't know," he replied, and I tamped down a surge of frustration. "But you are the first female descendant of the Primal of Life—the most powerful being known. In time, you will become even more powerful than your father."

How I could be more powerful than my father was beyond me. Nor did I know why the female part mattered. Still, I got stuck on those two words.

Your father.

Ires.

Those two words left me uncertain. I swallowed, looking away. Whatever relief I'd felt when I learned that Malec wasn't my father had been short-lived. My father was a cave cat I'd seen as a young child and again in Oak Ambler, at Castle Redrock. But the only father I remembered was Leopold. Still, anger hummed through my blood, mingling with the eather and warming those cold, hollow places scattered throughout. I would free him, too. "How long has Ires been held captive?"

"He left Iliseeum while we slept, after waking one of the draken to accompany him." The line of Reaver's jaw flexed as he stared ahead. "I don't know why he left or exactly when. I only became aware some eighteen years ago when the Primal awakened."

My brows knitted as Delano sank onto his haunches beside me. "Why did Nyktos awaken?"

Reaver's head swung in my direction. Those ultra-bright eyes were unnerving even with the distance between us. "I believe it was when you were born. It was *felt.*"

I hadn't known that.

He returned his gaze to the sky. "That was when we learned that both Malec and Ires were gone. As was...Jade."

It took me a moment to realize that he spoke of Jadis—Nektas's daughter.

Tension bunched the muscles along his shoulders. "I don't know why Ires took her. She was young when we went to sleep. And when she was awakened, she would've been untested. It wouldn't have been safe for her."

I felt the strange urge to defend a man I didn't know. "Maybe he didn't think it would be dangerous."

Reaver huffed, and I swore I saw faint wisps of smoke coming from his mouth. "I think...I think he knew something had happened to his brother and went to look for him. Malec was lost to us long before we realized," he said, his words similar to what Nektas had told me. "But Malec was Ires's twin. So alike as children, you couldn't tell them apart. As they grew older, their differences became clear," he said, his rough, unused voice turning distant. "Ires was cautious and thoughtful in everything, while Malec was reckless and didn't often stop to think of what he'd done until afterward. Ires was content in

Iliseeum, but Malec had grown restless, visiting the mortal world as the deities slowly built Atlantia. Because both he and Ires were in born this realm, he could come, but that was not without its limitations. The longer he stayed, the more his power lessened. Still, he chose to stay, even knowing what he would have to do to stay strong."

That lessening of his power must explain why no Primal *notam* existed between Malec and all the wolven like they had with me. "How did he stay strong?"

"He had to feed, *Liessa.*" One eyebrow rose as Reaver looked down at me. "He had to feed *often.* Any blood would do for a god or a Primal, whether it be mortal, Atlantian, or another god." A pause. "Wolven. Anything but a draken. You cannot feed from a draken."

Surprise rolled through Delano and me. Atlantians could feed off mortals, but it did nothing for them. Apparently, however, the world was one giant buffet when it came to gods and Primals. However, this piece of news meant…

I had to feed.

"Do you…?" I swallowed hard. "Do you know how often?"

"Probably not as often as Malec once you come into your power. Unless injured. But until then, you will need to ensure you do not weaken."

"Wait. I've Ascended—"

"Yes, I know that. Thanks for pointing it out," he interrupted, and my eyes narrowed. "But you haven't finished your Culling."

Delano's head cocked, and it felt like my brain did the same.

My abilities had begun to change over the last year, as I became of age to enter the Culling. Before that, I had only been able to feel— *taste*—the pain of others. But that had grown, allowing me to read all emotions. My ability to ease pain had also changed to one that could heal injuries. But after…*he* had saved me by giving me his blood—thus Ascending me—I had been able to bring the young girl back to life. So, I'd thought the Culling had run its course. "How do you know?"

"Because I would feel it," he said, as if that explained everything.

It really explained nothing, not even touching on why I was different than Malec. But those questions were lost in the realization that I would have to feed. I hadn't felt the need yet. I didn't even know what to think about what would happen if I had to do it before I freed…*him.* That was yet another thing I didn't want to stress about.

Delano nudged my limp hand with the side of his face. I reached over, gently petting the back of his neck. I wished my hands weren't gloved so I could feel his fur. I knew that his coat was thicker and softer than even Kieran's.

"Why can't I feed from a draken?" I asked and then wondered if that was a rude question.

"Because it would burn the insides out of most. Even Primals."

Oh.

All right, then.

I shook that disturbing image from my mind. "What exactly would weaken a god? Besides being injured?"

Reaver's head tilted once again. "You do not know much about yourself, do you?"

My lips pursed. "Well, this whole god thing is relatively new, and, you know, there aren't any gods standing around ready to educate me. Nor are there any texts I can simply read."

He made a harrumphing sound as if those weren't good enough reasons. "Most injuries would only weaken you unless they were serious. Then you will weaken more quickly. Using the essence of the gods can, over time, also weaken you if you haven't completed the Culling. Which, as I said, you have not."

Delano's ears flattened. *That's not ideal.*

No, it wasn't. Using the eather meant that I could fight like a god, but if it weakened me… My stomach dipped. "I didn't know that."

"I'm shocked to hear that."

Even Kieran would've been impressed by the level of sarcasm in Reaver's voice. "How will I know when the Culling is complete?"

"You'll know."

I resisted the urge to pick up one of the small rocks and throw it at him. "What good is having that kind of power if it inevitably weakens me?"

"It is a balance, *meyaah Liessa*," he said, and I blinked. I hadn't expected to hear him call me *my Queen* like the wolven did. "Even we have weaknesses. The fire we breathe is the essence of the Primals. Using it tires us. Slows us down. Even the Primals had their limitations. Weaknesses. Only one is infinite."

Nyktos.

He would be infinite.

"From what I can remember, it varies how much using the essence weakens from god to god," he continued. "But as I said, you carry the Primal essence within you. I imagine it will take longer for you to weaken that way, but you will know when it happens." His head turned in the direction of the camp. "Your wolven comes."

A sugary ripple of amusement came from Delano as I looked over my shoulder, seeing a distant figure among the broken stone and tall grass. "If you're talking about Kieran, he's not my wolven."

The wind lifted the strands of Reaver's hair away from his face, revealing the bland set to his features. "Is he not?"

"No." I ignored the quiet huffing sound that Delano made as I rose. "None of the wolven are mine." I glanced up at him. "The wolven belong to no one but themselves. The same goes for you and the other draken."

There was a pause. "You sound a lot like...*her*."

Noting the softening of his tone, I looked up at him, opening my senses. As before, I felt nothing. In my chest, the essence of the gods hummed, and the urge to push, to see if I could shatter his walls was almost as hard to resist as not throwing a rock at him had been. "The Consort?"

A brief smile appeared, and my gods, it was a breathtaking transformation. The chilly hollowness to his features vanished, turning him from someone uniquely appealing to a stunning, otherworldly beauty. "Yes. You remind me very much of the...*Consort.*"

The way he said that was more than a little odd, but I thought of what Nektas had said. A reminder that this wasn't just about *him*. "Will the Consort really wake upon Ires's return?"

"Yes."

"And what does that mean for the other gods?" *For us*, I wanted to add, but I wasn't sure if I truly wanted to know the answer to that at the moment.

"I imagine they will eventually wake."

I wondered why the Consort being awake had anything to do with the other gods. Or if it really had to do with Nyktos—that if his Consort had to sleep, he chose to be with her, which caused the other gods to sleep. I was also tired of calling her the Consort. "What's her name?"

His smile vanished, and his features sharpened as he stared down at me from his perch. "Her name is a shadow in the ember, a light in the flame, and the fire in the flesh. The Primal of Life has forbidden us to speak or write her name."

Disbelief flooded me. "That sounds incredibly controlling."

"You don't understand. To speak her name is to bring the stars from the skies and topple the mountains into the sea."

My brows inched up my forehead. "That's a bit dramatic."

Reaver said nothing. Instead, he rose so quickly I didn't have a chance to even look away. Thankfully, I saw nothing I shouldn't see because tiny silvery sparks erupted all along his body as he leapt from the pillar and *changed*. My mouth dropped open as a long, spiked tail formed, and then purplish-black scales appeared. Thick, leathery wings unfurled from the shimmer of light, briefly blocking out the muted glare of the sun. Within seconds, a draken swept through the air, high above.

A springy, featherlight sensation brushed against my thoughts as I stared up. *As I said before and will likely say again,* Delano's voice whispered, *he's an odd one.*

"Yeah," I said, drawing the word out. "What do you think about what he said, though? About what would happen if we spoke the Consort's name?"

I really don't know, he answered as we started across the foundation. *Could she be that powerful? As powerful as Nyktos? Because that's what it sounded like.*

It really did, but none were more powerful than Nyktos. Or his equal. Not even the Consort. I didn't like thinking that, but it was what it was.

Delano stayed at my side as we crossed the ruins, carefully making our way through the wispy reeds and broken stone toward the small group headed our way. Emil and the dark-haired Perry, whose skin was a warm brown in the sun that broke through the pines, flanked Kieran. The wolven was the only one who didn't wear the gold and steel armor—because of...*reasons*.

Kieran carried something. A small box. As we drew closer, Reaver landed among the wildflowers, shaking the nearby half-standing walls. His horned head swiveled in the direction of the approaching group. Emil and Perry wisely gave Reaver a wide berth while Kieran ignored the draken's presence.

I knew something had happened the moment I saw the tension bracketing Kieran's mouth, but I picked up nothing from him.

His emotions were shielded, and that wasn't normal at all.

I looked at the others more closely. There was no half-wild grin or teasing glint in Emil's golden eyes either. Tart uneasiness drifted from Perry. When Emil didn't pause to make an elaborate display of kneeling, the unease tripled.

I glanced at the box again, and everything in me slowed. My heart.

My breathing. The wooden box was no bigger than the length of the wolven dagger sheathed to my thigh but adorned with blood-red rubies. "What's that?"

"A Royal Guard brought it to the Rise of Massene," Emil answered, his knuckles bleached white from clutching the hilt of his sword. "He was alone. Said he traveled day and night from the capital. All he had was that small chest. He said it was for the Queen of Atlantia, from the Queen of Solis."

The back of my neck tightened. "How did she know we were here?" I looked between them. "There's no way word could've traveled to Carsodonia that quickly."

"Good question," Kieran said. "It would be impossible for her to know."

But she did.

My gaze flicked to the box once more. "And where is the Royal Guard now?"

"Dead." An icy blast accompanied Emil's lingering shock. "As soon as he finished speaking, he stood right there and slit his damn throat wide open. I'd never seen anything like that."

"That doesn't bode well." Tiny bumps erupted all over my skin as my gaze fell to the wooden box. A gift? "Have you opened it?"

Kieran shook his head. "The Royal Guard said only your blood could open it."

I frowned as Reaver stretched his long neck, eyeing what Kieran held.

"He had to be talking about old magic—Primal magic." Perry's handsome features were drawn tight by tension. "If one knew how to use Primal magic, they could create wards or spells that would work in a way that only responded to certain blood or bloodlines. They could use the magic for almost anything, really."

"It's the same kind of Primal magic that created the Gyrms," Kieran reminded me.

I suppressed a shudder at the image of the faceless creatures made of eather and dirt that were conjured forth. The Unseen had created them, but it was now abundantly clear that the Blood Queen had gained knowledge of the old magic—how to tap into the Primal essences that created the realms and was around us at all times.

My muscles tensed even further as I stared at the box. Malec would've known all about old Primal magic that was now forbidden. "What am I supposed to do? Cut a vein and bleed on it?"

"Let's not cut a vein open," Kieran advised.

"A drop or two of your blood will probably suffice," Perry suggested as Delano moved between us, brushing against the Atlantian's legs. Perry reached down, running his hand along the length of Delano's back.

"How do you know so much about Primal magic?" I asked as I reached for the box. Kieran held on, clearly reluctant to let go. My gaze flew to his, my senses opening. Then I felt something from him. It was tart in the back of my throat. Unease. A muscle flexed in his jaw as he let go of the surprisingly lightweight box.

"My father," Perry answered, and I thought of Lord Sven as I turned, looking for a flat surface on which to place the box. I found a portion of wall that stood about waist high. "He's always been fascinated with the old Primal magic, collecting anything written about it that he could get his hands on." There was a rough chuckle. "Spend any amount of time with him, and he'll start telling you how there used to be spells that could guarantee a successful yielding of crops or make it rain."

"Has he ever tried to use Primal magic?" I sat the box on the flattest section of a nearby wall.

"No, Your Highness."

A shaky breath left me as I glanced at Perry. "You don't have to call me that. We're friends."

"Thank you, Your—" He caught himself with a faint smile. "Thank you, Penellaphe."

"Poppy," I whispered absently.

"*Poppy*," Perry repeated with a nod. "My father, he wouldn't dare anger the Arae or even the sleeping gods by using such magic."

"The Arae?" It took a moment for the image of Priestess Analia and the heavy tome called *The History of The War of Two Kings and the Kingdom of Solis* to creep into my thoughts. I remembered. "The Fates."

"Yes," Perry confirmed.

I remembered Tawny and I once talking about them, and the whole idea of beings that could either see or control the outcome of the lives of every living creature seemed utterly unbelievable to both of us. But then again, I hadn't believed in Seers or prophecies either.

I turned back to the box. "Lord Sven's knowledge of Primal magic may come in handy. He'll be arriving with Valyn, won't he?"

"Yes."

Kieran stepped in close, his earthy scent surrounding me,

reminding me of the woods between Castle Teerman and the city Atheneum. "I don't know about this, Poppy." He touched my arm. "There could be anything in that box."

"I doubt she placed a venomous viper in there," I replied as I tugged the glove off my left hand, shoving it into the pocket of my sweater coat.

"She could've placed any manner of venomous or poisonous things in that box," he countered, his voice low. "I don't like this."

"I don't either, but…" I turned my left hand over, revealing the golden swirl across my palm. The marriage imprint. Then I withdrew the wolven dagger from its sheath. "I need to know." I lowered my voice as I met Kieran's stare. "I *have* to."

The hard press of his mouth tightened, but he nodded. Reaver's shadow fell over us as he watched. The bloodstone shone a deep red as I quickly dragged the tip of the sharp blade over my thumb. I gritted my teeth at the brief, stinging pain. Blood welled as I sheathed the dagger.

"Where do you think I should place my blood?" I asked, my hand steady.

"I would try the latch in the center," Perry suggested, inching closer.

I didn't hesitate, smearing my blood over the small metal latch shaped very much like a keyhole—without a hole. I pulled my hand back and waited.

Nothing happened.

Perry leaned in. "Maybe try—"

Then *something* happened.

A faint, reddish-black *shadow* seeped out from the seam as the box cracked open. Emil cursed…or maybe said a prayer. I wasn't sure. He lurched forward as Kieran threw out his arm as if he sought to edge me away, but the rippling shadow quickly disappeared. The Atlantian halted as the lock unlatched with a click, and the lid cracked open.

My stomach dipped. In the back of my mind, I acknowledged that the sight of such a thing a year ago would've had me backing up and praying to gods I had no idea still slept. I reached for the box.

"Careful," Kieran murmured, his hand now hovering near mine.

I had a feeling if a viper *did* spring out of the box, Kieran would catch it with his bare hands.

And I would also scream.

Slowly, I lifted the lid the rest of the way. A pillow of crimson satin appeared within, and nestled in the center was—

I jerked back, stumbling. Icy shock coated my throat. No one spoke. No one else moved. Not even Kieran, who stared into the box, his hand still hovering over it. Not even me.

My heart started pounding. My breath quickened. Kieran's hand trembled and then closed into a fist.

The wedding band made in Spessa's End shone a lustrous gold, matching the one I wore.

ALWAYS AND FOREVER.

The same message was inscribed on both. Neither of us had removed our rings since the ceremony.

And this one hadn't been now, either, for it remained on the finger I had placed it on.

That was *his* ring.

That was *his* finger.

That was a piece of *him*.

Kieran shot forward, smacking a hand down on the lid, but I still saw what lay inside. I would never *not* see it. Not if I lived thousands of years. I wouldn't forget.

Piercing howls echoed from within Massene, shattering the stunned silence as I stared at the ruby-adorned box. Someone spoke, but I couldn't make sense of the words. The shock and bitter-tasting horror pressed against my humming skin. I had no chance to shut down my senses. My icy disbelief and anguish crashed into others', but it was what lay under the agony that choked me—the sour, suffocating churning of guilt that was mine. All mine.

Because I had caused this.

It had been my message that had antagonized the Blood Queen. My hand that held the blade that'd severed King Jalara's head. My actions that had guided the Blood Queen's hand. I had taken the risk, believing she wouldn't harm him. Not when she needed him. I'd been mistaken.

I had brought this onto *him*.

The crack in my chest was a crevice that fractured and broke wide open. The flood of eather spilled from the chasm, brimming with unfettered rage and endless agony. The charged energy hit the air around me. Ancient power surged, rising once more, deep from the agony, absolute and final. A silvery-white aura crowded the corners of my vision as I sparked light and…

Tendrils of dark light arced and pulsed through the silvery aura as the eather manifested around me. Light lanced with shadows gathered near the ground, churning around my legs.

Delano edged Perry back—*away* from me. The wolven sank low to the ground, his ears flattening as Reaver stretched his head to the sky, emitting a strange, staggered sound.

In the back of my mind, I knew I was making them uneasy—that the raw anguish was calling the wolven to me. I might even be scaring them, and I didn't want that. But all…

All I saw was his ring—his *finger* in that box.

I shuddered, and from that cold, hollow fracture in my chest, icy wrath and vengeance poured out.

That was all I became.

Not Poppy.

Not the former Maiden and now the Queen of Atlantia.

There would be no more waiting. No carefully laid plans. No hesitation or thought. I would tear through Solis, sweeping across the kingdom like the plague *she* was. No city would be left standing. I would rip the Blood Forest apart to find her precious Malec, and then I would send her the gift of *her* love in tiny *pieces*. There would be no place for her to run. Nowhere she could find shelter.

I would lay waste to the entire realm *and* her.

Turning stiffly, I splayed my fingers wide as I started walking toward Cauldra Manor—toward the waiting horizon of Oak Ambler. The reeds and tall stems of lavender parted, shrinking back. The pines trembled.

"Poppy!" a voice shouted, and my head snapped in the direction of the sound. The wolven halted a few feet from me, his wide eyes fixed on me, the blue now luminous, his pupils no longer black but glowing a silvery-white. "Where are you going?"

"Carsodonia," I spoke, and my voice was full of…smoke and shadow. Full of death and fire. "I'm going to slice every finger from the Blood Queen's hands, one by one. I'm going to peel the flesh from her body." A shiver of anticipation swirled over my skin. "Then I will rip her tongue from her mouth and tear her eyes from her face."

"That sounds like a damn good plan." Kieran's voice had changed, too, roughening as he took a step toward me. "And I want to be right there beside you when you do it. I would love nothing more than to help you."

"Then help me." My voice…it *slithered* with the wind, carrying far as the shadow-laced light rippled along the ground. Through the tall, bushy weeds and flowers, sleek, dark shapes raced toward us. The wolven. They too would swarm the cities, a sea of claws and teeth and death. "You can all help me."

"We can't," Kieran said, the tendons in his neck standing out in stark relief. "You can't. You can't do this."

I stopped. Everything stopped. The faint trembling under my feet. The wolven, who halted in their tracks. I stared at the one before me. "I *can't?*"

He stretched his neck, his chest rising and falling. "No, you can't."

My head tilted. "You think you can stop me?"

A dry laugh rattled his body. "Fuck, no. But that doesn't mean I won't try. Because I can't let you do this." He edged closer, foolishly brave. Foolishly *loyal*. Because he wasn't just a wolven. My fingers curled inward as I forced myself to focus on Kieran, on what he was saying. On what he meant to me. Advisor. Friend. More in the past weeks. "I know you're in pain. That you hurt and are angry. You're afraid for Cas—"

The silver-tinged shadows pulsed around me. *Cas. He* loved it when I called him Cas. Had said only those he trusted most called him that. That it reminded him that he was a person. I shuddered, the back of my throat burning with the rage, the guilt, and the agony.

Kieran was within reach now, mere inches from the swirling mass of power radiating from me. Tension had gathered in him, tightening the lines of his face. "You want to make her pay for what she did. I do, too. We all do. But if you do this—if you go anywhere like *this*—people will die. Innocents you want to help. People Cas wants to protect."

Fiery anguish twisted my chest. *Cas.* Who was protecting *him*? No one. A tremor coursed through me, hitting the ground. The pines shook harder. "I don't care."

"Bullshit. You care. Cas cares," he said, and I flinched. Not at the sound of the name but at the truth. "That's what both of you have been trying to avoid. That's why we have plans. But if you do this? Those you don't kill will be terrified of you—of all of us. If they even saw you like this now, they would never see you as anything else."

I glanced down at the whirling shadows and the light dancing over my skin. *In* my skin. The next breath I took was too tight. "She *hurt* him."

"I know. Gods, I know, Poppy. But there will never be peace if you do this," he rasped, his lips pressing back against his teeth. "Even if you destroy the Blood Crown and end the Rite, you will become what mortals *and* Atlantians fear, and you will never forgive yourself."

I felt no fear from him as he lifted his hands, piercing the thrumming aura of power around me without hesitation. What bloomed in the back of my throat, easing the burn building there, was soft and sweet. The eather slipped over his hands and crawled up his forearms as his palms pressed against my cheeks—against the ragged scar along my left one.

His hands...they trembled. "What you're feeling is you, but what you want to do isn't. It's *her*. It's something the Blood Queen would do. It's something she'd want you to do. But you are not her."

I wasn't anything like her.

I wasn't cruel or abusive. I didn't take pleasure in others' pain. I didn't lash out in anger...

Actually, I did tend to lash out with sharp objects when angry, but I wasn't *spiteful*. I wouldn't have done what she had, taking all the pain and hurt she felt after the loss of Malec and their son, all that hatred toward the former Queen of Atlantia, and turning it on not just Eloana's sons but also an entire kingdom—an entire *realm*.

And that would be exactly what I'd be doing. I'd leave nothing but haunting graveyards behind. And I wouldn't be like my mother.

I would be something far worse.

Kieran's hands shook. His entire body rattled as if the ground were shaking, but it was him.

Concern rose, beating back the brutal tide of emotions. "W-why are you shaking? Am I hurting you?"

"No. It's the...it's the *notam*," he bit out. "It's making me want to shift. I'm fighting it."

My gaze searched the taut lines of his face. "Why is it making you want to do that?"

A strained chuckle left him. "Do you think that's an important question right now?" He gave me a short shake of his head. "Because I can protect you better in that form. And, yes, I know you don't need our protection, but the *notam* recognizes the kind of emotion you feel as a—a call of alarm. I...I don't think I can fight it much longer."

My attention darted over his shoulder to where I saw the forms of many wolven among the weeds. There was no way all of them could've already been in their wolven forms. They had been compelled to do that.

I'd forced them, and that made my stomach hurt.

Ice drenched my skin, and the chill quelled the fire. I squeezed my eyes shut. Control. I needed *control*. There was no threat to me. The one at risk was in Carsodonia. Losing it did absolutely nothing to help him, and Kieran was right. I repeated that over and over. I hadn't spent the past weeks planning for how to keep people safe only to turn around and be the cause of thousands, if not millions of deaths.

That wasn't me.

That wasn't who I ever wanted to become.

Another shudder rocked me as the vibrations in my chest eased and the hum receded from my skin. The rage was still there, as was the guilt and agony, but the wrath and the hunger for vengeance was banked, returning to those cold, empty places inside me where I feared it may fester.

"It's okay," Kieran said, and I was slow to realize that he wasn't speaking to me. "Just give us some time, all right?" There was a pause, and then he moved close as he guided my head down to his chest. I didn't fight it, welcoming the warmth and the familiar, earthy scent. He spoke about the box, about what was in it. He cleared his throat. "Don't tell anyone about it. No…no one needs to know."

Someone neared us, and Kieran's hand slid to the back of my head as the other left my cheek. "Thank you," he said.

In the quiet that followed, a rush of wings brought a gust of lavender-scented air. A few moments later, something brushed against my legs. *Delano*. I kept my eyes closed tightly against the sting. I wanted to tell him that I was sorry if I'd worried or scared him, but I couldn't get the words past the knot in my throat. Kieran's chin lowered, resting on the top of my head. The quiet went on for some time.

And then Kieran said in a low voice, "You scared me a little, Poppy."

Pressure clamped down on my chest. "I'm sorry. I didn't mean to."

"I know you didn't." His chest rose against mine. "I wasn't scared of you. I was afraid *for* you," he added. "I…I've never seen that before. The shadows in the eather. And your voice? It was different. Like it was when you spoke to Duke Silvan."

"I don't know what any of that was." I swallowed thickly.

"Your abilities are still changing. Growing," he said, making me think of what Reaver had shared.

Was this—the shadows in the eather—a new manifestation due to me still going through the Culling? I didn't know. And at the moment, I couldn't spare the energy required to dwell on it.

"You know he's still alive," Kieran said after a couple of moments. Thoughts of the ever-changing abilities faded. "The imprint is still on your palm. He lives."

I closed my left hand, pressing it to Kieran's chest. "But she…" I couldn't finish.

"He's strong. You know that."

Gods, I *did* know that. But it didn't change what was done to him. "He has to be in so much pain, Kieran."

"I know, but he will get past this. I know it. And you will get past this." His hand tightened in my loose braid of hair. "He is still yours. You are still his."

Tears stung my throat, my eyes. "Always," I whispered hoarsely. I forced myself to take a deep, steady breath. "Thank you for…for stopping me."

"You don't have to thank me for that."

"I do." I lifted my head, and his hand fell to the middle part of my braid. "And I am sorry about worrying you—worrying all of them. I just…I lost it."

"Anyone would, Poppy." Kieran slid his arm away and brought his hand up so it was between us. He took my left hand and pressed something cool and hard into my palm. My breath snagged because I knew what he'd put in my hand. "In case you don't know this, no matter what's done to Cas, he won't regret his choice."

I tried to swallow again, to stop the words from coming, but I couldn't. "I do. I regret it every moment I—" A soul-crushing sense of loss rose once more, stealing my breath. It took everything in me not to collapse under it and let all the rage and pain consume me once more. To lash out and inflict all that ate away at me onto anyone who stood in my way.

To unleash all the pain until nothing but bone and blood remained.

"Why did he do it, Kieran? Why?" I whispered, my voice catching.

Kieran squeezed my hand. "You know why. The same reason you'd do just as he did if someone was hurting him."

Gods, I did know the answer. A tremor coursed through me. I would've done anything. Because I loved him. Because he was mine, and I was his. My other half. A part of me, even though I hadn't spoken his name in many weeks. I barely allowed myself to even think it because it hurt.

But his name was love.

It was power and strength.

It would never break me.

Casteel. A shattered breath left me. *Casteel.* I made myself say it over and over in my mind. *Casteel Hawkethrone Da'Neer.* My chest felt as if a bolt were tearing through it all over again, but I said his name to myself until it no longer made me want to scream. Until I could say, "Casteel isn't lost to us."

"No. He's not," Kieran agreed, slipping his hand away from mine.

Slowly, I opened my fist. His…Casteel's ring rested in my palm, strong and beautiful. There wasn't a trace of blood on it. Either Emil or Perry had wiped it clean when they took it from the box. "What did they do with the…?" I couldn't bring myself to say it.

"It's up to you." Kieran's voice was hoarse. "You can burn or bury it. Or one of us can. You don't ever have to see it again. You don't need to, Poppy. There's no reason to."

I didn't want to see it again. Forcing myself to do so did nothing but inflict damage. Glancing up at Kieran, I sensed that he had his emotions locked down once more. I knew he did it so it wouldn't add to what I was feeling.

Kieran was…he was too good.

"Burn it," I forced myself to say. "But I don't want you to do it. I don't want you anywhere near it."

He inhaled sharply and nodded.

I squeezed the ring. *Always and forever.* "Was there anything else in the box?"

"A card."

"Did you have a chance to see it?"

"Only briefly."

"What did—?" My stomach twisted with nausea. "What did it say?"

"It said that she was sorry to have caused you any pain," he told me.

There was something so, *so* wrong with her. But at once, I knew what I needed to do. I knew what had to come next.

Because I could no longer wait.

When I took my next breath, it was easier. "We have plans—ones that are important to Solis and Atlantia." The next words were hard to speak, even though they were true. "Plans that are bigger than...Casteel and me."

Kieran said nothing, but I knew he agreed. Even if Casteel stood beside me now, there would still be the Blood Crown. The Rites would continue. Children would be stripped away from their families, either to Ascend or become nothing more than cattle to the Ascended. Innocent people would still be murdered. Atlantia would still run out of land and resources.

All of this was bigger than us.

The Blood Crown had to be destroyed.

I brought the ring close to my chest as I lifted my stare to Kieran. "But Casteel is more important to me. I know that's wrong. I know I shouldn't think that, let alone say it out loud, but it's the truth."

Kieran said nothing, but he'd gone completely still.

"She's not going to release him." A breeze caught the loosened strands of my hair, tossing them across my face. "She will hurt him again." Anger flared inside me, threatening to ignite once more. "You know that she could be doing anything to him right now. You know what it did to him last time."

His jaw clenched. "I do."

"I can't let her have him for weeks and months. And that's how long it will take for us to take the Atlantian armies across Solis. Casteel doesn't have that kind of time. We don't have that kind of time."

Kieran stared down at me. "I know what you're thinking. You want to go to Carsodonia."

"*After* we take Oak Ambler," I amended. "The Blood Crown needs to be destroyed, and we need to do it the right way. I need to be here to convince Valyn and the generals that our plan is the right one. I need to be here to see that through."

"And then?"

"And then I will go to Carsodonia, and you will lead the armies to the other cities."

His pale blue eyes hardened. "And if you're captured in the process?"

"It's a risk I'm willing to take. I'll be fine. Isbeth doesn't want me dead," I reasoned. "If that was what she wanted, she had ample opportunity to do so. She...she needs me if she seeks to control Atlantia. This is what I need to do."

Kieran folded his arms over his chest. "I agree."

My brows flew up. "You do?"

"I do. Cas needs to be freed, but there's one problem with your plan. Actually," he said, frowning, "there are a lot of problems. Starting with the fact that I doubt you even have a plan beyond walking up to Carsodonia's Rise."

I opened my mouth and then snapped it shut. His look turned knowing. Frustration bore down on me. "I will come up with a plan that doesn't involve me walking up to the Rise of Carsodonia. I'm not a fool, Kieran."

"You're a fool if you think I'll be anywhere other than by your side," he shot back. "There's no way in hell you're going to Carsodonia without me."

"It's too dangerous—"

"Are you kidding me?"

"It's too dangerous for anyone else to go."

He stared down at me. "You do realize that we're at war? Therefore, any number of us, including me, could die."

I stiffened as the statement knocked the air from my chest. "Don't say that—"

"It's the truth, Poppy. All of us know the risks, and we're not here just for you. He is our King." He met my glare with his own. "Also, I don't believe that once you have a couple of minutes to think about this, you won't seriously reconsider taking on the entire damn Blood Crown by yourself."

Maybe he was right. But at the moment, I really wanted to. "Okay, I won't go alone. I will see who wants to make the trip with me. But I need you here. I trust you to make sure Valyn and the others follow our plans. Because there can be no truce this time. No stalemate. I trust you to make sure there is a chance for peace when we destroy the Blood Crown. As the Advisor to the Crown, they have to follow your orders."

"I appreciate your trust. Am honored. Flattered. Whatever," he said, and I didn't think he sounded honored at all. "But you can trust others to ensure that our plans are carried out."

"I do trust others. Your sister. Naill. Delano. Emil—I could keep listing names. But they hold no position of authority like you do as the advisor. You are an extension of the Crown. You speak on behalf of the King and Queen. None of the others have that kind of authority."

"But any of them can," he insisted. "You can make one of them a regent—a person that you, as the Queen, can appoint. Someone who will act on your behalf in your absence. Normally, that would be the Advisor to the Crown, but there is no law that states it has to be the advisor. The Crown Regent would temporarily act on your behalf, and their word must be followed no differently than if it were you issuing the orders."

"Oh." I blinked. "I...didn't know that. But—"

"There is no but."

"*But* there is." Panic started to creep in. "If something were to happen to you—"

"There would be nothing for Cas to forgive you for if something did," he cut me off. "He would expect nothing less than me being by your side."

I stared at him in disbelief. "If you'd let me finish a sentence, I was about to say *I* would never forgive myself."

His stare softened. "And I would never forgive myself if you went into the heart of the Ascended without me." He clasped the back of my neck. "Just as I haven't for letting Cas go all those years ago."

Oh, gods. "*Kieran*—"

"Don't forget what he means to me, Poppy. I've known him my whole damn life," he said. "We shared the same crib more times than not. We took our first steps together. Sat at the same table most nights, refusing to eat the same vegetables. We explored tunnels and lakes, pretended that fields were new, undiscovered kingdoms. We were inseparable. And that didn't change as we grew older." His voice roughened, and he dropped his forehead to mine. "He was and still is a part of me."

I closed my eyes against the burn accompanying the images that his words brought forth. Them toddling about together, Kieran on two legs and four. Holding each other as they napped. Coming home covered in dirt and the gods only knew what else.

"Where I went, Cas was there. Where he traveled, I followed. The only time we have ever been separated and couldn't get back to one another was when they held him captive—and now. But I was there for him afterward. I watched him night after night, waking in a panic and thinking that he was back in that cell. I saw what had been done to him. How he couldn't stand to be touched at one point. How even the sight of bathwater caused him to freeze up."

"Bathwater?" I asked, half afraid.

"They wanted him clean when they wanted him."

Oh, gods.

Nausea churned. I shook, caught between rage and despair and shock because my mother had been one of his abusers. How could Casteel even look at me—?

I stopped myself from going down *that* path. He knew who I was.

"What he means to me has nothing to do with a damn bond," Kieran said. "I need to go as badly as you do, and he needs me there just as badly as he needs you."

Casteel did need Kieran.

"I'm sorry," I croaked. "I forgot."

"It's understandable that you would."

"No, it's really not." My grief was mine, and it was potent. But it was no more devastating than what Kieran or anyone else who cared for Casteel was experiencing. "I won't forget it again."

Kieran's forehead slid against mine as he nodded. "We're on the same page then."

"We are." I blinked back tears.

"Then who will be Crown Regent, *meyaah Liessa?*"

It was hard to focus when all I wanted to do was hug Kieran and sob. I wanted to sit down and have a good cry, but there wasn't time for that.

I pulled away, forcing myself to think over what Kieran had suggested. Worrying my lower lip, I looked down at my closed hand. The ring had warmed to my skin. I didn't know what kind of shape Casteel would be in when I found him. He could be okay or not, but he would want Kieran to be with me and to be there for him. It couldn't be just Kieran and me or a handful of others. No Queen would travel across a realm without guards. But we needed the fire of the gods.

"I saw Reaver in his mortal form earlier."

Kieran arched a brow. "That...was random."

"He's blond."

"Thanks for sharing?"

"He was also completely naked while perched on a pillar," I added.

"I don't even know what to say to that."

"Me, neither," I murmured. "But the point is, we need to bring a draken with us. They can help. Not just with...with Casteel but also with my father. Nektas wants him back."

"I agree." He paused. "But I have a feeling I won't like what you're about to suggest. To bring Reaver with us. The other draken will be here soon. Aurelia shifted—"

"For only a few minutes. I at least know Reaver feels comfortable enough in his mortal form to do it for longer than that."

"Great." Kieran appeared as if he'd rather face down an army of skeleton soldiers again.

"He'll need clothing."

"Don't know why you're telling me this."

"You two appear to be about the same size."

Kieran stared at me and then cursed. "Whatever. I'll see what I have."

I grinned, and it incited a confusing mix of emotions. It felt odd. Even a little wrong. But it was also a relief to know that I could still find humor despite what I held in my hand.

Then I remembered what else Reaver had told me. "This may not be the best moment to bring this up, but when I talked to Reaver, I found out that I will have to feed eventually. And, apparently, because I'm a god, I can feed off anyone. Except the draken. Even mortals. Who knew?" I said, then told him what Reaver believed about how often I would need to feed. "But there's more. It seems using eather can weaken me. He doesn't know how much I can use before it has an effect. I don't think it includes anything I was able to do before—"

"Does feeding off anyone mean you can feed off wolven?" he cut in.

"Yes. Wolven would fall under the everything-but-a-draken umbrella."

"Then feed off me if you need to."

I sucked in a sharp breath. "Kieran—"

"I know you don't want to feed off anyone but Cas," he said, and the breath I took withered. "And I know that feedings can get...intense, but you'll be safe with me." His eyes searched mine. "You know damn well that Cas wouldn't want you feeding off anyone but me."

A strangled laugh left me. Casteel would probably rip the limbs off whoever I fed from—anyone but Kieran, anyway—leaving them alive only because he knew the blood was necessary for me.

"It's not that," I said, shoving a strand of hair back from my face. Feedings could be intense, and I wasn't sure if feeding off someone might cause the same kinds of wicked pleasure a bite could bring. But it wasn't that—well, it wasn't *completely* that. I hadn't even begun to wrap my head around the possibility that me feeding off someone other than my husband could bring them pleasure.

Could bring *me* pleasure.

And I wasn't about to start thinking about that right now. "I don't want you to feel as if you have to offer yourself."

"I don't offer because I *have* to." Kieran squeezed the back of my neck. "I offer because I *want* to."

"Really? You sure that's not the *notam*? That it's not your friendship with Casteel?"

"It could be partly because of the *notam*. And it is because of my friendship with Cas. But it's also my friendship with *you*. None of those things are mutually exclusive," he told me. "I would offer the same to Cas. I would offer the same to anyone I cared about. Just like I know you would for me if I needed that."

My breath stung. I *would* offer myself if he needed to feed, and the reminder of how far Kieran and I had come rattled me in an entirely different way. I was pretty sure he hadn't liked me when we first met. Or, at the very least, I'd annoyed him to no end. But now...? I blinked back the dampness gathering in my eyes.

Kieran started to frown. "Are you about to cry?"

"No."

"Doesn't look that way."

"Then stop looking, and it won't."

"That doesn't even make sense, Poppy."

A burst of sugary amusement gathered on the tip of my tongue. I glared at him. "This isn't funny."

"I know it shouldn't be." His lips twitched. "But it kind of is."

"Shut up," I griped.

The grin appeared briefly. "We're on the same page, right? When you need to feed, you'll come to me?" All traces of humor were gone now. "And you won't let it get to a point where you're weakened?"

"We're on the same page."

His hold on the back of my neck firmed once more. "What about the regent?"

A few moments passed. "Vonetta. I would make Vonetta the Crown Regent."

Approval hummed as he let his walls down around him, tasting of buttery cakes. "Good choice."

I nodded. "You know how to get into Carsodonia, right? I doubt you and Casteel walked through the gates of the Rise."

He snorted. "No. We went in through the Elysium Peaks."

My stomach dropped all the way to the tips of my toes. The Peaks were vast—all one could see to the west and south of Carsodonia. And they extended into the Willow Plains. They'd even built the Rise into the— It struck me then. "You all went in through the mines."

Kieran nodded. "The entrances to the mines are right inside the Rise. The tunnels are guarded, but not like the gates. Of course, that was also how Malik got in there. It was how Casteel and..." His mouth tightened. "That was how Shea got him out of Carsodonia. From there, he ended up on the beaches of the Stroud Sea."

Shea. There'd been anger before when I thought of her. Now, there was only sadness.

"Can we get out the same way we get in once we find Casteel and my father?"

Kieran nodded. "We could. But, Poppy, it will take time to get out of those mines. Besides the likelihood of them guarding those entrances now, Cas was in them for a while, searching for a way out. He may have made it sound like it took no time, but it did."

"Gods," I whispered, heartsick over a past I couldn't change. "Is there a better way?"

"Besides going through the gates in disguise, no. If we get caught in the mines, we can fight our way out and then disappear into the city far easier than if they discover us at the gates."

That was true. Carsodonia was a maze of narrow streets and vine-covered alleys that ran through districts and neighborhoods sprawled across rolling hills and valleys.

He took a breath. "I don't know how to say this other than to just say it. We don't know what kind of shape Cas will be in, but we know that your father will likely be worse off."

He didn't say anything else, but I knew what he meant. We couldn't free both of them.

"We will still free him," Kieran said quietly. "Freeing Cas doesn't end the war. We will have to go back to Carsodonia."

I nodded, hating the idea of being so close to my father and doing nothing. But he was right. Again.

"It's a plan, then?" Kieran asked.

"It is."

I took yet another breath, and it was less painful than all the ones before it because we would find and free Casteel. And I would make sure that any piece of him that he lost was found once more. He would know exactly who he was when I saw him again.

I would make sure of it.

Casteel

The relentless throbbing in my left hand had all but gone away, replaced by the gnawing ache that started in my gut and spread to my chest.

Tilting my head back, I managed a dry, scratchy-as-hell swallow and opened my eyes to the gloom of the cell. The flickering candles did very little to cast light, but it still caused my eyes to ache.

And that was a bad sign.

I needed… I had to feed.

I shouldn't. Not this soon after feeding from Poppy. That hadn't been too long ago, had it? We'd been on the ship, on the way to Oak Ambler. After I'd feasted on all that liquid heat between her pretty thighs as she read from Miss Willa's diary.

Damn. I loved that fucking book.

One side of my lips curled up. I could still hear her reading from the journal, her voice becoming breathier with each sentence, every lick. I could still see the flush in her cheeks, deepening with each paragraph, every wet kiss. The feeding had come after that when I'd tugged that luscious ass of hers to the edge of the desk, and my dick and fangs had sunk deep into soft, sweetly scented flesh, reminding me of a light mist of jasmine. Her blood…

Gods, nothing tasted like it—*nothing.*

I should've known the first time I tasted her that she was more than part Atlantian. The taste of her had been strong even then, too potent for someone only of Atlantian descent. But as she came into her power, especially after her Ascension? Her blood was a sultry aphrodisiac and produced a high stronger than any drug one could crush into a powder and smoke. My stare fixed on the candles, tracking the melting wax.

Her blood was pure power—the kind I instinctually knew I needed to be careful with. Because the taste of her, the way it made me feel, it could become the kind of addiction I would drown in.

The roof of my mouth throbbed as my mouth dried more. I could almost taste her now—ancient and earthy, thick and decadent.

Groaning, I bit out a harsh curse as I shifted. I needed to stop thinking about Poppy's blood. And I really needed to stop thinking about how she tasted between her thighs. A hard cock was so not appreciated at the moment.

How much time *had* passed? A couple of weeks? Close to a month? More? Time neither existed nor let up in the darkened cell, both an enemy and a savior. But so far, it hadn't been *that* bad. Last time, I may have escaped with all my limbs and appendages intact, but that was about all.

But what was a killer was the damp, dark quiet and the worry. The fear. Not for me. But for her. Last time, there had been Shea. And I had worried about her because I cared. I'd worried for my family then. But this was different. Poppy was out there, at *war*, and the need to have her back, to protect her even though she needed no protection, raked at my flesh with sharp, taunting nails.

Dull pain settled into my brow and temples as I squinted, letting my head roll away from the candlelight. I could go months without feeding if necessary. It was a risk to push it that long, but I could. Though, normally, I was actually eating enough to keep my energy levels up and didn't have my blood siphoned into small vials routinely.

Having the finger chopped off sure hadn't helped. I doubted the Craven bite did either.

I looked down at the bloodstained gauze wrapped around my hand and wondered if the Blood Crown had given up on using golden chalices. That was what they'd used to collect my blood before. I wiggled my fingers carefully. One of the Handmaidens had oh-so-kindly applied the bandage while that golden Rev named Callum had made sure I allowed it. Not that I would've stopped her. The damn stump of a finger bled like a stuck pig. Stains *still* streaked my chest and covered the thighs of my breeches. And every so often, fresh blood spread across the once-white and now-rust-colored wrappings, reminding me that the severed skin hadn't healed itself.

I wasn't as special as a Rev, who would've apparently grown the damn finger back. But the skin should've closed over the wound by now, at least.

Yet more proof that I needed to feed.

My gaze flicked to the metal hip bath that had been brought in at some point today by a small legion of Handmaidens. The damn thing had looked heavy as hell. They had filled it with steaming, hot water that had long since cooled. The Rev Callum had done something to lengthen the chain, allowing me to reach the tub and bathe.

Fuck that.

I knew better than to make use of it, even though I was beyond filthy. The bath was one of two things: a reward or a prelude to punishment. And since I hadn't done a damn thing to earn it, that left option two. The last time they'd offered me baths was when the Blood Queen's friends wanted to *play* with something fresh and clean. Something that didn't resemble a dirty, chained animal.

So, I would sit in my filth. Gladly.

I lowered my hand to my lap. The breeches were stiff with dried blood. Staring at my hand, seeing the dirtied bandages and what they meant, my heart thudded. Anger trenched itself deep, turning my cold skin feverish. I slammed my bare foot down on the damp, uneven stone. The act served no purpose other than to cause the shadowstone shackles to tighten and for my foot to throb.

I didn't give a fuck about the finger. My entire hand could be gone for all I cared. It was the ring that was now gone that bothered me. It was what I knew that bitch had done with it and the finger.

She'd sent it to Poppy.

My right hand closed into a fist as my lips peeled back over my fangs. I would rip out her entrails and feed them to her because I couldn't…

Pressing my head back against the wall, I shut my eyes. Neither did anything to erase the knowledge that Poppy must have seen *that*. She had to know what that bitch had done, and there was nothing— absolutely, fucking *nothing*—I could do about it.

But she has Kieran. He would be there for her. And she would be there for him. Knowing that made it a little easier to breathe. To let go of some of the rigid tension in my body. They had each other, no matter what.

Slowly, I peeled back the edge of the soiled gauze, just enough to reveal the faintly shimmering golden swirl across my palm. I exhaled roughly at the sight—at what it meant.

She lived.

I lived.

The sudden click of heels echoed through the dark hall outside the cell. Alert, I let go of the gauze and looked to the rounded entryway. The sound was strange. No one, not even the free-roaming Craven, made that much noise. The Handmaidens were like silent little worker bees. *Isbitch's* steps were much lighter, only audible when she was right near the cell. The damn golden Rev was generally as quiet as a wraith. This sounded like a barrat in heels—a barrat in heels that *hummed*—very poorly.

What the...?

A moment later, *she* swept into the cell, the clacking of her shoes almost overpowering whatever she was trying to hum. Or maybe she was actually groaning because the sound she made carried no tune. She held a lantern—well, she *swung* a lantern much like a child would, sending light dancing across the walls.

I recognized her immediately, even though I'd seen her only once, and reddish-black paint shaped like wings had covered her cheeks and most of her forehead as it did now. It was her height. She was shorter than the rest, and that stood out to me because I'd seen how easily she'd handled Delano, a wolven who was at least a foot and a half—if not more—taller than her in his mortal form. It was also her scent. Not the rotten blood smell I picked up from her, but something sweeter. It was familiar to me. I had even thought that when we'd been in Oak Ambler.

It was the Rev who had been at Castle Redrock. No one else followed her now. No Handmaidens. No Golden Boy. No Queen Bitch.

"Hello!" she chirped, giving me a rather jaunty wave as she plopped the lantern on a stone ledge halfway up the wall. Yellow light slowly beat back the shadows in the cell and drifted over the mess of tangled, inky black curls falling over her shoulders.

She turned to me, clasping her hands together. Her arms were bare, and I saw marks there—strange shapes that had to be drawn or inked onto her skin and not *in* her skin. "You don't look so well."

"And you can't hum for shit," I replied.

The Handmaiden stuck out her lower lip, pouting. "That was rude."

"I would apologize, but…"

"You don't care. It's okay. Don't worry. You're totally forgiven." She came forward, her steps far quieter now. My eyes narrowed. "I wouldn't care either if I was chained to a wall in an underground cell, all alone and—" She crouched before me, the sides of her gown parting to reveal a long, lethal dagger strapped to one thigh and a shorter dagger sheathed to the shaft of her boot. Both blades were black. Shadowstone. She gave the air a dainty sniff. "Stinky. You smell like rot. And not the fun kind that usually accompanies the Craven." She paused. "Or a night of bad life choices."

I stared at her.

Her gaze dropped to my bandaged hand. "I think you have an infection."

I probably did, but was it the hand or the Craven bite? "So?"

"So?" Her eyes widened behind the painted mask, causing the white to stand out starkly. "I thought you Atlantians didn't suffer from such mortal ailments."

"Do you expect me to believe that you haven't been around injured Atlantians before?" I held her stare. "That I'm the first you've seen here?"

"You're not the first, but I don't normally go near the Queen's pets."

My lips peeled back against my fangs. "I may be chained, but I am no pet."

The wing on the left side of her face rose as she lifted a brow. "I suppose not when you make such growly sounds. If so, you'd be the kind of pet one would need to put down."

"Is that why you're here?"

She laughed—and I stiffened. Her laugh. It sounded… "You are so suspicious. That's not why I'm here," she said, and I blinked, shaking my head. "Honestly, I'm kind of bored. And I made a promise." The Handmaiden rose swiftly, glancing at the hip bath. "If you think you're not in need of a bath, I hate to be the one to tell you, but you are."

"I have no plans to make use of that."

"Whatever. It's your life. Your stench."

"What kind of promise did you make?"

"An annoying one." The Handmaiden went to the other side of the hip bath and then lowered herself to her knees. She tapped her fingers over the surface of the water, creating small waves. "Though bathing may help with that wound of yours."

When I didn't answer, she tapped the water some more as she eyed me with those pale, barely blue eyes. "Is it because you need to feed?"

Could I feed off Revs? I didn't know if it would be the equivalent of feeding off a mortal. Hell, I wasn't sure if they were dead or alive. Or really what the fuck they were.

Her head tilted to the side, sending a mess of hair tumbling over an arm. "I bet that's it. Your brother gets cranky when he needs to feed."

Everything in me zeroed in on her. "Where is my brother?"

"Here. There. Probably everywhere instead of where he's supposed to be."

My jaw clenched because that sounded like the Malik I knew, but I was beginning to think that the process of becoming a Rev addled the brain and was why the other Handmaidens didn't speak. What was coming out of her mouth now was pure nonsense. "You must be around him a lot to know when he needs to feed."

Her head straightened. "Not really."

"Then that would be a strange thing to notice."

"I'm just observant." Those eyes... They were so dull, nearly lifeless. Fucking eerie to look upon for too long. "And I'm also not trying to get him killed, which would happen if I was around him a lot."

"Are Handmaidens not allowed to spend time with those of the opposite sex?"

She let out a not so delicate snort. "Handmaidens are allowed to fraternize with any members of any sex they see fit."

"Then is it because your Queen wants Malik all to herself?" My stomach churned.

"She has no interest in him." Her expression hadn't changed, but I noticed that she gripped the edges of the tub. Interesting. "Not in a long time."

I didn't believe that for one second.

The Handmaiden dipped her arm into the water and began scrubbing at her skin. The odd symbols were quick to disappear. She moved on to the other side.

"Did you know these tunnels and chambers have been here for hundreds and hundreds of years?" Rising from the tub, her fingers dripped water as she walked across the chamber. "They existed when the gods walked among men. Of course, they've been expanded, added to, and now travel the length of the city, but these walls…" She placed her palm against the damp stone. "These walls are ancient, and only a few have ever been allowed inside them."

I knew about the chambers underground beneath the Ascended's homes, but not any tunnels that traveled the length of the city. "I don't give a fuck about these walls."

"You should." She looked over her shoulder at me. "Gods walked these tunnels. As did the Primals. They walked other tunnels in other cities, connecting *doorways* and creating magical wards made of Primal essence that could keep things out—or *in*."

I watched her run her palm over the uneven stone, wondering exactly what in the hell she was talking about.

"A god born a mortal, carrying the blood of the Primal of Life and the Primal of Death upon Ascension was foretold," the Handmaiden whispered. "Or so they say—and they say a lot. Either way, *she* broke those Primal wards when she Ascended into her godhood."

It was clear that she was speaking about Poppy.

She rested her cheek against the wall. "And anything that was kept in can now get out." Eyes not so dull met mine. "Two questions remain. When and where. Not even he knows."

I didn't even know what to say to any of that, but I caught how her lip curled when she said *he*.

"Who?"

"Callum."

"The golden boy Rev?"

Her laugh was throatier, more real, and strangely familiar. "He's old. Real old. Be careful of that one."

"Fuck him." Impatient, I leaned forward—farther than usual because of the loosened chains. "What in the hell are you rambling on about? And what does it have to do with Poppy's Ascension?"

"I do ramble, don't I? Ian said Penellaphe rambles." She turned sharply, facing me as she leaned against the wall. "Is that true?"

My eyes narrowed. "Why? Why do you want to know that?"

Her shoulder lifted. "Just curious."

"Odd thing to be curious about."

"Is it true?" she persisted. "Does she ramble, too?"

I unlocked my jaw. "Her thoughts tend to wander about…out loud. Frequently and sometimes randomly."

The corners of her lips turned up as she toyed with an edge of stone by her hip. "I…I didn't know the Queen would do that to Ian. I—" Her jaw tightened. "I didn't expect that."

I believed her. Only because the look of shock on her face and on my brother's when that bitch had ordered Ian killed couldn't have been fabricated. "I would tell you that I would kill Isbeth for that, but my Queen is a *god*. She will kill her."

Her fingers stilled on the stone.

"Yeah, I figured that out in Oak Ambler," I told her. "She's going to kill that bitch for sure."

The faint smile returned, surprising me, and I didn't think anything could still surprise me. "I saw her afterward. Penellaphe."

My breathing. My heart… Stopped.

"I stayed behind, figuring she'd be angry upon waking. And she was. She came at Oak Ambler, and she is powerful. For a moment, I thought she was going to destroy the Rise and the entire city." She continued rubbing her fingers over the sharp edge of a stone. "But she stopped. Maybe she's not like her mother."

"She's not," I snarled. "There's no one like her."

"You're actually right when you say that." Her gaze flicked to me. "But you don't really know her. I doubt she even knows herself." Her chin dipped, and her stare chilled my skin. "She carries the blood of the Primal of Life and the Primal of Death."

"I know. She knows she's descended from Nyktos—"

"If you think that Granddaddy is the *true* Primal of Life and the *true* Primal of Death, then you know nothing."

My eyes narrowed. What was she up to? Nyktos *was* the true Primal of Life. The gods Rhain and Rhahar oversaw the dead, but Nyktos was the Primal. The King of Gods. That meant he was the true Primal of Death, too. "Then educate me."

"I'm not *that* bored." She pushed off the wall. "Plus, I have things to do. People to see. Kill. Whatever. I did as I promised." Turning, she started for the entrance but stopped. She looked down. "The Queen has her plans."

"The whole remaking the realms bullshit?"

"To remake something, one must first destroy it."

A cold wind hit the length of my spine. "The Blood Queen is not that powerful."

"She may not be." The Handmaiden's back was unnaturally stiff. "But she knew how to bring to life something that was."

Poppy

The conversation around me was nothing more than a hum as I sat in the receiving chamber. The others clustered around Hisa Fa'Mar, one of the Crown Guard's commanders, and the map of Oak Ambler she'd been working on.

Word of the remaining armies' advancement had come shortly after we returned to Cauldra Manor—in the form of nineteen draken cresting the Pinelands.

There had been a lot more running about and screaming from the locals. They'd only calmed when the draken had landed around Cauldra and in the pines surrounding the manor, doing nothing more than watching the mortals scurry about.

I couldn't help but wonder what the draken thought of the reaction. Had it been like that when they were awake before? Or had they been accepted? Then again, had they only remained in Iliseeum? I hadn't thought to ask Reaver.

Their arrival had momentarily distracted me from what I carried in the pocket of my sweater coat. The draken's arrival meant we could expect Valyn and the remaining armies tomorrow.

I exhaled long and slow. We were right on schedule. The day after tomorrow, we would take Oak Ambler, and then I would leave for Carsodonia.

For Casteel.

I'd met with Vonetta after the draken's chaotic arrival to speak about the Crown Regent position. She accepted, although she wasn't entirely happy about the idea of not joining Kieran and me. Still, I thought she looked forward to bossing some of the Atlantians around, especially a certain auburn-haired one, who would also remain with her.

I'd also spoken with Reaver about going to the capital. He'd been in his draken form and had nodded his large, horned head.

Vonetta and Naill were not among us now. They, along with Emil, had gone out into the pines to take care of what had been in that wooden box. But before that, we'd spent hours hashing out what was to come after seizing Oak Ambler.

We'd decided that moving with any type of large group would draw too much attention. Conversation grew...tense when I announced that only Kieran and Reaver would be traveling with me. None of the others were thrilled about that, each demanding they accompany us. But what we'd planned was too risky.

Isbeth wanted me alive.

That desire didn't extend to anyone else, and I already wasn't happy about endangering Reaver and Kieran. I wouldn't budge on this.

And being that I was Queen, I didn't have to.

Besides, I wanted Vonetta to have all the support possible in case she got any pushback. And given that Aylard wasn't part of any of these conversations, that was likely. She would have Naill and Delano, Emil and Perry, along with Hisa and the wolven, to support her. What she would be doing was just as important as what I would be embarking on.

What we all *did* agree on was that it was seriously unlikely that the Queen would hold Casteel in the same location as before. Isbeth was smarter than that.

Finding him would be one of the most difficult parts of our plan. Wayfair Castle itself was extraordinarily large, with similar underground chambers as Redrock. It was where I'd seen...my father when I was younger. But I didn't think Casteel would be held there, either. Explaining away what appeared to be a cave cat to a wandering noble or a young girl like me was easier than explaining a captive Atlantian King.

Then there was the Wayfair land with its gardens and grottos, sprawling estates, and protected forests. Not to mention the city itself, with its endless places to hide someone.

It would be like searching for a ghost.

Feeling the outline of the ring inside the pocket, I looked up to the hall.

All that you and those who follow will find here is death.

My fingers stilled as the Duke's words resurfaced. "Excuse me," I murmured, rising.

Both Kieran and Delano glanced over at me, but neither made any moves to follow. I knew one would eventually, though. I walked out into the drafty, dim hall and to the door at the other end of the manor.

I entered the small sitting area of the suite and into the bedchamber, sectioned off by heavy drapes. Moving to the small table, I saw the card from the box. I hadn't read it yet.

I did now.

BELOVED DAUGHTER,

IT PAINS ME TO KNOW THAT THIS GIFT WILL BRING YOU HEARTACHE. FOR THAT, I AM DEEPLY SORRY, BUT YOU LEFT ME NO CHOICE. WHAT'S DONE IS DONE. HE LIVES. DO NOT FORGET THAT WHILE WE LOOK TO THE MANY TOMORROWS TOGETHER BUT APART. THE FUTURE OF THE KINGDOMS AND THAT OF THE TRUE CROWN OF THE REALMS DEPENDS ON US.

LOVE,

MOTHER

The words didn't change, no matter how many times I read them. I didn't gain any sudden understanding of how she could do something like this and then apologize. Or how she could carry out such terrible deeds as if she had no control over them. She'd blamed me for Ian's death. And now, she blamed me for *her* hurting Casteel? I'd provoked her. I'd guided her hand. But it was still *her* hand.

Mother.

I couldn't believe she'd signed it that way.

Footsteps neared, and I looked up to see Vonetta sweeping the curtain that divided the chambers aside.

"Kieran said you were probably here," she said, letting the heavy cloth drift back into place. "It's been taken care of. We...burned it."

I inhaled through the sting. "Thank you."

"I wish you were thanking me for something else."

"Me, too," I said.

"Of course." Vonetta peered over my shoulder to look at the note. "There is something majorly wrong with that woman."

"I said the same earlier."

"It makes you wonder if she's always been like this. And if so, what in the hell did Malec see in her?"

"I don't know if she was always like this or if losing Malec and their son did this to her." I thought of what Reaver had said earlier. "I think it's possible that Malec was attracted to that."

"He seemed like a real gem," she replied, and a wry grin tugged at my lips. "I wanted to ask how you're dealing with...well, with everything related to her being your mother. But it's always seemed like a stupid question. You know? Like I know you're not *everything is fine* when it comes to her."

"It's not a stupid question."

"Really?" Two arched brows rose as she leaned against the wall.

I nodded. "To be honest, I don't know how I'm doing when it comes to her. All I know is that I...I don't think of her as my mother. Because she wasn't." I glanced down at the card. "I used to struggle with who she was to me and the monster she was to Casteel and everyone else. I don't anymore. Not after Ian." My chest tightened, and I swallowed. "You talked to him when he came to Spessa's End?"

"Yeah." Vonetta pressed her lips together. Several moments passed. "I haven't met a ton of Ascended. I can count the number I *have* on two hands. But he was nothing like I expected. He was polite— and not the fake kind. He was....*warm,* even if his skin wasn't. Does that make sense?"

Inhaling a shaky breath, I nodded.

"And he was kind of flirty, but not in a creepy way." A small smile appeared briefly. "When he came to Spessa's End, looking for you, the Guardians didn't want to let him leave, believing he was a threat. I watched over him, and he spent the time telling me a story about Stygian Bay and the Temples of Eternity—how many of the Temples in Solis had been around since the gods walked the realm. They weren't just places of worship but also places of profound power, able to neutralize gods. He also said they were gateways to Iliseeum, where gods ferried mortals through." She picked up a braid, running it between her fingers. "Which I don't think is remotely true. But what he said *was* interesting. He had a way of telling the story where you couldn't help but get invested in it. I mean, he had me totally hooked on this tale about a girl picking flowers who had been startled by a god, falling to her death from some cliff. Anyway, Ian told me that he used to tell you stories, too, when you were lonely or upset...or when he was bored—which he claimed was often."

I knew that story. Sotoria and the Cliffs of Sorrow. Ian had shared it with me in one of the letters he'd written after his Ascension. "He could spin tales at the drop of a hat. Take something common like an old, dull sword and transform it into one once wielded by the first mortal king." My laugh trembled. "He had the wildest imagination." I lifted my gaze to the gently rippling curtains over the windows. "I wonder if Coralena and Leo were his parents. But since she was a Revenant, I don't even know if she could *have* children. Hell, I'm not sure…" I opened my mouth, closed it, and tried again. "I don't know if my father was willing. If they put him in that cage before or after me."

Vonetta's disgust reached me, mirroring mine. "We will find him, too."

"We will." With my mind shifting from Ian to my father to…to Casteel, I summoned the eather, just a tiny spark that took little energy, then let it flick from my fingertips. There were no shadows in the silvery glow as it washed over the note. I let what remained of the card, nothing more than ash, fall from my fingers. "And we will make sure she cannot hurt anyone else."

8

I was dreaming.

Though not a nightmare from a long-ago night or one birthed from too-recent anguish and rage.

I knew that as soon as I drifted out of the nothingness of sleep and found myself in a different place. One that didn't even feel like something from a dream because every one of my senses was awake and aware.

Warm, churning water lapped at my waist and bubbled along my inner thighs. Heavy and humid air settled against the bare skin of my arms and breasts like a satin veil. Water fizzed around the cluster of rocks jutting from the surface of the heated pool. Wisps of steam danced in dappled sunlight, twining around lilacs that smothered the walls and stretched across the ceiling, perfuming the air of Casteel's cavern.

I didn't know why I dreamed of this place instead of something horrific, or how I'd even been able to reach such a deep level of sleep on the eve of battle. Maybe it was knowing that I would soon be on my way to Carsodonia, replacing the keening sense of desperation with purpose. Perhaps that had given me the peace of mind I'd needed to truly rest and dream of something pleasant and beautiful.

I skimmed my hand through the water, smiling as it tickled my palm. Closing my eyes, I let my head fall back. Water tugged on the tail of my braid as damp, sweetly scented air...*stirred.*

Awareness bore down on my shoulders, sending a shiver through me as my hands stilled and my eyes opened. Tiny bumps broke out all over my skin. I inhaled sharply—and the breath snagged as a different scent reached me. One that reminded me of...of pine and decadent spice.

"Poppy."

My heart stumbled. Everything stopped. That voice. That rich, deep *voice* that carried a slight musical lilt. *His voice.* I would recognize it anywhere.

I whipped around, sending the water into a hissing fury. My entire being tensed, and then a shudder rocked its way through me.

I saw *him.*

In the damp heat of the cavern, I saw his soft, black hair already beginning to curl against the slash of his brows, and the sandy-hued, high cheekbones—ones that appeared sharper than I remembered. But that full mouth... I shuddered again. His mouth was slightly parted as if he'd inhaled and couldn't take another breath. A shadow of a beard ran along his cheeks and his strong, proud jaw, giving him an unfamiliar, rugged, and wild look.

He stood before me, the water lazily swirling against those fascinating indents on his inner hips. He was as bare skinned as I was, the tightly rolled muscles of his abdomen and the delineated lines of his chest appearing more defined, starker than I remembered.

But it was him.

My first.

My last.

My *everything.*

"Cas?" His name came from the depths of my very soul, and it stung and burned the entire way past my lips.

His throat worked on a swallow. I'd never seen his eyes so bright. They were like pools of polished gold. "*Poppy.*"

I didn't know who moved first. If it was him or me or if we both moved at the same moment, but it was only a heartbeat—less than one—and then his arms were around me. The feel of his hot, wet skin against mine was a shock because I *felt* him, from the hard flesh of his chest to the coarse hair on his legs. Grasping his cheeks, I marveled at the sensation of the prickly growth against my palms, something I'd never felt on him before.

I *felt* him.

He held me tightly, leaving no space between us. Leaving no way for me to not *feel* that he trembled as badly as I shook. His hand slid up the length of my spine, leaving a series of hot, tight shivers in its wake. He sank his hand into my braid.

In the recesses of my mind, I knew this was only a dream, even if nothing about any of this felt like a dull replica concocted from my desperate, lonely mind. Not when the cold, achingly vast holes in my chest filled with the feel of him—all of *Casteel.*

"Poppy," he repeated, his breath against my lips. And then his mouth was on mine.

His lips—oh, gods, I drowned at the feel of them. I didn't think any memory could capture the unyielding hardness or the lush softness. I didn't think any memory could recreate the way he kissed.

Because Casteel kissed as if he were starving, and I was the only sustenance he'd ever desired. Ever needed. He kissed as if it were the first thing he ever truly wanted and the last thing he needed.

I slid my hands into his damp hair, shaking at the *feel* of the strands sifting through my fingers. The edge of a sharp fang dragged across my lower lip, heating my blood in the way only he could. I kissed him back, desire sparking and igniting as a pulsing twist of pleasure curled the muscles low in my stomach. The intensity of it caused me to jerk against him—against the hot, hard length of him—and frenzied need exploded.

Casteel groaned as his fingers curled into my hair, and those long, drugging kisses became shorter, rougher. His lips tugged at mine. My teeth clashed with his. These kinds of kisses tore through me, leaving little fires in their wake—flames sure to consume me, even in a dream. And I knew that was all this was. A dream. A reward I didn't think I deserved but would greedily take, nonetheless. Because I needed him. Needed to feel warm inside again.

And with Casteel, I was always like flesh and fire.

I looped my arm around his broad shoulders as I dragged my hand down his face, his throat, to where I felt his pulse pounding. My hand dropped to his shoulder. "Please. Touch me. Take me." The words that spilled from my mouth carried no taint of shame. There was no room for that in this fantasy. No awkwardness. No hesitation or second-guessing. Just need. Just us. Only these stolen minutes mattered, even if they weren't real. "Please, Cas."

"You know better, Poppy. You don't ever have to beg."

Another full-body shudder took me at the sound of his voice—at the words replacing the last ones and the hoarsely shouted pleas.

"You have me," he swore against my swollen lips. "Always."

"And forever," I whispered.

He shook even harder. "I needed to hear that. You have no idea how badly I needed to hear *you*." He reclaimed the distance between us, capturing my lips with his. "Did my need somehow conjure you into reality? I don't know. I can't think beyond *this*. Beyond the way you feel." His sharp fangs tugged against my lips once more, scattering my thoughts. "Not when you're here, in my arms."

The kiss deepened again as his tongue touched mine, sending a flurry of swirling, heated sensations through me. "Not when I can taste you. Feel you." His shaking hand slid over my arm, grazing the side of my breast and then my waist. He kept going, the rough calluses on his palms just as I remembered. His hand slipped under the water and closed around my hip, his fingers pressing into the flesh there. He dragged his hand back up, cupping it to my breast as a primitive, raw sound left him. I gasped.

"I feel this." He ran his thumb over the aching tip of my breast, and then his palm skimmed my waist again, delving once more under the water. When he gripped my hip this time, he tugged me up and against him and his rigid length. "Can you feel me? Tell me. Can you feel me, Poppy?"

"I feel you." My fingers tangled in his hair as I rocked against him. I wanted to feel him moving inside me. I wanted to feel that delicious tug and pull. "You're all I feel, even when you're not with me. I love you so much."

His hoarse cry swallowed mine as he pulled me down onto his thick length—

A shock went through me. The feel of him stretching me, filling me was pure pleasure with a wicked bite. An intense sensation that was...

I stiffened, my pulse racing. The feel of him, the enormous presence... Gods, it felt real.

Like *really* real.

I looked down at us—at the hardened tips of my breasts and the fine dusting of hair on his chest. At where my soft belly met his harder one. I watched him breathe quickly and raggedly. I watched him shake as he held himself still while deep inside me. I felt *him* twitch where we were joined under the churning water. I continued staring at us—at him and his body. The leanness to his frame that hadn't been there before. The thin marks that slowly appeared, spreading across his chest beside the numerous faded nicks and cuts of his old scars. My already pounding heart sped up.

"Is this…is this real?" I whispered.

Casteel lifted his head, his heated stare piercing mine. His arm tightened around my waist. "Your eyes," he said, his voice thick and husky. "There isn't just an aura behind the pupils. There are streaks of silver piercing the green." Confusion pinched the tense lines of his face. "I've never seen them like this."

The way he described them reminded me of something. Of *her*. The Consort. The back of my neck cooled rapidly. I breathed in deeply and caught the scent of something else beneath the lilac and Cas's lush, pine spice.

The musty scent of damp, stale air.

The chill in my skin spread, but his felt hotter. Feverish. "Do you feel that?" I shivered as goosebumps broke out. "I'm…I'm cold."

"I…" He trailed off as his head jerked at the sound of… It wasn't falling water. It was a heavier sound. A *clanking*.

My breath caught. I stared at him—*really* looked at him. The shadow of a beard. The hollows under his cheekbones. The cuts in his skin. I saw the moment the confusion cleared his radiant, golden eyes.

And wonder poured into them. "*Heartmates*," he choked out.

"What—?"

Casteel kissed me again. Hard. Consuming. He kissed me as if he could draw me into him. When his mouth left mine this time, he didn't go far. "Gods. Poppy, I miss you so bad it hurts."

Pressure clamped down on my chest. Tears rushed to my eyes. "Cas…"

He folded both arms around me and held me tighter than before, but I was even colder. He trembled as he dropped his head to my shoulder. His chest rose with an unsteady breath against mine.

"Poppy," he breathed, kissing my cheek, the space below my ear, and then my shoulder. He pressed his mouth to the side of my neck. "My beautiful, brave Queen. I could stay here, holding you, forever."

Oh, gods, I knew this was ending. Panic exploded. I wasn't ready. I wasn't. "Don't leave me. Don't leave us. I love you. *Please*. I love—"

"Find me again." His head lifted, and his eyes…they were no longer bright, his features no longer clear. Things were hazy, and I couldn't—oh, gods, I couldn't feel him. "Find me. I'll be waiting here.

Always. I—"

I woke without warning, my eyes widening as I gulped in air, my heart racing.

It took several moments for my thoughts to slow enough for me to recognize the moonlight-kissed canvas walls. A fine sheen of sweat dampened my skin, and I swore I could... I could still hear the fizzing water of the cavern.

I'll be waiting here. Always.

I shuddered, closing my eyes and trying with everything in my power to go back to the cavern. To him. But it didn't work. I couldn't put myself back into the dream, but I still felt him. The warmth inside me was still there, slow to fade, as was the acute throbbing. My hands tingled—my entire body did. As if the touch had been real. As if the feel of him, hot and hard against me and inside me, had been real.

But it hadn't been.

Slowly, I became aware of Kieran's weight beside me and his soft, muffled snores. He was curled against my back, asleep in his wolven form. Thank the gods my dream hadn't woken him. I turned my head, spying Casteel's ring on the nightstand, bathed in the faint moonlight. I started to reach—

A scent made its way to me.

One that didn't make sense.

Grabbing my loosely braided hair, I inhaled deeply. The scent was unmistakable.

Pine and lush spice.

And sweet, fragrant lilac.

Shock rolled through me. I jerked upright, startling Kieran. He lifted his head and looked over his back toward me.

His thoughts brushed mine, woodsy and rich. *Poppy?*

I couldn't answer him. Not when my heart thundered. I looked down at the section of braid that smelled of lilac. How was this possible? There were no lilacs around here. And if there were, that wouldn't explain how I could smell...Casteel. And I did. It couldn't be my imagination.

Concern stretched out from the wolven, and I felt the bed shift suddenly. Kieran closed his hand around mine. The touch of his very mortal skin against mine rattled me out of my thoughts. I looked at him, seeing a whole lot of bare skin.

"Poppy? What is it?" His gaze searched mine. "Has something happened? Talk to me."

I swallowed. "I..."

"Did you have a nightmare?"

"No," I said, and Kieran relaxed. "It was a dream. About...about Casteel. It wasn't a bad one, but it wasn't like any I've ever had."

"A sex dream?"

"*What?*" I dropped my braid.

"You had a sex dream."

I stared at his shadowed features, stunned for a second. "What makes you even think that?"

"I don't think you want me to answer that," he said. "It will embarrass you."

"How—?" Then it hit me. Wolven and their godsdamn sense of smell. I lifted my chin, *refusing* to be embarrassed. "Why do you think I've never had a sex dream before?"

Kieran lifted a shoulder. "I figure you don't have a lot of sex dreams."

I blinked. "Why?"

"So it *was* a sex dream?"

"Oh, my gods. Why are we even talking about sex dreams when you're sitting beside me naked?"

"Does my nudity bother you, *meyaah Liessa?*"

It didn't.

Well, not exactly.

At this point, I was getting used to the bare skin buffet that came with being around so many wolven—and, apparently, draken. But right now, when I could still feel Casteel inside me, Kieran's nudity felt...*different*. Not bad or wrong. Just different in a way I couldn't explain. But it made me think of what he'd witnessed when I awakened after my Ascension. He'd been in that room, stopping me from taking too much blood, holding me by the waist as I rode Casteel...

My breath and body *snagged*, and...dear gods, I really needed to stop thinking in general.

One side of Kieran's mouth curved up in response to my non-answer. A teasing grin I saw in the delicate dance of moonlight making its way through the window.

My eyes narrowed. "You're teasing me."

He reached over, gently tugging on the sleeve of my shirt—well, *his* shirt that I'd helped myself to while the one I slept in was still drying after being laundered. "I would never."

I crossed my arms. "I'm being serious. The dream was too real."

"Dreams can feel like that sometimes."

"This was different. Here." I grabbed my braid, shoving it toward him. "Smell my hair and tell me what you think it smells like."

"Not something I've been asked to do before, but there's always a first, eh?" Kieran took my braid, dipping his head and inhaling. I sensed the immediate change in him. "I smell…" He rocked back a few inches, still holding onto my braid. "I smell *Cas.*"

Air punched out of my lungs. "And lilacs, right? I dreamt of the cavern in Spessa's End, and he was there."

"I smell that and…and something…" He frowned.

"Musty? I did, too, before waking up. Everything felt real up until the end when I started to get cold and then noticed things about him. He appeared thinner. He even had several weeks' worth of facial hair on his cheeks. There was a moment when he…oh, gods." I swallowed. "I think he thought it was a dream, too, but then he somehow realized that it wasn't. He said my eyes looked different. That there was more silver in them. Can you see them now?"

"They look normal—well, the *new* normal. That aura behind your pupils is there," Kieran answered, lowering my braid to my shoulder.

"When he saw my eyes, that's when he, like, became aware that…that it wasn't a dream." I shook my head. "I know that doesn't make sense, but he knew it was about to end."

"Did he say anything?"

"No. Just that he…" *I miss you so bad it hurts.* The breath I took was broken. I couldn't speak that aloud. "He said '*heartmates*' but didn't explain why. He told me to find him again and that he'd be waiting."

"Heartmates," Kieran murmured, the skin between his brows puckering. He'd always suspected that Casteel and I were that—the rare union of hearts and souls that was rumored to be more powerful than any bloodline.

I hadn't believed Kieran at first, but the moment Casteel and I had stopped pretending, I'd stopped doubting.

Kieran's eyes widened suddenly. "Holy shit."

I jerked. "What?"

"I heard my father say something once about heartmates. I completely forgot about it." Kieran picked up my braid again and breathed deeply. When he spoke, his voice had become hoarse. "He said that heartmates could walk in each other's dreams."

Shock rippled through me. I didn't know what to think, but if it was real? Good gods…

But why would tonight have been the first time? Was it because I'd slept deeply enough, and the nightmares hadn't found me first? Or was it the first time Casteel had been able to find me?

And what if it was something we could do again? I wouldn't waste the opportunity. I could find out where he was being held—if he knew. I could make sure that he was okay—as okay as he could be. I would use the time for anything other than...

The heated words I'd whispered against his mouth filled my mind, causing my steps to falter. The way I'd spoken to him—how I'd begged him? My entire body flushed.

"What are you—?" Kieran stiffened at the same moment a wave of tiny bumps spread across my skin. An intense chill swept down my spine. The Primal essence roared to life, throbbing as a sudden dark and oily sensation settled over me, soaking into my skin and stealing my breath.

Kieran's head snapped back to me. "You feel that?"

"Yeah. I don't..." My heart lurched in my chest. I turned my left hand over, shuddering with a burst of relief. The golden swirl across my palm shimmered faintly. "It's not—"

Lightning streaked across the sky, so bright and intense it lit up the inside of the chamber, briefly turning night to day. A crack of thunder followed, rattling my chest and ears.

Kieran rose as I pulled my legs out from under the blanket and stood. The borrowed shirt slid down my thighs as I grabbed the dressing robe from the foot of the bed, pulling it on.

The sound of booming thunder eased off, giving way to nervous neighing from the nearby stables. I went to the window and pulled the curtains back. Thick shadows rolled across the sky, obscuring the moonlight and plunging the bedchamber into near darkness.

"This is odd," Kieran said as I turned, walking to the drapes that sectioned off the bedchambers. "It's not nearly warm enough for such a storm."

A howl came from outside, the scream of roaring air. Wind slammed into the manor, lifting the curtains at the windows. Air poured in under the gaps, icy as the darkest hours of winter, blowing through the entire room. The gust pulled strands of hair free from my braid, tossing them across my face. Another bolt of lightning streaked overhead, and the wind...it smelled like stale lilacs.

That was what Vessa had smelled like.

The heavy canvas billowed, and through the opening, I saw the maps of Oak Ambler that had been brought to the bedchamber earlier fly through the air like birds made of parchment.

"Damn it," I gasped, racing forward in the blast of thunder that followed. My sock-covered feet slipped over the stone floors as I darted past the chairs. I grasped a map and then another as slips of parchment whipped about.

Slamming the maps down on the low table, I grabbed a heavy iron candle holder and placed it so it kept the maps safe. Wind spun through the chamber, throwing the doors open as bolts of light continued ripping across the sky, one after another, each charging the air. The eather in my chest and my blood...it started to *vibrate*—

I looked down as the table under my hands began to tremble. Across from me, the table used for private dining shook, rattling the pitchers and empty glasses on the top. Chairs scraped across the floor, toppling over behind me as the rumble of thunder came from above *and* below.

An outline of a figure filled the chamber's opening as lightning lit the sky, illuminating Naill's familiar features. "Are you all right?" he demanded.

"I think so!" I shouted over the rumbling. "Are you?"

"I will—" The manor shuddered, causing Naill to throw out his arms to steady himself. "I will be once the damn earth stops shaking."

Glancing at the window, I caught a brief glimpse of a darker, winged shadow gliding past. A draken landed outside the manor, its impact barely felt.

"We shouldn't be in here," Kieran announced, striding out from the curtained-off section.

I turned, stumbling. In a flash of light, I saw Kieran buttoning the flap on a pair of breeches. "Do you think it's safer outside?"

"The manor could come down," he said. "And the last thing I want to be is buried under tons of stone."

"Not sure that sounds worse than being hit by lightning," I said.

Kieran said nothing as he stalked past me, grabbing my hand. He kept walking, following Naill. We hurried down the seemingly nonending hall, out into the storm and the path of a large draken. Naill drew up short as Reaver swept his wings back, tucking them close to his sides.

I spun, seeing the rows of tents housing most of Aylard's division ripple violently. The draken turned his diamond-shaped head toward the sky. I followed his gaze, my heart stopping as the flashes of light revealed winged shapes.

"What are they doing up there? They'll be struck by lightning." Pulling free from Kieran, I charged into the heavy winds toward Reaver. The ground heaved violently, startling me as an entire section rolled like a wave. I wobbled along the unstable ground as dust and dirt exploded into the air. Naill caught my arm as my *will* swelled through me—the need for them to come down.

Reaver stretched out his neck, letting out a shrill, wavering sound that echoed. He made the call again, and thank the gods, the other draken heeded his order. They started to descend, two and then one more landing around the manor—

A bright flash of light erupted, but it came from below—from *inside* the manor.

"What the hell?" Naill gasped.

The boom the stream of light made while hitting the sky was deafening and stunning. The bolt arced and then *erupted*, splitting into several crackling streams of silvery-white light that raced across the entire sky and up into the clouds and the—

The draken.

Someone screamed. I didn't know if it was me or not as the lightning struck the draken above. The ground heaved, throwing me into Naill. Blinding light washed over the twisting and writhing shapes.

Pain flared in my throat. I was screaming, but I wasn't the only one. Horror swelled as the draken fell, wings limp and bodies twisting in the wind, slamming into the pines, tents, one after another after another after *another*—

Then it stopped.

All of it.

The earth ceased its trembling. The lightning vanished, and the clouds scattered, dispersing. The wind cut off. All of it just…halted as if fingers had been snapped. There wasn't even a breeze.

No draken were in the sky.

Reaver called out again, the sound mournful and low. I heard an answer, wavering and full of anguish.

"No. No. No," I whispered, pulling free of Naill and walking, then running, toward the nearest collapsed tent.

A nude body lay in the center. I wouldn't have known it was a draken if not for the patches of dark, charred flesh across the ankles, knees, and every other place there was a joint.

Shoving aside the folds of canvas, I dropped to my knees beside the dark-haired male. I channeled the throbbing eather in my chest as I placed my hands on his arm. I didn't hesitate. There was no time to think about what I was doing when I'd only seen three land and the rest fall. Heat rippled down my arms, spreading across my fingers as I pressed them into his biceps, feeling the faint but distinct ridges that were shaped like scales. A silvery glow washed over the draken in a veiny web of light and…and then rolled off, washing uselessly onto the tent.

My heart lurched as I tried again, pulling forth even more of the Primal essence and pushing it even harder into the draken.

It did the same, rolling right off him.

Kieran appeared on the other side, touching the draken's neck. His gaze lifted to mine. "He's gone."

I sucked in a breath. "I can bring him back. Like I did with that girl. I just need to try harder."

"You can't." The raspy voice sent a shudder through me. Kieran's eyes moved beyond me to where Reaver must've stood in his mortal form. "You can heal, but once the soul parts a being of two worlds, you cannot restore life."

Kieran rocked back, blinking rapidly before turning his head to another caved-in tent. To where soldiers and wolven gathered in multiple clusters around—

The anguished, warbling call came again.

"*No.*" I whipped toward Reaver and started to rise. "I can try with another."

"You cannot." Reaver knelt at the feet of the fallen draken, his head bowed.

"Why not?" I shouted, anger and disbelief crashing together. My heart was pounding, my breathing heavy.

"Only the Primal of Life can restore life to any being of two worlds." The finality in his words was a punch in the gut. "They're gone."

They're gone.

I stared at Reaver as those two words cycled, over and over. Only three had landed, joining Reaver. That meant…

A shudder rocked me. Sixteen had been in the air. Sixteen draken who'd just awakened from the gods knew how long to do nothing but die?

My hands opened and closed as I turned in a slow circle. "I'm sorry. I'm so sorry."

"This wasn't your fault," Kieran argued, standing.

But I'd woken them. I'd brought them here. They'd followed me—

All that you and those who follow will find here is death.

I stood on trembling legs, eyes and throat burning as I saw the cracks in the ground, some thin and others thick enough to trip someone up. The fissures spread across the land like a fragile web and continued along the walls of the manor. The roof had no damage that I could see in the moonlight. It was as if no arcs of light had pierced it.

Slowly, I turned to where Naill and several soldiers stood, staring beyond the collapsed tents. Skin pimpling with another chill, I followed their stares. Beyond the encampment, the pines no longer reached for the stars. The trees and the heavy, needled branches were bent forward, touching the ground. It looked like a massive hand had come down upon them, forcing them to bow. I looked at Kieran.

"I don't know what caused this." He dragged a hand down his face. "I've never seen anything like this before."

"But we've felt it," Naill uttered, his amber eyes bright. "After those bastard Unseen tried to kill you, and Cas had you in that cabin. That happened when you woke up," he told us, and I remembered seeing the trees outside the cabin. They, too, had been bent to the ground. "The same kind of storm happened when you Ascended to your godhood."

"This was not a storm," Reaver said, and I turned to him. "It was an…awakening."

"Of what?" I asked.

He lifted his head, and his eyes…they weren't like earlier. They were still a vibrant shade of blue, but the pupils were thin, vertical slits. "Death."

My entire body jerked as Vessa's words came back to me. "*You*," she'd said. "*I wait for you. I wait for death.*"

Numbly, I stumbled back to the manor and started walking. My pace picked up. The dressing robe streamed out from behind me as I ran.

"Poppy!" Kieran shouted.

I flew through the door into the manor, racing toward the Great Hall—to the chambers two doors away.

Kieran caught up to me. "What are you doing?"

"Her." My steps slowed as we passed the dark room. Behind us, I knew Naill and others followed. "Vessa."

Reaching the door, I grabbed the handle. Like with the chains at the gates of Massene, I melted the locks. The handle turned, and the door swung open, letting the potent stench of stale lilacs slam into me.

I rocked to a halt, inhaling sharply.

Reddish-black smoke filled the chamber, swirling around the robed figure of Vessa—the same kind of shadowy smoke that had drifted from the ruby-adorned box Isbeth had sent.

"What the fuck?" Kieran threw out his arm, blocking me.

Vessa's milky-white eyes were wide as she stared at a scorch mark on the ceiling, her arms spread. She stood in the center of a circle drawn not of ash but blood—hers. It dripped from her mangled wrists. Through the churning, thick tendrils of smoke, I saw a sharpened chunk of rock lying near her bare feet.

A thick, oily feeling seeped through my skin, and the eather in my chest pulsed. In the hall, I heard low snarls of warning from the wolven.

"You," I breathed, the essence colliding with the building anger. Energy flooded my veins. "You did this."

Her laughter joined the cyclone of smoke.

The corners of my vision turned silvery-white as I brushed Kieran's arm aside and stepped into the room.

"Careful," Kieran warned, his hand fisting in the back of my dressing gown as the pulsing smoke whipped past my face, blowing strands of my hair back. "This is some bad shit."

"Magic," Perry rasped from behind us. "This is Primal magic."

"*Harbinger*," she cooed, her frail body shaking as the reddish-black smoke whirled. "You were told when you entered this manor, Queen with a crown of gold, that all that you and those who follow will find here is death." The reddish-black smoke spun faster, spreading. "You will not harness the fire of the gods. You will win no war."

My breath scorched my lungs and throat as realization swept through me. "Isbeth," I hissed, chin lowering as the essence sparked from my splayed fingers. I didn't know how she was able to do this, but I knew why. "You did this for her."

"I serve the True Crown of the Realms," she yelled.

The floor began to shake as the smoke funneled, rising to the ceiling. That smell—the stale lilacs—grew until it nearly choked me. But it was not Vessa that caused the trembling.

It was *me*.

"I serve by waiting—"

"You *served*," I cut her off as the edges of my robe rippled. My will formed in my mind as I lifted my hand. Pure, ancient power spilled out from me, spinning down my arm. Starlight carrying the faintest tinge of shadow arced from my palm, slamming into the smoke. The eather rolled over the storm and cut through it, striking Vessa in the chest. She spun back as the flash of eather pulsed through the chamber, but only her robes fell to the floor. "And death has come for you."

I walked toward the receiving chamber, the dressing robe replaced by breeches and my sweater coat. It was the thick of the night, hours after the sixteen draken had been lifted onto hastily made pyres so Nithe, one of the remaining draken, could burn their bodies. I stood by the pyres until nothing remained but ash. Part of me felt as if I were still there.

Entering the room, I went to where Reaver sat, still in his mortal form, nude but for the blanket he'd wrapped around his waist as he sat on the floor, in a corner. Before I could speak, he said, "She smelled of Death."

"Well, that's because she was dead," Kieran replied.

"No. You misunderstand. She smelled of *the* Death," Reaver countered. "I thought I smelled it when we arrived here, on and off, but it was never strong. Not until tonight."

His pupils had returned to normal as he watched me lower myself onto the ground before him, the heavy length of my braid falling over my shoulder. It wasn't just the four of us. Those I trusted were with us, sitting or standing, drinking or motionless, still held tightly by shock. I swallowed the knot of sorrow gathering inside me—a mix of guilt and realization that I should've listened to Kieran. "What does that mean?"

"That was the essence of the Primal of Death. His stench. Oily. Dark. Suffocating," Reaver said, and I looked to where Kieran stood a few feet from me. That was exactly what we'd both felt. "It doesn't make sense."

"You mean Rhain?" Vonetta asked from where she sat on one of the chairs, her knees pressed to her chest.

Reaver blinked. "What?"

"Rhain," Emil started to explain, his hands on the back of Vonetta's chair. "The God of Common Men and—"

"I know who Rhain is. I knew him before he was known as the god you recognize today," he replied.

From the entry of the chamber, surprise flickered through Hisa, mirroring mine. "Who was the God of Death before him?" she asked.

"There was no God of Death before him. There was only the Primal of Death."

I remembered what Nyktos had shared with me. "Did Rhain replace one of the Primals that Nyktos said had become tainted and corrupt?"

"In a way." Reaver's head tilted to the side as he looked at the ceiling, his eyes closing. "There was only one true Primal of Death, and that—the storm and the woman—felt like him."

"Nyktos is both the Primal of Life and Death," Kieran said.

"Wrong."

Kieran knelt. "I'm not wrong."

"You are." Reaver lowered his chin, his eyes opening. "Nyktos was never the *true* Primal of Death. There was another before him. His name was Kolis."

"Kolis?" Naill repeated, stepping around Emil. "I've never heard that name."

"You wouldn't have."

"Erased history," I murmured, looking over my shoulder at the others. "Remember what I told you about what Nyktos said? About the other Primals and the war that broke out between them and the gods?" I faced Reaver. "That's why we wouldn't know his name, right?"

Reaver nodded.

"I cannot be the only person who's sitting here thinking that the name *Kolis* is awfully similar to Solis," Vonetta remarked.

She wasn't. It hadn't passed me by either.

"What happened to this Kolis?" Perry spoke up. The Atlantian had been quiet the entire time as he stood with a somber Delano. "Or the other Primals?"

"Some of the Primals passed on to Arcadia, a place very much like the Vale but which can be entered without death," Reaver said, and the confusion I felt from the others said they were as unfamiliar with Arcadia as I was.

"Some?" Perry prodded.

"Some," Reaver repeated. "Others were ended. As in they died. Were no more. A figment of a forgotten past. Dead. No longer—"

"I get it," I stopped him. "We all get it."

"Glad to hear," the draken retorted. "Kolis is as good as dead."

I didn't let his tone get to me. He'd just lost sixteen draken—some who had to be friends. Maybe even family. I knew so very little about Reaver—about any of the draken. And now, most of them were gone. A shiver slithered down my spine. "As good as dead isn't dead, Reaver."

"He's been dealt with. Entombed long ago. None of us would be here if he hadn't been," he insisted. "And the only thing that could've released him is the Primal of Life. That would never happen. They...they were the kind of enemies that go beyond blood and bone."

My heart rate settled a little. The last thing any of us needed to deal with was a randomly awakened Primal of Death.

"Wait." Reaver's brows knitted and then smoothed as his head jerked toward me. "Holy shit, I should've caught on to this. Admittedly, I don't always pay attention. You all talk a lot and do so in circles."

I started to frown when I heard what sounded like a choked laugh coming from Hisa.

"You spoke of these...creations your enemy has. Ones that can survive any injury?" Reaver asked.

"Yes." Kieran placed a hand on the floor.

"Do they come back to life?"

Kieran tilted his head. "What else does *survive any injury* mean?"

"Not the same as returning to life," Reaver shot back.

"Yes, they come back to life," I jumped in.

"Are they called Revenants?"

"They are." I looked around the room. "I'm sure I've said that before when you were around. More than once."

"Like I said, I don't always pay attention," he admitted. "Let me guess. They're the third sons and daughters."

"Yes." Emil drew out the word. "That would be correct. You know what these things are?"

"Revenants were Kolis's pet project. His crowning achievement," Reaver said. "He used magic to create them—the kind that only worked on them."

Vonetta straightened as I thought of the ledgers. "Why only them?"

"Because the third sons and daughters carry embers of eather in them."

"I don't understand," Kieran said. "And I don't think I'm the only one who doesn't."

"Everything in every realm descends from a Primal—well, besides the draken. We come from nothing. We just are and have always been," Reaver said, and I had no idea what to make of that—any of it.

"And mortals descend from a Primal and a draken," I finished for him.

"From Eythos, the first Primal of Life—also known as your great-grandfather." He pointed at me, and my eyes went wide. "What? Did you think Nyktos was hatched from an egg? He wasn't."

I hadn't thought *that*. I just hadn't realized there was another before him.

"Anyway, Eythos had a habit of creating things. Some would say it was out of curiosity and a thirst for learning, but I imagine it came from boredom. Who really knows? He's been dead for a very long time. Anyway, he was close to Nektas, even before we were given mortal forms. One day, for whatever reason—and I'm still going with boredom—they decided to create a new species. Eythos lent his flesh, and Nektas gave his fire. The result was the very first mortal. Of course, they ended up creating more, and those, and the ones spawned by them, are, for the most part, ordinary. But what Eythos and Nektas did meant that an ember of essence exists in all mortals. It's…dormant, for the most part."

Reaver leaned forward. "Except for in the third sons and daughters. The ember is not always dormant then. Why? I don't know. Perhaps it's just a pure-numbers game that, after so many births, the ember would be stronger. Who knows? It doesn't matter."

Perry appeared as if it mattered a lot to him.

"Either way, those mortals often have unique talents, much like your gift of sensing emotions. It wouldn't be as strong as yours. Most wouldn't even realize they were different. They're not immortal. They don't need to feed. They live and die like mortals."

My assumptions on what I had seen in the ledgers were correct. "The Ascended copied the Rite, then."

Reaver nodded, and a ripple of surprise was felt throughout. "At one time, it was an honored tradition for the third sons and daughters to enter Iliseeum to serve the gods. And because the ember was strong in them, they could be Ascended if they chose, thus earning their immortality."

"They had a choice?" Naill asked.

"Eythos always gave a choice," Reaver said. "But Kolis took those third sons and daughters and made them into something neither dead nor alive—something else entirely. It was his essence—*his* magic as your friend would say." He nodded in Perry's direction. "I was young then when all of this came to a head. When what Kolis had done was discovered, and the war unfolded, I was hidden among other younglings. He was dealt with, but now... Now, someone has learned how to harness his essence."

"Isbeth," I said, anger pumping hotly through my veins. "Both the Duke and Vessa knew about the prophecy, and Vessa said she served the True Crown—the Ascended. Isbeth must have shared the knowledge with her—knowledge she could've only gained from one person."

"Malec," Kieran surmised with a growl.

Reaver closed his eyes. "For him to share such secrets...it is a betrayal of the highest order. For he has given this Blood Queen the power to kill my brethren." The angles of his features sharpened. "Just like she most likely killed Jade."

I stiffened. "She may not be gone, Reaver. My mother—" I closed my eyes, correcting myself. "Coralena was the Handmaiden who tried to bring me to Atlantia when I was a child. She was a Revenant, but Isbeth said that she killed her. That means Isbeth must have had a draken then—had access to the fire of the gods. That wasn't that long ago."

"Yeah, I want to believe that, but the fire of the gods isn't just talking about the fire we breathe." A muscle ticked along his jaw. "The fire is our essence—our blood. Not even a Revenant is immune to that. All the Blood Queen would need is a drop of a draken's blood, no matter how old it was, to kill a Revenant."

I rocked back, my heart sinking.

Reaver's eyes met mine. "That kind of magic, that kind of power this Blood Queen has learned? You just saw what it is capable of. It can only be used for death and decay." Reaver's pupils thinned and stretched vertically. "She is a far more dangerous foe than I think anyone has realized."

Later, I sat on the bed as I held Casteel's ring between my fingers. My head spun as I turned everything over. And it was a lot. The dream that might not have been a dream. Vessa. The loss of all those draken. The knowledge that the Blood Queen had learned how to use the essence of this Primal, Kolis. Reaver's belief that Jadis was already gone.

I looked over at Kieran. He sat across from me, sharpening a blade. "I lost seventeen draken tonight."

"*We* lost those draken," he corrected softly.

"I awakened them. I summoned them. And within a month, they're dead." A knot burned the back of my throat. "You were right."

"I know what you're going to say," he said. "What happened to the draken wasn't your fault."

"It is you who are being too kind now." The knot of sorrow expanded. "If I had listened to you and gotten rid of her, she wouldn't have been here to do this."

Kieran didn't say anything for a long moment. "There was no way you could've known that she was capable of such a thing," he started, hands stilling as he lifted his gaze to mine. "Your kindness is part of who you are. It is one of the things that will make you a great Queen and god. You just need to learn when *not* to be kind."

Nodding, I drew in a shaky breath as I looked down at the ring. This was a horrible way to learn such a lesson. The draken had paid a terrible price for me to learn it.

I briefly closed my eyes. Several moments passed. "You heard Reaver when he said my touch doesn't work on beings of two worlds?"

He looked up once more. "I did."

"That could mean I can't bring wolven back to life."

Sitting the blade and stone aside, he leaned forward. "It's okay."

"How is that okay?"

"How can it not be?" Kieran asked, his face inches from mine. "I've lived my entire life without there being this…this second chance. Someone with extra-special hands."

"But I want that second chance to be an option. I know I

shouldn't. What happened with that young girl was an accident. I didn't know what I was doing. I know I'm not the Primal of Life and don't have that kind of authority, but…" My fingers curled around Casteel's ring. "If something were to happen—"

"Then it happens." Kieran's gaze searched mine. "All of us who are here know that our lives can end at any minute. We've all lived never counting on a second chance, and none of us expects it to be any other way."

"I know—"

"And you shouldn't either."

I knew I shouldn't, but the idea of losing him? Vonetta? Delano? My insides went cold—colder than they'd ever been. And that place in me, the empty one, it grew.

I didn't know what I would do if I lost them.

But as Kieran fell silent and eventually dozed off after placing his blade aside, I thought about the one thing that would prevent something from happening to Kieran. The one thing that would tie his lifespan to mine so neither Casteel nor I would ever have to say goodbye to him.

The Joining.

10

Standing in the bedchamber, I drew my finger across the ring. It now hung from a simple gold chain that Perry had given me. He'd used it for some sort of medallion, which he'd now sewn into the inside of his armor. The gift was beyond kind and allowed me to keep Casteel's ring safe and close to me.

Nervous energy hummed through me. Valyn and the generals would be here soon, and the hardest part of carrying out our plans would take place—convincing them to go along with it. With all of it.

Antsy and finding the woolen material of the more form-fitted tunic scratchy, I wasn't sure if it was my clothing or just anxiety. This was the first time I'd worn the tunic trimmed with fine gold thread at its knee-length hem and along the slits on either side. It was nearly identical to the one Kieran wore. His was shorter, hitting at the thigh, but it too had the golden scrollwork at the neck and across the halves of the tunic.

I thought about what I'd had Naill create for me. Come to find out, he was rather skilled with a needle and thread. Now *that* would be uncomfortable to wear.

But it would serve a purpose.

"Poppy," Kieran said from the other side of the chamber. I looked over my shoulder to see that his sister had joined him.

"They've arrived. Roughly two hundred thousand," Vonetta announced as I faced the siblings. "The remaining armies are stationed at Spessa's End in case the Blood Crown turns their attention there, along with the Guardians and the younger draken who remained. I spoke with Valyn briefly and gave him a heads-up about what happened to the draken."

"Thank you," I murmured, slipping the ring back behind the collar of my tunic, where it rested between my breasts. I stepped forward to leave for the receiving chamber that had been prepared for their arrival.

"Wait." Vonetta glanced up, her gaze flicking over the thick braid lying over my shoulder. "Where is the crown?"

Brows knitting, I gestured behind me. "It's in the chest."

"You should wear it."

"I don't need to wear a crown for them to remember I'm the Queen."

"But it serves as a good reminder," Kieran stated. "There will be generals here you've never interacted with before. For many of them, this will be the first time they've been in your presence outside of the coronation."

In other words, they may be like Aylard. Distrustful and standoffish. I sighed, more annoyed than bothered by the idea of so many of the upper echelon of the army most likely being cold and wary of me.

"I guess I should retrieve the crown, then." I turned, crossing the short distance to where the chest sat on the table beside a hairbrush that had seen much better days. The container was simple with no adornments or engravings, having previously been used by Perry to store cigars. The ruby and diamond crown that had once belonged to King Jalara was being kept in a crate that sat in the corner of the bedchamber under a muddy pair of boots—a fitting place for it.

Throwing the small latch, the rich scent of tobacco still lingered, faint but oddly pleasant as I slowly opened the lid. The gold crowns sat side by side, cushioned by a mound of cloth. The twisted bones, once a bleached, dull white, now shone, even in the low light. They were identical. One for a Queen. The other for a King. I didn't think that they should ever be apart from each other. Maybe that was why I hadn't worn the crown since the night I'd ended King Jalara's life. It didn't seem right to wear it while Casteel's remained closed away in this chest and not upon his head.

"Allow me?" Vonetta touched my arm.

I didn't realize I hadn't moved until then—that I was frozen, unable to touch them. I nodded.

Vonetta reached inside, picking up the crown to the left. She brushed a shorter strand of my hair back, and my chest twisted as I thought of Tawny. How many times had she helped pin back the length of my hair so it wouldn't be visible under the veil? Hundreds? Thousands? I swallowed hard.

Gods, I couldn't let myself think of that right now. There was so much I couldn't let myself think about. If I did, I truly wouldn't be *okay*. I wouldn't be strong. And I needed to be fearless right now.

Vonetta placed the gilded crown on my head, the weight lighter than I expected. The thin, golden teeth along the bottom of the crown caught in my hair, helping hold it in place. "There," she said, smiling. But I tasted the tangy bite of sadness when I looked at her. "Perfect."

I cleared my throat to ease the stinging. "Thank you."

Her bright eyes warmed as she clasped my hands in hers and squeezed. "They will be here any moment."

"I don't want anyone to know what Isbeth sent," I reminded them.

"We know," Kieran assured me. Of course, they knew.

I took another breath. "I'm ready."

Vonetta's smile was less sad now, a bit stronger as she let go of my hands. I turned back to the small box. The sight of the lone crown twisted something in my chest as I carefully closed the lid. *Soon*, I promised myself and smoothed a hand over the wood. Soon the crown would sit upon Casteel's head again. He would be beside me once more.

Nothing would stop me. Not the Atlantian generals. Not the Blood Queen. And not her stolen magic.

Emil had arrived, bowing his head as I walked into the much airier space of the receiving chamber. I stopped, glancing to where Reaver waited in his draken form.

Even I had no idea how he'd gotten into the chamber.

Loosely clasping my hands together, the nervous edginess ramped up as the sounds of clinking armor drew near. Reaver lifted his head, his curved horns brushing the ceiling as his nostrils flared.

Valyn Da'Neer was the first to enter, cradling his helmet under his left arm. Momentarily distracted by Reaver's presence, he quickly lowered to one knee, bowing his head. Hisa did the same, even though she'd been with us since the beginning, her single, thick, dark braid sliding over an armored shoulder. There were others behind them, too, but when Valyn lifted his head, I was unable to look away, even though I wanted to.

Even though it *hurt.*

There was no preparing myself. He was fairer-haired than his youngest son, who shared the dark hair and golden-bronze skin of his mother, but the cut of his jaw, the straight nose, and the high cheekbones were unmistakably familiar.

All I saw when I looked upon Valyn were parts of Casteel. But I breathed through the hurt and forced my gaze on the others. Three men and two women entered with Aylard. I recognized Lord Sven, Perry's father. The thick beard was new, giving his warm features a hardened edge. As they lowered themselves to their knees, I saw that Naill and Delano had joined us. The usual striking smile was absent from Naill's face as he kept a close watch on the generals—as did the pure white wolven now stalking the chamber's sides. Neither Delano nor Naill were being paranoid. The Unseen still posed a threat.

The slight brush of Kieran's shoulder against mine called forth instructions that Casteel had once given. "You may rise."

Valyn rose as I opened my senses, reaching out to my father-in-law. I brushed against what I imagined to be an iron and stone mental shield as strong as a Rise. That ancient hum of power in my chest told me I could break through it if I wished, shattering those shields. But there was no reason to do that.

There was no reason to even consider it.

With the advice Kieran had given me in the past echoing in my mind, I used my senses for my benefit. Curiosity and something warm surrounded me as I glanced at a fair-skinned woman with chin-length, icy-blond hair, and wintry-blue eyes. Determination tasted salty in my throat.

The generals had a wolven among them.

Happy to see that, I turned my attention to the others. Lemony uncertainty mixed with the same steadfastness as the wolven general reached me, which was expected. But there were…sharper, more biting undertones of unease that came from a dark-haired man and a brown-haired female with bright amber eyes. Their uncertainty was very much like Aylard's, venturing into distrust. And it was deep, tangling with the thrum of power at my core. I had a feeling their misgivings extended beyond me to the wolven by my side and those who had entered behind them—to what we now represented. The Crown. Power.

We'd need to keep an eye on them.

From his corner, Reaver watched the former King approach me. Valyn clasped my hands in his, squeezing gently. He said nothing, but the gesture meant a lot to me despite still being furious with Eloana and having no idea if Valyn had been unaware of who the Blood Queen was.

"We heard about the draken," Valyn said, turning to look in Reaver's direction. "You have our sincere condolences."

Reaver gave a slight nod of acknowledgment.

"If the Blood Crown is responsible, we will do everything in our power to make them pay tenfold," he swore, releasing my hands and stepping back. Only then did Reaver lower his head.

"I hope the journey here was uneventful," I said.

"It was, Your Highness," Valyn answered.

I was a heartbeat from advising Valyn that he didn't need to call me that, but using the formal title while in front of others or when business concerning Atlantia was being discussed was a sign of respect. "Would you care for something to drink?" I offered, gesturing to the table. "There is mulled wine and water."

A quick smile appeared on Valyn's face, hinting at the deep dimples his son shared. "That I would." He glanced over his shoulder. "I'm sure Sven would also enjoy a glass."

"Always," the Atlantian Lord replied. I wasn't quite sure how old Perry's father was, as the visible, rich brown skin showed little signs of aging. He appeared to be in his third to fourth decade of life, but that could also mean he was seven or eight hundred years old. I reminded myself to speak to him later about his knowledge regarding old magic.

Emil turned to the table. "Would anyone else like a glass?"

There were nods from all except Aylard and the female Atlantian. As Emil poured, Kieran dipped his head toward mine. "The wolven is Lizeth Damron. The general between her and Sven is Odell Cyr," he advised quietly, referring to an Atlantian with dark hair and skin that reminded me of the beautiful, smoky quartz Duchess Teerman liked to wear in her rings. "The one standing with Aylard is Lord Murin—a changeling."

That was one of the males I had felt distrust from. "The female beside Murin?" I asked as Emil handed Valyn a glass of wine.

"That's Gayla La'Sere."

I turned to him as my gaze met Vonetta's and said in a low voice, "La'Sere and Murin do not trust us."

"Noted," Vonetta murmured, her attention fixing on them.

Stepping forward, I affixed what I hoped was a welcoming smile on my face and not false like it felt. "I imagine all of you must be tired from traveling, but there is a lot we need to discuss. Namely, our plans regarding Oak Ambler."

"Our plans?" Murin queried. His eyes were a fascinating color— sea glass. "I was unaware that plans had already been made, Your Highness. Then again, we were also unaware that you'd seized Massene."

"Which is why I hope none of you are too fatigued from travel so we can discuss these plans," I replied, his answering annoyance prickling against my skin. I met his stare. "This upsets you, which I can understand," I told him, now tasting his icy surprise. He'd either forgotten what I could do or hadn't expected me to use the ability. "But we could not wait to take Massene. They were turning innocent mortals, and they killed three of the wolven. Not only that, the Blood Crown has your King. We don't have time to waste."

"No, we don't." Valyn lowered his glass as Murin's jaw hardened. "What are these plans?"

"We know that Oak Ambler is a vital port city for Solis. Goods are shipped there and then transported to most of the northwestern cities since it's far safer to move with such large cargo by sea rather than attempting to cross the Blood Forest." I kept my hands clasped to stop them from trembling as I glanced at Hisa. The commander gave me a small nod of encouragement. "It's also the largest city in the northwest, next to Masadonia and Three Rivers."

"It is," Valyn said. "Oak Ambler is a lifeline to the eastern regions of Solis."

"We want to make sure they cannot use the ports for their armies. If we secure Oak Ambler and the coast along the Wastelands, they will be forced to take the slower route to defend any of their other cities," I began. "Admittedly, I don't know much about battle strategy, but I imagine that the Blood Crown will attempt to move their forces from Eastfall," I said, referencing a district within Carsodonia where the soldiers and guards trained. "And from the Willow Plains, where the bulk of their armies are stationed."

"But thanks to the Blood Queen, we know that they have several thousand Royal Knights," Kieran tacked on. "Vamprys that will not be able to travel during the day. Because of that, it's likely they will keep the knights at the capital, moving forces consisting of mortals and possibly Revenants through Niel Valley."

Approval hummed from Lizeth as Hisa said, "Other than Pensdurth and Masadonia, which have ports, we will be able to control supply to the cities and prevent their fleets from entering. It will be far harder for them to launch an attack from sea than it will be for us to defend on land."

Cyr nodded. "Agreed."

"You say control supply," Gayla said, creases forming between her brows. "Would we not be cutting off supplies to those cities, as well?"

I focused on her. "Cutting off supplies such as food and other necessities does nothing to aid us. We cannot starve them out. The Ascended are secure within the Rise *with* their food source. All that would do is harm the innocents, and I don't believe any Atlantian wants that."

"We don't," Sven confirmed as a deepening pinch to Gayla's features appeared.

"But would that not create instability in the cities that we could then exploit?" Aylard suggested, and that earned sharp agreement from the changeling, Murin. "Force the mortals to stand up for themselves and turn on the Ascended?"

"How many mortals do you know who have lived the majority of their lives under the Ascended's rule?" I asked.

Aylard frowned. "I don't believe I know many, but I don't see what that has to do with wanting the mortals to fight for their freedom as fiercely as we will fight for them."

"Perhaps you believe the mortals won't fight the Blood Crown." Murin's gaze moved over my features, lingering on the left side of my face—on the scars. It used to bother me when someone saw them for the first time, but that was before I'd come to understand that they represented strength and survival—two things far more important than flawless skin. "I imagine you would know, as you spent the majority of your life as one of them."

An acidic burst of irritation rolled off Vonetta as I carefully considered my response. I decided that honesty was the best approach instead of telling him to shut the hell up. Which I wanted to do. "There was a time when I didn't doubt what the Ascended told me. Not enough to take notice of the inconsistencies or to truly question any of them. I didn't even realize that the veil I wore and the chambers they kept me in were nothing more than a cage," I said, aware that Valyn watched me closely, his drink forgotten in his hand. "But I did begin to question things, even before I met your King. It was all these little things that didn't add up. It was how they treated their people and each other. It was how they lived. Questioning these little things began to unravel everything else, and it was not only overwhelming but also terrifying to begin realizing that *everything* I believed in was a lie. That's not an excuse for not opening my eyes to the truth sooner, or for not being brave or strong enough to do so. That's just reality."

Delano edged around Emil, nearing Vonetta as I scanned the generals. "And that is the same reality for the millions who were born and raised under the Ascended's rule and who weren't afforded the privileges I had. Generation after generation are taught not only to fear the return of the Atlantians but to believe that any loss or strange death that takes a loved one in the middle of the night is their fault or that of their neighbors. That they brought the wrath of an angry god upon themselves or those around them."

Gayla remained silent, shifting uncomfortably as Cyr finished off his wine in one gulp, clearly troubled. "To them, the Ascended *are* an extension of the gods. And questioning them, let alone fighting back, is like striking out against gods they believe will and already do retaliate in the most vengeful, spiteful ways. Not only that, they've seen what happens to those even suspected of being Descenters or for simply questioning the Rite or an unfair tax. There are no legitimate trials. No real evidence is required. Punishment is swift and final. I ask how we can expect them to fight back while they're trapped with those who will brutally strike—and have struck out—against them."

"We couldn't." Cyr rubbed a hand along his jaw as his golden eyes narrowed.

"Not until they know they have support," Kieran added quietly. "Not until they know they're not alone in this fight for their freedom. If we can convince them that we are not the enemy—that we have come to help them by removing the Blood Crown from power and stopping the Rite—I imagine they will find the strength to fight back."

"And how would we do that when we're about to seize their cities?" Murin asked.

I smiled at him even though his blue-green eyes were hard as chips of ice. "One way is by not starving them."

Murin's lips pressed together into a thin line.

"Another way is doing everything possible not to harm them during the siege," I added. "Or cause them to suffer loss."

A rough, short laugh came from Aylard. "I mean no disrespect, Your Highness, but you did say you knew very little of battle strategy. One would expect that with you being so...*young*," he said, and I arched a brow. "People will suffer loss. We lucked out with Massene, but innocent people will likely die when we take Oak Ambler. That is not only expected but unavoidable."

"Is it?" I queried.

"Yes," Aylard confirmed.

"Perhaps my *youth* allows me to be a bit more optimistic." I tilted my head slightly. "Or maybe it just allows me to think differently. Either way, no one on the Council of Elders wants war. Neither do I. Nor does your King. We want to avoid that, but war is inevitable. The Blood Crown cannot be reasoned with, even if some Ascended can be. But that doesn't mean there has to be a great loss of life and property. Which is what *will* happen if we make war like before and ride through the cities, tearing through the people as they try to run for safety."

"No one wants to do that," Gayla argued. "But what I haven't heard is how you plan to avoid that and be successful. Our previous methods may have been brutal, but they were effective."

"Were they, though?" I countered.

A cool burst of surprise rippled from many of them, but Valyn lifted his brows. "Considering where we stand today, the answer would be no. We retreated. We didn't win." He glanced at the generals. "And we need to remember that."

I fought a wider smile, knowing that wouldn't help win the generals over. "To answer your question, we've given the Duke and Duchess of Castle Redrock a chance to avoid a siege if they agree to our demands."

A muscle flexed along Murin's jaw. "What were your demands?"

"They were quite simple. Only five," I stated. "Denounce the Blood Crown and all that involves the Rite. They were to agree to no longer feed from the unwilling and order all Ascended and guards—mortal and vampry alike—who answer to them, to stand down. Finally, they had to agree to forfeit their positions of authority over mortals and cede them to Atlantian rule." *Temporary* Atlantian rule, but I left that part out. I didn't think we had any business ruling over mortals, but that was something I needed to discuss with Casteel.

"And how did they respond to the demands?" Murin demanded.

I glanced at Kieran, who pulled the missive from the breast pocket of his tunic. He handed it over. I unfolded the parchment, the one-sentence reply clearly visible.

WE AGREE TO NOTHING.

"Of course." Murin sneered.

"Their response was disappointing but not unexpected." I glanced down at the slip of paper, calling forth the Primal essence. Just an ember of energy sparked from the tips of my fingers and swept over the parchment. Within a heartbeat, ash fell to the ground. Knowing I was showing off, I lifted my gaze to the generals. Many stared at the dusting of ash, their eyes wide. "Was it, Kieran?"

"No," he confirmed. "That is why a few stayed behind after Emil delivered the missive. They watched, speaking with mortal business owners and those who displayed tendencies of a Descenter. They spoke to as many mortals as possible, warning them that if the Ravarels didn't accept our demands, we would take the city come tomorrow."

Another wave of disbelief screamed from the generals as Aylard muttered, "I didn't agree to any of this, by the way."

I really disliked that man.

Valyn's features had locked down. "I'm not sure if that was a wise move." He looked at Hisa. "You agreed with that?"

"I did." Hisa nodded. "It gives the people a chance to leave the city before they get caught between our forces."

"But"—Gayla stressed the word—"they now know we're coming."

"They've known that for quite some time," I replied.

Sven scratched at his beard as he drifted away from the generals, nearing the other table that had a rough map of the city drawn up. "The Royals would've already started preparing for an invasion the moment our Queen relieved them of a King."

"Except now they know exactly when we will take their city," Murin reasoned.

"It is a risk," I agreed. "One that we decided was worth it."

"That map?" Lizeth followed Sven, glancing at Hisa as she gestured at the drawing. "This is your work?"

A brief grin appeared. "It is."

"Knew it," the wolven general murmured.

"So, let's say your plan works. The people flee the city, leaving it somewhat open to us." Valyn joined the others at the map. "Where would the Ascended be found?"

"Anytime the Ascended were under threat in Masadonia or in the capital, they retreated to the Royal Seat, where they would be protected by the interior Rise." I walked over to them, Delano at my side and flanked by Kieran and Vonetta. "I imagine many, if not all, will be in Castle Redrock when we take the city during the day."

"When they will be at their weakest." Murin nodded, having finally made his way over.

"Any Ascended who attacks should be killed," Hisa continued on to another part of the plan that would also likely not sit well. "Any who stand down and do not fight should be captured and left unharmed."

"They will need to be spoken to, and it will need to be determined if they can be trusted to abide by the demands," I said. "Not all Ascended are bloodthirsty monsters. I know this. My brother wasn't."

Murin looked up, his brows lifting. "And what of our King? Would he agree with that? With any of this?"

My fingers curled inward, digging into my palms. "If you have to ask that question, then you do not know your King at all." I held his stare until he looked away. And I held myself still until I was confident that I wouldn't do something rash and very unbecoming of a Queen.

Like stab him in the face.

Murin's jaw worked. "Are there any more unexpected guidelines?"

"There are." I smiled at him, enjoying the little prick of acidic anger that came from the Lord. "If possible, no homes or buildings should be damaged. The people who flee will need places to return to. And the outer Rise? It must remain intact. It protects the people from the Craven." Guilt slithered like snakes in my veins. Wasn't I a hypocrite to stand here and speak of the importance of the Rise when I had nearly taken down an entire section of the very structure in a fit of rage? I exhaled slowly. "They will need that protection once we are finished. We'll take down the gate. That will be enough."

"It will be better for us not to funnel through one opening," Murin argued. "Hell, it would be better if we just sent what draken remain and have them handle this."

Reaver's eyes narrowed, obviously not impressed by the statement. Neither was I.

"Winning the mortals' trust won't be easier if we take down their Rise," I said, surprised that I even had to voice that. "Yes, it would be easier for us, but if we did that, then a larger portion of our army would need to remain to protect Oak Ambler from the Craven or anyone who seeks to exploit the failure of the Rise instead of blocking any western advancement."

There were murmurs of understanding, but hot, acidic anger brimmed beneath Aylard's surface and filled my throat. "I don't think mortals—their trust or general welfare—should be our concern right now," Aylard argued. "We need Oak Ambler. We need—"

"We *need* peace when this is finished." I let a bit of the humming energy come to the surface as I fixed my stare on Aylard. The moment the tinge of silver filled the corners of my vision, he took a step back. "We may need many things, but we are not conquerors. We are not *takers*. We will use what power and influence we have to destroy the Blood Crown and free your King. We need to live side by side in peace with the people of Solis when this is finished. That will never happen if we prove what the Ascended have claimed about us to be true by leaving them defenseless and burning down their homes in the process."

His pale cheeks flushed. "With all due respect, Your Highness, I fear that you remember too much of what it's like to be mortal. You're far more concerned about them than you are with securing the future and safety of *your* people."

Delano's lips peeled back in a low growl as the eather in my chest hummed, and I welcomed the essence, letting the power come to the surface as I stepped forward. Gasps echoed around me as silvery light edged the corners of my vision, followed by icy darts of shock. In the back of my mind, I realized this was the first time most of the generals had ever seen this.

Witnessed who I really was.

They knew, but seeing was...well, I imagined it was something else entirely. "Showing concern and empathy for the mortals doesn't mean I have no concern for my people. Thinking of their futures means I'm thinking of *our* future, for they will be intertwined, whether wanted or not. It *is* the only successful path forward as we will not retreat beyond the Skotos Mountains. This war will be the last one."

Energy charged the space inside the chamber. Aylard had stiffened, his golden eyes wide while Lizeth slowly lowered to one knee. She placed one hand over her heart, and the other flat against the floor.

"*Meyaah Liessa*," she whispered, a slow smile spreading across her face.

They all followed, lowering before me—the generals, Hisa, my father-in-law, Naill, Emil, and the Contou siblings. Primal essence spilled into the space around me. Reaver's strong, leathery wings unfurled, sweeping over the generals' heads.

I stared down at Aylard. At all of them. "I was born with the flesh and fire of the Primal god in my blood. Make no mistake, with each passing day, I feel less like a mortal than I did the day before."

The truth of my words entrenched deep in my bones. Into those empty, hollow places inside me. And each time those holes spread, I felt...colder and more detached, less mortal. And I had no idea if that would change or grow. If that was because of Casteel's absence and everything there or something else. But at the moment, I truly didn't care.

"I am not mortal. Neither am I Atlantian. I am a god," I reminded them. "And I will not choose between the mortals and the Atlantians when I can choose both." I pulled the eather back in, and it wasn't easy. It seemed as if it had a mind of its own and wanted to lash out. To show all of them exactly how much I wasn't mortal.

But a part of that was a lie.

The essence of the Primal wasn't uncontrollable. It was an extension of me. What it wanted was a desire I had. It was what *I* wanted.

Left uneasy by that, I banked the power and closed off my senses. The silvery glow receded, and the air settled. Reaver tucked his wings back, close to his sides. "I imagine that is what a god would do, would they not? They would choose all."

Lizeth nodded slowly. "I would think so."

"Good." I smoothed my hand over my tunic, feeling the toy horse in its pouch at my hip as I concentrated on the brand of the ring between my breasts. "I want your support because what we do at Oak Ambler will set the tone for what is to come. How we treat the mortals and the Ascended who agree to our demands will be spoken of in other cities. And *heard*. That will aid us, long after the war is finished. It will show that our intentions are good in case..."

I looked at those gathered, realizing I needed to do as Cas had taught me. "You may rise."

"In case of what?" Valyn asked quietly, the first to get to his feet.

I met his stare as pressure landed on my shoulders. "In case our intentions have to change."

Gayla's focus sharpened on me, and there seemed to be some sort of understanding there. As if she knew that I recognized that this was the best-case scenario.

That I knew all of this could go south and there could be untold losses of life on both sides. But I, with their help, would do everything to prevent that from happening.

The tension slowly eased from the room as we discussed how we planned to take Oak Ambler and then how we believed the Blood Queen had discovered a way to harness Primal energy. But when Valyn turned to me, I knew it would only be a short reprieve. "What will happen after we take Oak Ambler?"

"We might as well all get back on our knees," Emil said with a sigh. "Because you're not going to like this either, and then she's going to go full god on us again."

Vonetta shot him a narrowed-eye glare.

"I would like to go on record now," Hisa spoke, and I sent her a look identical to the one Emil had received from Vonetta. Undaunted, Hisa lifted her chin. "This is a new part of the plan that I don't agree with."

"We will have to confront the Blood Crown on many different fronts," I said. "Atlantia will need to hold Oak Ambler while a sizable force travels westward, securing the cities between here and Carsodonia."

"Sounds good." Valyn hadn't taken his eyes off me. "But what are *your* plans?"

There had been some uncertainty about sharing what I planned, especially since we couldn't be sure we didn't have a traitor in our midst. But according to both Kieran and Hisa, for them to accept Vonetta as Crown Regent, I needed to officially announce the appointment. A proclamation that would inevitably lead to questions.

The information had to be shared. "Once Oak Ambler is secured, I will leave for Carsodonia with a small group. But I'm not going there for the Blood Queen or to take the capital. I'm going for our King. I'm bringing him back with me."

Aylard stiffened. "I didn't know this."

"No one is remotely surprised to hear that," Murin snapped.

"I cannot agree to this," Valyn said. "You are the Queen, but—"

"You will not be without leadership. Vonetta will be assuming the role of Crown Regent, acting on my behalf," I announced, much to the surprise and even displeasure of a few of the generals. "Her word will be obeyed as mine would."

"I don't give a damn about leadership right now. It's *you* that I'm concerned about," Valyn said, and my head jerked toward him. "You are the Queen, but you are also my daughter-in-law."

Surprise rose, momentarily leaving me speechless. "And it is *your son* who's being held captive in Carsodonia."

"Haven't forgotten that." Valyn moved closer. "Think about that every waking moment because *both* of my sons are there."

My heart twisted. "Then you, more than anyone, shouldn't want to stop me. The longer she has him, and the more cities we take, the more he's in danger." *More than I already endangered him.* "I cannot risk that."

"I, more than anyone, understand why you feel the need to do this. The gods know I want my sons here. I want them both safe and healthy. But not a single member of my family has ever entered Carsodonia and returned as they were when they left—if they returned at all." Valyn's stare met mine. "I will not have that happen to you."

My family.

Valyn considered me part of his family. My throat constricted as a wealth of emotion threatened to rise unchecked. I tamped it down. I had to.

"She will not be alone," Kieran spoke quietly. "I, nor any of us, will allow anything to happen to her. Neither will she."

Valyn's amber eyes flared as he looked at Kieran. "You not only support this but plan to go with her? As the advisor? I would've expected different from you."

"My support of this has little to do with being Advisor to the Crown," Kieran stated. "Unlike last time Cas was taken, I will not stand by. And I will not try to stop her and fail, only to have her go off by herself. No way either of those things are happening. And maybe that makes me a poor choice as advisor. I don't know. And I don't care."

I blinked away the burn in my eyes and cleared my throat. "I know what kind of risk this is, but I'm willing to take it. I can't wait until we cross Solis." I pressed a hand to my chest, feeling the ring under my tunic. "*He* cannot wait for that."

Valyn shook his head slowly as the others looked on. "Penellaphe," he said softly. "I know you care for my son greatly. That you would do anything for him. And I know that you are powerful— more so than the whole of our armies. But this is too much of a risk. One my son would never want you to take."

"You're right. Casteel would never want me to take such a risk, not even for him. Not even when he would do the same if it were me who had been taken. But he also wouldn't try to stop me."

Valyn's eyes slammed shut for a brief moment. "Then I will go with you."

"Absolutely not," I said, my heart stopping. His eyes flew open. "You know exactly what she will do if she has you in her grip. Eloana knows exactly what the Blood Queen will do."

Silence fell around us as Valyn stared back at me. He knew that I spoke the truth. Not only did Isbeth blame both of them for her son's death and Malec's entombment, but she would do it just to lash out at Eloana. I would *not* have his blood on my hands.

"As your Queen, I forbid it," I stated, and he turned his head, a muscle ticking under his temple at the outright demand—the pulling of rank. "At noon tomorrow, we will take Oak Ambler, and then I will leave for Carsodonia while the Atlantian armies continue on as planned," I told him—told them all. "My mind won't be changed."

Casteel

One more time.

Exhaustion dogged me as I braced a hand on the wall and slammed my foot down as hard as I could.

Bone cracked and gave way.

"Thank fuck," I muttered, breathing heavily.

The Craven that had found its way into my cell this time had been nothing but skin and bones—brittle bones.

I lowered myself to the floor. Or my legs gave out. One or the other. Dizzy, I reached into the gore, pulling the shin bone free. One end was more jagged than the other. Perfect. I could sharpen it even further on the edges of the chains, where the hardened spurs were.

The weapon wouldn't do much when it came to the Revs or even Isbeth. A false god was a god for all intents and purposes, but it could do some damage. Bloody damage.

I kicked the remains away, knowing that whatever Handmaiden would eventually show up and remove it before it revived wouldn't look too closely at the Craven.

Leaning back against the wall, I took a breather. Only a few minutes. I needed to stay awake, even though I wanted nothing more than to sleep. To dream of Poppy.

But that hadn't been a dream. At least, not a normal one. I should've known that it was something different. Poppy had looked far too real. *Felt* too real—too soft and warm. It hadn't occurred to me that we were dream walking until I saw her eyes.

Saw how they were different.

By then, we'd begun to slip away from each other, and I had wasted the opportunity to tell her...

What would I have told her? Where I might be held? Which was somewhere...*underground*. Not really helpful information there, but I could have told her what Isbeth was. Someone may know if a demis had the same weaknesses as a god or goddess. I could've...

A spasm ran through me, tightening my muscles painfully.

I needed to feed.

The barbed ache of hunger chewed away at me, and with the only sound the trickle of water, my eyes drifted shut. I must've dozed off. Or passed out. Either was possible, but the sound of footsteps pulled me from the nothingness. My eyes snapped open, taking far longer than usual to adjust to the dimness of the space as I shoved the Craven bone behind me. The steps weren't the shuffling click and drag of a Craven, nor obnoxiously loud as that Handmaiden's had been. The rhythmic, lazy *stroll* ceased as I focused on the void of the entryway. At first, I saw nothing but shadows, but the longer I stared, I realized that the shadows were too thick. Too solid.

Awareness prickled over my flesh as I began making out the figure in the darkness. Tall but otherwise shapeless. The shadow drifted forward into the weak glow of the candlelight—the *cloaked* shadow.

I stared, heart starting to pound. The cloak was black and long, more like a shroud, and the hood was situated so the face was nothing but darkness. Much like the one I'd worn in Solis when I hadn't wanted to be seen. The one that had given me the moniker of the Dark One.

This wasn't a Handmaiden that stood before me. And the cloaked figure was too tall to be Callum.

It didn't move.

Neither did I as acid churned in my gut.

The cloaked figure lifted hands to the hood, lowering it.

Every part of my being tensed.

I'd seen the life go out of men's eyes. I'd stood in gore of my making, hands and face slick with blood as I stared upon something that had become unrecognizable. I'd seen all manner of shit that would haunt most, but I'd never wanted to look away. Not until the night Poppy had learned who I truly was. The horror and betrayal dawning in those beautiful green eyes and the way I saw her fragile trust shatter made me sick.

And I felt that now. Sick. Wanting to look away. But just like that night with Poppy, I made myself see what was before me. Something else that had become unrecognizable.

My brother.

What I felt was nothing like that night with Poppy when I had been choking on shame. I felt a brief burst of relief to see that he was alive, but that was quickly snuffed out. Now, there was only anger, and it crowded out any chance for denial to take root.

"Motherfucker," I growled.

Malik smiled. It wasn't a smile I knew. Wasn't real. "Yeah…" His arms fell to his sides.

Several long moments passed. We just stared at each other. I didn't know what the hell he saw. Didn't care.

"You look well for someone who's been held *captive* for a century," I bit out.

Malik did look well. The light brown, shoulder-length hair was longer than I remembered him wearing it but clean. It even fucking shone in the candlelight. There was no gaunt paleness to his golden-bronze skin. No dullness to his amber eyes. The cut of his cloak was fine, the material sable in color and clearly tailored to the width of his shoulders. Closer now, I saw that he was thinner, but while Malik was a handful of inches taller than me, I'd always been broader.

"Can't say the same about you," he replied.

"Suppose not."

He fell silent again. Just stood there, his expression unreadable. Poppy's ability to read emotions would've come in handy. Unless he'd put shields up. Had he known to do so when we met in Oak Ambler? There had been no time to learn if she had picked up *anything* from him. To know if he was as empty on the inside as he appeared.

"Is that all you have to say to me?" Malik asked finally.

A dry, wracking laugh shook my shoulders. "There's a lot I want to say."

"Then say it." Malik came forward, brushing aside his cloak as he knelt. The shafts of his leather boots were remarkably clean. They'd never been spotless before, always splattered with mud or covered with pieces of straw he inevitably tracked from the stables through the palace. He stared at my wrapped hand. "I'm not going to stop you."

My lip curled. "I haven't *earned* your visit. So, what did *you* do to earn it, *brother?*"

"I did nothing, *Cas.*"

"Bullshit."

His gaze flicked up from my hand. That mockery of a smile returned, hinting at the one dimple in his left cheek. "I'm not supposed to be here."

There was a moment, a quick one, where hope took form. Just like that Handmaiden had said, Malik was never where he was supposed to be. Growing up, we had to hunt him down when it came to our lessons, something that had become sort of a game for Kieran and me. We'd made wagers on who would find Malik first. Come suppertime, he was always late, usually because he'd been fucking with the food or drink—or simply *fucking*. On more than one occasion, I'd heard our mother telling Kirha that she had a feeling she would become a grandmother while still Queen. She'd been wrong, much to the surprise of all. Even me.

But hope fizzled out. His inability to be where he shouldn't be wasn't a sign that my brother, the one I knew and loved, was still in this shell of a man. It was evidence of something else entirely.

"You and the bitch that close now?" The band at my throat tightened. I forced my body to relax against the wall. "That you don't worry about being punished?"

The divot in his cheek disappeared. "What I do and don't worry about doesn't change that we're still brothers."

"It changes everything."

Malik went quiet again, his gaze lowering. Another long moment stretched between us, and gods, he looked like my brother. Sounded like him. I'd spent decades fearing I'd never see him again. And here he was—yet wasn't.

"What did she do to you?" I asked.

The skin around his mouth pulled taut. "Let me see your hand."

"Fuck off."

"You're starting to hurt my feelings."

"What part of *fuck off* gives you the impression that I'm worried about your feelings?"

Malik chuckled, and the sound was familiar. "Man, you have changed." He grabbed my left wrist, and I started to pull away, as pointless an endeavor as that was in my current state. His eyes narrowed. "Don't be a brat."

"Haven't been one of them in a long time."

"Doubtful," he murmured, beginning to unwrap my hand. His fingers were warm and callused. I wondered if he still handled a sword, and if Isbeth would allow that. He uncovered the wound, letting the bandage slip to the stone. "*Fuck.*"

"Attractive, huh?" My laugh was cold, even as I thought of all the times he'd inspected some minor scrape when we were young. When I *was* a brat. "Is this the *truth* she opened your eyes to?"

His gaze flew to mine, his eyes brighter than before. "You don't know what you're talking about."

I pitched forward, ignoring the band as it started to squeeze. My face was suddenly in his. "What did she do to break you?"

"What makes you think I'm broken?"

"Because you aren't whole. If you were, you wouldn't stand beside the monster you came to free me from. The same piece of shit that—"

"I know exactly what she did." His stare held mine. "Let me ask you a question, Cas. How did it feel when you realized that our mother—and likely our father—lied to us about who Queen Ileana was?"

Anger pulsed hotly within me. "How do you think?"

"Furious. Disappointed," he said after a moment. "Even more pissed. That was how I felt."

Yeah, that about summed it up.

"Is that why you're with Isbeth? Betrayed everyone and your kingdom?" I asked. "Because Momma and Papa lied to us?"

His lips twisted into a thin smile. "Why I'm here has nothing to do with our parents. Though, if they had been honest, I have to wonder if either of us would be here."

Knowing who the Blood Queen truly was could've changed everything. "Yeah."

"But none of that changes that your wound is infected."

"I don't give a shit about the wound."

"You should." A muscle ticked in his jaw, in the same place it did in our father's, right below the temple. "This should've healed by now."

"No shit," I spat as the band dug into my windpipe.

"You need to feed."

"Dare I be repetitive and say *no shit?*"

A slight upward curve of his lips appeared. "Dare you continue choking yourself?"

"Fuck you." I sat back, taking shallow breaths as the band slowly loosened.

"You curse more than you used to," he remarked, looking back down at my hand.

"Does it offend your newly found sensibilities?"

He laughed. "Nothing offends my sensibilities anymore."

"Now that I believe."

Malik raised a brow. "If I give you blood, my visit will be discovered."

"So, you do worry about being punished?"

Those cold eyes lifted. "It's not me who'd be punished."

Disgust churned in my empty gut. "Is that supposed to mean you care about what she does to me? Even as you stand by her side?"

"Believe what you want." He reached into the folds of his cloak, tugging on a strap. He pulled a narrow leather satchel forward, the kind Healers often carried with them. "Figured you'd need aid."

I said nothing, just watched him pull out a small bottle. What that Handmaiden had said came back to me. She'd claimed to have made a promise when I asked why she was here. And said that she was bored. But she'd known my hand was infected.

And by the looks of it, Malik had come prepared because of that knowledge.

Had he asked her to check on me? Or had she gone to him?

"Without blood, your body is about as useful as a mortal's," he remarked. "The infection will spread and get into your blood. Won't kill you, but you'll end up where you don't want to be even faster."

I knew exactly *where* that was. I'd been at the edge with Poppy in New Haven, but I'd toppled over that cliff when I was held before.

Malik unscrewed the lid, and an astringent scent filled the space. "This is going to sting like the fires of the Abyss. Hope you don't scream and cry like you used to." He took my wrist in a firm grasp. "It won't end well for you if you do."

"I didn't scream when the fucker cut it off, so what do you think?"

That muscle flexed under his temple once more. "You might want to take a deep breath then."

I did, only because I knew what was coming. Malik poured the liquid over the partly exposed bone and nerve, his gaze locked on mine. And, fuck, I wanted to scream like holy hell. The breath I took did nothing to ease the fiery burn. I gritted my teeth so hard, it was a wonder my molars didn't crack. The pain made it difficult to breathe or understand what the hell Malik was saying, but he was talking because his lips were moving, so I made myself push past the torment and focus.

"Stings like a bastard, doesn't it? The pain is worth it. Shit's a miracle. Not even sure how she created it. Didn't really want to ask." A wry grin came, and even in scorching agony, I recognized that lopsided grin that revealed one fang. That was *real*. "But it will force the infection out and get your skin healing." He paused. "Yeah, it's working."

Jaw aching, I watched the liquid bubble across my hand and foam along the knuckle. The pain lessened enough that I no longer wanted to bash my head into a wall. From the froth, a thick, whitish-yellow pus oozed out, stinking about as bad as the damn Craven I'd kicked into the corner.

"You didn't even flinch." Malik sounded surprised. "I guess you've felt worse." Another heartbeat of silence. "And you've probably inflicted far worse pain on others."

"You heard?" I replied hoarsely.

"I have, but I'm not talking about what you did to the Ascended. Or to that Craven over there. Got a little messy, didn't you?" He stared down at my hand. The pus had slowed, no longer a steady, disgusting stream. "You know what I've been thinking about lately?"

"How fucked up you've become?" I suggested.

He barked out a sharp laugh. "I should probably clarify. I meant to say—you know *who* I've been thinking about lately?"

"Options are limitless."

"Shea."

Her name was a surprise. Worse than a curse. A once-welcomed memory that had become nothing more than a waste.

"I know what she did. They told me. Didn't believe it at first, but then I remembered how much she loved you. More than I think you even knew or deserved." He tipped the bottle over the stump of the finger.

I hissed as the liquid hit my flesh and foamed once more, but not as intensely as before.

"Then I knew they didn't lie. She set me up," he continued with a short laugh. "You kill her?"

Unlocking my jaw, I forced out, "Yeah."

"Sorry to hear that."

I wanted to believe that he was. I didn't.

He set the bottle aside. "Knowing you, you kept what she did a secret, didn't you? Bet only Kieran knows."

The stench from the wound wasn't so bad now. Neither was the pain. "Does it matter?"

"Not really." He let go of my hand. "Just that we've all had to do some messed-up shit, haven't we?"

"Well, if anyone has been keeping score of messed-up shit, you've won," I told him.

"Looks like it's you who actually won, little brother." He pulled out a small cloth from the satchel. "Found love." Turning my hand over, he revealed the imprint. "Became a King." He drew his thumb over the swirl. "You have the life I once thought I'd have."

The rage returned, as fiery as the pain had been. "Poppy never would've been yours."

"She could've been," he murmured. His grip on my hand tightened. "You look like you want to punch me. Hard."

"Sounds about right," I snarled.

He smirked as he dabbed the cloth along the knuckle. "It's funny."

"What is?"

"You're angry with me, when you've spent the last century living your life—your *best* life as it appears."

"Living?" I seethed. "I spent those years trying to find a way to free *you*. Not just me. Kieran, Delano, Naill. Countless others. Many who gave their fucking lives to bring you home—good men and women you don't even know, gave everything to free you. And this whole time, you were a *willing* pet." Unholy fury swamped me as he dropped the cloth and pulled out some fresh gauze, unfazed by my words. That pushed out what I said next. "Do you even wonder what happened to Preela?"

Malik went rigid, his pupils dilating.

"Because I have. The bond weakened her, and yet she still tried to save you. No one could stop her. She snuck out one night, and we never saw her again. But we knew. She died, didn't she?" I searched his face for a hint of something—guilt or sorrow. Anything. Preela was his bonded wolven, and they had been as close as Kieran and I were, which was why he had forbidden her from accompanying him when he left to look for me. "You would know exactly when she passed."

I saw it—godsdamn, I saw the reaction. If I'd blinked, I might have missed it. A flinch.

"She died." That muscle below his temple ticked even faster. "But not before she made it all the way to Carsodonia. I don't know how she managed it, but Preela made it all the way here, just to be captured." He leaned in. "The beast who's currently missing a head thanks to your wife killed her. Not quickly. Not before he had his fun. Not before many, *many* others had their fun."

Shit.

"I know this because I got a front-row seat. I got to see what he did afterwards when he carved her up, broke her bones into pieces that were eventually hardened and melded to bloodstone." Only a thin strip of amber was visible as he stared at me. "He made seven wolven daggers out of her bones. I found six of them, and I know exactly where the seventh one is." He nodded slowly. "Yeah, I know who has it."

I couldn't even focus on the possibility that Poppy's dagger had been crafted from Preela's bones. It was the answer to my question.

What had broken him.

This was it. And it had happened far before I ever imagined.

I couldn't blame him.

It was then that I realized that Malik hadn't been completely unaffected by what had gone down at Castle Redrock. Malik *had* shown some sort of emotion there. Twice. When Isbeth had summoned that Handmaiden and had one of her knights stab her, he had made a move as if to step forward. He'd been clenching his jaw, too, like he had when Alastir and our father spoke of war with Solis—something he'd been adamantly against. And he'd been shocked when Isbeth had killed Ian. He hadn't expected that.

This was the third time I'd seen him affected.

"She told you my hand was infected, didn't she?" I asked. "The Handmaiden."

Those pupils expanded once more.

"She said some wild stuff while she was here."

Malik didn't blink as he locked stares with me. "Like what?"

"Like some nonsensical shit about things awakening, and Isbeth creating something powerful enough to remake the realms."

He'd gone completely still, all except that ticking muscle.

Cold fingers of unease brushed the back of my neck. "What was she talking about, *brother*?"

Another long moment passed. "Who knows what she was saying. She's a…"

I watched him closely. "A bit odd?"

Malik laughed, and it was a punch to the gut because it too was real. The amber in his eyes became more visible. "Yes." He dragged his teeth over his lower lip. "I know you hate me. I deserve it. More than you realize. But you have no reason to hate her."

"I don't give a fuck about her."

"Didn't say you did, but she hasn't done anything to you, and she took one hell of a risk searching for you and seeing what kind of mess you'd become. I know you don't have any reason to protect her, but if anyone finds out that she was down here and talking to you? It will not end well for her."

"Why should I care?" I challenged, wanting to know why *he* cared.

"Because, just like your beloved," he said, his voice low as he held my gaze, "she's had very little choice when it comes to her life. So, don't take it out on her. That's all I ask, and I've never asked you for anything."

He never had.

It had always been me asking things of him. But that was a different life.

I searched those shielded eyes. If I weren't so weak, I could use a compulsion—something Malik had never been good at. "You care for her."

"I'm incapable of caring about anyone anymore," he replied. "But I owe her."

The flatness in the way he'd said that left a chill in my chest. I slumped against the wall. "I never gave up on you, Malik," I said wearily. "And I didn't live."

"Until now." He began wrapping my hand. "Until Penellaphe."

"This has nothing to do with her."

"Everything has to do with her," he murmured.

"Bullshit." I shook my head. "Why do you think I even entertained the idea of meeting with the Blood Queen after what she did to me—what she'd done to you? It wasn't just about Atlantia. It wasn't only about what the Blood Crown was doing to mortals. Those were secondary things. It was always about you. I came to Oak Ambler, prepared to negotiate for you. Poppy came to Oak Ambler, prepared to do the same, and she didn't even know you."

A strange look crossed his features, pinching his brow. "No, she didn't know me." He folded the gauze, covering the wound. "Or at least that's what she remembers."

My head tilted. "What does that mean?"

"You'll understand soon enough." Malik tucked the tail of the gauze under the wrapping. "I have a feeling you will be reunited with your Queen sooner rather than later."

Poppy

Running my fingers over the cool handle crafted from wolven bone, a faint smile tugged at my lips as I thought of the man who'd gifted me the dagger on my sixteenth birthday.

Neither Vikter nor I had known exactly *when* my birthday was. He'd said the same thing as Casteel: Pick a day. I'd chosen April twentieth.

I had no idea where he'd gotten such a blade. I'd never seen another. When he gave it to me, he'd placed his hand over mine and said, *"This weapon is as unique as you. Take good care of it, and she will return the favor."*

My smile grew, relieved that I could think of Vikter without drowning in grief. The sorrow was still there. It always would be. But it had gotten easier.

"I hope you're proud of me," I whispered. Proud of my choice to lead the Atlantian armies, to take the same risks as the soldiers and weather whatever *marks* this war left behind. After all, *he* had taught me the importance of that.

Like when I'd accidentally discovered what those white handkerchiefs tacked to the doors of homes in Masadonia meant, and how Vikter had helped those families inside, those who couldn't carry through on what needed to be done. He gave those cursed—those infected by a Craven's bite—a quick, honorable death before they became a monster that would attack their family and anyone else who came near them. A peaceful death instead of the public execution the Ascended liked to carry out for the cursed.

I'd asked him once how he could be surrounded by so much death and remain untouched by it. For the longest time, I didn't understand his answer.

"I'm not untouched by it. Death is death. Killing is killing, Poppy, no matter how justified it is. Every death leaves a mark behind, but I do not expect anyone to take a risk that I would not take. Nor would I ask another to bear a burden I refused to shoulder or feel a mark I haven't felt myself."

I eventually understood what he meant when I saw the true extent of how many—young and old—were really infected. There were a couple of dozen executions a year, but in reality, hundreds were infected. Hundreds of mortals cursed while doing what the Ascended would not do for themselves, even though they were stronger, faster, and far more resistant to injury than a mortal.

I thought I understood. But now? I sheathed the wolven dagger to my thigh. Now, I realized that Vikter's words had meant far more than just aiding the cursed. He wasn't a Descenter, but looking back, I suspected that he had been talking about the Ascended. The Blood Crown, who asked so much of those they were supposed to serve while doing so very little *for* them.

Whether I was a Maiden or Queen, a mortal or a god, I would never allow myself to become someone who would not take the very same risks I asked of others. Nor would I refuse to carry those *marks* Vikter had spoken of while expecting others to bear that kind of weight.

Tightening the thin strap that lay diagonally across my chest, I picked up a short sword made of iron and bloodstone. Far lighter than the golden Atlantian weapons, I slid the blade into the scabbard secured against my back so the grip was facing downward, near my hip.

Laid across the map, the remaining weapons beckoned in the early morning sunlight streaming in through the window. I planted a booted foot on the chair and reached for a steel blade. My fingers skimmed the straps holding my shin guards in place. I slid the dagger into the shaft of my boot and switched feet, placing a matching one in the other. Then I picked up a slender spike of bloodstone with a hilt no wider than my arm. I slid that into a forearm sheath. It was a favorite of Vonetta's. She normally carried one on each arm while in her mortal form. I secured the second short sword, strapping it to my back so it crossed the first, and the pommel sat at my left hip. Picking up the final blade, a brutal, curved one, I glanced down at myself, wondering exactly where I would place it.

"Do you think you have enough weapons?"

I looked up to see Valyn standing in the doorway. I hadn't seen him since he'd left yesterday.

Throat warming, I glanced down at myself. "I don't think you can ever have enough weapons."

"Normally, I would agree with that statement," he said, his hand resting on the hilt of one of the three swords I could *see* on him. I was sure the gold and steel armor hid more. "But you will be the deadliest weapon on that battlefield."

My stomach tumbled a little as I lowered the sickle-shaped blade. "I hope I won't have to use that kind of weapon."

Valyn's head cocked in a painfully familiar way that twisted my heart as he eyed me. "You really mean that."

"I do." I wasn't sure why, but Valyn's observation nagged at me. Why had I picked up so many weapons? My brows knitted as I tried to understand my apparently unconscious choices. "I just… The abilities I have can be used to heal. I'd rather use them for that." I looked up at him as I hooked the sickle blade to my hip. "Unless I have to use them to fight. And if I do, I won't hesitate."

"I didn't think you would." He continued staring, though not at the scars. "You look like…"

I knew how I appeared.

My lip curled as I eyed the sleeve of my gown—the *white* gown. The night in New Haven, when I decided that I could no longer be the Maiden, I'd made promises to myself. One of those was that I would never be garbed in white again.

I'd broken that promise today with the aid of Naill and the wolven, Sage. The linen gown was one of two that had been constructed from one of Kieran's tunics, the hem ending at the knees and the sides left open to allow me to reach the wolven dagger strapped to my thigh. Under it, I wore a pair of thick tights that I'd borrowed from Sage. The stitches had been loosened, as the wolven was at least a size or two smaller than I, and then reinforced. Both were a *pure*, pristine white, as were the armor plates at my shoulders, and my breastplates. Naill had even managed to tack white cloth over the thin armor. He'd done an amazing job, providing exactly what I'd asked for, and then he'd doubled it. There was another gown. Another pair of tights.

I hated it with every fiber of my being.

But what I wore would serve a purpose. I was not the Queen any mortal would recognize. The gilded crown meant nothing to them.

The white of the Maiden did.

"How you imagined the Maiden looked?" I finished for him. "Except, normally, I wore a veil instead of armor and..." My cheeks warmed again. "And not nearly as many weapons."

He gave a quick shake of his head, causing a strand of hair to slip free from the knot he'd tied the rest back in. It fell across his cheek. "I was going to say you look like one of my favorite paintings."

"Oh." I shifted a bit awkwardly.

"Of the goddess, Lailah, to be exact. Not in physical appearance, but the armor and straight spine. The strength. There's actually a painting in the palace. Not sure if you had a chance to see it, but it's of the Goddess of Peace and Vengeance. She wore white armor."

"I haven't seen it."

"I think you would like it."

I couldn't help but think of Casteel and what he would think if he saw me like this. He would approve of the weapons. Greatly. The gown?

He'd probably tear it off and set it afire.

Thoughts of Casteel made me think of the dream—and what it could mean. "There's something I wanted to ask you."

"Ask away."

"Kieran thought you may know if it's possible for heartmates to walk in each other's dreams."

"I remember reading something that made that claim. They actually called it..." Valyn's brow creased. "Soul walking. Not dream walking. Said that the souls could find each other, even in dreams." His expression smoothed out. "Did something like that happen?"

It took everything in me not to allow the dream to form in any sort of detail. "I had a dream that was incredibly vivid. It didn't feel like a normal dream, and I think Casteel realized it was different, too, right before I woke up. I mean, I could be wrong, and it could've just been a dream."

"I think it's exactly what you believe. Soul walking between heartmates," he said. "My son said he believed you were his heartmate—not that he needed to tell me that. I saw it for myself after the attack at the Chambers of Nyktos when he awoke to find that you'd been taken. I saw it in your eyes and heard it in your voice when you spoke of your plans to go to Carsodonia. You two have found something so very few ever experience."

"We have," I whispered, my throat tightening.

Valyn smiled, but the faint lines of his face seemed deeper as he let out a rough breath. "I passed Kieran on the way to see you," Valyn stated, much to my relief. "I could tell he worried about why I wanted to speak with you. Other than his family, the only other person I've ever seen him this loyal to is Casteel. And that kind of loyalty goes beyond any sort of bond—even a Primal *notam*." He turned his head toward me, his golden eyes sheltered. "He's good for you. For both of you."

"I know." I opened my senses to Valyn and brushed up against what reminded me of a Rise. The urge to find the cracks I knew had to be in his shields hit me again. Reaching for the pouch at my hip instead of the ring, I squeezed the toy horse and pushed past the need. "If you're here to try to convince me not to go to Carsodonia, I...I appreciate your concern—more than you probably realize," I admitted. "But I have to do this."

"I wish there was something I could say that would change your mind, but you're stubborn. Like my son. Like both my sons." He touched the back of a chair. "Do you mind if I sit?"

"Of course, not." I moved to the seat across from him and sat in the thick, upholstered chair.

"Thank you." The armor creaked as he lowered, stretching out his right leg. "I know I can't change your mind, but I'm worried. A lot can happen. A lot can go wrong. If we lose you in addition to them—"

"They're not lost. We know where they are. I'm going to find them," I told him. "And maybe Malik is—" I drew in a deep breath, squeezing the horse again. "Maybe Malik is lost to us. But Casteel isn't. I will get him back, and I will do as you asked before if necessary."

A ragged breath left him, and he appeared to take a few moments to collect himself.

Slowly, I extended my left hand and showed him my palm—my marriage imprint. "He's alive. Sometimes, I need to be reminded of that," I whispered. "He lives."

Valyn stared at my hand for what felt like a small eternity, then his eyes briefly closed. I'd kept my senses open, and for a moment, I picked up on something from him—something that reminded me of the sour green mangos that Tawny had enjoyed with breakfast every so often. Was it guilt? Shame? It was too brief to know for sure.

"With everything that has been happening, there hasn't been a lot of time, but there's something we need to talk about. And I have walked this realm long enough to know there's not always a later," he said, and my chest clenched. I knew anything could happen, but I didn't want to think about *that* happening to him. "I know what you discussed with my wife upon your return to Evaemon," he announced.

Every muscle in my body tensed, but my grip on the toy horse loosened.

He leaned back in the chair, rubbing his knee. "I know that you were angry with her."

"I still am." I slid my hand from the pouch before I did something stupid, like accidentally set it on fire. "That is not in the past."

"And you have every right to be. As does Casteel and Malik if he…" He exhaled roughly. "I'm not here to speak for Eloana, only for myself. I'm sure you've wondered if I knew the truth about the Blood Queen."

I flattened my hands on my thighs. "I have. It's one of the things I think about when I can't sleep at night," I shared. "Did you know? I'm willing to bet Alastir did."

"He did," Valyn confirmed, and if Alastir hadn't already been ripped to pieces and most likely consumed by the wolven, I would've dug up his body just so I could stab him again. Repeatedly. "He knew before I did."

Surprise flickered through me, but I didn't trust my reaction. "Really?"

"I had assumed that she died, either before the war or during it. I believed that for many years," he said, and I kept myself quiet and still. "Eloana never spoke of her or Malec, and I let it be because I knew it was difficult for her. That a part of her loved him, although he wasn't deserving of such a gift. That a part of her would always love him, even though she loves me."

Now that *did* surprise me. Valyn knew what Eloana had admitted to me, and I didn't think for a moment that knowledge lessened how much Valyn loved her. A measure of respect grew in me for the man. Because if Casteel felt that way for Shea, I would be consumed by irrational jealousy.

"It wasn't until she took Casteel the first time that Eloana told me what she had learned about the Queen of Solis," he continued, the muscle under his temple ticking again. "I was…" A dry laugh left him. "Furious doesn't quite capture what I felt then. If I had known the truth, I never would've retreated. I would've known that we couldn't end the war that way. That there was too much personal history for there to ever be an end, and maybe that's why she kept it a secret for so long. Or maybe it was because the lie had somehow become an unbreakable truth that held things together. I don't know, but what I *do* know is that I need to tell the truth now. I didn't know from the beginning, but I knew the truth about her for long enough. The whole situation is…hard and complicated."

"That's not an excuse."

"You're right," he agreed quietly. "It just *is*."

Anger simmered in my blood and at the core of my chest, seeping into those cold, empty parts of me. "You knew long enough to have warned Malik. To tell Casteel and me. If we had known the truth, we could've been better prepared. We could've decided there was no reason to attempt to negotiate with Isbeth," I said, and tension bracketed his mouth at the mention of her name. "If we had known, we could've located Malec and gotten leverage. At any point, either of you could've done that. But doing that would crack the foundation of Atlantia's lies. So, I don't remotely care how complicated and hard the situation was. Neither of you told the truth because you were both afraid of how it would affect you—how people looked upon you. Whether you would still have the support of the people if they learned that the Queen of Solis was the mistress *their* Queen had tried to kill. That Isbeth was never a vampry. She wasn't the first Ascended. Atlantia was built on lies, just like Solis."

"I…I cannot disagree with any of that," he said, holding my gaze. "And if we could go back and do the right thing, we would. We would've told the truth about her."

"Her name is Isbeth." My fingers dug into my legs. "Not speaking her name doesn't change that it is her."

Valyn lowered his chin, nodding. "Nor does that make it any easier to speak her name. Or think that she is your mother. Truly, we believed that you were possibly a deity, a descendant of one of the mortals Malec had an affair with. We didn't know what he was until you told us." He paused. "Though I am grateful to have learned that he's not your father. *Twins*. Malec and Ires. That explains why you share some of his features."

The shock Eloana had felt when I told her that Malec was a god had been too vivid to have been fabricated. I'd wanted to ask if that knowledge would've changed what they would've done with the truth regarding Isbeth, but I didn't. What was the point? His answer would change nothing.

"Did Eloana tell you about Isbeth and Malec's son?" I asked, remembering what Eloana had told me.

"She did." He dragged a hand over his chin. "And I believed her when she said that she was unaware of the child until Alastir told her."

I wasn't sure if I believed that. Because they had known that Alastir had located what they believed to be a descendant of Malec's, and that their advisor—their *friend*—had left that child, who happened to be *me*, to be killed by the Craven. They had made peace with such a horrific act because they had believed Alastir was acting in the best interests of Atlantia.

I hadn't blamed them for what Alastir had done. I still didn't. I held them responsible for what they knew and what they chose to do with that knowledge—or not do.

"I have a lot of regret," Valyn said roughly. "So does my wife. I don't ask for forgiveness. Neither would Eloana."

That was good to know because I wasn't sure how I felt about either of them. But forgiveness was never the issue for me. That was easy. Sometimes, too easy. It was understanding and accepting why they did what they did, and I hadn't had time to come to terms with that. "Then what is it you're asking for?"

"Nothing." His gaze met mine again. "I just wanted you to know the truth. I didn't want that to go unspoken between us."

I thought there may be another reason that went beyond clearing the air with me. He wanted me to know in case he never saw his sons again. So I would be able to tell them what he'd shared with me.

Silence stretched out, and I didn't know what to say or do. It was Valyn who broke the quiet. "It's almost time, isn't it?"

"It is," I said. "I expect to see you on the other side of this."

The smile returned, lessening some of the deep lines. "You will."

We left the manor then, Emil and a small horde of Crown Guards who seemed to have appeared out of thin air flanking me. Valyn reached out, clasping my shoulder briefly as we neared the armies waiting at the edge of the property, then he walked ahead.

As the soldiers became aware of my arrival, they placed their sword hands to their hearts and bowed. The pressure of their gazes, their trust, weighed down my steps. My entire body hummed, but the salty, nutty flavor of their resolve calmed my nerves. There would be no big speeches—no pomp or display of authority. They knew what to do today.

I joined Kieran at the front, where he stood beside Setti and another horse. Only Emil followed now. The Crown Guards joined the divisions.

The wolven looked over his shoulder. A cool splash of surprise reached me as he turned, watching my approach.

"What?" I asked.

"Nothing," he replied, clearing his throat. "I hate what you're wearing."

"Join the club."

"It's a club I want no part of." He looked away, eyeing the former King as he joined Sven and Cyr. "Is everything all right? I saw Valyn enter your room."

"It is." I took Setti's reins from Kieran and then gripped the saddle, hoisting myself onto him. As I got seated, the sight of the wolven general snagged my attention. Lizeth cut through the rows of soldiers, making her way toward the Commander of the Crown Guard. Hisa would remain with Valyn and the generals to ensure that our plans were followed.

Hisa turned from her horse, clasping the back of Lizeth's head. Her fingers tangled in the blond strands. Concern radiated from her. "Be careful."

The female wolven pressed her forehead to Hisa's. "But be brave," she replied, kissing her.

"Always," Hisa confirmed.

"But be brave," I whispered, looking away. I liked that. Be careful but be brave.

And we would all be that today.

13

The short journey into the Pinelands surrounding Oak Ambler, beyond the initial rows of bowed trees, was quiet. The only sounds were the snapping of needles and twigs scattered across the road. The dappled sunlight lent a peacefulness, one completely at odds with what was to come.

I sat stiffly in the saddle, holding Setti's reins just as Casteel had taught me. The armor was thin and formfitting, especially the cuirass covering my chest and back, but not exactly the most comfortable thing I'd ever worn. The armor was a necessity. I may be able to survive most wounds, but I didn't plan on being unnecessarily weakened, especially if I ended up needing to use the eather.

Emil rode to my left and had never looked more serious than he did now, continuously scanning the thickly clustered trees. Kieran was to my right. It was just the three of us riding toward Oak Ambler.

Or so it appeared.

I wanted to give those at the Rise a chance to make the right decision. Showing up with an army would immediately put them on the defensive, making it unlikely they'd open the gates and allow anyone who wished to leave to do so.

But we were not alone.

The wolven had spread out through the forest, moving quietly as they looked for Solis soldiers possibly hidden among the pines.

Weight pressed down on my chest, stirring the pulsing eather in my core as Setti crossed a narrow creek that had overtaken the road, kicking up water and loose soil. We'd been on the brink of war when the Blood Queen killed Ian and took Casteel. The war had started when I killed King Jalara. But this...*this* was the first battle. My hold on the reins tightened as my heart thumped heavily.

This was really happening.

For some reason, it hadn't struck me until now—that this felt different than Massene. This was actual *war*. All the planning and waiting, and *now* it felt surreal.

What if no one took the chance to trust us? What if they all remained in the city, even the Descenters? My heart began thumping heavily as the potential for the kind of carnage I wanted to prevent became more and more likely with each passing minute.

I couldn't help but think that if Casteel were here, he would say something to lighten the mood. He'd bring a smile to my face, despite what awaited us. He would also probably say something that annoyed me...and also secretly thrilled me.

And he would definitely, *definitely* like the armor and weapons.

"There," Kieran advised quietly. "Ahead and to our left."

Too afraid to allow my mind to speculate about what he'd seen, I scanned the fractured sunlight.

"I see them," Emil confirmed at the same moment I saw.

Mortals.

They walked along the sides of the dirt road, several dozen—maybe even a hundred. They slowed as they spotted us and moved farther away from the trodden path, giving us a wide berth. I tried to dredge up some semblance of relief, but the group ahead wasn't nearly big enough when tens of thousands lived in Oak Ambler.

The deep breath I took erased the disappointment I felt settling into my bones. A hundred was better than none.

Emil guided his horse closer to Setti as we neared the group of mortals, many of which carried large sacks upon their backs and in their arms. Out of the corner of my eye, I saw that he had slid his gloved hand to the hilt of his sword. I noticed Kieran tense beside me. I knew he too had moved a hand closer to a weapon.

I opened my senses to them and almost wished I hadn't. All I tasted was a nearly overwhelming mixture of thick concern and fear-coated dread. Their drawn features mirrored what they felt—twisting faces of those most likely only in their second or third decades of life. Mortals who had lived so many years under the Ascended's rule.

They slowed and then stopped, staring in silence as we rode past. Their gazes pressed upon me, and a few in the crowd were so worried that they projected their emotions, thickening the air around us. I managed to close down my senses.

After spending so many years forbidden to be looked upon and veiled, I still wasn't used to this. To being *seen*. Every muscle in my body felt as if it would start twitching under so many open stares, and it took all my effort not to start squirming.

I didn't smile as I looked down at them. Not because I worried that I looked foolish—which would've concerned me in any other situation—but because it didn't seem right when none looked me directly in the eye, either out of fear or uncertainty.

None except a small child toward the edge of the group.

The young girl's gaze met mine, her cheek resting on what I assumed was her father's shoulder. I wondered what she saw. A stranger? A scarred Queen? A face that would haunt her sleep? Or did she see a liberator? A possible friend? Hope? I watched the mother, who walked close to the two, place her hand on the little girl's back, and then I wondered if that was why they'd taken this risk. Because they wanted a different future for their daughter.

"Poppy," Emil warned quietly, drawing my attention. I slowed Setti.

Farther down, a man had stepped away from a pale-faced woman who held a boy barely reaching the waist of her cream, woolen coat.

"Please. I mean no harm," the man spoke thickly, words spilling from his trembling lips in a rush. "M-my name is Ramon. We just had a Rite. Less than a week ago," he said. My stomach clenched as he glanced at Kieran and then Emil. "They took our second son. His name is Abel."

My stomach tightened even further. Rites were held at the same time throughout Solis—when they actually took place. Sometimes years and even decades passed between them. That was why second sons and daughters were given to the Court at varying ages. The same as the third-born, who were given to the Priests and Priestesses. I had never known two Rites to be held within the same year.

"Abel…he would be with the others. In the Temple of Theon," the man continued. "We couldn't get to them before we left."

Understanding dawned. Knowing what he feared, what many others in this group likely feared, as well, I found my voice. "We will not besiege the Temples."

The man's relief was so potent, it broke through my shields, tasting of spring rain. A shudder rocked the man and echoed in my heart. "If...if you see him— He's only a babe, but he has hair like mine, and brown eyes just like his momma." His gaze darted between the three of us as he shrugged off the strap of a sack and tore it open.

I lifted a hand, stilling Emil as he went to withdraw his sword. Unaware, Ramon dug around in the sack. "M-my name is Ramon," he repeated. "His momma's name is Nelly. He knows our names. I know that sounds silly, but I swear to the gods he does. Can you give him this?" He pulled out a fluff of stuffed, brown fur. A small, floppy teddy bear. Leaving the sack on the ground, he approached, nervously glancing at Kieran and Emil, who tracked his every movement. "Can you give this to him? So he can have it until we can come back for him? Then he'll know we haven't left him."

His request burned my eyes and stole my breath as I took the floppy bear. "Of course," I whispered.

"T-thank you." He clasped his hands together and bowed, backing up. "Thank you, Your Highness."

Your Highness...

It sounded different coming from the mortal. Almost like a benediction. I looked down at the bear, its fur patchy but soft. The black button eyes were stitched tightly. It smelled of lavender.

I wasn't their Queen.

I wasn't an answer to their prayers because those prayers should've been answered a long time before me.

"Diana," someone yelled from behind Ramon, and my head jerked up. "Our second daughter. Diana. They took her during the Rite, months ago. She's ten years old. Can you tell her we haven't left her? That we'll be waiting for her?"

"Murphy and Peter," another shouted. "Our sons. They took them both in the last two Rites."

Another name was yelled. A third daughter. A second son. Siblings. Names were shouted to the needled branches, echoing around us as Emil's and Kieran's expressions hardened with each name yelled. There were so many names that they became a chorus of heartbreak and hope, and when the last one was cried out, my heart had withered.

"We will find them," I said. And then louder, as a part of me deep inside, next to that cold, hollow place shriveled, I repeated, "We *will* find them."

I gripped the bear as shouts of gratitude replaced the names—

names I suddenly saw carved into a dimly lit, cold stone wall.

"There are others," a woman toward the back said as we passed her. "There are others at the gates trying to leave."

All those names overshadowed what relief that brought. My shoulders tensed. A knot lodged in my throat as I nudged Setti forward. I didn't want to consider what drove the Blood Crown to hold two Rites so close together.

What that meant.

We traveled several yards before Emil spoke. "I don't know what to say about that." His amber eyes were glassy. He cleared his throat. "Two Rites back-to-back? That's not normal, right?"

"It's not," I confirmed, placing the bear in a satchel strapped to Setti.

"That can't be good." His jaw worked.

No, it couldn't be.

"Nothing should've been promised to them," Kieran stated quietly.

"I promised that we would find them." My voice was thick as I reached for the pouch at my hip and squeezed until I felt the toy horse inside. "That is all I promised."

Kieran looked over at me, catching my gaze. "We will save as many people as we can, but we cannot and will not save everyone."

I nodded. But if they'd held a Rite just a week ago, there was hope. A chance that the children were still alive.

That was what I kept telling myself.

Through the thinning trees, small farms and cottages stood eerily silent, doors and windows boarded up. There were no animals in sight. No signs of life at all. Did the owners remain inside? Or had they already been taken in a Craven attack as they lived outside the Rise, risking their lives every night to provide necessities to those inside the city?

After a few more moments, I saw the Rise. Constructed from limestone and iron mined from the Elysium Peaks, the massive wall encircled the entire port city. The portion I'd destroyed before the Handmaiden stopped me became visible. Relief filled me when I saw that it wasn't a complete loss. About ten feet of it stood, and scaffolding already lined the upper destroyed portion. Still, guilt scalded my insides once more. I forced it aside. Wallowing in my remorse would have to come later.

Closing my eyes, I searched for the unique, springy and

featherlight imprint that belonged to Delano. Finding it, I opened the pathway. Delano's response was immediate, a touch against my mind. *Meyaah Liessa?*

We are nearing the gates now, I told him.

We are with you.

I opened my eyes. "Delano and the others know where we are."

Both Emil and Kieran lifted shields from the sides of their horses. A handful of guards visibly patrolled, but I knew there were more, likely on the ground below the Rise. But for those on the battlements, the glare of the sun was directly in their path. They had yet to become aware of us.

That would soon change.

"Hear that?" Kieran inclined his head with a frown.

At first, I didn't hear anything except the flutter of wings in the trees above and the call of birds, but then I heard the distant yelling and then shouts of *pain*.

My heart sped up. "It must be those still trying to leave."

"Sounds like a sizable crowd, which explains why so few guards are on the Rise," Emil noted, lifting his helmet and sliding it on. "For now."

Kieran looked over at me. "You still want to give them a chance?"

No.

I really didn't.

That taste had gathered in my mouth again. The one that came from that shadowy, cold place inside me. The taste of death. It coated my throat as I looked up at the guards. They had to know what was being done to cause those pained shouts. I wanted to strike out.

But that wasn't the plan.

"Yes." I nudged Setti forward, and they followed, shields at the ready as we broke through the trees, entering the cleared land below the Rise.

A guard near a tower spotted us quickly. He swung an arrow in our direction. "Halt!" he shouted, and several guards whipped around, nocking arrows stored in the parapet. "Do not come any closer."

Setti pranced restlessly as I guided him to a stop. Adrenaline coursed through me, ramming my heart against my ribs. My skin hummed as the eather throbbed in response, sending a series of shivers across the back of my head and over the nape of my neck. Somehow, I managed to keep my voice steady, even as dread, anticipation, and fear collided. "I want to speak with the Commander of the Rise."

"Who the hell are you to make such a demand?" another guard yelled as I opened my senses, letting them stretch toward the guards.

"Perhaps they do not see the crests on the shields," Kieran murmured, and Emil's shield muffled his snort. "Or you should've worn your crown." A pause. "Like I suggested."

The crown was where it belonged, beside the one meant for the King.

My hand tightened on the reins. "Tell your commander that the Queen of Atlantia wishes to speak with him."

The guards' shock was an icy splash against the roof of my mouth. "Bullshit," one of them exclaimed, but I also sensed great unease. They recognized the white of my clothing and what that symbolized. They had to know we were coming. "No Queen would be stupid enough to march right up to our gates."

Kieran glanced over at me, his brows raised.

"Perhaps none would be so daring," I suggested.

"Nah. You ain't no Queen. Just two Atlantian bastards and one Atlantian bitch," the light-haired guard said.

"At some point," Emil said under his breath, "I hope we kill that one."

The snap of the bowstring was deafening, silencing my response.

Kieran moved quickly, his reflexes far more honed than any mortal's. He lifted his shield within the span of a heartbeat. The arrow smacked off its surface.

"They shot at you!" I exclaimed.

"Yes, I'm aware of that." Kieran lowered his shield.

My head swung back to the Rise, anger building. "Do that again, and you will *not* like what happens."

"Stupid bitch." The guard laughed, reaching for another arrow. "What are you going to do?"

"Stop!" A guard raced across the battlement, grabbing the archer's arm. He yanked the arrow from his hand. "You jackass," he said as the guard pulled his arm free. "If that's really her, it'll be your head on a spike."

If he fired another arrow, he wouldn't live long enough to be impaled to any spike.

"I want to speak to the commander," I repeated.

"You have my attention," a voice boomed a second before a man appeared at the top of the Rise, the white mantle flowing from his shoulders a symbol of his position. "I'm Commander Forsyth."

"Well, look at that," Kieran said. "He came with friends."

He'd arrived with a lot of his friends. Dozens of archers rushed the battlement, arrows at the ready.

"The Queen of Atlantia?" Forsyth dropped a booted foot on the edge of the Rise and leaned forward, resting an arm on his bent knee. "I heard rumors you were in Massene. Not sure I believe it then or now."

When I wore the veil of the Maiden, no one knew that I was scarred. But after I went missing, news of my appearance traveled far as a means of identification. From their position, it was unlikely they were able to see my scars, especially since they had faded a bit after my Ascension.

"That's her," one of the newcomers said, an archer farther down the battlement. "I was here the night she damaged the Rise. I know her voice. Never will forget it."

"Looks like you left an impression," Kieran commented.

I had a feeling I would leave another as wind whirled through the meadow, carrying the stench of the city. "Then you know what I'm capable of."

Forsyth abandoned his relaxed pose, standing straight. "I know what you are. You've got these people in here believing you've come to either free or terrorize them. Caused quite a bit of drama by spreading the word, telling them they needed to leave the protection of the Ascended. Because of you, many of them will die in the streets they called home. Because of your lies."

The essence flared once more. I concentrated on the commander, letting my senses reach him. What I tasted was the same as I'd felt when I passed our soldiers before riding for Oak Ambler. Salty resolve.

"You would think that the Duke himself would be out here, defending his people," Kieran countered.

"The Ascended honor the gods by refusing the sunlight," Forsyth shot back. "But you, being of a godless kingdom, wouldn't understand that."

"The irony," Emil drawled quietly, "is painful."

"You know why they don't walk in the sun," I said, doubting that the Commanders of the Rises were unaware of exactly what they protected. Forsyth's head tilted back, and I picked up the faint trace of something sour. Guilt? I seized on that. "But it's you who is out here. You and your guards—protecting the people. Those who wish to leave the city, by the sound of it. The reason shouldn't matter, should it?

They should be allowed to leave."

"Both you and I know that's not the case, *Harbinger*," the commander replied, and I sucked in a sharp breath as Emil's gaze cut to me. "Yeah, like I said, I know exactly what you are. The Harbinger, Bringer of Death and Destruction. Some of these people may have been convinced otherwise, but I know better. Many of us do."

Dear gods. If the people of Oak Ambler—of Solis—had been told about the prophecy... I couldn't allow myself to think of the ramifications at the moment. "You believe in prophecies?"

"I believe in what I know. You already attacked us once," Forsyth said. "You are no savior."

In the back of my mind, I knew there would be no reasoning with him. That there may not be any reasoning for any who believed I was the Harbinger. But I still had to try. "No harm will come to those who wish to leave. Abandon the Rise," I ordered, while silently begging that they listened to me. "Open the gates and allow the people to choose what they want—"

"Or what? If you could take down the gates, you would've already," the commander barked. "There's nothing that can take down these gates." He turned away.

Feeling Emil's and Kieran's gazes on me, I looked at the archers, saw that many exchanged nervous glances, but no one moved. I could already feel those *marks* cutting into my skin. My heart hurt for what was to come.

"So be it," I said, letting my *will* swell inside me.

A distant rumble answered, echoing with the wind.

14

Commander Forsyth stopped as a flock of birds suddenly scattered into the sky, then turned slowly. All along the Rise, guards quieted, looking up as a shadow glided over the pines. Shouts of alarm rang out as the draken broke through the tree line, becoming visible.

With scales the color of ash, Nithe was roughly the size of Setti, a little bigger than the steed. He extended wings the shade of midnight, slowing his descent. A deep roar came from him, like a crack of thunder, sending the guards and the commander into a frenzied retreat.

"Too late for that," Emil murmured.

I didn't look away.

I wanted to.

But I made myself watch the end result of my *will*.

A funnel of fire and energy turned the world bright as Nithe swept forward, striking the air above the battlement. For a moment, the commander and the guards were merely twisting, writhing shadows. And then, when the flames receded, they were nothing.

Nithe rose, arcing swiftly as a much larger shadow fell upon us. Reaver dipped low, a third draken following, its greenish-brown body almost as large as Reaver's. Aurelia flew down the length of the wall, releasing a stream of fire above the Rise, catching the guards before they had a chance to reach any of the stairs. Shouts rose. *Screams*. I didn't look away.

Reaver landed before us, his impact causing our horses to take several steps back. He stretched out his neck, releasing a burst of fire that struck the gates. Heat blew back at us as a wall of silver flames swept over the iron and limestone. Reaver moved, stretching his wings as he continued pouring fire upon the gates.

Then the flames waned. Reaver swept his wings back as he lifted into the air, revealing only scorched earth where the gates had once stood.

My gaze fixed on the smoke-filled opening as the draken landed on the Rise, their thick talons digging into the stone as they stared into the city beyond. There was quiet now. No screams. No shouts.

Then horns sounded from the city's Citadel, the blare shocking in the utter silence. Reaver's head whipped in the direction, but he waited. So did Nithe and Aurelia. Because *we* waited.

"Through the smoke," Kieran said. "Ready yourselves."

Heart thumping, I reached for the sword at my hip as several shapes appeared in the smoke, but Aurelia let out a soft trill. I halted. Whatever that sound was, it was gentle, not one of warning.

"Hold," I said, searching the smoke as it slowly lifted, revealing... "*Gods.*" My breath snagged in my chest as the crowd beyond the gates, within the smoke, was revealed. "Thousands," I whispered, my throat thickening as tears pricked my eyes. I knew I shouldn't be so emotional. Now was not the time, but I couldn't help it.

Kieran reached over, placing his hand on mine. He squeezed. "*Thousands,*" he confirmed. "Thousands will be saved."

Potent relief roared through me as they began shuffling forward, some carrying all they could in their arms and on their backs like the ones who had left earlier. Some only cradled their children. Others bore the burden of the older mortals and the ill. The injured with fresh blood and bruised skin. Their steps were hesitant under the draken's watchful eyes as they approached us slowly. Fear sickened the air, its bitter taste gathering in the back of my throat. Uncertainty followed, tart and lemony as many trembled, catching their first sight of the draken's shadowy forms, partially obscured by the rising smoke. There was also...something lighter. Fresher. *Awe.* Then I heard the whispers.

Maiden.

Chosen.

"It's okay," I assured them, my voice hoarse. "Walk toward Massene. You will be safe there."

I wanted to say more, to *do* more, but I couldn't take their fear, even though it was so similar to pain. Not all of them.

"Momma! Look!" a young boy cried out, pointing at the draken. His eyes were filled with wonder not fear as he stretched and tugged on his mother's hand, trying to see as they rushed past us. "Lookit!"

It took a blessed eternity for the last of the mortals to clear the Rise and begin crossing the meadow to enter the woods. Then, I felt that springy brush against my thoughts. Deep in the woods, a murmur of unease sounded from those who'd fled the city. I looked over my shoulder. A piercing howl penetrated the stillness, followed by another and another, rattling the needled branches. Yips and calls rang out in the air as the wolven ran through the trees and past the frightened mortals, where many had frozen where they stood, cowering close to the ground.

"I believe that is all of them, Your Highness." Emil shifted his hold on the shield.

The sound of pounding hooves, the armies now nearing the Rise, matched the tempo of my heart. My attention rose to where Castle Redrock beckoned in the distance. Where it sat near the cliffs, glinting like burnt blood in the sunlight.

The wolven broke through the tree line, an army of claws and teeth. Sage cut between Emil and me, her fur gleaming like polished onyx. Arden followed. Vonetta and Delano joined them, leading the wolven into the city.

The breath I took barely filled my lungs as I tightened my grip on Setti's reins. Beside me, Kieran shifted forward as he withdrew one of his swords. He looked at me. Our gazes met, and he nodded. I unhooked my crossbow.

"It's time." I squeezed my knees into Setti's sides, and his powerful hooves kicked off the ground.

We raced forward, streaking through the cleared gates and into Oak Ambler, into one less city that stood between the Blood Queen and me.

Large shadows fell over us the moment we cleared the Rise. I glanced up to see Reaver gliding above us, flanked by Nithe and Aurelia. They flew at the height of the buildings, their wings nearly grazing the tops of the structures.

And then the *sound* came.

Horns blared in the distance. Thousands of horses bearing down on the city behind us as the Atlantian armies funneled through the gate, their hooves thundering off the cobblestone streets, and their heavy, short breaths huffing. The wind whipped up by the draken's wings whistled above us. Distant, faint shouts rang out. I'd never heard anything like it.

My heart pounded sickeningly fast as I held Setti's reins and the crossbow. The force of the horse's speed tore at the shorter strands of my hair, blowing them back from my face as we raced through the narrow, winding streets crowded by businesses and ramshackle homes. The buildings were mostly a blur, but I caught a few brief glimpses of people scurrying into narrow alleys—and those who stood in front of their businesses holding wooden swords or clubs and pitiful shields, prepared to die to protect their livelihoods as we rode past them, the wolven leaping over forgotten wagons and carts. We swarmed the lower district of Oak Ambler with one target in mind. Castle Redrock.

The twisting streets widened, becoming less crowded, and the wolven quickly spread out, their claws digging into soil and stone now. Near the inner part of Oak Ambler, the homes were larger and more spaced out, businesses established in newer buildings. Lampposts dotted the streets. Cobblestones gave way to lush lawns and narrow creeks that all sat in the foothills of the glistening, black Temple of Theon and the crimson stone of Castle Redrock.

And the horns—the godsdamn horns—kept blaring.

Ahead, a stone bridge glistened like polished ivory in the sunlight, and on the other side of a wide but shallow creek, the sun glinted off...*rows* of shields and swords. The mass of guards and soldiers. They'd been waiting. The bulk of the guards and soldiers protected the Ascended's homes and the wealthiest of Oak Ambler.

Leaving everyone else to fend for themselves.

My mouth dried and my stomach twisted as dread collided with adrenaline, bouncing and spinning off one another until nothing but instinct guided my actions.

"Shields up!" Hisa shouted from behind. "Shields up!"

A volley of arrows shot into the air, oddly reminding me of the birds that took flight from the pines. Everything slowed down—my heart, my body, and the world outside it. Or, everything sped up so fast that it *felt* slow. The draken above us rose out of reach of the arrows as we rode toward where the Solis soldiers and guards had entrenched themselves on the other side of the bridge, beyond the reach of the arrows that arced and plummeted down, smacking off stone and shield and—

I shut my senses down, locking them far away as the wolven hit the creek. We followed, sending water spraying into the air.

"Shit!" Kieran leaned back as the line of soldiers on the other side of the creek moved into formation, slamming the blood-red shields into the ground, staking them side by side so they formed a wall under a line of swords that would pierce the flesh of the horses and wolven alike.

My gaze found Vonetta and then Delano in the mass of wolven and through the spray of water, ahead of the others and nearly halfway across the creek. They didn't slow. They showed no fear as they forged on, toward what would be certain injury and possibly even death for some.

I couldn't allow that.

I glanced up at the draken, and they responded before my *will* could even finish as a thought.

Nithe cut away from the others, making a sharp turn. He swooped down in front of the wolven. A flash of intense, silvery light followed, and then a stream of fire swept over the line of soldiers.

The *screams*. The *sight* of the soldiers as they dropped their shields and weapons, stumbling back and flailing as the fiery energy burned through their armor and clothing, their skin and bone, was horrific. Nithe lifted as a larger funnel of fire rained down, cutting through the second and third line of guards, clearing the path and leaving nothing but a cloud of ash and embers as we crossed the creek. I couldn't think about what the fine coating of ash settling on my hands and cheeks and the wolven's fur was made of. That would have to come later.

Another volley of arrows went up, angled lower. Reaver cut away sharply, kicking up wind with a snap of his barbed tail. The arrows sliced through the air as Kieran drove his steed toward Setti and leaned over, lifting his shield. My world went dark, and my heart lurched at the sound of arrows hitting Kieran's shield.

"Thanks," I gasped.

Kieran gave me that wild grin as he straightened, only to stretch down to grasp a fallen spear scorched by the draken's fire. "It's about to get messy, *meyaah Liessa.*"

And it did.

The grounds of the Temple of Theon, the imposing fortress-like Citadel, and the lands between them and the inner Rise surrounding Castle Redrock became a battleground.

Wolven leapt onto soldiers and guards, knocking their shields and swords aside as they took them to the ground, cutting off high-pitched screams. The Atlantian soldiers poured across the land, their white-

and-gold mantles a stark contrast to the shadowstone Temple. Their golden swords clashed against iron as they swarmed the Temple's courtyard.

In the back of my mind, I saw that this was a different kind of slaughter. Oak Ambler's forces were grossly outnumbered.

The Ravarels had scouts, they had to have some idea of the size of our armies. They had to know how fruitless this was for them. Yet they'd allowed this instead of surrendering.

Emil and Kieran struck out with their swords as we pressed forward, the draken following. Soon, Vonetta and Delano joined us, as did Sage and several other wolven. We crossed the road and began the climb, cresting the tree-heavy hill that Castle Redrock sat upon. Soldiers and guards rushed through the gates of the inner Rise.

"Archers," Emil shouted, lifting his shield as a volley of arrows came down from the battlement of the inner Rise, slamming into the road and shields and bodies. My breath caught at the yelps as the arrows struck true.

"Take cover!" I shouted at the wolven as Reaver glided ahead, his shadow falling upon the guards as they frantically tried to close the gates on the inner Rise. Nithe and Aurelia followed as several of the archers stationed there turned to the sky.

Some of the wolven bolted for the trees, dodging arrows while others huddled by those who'd fallen. Instinct fueled my actions. I tapped into the eather whirling through my chest. The essence responded at once, flooding my veins and burning away the near-sickening jolts of adrenaline as several of the archers took aim at the wounded wolven and those guarding them.

I didn't worry about how much using the essence would weaken me or allow myself to consider who the archers on the wall were. This was war. I kept reminding myself of that. This was war.

A silvery webbing of eather formed in my mind, draping over the archers on the wall and moving into them. I didn't know exactly what it did—what *I* did—as that metallic taste pooled in my mouth. All I knew was that I wanted it to be quick and as painless as possible. And I thought it was. They made no sound as they collapsed where they stood in the arrow loops, falling backward and forward, dead before they hit the ground outside the curtained wall.

That kind of power...

It stunned me a little as I pulled the eather back, but there was no time to dwell on it. The gates closed while a smattering of guards and soldiers outside rushed toward the wolven.

There were at least four times as many soldiers and guards at the inner Rise, protecting Castle Redrock and the Ascended—who didn't care about anyone left outside. They'd try to ride it out behind walls as thick as the outer Rise—stone that protected them from invasions and the people they lorded over, allowing the gods knew what to go on behind them.

I thought of the palace at Evaemon, where no wall separated the Crown from its people, and my sense of wonder upon seeing how accessible the Crown was.

A glimpse of fawn caught my attention. I lifted the crossbow, leveling it as Casteel had instructed me on the road to Spessa's End. I took aim, firing the bolt thicker than an arrow.

It struck true, snagging one of the guards before he could reach Vonetta. She raced past him as he fell backward and then leapt into the air, taking down another guard. I found Reaver in the sky. "Take it down," I murmured, aiming the crossbow at a soldier streaking across the land, heading for Delano. "Take the inner Rise down."

I fired, striking the man. His legs went out from under him as the white wolven latched onto the arm of a guard who was swinging his sword down on a wounded wolven. Delano yanked the howling man back, twisting his head sharply. Red sprayed and stained the snowy fur.

"Fall back," Kieran shouted to the wolven as I reached out to as many of them as I could through the *notam*. "Fall back!"

The wolven skirted the wall, backing off as Reaver broke through the glare of the sun, diving sharply above the inner Rise. A funnel of intense fire spilled forth, slamming into the stone. Chunks of rock exploded under its power. Another stream of fire came from above, and then a third as the draken flew over the length of the wall the Ascended hid behind, obliterating the structure so nothing remained between Castle Redrock and the people—as it should be.

As the smoke and debris settled, I nudged Setti forward. The wolven streamed out from the trees, and as silly as it was, I held my breath until we crossed into the splattered stone courtyard. Exhaling raggedly, my gaze swept the soldiers and guards rushing across the yard, moving to the main castle doors, sealed by iron—

Kieran drew his horse to a halt and leaned over, gripping Setti's reins. My head jerked around just as a greenish-brown draken landed in the courtyard directly before us, her tail whipping out mere inches from our horses' noses. "Good gods," he rasped. "They have no sense of spatial awareness."

They really didn't.

Aurelia's large wings swept back as she extended her head forward, letting out a burst of silvery fire at the guards, taking out a huge chunk of them. The draken had to be tiring, and I had no idea how they recovered.

Probably should've asked that question.

Several dozen more guards rounded the castle, swarming the courtyard. "I'm calling the draken back," I said, and Kieran didn't question why as Aurelia turned her head toward me.

"Go," I urged. There was no threat from archers, as no arrowslits could be seen in the front-facing towers of Redrock. And any who had been in the inner Rise…well, they were no longer a concern. "Find a safe place to rest."

She made a rough, deep harrumphing sound but lifted. I saw Reaver and Nithe do the same, but they didn't go far. Nithe and Aurelia retreated to the massive oaks and the jutting rocks and boulders along the sea-facing cliffs of the courtyard. But Reaver…

He flew up to one of the crimson spires, sinking his talons into the stone, sending a fine mist of dust exploding into the air as he curled his body around the tower. Stretching his neck, he peered down on the courtyard, letting out a deafening roar that caused many of the soldiers to scatter in different directions, and others to stop where they were, covering their heads with their shields.

"Find someplace to rest?" Emil looked over at me, his gold eyes wide. "And he chose *that?*"

"That wasn't exactly what I'd had in mind when I said that, but Reaver's…going to be Reaver."

Kieran snorted as my gaze lifted to the soldiers who had taken up their stations in front of the wide steps leading to the doors of Castle Redrock. There had to be a hundred at least, shields held side by side and spears at the ready. They didn't move as the wolven prowled forward, over what remained of the wall.

Behind us, our armies crested the hill and flowed into the courtyard. I caught sight of Valyn, his armored chest splattered with blood. Hisa rode beside him, her chest rising and falling heavily. Relief swamped me at the sight of them.

Kieran guided his horse forward, sword at the ready. "Our fight is not with you. It's with who is behind those doors. Surrender, and no harm will come to you. Just as no harm has come to those who left the city."

I turned back to the shields and spears, keeping my crossbow leveled. "We swear that to you."

The guards and soldiers made no move, but I saw a few lower their spears. *Please*, I thought. *Please, just listen.*

From the spire, Reaver let out a smoky breath and a rumbling growl that matched that of the wolven on the ground, who snapped and bared sharp, blood-streaked teeth as they paced before soldiers who had faces far too young to belong to those holding the line. They didn't need to die today.

A lot of those who already had hadn't needed to.

Opening my senses to them, I immediately tasted the saltiness of distrust, and the bitter bite of fear as they stared at me—looking upon someone they likely believed to be a false god.

"I was once the Maiden, the Chosen, but no gods chose me," I told them, hooking the crossbow onto one of Setti's straps. "The Ascended did because they knew what I was."

I'd worn white to remind the people of who I was.

It was time I showed them what I'd become.

Allowing the essence of the Primal god to surface was like having the golden chains removed, and the veil lifted. The more I allowed it to happen, the more it felt...natural. I didn't think this would weaken me because it felt like I was no longer hiding who I was. It was almost a relief.

The hum in my chest pulsed and pounded through my veins. The thrum of power moved to my skin, where a silvery-white aura appeared.

A wave of surprise fell like freezing rain, rippling over those before me. "I am not the Harbinger. I carry the blood of the King of Gods in me, and those who reside in these walls do not speak to any god—or for them. They are your enemy. Not us."

No one moved.

And then...

Shields and spears clattered off the stone steps as they *surrendered*.

The wave of relief I felt was so potent, it was a little dizzying. Pulling the eather back in, I rubbed the side of Setti's neck and then swung my leg over the saddle, dismounting. Emil and Kieran quickly followed as I walked forward, my thighs aching from how tense I'd been the entire time.

Under the watchful eyes of the wolven and Reaver, the men stared as I approached them. A few had lowered themselves to their knees, placing trembling hands across their chests and on the ground. Others stood as if in a daze.

"All I need to know right now is where the Ravarels and the Ascended are located in the castle," I said.

"The chambers." A young man wearing the black of a Rise Guard quavered as he spoke. "They would've gone into the underground chambers."

As Vonetta, along with several others, went to secure the Temple of Theon—and hopefully locate the children—I descended into the chambers under Castle Redrock with Kieran, Emil, and some of the wolven, while Valyn searched Redrock with Hisa and several of the soldiers.

I didn't look past the crimson banners bearing the Royal Crest and the hallway that led toward the Great Hall. I couldn't. The last thing I needed to be reminded of was where Ian had taken his last breath.

And where I'd last seen Casteel.

So, we went straight for the hall the Handmaiden had led us through the last time we were here. The Rise Guard who'd spoken up outside led the way, while my mind lingered on what I'd seen in one of the underground chambers.

The cage.

My *father*.

I knew it was highly unlikely that he was still there. I didn't even understand why Isbeth had brought him with her in the first place, but I doubted she would've left him behind.

"Keep walking," Emil advised coolly when Tasos, the guard, slowed as we traveled down the narrow stairwell.

"S-sorry." Tasos picked up his pace as Arden, in his wolven form, nudged him. "It's just that there should be guards here." He swallowed. "At least ten of them."

I glanced at Kieran. That was odd. "Could they have joined the fight outside?"

"No. They were given orders to block the stairwell," Tasos told us. "It's the only way into the underground chambers from the inside."

Is it possible they moved to the section we snuck through? Delano's question whispered through my thoughts as we rounded a bend in the stairwell.

And then the stench hit us.

The sickly-sweet scent of death.

"What is...?" Tasos trailed off as we stepped into the narrow, torch-lit hall.

"Hell," Kieran muttered as I reached for the wolven dagger on my thigh out of habit instead of going for the swords.

Red. So much red. It streaked across the stone floor, splattered the walls, and pooled under the bodies.

"Well," Emil drawled as he looked down at a fallen bloodstone sword. Several of them were scattered about. "I'm assuming these are the guards."

"Yeah," Tasos croaked as he stood there, arms stiff at his sides.

"Would the Ascended have done this?" Emil asked, glancing back at me.

Tasos' head cut sharply in his direction, his surprise an icy burst in the back of my throat. It was clear that he had no idea what the Ascended were.

"I don't see why they would've done this." I walked forward, not even trying to avoid the blood. It would be impossible. Emil, as always, followed closely behind.

Kieran knelt by one of the fallen guards. "I don't think this was the work of a vampry."

"Vampry?" Tasos whispered.

There wasn't enough time in the realm to explain what the Ascended were. None of us bothered.

"Look at this." Kieran picked up a limp arm as Delano joined them. The black uniform was torn and ripped, revealing skin that hadn't fared much better.

I stiffened. Even in the flickering torchlight, I recognized the wounds. I saw them on my body. Jagged bite marks. Four sets of fangs. I turned, scanning another body. My stomach roiled, and I swallowed hard. The man's chest had been *clawed* into, revealing ropey pink muscle and tissue.

Tiny hairs rose all over my body as I unsheathed the wolven dagger.

Arden's ears flattened and he let out a snarl that reverberated through the hall as he prowled forward, one step and then two. At the same moment, Kieran's head snapped in the direction of where the hallway split. Delano's lips peeled back as he growled low in his throat.

They sensed it before we saw it—wispy tendrils creeping out from the corridor ahead and spilling into the hall.

The *mist*.

And only one thing could be within it. The same thing responsible for these wounds.

The Craven.

15

Vikter once told me that he believed the mist was more than just a shield that cloaked the Craven. It was what filled their lungs since no breath did. It was what seeped from their pores since they did not sweat.

It never made sense to me then, but now, after seeing the Primal mist in the Skotos Mountains and again in Iliseeum, I had to wonder if Vikter had been onto something. If this Primal mist was somehow related to what surrounded the Craven.

I would have to think about that later, when the mist wasn't filling the end of the hall, rising halfway up the walls. Inside it, dark shapes could be seen. Many dark shapes—

Arden lunged forward, taking off for the mist.

"No!" I shouted.

But it was too late. The mist swallowed him, his snarling growls lost in the skin-chilling shrieks.

"Shit!" Kieran grabbed a fallen bloodstone sword as he kicked one over to Emil. He rose.

I grabbed hold of Tasos' collar, pushing the weaponless guard back as Emil snatched up a spear with a bloodstone blade. "Stay back," I ordered, not trusting the guard to pick up a weapon and use it on a Craven versus one of us.

A Craven shot forward—incredibly fast, and incredibly *fresh*. Under the blood-smeared face, the male's skin carried the gray pallor of death, and shadows had already formed under its crimson eyes. But the black tunic and trousers weren't ragged. Another broke free of the mist, letting out a shrill howl. This one was a woman, dressed the same as the man. Then another and another. None were missing clumps of hair or had patches of skin missing or hanging.

All had gaping, terrible wounds at the throats.

"Mother—" Emil changed up his grip on the spear. "—*fucker.*" He threw it, striking the male Craven in the chest.

The creature pinwheeled, falling backward. Another took its place as I raced forward, shoving my arm under the Craven's chin. Blood-streaked teeth snapped at me. The woman…gods, she had to be my age, maybe even younger. She would've been pretty if not for the dark veins spreading out from the *bite* on her throat, covering the side of her cheek.

And for the fact that she was basically dead.

I shoved the bloodstone into her chest just as hot, burning pain *slammed* into me. Pain that was not mine. *Arden.* Yanking the dagger free, I jumped back as Emil tossed a headless Craven aside.

Delano leapt over Emil as the Atlantian bent to retrieve a bloodstone sword, landing on a Craven's chest. He tore into it with his claws as I desperately searched the mist for any sign of Arden. I couldn't hear him over the godsforsaken screeching.

Heart thumping, I thrust the dagger into a Craven's chest as I let my senses stretch out, looking for Arden's unique imprint. It was salty like the sea and reminded me of Saion's Cove. I couldn't find it. I couldn't sense him. Panic blossomed.

Kieran cursed as he cut through a Craven, twisting as another bounced off the wall, rushing him. Shooting forward, I swung my leg out and up, planting my booted foot in the Craven's midsection. I tried not to think about how it didn't cave under the force like a rotted Craven's would—about how this older male with bloody smile lines creasing his face must have been alive the day before. I kicked the Craven into the wall. It screamed while I rushed it, cutting the sound off with a direct blow to the head. I spun around, stirring the mist at my hips.

"Thanks," Kieran grunted.

"We need to find Arden." I shot past him, sucking in a sudden breath as a Craven grabbed for me. I ducked under its arm and then twisted, jabbing the dagger through the base of the creature's neck, severing its spinal cord. I spun, searching the thick, churning mist.

Three Craven were on their knees, crowded together on the floor, over something once silver and white but now…red.

My heart stopped. No. No. No.

Horror propelled me forward. Grasping a fistful of hair, I yanked one of the Craven back as I jammed the blade into the back of her neck. Her slackened mouth glistened with blood. Choking on a cry, I grabbed another, throwing it aside. Kieran was there, thrusting his sword into the Craven's head. Emil shot forward, his blade cleaving through the neck of the third Craven as I dropped to my knees beside Arden.

"Oh, gods," I gasped, dropping the dagger. Arden was breathing too rapidly, and the wounds, the bites—

"Guard her," Kieran instructed as he dropped to the blood-slick floor across from me.

Delano pressed against my back as Emil circled us. I sank my hands into Arden's thick fur, feeling his chest rise and then stop. No inhale. Nothing. My heart made a tripping motion. My gaze flew to his head as the mist slowly dissipated around us. Arden's eyes were open, pale blue and dull. His gaze fixed.

"No," I whispered. "No. *No.*"

"Fuck," Kieran exploded as he rocked forward, placing his hand on Arden's neck. "*Fuck.*"

I knew what Reaver had said, but I had to try. I had to because I couldn't be too late. Sharp, warm tingles ran down my arms, spreading across my fingers as I summoned the Primal essence. A silvery-white glow sifted through the fur—

The remaining Craven wailed, the sound higher and louder than before. Emil grunted as I felt him stumble and then catch himself. A body hit the floor beside us and then a head. Channeling the eather into Arden's body, I focused all my will on him. *Breathe. Live. Breathe.* Over and over, I repeated those words, like I had with the small girl who'd been struck by the carriage. The aura spread over his body in a glittering web of eather and then sank through the matted fur and into the torn skin and tissue. I wasn't too late. I couldn't be. *Breathe. Breathe.* I funneled every wonderful and happy memory I had into my efforts. Ones of Ian and me on the beach with the people who would always be our parents. How I felt on my knees in the loamy soil as a ring was slipped onto my finger while I stared into beautiful, golden eyes. My entire world behind my closed lids became silver and white as the eather pulsed and flared deep within me—

"Poppy," Kieran whispered.

Nothing was happening.

The shrill shrieking stopped.

Heart cracking, I looked at Arden's eyes. They remained vacant and without life. His chest didn't move. I pushed harder, hands trembling as the mist receded and cleared. Blood. There was so much blood.

Kieran's hand slid off Arden and folded over mine. "*Poppy.*"

"I wanted it to work. I wanted—" A ragged cry parted my lips.

"*Stop,*" Kieran ordered quietly, lifting my hands—my blood-smeared hands. He pressed his lips to my knuckles. "He's gone. You know this. He's gone."

I shuddered as Delano turned, nudging Arden's paw with a whimper. Anguish built in my throat, tart and tangy. It came from them. It came from me as the fur thinned out, and pale, blood-streaked skin appeared. Arden returned to his mortal form.

Pulling my hands free, I rocked back, closing my eyes. Tears burned my throat. I didn't know Arden as well as a few others, but in Evaemon, he'd become my shadow. I had been getting to know him. I liked him. He didn't deserve this.

The others backed off a little, all but Kieran and Delano. They stayed with Arden and me as I knelt there, eyes closed as the sorrow—*ice, ice*-cold—and that hollow place in me—chilly and dark—heated.

"These Craven were servants," Emil said, his voice rough. "Weren't they?"

"They were," came Tasos' answer. "That's Jaciella. And Rubens. They were both alive yesterday. So was…" Tasos continued, rattling off the names of those who'd served the Ascended.

"They did this," Kieran said quietly. His anger, hot and yet cold, reached out to me, colliding with my building fury.

Running my hand over Arden's arm, I opened my eyes. They were dry. Barely.

The white aura behind Kieran's pupils glowed vividly, and that taste built in my mouth again. This time, it throbbed in my chest, in my heart, and at the very core of my being. "Locate them," I bit out, reaching for and finding my dagger. "Find them and bring them to me."

More servants had been turned, but they'd made it out of the underground chambers, somehow avoiding the sunlight. Valyn and Hisa had dealt with several on the second and third floors of Castle Redrock.

We'd been lucky to have missed them when we entered the stairwell.

Until we weren't.

I stared at where Arden lay, shrouded in white, next to the guards and the deceased Craven. I counted them. Eighteen. The Ascended had turned eighteen mortals. Some of them looked as if they had fought back. I saw it on the bruised knuckles and broken nails. The turned mortals would be given the same honor as anyone else.

Footsteps echoed through the hall, and I turned from the bodies, seeing Emil and Valyn. "Did you find the Ascended?"

Valyn shook his head. "I believe they abandoned the city."

Kieran cursed as Emil nodded. "The bastards turned the servants, set the trap, and left."

My lips parted. "How can we be sure?"

"We've checked all the chambers down here, and the homes near the interior rise are being searched to see if any are underground," Valyn said, his features tense. "But I believe they left."

Every part of me focused on him, and when I reached out with my senses, the shield around him was even thicker. "What did you find?"

Neither answered for a long moment and then Valyn said, "What I can only imagine to be a message."

"Where?"

"In the chamber at the end of the left hall," he answered, and I started walking, Delano close behind me. Valyn caught my arm as I moved past him. "I don't believe you want to see it."

Dread blossomed. "But I need to."

He held my gaze and then released my arm, saying quietly to Kieran, "She shouldn't see this."

Kieran didn't try to stop me, only because he knew better.

The hall was quiet as I walked to the open chamber, softly lit by several candles I could already see placed on the floor. My steps slowed as I neared the mouth of the chamber, and I stopped as I saw inside it.

I saw legs first.

Dozens of legs, swaying gently among crates of what appeared to be wine. Slowly, I looked up. Slim calves. Bite marks at the knees, the inner thighs. I shuddered. Wrists torn open. Breasts mauled. The gauzy white of a veil. Gold chains holding the veils in place—gold chains secured to the ceiling, holding *them* in place.

Kieran had gone rigid beside me as Delano pressed against my legs. I couldn't breathe. I couldn't think or feel anything but the stirring eather, the simmering rage. These people…these *girls*…

I pressed a shaky hand to my stomach as I saw the words on the wall behind them, lit by rows of candles. Words written in dried, rusty-colored blood.

All you will liberate is death.

The hand of one of the girls twitched.

I took a jerky step back, and Kieran moved then, curling an arm around my shoulders. He gave me no choice, guiding me from the chamber and away from the doors. I wouldn't have fought him because that was…

Pulling away from Kieran, I leaned against the wall and closed my eyes. I still saw them, the bodies drained of blood.

"Poppy." Kieran's voice was too soft. "They will—"

"I know," I bit out, stomach churning. They would become Craven. They had to be close to it already.

"We'll take care of it." Emil's hoarse voice reached me. "We'll cover their bodies and then make it quick. They will find peace soon."

My mouth felt too wet. "Thank you."

There was nothing but silence as I focused on shoving the essence—the rage—down. It pushed at my skin, and for the briefest moment, I imagined it erupting, leveling the castle. The city. Even then, that explosion of energy would do little to assuage the fury. I swallowed hard, closing myself down. It wasn't easy. A tremor coursed through me.

Delano leaned against my legs, his concern gathering around me. *Poppy?*

"I'm okay," I whispered, reaching down to touch the top of his head. I took a deep breath, opening my eyes only when I…

When I felt nothing.

"Why did you lie back there? To Delano?"

I stopped at the foot of the circular steps of the Temple of Theon and looked up at Kieran. *Back there.* In those chambers underground, where Arden had taken his last breath. *Back there*, where the servants had been fed upon and left to turn into Craven. *Back there*, where those girls had been left with that message.

Back there had left several *marks.*

And I had a feeling there would be more that would cut into my skin before the day was over.

"What do you mean?" I asked, noting that Valyn had already climbed the steps, speaking to one of the soldiers. I had no idea where Delano had gone.

Kieran crossed his arms. "Poppy."

I sighed, looking up at the entrance to the Temple. Valyn had walked ahead and was speaking with Cyr now. The large circular structure only had a few long and narrow windows. "I'm…"

I felt a little sick. Not physically. I was tired. Again, not physically. And I felt like I…like I needed to bathe—no, I needed to *shower.* To wash away the seconds, the minutes, and the hours of this entire day. I was worried and full of concern as I stared at the smooth surface of the black doors. I was also afraid of what waited beyond. What Vonetta and the others had found.

Most of all, I…I wanted Casteel to be here with me so I could tell him how I felt. To shoulder some of the weight. To receive some of these marks. To make me smile and even laugh despite the horror of the day. To distract me and take away the aching coldness.

"I'll be okay," I said hoarsely.

His gaze searched my features. "What they did back there to those girls? That message? It's all to mess with your head. You can't let it."

"I know."

Except it had. Because it didn't seem to matter that I wasn't the one who'd killed the mortals at Massene, the wolven or the draken, the servants or those girls. They still died because of me.

I squinted as the late-afternoon sun glinted off the shadowstone. I looked beyond the Temple to where I could see the golden armor of several of the Atlantian soldiers outside a grand manor. So far, all the estates had been free of vamprys. "Do you think it's possible that all the Ascended left?"

"I don't know." Kieran nudged my arm with his. "But we're going to need to be prepared in case they're holed up somewhere."

"Agreed," I whispered. "We should head in there."

"Yeah." Kieran followed my gaze, exhaling heavily. "We should."

Opening my senses, I let them stretch out. I tasted the tanginess of sorrow and something heavier, almost like concern. I tasted dread. Kieran wasn't looking forward to what might await in the Temple. "Are you okay?"

"I will be."

My eyes narrowed.

A faint grin appeared, a hint of teasing before it disappeared again. We said nothing else as we joined Valyn at the top of the Temple stairs.

"There are tunnels under the Temple," Valyn announced, nodding at one of the soldiers I recognized as being part of Aylard's regiment. "Lin was just telling me about them."

Lin's throat worked on a swallow. "There was a hidden entryway in the chamber beyond the sanctum," Lin explained. "It led to a tunnel system underground—a pretty extensive one. There were chambers there."

I had a sinking feeling those tunnels connected to the ones under Redrock, which led straight out to the cliffs. We had suspected upon our first visit to Oak Ambler that they were using the tunnels to move mortals about without them being seen by others. Which could also mean that the Ascended, if any remained, could use them to travel unseen.

"They were…chambers, Your Highness. But…" Lin trailed off.

"What?" Kieran asked as I opened my senses, tasting…tartness. Unease.

"What did you see?" Every muscle in my body tensed. If they found anything like what we had seen in that other chamber, I didn't think I could take it. "Did you find any children?"

"Not yet, but we did find men and women in white robes."

Likely Priests and Priestesses. "Where are they?"

"We have them in the sanctum." Lin dragged a hand over his face as I came up the steps. "The tunnels and chambers are still being searched."

My hands curled into fists as two soldiers opened the doors. We entered the receiving chamber of the Temple, passing another soldier who stood off to the side, her features stark as she stared at the wall.

Beams of narrow sunlight streaked in from the thin windows and crept across the shadowstone floors. Dozens of gold candelabra lined the walls, their flames rippling gently as we entered the mouth of the sanctum. There were no pews. Only a platform framed by thick, black columns.

They sat in front of the platform. Six of them, wearing the white robes of the Priests and Priestesses of Solis. Their heads were bowed. Two females. Four males. Those who had hair wore it either shorn or pulled back in a lacy, white cap. The shapeless robes covered their bodies except for the face, hands, and feet.

A bald head lifted, glancing past me and then bouncing back. His eyes widened as he watched my approach. "I know who you are."

I stopped in front of him, silent as the remaining Priests and Priestesses lifted their heads. The visage of someone I hadn't given much thought to took shape in my mind. *Analia.* The Priestess in Masadonia, who had been responsible for my *teachings* but preferred to use her hand as a form of education. There had been a singular cruelty to that woman, and I didn't know if those before me possessed the same vicious streak. But I didn't doubt that Analia or any who served in these Temples knew the truth about the Ascended and the Rite. "What is your name?"

"I am called Framont," the Priest answered. "And you...you are the one they call the Queen of Flesh and Fire. We've been waiting for you since before you were born."

"What in the hell is that supposed to mean?" Valyn demanded, having come up behind us.

The Priest didn't look at him. He didn't take his eyes off me as tension compressed my spine. I had a feeling I knew what he referenced. "The prophecy."

Framont nodded as Kieran drew closer to me. "It's time for you to fulfill your purpose."

"My *purpose*?" I repeated. "My purpose is to destroy the Blood Crown—"

"And remake the realms as one." His words chilled my skin. Vessa had said that I would remake the realms. An almost childlike smile crept across his rounded face. "Yes, that is your purpose. You are the Chosen, spoken of long before your birth. You were foretold. Promised."

"What in the utter hell is he talking about?" Cyr muttered from behind me.

Kieran sent a quick look at Valyn. "The tunnels under Redrock— they likely connect to this Temple. They should be guarded immediately." There was intention in Kieran's words, one heavier than what he spoke. "They lead out to the cliffs by the sea."

Valyn picked up on the meaning. The former King pivoted on his heel. "I want all of you to make sure that Redrock is secure. Check every tunnel under the castle and seal off those pathways."

Within moments, Valyn had cleared the Temple of all the generals and soldiers. Only Hisa remained, and that was a smart move. Although Valyn and Hisa had ferreted out any members of the Unseen from their ranks, their methods weren't perfect. We knew that because of the attack the Unseen had launched on us on the road to Evaemon. But beyond that, anyone who heard the prophecy would assume that it was about me.

"You speak of prophecies," I said, refocusing on the Priest. "Of the great conspirator—"

"Who is '*birthed from the flesh and fire of the Primals*,'" he finished. "And '*will awaken a*s the Harbinger, the Bringer of Death and Destruction—*'"

"I have birthed nothing," I cut him off.

The smile grew, flushing his face. "Not in a physical manner."

"How? How has a Priest in Solis heard a prophecy spoken by a god eons ago?" Valyn pressed, even though he already knew. Isbeth. "A prophecy that only a handful of Atlantians have heard?"

"Because we have always served the True King of the Realms." Then, and only then, did Framont look at Valyn. His smile turned into a sneer. "And the Atlantians have always served a lie."

Valyn stiffened and then moved as if to step forward. I held up a hand, stopping him. "The True King?"

"Yes." Framont spoke the word as if it were a benediction.

The Priests and Priestesses might believe they served the gods, but they answered to the Blood Crown—what I was sure they called the True Crown. And what they believed about the gods had been fed to them by the Ascended. Which meant that the person Framont believed this True King to be, was who Isbeth believed it should be.

And that could only be one person.

My upper lip curled as anger pulsed through me. "The Blood Queen spoke of the True Crown in her summonses," I explained to Valyn. "Who do you think she would believe to be the True King?"

"Malec," Valyn seethed.

It made sense, especially since she now knew that Malec was alive. A sudden chill swept through me. What if Isbeth had discovered where Malec was entombed?

Gods couldn't be killed in the same manner as the deities who were held under the Chambers of Nyktos, but they wouldn't be able to feed. And according to Reaver, Malec would've needed to feed more than a normal god. He would've weakened to a point where he most likely no longer resembled anything close to who he was. I imagined at some point he would've lost consciousness.

What if Isbeth hadn't used Kolis's essence to create the storm? What if it had been Malec? That sounded impossible, but...

"Keep a close eye on them," I said to Hisa and then motioned for Valyn to step back several feet from the Priests and Priestesses. Kieran followed, listening intently as I spoke in a low voice. "I don't know how much of what he said is true or not. But what do you know about how Eloana entombed Malec?"

"She used old magic—what kind exactly, I don't know—and bone chains," he said, and I suppressed a shudder as memories of the twisted chains of sharp bones and ancient roots surfaced. Nyktos had created the method of incapacitating any being that carried eather in them, bestowing the bones of dead deities with such power. I didn't need to think hard to remember what they had felt like digging into my skin. "The only way he could've escaped them is if someone removed them."

It was possible that Isbeth had figured out where Malec was entombed. I needed to be sure. Malec was the ace up my sleeve. It was what kept Casteel alive. "We need to know exactly where Malec was entombed and any other safeguards Eloana may have put in place."

Kieran frowned. "Even if the Blood Queen had located him, they would need to get past the Craven. Which would be difficult—even for whatever she is."

"And after all that time? Hundreds of years?" Valyn added. "He wouldn't be conscious. I doubt he would remember himself, let alone be able to seek retribution against Atlantia."

"We would think that, but he...he *is* a god. The son of the King of Gods and his Consort. We have no idea what he would be capable of if he somehow woke and had time to recover." And blood, lots of blood. I glanced back at those in white. Framont still smiled as if a hundred of his wishes had all come true at once. There was no telling what the Blood Queen had told the Priests and Priestesses to evoke this kind of faith. "Everything he's saying could be nothing more than mind games. But…"

"But we need to be sure," Valyn agreed. "I will get word to Evaemon as soon as we're done dealing with this."

Nodding, I turned back to the task at hand while many things picked at my thoughts. Malec possibly being this great conspirator that the prophecy warned about made sense—and yet, didn't. For many reasons. Starting with: what could I possibly have to do with him waking? When I asked Framont, he only smiled blissfully up at me. And with no one present who could use compulsion, I knew we wouldn't get any more information from him regarding this.

Besides, there was something that felt far more important that I needed to deal with. I shoved all the other stuff aside for now. "I want to know where the children are."

"They're serving the—"

"Don't," I cut him off. "Don't lie to me. I know the truth behind the Rite. I know those taken don't serve any gods or the True King or Crown. Some are changed into things called Revenants. Some are fed upon. None of that involves an act of service."

"But it does," Framont whispered, a glint of eagerness in his gaze. "They serve. Just as you do. Just as you will also—"

"I would think very carefully about what you say next," Kieran warned.

Framont glanced at him. "Will you harm me? Threaten me with death? I fear no such thing."

"There are things far worse than death. Like her when she's annoyed." He jerked his chin in my direction. "She likes to stab things then. But when she gets angry? You'll see exactly what a god is capable of."

The Priest's eyes darted to me, and I smiled tightly. "I do get stabby. And I'm already annoyed by a whole list of things. Where are those given over in the Rite?"

He didn't get a chance to answer.

"We have two more of them," Naill announced as he entered through the side door. "And they're not mortal. They're Ascended."

I locked my jaw. "You had Ascended hidden with you?"

"Ascended serve in the Temples—serve the True King," Framont said. "They always have."

"You didn't know that?" Valyn asked.

I shook my head. "I wasn't around many of them," I told him. "Who all knew the Ascended were among you?"

"Only the trusted." He looked up at me with a sort of wonder that was really beginning to border on creepy. "Only the Crown."

Then the Duchess would've known. They were a part of the Crown.

Kieran tilted his head as Vonetta came through the doorway, leading another Priestess. "Where is the other?"

"He wasn't very happy about being discovered," Vonetta said with a sneer.

The Priestess Vonetta had a grip on suddenly stumbled forward into a beam of sunlight. The woman shrieked, jerking back. Faint smoke wafted from her robes, and the scent of burnt flesh hit the air. I turned to Vonetta.

"What?" Her brows rose. "I tripped."

I stared at her.

Vonetta sighed. "She tried to bite me." Grabbing hold of the Priestess's arm, she yanked the vampry back and shoved her toward the others. "More than once."

"Did you find any…?" I asked.

She gave a curt shake of her head. "A few others are still down there, looking."

"I'll show you." A female Priestess spoke up, and my head snapped in her direction. "I'll take you to them."

16

"If this is some sort of trap," Kieran warned, "you won't like what happens."

"It's not." Her head finally lifted, and I saw that she was young. Gods. Not much older than I. Her eyes were a pretty cornflower blue. They were wide and eager like Framont's.

Cracking open my senses, I reached out to her. I didn't feel fear. I didn't know what I felt. It wasn't…nothing. It was just an emptiness that wasn't very different from what I felt when I tried to read an Ascended.

"Why would you agree to take us to them now?" I asked.

"Because it is time," she said softly.

My heart tripped as I stared at her, more than a little unnerved by the response—by *all* of this. "Show me."

The Priestess rose and walked past the others still on the floor, her head bowed. Vonetta and Naill left the Ascended above with Valyn and the soldiers who'd been waiting outside. They joined us, along with Hisa and Emil, who'd arrived just as we started leaving the sanctum. All of them had their swords out as we entered the empty chamber and stepped through the narrow, tall break in the wall that became visible.

Torches lined the wall, casting an orangey glaze along the steep, earthen steps and wide-open chamber at the foot of them. Beyond them, nine tunnels connected to the opening, each lit by the faint glow of fire.

"It's like a hive," Hisa murmured as she scanned the circular space and the many openings.

The only sound was that of the Priestess's robes whispering across the packed dirt that gave way to stone as she took a tunnel to our right, and that corridor branched into two more. Halfway through them, we met up with the others, who I had a feeling might've been a bit lost based on the earthy bursts of relief I felt from them. The temperature dropped significantly as we descended farther underground to the point where I found it difficult to believe that any mortal could survive long in this kind of cold. The air was dry, but it chilled the skin and sank into the bones. My fingers began to ache from it.

The Priestess reached for one of the torches on the wall. Naill stepped in close to her, keeping his sword poised in case she did something foolish.

But all she did was walk forward and then touch the torch to another. The joining of flames cast a brighter light upon the wall. I stopped. So did Kieran. The rock had marks carved into it—rock that was a reddish-pink color.

He reached out, tracing his fingers over a carving, following the shape—

The Priestess touched another torch with the one she held and set off a chain reaction. An entire row of torches flamed to life, filling the air with the pungent scent of flint. The underground system was suddenly bathed in rippling firelight.

"What in the gods' names?" Kieran uttered, staring ahead.

I brushed past Vonetta, stepping down into a wide, circular opening. Water or something must have run through the cavern before, carving jagged formations out of the ceiling and depositing what appeared to be some sort of reddish mineral all along the spiraling and bizarre formations stretching down.

"Stalactites," Naill said, and several gazes turned to him. He nodded toward the ceiling with his chin. "That's what they're called."

"That sounds like a made-up word," Emil said.

Naill arched a brow. "It's not."

"You sure about that?" Emil challenged.

"Yes," Naill replied flatly. "If I were to create a word out of thin air, I would choose something more…interesting."

Emil let out a short laugh. "More interesting than *stalactites*?"

"Careful," Vonetta warned as what sounded like twigs snapped under my steps when I walked forward. "I don't think those are rocks or branches on the floor."

I looked down. There were chunks of something ivory in color, shards here and there, mixed with slender, longer, and darker-colored—bones. They were definitely bones.

Oh, gods.

Kieran made a sound of disgust as he toed aside a piece of rag, revealing what appeared to be a partial jawbone. "These didn't come from animals."

"Animals do not serve the True King," the Priestess said, drifting forward.

Stomach churning with anger, I started to speak, but what the Priestess walked past caught my attention.

It was like the ground had erupted, and snake-like roots spilled across the floor of the cavern from a deep, dark hole. The roots wormed their way through the discarded bones—bones that were too small. I carefully made my way forward, avoiding the scattered remains as much as I could. Something was on the roots *and* under them. Something dry and rusty-hued. And it was everywhere, splattered across the floor and pooled in thick, dried puddles. It was what had stained the walls and the bizarre rock formations that pinkish-red.

Kieran's arm brushed mine as he crouched, running a finger through the substance. His jaw clenched as he looked at me. "Blood."

The Priestess reached the other side of the cavern and touched her flame to the wall. Once more, a series of torches lit. Light splashed across a narrow opening and another sunken chamber.

And then we saw…

"Good gods," Hisa rasped, bending at the waist.

I opened my mouth, but I was beyond words. I'd believed the sight of those impaled on the gates, and the murdered girls from earlier, had been the most horrifying things I'd ever seen.

I'd been wrong.

I couldn't look away from the pale, bloodless limbs—some long and some so, so *tiny*. The piles of faded clothing, some white and some red, barely holding together dried-out husks where patches of hair remained, and legs and arms curled. Withered. Some dropped side by side in the ceremonial red of the Rite, their clothing fresh, their decay not even begun to take hold. Dimly, I wondered how there could be no smell—perhaps it was the cold or something else.

My heart started pounding as I stared into the sunken…*tomb*. And that was exactly what this was. A tomb that had been in use for only the gods knew how long, full of remains haphazardly left about.

The Priestess quietly placed the torch into a holder jutting from the wall and then clasped her hands loosely at the waist. "They have all served a great purpose."

Slowly, almost painfully, I turned to her. The eather pulsed in my chest and swelled, pressing beyond me and brushing against the walls. The air thickened as if filled with choking smoke, but there was no fire. Not outside of what burned inside of me.

"Just like we all do," the Priestess continued softly, *joyfully*, and her face lit up as if she spoke of a glorious dream. "As will you, the one whose blood is full of ash and ice."

I stepped forward, skin sparking with Primal essence, but an arm blocked me. "Don't," Kieran seethed. "Don't waste any energy on her. It's not worth it."

My hands closed around air as the Priestess smiled, and her eyes closed. Peace. That was what I tasted from her. Soft and airy like sponge cake. *Peace.*

The breath I took was full of daggers. "Give her what she so eagerly awaits."

I stepped back and turned stiffly, walking away. The only sound I heard was that of a sword meeting flesh.

"Is that all of them?" I asked.

"The Temple is empty," Valyn answered stoically, staring at the bodies carefully placed on the ground—the too-small bodies wrapped in rags with sunken stomachs and shriveled, pale skin. Bodies treated worse than diseased cattle.

"Seventy-one," Kieran stated. "There are seventy-one that are…"
Fresh.

Seventy-one that must have been taken in the unexpected last Rite and the one before. That number had to include the second and third sons and daughters. Which meant none had been given over to the Court as was normal for the second-born. It also meant that those who carried that not-so-dormant ember of life had been slaughtered.

Even worse was that the soldiers had carried outside what had to be…hundreds of older remains.

I'd never seen *anything* like it.

The underground chamber in New Haven, with all the names etched into the walls of those who'd died at the hands of the Ascended, paled in comparison to *this*.

Because most of these bodies belonged to *children*. Only a few may have been older, like the ones in the chamber under Redrock. But these were innocent children. In some cases, *babes*. I couldn't stop myself from thinking about that floppy, stuffed teddy bear that smelled of lavender.

The back of my throat burned as a knot gathered there, tasting of hot anger and bitter agony that wasn't just mine. I searched out the source, finding Casteel's father. His features gave nothing away, but his emotions had broken through his shields and projected outward, crashing through mine.

"That opening in the floor in there?" Naill cleared his throat, taking a step back as if the distance could somehow erase what he'd witnessed. "It looked like some sort of well. It goes deep. *Real* deep. We dropped some rocks down it. Never heard them land."

Meaning, there could be more. Bodies that had either been dumped or had fallen into the well. Gods.

Opening my eyes, I looked behind me to where many of the Atlantian soldiers stood in silence, and I knew what I would feel if I let my senses stretch. Horror. Horror so potent, I would never be able to wash it away. They all knew what the Ascended did, what they were capable of, but this was the first time that many of them were *seeing* it.

"What will we do with this place?" Vonetta asked, her back to the Temple.

"There is only one thing." I lifted my chin, searching the sky. A few heartbeats later, a purplish-black draken broke through the clouds. The shouts of surprise from those who had remained in the city echoed through the valley as Reaver stretched out his large wings, gliding overhead. "Burn it," I said, knowing he would carry through, even though he couldn't hear me. "We will burn it to the ground."

Reaver swept up with a powerful lift of his wings as Valyn asked, "And what of them?"

I turned to the Priests and Priestesses clothed in white. The two Ascended had already been *dealt* with. I opened my senses wide then.

None of them felt guilt or even regret, and those were two vastly different things. Regret came when it was time to face consequences. Guilt was there no matter if one paid for their sins or not. I wasn't sure if it would have changed anything if they *had* felt either of those things instead of what I sensed from them.

Peace.

Just as with the Priestess, they were at peace with their actions.

They hadn't just stood by, doing nothing. They weren't merely another cog in a wheel they couldn't control. They were a part of it, and it didn't matter if they'd been manipulated into their faith. They had been taking children, not to service any god or True King, but to feed the Ascended.

"Put them on their knees." I walked forward, reaching for the wolven dagger at my thigh. "Facing the bodies."

Valyn followed as the soldiers obeyed. "You don't have to—"

"I will not ask any of you to do what I would not do myself." I stopped in front of the kneeling Framont. His eyes were shut. "Open your eyes. Look at them. All of you. Look at them. Not at me. *Them.*"

Framont did as I demanded.

A flash of silvery fire lit the darkening sky as Reaver circled the stone Temple, unleashing his wrath. "I want them to be the last thing you see before you leave this realm and enter the Abyss, for that is surely where each of you will find yourselves. I want their bodies to be the very last thing you commit to memory, as it will be the last thing the families who claim their own will ever remember from this day forward. Look at them."

The Priest's eyes shifted to the bodies. They weren't filled with awe this time. They weren't filled with *anything*. He stared at them and smiled.

Smiled.

I swung out my arm. Red sprayed the white of my armor as I dragged the bloodstone blade across his throat.

The receiving hall and banquet chamber of Redrock had become an infirmary by nightfall. Injured soldiers and wolven had been laid out on cots. Banners baring the Blood Crown Royal Crest had already been stripped from the chamber and throughout the castle.

No Oak Ambler guards or Solis soldiers had been merely wounded. No survivable injuries. Those who had surrendered were under guard at the Citadel's jail, and I tried not to linger on thoughts of exactly how many lives had been lost as I made my way through the now-mostly-empty cots. Just as I tried not to think about what had been under the Temple of Theon—what had been done to the children.

I…I just couldn't think about it.

So, I'd gone from one wounded to another, healing them. I did it, thinking that since it was an ability that had developed before I Ascended, it couldn't weaken me too badly.

That, of course, could be dangerously faulty logic, but it gave me *something* to do that was helpful, while a group went to inform the people of Oak Ambler that they would be able to return to their homes tomorrow.

I planned on speaking to everyone in the morning. All of them. The families. Ramon and Nelly. My steps felt heavy.

"You look tired, *meyaah Liessa*," Sage noted as I approached her, the last of the injured. Sprawled out on the cot, her short, dark hair was a spiky mess. A thin sheet was tucked under her arms, covering her body entirely except for the leg that an arrow jutted from. It had been left in to prevent additional bleeding, and I knew it had to hurt something fierce. I'd tried to come to her sooner, but she continuously waved me off until everyone else, including those with much less severe injuries, were treated.

I lowered myself onto the floor beside her, grateful to no longer be wearing the armor. "It's been a long day."

"And then some." She leaned back on her elbows. A fine sheen of sweat dotted her brow. "We'll have more days like this." Her gaze shifted away from me. "Won't we?"

I knew where she looked. They'd brought in a wolven named Effie. He'd been in bad shape, having taken a spear to the chest. I'd known he was gone when I knelt beside him, but a desperate sort of childish hope had driven me to try. My abilities had worked on the Atlantian soldier who had passed. A young male who only Naill and I had seen take his last breath. He'd come right back, a little groggy and disorientated but alive. Not so for the wolven. *Or Arden.*

I hadn't misunderstood what Reaver had said. Only the Primal of Life could bring back those of two worlds.

We'd lost five wolven and close to a hundred Atlantian soldiers. We would've lost more if their injuries had been left untreated. But still, any loss was too much.

"I'm sorry," I said, my heart twisting as I thought about what Casteel had once told me. Nearly half of the wolven had died in the War of Two Kings. They had only begun to reclaim those numbers. I didn't want to lead them into that many deaths again.

Her gaze cut to me. "I'm sorry, too."

Chest heavy, I shoved at the long sleeves of the white top. They kept slipping down. "Naill?" I glanced over my shoulder. "I need your help."

"Of course." He lowered himself beside me, far more graceful than I, and he still wore his armor. Weariness I felt in my soul etched into the lines around his mouth as he carefully gripped the arrow. He knew the drill by now. "Let me know when."

I met Sage's eyes. "This will hurt."

"I know. This isn't the first time I've been hit by an arrow."

My brows rose.

A grin appeared. "It involved a dare that went horribly wrong. Long story. Maybe I'll tell you about it later?"

"I would like that." I was very curious about a dare that involved an arrow. "I will take the pain as fast as I can, but…"

"Yeah, I'm going to feel it when he pulls it out." Sage dragged in a deep breath. "I'm ready."

Placing my hands on either side of the arrow, I summoned the eather and got down to business. "Now."

Naill yanked the arrow free with a quickness born of experience. Sage's entire body spasmed, but she made no sound. Nothing until I heard a sigh of relief and the jagged hole in her thigh stitched itself together, the skin now a bright, raw pink.

"That was"—Sage's round eyes blinked—"intense."

"Better, though?"

"Unbelievably so." She gingerly curled her leg and then straightened it. "I've watched you do this, over and over. And still, it's…intense."

I smiled faintly, rocking back. "I'm no Healer, so I don't know how much of the wound heals immediately. I would take it easy for the next couple of days."

"No running around or dancing…" She trailed off, her eyes widening as her gaze fixed over my shoulder. "What the…?"

Naill and I followed her gaze. My mouth dropped open as the Atlantian made a choked sound.

Walking through the hall was a tall blond wearing what appeared to be a sheet knotted at the hips—*barely* knotted. With each long-legged step, the sheet appeared mere centimeters from slipping away.

"Reaver," I whispered, a little rattled by the sight of him.

Naill made that sound again.

"That's the draken?" Sage asked, and I realized she must not have seen him in his mortal form before.

"Yep."

"Really?" She eyed him. "Yum."

Naill looked down at her, his jaw slack. "He can breathe fire."

"And that's a bad thing?"

Thankfully, Naill didn't answer because Reaver had reached us. He nodded at the other two and then bowed slightly in my direction, causing the sheet to slip a little more.

"We need to find some clothing for you," I said, remembering what I had asked of Kieran. I doubted Reaver would fit into anything the Duke had worn. "Like as soon as possible." Then I thought of the other draken. "We need to find a lot of clothing."

"You people and your concerns about nudity is tiresome," Reaver replied.

"I have absolutely no problem with nudity," Sage announced. "Just thought I'd share."

Reaver grinned.

And my heart gave another shaky skip because I hadn't been wrong when I'd thought the upward curve of his lips took all those interesting features and made them into something stunning.

I gave my head a shake. "Is everything okay?"

"It is." Reaver faced me. "I wanted to let you know that Aurelia and Nithe returned to Thad," he said, referencing the remaining draken who had stayed back at the encampment. "They will return to Redrock tonight when it's less likely they'll be seen by mortals."

"Good thinking." I hadn't thought of that. "Will you…?" I rose, and a *whoosh* went through me. The floor stumbled. Or I did. "Whoa."

Naill was immediately by my side, his hand on my arm. "Are you okay?"

"Yeah. Just a little dizzy." I blinked the bright, flashing lights from my eyes in time to see that Sage had also stood. "You should still be sitting. I'm fine."

She watched me, making no move to sit.

"It's been a long day," I reminded her. I *was* tired. We all were.

"Have you eaten?" Reaver asked, drawing my attention to him.

I frowned. "I haven't had a chance since morning. Been kind of busy."

"You should make time for that," he advised. "Now."

Considering how the world had gone topsy-turvy, I couldn't really argue, so I ended up in the kitchens with a draken dressed in only a sheet hanging on for dear life, sharing a plate of sliced ham that must've been left over from the day before.

Come to find out, draken did eat actual food. Thank the gods.

With Naill feeling confident that between Reaver and I, we were more than capable of handling ourselves, he'd gone off to check in with Hisa. It was quiet. Probably because I was stuffing my face.

And where was Kieran to not witness this and comment on how much I was eating?

I hadn't felt this hungry since the first time I'd been to Castle Redrock.

But thinking of everything that still needed to be done tamped down my appetite. I needed to talk to the people. The families of the poor children. The imprisoned soldiers. The list went on. It was…a lot.

A lot of *responsibilities* that I had no experience with.

I looked around the kitchens, trying to imagine what the space looked like with cooks at the counter, steam rolling off the stoves, and people rushing to and fro. And then that made me wonder if the servants had any clue about the Ascended. Had they been completely blindsided? Or had some helped ferry in mortals, preparing them instead of roasted ham?

Gods, that was a dark thought.

"Does it not make you feel odd to be eating in here—eating their food? Like we took their city and now we're taking their food?"

Sitting beside me on the counter, Reaver cocked his head. "I hadn't even thought of that."

"Oh." I stared at a chunk of ham. Perhaps that wasn't an entirely normal concern to have. It probably wasn't. But I knew why I was thinking about that instead of where my mind wanted to go. I stopped fighting. "I can't stop thinking about the girls under here and those children. I can't unsee either thing. I can't understand how those who served in the Temple were at peace—how anyone, mortal or Ascended or whatever, can do those kinds of things."

"Maybe we're not supposed to," Reaver said, and I glanced at him. "Maybe that's what truly separates us from them."

"Maybe," I murmured. "Framont—the Priest—spoke of a True King of the Realms, as if the children had been killed in service to him."

"The True King of the Realms is Nyktos, and he would not approve of such a thing."

"Didn't think so." I finished off the piece of ham and reached for a linen. "I don't think he was talking about Nyktos, though. But maybe…Malec?"

Reaver's brows shot up. "That would be unfortunate if he believed that."

I grinned, but it quickly faded. Several moments of quiet passed between us, and in that time, I saw Arden and Effie. The soldiers and mortals whose names I didn't know. "People died today," I whispered.

"People always die." He reached over and picked up an apple from the bushel. "Especially in war."

"That doesn't make it any easier."

"It just makes it what it is."

"Yeah." I wiped my hands. "Arden died today."

He lowered the apple. "I know."

"I tried to bring him back to life."

"I told you it wouldn't work on anyone of two worlds."

"I had to—"

"You had to try anyway," he finished for me, and I nodded. He took a bite. "She doesn't like limitations either."

"Who?"

"The Consort." Turning the apple, he went to work on the other side.

"I have no problem with limitations."

Reaver slid me a long look. "I haven't known you for long, but I know you don't like limitations. If you did, you wouldn't have gone on and tried to restore life to another wolven, even after knowing you couldn't."

He had me there.

Reaching for the tankard, I took a drink. "I'm guessing the Primal of Life probably isn't thrilled with me restoring life, huh?"

He laughed, the sound hoarse and untried.

"What's so funny?"

"Nothing." Reaver lowered the apple. "Nyktos would be conflicted over your actions. On one hand, he would never not be happy about a renewal of life. On the other, he would worry about the nature of things. The course of life and death and how such an intervention alters the balance—the *fairness*." The corner of his lips tilted up, softening the sharp features. "When it comes to the Consort and choice to act or not, she would weigh the concerns, toss them aside, hope no one was paying attention, and just do it." Dusky lashes lifted as he gave me a sideways glance. "Sound familiar?"

"No," I muttered, and Reaver chuckled, the sound just as rough as the laugh. "Why does the Consort sleep so deeply when Nyktos doesn't?"

Reaver looked down at his apple, not speaking for several long moments. "It's the only way to stop her."

17

My brows flew up. "Stop her from what?"

"From doing something she'd regret," Reaver said, and my stomach lurched. "Both of her sons were taken from her. Neither may be dead, but neither are really alive, are they?"

No. They really weren't.

"She's angry. Furious enough to forget who she is. Enough to cause the kind of harm that cannot be undone."

I didn't know what it was like to be a mother and to have a child taken from me, but I knew what I'd done when Ian died. I knew what I'd done when I learned Casteel had been taken. So, in some small way, I could understand her anger.

His gaze flicked to the rounded archway. "When will we leave for the capital?"

"I will speak to the people tomorrow." My throat dried. "And the families."

"That…that will not be easy."

"No, it won't be." I lowered the tankard to the counter. "We'll leave the day after."

"Good." He paused. "We must not forget about Ires."

"I haven't."

"He must return home." His gaze remained fixed on the entrance. "Here comes your wolven."

"As I said before, he's not *my* wolven," I snapped, just as Kieran appeared in the doorway.

He stopped mid-step, his eyes widening slightly.

"Surprised?" Reaver asked.

Kieran's expression settled into one that could only be described as bland boredom. "I'm unused to seeing you not picking your teeth with your claws."

"I can do that now if it makes you feel better," Reaver remarked and then bit into the apple again.

"Not necessary." Kieran gave him the once-over, his eyebrow rising as he turned to me. "He's wearing a sheet."

"And that's why I said he needed clothing."

Reaver frowned around his apple. "Do you expect me to wear *his* clothing?"

"What's wrong with my clothes?" Kieran demanded.

A fair brow rose as Reaver mimicked Kieran's earlier look. "I don't believe they will fit me. I have broader shoulders."

"I don't think so," Kieran replied.

"And chest."

Kieran's arms crossed. "You definitely do not have that either."

"And my legs are not thin twigs that could snap under a breeze," Reaver continued.

"Are you serious?" Kieran looked down at himself. He didn't have...twig legs or whatever.

"Reaver." I sighed.

He lifted a bare shoulder. "Just saying."

"You're just saying nonsense. You both are nearly the same height and size," I said.

"I believe your vision could use improvement," the draken responded, and I rolled my eyes.

"You could use an attitude improvement," Kieran retorted.

"I ate a lot of ham," I announced to Kieran before Reaver could fire back another barb. Both males looked at me. "A lot. You'd be proud."

"While I'm glad to hear that," Kieran began, "that was a little random, Poppy."

"Yeah, well, I'm feeling random." I scooted off the counter. "Were you looking for me?"

"What else would he be doing?" Reaver asked.

Kieran's eyes narrowed on the draken. "Literally anything that doesn't include sitting in nothing but a sheet and eating an apple."

"So, not much, then?" Reaver quipped.

"Reaver," I said, shooting him a look. "Stop antagonizing Kieran."

"I have done no such thing," the draken denied. "He is just overly sensitive…for a wolven."

Kieran's arms unfolded as he stepped forward.

I held up a hand. "Don't start."

"Start?" He turned to me. "What exactly have I started? I just walked in here."

"See?" Reaver tossed the apple core into a nearby bin. "Sensitive."

"And you need to stop," I said, planting my hands on my hips. "I get it. Kieran almost stepped on your tail." I turned to the wolven. "Reaver almost bit your hand. Stop whining and get over it."

"He almost stepped on my entire leg," Reaver corrected. "Not my tail."

"And he almost bit my arm off." Kieran's eyes narrowed. "Not my hand."

I stared at them. "You two are…I don't even know." I narrowed my stare on Kieran when he started to respond. He wisely closed his mouth. "So, were you looking for me?"

"I was," he said, and Reaver wisely kept his mouth shut. "I need your special hands."

In other words, someone needed to be healed. It wasn't him. I picked up no signs of pain from him. Only acidic annoyance. "Who's injured?"

"Perry."

"Perry? Did something happen in Massene?" I took a deep breath. At least now I knew where Delano had disappeared off to. "He didn't remain at Massene, did he?"

"Nope."

"Gods." I started forward. "How badly is he injured?"

"Took an arrow in the shoulder, clean in and out," Kieran told me. "He says it's just a flesh wound, but from the looks of it, it's not. He'd heal from it in a day or two, but Delano's worried."

I started to ask why Perry didn't just feed, but then I remembered Casteel's unwillingness to do so from someone when he needed to. What he had felt for me, before he was even willing to acknowledge it, had become a mental block that he hadn't been able to get past until I'd Ascended and needed to feed upon awakening. It could be the same for Perry.

"Let's go," I said.

"She was dizzy earlier," Reaver announced. My head jerked in his direction. He looked utterly unapologetic. "After healing all those who were injured."

"What?" Kieran looked down at me, his pale eyes sharp.

"I'm fine. I hadn't eaten, which is why I devoured what probably accounts for half a pig."

Kieran wasn't assured. "Maybe you should sit this one out. He'll heal eventually—"

"I don't want him to suffer or for Delano to worry about him. I'm fine. I would tell you if I wasn't."

A muscle ticked along his jaw. "I have a feeling that's a lie."

"Something I think we can agree on," Reaver chimed in.

"No one asked you," I shot back.

"So?"

I exhaled slowly. "I think I like you better in your draken form."

"Most would agree with you on that." Picking up another apple from the bushel, Reaver brushed past us in his sheet. "I think I will take a nap." He paused at the archway. "I know you're not nearly as graceful as most wolven, but please do not step on me while I'm sleeping." And with that parting shot, Reaver left the kitchens.

"I really don't like him," Kieran muttered.

"Never would've guessed that." I turned to him. "Where's Perry?"

It took him half a minute to drag his attention from the entryway. I had a feeling he used that time to convince himself not to go after the draken. "You were dizzy?"

"Barely. I stood up quickly, and it's been a long day with little sleep and not enough food. It happens."

"Even to gods?"

"I guess so."

Kieran eyed me closely, in a way that was almost as intense as Casteel would look upon me. As if he were trying to ferret out things I wasn't saying. "Do you still feel hungry after eating nearly an entire pig?"

I never should've said that, but I knew what he was getting at. "I don't need to feed. Can you take me to Perry?"

Kieran finally relented and led me out to a back stairwell. "Perry can fight," he said after I asked why Perry hadn't stayed behind. "He's trained with a sword and bow. Nearly all Atlantians are after the Culling."

I hadn't known that.

There was a lot I still didn't know about the people I now ruled and was responsible for. And, gods, didn't that make my heart start racing?

"And that goes for changelings and those of mortal birth?" I asked. "Is it a requirement?"

"It goes for all who are able to do so." Kieran kept his pace slow as we climbed the narrow, windowless stairs. "But they're not required to join the armies. That is their choice. This is so all can defend themselves. Perry's as skilled as any soldier. A bit rusty, but his father wanted him to focus more on the land they owned and shipping."

"Is that what Perry wants?"

"I think so." Kieran opened the door on the second floor to a wide hall lit with gas lamps. "But I don't think he wants to stay back when everyone else is fighting."

But everyone else wasn't fighting. Younger Atlantians served as couriers and stewards. Helped prepare meals and run a slew of errands.

Kieran led the way down the hall, stopping before a door left ajar. He rapped his knuckles off the wood.

"Come in," came the muffled response I recognized as Delano.

Pushing open the door, Kieran stepped inside. I followed, giving the space a quick scan. The chamber was small and outfitted with the necessities, but airy with a large window overlooking the cliffs that allowed the rapidly approaching night to seep inside. There was an adjoining bathing chamber that had to be a welcome addition after nearly a month of living in an encampment and then the manor in Massene, which hadn't felt much different than the tents.

Perry lay stiffly on a bed, propped up by a mound of pillows. Gauze packed the wound on his bare shoulder, the material turning pink. One look at the tense set of his jaw and the fine sheen of sweat on his brow, and I knew he was in pain. It scratched hotly at my skin as Delano looked over his shoulder from where he sat in a chair beside the bed. His relief became earthy and rich upon seeing me.

"You didn't have to tell her," Perry said, his amber gaze shifting from Kieran to me. "I'll be fine. I told him that." He looked at Delano. "I told you that."

"I know, but I'm here. There's no reason for you to be in pain when I can help."

"There's no reason for you to be bothered with me when you have so much to do," the Atlantian argued.

"I will always have time to help my friends." I walked up to the bed, realizing Delano had a book open on his lap. "What are you reading?"

Two pink splotches formed in his cheeks. "Um, it's a book Perry found in the ship cabin you and Cas stayed in, actually."

My eyes went wide as they shot back to what lay in his lap. There was only one book that would've been on that ship.

That godsdamn journal.

"Willa has lived quite the interesting life." Perry grinned weakly from the bed. "Didn't know how interesting, though."

"You brought that sex book with you on the ship?" Kieran asked from where he now stood by the window.

"I did not bring it with me. Casteel brought it."

"Likely story," Kieran murmured, eyes glimmering with a hint of amusement.

"Whatever," I muttered, making my way to the other side of the bed, where I sat carefully and did everything in my power not to think about how Casteel had me read from the journal as he enjoyed his *dinner*.

"I have a question," Perry said as I reached for him. "Did you read this before you met Wilhelmina?"

"I did. The journal was in the city Atheneum in Masadonia, and the Ladies in Wait were always whispering about it," I said, breathing through the pinching sadness for Dafina and Loren. "I didn't even know that she was an Atlantian, let alone a changeling and Seer. Neither did Casteel. So, you can imagine the shock when we met her in Evaemon."

"I can only imagine." He chuckled softly, wincing. "I bet Cas had a field day with that."

A faint smile tugged at my lips as I placed my hands just below the bandage. The essence pulsed intensely, flowing toward my *special hands*. I watched the light move from my fingers and disappear. The silvery glow gave his brown skin a cooler undertone than usual. The tight muscles of his arm loosened within seconds. I lifted my gaze to his face, seeing his lips part with a deeper, longer breath.

Delano moved, stretching to reach for the bandage. He gingerly lifted it. Then, he took a deeper, longer breath. His eyes met mine, and his lips spoke a silent, "*Thank you.*"

I nodded, easing my hands from Perry as Delano clasped his cheek with one hand. He stopped to press his forehead against the Atlantian's and then kissed him. With my senses still open, the sweet and smooth taste I hadn't recognized the first time danced across my tongue. Chocolate and berries.

Love.

I couldn't stay asleep, jerking awake every hour on the hour, seeing those guards torn apart in the hall by the Craven who'd been mortals hours before. I kept seeing Arden charging forward and then finding him, his fur more red than silver and white. Gently swaying legs and veiled faces haunted me. And those bodies. All those bodies being carried out by the soldiers. It all replayed, over and over.

Along with the Craven's shrill shrieks. I lay on my side and stared at nothing. My skin was cold. My insides felt as chilled as the tomb underground. I tried to focus on the warmth pressed against the back of my legs, where Kieran slept in his wolven form, but my mind latched onto other things.

Who were those girls? I didn't think they were taken in the Rite. If so, wouldn't they have been in the Temple? Were they children of the servants slaughtered here? Had they been stolen from their homes?

And the ones we'd found under the Temple, had their souls been trapped there? It was believed that bodies must be burned for a soul to be released to enter the Vale. I didn't know if that was true, or if the ceremonial burning of the body was more for the mourners than the deceased. But all I could think about was those poor children lost under there, alone and scared and so very cold—

I sucked in a shaky breath as I reached up, clasping Casteel's ring. How could anyone take part in something like that? What could they believe in so fully, so completely, that they were able to justify that? What allowed them to live each day? To breathe and eat and sleep? How could *she* do something like this? She was a part of this. The cause. She'd convinced those Priests and Priestesses to do her bidding. Made sure the Ascended were made and turned into something just as horrid as the Craven.

How could I be a part of Isbeth? I was. I shared her bloodline, no matter how desperately I wanted it not to be true. How could *that* be my mother? Had she always been like this? When she was a mortal? Had the loss of her son and heartmate done this? Had the pain of such a loss truly shaped her into a monster utterly incapable of caring about anything but revenge?

My throat dried as I held Casteel's ring tighter. Could I become like her? If something happened to Casteel? If he...if he were killed, would I become nothing more than wrath and poison that only liberated death?

I'd already been close.

So close to losing myself in that pain. And he was still alive. Was that the impact of her blood in me? Did it mean I was more likely to become like her? Or was it the heartmate bond? Was that what became of those who lost their other halves—if they simply didn't give up and die like the ones Casteel had spoken of?

In the dark, silent moments of the night, I could admit that it was possible. I could become just like her. But what terrified me more was the knowledge that I could become something far worse.

Maybe that was what she wanted. Perhaps that was what she planned, and I truly was the Harbinger. The Bringer of Death and Destruction.

And maybe it wasn't just Isbeth's bloodline. Perhaps it was also the Consort's. She slept until at least one of her sons was returned to her because of what she might do if awake. In those strange glimpses I'd gotten of her, I'd felt her rage. Her pain. It'd felt like the kind that...*undid* things.

And when *I* felt rage, I tasted death.

Squeezing my eyes shut, I lifted my closed hand to my lips. The ring dug into my skin as I opened my mouth and screamed without sound—yelled in silence until the corners of my mouth hurt, my throat burned, and my entire body shook with the force of it. I screamed until whatever Kieran felt from me through the *notam* had not only awakened him but also caused him to shift into his mortal form. A heavy, warm arm covered mine.

Kieran didn't speak as he worked his other arm under my stiff shoulders and folded his upper body over mine. He didn't say a word as I lifted my hands, ring and all, to my face, covering my mouth and eyes as he tucked my head under his chin. I stopped the silent screaming, but I didn't cry. I wanted to. My eyes ached, and so did my throat. But I couldn't. If I did, I didn't think I'd stop. Because a sinking sort of horror settled into me. The same sort of foreboding dread I'd felt when I heard Duke Silvan say that I would fill the streets with blood.

I didn't know how long we lay there before it hit me—before I realized what I needed to do. Then, the trembling ceased. The fire in my throat eased.

I lowered my hands, still holding onto the ring. "I need you to promise me something."

Kieran was silent, but his arms tightened around me, and I felt his heart beating against my back.

"You're not going to like this. You may even hate me a little for it," I began.

"Poppy," he whispered.

"But you're the only person I trust to do this," I continued. "The only person who can." I took a breath. "If I...if we lose Casteel, if something happens to him—"

"We won't. That will not happen."

"Even if it doesn't, I could still...lose myself. If I become something capable of the kind of devastation we saw yesterday—" I whispered.

"You won't. You won't become like that."

"You don't know that. *I* don't know that."

"Poppy."

"What I said, about feeling less mortal with each day? I wasn't lying, Kieran. There's like this...this line inside me that, once crossed, makes me something else. I've done it before. At the Chambers of Nyktos. I could've destroyed Saion's Cove," I reminded him. "I could've destroyed Oak Ambler when I woke to find Casteel taken. I wanted to."

"I will reach you. Cas will," he reasoned.

"There won't always be someone there." I forced my grip on Casteel's ring to loosen. "There may be a time that no one will be able to reach me. And if that happens, I need you—"

"Fuck."

"I need you to put me in the ground. Casteel won't be able to do it. You know that. He can't," I forged on. "I need you to stop me. You know how. There are bone chains under—"

"I know where the chains are." His anger was hot in my throat but not nearly as bitter as his anguish. And I hated myself a little then.

I hated myself a lot. But there was no other choice. "And if we haven't discovered all Eloana did to entomb Malec, you need to find out. Put me in the ground and do whatever she did. Please. He…Casteel will be angry with you, but he'll understand. Eventually."

"The fuck he will," Kieran said on a growl.

"But he won't kill you. He would never do that to you." I swallowed as my throat constricted. "I'm sorry. I am. I don't want to ask something like that. I don't want to put that on you."

"But you are." His voice had turned hoarse. "That's exactly what you're doing."

"Because I can't become something capable of leveling cities. I couldn't live with myself. You know that. You couldn't live with allowing me to become that. Neither could Casteel." I folded my hand over his arm. "Maybe that will never happen. I will do everything I can to not let it. But if it does? You would be doing the right thing. You know that. You would be doing the thing that needed to be done."

Kieran's hold tightened even further. He didn't respond. Not for a long time. "I don't think you give yourself enough credit, Poppy. I don't think *you* will allow it to happen," he told me, shifting his arm so my hand slipped into his. He tangled his fingers with mine. "But if I'm wrong…"

I held my breath.

"I will do it," Kieran swore with another shudder. "I will stop you."

18

"The people of Oak Ambler are waiting," Valyn told us as we climbed the tower of Castle Redrock the following afternoon. "They appear rather calm, so that's good."

I wanted to agree, but the sobs of grief from the parents we'd met on the road to Oak Ambler clogged my throat. They'd been brought into the city ahead of the others and then led to the Temple, where the remains had been carefully wrapped in shrouds. And then all I could do was watch as their hope gave way to despair. As each of their worlds shattered. The sounds they'd made each time one found their child on the pyres—the raw, pain-filled screams coming from the depths of their shattered beings didn't even sound like something a mortal could give voice to.

I couldn't stop seeing, hearing, or tasting it.

I'd given the stuffed bear back to Ramon and Nelly. I'd said I was sorry. I'd said that nearly a hundred times, and it meant nothing. It did nothing. I'd promised this would never happen again, and I'd meant that. But that also did nothing for them.

"Everyone's present?" Vonetta asked as we entered the small chamber at the top. Naill lingered in the narrow doorway, blocking it as if he expected something to rush up from the stairs.

"As far as we can tell," Lord Sven said as I walked to one of the small, square windows that faced the oaks along the bluff. Through the trees, I saw glimpses of the draken. "I have one of my men going through the records at the Citadel to see if we can get a better than rough estimate of how many people lived here."

"A small group of mortals was at the Rise this morning—some of those who remained," General Cyr said. "They've expressed a desire to leave the city."

"Then they should be able to leave," Vonetta replied.

"Agreed," Emil said.

In the ensuing silence, Kieran touched my shoulder. He'd been quiet all morning. He wasn't angry because of what I'd asked of him last night. I didn't pick up any of that from him. Nor did I think he'd lied when I'd asked him five hundred and five times since I woke if he was. He was tired and *troubled*.

I cleared my throat as I turned from the window. Sven and Valyn looked at me, waiting. "They should be allowed to leave if that is what they want."

Neither Valyn nor Cyr appeared entirely thrilled by that.

I swallowed again, pushing the knot further down. "If anyone wanted to leave their city to move closer to family or seek better opportunities, they'd have to gain permission from the Royals," I told them, remembering the requests that had been brought before the Teermans during the City Council meetings held weekly. "It was rarely approved. People should have that basic freedom in Solis, just as they do in Atlantia."

"I agree, but during a time of war? And with the Craven?" Lord Sven began. "It may not be the best time to allow that freedom."

"I understand the hesitation to allow this. I would rather no one choose to leave because of the dangers that choice incurs. But if we prevent that, they have no reason to believe that it would be temporary or that we have no intention of continuing to suppress their rights." I looked to the dark-haired general. Cyr would remain in Oak Ambler to protect the port and the surrounding lands with a part of his regiment. The remainder of his force would be absorbed into Valyn's. "They should be reminded of the risks, but if they insist, then we allow it."

Cyr nodded. "Of course."

"What we do here will be heard in other cities," I reminded him—reminded all of them. Including myself. "This is how we gain the trust of the people of Solis."

The group nodded, and I looked to the doorway of the balcony. I could hear the hum from the crowd gathered in the courtyard below and in the meadow of Redrock. My heart tripped over itself. "It's time I speak with them."

"We'll wait for you outside." Sven bowed and then made his way out onto the balcony. Cyr and Emil followed.

"You sure you want to do this now?" Valyn asked, having stayed behind.

"Do you think I shouldn't?"

"I think you should do what you feel you can," he said rather diplomatically. "But I also think what you've already done today is more than enough."

He was speaking of the meeting with the families. I pressed the heel of my palm against the pouch, feeling the toy horse. Valyn had been there when I spoke to the families. So had Kieran and Vonetta. They'd borne witness to that painful desperation. "Is all of this not the duty of a Queen?"

"It doesn't have to be. There's no rule that says that." Valyn's response was as soft as his gaze. "There's no policy that dictates you must shoulder all the responsibility. That's why you have an advisor." He then nodded at Vonetta. "That's why you have a regent."

Kieran lifted a shoulder when I glanced at him. "He's right. Any number of us can speak to the people."

Anyone could—and probably do a much better job of it than me—but... I looked back up at my father-in-law. "If you were still King, would you have allowed someone else to speak to those families? Speak to the people?"

Valyn opened his mouth.

"Truly?" I prodded.

He sighed as he dragged a heavy hand through his hair, shoving it back from his face. "No, I would've done it myself. I wouldn't have wanted anyone else to—"

"Bear those marks?" I murmured, and his head tilted in *that* way. The corners of my lips curved up faintly. "I appreciate the offer." And I did because I thought it came from a good place. "But this has to be me."

Something akin to pride settled into his features. "Then it shall be you."

I drew in a breath, but it didn't go very far. Nervousness swamped me. "I...I've never spoken to such a large crowd before." My palms felt damp, and I couldn't help but think if Casteel were here, he would've taken the lead on this until I felt comfortable. Not because he'd doubt that I could do it or think that he would be better at it, but because he knew it was something I had so very little experience with. I glanced at Valyn, who had waited behind. "I'm not sure what I should even say to them."

"The truth," Valyn suggested. "You tell them what you told us when we arrived. That you're not a conqueror. That you're not here to take."

My chest loosened a little, and I nodded, facing the door.

"Penellaphe," Valyn called, stopping me. "My son is truly lucky to have found you."

The knot came back but for a very different reason. But when I took a breath this time, it filled my lungs. "We're both lucky," I told him, and I swore the ring warmed against my skin.

I turned back to the door, lifting my shoulders as Vonetta leaned in, speaking quietly. "You got this."

Reaching down, I took her hand and squeezed it. "Thank you."

Vonetta squeezed back, and then I went forward, stepping out into the cool air and the bright afternoon sun. My heart pounded as I walked toward the stone railing, followed by the others. The crowd quieted in a wave that extended beyond the courtyard, the meadow, and farther, into the packed and crowded streets. My hands trembled slightly as I placed them on the stone, every fiber of my being aware of thousands and thousands of gazes turned upward, seeing me in the white of the Maiden and the gold mantle of the Atlantians. I wore no crown because I was not their Queen.

And then I told the people of Atlantia what I had told the generals in a voice that trembled but was loud. In a voice that was heard. "We are not conquerors. We are not *takers*. We are here to end the Blood Crown and the Rite."

Much later, after addressing the people of Oak Ambler and meeting with the generals to firm up plans for tomorrow and beyond, I paced the length of the sitting area adjoining the bedchamber I'd slept in the night before. Valyn had joined us some time ago, sharing a glass of whiskey with Kieran. Mine sat untouched on the table. My head was too full of thoughts, and my stomach churned, even though it was full.

"Can you sit?" Kieran asked from the chair he was seated in.

"No."

"Your pacing won't make tomorrow come any sooner," he said, and leaving tomorrow wasn't even one of the top reasons I was wearing a path in the stone floor. It was the grief that I still tasted from that morning. It was the tentative hope I still felt from the people of Oak Ambler. It was also their awakening rage that lingered in the back of my throat. "And it's making me nervous."

I stopped, facing them. "Really?"

"No." Kieran lifted his glass to his lips as he kicked a booted foot onto the ottoman in front of him. "It's just really distracting, and I feel like if I drank any more, your constant back and forth would end up making me sick."

"Why don't you stop drinking then?" I suggested, tone dripping with acid. Sugary amusement radiated from where Hisa stood at the archway of the chamber.

Valyn raised his brows as he lifted his glass, surely hiding his grin as I did, in fact, plop very loudly into the chair across from Kieran. "Happy?"

"Sounded like you may have hurt yourself," he observed dryly.

"It's about to sound like you're hurt because I'm a second away from punching you," I retorted.

Kieran grinned. "You mean, a love tap?"

My eyes narrowed.

"So, I've been thinking about what that Priest said. What you all told me about the woman in Massene," Valyn spoke, wisely changing the subject. "If they really were speaking about Malec, do you think Isbeth is the conspirator?"

"I don't know. I don't know if it's her, or Malec, or if this is all just nonsense," I said, blowing out an aggravated breath. "I don't know how any of that plays into why they had another Rite. Or why she created the Revenants, or how any of them believe I play a role in this. None of them can seriously think I will go along with her plans."

"Remaking the realms could mean taking Atlantia," Valyn surmised after a few moments. "After all, that's what we're doing in a way—bringing the two kingdoms together. That could be what Framont was speaking of."

It could be, but I felt as if I were missing something.

"I've sent word back to Evaemon. I hope to have a response by the time we're reunited," he said, and I nodded. "You still plan to travel through the Blood Forest?"

"We will come close to it," Kieran said. "It's the safest way. We want to get as close to Carsodonia as possible before we're seen. We want that advantage."

If we traveled straight through New Haven and Whitebridge, it added to the risk of being seen. So we planned to travel up the coast, skirting the edge of the Blood Forest and then cutting between Three Rivers and Whitebridge, making our way to the Willow Plains through a portion of the Niel Valley, where we would then enter the Elysium Peaks. The armies would be following behind us, taking those cities under Vonetta's leadership.

"The path you take won't be without danger," Valyn pointed out. "News of our siege of Oak Ambler will reach the capital soon. The Blood Crown will move their armies. There will be patrols."

"We know," Kieran stated. "Nothing about what we're about to embark on is safe."

Valyn shifted, bending his leg. "If your estimates are right, it will take you about a fortnight to reach Carsodonia."

"Give or take a day," he answered. "That's if we're able to push hard."

"By then, we should be at Three Rivers," he continued. "Where we'll meet with you and—"

"And Casteel. He will be with me," I promised.

His exhale was one of hope. "I believe that. Because I believe in you," he added, holding my gaze. "I want to make you a promise. I will make sure your wishes are carried out on our end. The regent will have no issues from any of the generals. We will not take down any Rises. We will not be the cause of innocents losing their lives."

Now my exhale was hopeful. "Thank you."

He nodded. "What are your plans once you get into Carsodonia? How will you find him?"

"We're still working on that," Kieran shared, and I almost laughed because *working on that* could easily be translated into, *we don't know.*

The thick, cream-like taste of concern gathered in my throat, and my gaze shot from Kieran to Valyn. The burst of worry had come from him, and that was…well, it was rare to pick up anything from the man.

"It's been a long, long time since I've even been close to

Carsodonia," he began. "And it was a big city then. That's a lot of ground to search. A lot of Ascended. A lot of Royal Knights."

"We know," Kieran said, his drink forgotten in his hand.

"And then you have the Blood Queen to deal with," Valyn continued, undaunted. "You're not going to have free roam of that city."

"We know," the wolven repeated. "We've talked about capturing a high-ranking Ascended, and even Handmaidens, and getting them to talk. One of them would have to know where Cas is being held."

We'd also talked about the fact that the Handmaidens rarely strayed far from the Blood Queen. And we also discussed that we'd have to find a high-ranking Ascended who was completely on board with everything the Blood Queen did, which also meant they'd probably be more afraid of disobeying their Queen than the threat of death.

We had ideas regarding what to do, but nothing we came up with was a magical fix for how to find him in a city of millions—

Magical.

I launched to my feet, startling both Valyn and Kieran. "Magic."

"Magic?" Valyn repeated, brows lifting.

"Primal magic." I spun toward Hisa. "Do you know where Sven is?"

"I believe he's visiting with his son in one of the chambers down the hall."

"What are you thinking?" Kieran set his drink aside.

"Perry said his father knows a lot about Primal magic, remember?" I said, relieved when understanding flickered across his features. "And that almost anything is possible with it. Why wouldn't there be some sort of magic that could help us locate Casteel?"

As Sven sat in the chair across from his son, I wanted to smack myself. How had I not thought of Primal magic until now?

"I remember reading about old spells used to locate missing

items," Sven said after I'd burst into the chamber and asked if he knew of a spell that could be used to locate a person. He rubbed at the beard on his chin. "Let me think about this for a moment. Missing items like a cherished ring are vastly different than a person. But I just need to think for a bit. I've read a lot of books. A lot of journals. And those old spells were scattered throughout them."

"Yes." I nodded, pacing once more. But this time, I was doing it between Kieran and Valyn, who'd followed me to the chamber that Hisa had led us to. "Think for as long as you need."

Sven nodded as he continued fiddling with the growth on his chin. Seconds turned into minutes as the Atlantian Lord murmured under his breath, eyes squinted. I had no idea what he was saying.

His son rose, going to a serving table and a bottle of amber liquid. Pouring a glass, he moved as if he hadn't taken an arrow to the shoulder the day before. He brought it to where his father sat. "Here. This usually helps."

Sven grinned as he took the short, crystal glass. He glanced at me, noticing that I'd stopped pacing. "Whiskey warms the stomach and the brain," he said, taking a deep drink that caused his lips to pull back over his fangs. "Yeah, that's definitely going to do some warming."

Perry chuckled as he dropped back into the chair next to Delano.

I wasn't sure if warming the brain was a good idea. I started to pace again, but Kieran dropped his hand on my shoulder, stopping me. Shooting him an arch look, I folded an arm across my waist and began rocking back on the heels of my boots.

"See, I keep thinking of the location spell," Sven spoke, and I stopped rocking. "I remember it because I almost used it once to find some old cufflinks I misplaced. I didn't, though." He glanced up. "Primal magic is forbidden. It can change the threads of fate for a person. Not all Primal magic does, but some can, and you don't want to mess with the Arae—not even for a pair of cufflinks. Never did find them."

I had no problem potentially messing with the Fates—if they actually existed. The Unseen and the Blood Queen had used Primal magic and hadn't seemed to incur their wrath.

"What about that spell, Father?" Perry asked with a wink in my direction. "Why do you keep thinking about it? Can't just be the cufflinks."

"It's not." One side of his mouth curled up. "It's the language of the spell. It's old Atlantian, and that means the language of the gods.

But it was written something like..." His fingers stilled. "To find what was once *cherished*—to locate what is *needed*." His gaze lifted to his son. "It doesn't specify that it only refers to an object."

"A set of cufflinks and a person could both be cherished and needed," Perry agreed, and I willed myself to stay quiet. There seemed to be a process to Sven recalling these things, and his son knew it well. "Do you remember what that spell called for?"

Sven didn't answer for a long moment. "Yeah, it was a fairly simple one. Only a few items needed. A piece of parchment to write upon. The blood the item belonged to—or in our case, the person—and another cherished item belonging to the same person."

"Well, those items will be a bit hard to come by," Kieran stated. "Starting with the fact that we'd need Cas to get his blood."

"Not necessarily," Sven objected. "The blood doesn't have to come from his veins."

"It could come from someone who has fed from him," I said.

Sven nodded. "That, or a relative—any relative. But your blood will work."

Relief shuddered through me, though it was brief.

"But we also need a cherished item," Delano said, leaning forward.

"Poppy?" Kieran suggested and then quickly added, "Not that I think you're an item or that you belong in that kind of way to Cas, but—"

"It would have to be an actual item," Sven stepped in. "Something that belongs to them."

"The journal?" Perry suggested.

"Journal?" Valyn repeated.

My face heated as I quickly spoke, preventing anyone else from going into detail. "While I believe he cherishes that, it's not technically his. It belongs—*wait*." Unfolding my arm, I reached to where the pouch was secured at my hip. My heart started racing as I pulled it free. "I have something of his." I swallowed as I tugged open the strings keeping it closed and pulled out the tiny wooden horse. "This."

"Gods," Valyn rasped. "I haven't seen that in ages."

Kieran stared at it. He hadn't known what was in the pouch. He'd never asked. His voice was rough when he said, "Malik made that for him. He...he made one for me at the same time."

"I don't know why I picked it up when we left the palace." I held the toy horse tightly. "I just did."

"That should work," Sven said. "You'll need to be in the general vicinity of where you think he may be. A building. The neighborhood. I know we don't know where he's being held, but if we can narrow it down, this spell should help."

The spell wasn't the answer to finding Casteel, but it was something. Something that would definitely help if we could narrow things down.

If I could reach Casteel again in our dreams, maybe I could get that information.

I stared at the horse, no longer entirely convinced that the Arae weren't real, and unable to stop myself from wondering if the Fates had played a hand in this.

Either way, I had hope, and that was such a remarkable, confusing thing.

Fragile.

Contagious.

Breakable.

But, ultimately, beautiful.

A throat cleared from the entrance, drawing our attention to where Lin now stood next to Hisa. "I'm sorry to interrupt, Your Highness, but someone's arrived at the gates, asking to speak with you. They say they've come from Atlantia, but I do not recognize either of them."

Hisa frowned as I glanced at Kieran. "Did you get any names?"

He shook his head. "I'm sorry. If any were given they were not shared with me."

Curiosity rose. I had no idea who could have arrived from Evaemon. "Where are they now?"

"They've been escorted to Redrock and should be arriving any moment."

Turning to Sven, I thanked him for his help and then left the chamber. Kieran and Delano followed close, as did Valyn.

"This is odd," Kieran remarked.

"Agreed." Hisa led the way with Lin as we entered the wide hall. "I cannot think of any who would travel from Atlantia that weren't already with us."

Guards opened the doors, and we stepped out into the fading sunlight. My gaze swept over the tents that had been set up and the piles of rubble from the destroyed inner walls, stopping on two people walking around a small horse-drawn wagon. I recognized the warm blond hair, golden skin, and the unique beauty of Gianna Davenwell. The appearance of Alastir's great-niece was a shock. She was one of the few wolven who remained in Evaemon to guard the capital, but when the one who walked with her lowered the hood of the cloak all the air went out of my lungs at the sight of rich, warm brown skin and the mass of tight, snow-white curls.

"Holy shit," Kieran muttered.

My heart stuttered and sped up as I stumbled away from Kieran. "*Tawny?*"

I was rooted to where I stood, and then Tawny *smiled*.

And *spoke*. "Poppy."

Springing forward, I was only distantly aware of Kieran reaching for me, but I was fast when I wanted to be.

I raced across between the tents, and I didn't stop. For what almost felt like the first time with her, I didn't hesitate to think about anything. I threw my arms around her as she did the same, and for several moments, that was all I could focus on. Tawny was in my arms. She was upright and *talking*. She was alive and here. Emotion clogged my throat as I fisted my hand in her hair, squeezing my eyes shut against the rush of tears.

"I missed you," I said, voice thick.

"I missed you, too." Her arms tightened around me.

I sucked in a shaky breath, becoming aware of several things all at once. Kieran was near. I felt Delano pressing against the side of my legs, and inadvertently, Tawny's. His wariness confused me, as did Kieran's reaction—his attempt to stop me—but it was how Tawny felt that was of greater concern. She was slimmer than before, in her shoulders and through her body, and she'd already been slender. With as long as she'd been asleep, the loss of weight was no surprise, but it was her skin that shocked me most. The coldness of it seeped through the long-sleeve tunic.

I drew back, my gaze lifting to her face. Whatever I was about to say fell to the wayside. "Your eyes," I whispered. They were paler than a Revenant's, nearly white with the exception of the pupil.

"*My* eyes?" Her brows shot up. "Have you seen the glow behind your pupils?"

"Yes. Mine are different, too. It's the—"

"The Primal essence," she said, glancing behind me to where Kieran hovered. "I know what it is."

"How...?" I looked to where Gianna lingered. I didn't think the wolven had seen my eyes like this. "Did someone tell you about them? About the essence?"

"Yes, and no." Tawny's cold, cold hands slid down my arms to clasp mine. "And my eyes? My hair? I don't really know why any of it's like that. I'm guessing the shadowstone, but I can see fine. I feel fine." Her head tilted, and a white curl fell against her brown cheek. "I feel so much better now that I'm here." She glanced down at Delano, who watched her closely. "Even though he looks like he wants to eat me, and not in the fun way."

A short laugh burst out of me. "Sorry," I said, reaching out through the *notam* to let him know he had nothing to worry about. "The wolven are very protective of me."

"Gianna said as much," Tawny said, and the wolven gave me a short, awkward wave I felt in my bones.

I glanced over my shoulder to where Kieran stood. He wasn't looking at me. His body was tense. His focus on Tawny. Tart wariness gathered in the back of my throat. He wasn't the only one who stood close. Hisa and Valyn were right behind him. Unease was a heavy cloud, and—*wait*. Slowly, I turned back to Tawny, opening my senses to her. I felt...

I felt nothing.

And I knew Tawny wasn't shielding from me. She was never good at that. Her emotions were always close to the surface, if not plainly written across her face. My heart skipped a beat as I pressed a little harder, finding nothing, not even a wall.

I tightened my grip on her hands. "I don't feel anything from you."

Her milky-white eyes flicked back to me, and I didn't feel it, but I saw the pinch of concern settling into the fine lines of her brow. "I don't know why. I mean, I do, but—" Her eyes closed briefly. "None of that matters right now. There is something that I do know." Her chest rose with a deep breath. "There's something I need to tell you in private. It has to do with Vikter."

Blinking, I drew back. "Vikter?"

Tawny nodded. "I saw him."

Private wasn't exactly private.

Tawny and I had retreated to one of the receiving chambers, and I wasn't sure if Nyktos himself would've stopped Kieran from being there. He sat beside me while Delano remained in his wolven form, sitting at my feet. Gianna stood behind, appearing to be genuinely concerned for Tawny's well-being. Tawny hadn't protested either's presence, but she was clearly nervous, her knees pressed tightly together as she continuously twisted a curl around her finger, a habit she had whenever she was anxious.

Delano and Kieran's rigid posture and quiet watchfulness probably had a lot to do with that. Kieran had stopped me before we entered the chamber, pulling me aside. He'd spoken low, but the words still echoed like thunder as I looked at Tawny. "She doesn't feel right," he'd said. "All of us can sense that."

And he was right.

Tawny *didn't* feel right, but it was her. The hair and eyes, the cold skin, and my inability to read her wasn't who I remembered, but everything else was her. And just because she didn't feel right, didn't mean she was *wrong* somehow. It just meant she had changed.

And I, more than anyone, understood that.

"As soon as I woke, I knew I needed to find you," Tawny said as she clutched a glass of water. "I think everyone thought I was a bit out of it. Willa, Casteel's mother," she said, glancing at Kieran. "I can't blame them for feeling that way. I was a bit—"

"Hysterical?" Gianna supplied for her.

Tawny cracked a grin. "Yeah, a little. They didn't want me to leave, but you know I can be pretty insistent when it comes to doing what I want."

Boy, did I ever.

"Anyway, Gianna actually volunteered to travel with me," Tawny added.

"She was going to do it with or without someone." Gianna sat on the arm of the settee. "It was too dangerous to make such a journey alone, especially when no one had any idea where you'd be."

"Thank you," I said to her, feeling a little bad about having threatened to feed her to barrats.

Gianna nodded.

"How is it that you woke up?" Kieran asked of Tawny. "Was it something Willa or Eloana was able to do?"

"I...I don't really know, other than I don't think I was supposed to—wake up, that is." Tawny's hand trembled, sloshing the steaming liquid in her mug. "I know that doesn't make sense, but I felt like I was dying. I *knew* I was dying, until I saw Vikter. I think either he or the Fates did something to prevent that."

"The Fates," I murmured, almost laughing. "You mean the Arae? You've never believed in them."

"Yeah, well, that has definitely changed," she admitted, widening her eyes.

My breath snagged again. "How did you see Vikter?"

"I saw him in a dream that wasn't a dream. I don't know how else to explain it other than that." Tawny took a drink. "I remember what happened in Oak Ambler—the pain of being stabbed. And then there was nothing for a long time until there was something. A silvery light. I thought I was entering the Vale until I saw him. Vikter."

A fine tremor ran through me.

Delano leaned into my legs as Kieran asked, "And how do you know it wasn't just a dream?"

"He confirmed who you are—that you're a god—and I knew that. Isbeth had let that slip, but I hadn't believed her, even though Ian did. And, gods, Poppy, I'm so sorry for what happened to him."

"Yeah," I breathed through that burn. "Me, too."

"What exactly do you know of Isbeth and her plans?" Kieran jumped on that.

"Not much other than she believed Poppy would help her remake the realms," she said, and I inhaled sharply at hearing those words once more. "And I didn't understand what that meant. I wasn't around her that much. I didn't even truly understand why I was being summoned to Carsodonia other than they said they feared that I would be taken, too, because it was known how close you and I were. That didn't make sense, but once I got to Wayfair and saw those…Handmaidens and the Revenants," she added with a shudder, "nothing about the place felt okay. And when Isbeth told me you were her daughter, I thought that she wasn't in her right mind," Tawny said with a shake of her head. "But Vikter told me things that I couldn't have known. Like a story about a god who had awakened long enough to prevent you from being harmed in the Skotos Mountains. He said that your suspicions were correct. That it was Aios who stopped you. He also told me it wasn't just Nyktos who gave his approval for your marriage. That it was him *and* the Consort."

I opened my mouth, but I couldn't find the words.

"I also approve. Not that anyone asked." Tawny gave me a quick, teasing grin that was so familiar, it eased something in me. It faded quickly. "Vikter also told me that he—that Casteel was taken?"

The burn in my throat increased. "He was, but I'm going to get him back—"

"You're going to travel to Carsodonia and free him," she interrupted, and I blinked. "I know. Vikter said you would."

"Okay." I took a deep, shuddering breath. There was no way Tawny could've known all of that. "Was Vikter a spirit?"

"No." Tawny shook her head. "He's a *viktor*."

I jolted. Something about the way she said that tugged at a memory that lingered just out of my reach. "What do you mean?"

"I hope I can explain this well enough to be understood." Tawny blew out a breath. "A *viktor* is born with a goal—to guard someone the Fates believe is destined to bring about some great change or purpose. I got the impression that not all are aware of their duty, and they end up being there for that person anyway—like the Fates bring them together. I think other *viktors* are aware and are involved in the lives of the ones they're protecting. Once they die, either while carrying out their purpose or from any other cause, their souls return to Mount Lotho."

"Where?" My brows lifted.

"It's where the Arae reside," she explained. "Their souls return to Mount Lotho, where they wait to be reborn."

"It's a place written to be in Iliseeum," Kieran told me, but all I could do was stare at Tawny.

"And you said Vikter was one of these?" When Tawny nodded, my thoughts began to race. "Does that mean he knew I was a god the whole time? What happened to him?"

Tawny tipped forward, placing her glass on the small table. "How Vikter explained it to me was that when *viktors* are reborn, they have no memories of their previous lives like they do when their souls return to Mount Lotho where they are once more given mortal form. But some *viktors* are basically, um, predestined to figure out what they are, and who they are sent to either protect or lead. Like Leopold. Viktor said that he figured it out, and that was why he sought out Coralena before you were even born."

Another shock rippled through me, once more tugging at a strange feeling in the back of my mind. The sensation that I somehow knew this already. But I didn't. "So, they weren't together because they loved one another?" I asked.

"I don't know, but they had Ian together. Ian told me they were his parents," she said. "That doesn't mean they were in love, obviously, but there was definitely something there, and I don't think that being a *viktor* means you can't love."

I nodded slowly. I knew that Vikter had been in love with his wife. The grief he'd felt whenever he spoke of her was far too real to have not been birthed from love. And in that moment, I chose to believe that Coralena and Leopold—my parents—did love one another.

"Vikter had to know, though." Kieran's eyes met mine. "He became a Royal Guard—became your personal guard, and he made sure you could protect yourself. That you could fight better than most Rise Guards. Besides all of that, his name couldn't be a coincidence."

I'd always believed that Vikter had trained me because he knew I never wanted to be as helpless as I had been the night in Lockswood, but he could've been ensuring that I knew how to keep myself alive until I Ascended and completed the Culling.

"If he did know what his purpose was, why didn't he tell her?" Kieran turned back to Tawny. "Could've made things a lot easier."

"If he knew, he couldn't because even though *viktors* are there to protect their charges, they cannot reveal their reasons. There was a lot of things he couldn't tell me, saying it had to do with the Fates and balance, so he was very careful and deliberate with what he said," Tawny said with a shrug. "It's the same reason they're born without memories and from what I gathered, even mortals who are bound to do some terrible stuff may also have *viktors*. He would've been unable to speak the truth."

I didn't know how to feel about the fact that Vikter could've known who I truly was or knew that Hawke was really Casteel. Or that he came into my life with one purpose: to protect me. Some of his last words came back to me then, squeezing my heart into pieces. *I'm sorry for not protecting you.* His belief that he'd failed me took on a whole new meaning now. I reached out, running my fingers between Delano's ears when he rested his head on my knee. "Did he look well? Like, did he look the same?"

"He looked…" Tawny dragged her gaze from Delano. "He looked like I remember. Not the last time we saw him, but before that." Tawny smiled, and it was only a little sad. "He looked good, Poppy, and he wanted me to tell you that, yes, he was proud of you."

I sucked in a shaky breath as raw emotion rose, clogging my throat. I closed my eyes, struggling to keep the tears at bay. "Did he tell you anything more?"

"Yes, and no," she answered.

"That's not really helpful," Kieran replied.

Tawny's blanched eyes drifted to Kieran and the look she gave him was one I'd seen her give many Lords in Wait in the past. One that said she was sizing him up and wasn't sure if she was impressed or not by what she saw. "No, it's not."

"So, Vikter was able to tell you all about *viktors* and update you on things that have happened in Poppy's life, but he wasn't able to say anything of importance regarding the Blood Crown's plans?"

"I'm not sure if you were listening or you just didn't understand when I said that there were things he couldn't say because of the balance and the Fates," Tawny said in a tone I also recognized. Gianna pressed her lips together to hide her smile, while I didn't even fight mine. "So, he obviously couldn't spill all the secrets."

Kieran's eyes narrowed. "Obviously."

Tawny lifted her brows at him.

"What was he able to say?" I asked before the argument I sensed brewing could really take off.

"He told me about the prophecy the goddess Penellaphe spoke about."

Frustration rose, as did dread. I was so damn tired of that prophecy. "I know what the prophecy is."

"But do you know what the whole prophecy is?" Tawny asked. "I don't think you do. Or at least I don't think Vikter believed you did."

Again, it was a shock to hear Vikter's name and to be given proof again that Tawny had spoken to him or someone who knew a whole hell of a lot. "What were you told?"

"I remember it completely. How, when I normally can't remember what I had for supper a few hours after I eat it, I have no idea," she said, and her memory was notoriously subjective. "'*From the…from the desperation of golden crowns and born of mortal flesh, a great primal power rises as the heir to the lands and seas, to the skies and all the realms. A shadow in the ember, a light in the flame, to become a fire in the flesh. When the stars fall from the night, the great mountains crumble into the seas, and old bones raise their swords beside the gods, the false one will be stripped from glory until two born of the same misdeeds, born of the same great and Primal power in the mortal realm.*'" She took a deep breath. "'*A first daughter, with blood full of fire, fated for the once-promised King. And the second daughter, with blood full of ash and ice, the other half of the future King. Together, they will remake the realms as they usher in the end. And so it will begin with the last Chosen blood spilled, the great conspirator birthed from the flesh and fire of the Primals will awaken as the Harbinger and the Bringer of Death and Destruction to the lands gifted by the gods. Beware, for the end will come from the west to destroy the east and lay waste to all which lies between,*'" Tawny finished and twisted a pure white curl. "That's it."

"Yeah," Kieran murmured, clearing his throat. He looked to me. "That is much longer."

It was. "A first and second daughter? I've been called the second daughter, but who is the first? And in what context?"

"I don't know. I'm sorry." Tawny's brows pinched. "He couldn't tell me what it meant, only that you needed to hear it. He said that you would figure it out."

A choked laugh left me. "He's giving me way too much credit, because I…" I trailed off, my thoughts centering on one part of what she'd said. "Wait. The once-promised King?"

Kieran drew back. "Malik?"

"When you were in Carsodonia, did you ever see Malik?" I asked.

Tawny shook her head. "No. I don't know a Malik."

"It has to be him if the second daughter part is about me," I said. "Casteel is the King."

Kieran nodded. "Yeah, but what is this blood full of ash and ice?"

I thought of the coldness in my chest, mingling with the eather. "I don't know what that means or how I will remake the realms and usher in the end, alone or with anyone. I'm not going to usher in anything."

"I don't know either," Tawny said. "Or who the false one is."

Something occurred to me, and I stiffened. "You said that *viktors* will even guard those who are destined to do something—"

"I know what you're about to say," Kieran cut in, and I knew he thought of what I'd asked him the night before. "You're not destined to do anything terrible."

"He's right," Tawny said quickly. "I didn't get the impression from Vikter that he believed you were destined to do anything evil."

I nodded, feeling Kieran's stare. I cleared my throat. "And that was all he said?"

"No. There was one more thing, but he told me it was only for you to hear and no one else." She glanced at Kieran and then Delano. "I'm sorry."

A muscle ticked along Kieran's jaw. "I don't like this." He quickly glanced at Tawny. "No offense."

She lifted a shoulder. "I wouldn't like it either. I'm way too nosy."

A wan grin tugged at my lips. "I need to hear what this is. Vikter wouldn't have told her anything that would hurt me."

"And if he had—which he didn't—I wouldn't repeat it," she added and then pursed her lips. "Unless it was something she needed to hear. Like when she was about to make a bad life choice by not going back to the Red Pearl to find Hawke—er, Casteel. Whoever. Anyway, I did tell her to do that."

"Oh, my gods, Tawny." My head snapped toward her.

Kieran's head cocked. "You weren't actually going back to—?"

"Nope." I gave him a small shove. Gianna grinned as she rose, along with Delano. "We're not getting into any of that now. Sorry. Everyone out."

Kieran arched a brow. "Is that an order?"

"Yes," I said. "And you know it was."

"Whatever," he muttered as he rose. "I'll be waiting outside."

"Okay."

"So," Tawny drew out the word. "Why is it that he behaves as I would expect from your husband?"

Heat crept into my cheeks. "He's the Advisor to the Crown."

Tawny stared at me.

"And a friend. A close friend—but not like that," I quickly added as interest sparked along Tawny's features. "Honestly, I don't know what it's like. It's complicated."

"I would say," she murmured. "And I cannot wait to hear all about this complication in excruciatingly painful detail."

I laughed and realized I was close to crying because this was Tawny. My Tawny. "I'll tell you everything."

She nodded. "But later?"

"Later. I have to leave tomorrow," I told her, hating that I would, and we'd have little time together. It didn't seem fair, but I was grateful that she was here now. "I need to free Casteel."

"I understand." Her eyes searched mine. "I'm just glad we reached you when we did."

"Me, too." I started to speak, then stopped and tried again. "Did you learn about the Ascension? What really happened to the third-borns?"

"I did," she whispered. "Ian told me after I arrived in Wayfair. You know, I didn't want to believe him. I didn't want to admit that I bought into this horrific lie—that I was a part of it."

"But you didn't know. None of us did."

"Doesn't seem to make it better, though, does it?"

Meeting her gaze, I shook my head. "No, it doesn't."

Tawny scooted forward until her knees pressed into the coffee table. "I think I know why you can't sense anything from me. I think it's because I was dying, Poppy. Whatever the Arae or Vikter did could only stop the process. But look at me. My hair. My eyes. My skin is so cold. I think I'm dead but...not."

My heart stuttered. "You're not dead, Tawny. You breathe, right? Eat? Think? Feel?" When she nodded, I took a deep breath. "Then you're alive in all the ways that matter."

"True," she murmured. "But the Ascended can do all of those things."

"You're not an Ascended." My gaze searched the beautiful, fine lines of her features. "We'll figure out what happened to you. Someone has to know."

"We will." She inhaled sharply, meeting my gaze. "Vikter told me why no one was allowed to know the Consort's name, and why those who did were not allowed to repeat it in the mortal realm."

My lips parted. "Okay, I was not expecting that."

Tawny laughed. "Yeah, me neither, but Vikter said that her name is power, and that to speak it is to bring the stars from the skies and topple the mountains into the sea."

I stilled as she basically repeated what Reaver had said.

"But only when spoken by the one born as she and of a great primal power."

"I'm...I'm not a Primal," I said, still not understanding why or how the Consort could be so powerful that no one dared to utter her name in the mortal realm.

"I don't know. I wish Vikter could've told me more, but he told me this." Tawny leaned in even closer then, over the table. "He told me you already knew her name."

The sky was overcast when I walked out of Castle Redrock the following morning, the toy horse secured in its pouch, a piece of parchment and pencil tucked within a satchel, and the words Sven had said I would need to speak to cast the Primal spell committed to memory. My hair was braided and pinned beneath a wide-brimmed cap. We were all dressed in the brown usually worn by the Huntsmen of Solis, our cloaks that bore the crimson crest of the Blood Crown—a circle with an arrow piercing the center—taken from the Rise Guards. The crest was supposed to represent infinity and power, but it was more a symbol of fear and oppression.

I hated wearing it as much as I did the white of the Maiden, but the Huntsmen were one of the only groups who were seen moving freely through Solis, ferrying messages from city to city or transporting goods.

The wolven paced restlessly, their agitation at not accompanying us tart and lemony. I hated that our plans left them uneasy, but even if they were all in their mortal forms, it would be too noticeable and too risky.

Isbeth would have them slaughtered.

I turned to where Tawny stood beside me. We'd spent the remainder of yesterday together as I caught her up on everything she hadn't already been told, and she'd talked to me about what it had been like when she saw Vikter. It reminded me a lot of how it had been when I too had been at the Vale's door and had dreamed of the Consort. I still had no idea why Vikter would think I knew the Consort's name.

Tawny smiled at me. "You're going to be careful."

"Of course."

She took my hands in hers. The coldness of her skin seeped

through my gloves. "As careful as you were when we snuck out of Castle Teerman and would go swimming as naked as the day we were born?"

"Even *more* careful than that." I grinned. "And you? I want you to stay close to Vonetta and Gianna."

She glanced to where Vonetta waited. "I'll probably get on her nerves."

"No, you won't." I squeezed her hands. "Vonetta is very nice. You'll love her."

Tawny stepped in, lowering her voice. "Have you gotten used to them? And I don't mean that in a bad way. I've seen Gianna shift about a dozen times now, and other than a whole lot of nakedness, I can't wrap my head around how all of that works."

I laughed. "You saw Vikter—who died in front of us—and you can't wrap your head around a wolven?"

She pinned me with a knowing look.

"Okay, no, I'm still sometimes caught off guard by it. But wait until you see a draken do it."

Tawny's eyes widened. "I can't wait."

She'd yet to see any of the draken, as they remained out of sight, and Reaver was in his mortal form. That would change soon.

"You should be going," she said, her lower lip trembling.

"Yeah," I whispered, pulling her in for an embrace. "This won't be like before."

"Promise?"

"Yes." I started to pull back and then stopped, holding her tighter. "You've always been a great friend to me, Tawny. I hope you know that. I hope you know how much I love you."

"I know," Tawny whispered. "I've always known."

Parting ways with Tawny was hard, but I had to. Kissing her cool cheek, I promised to see her in Three Rivers and then walked to where Vonetta waited with Emil. I caught sight of Reaver, wearing black breeches and a simple tunic sweater he'd apparently borrowed from Kieran, securing an additional horse to the wagon, where several crates of whiskey had been placed in the back under a cover that also hid a small arsenal of weapons. The liquor had been Emil's idea. The whiskey could be used as a distraction for those who pried too closely or asked too many questions.

"I hate that I'm not going with you." Vonetta clasped my arms. "You know that, right?"

"I hate it, too, but I trust you to lead in my absence."

"Hey," Emil cried, pressing his hand to his chest. "I'm standing right here."

"As I said, I trust you to lead in my place," I repeated to Vonetta with a small grin.

Emil sighed. "Rude."

Vonetta rolled her eyes. "He's a mess."

"You like my kind of mess," the Atlantian said.

"I wouldn't let Kieran hear that," I teased, wanting to hug her. And since I wanted that, I did it instead of thinking about how much I wanted to. "Take care of Tawny, please?"

"Of course." Vonetta returned the embrace without hesitation. I closed my eyes, soaking in the feel as I did with Tawny. "I will see you in Three Rivers."

"You will."

Pulling back and wondering why I suddenly wanted to cry, I turned to Emil, and he gave me an elaborate bow. "Really?"

"Really." Upon rising, he took my hand in his and stepped into me. He dipped his head, pressing his lips to my forehead. "Go get our King, my Queen," he whispered.

My breath snagged then. I nodded, stepping back when he let go. Turning away as Kieran spoke to his sister was hard, as was stopping to say goodbye to Delano, Naill, and Perry. Delano gave the best hugs. Anything could happen between now and when I saw them in Three Rivers. *Anything.*

I went to my horse, picking up the reins. His name was Winter. The steed was large and white, beautiful, but he wasn't Setti. I didn't think it was wise to bring him to Carsodonia. I glanced at the entrance to Redrock, relieved to see Vonetta speaking with Tawny and Gianna. Tawny would be okay. They would all be okay.

Kieran came up behind me, touching my arm. "You ready?"

"I am," I answered, lifting myself onto the saddle. My gaze swept past the group—past my friends—and made its way to the valley below, where the stately manors sat. As we rode out of Oak Ambler and beyond the Rise now draped with Atlantian banners, a part of me hoped I never returned. That might make me a coward, but I never wanted to step foot in the city again, even though I knew I would never really leave.

A part of me would remain in the still-smoking ash of the Temple of Theon. Charred and ruined.

Casteel

I opened my eyes at the sound of fizzing water and the heavy, sweet scent of lilacs. Thick, purple blossoms climbed up the walls and stretched across the ceiling. Steam rose in the pinpoints of sunlight. Water churned restlessly among the boulders.

I hadn't remembered falling asleep. I'd been sharpening the bone until I grew tired. Either way, I wasn't there now. At least, not mentally. I was in the cavern. What Poppy called my cavern. But it was *ours* now. A paradise.

My heart started pounding fast, shocking the hell out of me. It hadn't beat like this in days. Should be concerned about that. It was a warning I needed to heed, but I couldn't. Not now.

Twisting at the waist, I scanned the swirling surface of the water and the wispy steam. "Poppy?" I rasped, forcing a dry swallow.

Nothing.

My damn stomach started thumping in tandem with my heart. Where was she? I turned again, swaying in the warm water and the humid air. Why was I here without her? It was almost too cruel to wake and find myself here alone. Was this some new form of punishment?

Punishment for the sins I'd committed. The lies I'd spun. The lives I'd forfeited. The lives I'd *taken* with my own hands. I'd always known those deeds would come back to reap what I'd sown, no matter my intentions. No matter how much I wanted to be *better*.

To deserve someone like Poppy—someone so incredibly strong, so curious and intelligent and unbelievably *kind*. Someone who deserved another as equally good as her. That wasn't me. My eyes closed as my chest clenched. That would never be me. I knew that. Had always known that. From the moment I realized who I had under me at the Red Pearl.

I knew I was where I had no right to be.

Someone like me—someone capable of killing the woman who loved me—wasn't worthy of a *goddess*. It didn't matter that Shea had betrayed me or her kingdom. Decades later, and no matter the reasons, that shit and all the what-ifs still ate at me. My chin dropped, and my eyes opened, my gaze falling to my hands—hands whole in this piece of paradise but still nicked and scarred. Two hands that had taken Shea's life and so many others, it was a wonder they weren't forever stained by blood.

But I was forever Poppy's.

I'd been coming for her, but she'd found *me* at the Red Pearl. I'd been planning on taking her, but she'd captured me on the Rise surrounding Masadonia. I'd been ready to use her, but under the willow, she had wrapped me around every single one of her fingers without even trying. I'd been prepared to do anything, but she'd become everything to me when she asked me to stay the night while in New Haven.

She'd claimed me.

And she'd kept me, even after knowing what I was, who I was, and what I'd done. She *loved* me.

A better man, one not steeped in the kind of blood I was, would've walked away. Would've left her to find someone *good*. Deserving.

But I wasn't that kind of man.

"Cas?"

Good gods, my entire body jerked at the sound of her voice. My damn breath actually seized in my lungs. I couldn't even move at first. I was so locked up. Just her voice did that. *Her voice.*

Control rushed back into my body, and I spun in the bubbling water. I saw her then, and the sight of her...

She stood there, the water frothing around rounded hips and teasing the soft dips and rises of her belly. My lips tingled with the memory of tracing those faded claw marks above her navel, and the need to drop to my knees and pay homage to them almost drove me underwater.

I took in the faint pink marks streaking across her left temple and cutting through the arched brow—healed wounds that were as beautiful as the freckles dancing across the bridge of her nose. Scars that only spoke to the strength of the delicate sweep of her cheekbones and her proud brow. And those eyes…

They were wideset and large, heavily lashed, and they had been stunning before, reminding me of glistening spring grass. Now, the silvery glow behind the pupils and the thin wisps streaking through the green were striking. Her eyes… Hell, they were a window to my soul.

I drank her in, my lips parting on a breath that never left me. All that beautiful red-wine hair cascaded over her shoulders and skimmed the water. The heavy swell of her breasts parted the tangled mass of curls and waves, offering a tantalizing glimpse of rosy-pink skin. My heart stuttered—actually skipped a godsdamn beat as I continued soaking in the sight of that stubborn, slightly pointed chin and those fucking mind-blowing lips that were dewy and ripe like sweet berries. My cock hardened so quickly it finally kicked the air out of my lungs. Those lips…

They were a torment in the best possible way.

Never in my life had it taken me so long to find my voice. "I've been waiting for you."

That mouth…the corners tipped up, and the smile that raced across her face owned me.

Always.

And forever.

Poppy lurched forward, and I pushed through the water. It swirled in a frenzy as we cut through it, reaching each other at the same moment.

I took her in my arms, and the contact of her warm, soft flesh against mine nearly stopped my heart. It might've. I didn't know.

Fisting a hand in her silken hair, I dropped my head to hers and held her. Held her tightly as she wrapped her arms around my waist. "My Queen," I whispered as the crown of her head brushed my lips. I inhaled deeply, finding a hint of jasmine, the scent of her, underneath the lilac.

"My King." Poppy shuddered, and I managed to find a way to press her even closer to me.

I closed my eyes. "You shouldn't call me that." I kissed her head again. "I'll get an overinflated sense of self-importance."

She *laughed*. Gods, her laugh did just as I'd warned. It made me feel important. Powerful. Because I could make her laugh when the sound had been so rare.

"Then you shouldn't call me your Queen," she said.

"But you are important." I forced my grip on her hair to loosen. I ran my fingers through the strands, marveling at the feel. The realness. "A goddess. Which, by the way, just want to point out...I knew it. Maybe I should call you—"

She jerked back, her eyes going wide as she tilted her head back and looked up at me. "You...you know?"

Gods, those eyes... The green with the wispy tendrils of silver was enthralling.

"Casteel?" She pressed a hand—a warm palm a little callused from handling a sword and dagger—against my chest.

"Your eyes..." I slipped my hand to her cheek. "They're mesmerizing," I told her. "Almost as much as those plump little—"

"*Casteel.*" Her cheeks blushed a pretty shade of pink.

I chuckled, and I wanted to do it again when I saw how her lips parted at the sound. "Yeah, I know you're a goddess."

"How?" The softness vanished from her features instantaneously. Her jaw hardened under my palm. So did her eyes. They became fractured emerald jewels. The transformation was shocking...and really *hot*. "The Blood Queen."

"I knew the moment she said Malec was a god. That would mean you're one, too."

"Malec's not my father. It's Ires," she said. "Malec's twin. He's the cave cat—the one we saw in the cage."

Surprise blasted through me, but it made sense. Isbeth had no idea where Malec was. She hadn't even realized that he was still alive—at least technically. I should've caught onto that when Isbeth asked about where Malec was.

"She's taken my father and you," Poppy said, her throat working on a swallow. "She's taken—"

"She is nothing to us," I said, hating the pain building in her eyes. "*Nothing.*"

She searched my face closely as her fingers curled against my chest. "This is real," she whispered.

I nodded, dragging my thumb over the jagged mark on her cheek. "Heartmates."

Her lips trembled. "I have so many things I want to say. So much I want to ask you. I don't know where to start." Her eyes briefly closed. "No. I do. Are you okay?"

"Yes."

"Don't lie to me."

"I'm not." I totally was.

She reached for my wrist, and I knew why. I knew what she wanted to see, and what she would see wasn't real. "Don't," I told her as she froze, her eyes dampening. "Are you okay?"

"Are you seriously asking me that?" Disbelief filled her voice. "I'm not the one being held captive."

"No, you're just the one at war."

"Not the same thing."

"We'll have to agree to disagree on that."

Her eyes narrowed. "I'm okay, Casteel, but I got what she sent—"

Fury entrenched itself deep within me at the thought of what she must have felt. "I'm here. You're here. I'm okay, Poppy."

I could see it—the struggle. The battle that she won because, of course, she would. She was that damn strong.

Her chin lifted. "I'm coming for you."

Those four words set off a conflicted flurry of emotions. Anticipation. Dread. The need to really have her in my arms and hear her voice outside of this dream. To see her smile and listen to her questions, her beliefs, her *everything*. It battled with a great sense of alarm—that we didn't know exactly what the Blood Queen planned. What it really had to do with Poppy.

"We're close to Three Rivers," she told me.

Holy shit, she *was* close.

"Kieran is with me," she said, and my heart—fuck, it was beating fast again. "And I have the draken." Her face tensed, paling. "Actually, only Reaver is with me. But I also have this Primal spell—"

"Wait. What?" I stared down at her, my thumb stilling just below her lip. "The draken? You have them now?"

"Yes. I was able to summon them."

"Holy shit," I whispered.

"Yeah." She drew out the word. "I think you'll like Reaver." Her nose scrunched in that adorable way of hers. "Or maybe not. He tried to bite Kieran."

My brows lifted. "A draken tried to bite Kieran?"

She nodded.

"My Kieran?"

"Yes, but at this point, if Reaver tries to bite him again, Kieran has it coming. All of it is a long story," she quickly added. "We've...we've lost so many—" Her breath caught, and my chest ached at the sight of the pain in her eyes. "Draken. Wolven. Soldiers. We lost Arden."

Damn it.

I pressed my lips to her forehead. Arden was a good man. Damn it. And to hear that draken had already fallen? Gods.

She took another breath and then pulled back. "Can you tell me anything about where you're being held? Anything?"

"I..."

"What?" She bit down on her lower lip, drawing my attention. "Are you about to leave me again?"

"I never left you," I said at once.

Her stare softened as she leaned in to me. My arm tightened around her lower back. "Can you tell me anything? Even the smallest detail, Casteel."

Uncertainty built. "I don't want..."

"What?"

"I don't want you anywhere near Carsodonia," I admitted. "I don't want you anywhere near—"

"I'm not afraid of her," Poppy cut me off.

"I know." I slid my thumb over her brow. "You're not afraid of anyone or anything."

"That's not true. Snakes scare me."

My lips twitched. "And barrats."

"Those, too. But her? Absolutely, not. I'm coming for you, and don't you dare hide information from me out of some chauvinistic need to protect me."

"Chauvinistic?" I grinned. "I was thinking it was love that fueled my need to protect you."

"Casteel," she warned.

"I think you want to stab me."

"I would, but since you like it when I do, it doesn't have the desired effect I'm going for."

I laughed, and then my damn breath caught as she did it again. She softened at the sound. She *yearned* at the sound. I saw it in the set of her mouth and in her eyes.

Damn it.

"I'm underground. I don't know where exactly, but I think—" I thought of the Handmaiden. "I think it's part of a tunnel system."

Her nose scrunched. "Remember the underground paths that led to Redrock from the bluffs? There were tunnels under the Temple of Theon in Oak Ambler, too. A pretty large network that connected to Castle Redrock and some of the estates," she told me and then quickly shared how she'd discovered it. "Could they be like that?"

"Could be." My jaw tightened at the feel of icy fingers brushing the nape of my neck. A bolt of panic cut through me. I dipped my head, kissing her. The touch of her lips. The taste. She was a drug.

"*Cas*," she murmured against my mouth, and everything in me tightened. "We should be talking."

"I know. I know." There were things to be discussed. Important things. I wanted to know what her days and nights had been like. How Kieran was. I wanted to know more about her siege of Oak Ambler. Who she'd stabbed—because, surely, she *had* stabbed someone. Lots of someones. I wanted to know that she was okay. That she wasn't afraid. That she wasn't punishing herself. But she was here, in front of me, and I could feel it, the coldness sinking into my skin. It was just a chill, but one of us was waking, and I knew how fast it could happen.

I kissed her again.

There was nothing soft about it. I kissed to feel her. To show her how much she'd claimed me. And when I prodded at the seam of her mouth with the tip of my tongue, she opened for me. She let me in like always, and it was almost as good as the real thing. *Almost*. I kissed until I felt the cold kiss at the nape of my neck, and then I lifted my head.

The daze slowly cleared from her eyes as she looked up at me, and I saw the moment she knew. She realized that this was coming to an end.

"No," she whispered.

My heart cracked as I dropped my forehead to hers. "I'm sorry."

"It's not your fault."

I shuddered, knowing we didn't have much time left and that there was something I needed to tell her. "I know what Isbeth is. A demis."

"A what?"

"A false god. Ask Kieran. Or Reaver. The draken must be old. He may know what her weakness is. A demis is like a god…but not."

"Okay." She nodded. "She's also learned how to harness Primal energy—I don't know now if it's because of what she is or something Malec told her. But be careful. That magic is what killed the draken."

"I'm always careful." I pressed my lips to the tip of her nose as the chill spread down my spine, and a pang of hunger ripped through me. "Two hearts. We're two hearts." I brushed my lips over her brow, closing my eyes. "One soul. We'll find each other again. We always will—"

The dream fragmented, shattering no matter how hard I tried to keep it together—to keep Poppy in my arms. I awoke shivering in the cold cell, alone and *starving*.

Poppy

"Demis," I announced. A faint, misty cloud followed my words. The air wasn't as chilled as it had been along the coast. Soon, when we crossed between Whitebridge and Three Rivers, it would be warmer, but we couldn't risk a fire.

We were too close to the Blood Forest.

This was our second night camping near the cursed lands. So far, there'd been no sign of the mist or the Craven, but our luck could change at any second. Because of that, we rested in shifts, and very few of us slept deeply.

But, somehow, I'd managed to sleep after being on the road for six days. After not reaching Casteel for nine nights, I'd finally drifted off. But I'd been tired. *Really* tired. In a way I thought had nothing to do with our hard pace. Something that concerned me greatly and also made me think about how hungry I'd been over the last day or so. How dry my throat had felt no matter how much I drank. I didn't want to think about any of those things right now while speaking to the side of a wagon.

There was no answer.

Biting back frustration, I rapped my knuckles off the side.

"*What?*" came the gravelly reply.

"I just woke up," I said, plopping down on the ground outside of the wagon.

"Okay." The tarp muffled Reaver's voice. "What am I supposed to do with that?"

"She had a dream," Kieran explained, having followed me. He lowered himself far more gracefully onto the cold, packed ground beside me. "About Cas."

"And?"

Kieran shot me a look that warned he was a second away from toppling the wagon. Which would be funny but not worth the ensuing drama.

"He was able to tell me a little bit about where he's being kept," I told Reaver. "He's underground and thinks it's some sort of tunnel system—possibly something like what was in Oak Ambler. And he told me what Isbeth is. A demis. A false god. He told me to ask Kieran, but all he could remember was some sort of old wives' tale."

There was a gap of silence, and I was half afraid that Reaver had gone back to sleep. "And what is this tale?"

"Do I really need to repeat it?" Kieran asked. "To a *wagon*? And why are you even sleeping in there anyway? You have a tent you could have set up."

"I find tents to be…suffocating."

"But you don't feel as if sleeping under a tarp is suffocating?"

"No."

Okay. That didn't make any sense but was beside the point. *"Kieran."*

He sighed. "Whatever. There was this old story my mother used to tell Vonetta and me about a girl who had fallen in love with another who was already mated. She believed that she was far more worthy, and so she prayed every day. Eventually, a god who claimed to be Aios came and promised to grant her what she desired, so long as she gave up something in return—the firstborn of the family. Her eldest brother. So, she had to kill him or something. And she did. But, of course, it wasn't Aios. It was a demis who had tricked her into killing her sibling."

"Even after hearing that for the second time, it still makes little sense," I said. "Like, I get the message. You can't make someone love you, right? Not even a god could or should do that. But why would a demis do that? Why make the woman kill her brother?"

"I guess because the demis can?" Kieran said with a shrug. "No idea. All of that was never really explained, and again, I didn't think any of it was rooted in truth."

I reached for the ring, finding the chain beneath the collar of my coat. "This fable could really use some fleshing out."

"Well, I'm sure the writer of such a story cares about your opinion," a rough voice intruded from the recesses of the wagon. "Actually, no, they probably don't. The demis are real but very rare," Reaver said. "So rare that I've never seen one."

"But what are they exactly?" I asked.

"A god who was made and not born. A mortal Ascended by a god but not a third-born and considered Chosen. The few who existed were considered false gods," he explained.

Kieran sent me a quick glance. "Do you know of their weaknesses?"

"As I said, I never knew any. The act of Ascending a mortal not Chosen was forbidden, and few dared to break that law." There was another pause. "Most didn't survive the Ascension, but those who did, for all intents and purposes, were gods. I assume their weaknesses would be the same as any god's."

"Meaning they could only be killed by another god or a Primal or by shadowstone through the head or heart." I sat back. "That's good news."

"It is." Kieran's gaze met mine. "We now know how to kill Isbeth."

It was good news, but if Isbeth was basically a god, she had far more years of experience when it came to using the eather—and, well, everything else.

"Great. Now you two can go chat elsewhere, and I can go back to sleep," Reaver said.

Kieran's eyes narrowed. "Why don't you find someplace else to sleep?"

"Why don't you go fu—?"

"All right," I cut in as Kieran emitted a low growl. A dull ache had started in my forehead. There'd been headaches on and off for the last couple of days, but I wasn't sure if this one was due to speaking with Reaver or something else. "That's all I needed to know."

"Thank the gods." Reaver's hands suddenly appeared above the wagon. He shook them as if he were in joyous prayer.

I took a deep breath, rising. Kieran followed as we made our way across the short distance to the tent we'd shared. I thought everything over. Knowing that Casteel believed he was being kept under Carsodonia and not in the mines or some other place was information we hadn't had before. As was the knowledge that Isbeth was a demis—

a false god that could be killed like any other god.

I stopped before reaching the tent. Kieran had been on watch duty, but I knew I wouldn't be going back to sleep. I turned to him. "I can take over from here."

He nodded absently, his gaze fixed on the star-strewn sky. "How was he?" he asked, having not gotten a chance to ask that before. "How did Casteel look?"

"He looked good. Perfect," I whispered, chest squeezing. I hadn't seen those new cuts on his skin like I had the first time. In this dream, he didn't appear thinner. There was no scruff on his cheeks. He looked exactly as I remembered when I last saw him in person, thirty-nine days ago. But I knew it was a façade. That part hadn't been real at all, and I wasn't sure if he'd been able to present himself differently this time because he was aware that we were soul walking. "He told me he was okay," I said.

Kieran smiled, but I didn't taste relief from him. Because he knew, just like I did, that Casteel couldn't be okay.

I touched the ring, closing my eyes.

"Hell," Kieran muttered. "Look."

Opening my eyes, I followed his gaze to the empty land between the Blood Forest and us, where thick trails of mist gathered and swirled across the ground.

"Craven." Our luck had changed. I reached for my dagger.

"For fuck's sake," Reaver shouted, tossing the tarp aside as he rose...completely naked. He jumped from the wagon, landing in a crouch. "I got this."

"What does he think he's going to do buck-ass na—?" Kieran bit off as sparks of light erupted all over Reaver, and he shifted into his draken form. "Well, okay, he's going to do *that*."

A shrill wail of a Craven pierced the silence, and then a funnel of silvery-white fire lit up the night, cutting through the darkness and the gathering Craven.

Casteel

Icy water splashed over my head, sending a painful shockwave through me as I jackknifed off my side. Eyes flying open, I dragged in air, even as my lungs locked from the cold drenching my skin.

"He's awake now," came the dry voice.

"Took long enough," a softer, throatier voice replied. I tensed, recognizing *that* voice. The annoyance.

The Blood Queen.

Feeling the sharpened bone behind my back, I blinked away the cascading water and waited...and waited for my vision to make sense of the shapes in front of me. To pull them into focus.

Callum knelt beside me, a bucket by his knee. His features were still blurry, but I could see the disgust in the curl of his lip. "He's not looking too well, Your Majesty."

My attention shifted to who waited behind him. The Blood Queen stood tall and straight, the thin material of her midnight gown clinging to her narrow hips. I had to blink again because I was almost positive upon first glance that she wore no top. I was wrong. Sort of. The bodice of the gown was cleaved in two, the thicker panels of material held together by sheer lace only covering the fullest parts of her breasts. Disgust filled my gut.

"He stinks," Isbeth replied.

"Fuck off," I muttered, righting myself enough and slipping my right hand to my hip, close to the bone.

"I would love to do just that." Her head tilted, and the hair piled on top glinted a deep auburn in the firelight. Almost like Poppy's. *Almost.* "However, it's become highly apparent that you've refused to bathe or eat."

Eat? When had food been brought in? I saw a plate then, several feet from me. There was a hunk of cheese and some stale bread on it. I had no idea when that had arrived.

From the cloud of my thoughts, what Poppy had told me in the dream broke free. I loosened my jaw, wincing. The son of a bitch ached. My whole face did. Teeth. Fangs. They throbbed as my gaze focused on the Queen. My time with Poppy in the cavern was the only time the need had vanished—the only time I felt like myself.

"I've been thinking," I said, latching onto a moment of clarity. "About what I saw in Oak Ambler."

Isbeth raised a brow.

I forced a painful, dry swallow. "A large gray cat kept in a cage."

Her nostrils flared on a sharp inhale, and she took a step forward. "When did you see that?"

"Oh, you know,"—I leaned forward slightly—"when I was touring Castle Redrock."

"And was anyone else sightseeing with you?"

"Maybe." I watched her. "Why the fuck do you have a cat caged? Is that one of your...*pets*?"

Her blood-red lips twisted into a thin smile. "Not my favorite. That would be you."

"Honored," I growled, and the smile deepened. "The cat didn't look like he was doing too well."

"The cat is fine."

The edges of my fingers brushed the bone. "But it must be old. If it's the same one Poppy spoke of—the one she saw as a child."

Isbeth went completely still.

"She once told me she saw it under Wayfair Castle."

"Penellaphe was a curious child."

"You still have it?"

Her stare fixed on me. "He's right where he was when Penellaphe saw him all those years ago," she said, and it took everything in me not to smile at the savage rush of satisfaction I felt. "But he may be hungry. Perhaps I will feed him the next finger I take."

"Why don't you come take it now? Not your golden boy."

Callum frowned. "I am not a *boy*."

"Or one of your Handmaidens," I continued, holding her stare. "Or are you too afraid? Too weak?"

Isbeth tipped her head back, laughing. "Afraid? Of you? The only thing about you that frightens me is your stench."

"So you say," I murmured. "But I know the truth. Everyone here does. Your courage comes from keeping those stronger than you in chains."

Her laughter ceased. "You think you're stronger than me?"

"Fuck, yeah." I smiled then, closing my hand around the bone. "I am, after all, my mother's son."

Isbeth stared down at me and then shot forward, just like I knew she would because some things never changed. Her fragile ego was one of them.

I wrenched the bone out from behind my back, thrusting it up as her hand closed around my throat, just above the shadowstone band.

Isbeth's eyes went wide as her entire body jerked.

"That's for Poppy's brother," I bit out.

Slowly, Isbeth lowered her chin and looked down to where the bone protruded from the center of her chest. Missed her godsdamn heart by an inch, if that.

Her gaze lifted to mine, the glow in her dark eyes bright. "Ouch," she hissed, shoving me back. Hard.

My head cracked off the wall, the pain exploding behind my eyes in a hundred starbursts. Sliding sideways, I caught myself before I toppled over.

"That was really unnecessary." Isbeth's chest rose as she reached down, gripping the bone. The Handmaidens had moved in, but she stopped them. Only Callum remained where he knelt, his eyes fixed with captive interest. "All it served to do is anger me."

"And ruin your gown," I added. The pain in my head intensified the hunger—the need to feed and heal whatever recent damage had been inflicted.

Her lips pulled back, revealing blood-coated teeth. "That, too." She pulled the bone free, tossing it aside. "Contrary to what you may think, I don't want to kill you, even though it would make me feel very, very happy to do so at the moment. I need you alive."

She continued speaking, but I only caught parts of it. Her heartbeat had sped up. The scent of her blood was strong. I even heard the golden Rev's heart. I felt the steady thump of the Handmaidens', who stood quietly behind her.

"He needs blood," Callum stated.

Thump. Thump. Thump.

"He needs an attitude adjustment," she retorted.

Thump. Whoosh. Thump. Whoosh.

"Can't argue with that. But look at his eyes. They're nearly black." Callum started to rise. "If he doesn't get some blood in him soon, he will—"

"Rip your fucking throat out?" I finished for him. "And shove your entrails down the gaping hole?"

Callum's lips pursed as he eyed me. "That painted a lovely picture. Thank you."

"Fuck you," I growled.

"Well, we know what your favorite word is today." Isbeth sighed, wiping at the blood that ran down the center of her stomach. "I don't know why you're being so difficult. I've given you food, clean water, a"—she glanced at where a downed Craven lay—"somewhat safe shelter. All I've taken from you is a finger. And yet, you stab me."

The absolute *fuckery* of her statement cleared a little of the haze of impending bloodlust.

"Meanwhile, my daughter has taken my port city from me," she continued, and my entire body tightened. "Ah, I see that has your attention. Yes. Penellaphe seized Oak Ambler, and I have a feeling I'm now a few Ascended short of what I was before."

I felt my lips start to curve upward.

"Smile all you want." Isbeth bent at the waist, her heavily lined eyes shrewd. "Do I look remotely bothered by the news?"

It took a moment to focus. No, she did not.

"Oak Ambler would always fall," she said, her voice dropping to a whisper that I barely heard over her heart. "It had to."

A low rumbling sound filled the cell, and she straightened suddenly, her crimson lips thinning. My lips had peeled back, and that sound…it was me.

"Oh, for godssake." Isbeth snapped her fingers, motioning one of the Handmaidens forward. Something was in her hand. A chalice. "Hold him."

Callum moved fast, but I saw him. I lurched to the side and to my feet, throwing out my elbow and making contact with the Rev's chin, startling the bitch. The golden boy grunted as he stumbled back. There was no time to relish either of those things. I launched myself at her. The chain tightened around my throat, jerking my body back. I shot forward again, past the point of caring how tight the band around my throat clamped down. Past the ability to register the pain from the shackles digging into my ankles. I pulled hard against the chains, stretching out—

An arm clamped around my chest, hauling me back. "That hurt," Callum muttered as he slammed his booted foot into my calf. The move, one I *should've* known was coming, took my damn leg out from underneath me.

I went down, my knees cracking off the stone floor as one of the Handmaidens gripped the chains securing my arms and twisted. She forced my arms to cross over my chest, pinning them there as fingers dug into my jaw, yanking my head back.

"Get this over with," Isbeth ordered.

Another Handmaiden briefly appeared in my line of sight as I bucked against the Rev's hold, my feet slipping over the floor as I threw my head back. The hiss of pain brought a wild, choked laugh to my lips as Callum's head snapped back. I pushed my weight into him, slamming him into the wall as I dragged the Handmaiden holding the chains forward.

"Gods," Callum groaned, shifting his hold from behind me. "He's still strong."

"Of course, he is," Isbeth commented. "He's of the Elemental bloodline. They are always strong. Fighters. No other bloodline would've been brave—nor idiotic—enough to stab me. Even when they're mere hours from becoming nothing more than a blood-starved animal. And I bet he also has the blood of my daughter in him."

And then everything was a blur of black and pain and something earthy and *charred*. Of fingers digging into my jaw and forcing my mouth open. Someone shoved a chalice in my face, under my nose, and a brief, iron-rich scent hit me before landing on my tongue, filling my mouth, and pouring down my throat.

I choked, gagging on the warm thickness, even as every cell in my body opened up, becoming raw and screaming in need.

"I must confess something, my dear son-in-law." Isbeth's voice was a lash of flames. "You know what I never wanted to be? A Primal. I never wanted *that* weakness."

She was closer. Probably close enough for me to get to her again, but the blood hit my gut, and my entire body spasmed.

"A god can be killed just like an Atlantian. Destroy the heart and the mind. But a Primal? You have to weaken them first. And do you know how you weaken a Primal? It's rather cruel. Love. Love can be weaponized, weakening a Primal and becoming the blade that ends their existence." A soft laugh echoed around me. Through me. "I wonder how much you even know about Primals. I must admit, I knew very little myself. If it weren't for my Malec, I never would've learned the truth. I never would've known that a Primal could be *born* to the mortal realm."

A Primal born to the mortal realm?

"When the gods you know now Ascended to rule over Iliseeum and the mortal realm, forcing most of the Primals into their glorious eternities, it created a ripple effect that caught the eyes and ears of the Fates. They made sure that a spark was left—a chance for rebirth of the greatest powers. An ember of Primal life that could only ignite in the female lineage of the Primal of Life."

My head jerked up, and I saw Isbeth in sudden, sharp clarity. What she was saying, *suggesting*... She hadn't given birth to a god. She'd birthed a—

Muscles tightened to painful rigidity as the blood then kissed my veins. It was like something on the verge of catching fire, but it lit up my senses, pulling me back inch by inch from the brink—

The chalice disappeared, and a ragged groan of pain punched out of me as my throat worked to swallow more, but there was nothing else. That was it.

But it wasn't enough.

It wasn't nearly enough.

Isbeth had drifted even closer, the feel of her stare like rusted nails against my flesh. "The color is already returning to his skin. This will do. For now."

I looked for her, only to realize my eyes had closed. Forcing them to open, I lifted them to her.

She smiled, and it was a tear to the chest because it was a small curve of the lips. An almost bashful, innocent smile, the same as I'd seen on Poppy.

The ache in my stomach exploded once again, more intense than before. What little blood trickled through my veins only took away the numbness. That was all. And it was no reprieve.

She knew that. She knew exactly what that small taste of blood would do.

My hand burned. My legs. The numerous cuts stung as if I'd been swarmed by hornets. And the hunger...it ramped up until it swelled.

I launched off the floor, pulling at the chains as the growl vibrating from my chest rumbled into a howl. I started to come apart at the seams, shattering into pieces that were no longer grounded in any sense of self.

Hunger.

That was all I was.

Hunger.

21

Poppy

Unable to sleep the following night, I sat on the boulder outside of the tent, feet dangling above the ground as I watched the limbs of the blood trees sway in the distance. Nightbirds called from the smattering of oak trees we'd hidden our little cluster of tents and wagon under. Just inside the tent, Kieran dozed in his mortal form. I had been relieved to see that when I looked in on him a little bit ago. He didn't need to lose sleep simply because my mind wouldn't shut down.

I was restless.

Hungry again.

And thirsty.

My gaze crept across the landscape. The Blood Forest was oddly beautiful, especially at dawn and dusk, when the skies gave way to paler shades of blues and pinks. It was vast. I didn't think many people realized just how large it was, encompassing the distance between Masadonia and the outskirts of Carsodonia. Basically, it was the length of the Niel Valley, and Malec was entombed somewhere in there.

Hopefully.

The forest was beginning to thin out, though. Through the trees, I caught tiny glimpses of the horizon. And beyond that, the capital.

Where Casteel waited.

Forty days had passed since I'd last seen him in person. Felt so much longer than that, each day a week. At least I should be grateful that my monthly menstruation had ended while in Oak Ambler and I wasn't dealing with that out here in the woods.

This would be our last night camping outside the Blood Forest. Tomorrow, we would reach the Western Pass. Then, we were roughly a two-day ride to where the Elysium Peaks began in the Willow Plains. According to Kieran, it would only take about a day—maybe two—to travel through the Peaks and reach the other portion of the mines that connected to the Rise. My heart lurched with a dart of anticipation.

But from here, if we kept traveling southwest, we'd reach the Niel Valley in a day and then the rise of Carsodonia in a day and a half. From here, we were no more than two days from being in the same city as Casteel. Not four.

We couldn't keep going straight, though. There would be no way to get past the gates. We had a better chance if we took the extra days.

Then, we would be in Carsodonia, and—

A sudden chill erupted along the nape of my neck, sending a rush of goosebumps across my skin. It wasn't just the cold air. More like the heavy press of *awareness*. The Primal essence throbbed in my chest.

I slid forward, lowering my feet to the ground. Scanning the Blood Forest for any hint of the mist, I reached for my wolven dagger and slid it free. I stepped forward, my footfalls silent as I searched and searched. There was no mist, no shrill shrieks of the Craven shattering the silence, but that feeling was still there, pressing down on the back of my neck.

Wait.

It was completely silent. The trees that had been swaying moments before had stilled. I looked up at the elms. No nightbirds sang. Everything was still. But that sensation, that heavy awareness, prevailed. A kiss of coldness brushed the nape of my neck. I reached behind me, folding my hand over my skin. It felt as if a hundred eyes were upon me.

Turning slowly, I scanned the thick shadows between the trees and beyond, still seeing nothing. Another shiver erupted over my flesh as I went to Winter's side where his head had risen from its droop. His ears were perked, nostrils flaring as if he, too, sensed something.

"It's okay, boy." I rubbed the side of his neck.

A breeze swept in, rattling the leaves above and taking with it that *oppressive* feeling of not only being watched but also not being *alone*. The same feeling I often felt in Massene and the Pinelands. The sensation lifted from my shoulders. The icy touch on my nape faded. A short, tentative trill echoed from a bird and, after a moment, was answered. Sound returned.

Life returned.

Uneasy, I moved closer to the tent, keeping my eyes on the reddish-black leaves of the blood trees. Minutes ticked by without more strange occurrences. If it hadn't been for the horse's reaction, I might have thought it was my imagination.

Not too long after, Reaver rose from his wagon to take over watch for the remainder of the night. I'd tried to tell him that he could sleep, but he simply pointed in the direction of my tent and then turned away.

I went but didn't enter. Instead of doing what I should be doing, which was sleeping, I started pacing again. My mind still wouldn't shut down, and I was really *hungry*.

And I knew what that meant.

I needed to feed.

Gods.

Closing my eyes, I tipped my head back. My body was telling me, even though I'd never experienced such hunger before. And I knew that if I waited, it would only worsen. I would weaken. And if I went past that? I remembered what that had done to Casteel. And while he hadn't fallen off that ledge, I would be of no help to anyone if I fell into any sort of bloodlust. I knew I couldn't delay this.

I groaned.

But I also felt about seven different kinds of awkward. Sure, Kieran had offered himself, and it wasn't because I felt that feeding from him would be wrong or uncomfortable. It was just that, well, the experiences I had with feeding—those that I actually remembered—involved…other things.

Things I only felt for Casteel—*with* Casteel.

What if Kieran's blood elicited the same reactions as Casteel's—which was nothing short of an aphrodisiac? *No*, I told myself. That was the effect of Atlantian blood. Casteel had never mentioned that wolven blood had the same effect.

My chin snapped down as something occurred to me. Did Casteel have that same kind of visceral reaction when he fed from other Atlantians? Like Naill? Emil?

I was really curious about that—for research purposes.

Fiddling with his ring, I brought it to my lips. Feeding had to be intense, no matter what. But what if I didn't like the taste of Kieran's blood? I wouldn't want to offend him—

"What are you doing?"

I swallowed a squeak of surprise as I spun at the sound of Kieran's voice, then lowered the ring. The muted glow of the gas lamp cast soft shadows across his face as he bent at the waist, barefoot in the entryway. One arm was outstretched, holding the curtain of the canopy back. "What are *you* doing?" I asked.

"Watching you pace for the last thirty minutes—"

"It has not been thirty minutes." I let go of the ring, letting it fall against the lapel of my coat.

"Your inability to realize how much time has passed is a little concerning." He moved aside. "You need to be resting. *I* need to be resting."

"No one is stopping you," I muttered, knowing damn well that it was I who was stopping him. If I slept, he did. If I was awake, so was he. Which meant I had to be at least three times more annoying than usual. Because of that, I stomped—loudly and heavily—forward and dipped under his arm, entering the tent.

"This should be a fun night," Kieran muttered.

He has no idea, I thought as I shrugged off my coat, letting it fall wherever it landed, and then all but threw myself down on the bedroll.

Kieran stared as he let the flap of the tent fall shut. He slowly approached me, having to walk half bent over. "What's up?"

"Nothing."

"Let's try that again." Kieran sat cross-legged beside the bedroll, utterly unbothered by the cold, packed earth. "I'm going to ask you what's up—"

"Which you already did."

"—and you're going to answer honestly." A moment later, I felt him tug on my braid. "Right?"

"Right." I turned my head toward him, feeling warmth creep into my cheeks and my stomach flip over and over as I focused on the collar of his tunic. "I'm hungry."

"I can get you—" Kieran's jaw loosened. "Oh."

"Yeah," I whispered, lifting my gaze to his. "I think I need to feed."

Kieran stared down at me. "So, that's why you flung yourself onto the ground?"

My eyes narrowed. "I didn't *fling* myself onto the ground. I flopped onto this bedroll. But, yes. That's why."

His lips twitched.

I narrowed my eyes even further. "Don't laugh."

"Okay."

"Or smile."

One side of his lips tipped up. "Poppy, you're being—"

"Ridiculous." I sat up so suddenly that Kieran jerked back. "I know."

"I was going to say cute," he replied.

I rolled my eyes. "There's nothing cute about needing to drink my friend's blood. Someone who also happens to be my advisor and my husband's best friend. It's awkward."

A choked laugh left him, and I reached over to punch his arm like the mature adult I was. He caught my hand. "There's nothing awkward about this, other than you *flopping* around."

"Wow," I muttered, tasting his sugary amusement in the back of my throat.

His wintry eyes glimmered as he leaned in, lowering his chin. "What you need is natural. It may not feel that way right now because it's new to you, while I've been around Atlantians my whole life. There's nothing awkward or bad about it." His gaze searched mine. "I'm actually proud of you."

"For what?"

"For telling me that you think you need to feed," he said. "I honestly didn't think you would. Figured you would wait until it got to the point where you were weakened or worse."

"Well, thanks," I said. "I think."

"It's a compliment." He slid his fingers from my wrist to my hand. "You know, I wish you had this much trouble asking me to entomb you."

"I didn't want to ask that of you. But—"

"I know," he said with a sigh. "You've fed from Cas, right? Other than when you Ascended?"

I nodded as my gaze dropped to our joined hands. His hand was the same size as Casteel's, the skin only a few shades darker. "On the ship to Oak Ambler," I told him. "I didn't feel like I do now—being hungry, throat dry or my head hurting—which I'm not even sure has anything to do with that."

"Cas would get headaches sometimes. Usually, before he got hungry."

Well, that explained that then. "He had me feed just in case. I'm lucky that he did because I probably would've needed to feed sooner."

"You have used the eather a lot, especially practicing with it while we were in Pompay." Kieran squeezed my hand. "I imagine without the training, you probably could've gone longer."

"I know that Casteel could go longer than a month without feeding if he wasn't wounded, was eating well, and—" I sucked in a shaky breath. "Do you think he's been allowed to feed?"

Kieran's eyes met and held mine. "He was the first time."

"But the first time, they kept him starving. To the point where he killed when he fed. We both know that. We both know what it did to him." I closed my eyes against the surge of pain. "The first time I dreamt of him—he was thinner. There were these cuts all over him. I didn't see him like that this time, but I think... I think he was able to change the way he appeared because he knew we were soul walking and didn't want me to worry."

"He fed on the ship, right?"

I nodded.

"Then, worst-case scenario, it's been forty days since he last fed," Kieran said.

My head jerked up. "You've been counting."

"Haven't you?"

"Yes," I whispered.

He smiled, but I tasted the tangy, bitter sorrow. "We know he's been injured, but we're close. We're almost there. He'll be okay. We'll make sure of it."

I squeezed his hand.

"I know you would rather feed from Cas, and I wish he was here. For a multitude of reasons, Poppy. But he's not, and you need to feed." He lifted his other hand, clasping the side of my cheek. His skin was warm. "Not just for Cas. He will need you when we free him, of course, but more importantly, for yourself. So, let's do this." He dropped his hand from my cheek. "Okay?"

"Okay." I could do this without making things awkward. I was a Queen. I straightened my spine. I was a god. My shoulders squared. I could do this without making it weird.

Or weirder than I'd already made it.

Kieran still held my hand as he reached for a dagger that lay in a pile of weapons. He picked up a slender steel one that he normally wore inside his boot.

"Feedings can get intense," he reminded me, drawing my gaze to his. "Whatever you feel or don't feel during this doesn't matter. What does is that you know that this—all of it—is natural. There's no shame here. No judgment. I know that. Cas knows that. You need to know that, Poppy."

All of this was new to me. Everything was, but I did know I never had anything to be ashamed of when it came to Casteel or Kieran. Tightness eased in my lower back, and then in my chest where I hadn't even realized tension had settled. Letting out a long, slow breath, I nodded.

"You're safe here."

And I knew that, too.

Kieran turned our hands over. My stomach gave a little flip as he placed the edge of the blade against the inside of his wrist. A part of me couldn't believe what I was witnessing—that this was my life now. And another bit was still the person from six months ago, who never would've even considered the act of drinking blood and who probably would've vomited a little in her mouth at the thought of feeding.

But that other me from the past didn't stop who I was today or from doing what I needed to do.

I wasn't used to feeding. I wasn't used to being a Queen or a god. I wasn't even used to being able to freely make decisions for myself, let alone for other people. There was a lot I still had to get used to, and like with everything else, there hadn't been a lot of time to come to terms with it.

I just had to do it.

Kieran didn't move as he pressed the blade into his skin, blood welling as he made a short, quick cut along his wrist. I flinched. I couldn't help it. I kind of wished I had fangs now. A bite had to be far less painful. Then again, since I had no idea what I was doing, a bite from me would probably be worse.

But that two-inch slice reminded me of what I'd seen on Casteel, and I wished I hadn't thought of that either.

Still holding my hand, Kieran lifted his wrist. My heart had started pounding at some point. When, I wasn't sure. The scent of his blood reached me, and there was no heavy, iron smell. No, Kieran's blood smelled of the woods—earthy and rich, just like his imprint.

I didn't know what to expect. My mouth to start watering? My stomach to growl? Neither of those things happened. What did was...*ordinary*. That was the only way I could describe it. Like a new instinct gently waking without alarm, quieting the concerns. Ancient knowledge took hold, guiding me. I lowered my head.

Tentatively, my lips and then the tip of my tongue met the warm blood, and it was a jolt—a rush almost as powerful as when I tasted Casteel. But Kieran's blood tasted like his imprint—like breathing in earthy, woodsy air. The moment his blood reached the back of my throat, the unrelenting dryness eased, and my chest warmed, reminding me of the first swallow of whiskey. That warmth beat back the coldness there—the chill I feared had very little to do with needing to feed.

My eyes drifted shut. The thick warmth slid lower, hitting my belly as the urge to clamp down on his skin and really feed hit me hard. I jerked as a sharp swirl of tingles darted through my veins and then hit my skin. It was like…like sensation was returning to my skin when I hadn't even realized it had vanished.

"You need to drink." Kieran's hand tightened on mine. "Not sip. And that's what you're doing. You're sipping."

He was right, which was annoying, but I gave in to that urge, closed my mouth around the wound and *drank*, pulling his blood into me. That was another jolt—a brighter one that was powerful in its own way. Different from Casteel's but still rattling. And it came with the strangest array of colors that moved behind my eyelids—greens and blues that swirled and whirled. Tension in my arms and legs faded as I swallowed. His taste was earthy and raw. *Wild.* I drank deeper. His blood—

An image came to me suddenly, birthed of the churning colors. Two young men. Shirtless and with their pants rolled up to their knees as they waded through murky water. *Laughing.* They were laughing as they bent, dipping their hands into the water as they grabbed for fish. Even though their frames were leaner, and their skin wasn't yet marked by their lives, I knew at once that it was Casteel and Kieran. A memory of them as young men—perhaps right before Casteel's Culling or just after.

Casteel jerked upright suddenly, a squirming fish between his hands. "Thought you were an expert hunter," he taunted.

Kieran laughed, shoving him, and somehow, they both went down in the water and the fish swam free.

The image crumbled and faded like smoke. I caught brief flashes of other images, the pictures coming in and out too quickly for me to make sense of them, no matter how hard I tried. And then I saw fire.

A bonfire.

The night sky, full of twinkling stars, heady, intoxicating music, and churning, twisting shadows. The beach—the one at Saion's Cove. I latched on to the memory. Driven by curiosity, I opened my senses wider, following the dancing stars and smoke until I saw...*me.*

I saw me on the beach, wearing that stunning cobalt blue gown that almost made me feel as beautiful as I did when Casteel looked at me in that way—the one that carried the heat and weight of his love. And I was in Casteel's arms, leaning against his chest.

My pulse pounded, and in the distant recesses of my mind, I knew I should close down my senses, find a way out of Kieran's memory. But I couldn't.

I...I didn't want to as I watched Casteel lower his head to my neck and saw his hand under the wispy folds of the gown, his fingers sliding between my thighs. My breath caught as I saw myself responding to his touch, moving my hips in tight circles. The image of us was as decadent as it was scandalous—lush and wanton and *free.*

Everything had felt *free* on that beach.

And Kieran...he hadn't just seen me watching him and Lyra. He'd *watched.* The spiciness of arousal filled my throat. My veins. My stomach tumbled in a way that reminded me of standing too close to the edge of a sheer cliff because that wasn't the only thing I saw...or *felt* in Kieran's memory. I saw Casteel nipping at the skin of my throat and lifting his gaze as he pressed his lips there to soothe away the sting. He'd watched, too, and that throbbing in my pulse hit my chest, my stomach, and—

"So nosy," Kieran murmured.

Losing my hold on the memory, my eyes flew open, and I peeked up at Kieran. His eyes were closed, the lines of his face relaxed. His full lips were parted in a slight, barely-there grin.

"Should've known you'd be nosy," he continued, but he didn't sound mad. He sounded amused, and as if he'd just woken up.

Dimly, I was aware that he no longer held my hand. I held his and his arm, just below where my mouth moved against his skin.

Thick lashes lifted, and heavily hooded blue eyes met mine. "There's so much silver in your eyes." He touched the side of my face with just the tips of his fingers. "I can barely see any green."

My senses were open, and under the taste of his blood, there was something smoky—something I wasn't sure had to do with the past or the present, and I knew I should've closed down my senses before this. I did so then and thought...

I thought I should stop. It was enough. The dryness in my throat was gone. The gnawing ache in my belly had vanished. Every sense felt heightened but also relaxed. Sated. I imagined Kieran had to know I'd taken enough, but he didn't stop me. Slowly, I realized that he wouldn't. Kieran would prevent me from taking too much from Casteel, just as he had before. But now? Just like Casteel, he'd let me feed and feed.

And a tiny part of me wanted to keep feeding. To drown in his earthy taste. But I couldn't. I didn't want to weaken him. I lifted my mouth from his arm. "Thank you," I whispered.

Kieran's chest rose with a deep breath. "You don't need to thank me, Poppy."

My heart was still thrumming. So was my body. I felt flushed, like the sweater I wore was almost too thick. Not as hot as it had been with Casteel, when I had ignited and caught fire. This was different. More like the pleasant haze seconds before falling asleep.

I still held Kieran's arm, and I didn't know what provoked me to speak what I saw. If it was the blood or the feeling of being lighter, warmer, and less empty. "I saw your memories. I forgot that could happen." I watched his face closely. "I saw you and Casteel when you were younger—"

"We were trying to catch fish with our hands," he finished for me. "Malik had dared us. I don't even know why I thought about that. Just popped into my head." He paused. "That's not all you saw."

"No."

There was no hint of embarrassment in his features. No shame. "You're going to be irritated."

I didn't think I was capable of feeling that at the moment. "Why?"

"When I realized you were in my head, I changed what I was thinking about," he said, and I wondered if those rapid, brief images I couldn't catch was him flipping through his memories. "I thought of the beach on purpose. Figured it would shock you."

"Jerk," I muttered.

"But the thing is," he continued as if he hadn't heard me, "I don't think it shocked you at all. I think it *intrigued* you."

I'd been wrong.

I *was* capable of feeling annoyance. I started to let go of his arm when I noticed that his wound still seeped blood.

Sliding my fingers closer to the cut he'd made, I felt a kind of tingling warmth dancing down my arms that wasn't all that different from how his blood made me feel. A soft, silvery glow radiated over his forearm, seeping into the cut he'd made.

Kieran jerked a little. "That feels...different."

I realized I had never healed Kieran before. "Does it feel bad?"

"No." His throat worked on a swallow.

"Let's hope you never have to feel that again." I let go of his arm, and he looked down at his wrist. There was nothing but a thin line of blood that he quickly wiped away, revealing a faint pink mark that would likely be gone by morning.

"You're not going to acknowledge what I said about you being intrigued?" he asked.

"Nope." I scooted back on the bedroll and lay down on my side.

Grinning, he looked up from his arm. "You going to pretend that you don't know I was watching the both of you and that you and Casteel were watching us?"

"Yep." I closed my eyes. My heart was slowing, so was the thrumming in my blood. "You're welcome, by the way. For healing your cut."

There was a soft snort as I felt him move. I heard the click of the lantern turning off and then the sound of him undressing. A few moments later, I felt him lay down beside me in his wolven form. Then I fell asleep and slept deeply.

But I didn't find Casteel.

22

The gray of dusk had long since given way to the sun as we continued riding west and to the south. The sunken earthen road known as the Western Pass was nestled between heavily wooded land that bordered the outer Rises of both Three Rivers and Whitebridge.

Kieran and I rode beside the wagon led by Reaver. We'd been silent most of the morning. All of us were alert, our muscles tense. We'd already passed one group of Huntsmen. I kept my head down, the wide-brimmed hat and cloak shielding my face as I kept my senses open, searching for any signs of suspicion. There had been none as they nodded and hurried on, more focused on getting to their next location than looking at us too closely. No one wanted to linger outside a Rise, not even with many hours of daylight left.

I glanced over at Kieran. He was staring into the woods. Nothing had been awkward or weird between us when I woke that morning. It wasn't like I was pretending I hadn't fed from him. It just wasn't a thing. Following his gaze, I squinted as I searched through the glistening leaves. It had rained that morning. Not long, but enough to leave puddles in the road. Through the trees, I saw that land had been cleared at the foot of the Rise for farming. We caught glimpses of people, their backs bent as they worked the fields.

"Are they children?" Reaver asked, having checked out what we were looking at.

They were too far away for me to tell for sure. "It wouldn't be uncommon if so."

"Should they not be in some sort of learning institute?"

"Not every child receives an education," I told him, realizing that Reaver would have no knowledge of what life was like in Solis. "Only those who can afford to send their children to school do, and that's not many. So, a lot of the children take on work, some as young as ten years of age. They end up in the fields until they can learn a trade or enter training to guard the Rise."

"That is…" Reaver trailed off.

"Awful?" I supplied for him.

"And Atlantia? Is it no different?"

"It's completely different," Kieran answered. "All children are educated."

"No matter their wealth?" the draken questioned.

"There's not a wealth gap like there is here in Solis. Atlantia takes care of their people, whether or not they can work or what skills and trades they have learned."

"What was Iliseeum like?" I led Winter around a rather large dip in the road.

"Depends on where you were," he answered. "Depends on what you found beautiful and what you found frightening."

I frowned, but before I could ask him to elaborate, he said, "I guess the mortal realm hasn't changed all that much since the last time I was in it."

My brows lifted. "You were here before?"

He nodded. "I was here when the area I believe we are riding to was known by the name Lasania."

"Lasagna?" Kieran's brows furrowed while I frowned. Where had I seen that name before?

"No. I didn't say lasagna. I said Lasania. La-sa-nee-ah," Reaver snapped.

"Sounded like lasagna to me," he muttered. "What was it like when you were awake? This *Lasania* you speak of?"

The angular features of Reaver's face were shadowed by the brim of his hat as he looked through the trees. "I didn't enter the mortal realm often. Only a few times. Only when necessary. But I think it was a lot like this. Like Solis. It's where the Consort was born. She was once the Princess, the true heir."

My jaw had to be on the muddy ground. "What?"

"The Consort was mortal?" Kieran's surprise matched mine.

"Partly mortal," Reaver corrected, his gaze following a swath of birds that flew overhead.

"How can anyone be partly mortal?" I demanded.

"Just like you were partly mortal," he pointed out.

Oh. Well. He had me there.

I leaned forward, staring up at where he sat on the driver's box. "How was *she* partly mortal, Reaver?"

There was a heavy sigh as if it were knowledge we should already have. "She was born with an ember of the Primal of Life in her."

"Well." I drew out the word. "That sounds far dirtier than I assume was intended."

Reaver snorted.

"What does that even mean?" Kieran asked, and I had to think it was possibly the nicest way he'd ever posed a question to Reaver.

"It means she was born with the essence of the true Primal of Life in her," he answered, which explained nothing. "And, no, I'm not talking the kind the third sons and daughters have. This was an ember of pure power."

I shook my head. "Why am I always more confused after speaking with you?"

"That sounds like a personal issue," Reaver stated.

Kieran made a noise that sounded an awful lot like a choked laugh. My head swiveled to him. He smoothed out his expression.

"Hold up," Reaver said, stiffening. "There is another group on this road."

I faced the road, seeing nothing in the dappled sunlight. "Is it more Huntsmen?"

"I don't think so." Kieran's head cocked to the side as he listened. "There are too many horses."

"How in the world do you hear anything?" I muttered, squinting at…nothing.

"This is definitely a far larger group," Reaver said as another cluster of birds took flight.

"Could they be soldiers?" I slowed Winter. We'd seen none so far, which meant the Blood Crown had to be moving them through the Stroud Sea, or they'd already arrived and were within the Rises. The only other option was unlikely—that the Blood Crown had abandoned the cities.

"Give me a few moments." Kieran handed his reins over to me. "I'll see if I can get close enough."

"Be careful."

With a nod, he quickly dismounted and disappeared into the trees and shrubs.

"I hope he's quieter than that," Reaver remarked dryly.

"He will be."

The handful of minutes that passed before Kieran's return felt like an eternity. "Definitely soldiers. About two to three dozen total," he said. My heart lurched. "They're roughly where the woods thin out."

My gaze cut to the road. Two to three dozen was a lot.

"I can just burn them."

My head swung toward Reaver. "No."

"But it would be quick."

"Absolutely, not."

"Let me take care of this." He started to dismount.

"Do not go all draken and start burning people, Reaver."

"Why not? It's fun."

"That's not fun for anyone—"

"It is for me."

"Stay on your wagon," I ordered. "You shifting and burning things will alert everyone that we have a draken with us. If Isbeth taught Vessa how to harness Primal magic, then she could also use it to kill the remaining draken," I reminded him. "As far as they know, we no longer have any with us."

"Whatever," he muttered.

"I have an idea," Kieran said. "It's not much, but if they get close enough to you, they're going to see that you're no Huntsman."

They would also see the scars.

Kieran crouched, and I watched in confusion as he dipped his hands into one of the puddles. "This won't be fun, but it'll offer some camouflage as long as they don't look too closely at your eyes."

The silvery-white aura behind my pupils was a bit hard to conceal, but this was better than nothing. I leaned down, closing my eyes as Kieran reached up. The feel and texture of the sludge wasn't pleasant as he smoothed it over my brow, along my cheeks, and then on my chin. I didn't dare breathe too deeply in case that wasn't just rain and mud.

Kieran did the same to himself. He didn't offer the same treatment to Reaver, and I wasn't sure if it was the look the draken sent him or the fact that it would be far more bizarre for all of us to be covered in mud.

"They're almost upon us," Reaver stated.

Kieran took the reins and returned to the saddle. He leaned over, tugging down the brim of my hat. Our eyes met. He spoke low. "What you said to Reaver. Does the same go for you?"

The essence pulsed intensely in my chest. "I hope it doesn't come to me having to make that choice, but I won't be as noticeable as Mr. Burn Everyone over here if it does."

Reaver snorted.

"I won't allow us to be taken," I told Kieran, holding his stare. "But remember what I asked."

He knew what I meant. That if I used the essence and got a little too murderous—if I didn't pull back—he would stop me.

Kieran's jaw was hard, but he nodded, straightening himself on his saddle. I kept my chin ducked as I lifted my gaze. Reaver's right hand casually rested on the hilt of the sword I knew was stowed between the two seats of the box.

"No matter what, don't shift." I looked at Reaver. "Don't reveal who you are."

He didn't look happy, but he nodded.

The sound of approaching horses drove my heart against my ribs, and the eather vibrated in response, whispering through my veins. Mud-splattered horses rounded the bend. I saw the soldiers' crimson and white armor, each bearing matching shields engraved with the Blood Crown's Royal Crest. The essence pressed against my skin, telling me I could stop this before it started. I could do it quietly, snapping their necks with just my will. We could ride right past them as if nothing had happened.

But something would've happened.

I would've killed men who had yet to prove a threat. An action that would be discovered and lead to questions—ones that could alert others to our presence. An action that made that hollow place inside me even colder.

"Halt," a soldier called out, his helmet adorned with a comb made of red-dyed horsehair. Knights wore the same, but for a mortal, it symbolized that he was of high rank. Most likely a lieutenant.

We obeyed as any Huntsmen would upon an order from a high-ranking soldier.

The lieutenant rode forward, flanked by three others who bore no combs on their helmets. A gaiter—a thin, black cloth—covered most of his face, leaving only his eyes visible beneath the helmet. He sent a cursory glance in Reaver's direction and then looked at us. "Where do you travel from and where to?"

"New Haven, sir. We are headed for the Willow Plains." Kieran didn't miss a beat. "Ordered to deliver the recent batch of whiskey."

I let my senses reach out as I focused on the lieutenant. Salt gathered in my throat, either distrust or wariness. Neither was uncommon.

The lieutenant remained by Kieran's side as another rode forward. "Three Huntsmen transporting whiskey? Seems like that's one too many."

"Well, sir," Kieran replied, "some would think double the amount isn't enough to guard something as valuable as these spirits."

One of the other soldiers chuckled roughly while another lifted the tarp on the back of the wagon. He nodded at the lieutenant.

I bit down on the inside of my lip as the soldier reached in, checking the crates. The weapons we'd stored in there were closer to the box, but if he found them, it wouldn't raise too many eyebrows.

"We hope to make it to the Willow Plains before nightfall," Kieran added, and I slipped my right hand under the fold of my cloak as the taste of wariness grew from the lieutenant. I grasped the handle of the wolven dagger—just in case.

The lieutenant urged his horse forward. "I bet you do."

I stiffened at the low, smoky rumble that Reaver gave. No one else seemed to have heard. I glanced at him, but his attention was fixed on the lieutenant.

My grip on Winter's reins tightened as the soldier gave Kieran a closer once-over. The man was older, possibly in his fourth or fifth decade of life, and that was unusual for anyone who spent any amount of time outside a Rise. "What happened to you?"

"Ran into some Craven in the middle of the night," Kieran answered. "Things got a bit messy."

The soldier nodded as the lieutenant drew closer, his gaze moving from Kieran to me. I held myself still.

"You're a shy one, aren't you? Too afraid to look up and meet the stare of your superior, and yet you're out here beyond the Rise?" The lieutenant tsked under his breath. "And young by the looks of it."

Unease blossomed as he continued to stare. Though my head was bowed, I felt his gaze.

His hand lashed out, snapping his fingers in front of my face. A rush of prickly heat swept over my skin. "Look at me when I speak to you."

Acidic anger crowded my mouth as my gaze lifted past the black cloth, to meet steely gray eyes.

A long, tense moment of silence stretched as the other soldier turned his horse around. The lieutenant held my stare, his eyes slowly widening. I knew then that he saw the glow behind my pupils. His emotions clogged my throat. Distrust gave way to a quick burst of bubbly awe and then the taint of bitter fear. "Good gods," he uttered, and I knew then that our paltry cover was blown. "The *Harbinger*—"

I snapped forward, unsheathing my dagger in one quick move. The lieutenant's reflexes were well-honed, but he was mortal, and I was not. He withdrew his sword, but that was as far as he got. I thrust the dagger through the neck of his gaiter and into his throat. His words ended in a wet gurgle.

"That was for snapping your fingers in my face." I jerked the blade free. The lieutenant grasped for his throat as he toppled from his saddle, hitting the muddy road on his side.

A sort of controlled chaos exploded as Reaver twisted at the waist, releasing a slender knife. The blade struck the soldier before the man had a chance to react to his lieutenant's demise. Kieran was off his horse in the blink of an eye and beside the other. He caught the soldier by the arm, tearing him from his mount.

"Can I burn them now?" Reaver asked as the remaining soldiers sprang into action. Several charged forward on their horses as Kieran leapt onto the back of a soldier's horse. A blade glinted in the sunlight as it swept across the soldier's throat.

"No." I swung off Winter, landing in a crouch as I sheathed the wolven dagger. "No burning."

"No fun, more like it." Reaver reached down, withdrawing a crossbow I hadn't even known was by his feet as I reached to my hip, pulling a short sword free.

Reaver rose from the box, crossbow in hand. He fired in rapid succession, taking out several soldiers with envious precision. Soldiers on foot raced behind the fleeing horses. I met the heavy swing from a much bigger, broader soldier. The impact of the blow rattled my arm. The soldier laughed. I grunted as the essence merged with my will. I used it to give the mountain of a man a little push. Nothing that required a large expenditure of energy, but the soldier skidded back several feet, his eyes above his gaiter flaring wide.

I did as Vikter had drilled into me through our hours of training. I shut it down. All of it. My senses. My fear that either Kieran or Reaver may misstep and be taken down. That they would be injured or worse before I could get to them. I closed down my emotions as the man caught himself before falling backward. I did what Vikter had taught. But this time, I fought as if each breath my friends took might be *their* last. Dipping low, I planted my free hand in the damp soil as I kicked out, sweeping the soldier's legs out from under him. He hit the ground with a groan.

Kieran was suddenly there, slamming his sword down, just above the breastplate as I rose. He gave the blade a quick twist as he met my gaze. "We need to get out of here."

"Agreed." I looked up to see Reaver striking down another soldier with a brutal blow to the head.

"Incoming," Kieran warned as he withdrew his sword from a soldier's back.

My head snapped forward. Up ahead, at the bend, a group rode hard, the white mantle of the Royal Guard streaming from their shoulders. Their presence was not remotely good. My mind raced through the possibilities. We had to get out of here fast, which meant abandoning the wagon. That could pose a problem down the road, but we'd have to deal with that later.

Prowling forward, I stepped into the attack, twisting under the swing of a sword. I spun back as an arrow whizzed past my head, slamming into the side of the wagon where the shaft vibrated. I shoved the sword into the man's chest between his plates of armor. Whirling around, I gripped a soldier's helmet, yanking his head back as I drew the blade across his throat. I released the man, letting him fall forward as another arrow cut through the air, hitting the ground before me.

I drew to a halt, the air punching out of my lungs as I saw the arrowhead—the shiny, black arrowhead—embedded in the ground.

Shadowstone.

My eyes shot to the Royal Guards as they descended on us. Another arrow streaked through the air, nearly striking Reaver. Fury exploded, mingling with the eather. Kieran whipped toward the Royal Guards, cursing as I summoned the Primal essence. It responded in an immediate rush, hitting my skin, and crowding the edges of my vision in silver as I lowered the sword, walking forward. Passing Kieran, I tossed the swords aside as the eather spilled out from me, flowing over the muddied earth in rippling light—light, and faint, churning *shadows*. My will merged with the essence of the Primal god as the first row of Royal Guards bore down on us, their swords raised.

Their heads jerked sharply to the side, one after another. Five of them. Their swords slipped from their suddenly empty grasps, and they fell with their weapons, dead before they even left their saddles. The horses galloped past me as Kieran shouted—

Red-hot pain exploded near my collarbone, knocking me back a step. I sucked in a burning breath as I looked down to see an arrow jutting from my shoulder.

The eather throbbed violently, matching the pumping wave of pain radiating from my arm. The Primal essence poured into every cell and space in my body, filling my throat with that shadowy, smoky-sweet taste. The taste of *death*.

And that was what I became.

Death.

The Harbinger the lieutenant had called me.

"Oh, shit," Reaver muttered from behind me.

I gripped the shaft of the arrow, feeling nothing as I tore it free. My lip curled as I caught sight of the shadowstone and the blood dripping from it—my blood. The essence sparked from my fingers and rippled across the arrow, burning the shaft first before seeping into the shadowstone tip, shattering it from the inside.

Under my feet, the road trembled and cracked open. Thick roots spilled out, unfurling, and then sinking deep into the mud. The scent of blood and rich soil grew heavy as the ground groaned. A shadow fell upon me as a blood tree grew, its bark a glistening gray. Tiny buds sprouted from the bare limbs, unfurling into bright red, blood leaves.

I heard shouts as Kieran reached for me. Calls to fire as Reaver clashed with the Royal Guards who streamed from between the trees. Another voice came from under it all. One that urged caution. Demanded the guards fall back. One I *almost* recognized.

Lifting my head, I scanned the soldiers, finding the archer to the side of the road, crouched at the trunk of a tree. My eyes narrowed as my will swelled once more. His neck twisted as did his body, bone cracking as he jerked sideways. The arrow released as he fell, finding a target in one of the Royal Guards. A sharp yelp of pain followed. The eather churned wildly around me, snaking between my legs, snapping off the ground, spreading toward the massive oaks. And that cold, aching, empty part of me grew and grew as I turned my attention to the others riding up on us. The bitterness of their fear, the hot acidity of their anger, and their salty resolve stretched out, filling that hollow space within me. I took it in. I took it all in as the shimmering cords stretched out in my mind, arcing across the road and connecting with each of them.

I turned it back on them, feeding them all that fear and anger. All the determination, fury, and...*death.*

They dropped their reins and weapons, clutching their heads as all that emotion poured into them. Their screams—their howls of pain—tore the air as I drifted forward. I *glided* between the anxious horses, their riders tumbling from the saddles both behind me and in front of me. They withered on the road, tearing at their hair as the churning mass of light and darkness pulsed, rippling out from between the prancing horses, searching and searching—

"That's enough," a shout rang out.

A voice that stopped me.

One I finally recognized.

I found it. Found *her* standing in the center of the road, a nightmare of crimson—a crimson coat like a second skin, buttoned from her waist to her chin. Inky black hair that fell over her shoulders, framing a face half-obscured by a mask of wings painted in a deep red.

But I knew it was *her.*

"You," I whispered, and that one word reached her in a wave of smoke and shadow.

The Handmaiden smiled. "We meet again."

She wasn't alone.

I didn't focus on the Royal Guards standing near her, their swords trembling. It was the *others.* The ones cloaked in the color of blood. Ten of them. None of their faces were visible. Nor were their hands, or any other parts of their bodies. But I knew in my bones that they were Revenants.

The Primal essence swirled and snapped around me, stretching out and then recoiling as it neared the Revenants. I felt the press of Kieran's body behind me and heard Reaver's low snarl. My attention remained fixed on *her.* "I'm not here for any of these cities," I told her.

Her pale, pale silver-blue stare met mine. "Yet."

"*Yet,*" I confirmed.

"I know what you're here for."

My fingers splayed at my sides, sparking embers of silvery fire and thick shadows. "Then you should know you won't stop me this time."

"Debatable."

Anger pulsed through me, silencing the little voice that wanted to remind me of what I'd felt when the Blood Queen had ordered her forward—that desperation and hopelessness. Two things I'd felt over and over every time Duke Teerman summoned me to his offices.

What she felt couldn't matter.

Reaver crept in close, his voice only for me to hear. "Can I burn *them?*"

The corner of my lips turned up, and I started to tell him yes.

"*She* will kill him," the Handmaiden spoke.

Everything stopped. Reaver's breath. The pulsing eather. Everything. My entire being focused on her as I felt Casteel's ring between my breasts like a brand.

"If you somehow, in the unlikely event, make it past us, *she* will know, and she *will* kill him," the Handmaiden said softly. "She'll tell you she didn't want to, and a part of her will be speaking the truth because she knows what that will do. What pain it will cause you."

"I'm no fool," I snarled.

Her head cocked. "Did I say you were?"

"You must think so if you believe I can be convinced that she actually cares about the pain she inflicts."

"What you believe is irrelevant. All that matters is that she believes it. Actually, it's not all that matters. Her killing him also does," she added with a half-shrug. "Doesn't it? She'll make a dramatic show of it, too. Send him back in *more* pieces this time. One at a time—"

"Shut up." I stepped forward, the essence whipping around me, lashing an inch from her face.

The Handmaiden didn't even flinch. "We've been waiting for you to make a move. To come for your King. We knew there were two paths you'd likely attempt. The Queen believed you would come straight for Carsodonia, right to the gates of the Rise, proving to the people that you *are* the Harbinger of Death and Destruction."

My stomach soured with returning dread. If the people were being told I was a Harbinger, the war and its aftermath would be so much more complicated.

"I didn't believe that," she continued. "I said you'd come in through the back door. The mines." The Handmaiden smiled, and Kieran cursed behind me, but there was something about her smile. Something familiar. "That's what *I* would do."

It was not entirely shocking that they suspected I would attempt something like this. We knew that. What *was* surprising was that this Handmaiden had assumed correctly.

At the moment, none of that was important. "She knows what I will do if she kills him. She wouldn't dare."

"But she would." The Handmaiden stepped forward. "I am her favorite…after you."

Again. There was something about the way she said that. It cracked the hold my fury had on me. I wasn't sure what it was, though.

"Poppy," Kieran spoke quietly behind me. "If she speaks the truth…"

I wouldn't risk Casteel.

Not again.

The breath I took tasted less of smoke, fire, and death. I pulled the eather in. The tendrils retracted, slipping over the grass and road as the hum in my blood calmed. The anger remained, only leashed. As the silvery glow faded from my vision, the deep throb in my shoulder flared to life, reminding me that one of them had managed to hit me.

I would have to deal with that later.

"What happens now?" I asked.

The Handmaiden's chin dipped. "We will escort you to Carsodonia, where you will meet with the Queen."

I laughed. "Not going to happen."

"I don't think you understand—"

"No, *you* don't understand." I crossed the short distance between us, stopping directly in front of her. Up close, I realized we were the same height. Her build was a little narrower than mine, but not by much. "Just because I won't kill you doesn't mean I will go along with any of your plans."

"That would be a mistake." Her eyes narrowed behind the paint. "Why do you have mud on your face?"

"Why do you have paint on yours?" I fired back.

"Touché," she murmured. "But that's not an answer."

The breeze stirred then, kicking up a scent—one of decay and…stale lilacs. My gaze flickered to the immobile Revenants. "They stink."

"That's rude."

I looked back at her. "But you don't."

"I don't," she said, and that was strange.

But it also didn't matter. "I think you just need to take your merry band of stinkers and get out of our way."

The Handmaiden laughed—it was deep and short but sounded genuine. "And let you and your merry band of extremely good-looking men pass?" She dipped her head to mine, speaking so quietly I barely heard her. "Not going to happen, *Penellaphe*."

Staring at her, I opened my senses to her and felt sugary amusement. That was all. And it didn't tell me much.

"You're out of choices, Queen of Flesh and Fire," she said. "If you're as smart as I hope, I would think you'd realize that you won't get into the capital unnoticed. Not through the mines or the gates."

I zeroed in on her word choice. She didn't say that I wouldn't *escape*. Only that I wouldn't get into the capital unnoticed. That was strange.

But also, she was right.

There would be no sneak attacks. I wouldn't risk Casteel by allowing Reaver to finally get what he wanted. This wasn't the best way into the capital. We would be under guard, but it was a way in.

"Let my people go, and I will not fight you on this," I told her.

"Absolutely, not," Kieran barked out, appearing at my side at once. "We will not be separated."

I turned to Kieran, but he cut me off before I could say another word. "Don't start. We're not leaving your side. At all." He said the last in the Handmaiden's direction. "It's not going to happen."

His loyalty was admirable, and I...

The draken stepped forward. "If you want the Queen of Flesh and Fire, the Bringer of Life and Bringer of Death..." he said—admittedly, I preferred his version of the title the prophecy had given me—"to *accompany* you to the capital, then you will allow her advisor and me to travel with her as a continuation of that good faith."

Kieran's gaze held mine, a clear warning in them that neither he nor Reaver would allow me to go alone. Swallowing the frustration and worry that this was far too dangerous for them, I turned to the Handmaiden. "That is your choice. Because contrary to what you think, I am not out of choices."

"Whatever," the Handmaiden replied. "I couldn't care less. It's not like you're prisoners."

Kieran's head snapped in her direction.

"What?" she asked, widening her eyes in feigned surprise.

"We're not prisoners?" I questioned.

"No. You will be *guests*." The Handmaiden bowed with the kind of flourish I'd only thought Emil capable of. "Honored guests. You are, after all, the daughter of the Queen, and a god. You and whoever *accompanies* you will be treated with the utmost respect," she said with a bright, overly wide smile. "And if they *didn't* want to join you, they could fuck right off for all I care."

I didn't believe the being-treated-with-respect part for one second.

"Either way, I do hope we'll be on our way shortly. The Queen wishes to speak with you about the future of the kingdoms and the True King of the Realms," she added, holding my stare and...

"You haven't blinked once. That's creepy," I told her, glancing back at the Revenants. They still hadn't moved. "Not as creepy as them, though."

She snorted. "You haven't seen creepy yet."

"Something to look forward to, I suppose."

"Then..." She stepped to the side, extending her arm.

A mixture of dread and anticipation rose. "I will..." A floral taste filled the back of my mouth as a whirl of tingles flowed from my throbbing shoulder, over my chest and down my legs.

Kieran grabbed my arm, but I didn't feel it. "Poppy?"

"I—" A sudden rush of dizziness swept through me, followed by the sharp rise of nausea. I twisted away from Kieran, half afraid I might vomit on him. My wide, stinging eyes connected with the Handmaiden's.

"*Shadowstone,*" I whispered hoarsely.

She stared at me, her lips moving, but I couldn't hear what she was saying. I couldn't hear anything. My heart lurched, and then my legs went out from under me.

And then...there was nothing.

23

"You've got to let go, baby. You need to hide, Poppy—" Momma stilled and then pulled away, reaching inside her boot. She pulled a slender, black blade free and then spun, rising so fast I could barely track her movements.

Someone else was here.

"How could you do this?" Momma stepped to the side so she partially blocked the cupboard, but I could see that a man was in the kitchen. Someone clothed in night.

"I'm sorry," he said, and I didn't know his voice.

"So am I." Momma swung out, but the cloaked man caught her arm…

And then they stood there, not moving. I was frozen in the cupboard, heart racing and sweating.

"It has to be done," the man said. "You know what will happen."

"She's but a child—"

"And she will be the end of everything."

"Or she is just the end of them. A beginning—"

Glass broke, and the air filled with shrieks. "Momma!"

Her head jerked around. "Run. Run—"

The kitchen seemed to shake and rattle. Darkness flowed into the room, sliding down the walls and spilling across the floor, and I was still frozen. Gray and dull things filled the chamber, dripping red. "Momma!"

Bodies snapped in my direction. Mouths with sharp teeth. Shrill howls ripped through the air. Bony, cold fingers pressed into my leg. I screamed, scrambling back inside the cupboard—

Something wet and smelly splashed across my face, and the cold fingers released *me. I started to climb farther back.*

The dark man filled the mouth of the cupboard. He reached inside, and there was nowhere to go. He grabbed my arm, yanking me out. "Gods, help me."

Panicked, I tugged at his hold as he swept out his other hand, knocking down the creatures as they came at him. My foot slipped in the wetness as I twisted sideways—

Momma was there, her face streaked with red. She was bleeding as she thrust the black blade into the man's chest. He grunted, saying a word I'd heard Papa say once. His grip slipped away as he stumbled backward.

"Run, Poppy." Momma gasped. "Run."

I ran. I ran toward her—

"Momma—" Claws caught my hair, scratched my skin, burning me like the time I'd reached for the kettle. I screamed, straining for Momma, but I couldn't see her in the twining mass on the floor.

I saw Papa's friend in the doorway. He was supposed to help us—help Momma—but he stared at the man in black as he rose from the mass of twisting, feeding creatures, and his bitter horror filled my mouth, choking me. He backed away, shaking his head, leaving us. He was leaving us—

Teeth sank into my arm. Fiery pain ripped through my arm and lit across my face. I fell, trying to shake them off. "No. No. No," I screamed, thrashing. "Momma! Papa!"

Deep, forbidding pain sliced through my stomach, seizing my lungs and my body.

Then they were falling all around me and on me, limp and heavy, and I couldn't breathe. The pain. The weight. I wanted my momma.

Suddenly they were gone, and a hand was on my cheek, my neck. "Momma." I blinked through blood and tears.

The Dark One stood above me, his face nothing but shadows beneath the hooded cloak. It wasn't his hand at my throat but something cold and sharp. He didn't move. That hand trembled. He shook. "I see it. I see her staring back at me."

"She must…he's her viktor," *I heard Momma say in a voice that sounded wet. "Do you understand what that means? Please. She must…"*

"Good gods."

The cold press was gone from my throat, and I was lifted into the air, floating and floating in the warm darkness, my body there but not. I was slipping away into the nothingness, surrounded by the smell of flowers. Of the purple blossoms the Queen liked to have in her bedchamber. Lilacs.

Someone else was with me in the void. They drew closer, a different kind of darkness before they spoke.

What a powerful little flower you are.
What a powerful poppy.
Pick it and watch it bleed.
Not so powerful any longer.

Waking was a chore.

I knew I needed to. I had to make sure my people were okay. There was Casteel. And that nightmare… I wanted to get as far away from it as possible, but my body felt heavy and useless, not even connected to me. I was floating somewhere else, and I drifted and drifted until I no longer felt weighed down. I took a sudden, deep breath, and my lungs expanded.

"Poppy?" A hand came to my cheek, warm and familiar.

I forced my eyes open.

Kieran hovered above me, just like…like the Dark One had in the nightmare. Kieran's face was only fuzzy around the edges, though, not unseen to me. "Hi."

"Hi?" A slow smile spread as a rough laugh left him. "How are you feeling?"

I wasn't sure as I watched his features clear even more. "Okay. I think. What happened?" I swallowed—and stiffened—at the earthy, woodsy flavor in the back of my throat, quickly becoming aware that I was lying on something impossibly soft. "Did you feed me? Again?" I didn't hear Reaver or anyone else. "Where are we?"

"One question at a time, okay?" His hand remained on my cheek, keeping my eyes on his. "That shadowstone arrow was coated in some kind of toxin. Millicent said it would only leave you unconscious for a few days—"

"Millicent?" My brows furrowed.

"The Handmaiden. That's her name," he told me. "Since I'd trust a pit viper over her, I gave you blood, just in case."

"You…shouldn't have given me more blood. You need it."

"The wolven are like the Atlantians. Our blood replenishes itself quickly. It's one of the reasons we heal so fast," he said, and I remembered Casteel saying something similar. "Does your arm hurt at all? The last time I checked, it looked healed."

"It doesn't hurt. Thanks to you, I'm sure." I started to turn my head, but his thumb swept over my chin, holding me there. My heart stuttered as something else he'd said came to the forefront of my mind. "How long have I been out of it?"

The way he looked at me sent my heart racing. "You were asleep for about two days, Poppy."

I held his stare, and I wasn't sure which thing hit me first. The salty breeze lifting the sheer curtains from a nearby window. The soft *bed* I lay upon that had always been big, no matter how small I'd been. The lack of the Huntsmen cloak and the muted gray, sleeveless tunic Kieran wore in its place. Or that the eerie rhyme I'd heard in my nightmare had been slightly different. I turned my head. This time, Kieran didn't stop me. His hand slid from my cheek to the bed. Beyond him, I saw a sweeping marble and sandstone ceiling higher than many homes—one painted in pastel blues and whites—between curved columns that flowed from the walls and along the dome-shaped...*tower* chamber.

The eather hummed in my chest as my gaze shifted to where I knew two pillars would stand, framing a door plated in gold. One that had often been left unlocked, but I seriously doubted was now. The chamber wasn't small or large, but it was as *lush* as I remembered. Pale gray canopies were tied back to the four posts of the bed. A thick, cream rug covered the floor between the bed and the pillars. A dainty, gold-trimmed table sat to one side with gold-adorned chairs. A sprawling wardrobe took up one wall—one that had once held more dolls and toys than it did clothing.

Kieran barely had a chance to avoid colliding with me as I sat up. "You should take it easy—"

Swinging my legs off the bed, I stood. I felt dizzy, but it had nothing to do with the shadowstone or the toxin. Disbelief flooded me as I crossed the circular chamber.

"Or not," he muttered.

I went to the window, my heart in my throat. Grabbing a fistful of the buttery-soft curtain, I yanked it aside, even though I knew what I would see.

The tops of covered breezeways that traveled across the manicured courtyard, which sat in the shadow of an inner wall taller than most Rises. The stately estates that sat nestled beyond yet another wall. My eyes latched onto the rows of bright, pinkish-purple jacaranda trees lining the road beyond the inner gates. I followed them into the rolling hills full of bright green trees, and the terracotta roofs, sitting side by side, covered in vines smothered by red poppies. I saw the Temples. They were the tallest buildings in Carsodonia—stretching higher than even Wayfair Castle, and both could be found in the Garden District. One was constructed of shadowstone, and the other was made of diamond—crushed diamond and limestone. I followed the vibrant trees straight to where the Golden Bridge glinted in the sun.

We were in Carsodonia.

I whipped around. "When did we get here?"

"Last evening." Kieran rose. "They brought us straight to Wayfair. Some golden fuck was waiting for us at the doors. He wanted to separate us. Said it would be inappropriate for us to be together or some shit, but I told him exactly how—in great detail—that wasn't going to happen."

I had no idea who the golden *fuck* was. "And Reaver?"

"The draken is in a chamber below. We're in the—"

"East wing of Wayfair. I know. This was my chamber when I lived here," I interrupted, and his jaw flexed in response to that piece of information. "Have you been in here this whole time? How do you know Reaver is okay?"

"They've brought him by when I demanded to see him. He was rather well-behaved, which was probably the most unnerving thing. But like me, they gave him clean clothing and food. He's under guard in his chambers." He smirked. "Well, as locked in as they think we are. They have no clue what he is. If they did, I doubt they'd just put him in a chamber, lock the door, and call it a day."

"And he truly stayed in his room?"

He nodded. "Even he seems to know better than to go off half-cocked when we're literally in the heart of enemy territory."

The Primal essence pressed against my skin, responding to the whirlwind of emotions. I felt as if *I* might go off half-cocked. "The satchel—"

"It's right there. I grabbed it." He nodded to the ivory-cushioned chair on the other side of the bed.

Thank the gods. "Have you…have you seen *her*?"

The Blood Queen.

Isbeth.

"No. I haven't even seen any Ascended other than a small army of knights. They're everywhere. Outside this room, in the hall, on every floor," he told me. "I half-expected them to be in the damn wardrobe. The Handmaidens and that golden dick have been the only ones to interact with us."

But she was here.

She had to be.

"Malik?"

Kieran shook his head.

I closed my eyes, taking a deep breath. "Who is the golden one you speak of?"

"Name's Callum. He's a Revenant. And there's something really off about him."

"There's something really off about all of this," I murmured. My head felt as if it were all over the place, bouncing from the confusing nightmare to the knowledge that we were in Carsodonia. Inside Wayfair. It was a lot to process—how much our plans had gone off the rails. How much control we'd either lost or never had. A fissure of panic bolted through me, threatening to sink its claws in deep. I couldn't let that happen. Too much was at stake. I had to deal.

My hands trembled as I closed them at my sides. "What about that Handmaiden? Millicent?"

"Haven't seen her since we arrived here."

I drew in a shallow breath. "Did you catch how she said we wouldn't get into Carsodonia unnoticed if we didn't go with her? Not that we wouldn't *escape*. Did that seem odd to you?"

"There's literally not one thing about her that I *don't* find odd."

Well, I had to agree with that.

Willing my thoughts to slow and focus, I placed my hands on the warm ledge of the window and looked out. Faint pink streaked the sky. My gaze immediately landed on the shadowstone spires of the Temple of Nyktos and then the shimmering diamond dome of the Temple of Perses. They sat across from one another, in different neighborhoods, one looking to the Stroud Sea and the other in the shadows of the Cliffs of Sorrow.

If Casteel was underground and in a tunnel system like the one in Oak Ambler, he could be under either of them.

So could my father.

I was where I wanted to be, but it wasn't how I'd wanted to get here. I focused on the distant Golden Bridge, which separated the

Garden District from the less fortunate areas of Carsodonia. My heart finally slowed. My thoughts calming as the eather settled in my chest. "This isn't entirely bad."

"It's not," Kieran agreed, joining me at the window. "We're here."

"It's not like we'll have free roam of the castle or the city," I reasoned. "We will be watched closely, and there's no telling what the Blood Queen has planned. She won't leave everyone in their rooms fed and clothed for long."

"No, that's not her style." Kieran's gaze followed mine.

Seagulls dipped and swayed over the Rise, where it began to curve and look out over Lower Town and then the sea, where the setting sun glistened off the blue waters. The soft glow settled over the rooftop gardens and pitched roofs, and even farther out, where the homes were stacked one upon another and there was barely room to breathe, warm light bathed the city. Carsodonia was beautiful, especially at dusk and dawn, just like the Blood Forest. Further proof that something so stunning on the surface could also be ugly underneath.

"Where do you think our armies are now?" I asked.

"The armies should be at New Haven or even Whitebridge by now," he told me. "They'd be three to four days out." His head tilted as he eyed me. "If we don't return to Three Rivers when we told Valyn, they'll come looking."

I nodded.

"How far were you able to communicate with Delano through the *notam*?"

"Pretty far. He was able to contact me from the Wastelands once, but I don't think I could reach him this far out."

"I don't think so either." He looked at the window. "But Carsodonia can't be much bigger than the distance between the Wastelands and Pompay, is it?" Kieran turned to me. "What if he was able to get close to the Rise?"

I stared at the massive wall that loomed in the distance. "I could reach him."

Sometime later, I stood, blank eyes staring at me from shiny, porcelain faces neatly lined up along the shelves on one side of the wardrobe.

"Please close that door," Kieran said from behind me.

"Scared of dolls?"

"More like I'm scared of those dolls stealing my soul."

A wry grin tugged at my lips as I closed the door. I'd been snooping, looking for anything that could be used as a weapon. I still had my wolven dagger on me, but they'd stripped Kieran's and Reaver's weapons. I'd offered Kieran the blade, but he'd refused. Neither of them was defenseless, but it would've made me feel better if he had taken the dagger.

"Did you actually play with them as a child?" Kieran stared at the closed wardrobe as if he expected a doll to crack open the door and stick its head out.

"I did." Turning to him, I leaned against the wardrobe.

"That explains a lot."

I rolled my eyes. "She...Isbeth used to give me one every year on the first day of summer until they sent me to Masadonia. I used to think they were beautiful."

Kieran's lip curled. "They are terrifying."

"Yeah, but their faces were smooth and flawless." I touched the scar running along my now-warm cheek. "Mine obviously wasn't, so I pretended I looked like them."

His features softened. "Poppy..."

"I know." My entire face felt like it was on fire. "It was silly."

"I wasn't going to say it was silly—"

A loud bang sounded on the gilded doors a second before they swung open.

It was her.

The Handmaiden.

Millicent sauntered into the chambers, her long-sleeved black tunic was without any adornment and ended at the knees, just above tightly laced boots. The winged mask was painted onto her face once more, this time in black. The contrast to her pale eyes was startling.

"Good evening." Millicent clapped her hands together as three Handmaidens entered behind her. They were dressed similarly, but they wore loose cowls that covered their heads and their mouths, leaving only their painted masks visible. Two of them had those nearly colorless blue eyes. One had brown. Something struck me then. It was possible that not all Handmaidens were Revenants, but it was clear that not all had those pale blue eyes. My mother…she'd had brown eyes.

"Glad to see you up and moving about." Millicent tipped her head at Kieran, and her hair caught my attention. It was a flat, midnight-black, but it looked…patchy and faded in areas. "Told you she'd be right as rain in a day or two…and a half."

I pushed off the wardrobe, immediately reaching out to read her. My senses brushed against a wall, sending a flare of annoyance through me. She was blocking me. "What was that toxin?"

"Something scraped from the insides of some creature." One shoulder rose. "It would've killed an Atlantian. Definitely a mortal. Only one guard carried those arrows. You know, as an insurance policy in case you wanted to continue on your godly Harbinger of Doom warpath."

"If you continue calling me a Harbinger, I will likely restart that godly warpath."

Millicent laughed, but the sound was nothing like the one on the road. It rang falsely. "I would strongly advise against that. Everyone is on edge right now, especially after the missive the Crown received."

"What missive?"

"The Crown got word that New Haven and Whitebridge have fallen under Atlantian control," she told us. "And we expect Three Rivers to be seized at any moment."

Vonetta and the generals were right on schedule. I smiled.

The Handmaiden's lips mimicked mine. "The Queen requests your presence."

My smile disappeared.

"Hot water is being brought to your bathing chamber," Millicent announced as she crossed the bedchamber and dropped into the chair by the bed. "Once you're presentable, you will be escorted to her."

"*We* will be escorted to her," Kieran corrected.

"If that's what makes you happy, then by all means, please feel free to join your much beloved Queen." She lifted a half-gloved hand. Another Handmaiden entered. A swath of white lay across one arm as she headed to the wardrobe.

"You can stop right there," I said. "I'm not wearing that."

The Handmaiden halted, looking at Millicent, who had readjusted herself so her shoulders were on the seat, and her legs against the back of the chair, crossed at the ankles. Her head hung off the edge of the seat, and I really had no idea why she was sitting like that or how she'd gotten into that position within seconds. She gave me an upside-down frown. "And why not?"

"She wants to put me in the white of the Maiden." I stared at the gown. "I don't care what her reasons are, but she will never have a say in what I wear again."

Those pale eyes watched me from behind the painted mask. "But that's the only gown I was given."

"Not my problem."

"It's not mine either."

I faced the Handmaiden. "Your name is Millicent?"

"Last time I checked."

My spine straightened. "I need you to understand something, *Millicent.* If she wants me to come to her, you will find me clothing that is not white. Or I will go to her as I am."

"You have dirt and blood and the gods only know what else on you," she pointed out. "Perhaps you've forgotten, but your *mother* has a thing for cleanliness."

"Do not refer to her as my mother." Eather vibrated in my chest as I stepped toward the Handmaiden. "That is not who she is to me."

Millicent said nothing.

"Either you find me something else to wear, or I go like this," I repeated. "And if that is unsuitable, I will go to her with nothing but the skin I was born in."

"Really?" She drew out the word.

"*Really.*"

"That would almost be worth letting you do, just to see the look on her face." Millicent was still for several seconds and then kicked her heels off the back of the chair. I crossed my arms as she half-rolled, half-flipped out of the chair onto her feet. She pivoted toward me, the flat, patchy hair half in her face. "Then it is my problem."

"Yep."

Millicent exhaled loudly. "I don't get paid enough for this." She grabbed the gown from the other Handmaiden. "Actually, I don't get paid at all, so it's even worse."

"Fucking weird," Kieran muttered under his breath as we watched her…*flounce* from the chamber.

The other Handmaidens remained, still and silent, their features obscured by their painted masks. How had I forgotten about them? I suppressed a shudder at the memory of them moving silently through the halls. And my mother, the only woman I knew as one, had been one of them?

"Do you all have names?" Kieran asked, watching them closely. Silence greeted him. "Thoughts? Opinions? Anything?"

Nothing.

They didn't even blink as they stood there between us and the open doors. I let my senses reach them. I found walls similar to Millicent's, and in my mind, I pictured tiny cracks in those shields. Just little fissures that filled with silvery-white light. I squeezed through the openings, feeling—

One of the Handmaidens gave a little jerk as I tasted something airy and like sponge cake. *Peace.* Surprised, I pulled out and almost took a step back. How in the world could they feel peace? That was nothing like what I'd picked up on from Millicent.

"Makes you wonder why the other one is so talkative," Kieran observed. "And these aren't."

"Because I don't think she's entirely like them. Is she?" I asked the Handmaidens as Kieran sent me a quick glance. "She's different."

"In ways other than the obvious?" Kieran drawled.

"She doesn't smell like them."

Kieran's brows pinched as he turned back to the other Handmaidens. "You're right."

Millicent returned shortly after that, carrying garments as black as the ones she wore. She stomped past Kieran and me, dropping the clothing onto the bed. "This is the best I could manage." Turning to me, she planted her hands on her hips. "I hope this makes you happy because it will surely annoy *her.*"

"Do I look like I care if she's annoyed?"

"You don't." She paused. "Right now." A chill swept down my spine as she went to the chair and sat, crossing one leg over the other. "You should get ready. I'll keep your...man company."

"Great," Kieran muttered.

"I want to see Reaver before I meet with the Queen."

"He's fine."

"I want to see him."

Her lips thinned as she stared up at me. "Is she always this demanding?"

"What you call demanding, I would say is asserting her authority," Kieran replied.

"Well, it's annoying...and unexpected." Her unblinking gaze latched onto mine. "She wasn't always like this."

"How would you know?" I asked.

"Because I remember you when you were as quiet as a tiny mouse, not making a single sound unless it was night, and bad dreams found you in your sleep," she said.

That chill returned, once more skating down my spine.

"I was here then. I feel like I've always been here," she said with a sigh. "I'm old, Penellaphe. Almost as old as your King—"

Before I even realized I had moved, I was in front of her, my hands on top of hers, pressing them into the arms of the chair. "Where is Casteel?" I asked, aware of Kieran coming up behind me as the other Handmaidens stepped forward.

When Millicent said nothing, the Primal essence throbbed in my veins as I lowered my head so we were at eye level. "Have you seen him?" The smokiness returned to my voice.

A long moment passed. "If you want to see him," she said, and I almost missed it—the quick, darting glance she sent in the Handmaidens' direction. "I suggest you get out of my face, get *your* face ready, and do it quickly. Time is of the essence, Your Highness."

I held her stare and then slowly backed off. Snatching the clothing from her, I went into the bathing chamber, quickly washing in the clean, warm water that someone had brought in. I could hear Millicent asking Kieran if he was a wolven and then her prattling on about how she'd never spoken to one. Kieran gave little to no response.

The clothing appeared to have come straight from her wardrobe. The chiton-style tunic was sleeveless and sat off the shoulder, resting where the wound from the shadowstone arrow should've been if the injury hadn't already healed, leaving not even a mark behind. The bodice was tight, but the leather bands around the waist and hips allowed me to loosen the material so it fit my fuller figure. The hem reached the knees and had slits on either side, allowing the wolven dagger to remain hidden but easily accessible. I managed to secure the pouch to one of the bands at my waist and let the ring lay behind the neckline, against my breasts. She'd brought a pair of breeches that I didn't think belonged to her, but they fit, so I really couldn't care less who they'd come from.

I moved to the vanity, my heart pounding as I stared at my reflection. The silvery glow behind my pupils was bright, and I thought the aura had grown a little. I blinked. No changes.

As I stood there, I thought about the dream—the nightmare. My...mother had said something to the Dark One. He was her *viktor*. That's why Tawny had said it sounded so familiar. I'd heard it before.

That night, and the gods only knew how many times in the nightmares I couldn't remember since. Leopold. My father. He was...he was like Vikter. The breath I exhaled was a little ragged.

My grip on the porcelain vanity tightened as my gaze tracked over the scars. They had faded a little when I Ascended, but they seemed more noticeable now than ever. I didn't know if it was the bright lamplight or just the mirror in this castle—in this *city*—that made them seem so stark.

My heart continued pounding as a mixture of dread and anticipation rolled through me. It kept coming in waves, ever since I'd woken to discover that we were in Wayfair. I was here. Where Casteel was. Where my father was. Where Isbeth was.

"I'm not afraid of her," I whispered to my reflection. "I'm a Queen. I'm a god. I'm not afraid of her."

I closed my eyes. In the silence of the chamber, my heart finally slowed. My stomach settled, and my grip eased from the vanity. With steady hands, I braided my still-damp hair.

I couldn't be afraid of her. I couldn't be afraid of anything. Not now.

For the first time, the scars on my arms and face were visible for all to see as we descended onto the main floor of Wayfair Castle.

It was a surreal feeling.

Millicent had taken me to see Reaver, and she didn't put up much of an argument when he followed us back into the hall. The draken was quiet, his head bowed and face obscured by his sheet of blond hair, but I knew he missed nothing as we crossed the atrium that had once seemed so much larger and so beautiful.

As a child, I used to find the vines carved into the marble columns and overlaid in gold to be appealing. I would trace the delicate etchings as far as I could, but the designs traveled all the way to the arched ceilings. Ian and I used to sneak into the atrium in the middle of the day and call out to each other, listening to our voices echo against the tinted glass above.

Now, I found it all to be…excessive. Gaudy. As if all the gold trim and artwork were trying to cover up the bloodstains no one could see.

But the fact that it felt smaller now could have something to do with the number of people who *escorted* us. Besides Millicent and the four Handmaidens, six Royal Knights flanked us, and what I could only assume was the additional arrival of Revenants based on their scent and what I'd come to learn was an eerily silent way of walking. The vamprys wore similar neck and face clothes, leaving only their eyes visible below their helmets. I wasn't worried about them. If they tried something, I could take them out. The Revenants would be an issue, but we had Reaver.

We entered the Hall of Gods, where statues of the gods lined each side of the corridor. I knew exactly where we were headed. The Great Hall.

Vases of lilacs were intermingled with night-blooming roses, a favorite flower of mine, and sat between the massive statues. None of the gods' faces had been captured in any detail in the statues. They were just smooth stone, turned upward to the pitched ceilings. This was another place where Ian and I would play, racing in and out of the statues one moment and then sitting at the feet of them the next as Ian made up grand adventures for the gods to take part in.

My chest tightened as I looked ahead to the smaller, domed atrium, where only two statues stood, both chiseled from rubies.

The King and Queen of Solis.

"Tacky," Kieran muttered upon seeing them.

Millicent stopped in front of us, and to our right, I saw two Royal Guards stationed outside a set of red-painted doors. The guards opened them, and sound rushed out from the side entrance of the Great Hall—murmurs and laughter, cries, and shouts of blessing.

Millicent looked over her shoulder, placing her finger to her rosy-colored lips before entering the Great Hall. The Handmaidens didn't follow. They stepped to the sides, leaving a path for us as Millicent walked out onto the alcove I remembered circling the entire Great Hall.

Pressing my palm against the pouch, I joined her. I didn't take in the crowd below or the Ascended that filled the other sections of the alcove. My attention went straight to the raised dais—its width and length the size of most homes. The thrones were newer versions, still diamond-and-ruby-encrusted, but their backs no longer bore the Royal Crest. They were now shaped to resemble a crescent moon. And both were empty.

But not for long.

Behind the thrones, Handmaidens parted crimson banners, and the Great Hall fell silent. Not a single word was uttered. Chairmen in gold robes appeared, their hold on the wooden rails firm as they walked out, carrying a caged litter, one that reminded me of a gilded birdcage. My brows lifted as I took in the red silk wrapped around each bar, and the gauzy layers of curtains on the sedan chair, obscuring who sat inside.

"You have got to be fucking kidding me," Kieran muttered as the chairmen lowered the litter to the floor.

I couldn't respond as the Handmaidens pulled the curtains aside, and the Blood Queen stepped out from the gilded litter. Cheers erupted, and thunderous applause echoed off the banner-covered walls and the glass-domed ceiling.

Every part of my being focused on her as she crossed the dais, garbed in white—a white gown that covered all but her hands and face. The crown's diamond spires atop each ruby hoop connected by polished onyx dazzled and taunted. Her dark hair shone auburn in the glow of the numerous sconces lining the dozens of columns holding the alcove floors and framing the dais. Even from where I stood, I saw that her eyes were heavily outlined in black, and her lips were a glossy, berry hue.

The essence twisted and tightened inside me as I placed my hands on the railing while she sat on the throne, her head tilting as she *basked* in the reception. It took everything in me not to tap into the roaring power filling my veins and lash out at her, right here, right now. My fingers curled into the stone, pressing into the golden scrollwork that swirled over the railings, the columns, across the floor, and along the visible sections of the walls.

"Son of a bitch," Kieran snarled from my other side.

I tore my attention from the Blood Queen to the dark man who'd joined her, standing to her left. My breath scorched my lungs. Golden-bronze skin. Brown hair touched by streaks of sun and pulled back from uncannily familiar features. High cheekbones. Full mouth. A hard jawline.

"Malik," I whispered.

The bitterness of anger grew in the back of my throat, tinged by tangy anguish. I lifted a hand, placing it on the one beside mine. Kieran gripped the stone just as tightly as I had. I closed down my sorrow and fury, channeling a bit of warmth and...and *happiness*. A tremor went through him, and under my palm, the tendons of his hand relaxed.

"*Prince* Malik," Millicent corrected softly. "Your brother-in-law."

My head cut to her. She was looking at Malik. As close as we stood, I saw tiny spots across her cheeks beneath the painted mask. Freckles. I squeezed Kieran's hand. She watched the Prince much like he'd watched her in Oak Ambler, jaw tight and motionless.

Reaver passed behind her, the muscles in his biceps and forearm taut. He didn't appear to be bothered by those in the alcove—the Ascended in their fancy silk gowns and glittering jewels. Though they were definitely looking at us with curious, midnight eyes.

No, it was the massive statue of the Primal of Life that had garnered the draken's attention.

It stood in the center of the Great Hall, chiseled from the palest marble. Like the other statues in the Hall of Gods, nothing but smooth stone appeared where the face should be, but the detail elsewhere was striking and hadn't faded in the years since I'd last seen it—not from the heavy-soled caligae or the armored plating shielding the legs and chest. He held a spear in one hand and a shield in the other.

The mortals gave the statue and the black petals, pulled from night-blooming roses and scattered around his stone feet, a wide berth.

"I doubt Nyktos would be pleased to know his statue remains here," I murmured.

"That is not a statue of Nyktos." Reaver's words were a low rumble.

"He's right," Millicent added.

The crowd quieted before I could ask what they'd meant, and then she spoke. "My people, how you honor me."

Her voice.

My insides went cold at the soft, warm tone that was so at odds with her special brand of cruelty.

"How you humble me," she said, and my fingers returned to pressing into the railing. Humble? I almost scream-laughed. "Even in times of such uncertainty and fear, your faith in me has never wavered."

Kieran slowly turned his head to me.

"I know," I muttered.

"And for that, I will not waver. And neither will the gods. Not in the face of a godless kingdom or the *Harbinger*."

24

The low sound of hissing rolled across the Great Hall's floor and through the alcove, coming from mortals and Ascended alike. The back of my neck tensed as Kieran and Reaver stiffened.

"'*The Harbinger and the Bringer of Death and Destruction to the lands gifted by the gods,*' has awakened," the Blood Queen said, and the hissing ceased. Silence greeted her words—silence and my rising disbelief. "It is true, the rumors you've heard about our cities to the north and east. They have fallen. Their Rises torn down. The innocent raped and slaughtered, fed from and *cursed.*"

I...I couldn't believe what I was hearing. Stunned, my gaze swept out over the crowd—over the pale faces as bitter fear scraped against my shields. What I dreaded was true. The prophecy was no longer a barely known cluster of words but a weapon.

An expertly wielded one that was nothing but horrific lies. Lies that were sold and bought without hesitation or question. Lies that had already become truth.

Eather burned from the center of my chest as my grip tightened on the railing. Anger pumped through my veins.

"And those left alive, now captives to barbaric rulers who have spent centuries plotting against us. The gods weep for us." She leaned forward on the throne, spine straight as more lies spilled from her berry-hued lips. "Our enemy wants to end the glorious Rite—our honorable service to the gods."

The hissing came again, as did cries of denial.

"I know. I know," the Blood Queen cooed. "But do not fear. We will not cave to them. We will not submit to the horror they have awakened, will we?"

The shouts were even louder now, a boom as powerful as any blast of thunder. Kieran slowly shook his head, and my skin started to hum.

"We will not live in fear of Atlantia. We will not live in fear of the Harbinger of Death and Destruction." The Blood Queen's voice vibrated as the essence did inside of me. "The gods have not abandoned us, and because of that, because of your faith in the Ascended, in me, they never will. You will be spared. That, I promise. And we will have revenge against what has been done to your King. The gods will see to it."

As the people roared their support in a false god, the Primal eather swelled and pressed against my skin. Under my hands, I felt a tremor in the railing.

Millicent looked down and then took a small step back. She turned her head to me and leaned in. "Calm yourself," she warned. "Unless you wish to alert the people to the fact that the Harbinger is among them."

My gaze shot to hers. "I'm not the Harbinger."

"You're not." She sent a pointed glance at the railing.

To the faint cracks beginning to appear in the marble.

"Poppy." Kieran touched my back as Reaver stepped in closer. "I hate to agree with her, but now would not be the time to do anything rash—no matter how justified."

"I'm thinking now is as good a time as any," Reaver commented.

I had to agree with Reaver, but I had no knowledge of where Casteel was being held. No knowledge of my father's whereabouts. The Blood Queen may be right before me, but that didn't mean either was located somewhere safe. If I lashed out at her, someone else could strike against them.

And this wasn't just about them or me. It was about the people on the floor who already believed I was this monster—the Harbinger. If I did anything right now, it would undo everything being done to free them.

A shudder went through me as I pushed the essence down. It took a couple of moments, but I felt Kieran relax, and Millicent turn back to the Great Hall. Eventually, I became aware of what was happening. The Blood Queen was speaking.

"You may come forward," she said.

"What in the hell is this?" Kieran muttered.

Slipping my hand from his, I looked down to see a frail young woman dressed in a beige gown that hung from sunken shoulders. An older couple aided her, all three under the watchful stares of the knights standing on either side of the wide, curved dais steps. The young woman reached the top, and the couple helped her to her knees. She lifted a shaking arm—

The Blood Queen extended hers, folding her pale, steady hands around the much smaller, trembling one. Only one ring adorned her fingers—a pink diamond that glittered under the light. I'd shut down my senses, but the moment the Blood Queen bowed her head, the young woman's joy burst through my shields, sweet and smooth.

And my stomach turned. "It's the Royal Blessing. I didn't know she was still doing this."

"Do I even want to know what that is supposed to be?" Kieran asked.

"Mortals believe that the touch of a Royal has healing properties," I told him. Tears ran freely down the woman's cheeks. My stomach continued to churn. "I remember them lining up for days to get a chance to receive the Blessing."

"They still do," Millicent remarked.

"I used to believe it. The Blessing seemed to work sometimes. I didn't know how. If it was just the power of the mind over the body or…" I watched the Blood Queen take a gold chalice from a nearby Handmaiden and lift it to the woman's lips. Isbeth smiled warmly, and when she did, she actually looked loving and caring as she tipped the chalice, allowing the woman to sip. My eyes narrowed. "Or if it's what's in that cup she has them drink from."

Kieran slowly turned his head to me. "Blood? Atlantian blood?"

It had to be.

"Gods," he growled. "It wouldn't heal someone suffering from some sort of terminal illness, but it could give them a reprieve. It could work long enough to convince the mortals that the gods had blessed the Blood Crown. That their touch could heal. That they and all the Ascended had been Chosen."

And it had.

After a few moments, the woman's coloring improved. Her features no longer appeared so gaunt. And then…she stood on her own. Her movements were jerky, but she *stood*.

Cheers erupted from the mortals packing the floor of the Great Hall. Many dropped to their knees, tears streaming down their faces as they clasped hands in prayer and gratitude. And the Blood Queen lifted her chin—raised those dark eyes to the alcove.

To me.

And she smiled.

"I don't like how they stare at you." Reaver's voice rumbled just above a whisper, swept away by the hum of conversation and the soft strings of music drifting to the high ceiling of the receiving chamber we'd been brought to after the Royal Blessing had ended.

"For once, I can agree with you," Kieran drawled from my other side.

Wealthy mortals weren't the only ones in attendance, standing in groups or sprawled across thick, crimson settees, their fingers and necks dripping with costly jewels, and their stomachs full of the treats served by silent servants.

The Ascended surrounded us.

Lords and Ladies existed among the others like empty voids, their jewels larger, their stares darker, and their stomachs likely full of a different kind of treat.

The mortals kept stealing curious glances in our direction, their stares lingering on the two beside me for reasons that had nothing to do with why they looked upon me. They were rather covert about it. Meanwhile, the Ascended gawked openly.

"They stare because they find you two appealing to look upon. They stare at me because I'm flawed," I told them. "And they cannot figure out why I would be among them."

"What the hell?" Reaver muttered, frowning.

"The mortal elite of Solis mimic the Royals, and the Ascended covet all things beautiful. Look at them," I advised. "They're all perfect in one way or another. Beautiful."

Reaver scowled. "That's the stupidest godsdamn thing I've heard in a while, and I've heard a lot of stupid."

I shrugged, a little surprised by the fact that I wasn't bothered. The idea of any of them seeing the scars had once been mortifying to consider, even though I had always been proud of them—of what I had survived. But I had been a different person then—someone who cared about the opinions of the wealthy and the Royals.

I couldn't care less now.

My gaze flicked to where the Royal Guards stood at the entrance. They too watched, as did the Handmaidens. Millicent had disappeared to the gods only knew where. Time was of the essence, she'd said, and it was. The eather pulsed in my chest. I was growing very impatient.

The Blood Queen knew I was here, and she kept me waiting. It was a silly power move. She'd put me in this chamber because she believed I would behave myself among so many mortals.

Mortals who had no idea a god was among them.

The urge to change that was hard to resist. I touched the ring through my tunic. If I had learned anything, it was that my actions could have unintended consequences. Ones that wouldn't only end with someone being harmed but could further brand me as the Harbinger. So, I waited. *Impatiently.* And while I did, I watched the knights. About half of them stood with the unnatural stiffness of the Handmaidens. Their chests didn't move too much. They didn't twitch or shift. They rarely blinked.

"I think there are Revenants among the Royal Guards," I quietly said.

"Would make sense," Kieran observed. "Less easy to pick out than having them run around in red robes."

Finally, the guards stepped aside and opened ornate gold doors. Two Handmaidens entered first, their cowls in place, covering their hair and casting their painted faces in shadows. The Blood Queen walked in behind them, still dressed in white.

I lowered my hands to my sides. Anger pulsed so furiously through me that I truly believed I deserved some sort of recognition for not unleashing my rage right there. For just standing still as the mortals and Ascended bowed to her. The three of us did no such thing, and that didn't go unnoticed. Shock fell like icy rain from the mortals as they rose. Whispers whirled through the chamber as the small orchestra continued playing from their corner.

Kieran stiffened beside me, and my attention briefly shifted to the man who'd entered behind Isbeth.

Malik.

I let my senses stretch to him, and like before, I hit shields as thick as his father's.

The Blood Queen drifted through the crowd, doling out pretty smiles and brief embraces. Her diamond and ruby crown glittered under the bright chandelier as she turned her head toward me, and her stare met mine.

My heart didn't pound.

My pulse didn't speed up.

My hands and body were steady.

There was no fear or anxiety. I wasn't nothing. I was just icy, banked rage which had infiltrated every cell of my being as she crossed the chamber, the hem of her gown trailing behind her. In other words, I was rather calm.

I held her stare as the cowled Handmaidens followed her and Malik. The guards had moved, taking up stations every so many feet, creating a staggered wall between us and those in attendance.

Isbeth stopped a mere foot from me, that warm and *caring* smile still upon her berry-red lips. Those dark but not endless eyes flickered over my attire. "This isn't what I sent you to wear."

Fury blasted off Kieran, so hot and intense I wouldn't have been surprised if it had ignited a fire. But I…I was *nothing* but that cold rage. "I know."

I saw a slight tightening at the corners of her lips as her eyes rose to mine. "What you wear isn't befitting of a Queen."

"What I wear will be my choice. What befits a Queen, I will decide."

"Now *that* was said like a Queen," she replied. "Unlike the last time we spoke."

"A lot of things have changed since then."

"Have they?"

"Yes. Starting with the fact that you rule over several cities less than you did last time," I answered.

"Is that so?" The Blood Queen lifted a hand. The pink diamond glittered as she snapped her fingers. "What was lost yesterday can easily be regained tomorrow."

My lips twisted into a thin smile. "I never thought you to be a fool."

Her eyes sharpened on me. "I would hope not."

"But you must be one if you think you will easily gain anything you have lost," I told her, aware that we held the rapt attention of the Ascended and mortals alike. They couldn't get close enough to hear us, though. The guards and Handmaidens prevented that.

"Hmm," she murmured, taking a glass of what appeared to be champagne from a servant who'd arrived. "Would you like a drink? Any of you?"

We didn't take her up on the offer, but Malik did, drawing Kieran's attention. "You look well, *Prince* Malik."

That half-smile that hinted at a lone dimple in his left cheek surfaced as he took a sip of his champagne, saying nothing.

Isbeth eyed Kieran. "And you look as scrumptious as you did the last time."

Kieran's lip curled. "I think I will vomit now."

"Adorable." Unbothered, she looked at Reaver, her delicate, dark brows lifting. "You, I do not recognize."

Reaver stared back, unflinching. "You wouldn't."

"Interesting." She gave him the once-over from above the rim of her slender flute. "Tell me, daughter, have you been able to resist the ample charms of the men you surround yourself with?"

"I'm not even going to dignify that with a response," I replied, and Malik's grin deepened.

"Smart move." She winked, and my stomach turned. "By the way, you are wrong."

"About?"

"Being unable to easily reclaim what I've lost," she said, lifting her chin. "I have you."

An icy shiver of anger swirled down my spine. "You only have my presence because I've allowed that."

"Ah, yes. You *agreed* to come. My apologies." She stepped in closer, and both Kieran and Reaver tensed. I did not. "Did you really think you would be able to sneak in here and free him? Come now, Penellaphe. *That* was foolish."

My insides burned from how cold I felt. "But I'm here now, aren't I?"

"You are, and I am glad." Her gaze searched mine. "We have so much to discuss."

"The only thing we have to discuss is Casteel's release."

She took another sip. "Do you remember what happened the last time you made demands?"

I ignored that. "And the release of my father."

The Blood Queen lowered her glass as the striking lines of her features tensed. "Your father?"

"I know who he is. I know you have him. I want both of them."

"Someone's been talking," she murmured. "Your father and your King are well. Safe where they are."

Safe? I almost laughed. "I want to see them."

"You haven't earned that," she replied.

Earned? The essence pressed against my skin, threatening the icy calm. "Do the people in this room know who I am?"

A curious look settled into her features. "Only a few in my Court know you're my daughter."

I stepped forward, and the Handmaidens moved. Isbeth held up her hand. "I'm not talking about that. Do they know I'm a god and not this Harbinger you speak of?"

She said nothing.

"What do you think will happen if I reveal that?" I asked. "What would've happened if I'd done so during your farce of a speech and the Royal Blessing?"

"Better yet, what do *you* think will happen if you do?" Isbeth countered. "Do you think they will drop to their knees and praise you? Welcome you? That they will no longer see you as the Harbinger the gods warned about?"

"The gods warned of no such thing," I said. "And you know that."

"What, my dear, do you think a prophecy spoken by a god to be, other than a warning spoken by a god?" Isbeth countered.

My nostrils flared. "I'm not the Harbinger."

She smiled as her gaze swept over my face. "My sweet child, I see one thing hasn't changed."

"My rampant dislike of you?"

Isbeth laughed softly. "You still haven't accepted who and what you are."

"I know exactly who and what I am," I said, ignoring the sudden burst of dread—of unease. "And soon, all those you have lied to will know the truth. I will make sure of it."

"Again, what do you expect of the people, Your Highness?" Malik asked. "For them to turn their backs on her? When she is all they know and trust? You were a Maiden they believe either dead or *changed*. A stranger from a kingdom they fear."

"Shut up," Kieran growled.

"I'm only speaking the truth," Malik responded. "They will fear her."

"Instead of fearing the false god in front of them? A demis who has stolen the essence of a long-forgotten Primal and used it to kill the King of Gods' guards? Who sanctioned the slaughter of countless children in the so-called, honorable Rite?" I arched a brow at Isbeth. Her eyes narrowed slightly. "I wonder how they will feel to learn that not even your name is real." I laughed softly. "Fake, just like the Blessing. Just like the Rite and everything that makes up the Blood Crown. False, just like the god you believe you are."

"Careful," Isbeth warned.

"What about the other Ascended?" I pushed. "Those who aren't favored by you? What do you think they will do if they learn you're not one of them? Should we find out?"

She stared at me, her glass forgotten in her hand as Malik edged into our space. "I wouldn't suggest doing anything so reckless, Your Highness," he said to me, placing his hand on the Blood Queen's arm. "You may be the one to walk out of whatever catastrophe you create, but many of those in this room and beyond won't. Is that what you want?"

I stared at his hand, momentarily stunned. Disgust built inside me, joining the cold anger. "How can you even touch her?"

Malik lifted a shoulder. "How can I not?"

"You fucking bastard," Kieran snarled, stepping forward.

I grabbed Kieran's arm, stopping him, somehow becoming the rational one.

The Prince eyed Kieran. "It's been a while since we were around each other for any amount of time, so I'll let that slide. You've apparently forgotten I can kick your ass from here to Atlantia without breaking a sweat."

Kieran's wintry eyes brightened. "I haven't forgotten shit."

"Good." Malik smiled. "Now you know that hasn't changed."

My eyes cut to Malik, to that bored, indifferent smile, and I let my senses reach out to him again. I brushed against those thick shields, and this time, I didn't pull back. I didn't stop the dark urge to find those vulnerable spots. I let the essence follow my senses, let the power gently wash over those walls, discovering the cracks.

Malik's gaze snapped to mine, and that lazy smile of his froze. I didn't stop myself. I sank the eather into those mental walls, digging in with claws, into those tiny slivers of weakness. Blood drained rapidly from the Prince's face as I tore those fissures wide. The glass slipped from his fingers as I shattered his shields.

Emotions poured out, raw and unfettered, as Malik stumbled to the side—a wild, spiraling mix that was almost too fast and too chaotic to make sense of. *Almost.* I caught the sugary residue of fleeting amusement and pooling, acidic anger. Malik shuddered, bending at the waist as his fingers dug into his hair. The Handmaidens stepped in, blocking him from the view of others as I continued to *pull* his emotions from him. I tasted hints of sourness and tart tanginess. Equal parts shame and sorrow, but it was the dagger-sharp bitterness that overpowered everything else. Fear that had grown into an ever-present panic.

I pulled back then, recoiling from the holes now left in his shields. He lifted his head. Blood trickled from his nose. His stinging pain eased off, becoming a dull, throbbing ache as he stared at me.

"Get him out of here," Isbeth ordered in a clipped voice. Two guards stepped forward. One of them took hold of his arm.

Malik shook them off. "I'm fine," he rasped, but he didn't fight them when they turned him. When he walked off, his steps were shaky.

"And someone clean up this mess," she snapped, her dark eyes flashing with a hint of eather. "That was not kind of you, daughter. He is, after all, your brother-in-law."

"He had it coming," Kieran said with a smirk.

"Maybe." Isbeth stepped to the side as a servant hastily cleaned up the shattered glass. She took a deep breath, and the faint glow faded from her eyes. The strain left her mouth. "As I was saying, there is much to be discussed. This war. The kingdoms. The True King. That is why *I* allowed you to enter the capital."

Still rattled by Malik's emotions, I said, "You want to have a discussion? That's not going to happen until you release Casteel and my father."

The Blood Queen's laugh was like wind chimes. "My darling, think of what you're asking. You want me to give up leverage—the only thing that keeps you from doing something incredibly reckless and foolish? Something you'd regret? You should thank me."

I drew back. "*Thank you?* Are you out of your—?"

"You are my daughter, Penellaphe." Her hand snapped out,

curling around my chin. This time, I warned Kieran and Reaver off with a raised hand. Her hold wasn't painful. Her touch wasn't warm, but it wasn't cold like an Ascended's. "I carried you in my womb and cared for you until it was no longer safe for me to do so. That is why I tolerate from you what I would not allow from others." Her eyes flashed once more. "That is why I will give you—*only you*—what you haven't even begun to earn. But you must make a choice. You either see your King or your father. Not both."

"I want both."

"That's not an option, Penellaphe." Her eyes bored into mine. "And soon, neither will be. So, make your choice and do so quickly."

I stiffened, hands curling into fists. "Casteel," I forced out, and guilt churned, bordering on shame. My father was important, but I couldn't choose differently.

Isbeth smiled. She had known who I would pick. She dropped my chin. "I will let you see your precious King, and then you and I will talk. And you *will* listen."

"Your Highness." The male in front of me bowed at the waist. He had to be the Revenant Kieran had spoken about. Callum. Everything about him was golden—his hair, skin, clothing, and the winged mask painted on his face. Everything except his eyes. They were the same milky blue as Millicent's. She'd resurfaced when they led us out of the chamber, along with a less pale but not-so-smug Malik.

From what I could see, the Revenant was handsome, the curve of his chin and cheeks almost delicate. Oddly enough, he reminded me of one of the porcelain dolls stowed away in the wardrobe.

"It is an honor to finally meet you," Callum said, straightening.

I doubted it was an honor, so I said nothing.

Callum smiled, nonetheless. "You wish to see your King?"

"Yes." Opening my senses, I brushed against thick, shadowy walls.

"Then follow me." Callum started to turn. "But only you. They cannot come."

"We're not leaving her," Kieran stated.

"I said I would let you see him," the Blood Queen spoke, surrounded by Handmaidens and silent Royal Knights, who also appeared to be a mixture of vampry and Revenant. "Not all of you. That is asking for too much, while thinking little of my intelligence. They will remain behind to ensure your behavior."

Reaver shook his head, his chin low. "You insult *our* intelligence if you think we will allow her to walk off alone."

The Blood Queen's gaze flicked to the draken and lingered far longer than was comfortable. "If you choose not to agree, then you will not see him at all."

Kieran stiffened, as did I. He knew what I would decide before I could even speak. "I agree," I said, meeting Kieran's stare. "I will be fine."

"Of course, she will," Callum confirmed.

I ignored him as I looked at the Blood Queen, catching and holding her gaze. The Primal essence burned in my chest, sparking. The air charged around me. "If anything happens to them, I will bring this entire castle down on your head, stone by stone."

"Goosebumps," Callum murmured, lifting his arms. "You've given me goosebumps. *Remarkable.*" His gaze flicked to me. "I haven't felt such power in, well…" The edge of his teeth dragged over his lip. "In a very long time."

Reaver's head swiveled in Callum's direction. "How long?"

"Long," he said.

I saw that Isbeth's features had tightened. "Yes. Remarkable." Her chin tilted. "Nothing will happen to them. Malik." She snapped her fingers, and he came forward like a loyal hound. "Show them to their rooms—and I do mean their individual rooms."

I reached down, gently squeezing Kieran's hand as several knights joined Malik. "I'll be fine." I turned to Reaver and then returned my gaze to Kieran. "Go with him."

A muscle throbbed in Kieran's jaw. "I'll be *listening* for you to return."

Meaning he would be in his wolven form, allowing me to communicate with him. I nodded and then stepped forward, stopping at Malik's side. He looked straight ahead, his body rigid. I could still taste his anguish. That sorrow could have come from many different sources, but I stopped myself from going down a road that would surely end in disappointment. I forced myself to walk past him.

"Ready?" Callum asked in a jovial tone as if he were questioning if I would join them for supper.

Leaving Kieran and Reaver with Malik and the knights was extremely difficult, but I didn't think Isbeth would attempt something wretched *yet*.

Millicent and the Blood Queen fell into step beside me as I followed Callum through the winding, crimson-banner-adorned halls, my hands clasped, much like I used to do when walking the halls of Castle Teerman as the Maiden. Except, this time, it wasn't because I had been instructed to walk as such. I did it to stop myself from doing something *reckless*.

Like strangling my mother.

"I can remember the last time you walked these halls," the Blood Queen started. "You were so quiet and quick, always running about—"

"With Ian," I cut in, noting the thinning of her mouth as we passed the kitchens. "Do you remember the last time he walked these halls?"

"I do," she replied as Millicent walked beside me, very much in the same manner as I did, hands clasped and alert. "I think about him every day."

Anger rose, scorching the back of my throat as I saw two Royal Guards ahead, opening heavy, wooden doors. At once, I knew we were headed underground. "I bet you do."

"You may not believe this," the Blood Queen said, her crown's shine dulling as we entered an older part of Wayfair where only gas lamps and candles lit the halls, "but very few things pain me as greatly as his loss."

"You're right. I don't believe you." My fingers curled inward, pressing against my palms as we descended the wide, stone stairs. "You killed him. You didn't need to, but you did. That was your choice, and he didn't deserve that. He didn't deserve to be Ascended."

"He didn't deserve to be granted a long life where he would not have to worry about sickness or injury?" Isbeth countered.

I choked out a harsh laugh. "A long life? You made sure that didn't happen." Feeling Millicent's gaze on me, I relaxed my fingers. "I don't want to talk about Ian."

"It was you who brought him up."

"That was a mistake."

The Blood Queen went quiet as we entered the underground hall. Even belowground, the ceilings were high, the openings to other paths rounded and meticulously cleaned. It was eerily silent—not a whisper of sound. My gaze roamed ahead, following the seemingly endless rows of sandstone columns rising to the ceiling to where it wasn't nearly as well lit, and shadows huddled at the edges of the columns. I could almost see myself now—much younger, veiled, and so very lonely as I crept down the hall.

Callum stopped, facing us. "We cannot allow you to see where we go. You will be blindfolded."

I didn't like the idea of being unable to see what any of them were doing around me, but I nodded. "Then do it."

Millicent stepped behind me as quiet as any spirit. A heartbeat later, I could see nothing but darkness.

The path we took was a silent and confusing journey. Millicent held my arm, steering me along for what seemed like an eternity. It felt as if I were walking straight and then making constant, continuous turns. I had to applaud her skill because I had no hope of ever retracing our steps.

I had the spell, though. And based on the length of time we walked, I knew I couldn't use it in the chambers under Wayfair. We had to be near or under the Garden District by the time Millicent stopped us, which meant we could possibly enter the tunnels via one of the Temples.

The air had grown colder, damp, and musty, sending a jolt of alarm through me as Millicent untied the blindfold. How could anyone be kept down here and be well? My heart sped up.

The cloth fell away, revealing Callum towering over me. Surprised, I took a step back, bumping into Millicent. The mustiness of the underground tunnels must've been strong to hide the sweet scent of decay. He was so close now, I saw a mole beneath the golden face paint, just below his right eye.

Callum smiled as his pale gaze tracked over my features—over the scars. "It must have hurt something terrible."

"Do you want to find out?" I offered, and that closed-lip smile of his went up a notch. "You will if you continue standing so close to me."

"Callum." The Blood Queen spoke from behind us.

The Revenant retreated, bowing slightly. His smile remained, as did his unblinking stare. Holding his gaze for a moment longer, I quickly looked around. I saw nothing but damp stone walls lit by torches.

"Where is he?" I demanded.

"At the end of the hall to your left," Callum answered.

I started forward.

"Penellaphe," Isbeth called out, the sound of my name dripping from her lips hitting my nerves like Craven claws against stone. "I promised the safety of your men. How you behave next will determine whether or not that promise is kept."

Her words…

A chill went down my spine as I slowly turned to her. Guards and Handmaidens surrounded her. Only Millicent stood off to the side, across from Callum. Isbeth's words were a warning, not just for what she'd do, but what I would soon find.

The Primal essence thrummed just beneath the surface of my skin. A hundred different retorts burned the tip of my tongue, filling my mouth with the smoke of promised violence. But once more, I pulled on all those years of silence—no matter what was said or done. I swallowed the smoke.

"Casteel has never been a…pleasant guest," she added, her dark eyes glimmering in the firelight. Guest? *A guest?* "And, unlike his brother, he has never learned how to make a situation easier for himself."

A burst of acidic anger hit the back of my throat, coming in a sharp, quick punch from Millicent. Not for one second did I believe the emotion stemmed from talk of Casteel. It was the mention of Malik. Her reaction was curious, as was his when we'd been at Oak Ambler. I filed that all away as I turned from the Blood Queen. And I didn't say anything as I walked forward. If I did, it would end badly.

Each step felt like twenty, and I lost any semblance of calm I might have had as I grew closer and saw the shadow-filled opening curved into the cell wall. My hands repeatedly opened and closed as fear for what I would see—what I would *do*—crashed into the anticipation and rage within me. This place wasn't even fit for a

Craven, and she had *Casteel* here?

A sound came from the recesses of the cell. It was rough and low, a snarl that didn't sound mortal as I hurried through the opening into the dim, candlelit space.

I spotted him then.

And my heart cracked under the weight of what I saw.

25

Limp, dark waves fell forward, shielding most of Casteel's face. All I could see was his mouth—lips peeled back, and fangs bared.

His growl vibrated from a chest that shouldn't have been so slender. The bones of his shoulders stood out as starkly as the twisted ones chaining him to the wall. Bonds I knew were made of the bones of long-dead deities. They hadn't been used to keep him chained. They did nothing to him.

The intent was to stop someone like me from breaking them.

Shadowstone shackles encircled his ankles, wrists…and his throat. His throat. His actual, *fucking* throat. And his skin—good gods, not an inch wasn't covered in thin, angry, red lines. Nowhere, from his collarbone to his breeches. The cloth along the calf of his right leg had been torn, revealing a jagged wound that looked too much like a Craven bite. The dirtied bandage on his left hand…

Gods.

I'd thought I had prepared myself, but I truly wasn't ready. Seeing what had been done to him was a horrifying shock.

"Casteel," I whispered, starting forward.

He launched to his feet, swiping out with curled fingers. I jerked to a stop, narrowly avoiding his reach as the chain at his neck snapped him back. His bare feet, dirty with dried *blood*, slipped over the damp stone. Somehow, he kept his balance. Fighting the bindings, the chains creaked as he threw his head back.

Oh, gods. His eyes…

I could only see a thin strip of gold.

My gift came alive, spilling out from me in a way that hadn't happened in a long time. I connected to him, flinching as his emotions swamped me, coming in a dark, gnawing wave of painful hunger.

Bloodlust.

He'd fallen into bloodlust. I knew in that moment that he had no idea who I was. All he sensed was my blood. Possibly even the Primal essence *in* that blood. I wasn't his Queen. His friend or wife. I wasn't his heartmate. I was nothing but *food*. But what cut deep and to the quick was that I knew he had no idea who *he* was.

My chest rose and fell rapidly as I tried to catch my breath. I wanted to scream. To cry.

Most of all, I wanted to burn the realm.

Those nearly black eyes darted to the opening, his growl growing louder, deeper.

"I wouldn't stand too close to him," Callum advised. "He's like a rabid animal."

My head jerked to the Revenant. Millicent stood behind him. "I will make sure you die," I promised. "And it will hurt."

"You know," he drawled, leaning against the stone as he crossed his arms and jerked his chin toward Casteel, "he said the same thing."

"Then I'll make sure he has the pleasure of witnessing it."

Callum chuckled. "So giving of you."

"You have no idea." I turned from him before I discovered how a Revenant survived decapitation.

Casteel was still staring at the Revenant. His focus had zeroed in on Callum, even though I was much closer to him. The way he fixated on the Revenant gave me hope that he wasn't completely lost.

That he was still in there, and I could reach him—remind him of who he was. Stop him before he became a *thing* instead of a person.

I sprang forward, clasping his arm. He swung his head to me, hissing. His skin was hot—*too hot*. And dry. Feverish. I stepped into him.

"Shit," Millicent exclaimed from the hall.

Casteel was like a viper. He went straight for my throat. But I'd expected the move and caught him by the chin, holding his head back. The rough, short hairs on his jaw felt strange against my palm. He had lost some of his body mass, and I was strong, but his hunger gave him the strength of ten gods. My arm shook as I tapped into the essence, letting my gift roar to the surface.

Silvery-white light sparked across my vision and from my hands, washing over skin that shouldn't be so dull and hot. I channeled every happy memory I could into the touch—memories of us in the cavern. When we stopped pretending. Us on our knees before Jasper, our rings clasped in our hands. The way he'd looked at me in that blue gown in Saion's Cove. How he'd taken me in that garden, up against the wall. I funneled the energy into him, praying that healing his physical wounds would ease some of the pain of hunger, calming him enough for him to remember who he was. It would hopefully be a temporary fix, at least. Easing the knife's edge of hunger so he could feed without doing real and painful damage. Because he would now if I let him. And that would hurt him. It would kill a part of him.

A spasm ran through Casteel's body. He went painfully rigid for a heartbeat, no longer pushing against my touch. Then he jerked away so fast, he completely broke free of my hold. I stumbled, nearly falling as he pressed back against the wall. The silvery glow faded from my hands, from *him* as he stood there, head bowed and chest heaving. The numerous, impossible-to-count cuts down his arms, across his chest, and on his stomach had faded to faint, pink marks. The candlelight didn't reach his lower body, and I couldn't see the wound on his leg now, but I imagined that it too had begun to heal. His hand, though… My abilities couldn't fix that.

Seconds stretched with the only sounds his ragged breathing and a muted, steady thump from above. Carriage wheels?

"Cas?"

He shuddered—his entire body and the chains moving. He lifted his head, and I saw that his face…it, too, was thinner. Like it had been in that first dream. The shadow of hair along his jaw and chin had darkened. Deeper hollows had formed under his cheeks and eyes.

But his eyes…they opened, and they were still that stunning shade of gold. "*Poppy.*"

Casteel

She stood before me, a bright flame that had beaten back the red haze of bloodlust. She was here. Real.

My Queen.

My soul.

My savior.

Poppy.

This was no dream. Not a hallucination like the ones that had plagued me in the last hours and days. Poppy had said that she would come for me, and now she was here.

I pushed off the wall. The bone chains rattled, pulling tautly. The band tightened around my throat, but Poppy was already moving. Before I could take my next breath, she was in my arms. Somehow, I ended up on my ass, but she was *still* in my arms. Warm. Solid. Soft. Holding me tightly. Pressing her cheek against mine. I was filthy. I must stink. The floor of the cell was rank. None of that stopped her from pressing a quick kiss to my cheek, brow, and the bridge of my nose.

I didn't want any of this filth to touch her, but I couldn't bring myself to separate from her. Her touch. The feel of her in my arms. The faint scent of jasmine that I breathed in.

Her gift had snagged me from the edge of nothingness and pulled me back, but it was her—simply *her*—who kept me from spinning to that brink again. I sank my fingers into her braid, my flesh coming alive at the sensation of those strands against my skin.

Poppy was…gods, she was grounding in a way only she could be. Her mere presence gathered all those fragmented shards that had broken off and floated away, piecing them back together once more.

I shook as she smoothed her fingers through my hair and then moved her hands to my cheeks. She stilled against the rough patches of hair and the dampness there.

"It's okay," she whispered thickly, sweeping away the wetness with her thumb and then her lips. "It's okay. I'm here."

I'm here.

I stiffened, my fingers clenching her braid. She truly was here. In this cell with me. And we weren't alone. My eyes snapped open, and I searched the space for Kieran.

Golden Boy waited at the entrance with that fucking smirk on his face. The Handmaiden was with him. She wasn't smirking. She stood with her arms crossed, silent and still. Beyond them, in the shadows, other guards watched. Knights with their faces covered in black.

My entire body went cold. This was no rescue.

I tightened my arm around Poppy's waist, shifting us as best I could with the damn chains. I could only get her body halfway shielded by mine.

I turned my head, pressing my mouth to the space by her ear. "What happened?" I spoke low, not taking my eyes off the entrance for one damn second.

"They caught us outside Three Rivers."

The kind of panic that had pierced my soul when I'd seen that bolt protruding from her chest slammed into me now, kicking my sluggish heart into a gallop.

And Poppy sensed it. I knew she did.

She kissed my cheek with warm, soft lips. "It's okay," she repeated, petting the nape of my neck. "Kieran and Reaver are with me. They're safe."

Reaver... It took me a moment to remember the draken, but the relief that came with knowing that she wasn't alone with these vipers was short-lived. "Have they hurt you?"

"Does she look as if she has been harmed?" Callum interjected.

"Does it look like I'm talking to you?" I growled.

"I'm actually surprised to see you speaking at all," the golden Rev replied. "Your Queen must be made of magic, considering that the last time I saw you, all you could do was foam at the mouth."

Poppy's head swiveled in the Rev's direction. "I changed my mind. I will kill you the first chance I get."

The Rev chuckled. "Not nearly as giving as I thought you were."

"How about we make a deal?" I said to Poppy, easing my fingers from her braid. I drew them down the thick length of her hair. "Whoever gets to him first, gets the honor."

"Deal," she said.

"Threats are unnecessary," came the voice I loathed most of all.

The Handmaiden stepped aside as the Blood Queen emerged from the shadows. My eyes narrowed at the sight of her, her body swathed in white. I pulled Poppy closer. I would've tucked her inside my damn body if I could have.

"And they are also pointless," Isbeth continued. "None of you, not even my dear daughter, can kill my Revenants. Your draken remain with your armies—well, whatever is left of them."

Poppy flinched, and the sight of that, the knowledge of the blow the Blood Queen had landed, nearly sent me straight to the edge again. Rage pooled in my empty gut.

"Fuck you," I spat.

"Charming," Isbeth replied.

As the Blood Queen and I locked stares, it occurred to me that they must not know that Poppy had brought a draken with her. Isbeth knew Kieran. She never would've met this Reaver. That alone should have raised suspicions…unless she had no knowledge that they could take mortal form—or she simply underestimated Poppy that much.

Very, very foolish of her.

I ducked my chin, hiding my smile against Poppy's cheek.

She must've felt the rise of my lips because she turned her head back to mine, seeking the smile. Her mouth closed over mine in a kiss that wasn't tentative or innocent. It was one of strength. Of love. And the taste of her mouth shook every part of me. I didn't even know until then that only a kiss could do that.

Poppy lifted her head. "He needs to feed," she said, hands clasping my cheeks. "And he needs food and fresh, clean water." She paused as I tensed. Her gaze flicked to the hip bath, and her chest rose with a sharp inhale. "To *drink*."

To drink.

Not to bathe.

She knew. Somehow, she'd figured it out. Or Kieran had told her. Probably Kieran, but still, she remembered.

"He has been given all those things," the Blood Queen answered. "And as you can see, he has made no use of all that fresh water provided to him."

Her eyes closed briefly. "He has only been given enough to survive. He needs food. *Real* food. And he needs—"

"Blood. Which he has also been provided. If he hadn't, you wouldn't be sitting in his lap right now. You'd be lying there with your throat torn open," Isbeth stated.

What she'd said was blunt. Cruel. But it was the truth. What little they'd given me had pushed me to the edge. But without it? I would be gone.

Poppy moved her hand down, bringing her wrist close to my mouth. Even in the faint light, I saw the pale blue veins under her skin. My lips parted. Muscles tensed painfully—

"I did not give you permission to bleed for him." The Blood

Queen's voice was closer, but I couldn't look away from that vein.

"I don't need your permission," Poppy spat.

"I would have to disagree."

Poppy's head cut in her direction. "Try and stop me."

There was a beat of silence. "And what? You bring this stone down on my head as you promised? If so, you will bring it down on all of us."

"So be it," Poppy hissed.

"She'll do it," I said, curling my right hand around her arm, forcing my eyes away from her wrist. "And I kind of want to see her do it."

Isbeth's lip curled. "You *would* want something so idiotic."

I smiled at her.

"Whatever." Isbeth threw up a hand. "Feed him and get it over with. This whole scene is tiresome."

Poppy twisted back to me, folding her hand around the nape of my neck. "Feed."

My gaze dropped to that vein again. I hesitated, even as my stomach clenched. Her blood…it was powerful, and she'd pulled me back from the edge before. But she needed her strength. I didn't know if she had learned if *she* needed to feed or not, and I wasn't about to ask that in our present company. I wouldn't risk her well-being.

I lowered my mouth to her wrist, dropping a kiss to that vein as I braced myself against the surge of need and hunger that rose. I didn't block the pain. I quieted it, knowing she would search for it. "I don't need to feed."

"Yes, you do." Poppy dipped her head. "You need blood."

"Your touch…it pulled me back. That was enough." I lowered her wrist.

Her breath snagged. "Cas—"

I groaned, feeling the sound of my name in a way she would likely find highly inappropriate given the situation. "It's better that I don't."

Poppy's brows creased with frustration. "Then food. I want food brought in. Now."

"Food will be brought to him," Callum answered, and it took everything in me not to laugh. Stale bread? Moldy cheese. Yeah, food.

"Then go get it," Poppy ordered. "Now."

I fought another smile. Oh, how she fought for me. "My Queen," I whispered, trailing my fingers along the curve of her jaw. "So demanding."

"Yes. That she is," the Blood Queen stated coolly. "She will also be leaving your embrace."

"No." She curled her arm around my shoulders. "I'm not leaving him. I will stay right here with him."

"That was not a part of the deal. You promised that you would speak with me."

"I promised to talk to you. I didn't agree to do so in any certain location," Poppy shot back.

"You have got to be kidding me," Isbeth muttered. "You expect me to stay down here?"

"I don't care what you do," Poppy snapped.

"You should. If you think I will allow you, my daughter, to stay down here, you are foolishly mistaken."

"You are holding a *King* here," Poppy exclaimed, her eyes flashing. "The man your daughter is married to."

"Oh, *now* you recognize yourself as my daughter?" Isbeth laughed, and the sound was like falling ice. "You are testing my patience, Penellaphe."

I knew what would happen. She wouldn't strike out at Poppy. The Blood Queen would go after someone else, just to inflict the kind of hurt that never really healed. I wouldn't allow that. And even though I didn't want Poppy out of my sight or my arms, I didn't want her down here in this hellish place either. I didn't want these walls, the smells, and the godsforsaken cold to join the nightmares that already plagued her.

"You can't stay down here," I told her, dragging my thumb across her lip. "I don't want that."

"I do."

"Poppy." I held her gaze, hating the dampness I saw growing there. Hating it more than anything. "I can't have you down here."

Her lower lip trembled as she whispered, "I don't want to leave you."

"You won't." I kissed her forehead. "You never have. You never will."

"My daughter is obviously still desperately worried about you," Isbeth spoke, derision dripping like syrup from her words. "I assured her that you were alive and well—"

"Well?" Poppy repeated, and that one word caused every instinct I had to go on high alert. It was her voice. I'd never heard it sound like that before. As if it were made of shadows and smoke.

The normally chatty Handmaiden unfolded her arms, her stare

fixing on Poppy.

Poppy turned her attention back to me. Her hands slipped to my cheeks and then my shoulders. In the waning candlelight, her gaze moved over my face and then lower—across the numerous, now-faded cuts. Her hand slid down my left arm, tugging until her fingers reached the edge of the bandage. Her chest stilled.

A ripple of static hit the air, drawing a hiss from the golden Rev. Slowly, her eyes lifted to mine, and I saw it—the glow behind her pupils. The power throbbed and then spread in thin streaks of silver across those beautiful green irises. The sight was fascinating. Stunning. That stubborn jaw of hers tightened. She didn't blink, and I knew that look. Fuck. I'd been on the receiving end of it, right before she plunged a dagger into my chest.

I wished we were someplace else. Anywhere I could show her with my lips and tongue and every part of me just how incredibly *intriguing* that display of violent power was.

A shiver went through Poppy—a vibration that sent another ripple of energy through the cell as she looked over her shoulder. "You have him chained and starved," she said, and that voice… Golden Boy straightened. The skin around Isbeth's mouth puckered. They heard *it,* too. "You have hurt him and kept him in a place not fit for even a Craven. Yet you say he is well?"

"He would be in far better accommodations if he knew how to behave," Isbeth remarked. "If he showed even one iota of respect."

That really pissed me off, but Poppy's skin now had a faint sheen. A soft glow as if she were lit from within. I'd seen it before. What I didn't remember was what I saw sliding and swirling under her cheek now. Shadows. She had *shadows* in her flesh.

"Why would he, when dealing with someone so unworthy of respect?" Poppy questioned, and I blinked rapidly, swearing the temperature of the cell dropped by several degrees.

"Careful, daughter," Isbeth warned. "I told you once before. I will only tolerate your disrespect to a point. You do not want to cross that line more than you already have."

Poppy said nothing, and the shadows ceased their relentless churning under her skin. Everything about her became still once more, but I felt it under my hands and against me, building and ramping up. The thing under her flesh. Power. Pure, unfettered power. An ache settled in my upper jaw. Fuck. Her essence. I could *feel* it.

"You are so very powerful, daughter. I feel it pressing against my skin. It's calling to everyone and *everything* in this chamber and beyond." The Blood Queen bent slightly at the waist, her pale face expressionless. "You have grown in the short time since we last saw each other. But you still haven't learned to quiet that temper of yours. If I were you, I would learn to do so quickly. Pull it back before it's too late."

There was no one in the entirety of the two kingdoms that I wanted to see dead more than the Blood Queen. No one. But Poppy needed to heed the warning. Isbeth was a cornered viper. She would strike when least expected, and she would do so in a way that would leave deep, unforgiving scars. She already had with Ian.

"Poppy," I said quietly, and those fractured eyes latched on to mine. "Go."

She shook her head fiercely, sending loose curls across her cheeks. "I can't—"

"You will." I couldn't bear to see her strength cracking like this. Fuck. It hurt. But seeing her weather whatever blow the Blood Queen would deliver next if she continued disobeying her would kill me. "I love you, Poppy."

She shook. "I love *you.*"

Tightening my arm around her, I hauled her close and kissed her. Our tongues tangled. Our hearts. I committed the feel and taste of her to memory to drown in them later. She was breathing just as hard as I was when our lips finally parted.

"From the first moment I saw you smile… And heard you laugh? *Gods,*" I rasped, and she shuddered, her beautiful eyes closing. "From the first time I saw you nock an arrow and fire without hesitation? Handle a dagger and fight beside another? Fight *me?* I was in awe. I'm never *not* in awe of you. I'm always utterly mesmerized. I'll never stop being that. Always and forever."

Poppy

Always and forever.

Those two words were the only things that allowed me to keep my *temper* in check as they escorted me back through the winding, endless network of tunnels. Barely. The trembling the rage had caused had ceased, but the anger hadn't lessened. How Casteel had been treated would haunt every breath I took, as would his choice not to feed.

Not a single part of me believed that my gift had been enough to stave off his hunger. I'd felt it. The gnawing ache was far worse than what I'd experienced or what I'd felt from him in New Haven.

He'd made the choice because he didn't want to potentially weaken me.

Gods, I didn't deserve him.

We stopped, and they removed the blindfold once we reached the vast hall beneath Wayfair.

The Blood Queen stood directly in front of me. I couldn't believe she'd allowed me to see Casteel like that.

But I remembered that she was a coldhearted bitch.

"You're angry with me," she stated as Millicent stepped to the side. Callum remained to my right, far too close for comfort. "With how you believe Casteel has been treated."

"I saw with my own eyes how he's been treated."

"It could've been easier for him," she said, the ruby crown glittering as she tilted her head. "He made it harder for himself, especially when he killed one of my Handmaidens."

My gaze flicked to where they stood silently. They each had the pale blue eyes of a Revenant, but not all had in the bedchamber—and neither had Coralena. "My mother had brown eyes, yet you said she was a Revenant."

"She was not your mother. She was Ian's, but not yours." Tension bracketed her mouth. "And she did not have brown eyes. Hers were just like the others."

"I remember them—"

"She hid them, Penellaphe. With magic. Magic *I* lent her." Just like she'd lent the essence to Vessa. "And I did so, only because when you were little, her eyes scared you."

Surprise rolled through me. Using the Primal essence for such a thing had never crossed my mind. "Why...why would her eyes scare me?"

"That, I cannot answer."

I'd buried the memories of the Handmaidens so deeply that it had taken Alastir speaking of them to trigger any recollection. Had I somehow been able to sense what they were and that had caused my fear?

"I didn't want to hurt Casteel," Isbeth announced, jerking me from my thoughts. "Doing so only serves to drive the wedge between us further. But you left me with no choice. You killed the King, Penellaphe. If I did nothing, it would've been a sign of weakness to the Royals."

The breath I exhaled felt like fire in my throat. Her words collided with my guilt. "What I did may have guided your actions, but it was still your hand. You're not absolved of responsibility, *Isbeth*. Just like how what happened to your son doesn't justify all you've done since."

Her nostrils flared as she stared at me. "If I kill Casteel, you would do worse than I ever could've imagined. And if that day ever comes, judge me then for my actions."

The wave of fury that swept through me was only cooled by the realization that she spoke the truth. That empty, cold part of me stirred. I didn't know what I would do, but it would be horrific, and I knew that.

That was why I'd made Kieran make that promise.

I looked away, shaking my head. "Will you send food to Casteel? Fresh food?" I took a shaky breath. "Please."

"Do you think you deserve that?" Callum asked. "Better yet, do you really think *he* does?"

Spinning around, I'd already grasped the dagger at his hip by the time he registered that I'd moved. I slammed the blade deep into his chest and into his heart.

A flicker of shock widened his eyes as he looked down at the hilt of the dagger.

"I wasn't speaking to you," I snarled, letting go of the blade.

"Dammit," he muttered, blood trickling from the corner of his mouth. He toppled over like a pile of bricks, hitting the floor. The back of his head met the stone with a satisfyingly loud crack.

Millicent choked on what sounded like a laugh.

"You just stabbed my Revenant." Isbeth sighed.

"He'll be fine, won't he?" I faced her. "Will you please send *fresh* food and water to Casteel?"

"Yes, but only because you asked nicely." The Blood Queen

flicked a glance at Callum. "Get him out of here."

A Royal Knight stepped forward.

"Not you." The Blood Queen threw a glare in Millicent's direction. "Since you find this so amusing, you can be the one who cleans it up."

"Yes, my Queen." Millicent stepped forward and gave such an elaborate bow it could only be a mockery.

The Blood Queen's lips pressed together in a thin line as she watched the Handmaiden. The interaction between the two was...different.

Isbeth turned her attention back to me, her head tilted. The light cut across her face, revealing a thin strip of slightly deeper-colored skin at her hairline. Powder. She wore some sort of powder to make her skin paler. To help her blend in with the Ascended.

"How have you kept your identity a secret from every Ascended?" I asked.

A brow arched. "Don't forget that vamprys were once mortal, Penellaphe. And while they have left many of those trappings behind, they still see only what they want to see. Because looking too closely at things often makes one uncomfortable. Unsure. Not even vamprys enjoy living like that. So, like those mortals upstairs," she said, tilting her chin up, "and in all of Solis, they'd rather be oblivious to what is right in front of them than feel doubt or fear."

There was some truth to her words. I, myself, hadn't pried too deeply. It was terrifying to start peeling back the layers, but others had the courage. "And what happens to the Ascended who *do* look closely?"

"They are dealt with," she answered. "Just as anyone else would be."

In other words, they were killed, as would be any Descenter. Disgust crowded my breath. "Why lie, though? You could pretend to be a god to the people."

The Blood Queen smiled. "Why would I need to, when they already believe I am the closest thing to one?"

"But you're not. So, why? Do you fear that they would see you as you are? Nothing more than a false god?"

Her smile didn't waver. "Mortals are easily influenced. They can be convinced of anything by nearly anyone. Take from them, then give them something or someone to blame, and even the most righteous will fall prey to that. I'd rather have them believe that all Ascended are godlike. That way, there are many instead of a few that they will not question. One person cannot rule a kingdom and keep the masses in line," she shared. "You should know that, Penellaphe."

"I know you shouldn't need to keep anyone in line or rule with lies."

Isbeth laughed softly. "That is a very optimistic way of looking at things, my child."

The patronizing tone struck every nerve in my body. "Your rule is built on nothing but lies. You told the people in the Great Hall that the cities to the north and east had fallen. Do you really think they will not learn the truth?"

"The truth doesn't matter."

"How can you believe that?" I shook my head. "The truth matters, and it will be known. I took those cities without killing innocents. Those who called those places home still do. They either know I'm not this Harbinger, or they will soon learn that—"

"And you think that will happen here? In Masadonia? Pensdurth?" Her eyes searched mine. "That you will be successful in this campaign when you, yourself, are lying?"

My hands curled into fists. "How am I lying?"

"You are the Harbinger," she said. "You just don't want to believe it."

Anger pulsed through me, quickly followed by a surge of apprehension. I looked at the long shadowy corridor, inhaling deeply. The musty scent was familiar, wiggling an old memory free.

I crept through the silent halls, where only the Royal Ascended traveled when the sun rose, drawn by what I'd seen the last time I'd snuck where the Queen told me I should not go. But I liked it down here. Ian didn't, but no one looked at me strangely here.

Click. Click. Click.

Soft light seeped from the opening of the chamber as I pressed against a cold pillar, peeking around the corner. A cage sat in the middle of the chamber that looked nothing like the rest of Wayfair. The floor, walls, and even the ceiling were a shiny black, just like the Temple of Nyktos. Strange letters had been etched into the black stone, the symbols shaped nothing like those I'd learned in my lessons. I reached one hand into the chamber, pressing my fingers against the rough carvings as I leaned around the pillar.

I shouldn't be down here. The Queen would be very mad, but I couldn't stop thinking about what prowled restlessly behind bleached-white bars, caged and…helpless. That was what I'd felt from the large, gray cave cat when I'd first seen it with Ian. Helplessness. That was what I'd felt when I could no longer hold on to Momma's slippery arm. But my gift didn't work on animals. The Queen and Priestess Janeah had said so.

The clicking of the animal's claws ceased. Ears twitched as the wild cat's big head turned to where I peeked around the corner. Bright green eyes locked on to mine, piercing the veil that covered half my face—

"Your eyes are your father's."

26

Her words pulled me from the memory. "What?"

"When he would get angry, the essence would become more visible. Sometimes, the eather would swirl through his eyes. Other times, they were just green. Yours do the same." Isbeth tipped her head back, her slender throat working on a swallow. The remaining Handmaidens and knights had backed off from us, leaving us in the center of the hall. "I didn't know if you knew that."

My eyes were…

Pressure clamped down on my chest and throat as I backed up, stopping when I bumped into a pillar. One hand fluttered to where the ring rested under my tunic. I didn't know why that piece of knowledge affected me so intensely, but it did.

It took me several moments to speak. "How did you capture him?"

Isbeth didn't answer for a long moment. "He came to me, almost two hundred years after the war had ended. He was looking for his brother, and the one who came with him could sense Malec's blood and led him to me."

"The draken?"

Tense silence followed, and in those moments, I thought about what I'd felt from the cave cat when I'd seen him as a child. Hopelessness. Desperation. Had he known who I was?

"Interesting that you'd know that," the Blood Queen finally said. "Very few know what traveled with him."

"You'd be surprised by what I know."

"Unlikely," she replied.

I lowered my hand to the cold pillar behind me. "Where is the draken?"

"The draken has been dealt with."

I briefly closed my eyes. I knew what that meant. Did she have any idea that she had killed the first draken's daughter? Probably not, and I doubted she cared.

"I knew Malec had a twin, but when I first saw him… I thought, *my gods, my Malec has finally returned to me.*" Her breath caught, and I tasted the tiniest bit of bitterness. Her emotions had briefly, for less than a heartbeat, punched through my shields. "Of course, I was wrong. The moment he spoke, I knew he wasn't Malec, but I let myself believe that for a little while. I even thought that I could fall in love with him. That I could just pretend that he *was* my Malec."

Bile crept up my throat. "You pretended by locking him in a cage and forcing yourself upon him?"

"I didn't *force* myself upon him. He chose to stay."

Gods, she was such a liar.

"He became intrigued by this world," she added. "He'd never really interacted with mortals. He was curious about the Ascended. About what his brother had been doing. I think Ires even grew to become fond of me."

"If my father showed up in the last two centuries looking for Malec, you would've been married at the time."

"So?"

My gaze flicked to where the Handmaidens stood motionless. I figured that many of the Royals had open marriages, but would Ires have grown interested in his brother's lover? Seemed kind of…gross, but that would be the least disturbing aspect of all of this.

"But then he wanted to return, and I wasn't ready to let him go." A pause. "And then I couldn't."

It took everything in me not to scream at her. She *couldn't?* As if she had no choice?

"He was angry. But when we came together to make you, he was not forced. Neither time."

A tremor ran through me. I couldn't trust myself to speak. The essence pulsed too violently.

"You don't believe me?" Isbeth asked.

"No."

"I can't blame you for that. It was not an act of love. Not on either of our parts. For me, it was necessary. I wanted a child. A strong one. I knew what you would be," she went on, and I thought I might vomit. "For him, it was just lust and hatred. Those two emotions aren't very different from one another once there's nothing but flesh between you." Another pause. "Perhaps it will please you to know that he tried to kill me afterward."

I shuddered, feeling sickened. "No," I whispered. "That doesn't please me."

"Well, that's a surprise."

The back of my throat burned, and I closed my eyes against a rush of tears. My stomach continued churning. Even if he was a…an active participant, she had already taken his freedom. There was no real consent there. And Isbeth was the worst sort on so many different levels.

"I used to wonder why it took Ires so long to look for his brother. Maybe because Ires slept so deeply. But Malec didn't die all those years ago like I believed, did he? That bitch entombed him. Now I know that he must've been conscious up to that point. Two hundred years, Penellaphe. And then he must've slipped away, as close to death as he could get for it to then wake Ires."

I opened my eyes. "You were heartmates. How did you not know he wasn't dead?"

"Because whatever Eloana did to entomb him severed that connection. The bond. You know what I'm talking about. That feeling—the *awareness* of the other," she said. And I did. It was an intangible sense of knowing. "It's like the marriage imprint but not on your flesh. In your soul. Your heart. I felt the loss of that, and a part of me died. That's why I believed he was dead and wished he was. For it took nearly two hundred years for him to lose whatever bond he shared with his twin. To become unconscious. Can you even imagine?"

"No." I thought of those deities in the crypts.

"Eloana may not have known that he was a god, but she knew what she was doing to a deity. That type of punishment is worse than death," she continued. "Your mother-in-law is not so very different than your mother."

"You're right," I said. "Except she's not nearly as homicidal as you."

The Blood Queen laughed. "No, she just murders innocent babes."

"And you haven't?" I fired back, not even bothering to tell her that Eloana had claimed to have no knowledge of Isbeth's son's death. She wouldn't believe me anyway. "Where is he?"

Her mouth tensed. "He is not here."

I stared at her, unsure that I believed that. If she had brought Ires with her when she traveled, I doubted he was far. "So, if I had chosen to see him instead of Casteel, would you have allowed it?"

"You never would've chosen anyone *but* Casteel," she replied.

Guilt churned in my stomach. "But if I had? You wouldn't have allowed it, would you?" When she didn't answer, I knew that I was right. Anger replaced the shame. "Why haven't you let him return to Iliseeum?"

"Other than the fact that he would be sure to return once he regained his strength? When he couldn't be so easily subdued?" Isbeth had drawn closer. "I need him to make my Revenants."

A ripple of understanding went through me. "You needed a god to Ascend the third sons and daughters. And you already had knowledge of Kolis's essence and how to use it, thanks to Malec."

Isbeth studied me. "I was wrong earlier. I didn't know that you would be aware of him. That is…curious."

My palm slipped on the pillar, and I turned, feeling an indentation in the stone. I shifted slightly, looking down. There were markings there, shallow and spaced every couple of feet. A circle with a slash through it, half off-center. Just like the bone and rope symbols in the woods near the Dead Bones Clan.

"What are these marks?" I asked.

"A safeguard of sorts," she answered.

I pressed my thumb against the markings. "More stolen magic?"

"*Borrowed* magic."

"How do they act as a safeguard?"

Isbeth's gaze lifted to mine, and she smiled. "They keep things in—or things out."

Casteel

Poppy was here.

I pulled harder on the chain, cursing when the hook refused to budge even a centimeter. How many times had I tried to loosen these damn chains since I'd been here? Countless. In the last couple of days, hunger had driven the frenzied attempts. Now, I was just as desperate, but for different reasons.

Poppy was here.

Panic sliced through my gut. She could take care of herself. She was a fucking goddess, but she wasn't infallible. No one was. Except for the Primal, who spent most of his time sleeping. I had no idea what the Blood Queen truly was or how Poppy was dealing with the knowledge of who Isbeth was to her. There were too many unknowns, and I needed to get out of here. I had to get to her before that red haze descended again. And it was coming. I could already feel it in the ache returning to my bones.

I struggled to ignore it. To focus on the task at hand and something Isbeth had said when she'd given me the blood. It had been a shock. Important. But it was on the fringes of my memories, existing just out of reach as I curled the chain around my forearm and pulled until my feet slid over the stone—

The sound of approaching steps stopped me. They were light. Quick. I heard them. Dropping the chain, I turned and then lowered myself to the floor, my back against the wall. I even heard blood pumping through veins before a shadow crossed the flickering candlelight. Hell. Whatever Poppy's touch had managed to do was already fading.

The Handmaiden.

Chains rattled as I leaned forward, the thunder in my chest and in my blood returning and growing louder.

She stepped into the light of another half-burnt candle. The winged mask on her face painted in black made her eyes even lighter. More lifeless.

But she had life in her.

Blood.

I could *hear* it.

Hungry, starving muscles tensed. My jaw pulsed. "Where is Poppy?"

"She was with the Queen." The Handmaiden knelt by the hip

bath, her stare not drifting far as she gripped the rim. She knew better than to take her eyes off me.

I growled.

"You don't like that, huh?" she asked, shoving the sleeves of her gown up.

I twisted my head to the side, fangs throbbing. Dread and anticipation collided with the fog of hunger. My skin tightened, pulling taut against the healed wounds. The shadowstone bands clamped down on my wrists and ankles. *Get it together. Get it the fuck together.*

It took everything in me, but the storm in my blood quieted as my chin dropped. "If…if she has been harmed, I will kill all of you." The words scratched their way through my dry throat. "I will rip your fucking throats out."

"The Queen won't touch a hair on your precious *Poppy*." She inched back, moving to the other side of the hip bath. "At least, not yet."

The sound that came from me was the promise of violent death. "She'll hurt others to hurt her."

She stared for a moment, motionless. "You're right."

My head snapped toward the cell's opening. I didn't want that monster anywhere near Poppy, and Kieran was here, too. If either of them was harmed… The shackles weighed more than ever suddenly. Water splashed, jerking my attention back to the bath. The Handmaiden had dipped her hands into the water.

The fog of impending bloodlust waited at the edges of my being as I watched her grip the sides of the tub and bend over the water. "You going to bathe?"

She glanced up at me. "You got a problem with that?"

"I don't give a fuck what you do."

"Good." She plucked up a matted curl. "I've got blood in my hair."

The Handmaiden then tipped forward. She straight-up dunked her head into the tub. The once-clear water immediately turned an inky black.

What in the hell? I stared into the gloom as the Handmaiden scrubbed her fingers through her hair, washing away what seemed to be some sort of dye, revealing a shade of blond so pale it was nearly white—

Claws scraped over stone. I tensed as a Craven let out a low-pitched shriek. The Handmaiden tossed her hair back, sending a fine mist of water across the floor as she grabbed a blade from the shaft of her boot. Spinning on her knee, she threw the weapon, striking the creature in what was left of its face as it rushed into the cell. Knocked back, the Craven fell into the hall.

"The Craven are so annoying." The Handmaiden cocked her head. Streaks of black dye ran down her cheeks, cutting through the painted mask and over her teeth as she smiled broadly. "I feel so pretty right now."

"The fuck?" I muttered, beginning to think this was some sort of bloodlust-induced hallucination.

She giggled, turning back to the hip bath. "You know the Queen won't send you food or water."

"No shit."

Shoving her hands into the tub, she splashed her face and commenced scrubbing as black dye slowly tracked down her arms. "I have something to tell you. Something very important." Her hands muffled her words. "And it will hurt your little heart."

I was barely paying attention to what she said because I was transfixed by what she was doing.

By what I saw transforming before me.

The sooty facial paint was almost all gone now, revealing her features—what she truly looked like. And I couldn't believe what my eyes were telling me.

The hair wasn't the right color, and the curls were tighter, but the face was the same oval shape. The mouth full and wide. She had the same strong brow. I saw freckles over the bridge of her nose and all over her cheeks—much more prominent and plentiful. The way she now looked back at me with a slight tilt of a stubborn jaw…

Good gods.

All of it was familiar. *Too* familiar.

The Handmaiden's smile was slow and tight. "Do I remind you of someone?"

"Gods," I rasped.

She rose, the shoulders of the simple black tunic she wore now soaked. Hair the color of silvery-white moonlight hung all the way to the multiple rows of leather encasing her waist, exaggerating hips that didn't need the aid. She was leaner, not so amply shaped, but she stood there in a way…

Disbelief flooded me. "Impossible."

Water dripped from her fingertips as she silently walked toward me. "Why do you think what you're seeing is impossible, Casteel?"

"*Why?*" A hoarse laugh parted my dry lips. There was no logical reason, other than the fact that my mind couldn't accept that this Handmaiden—this *Revenant*—was almost a mirror image of Poppy. But I couldn't deny it. There was no way she wasn't related to my Queen.

"Who are you?" I choked out.

"I'm the first daughter," she said, and shit if that wasn't another shock. "I was never meant to be. Neither was the second. But that's neither here nor there at the moment. I prefer to be called by my actual name—Millicent. Or Millie. Either works."

"Your name means brave strength," I heard myself say.

"So I'm told." *Millicent* stared down at me, once again unblinking. Eerie. "Is that all you have to say?"

Hell, no. There was a lot I had to say. Fuck. I felt like Poppy because I had a lot of questions. "You're...her sister, aren't you? Full-blooded."

"I am."

My thoughts raced. "Ires is your father, too."

She nodded.

And that also meant... "You're a goddess."

Millicent laughed darkly. "I'm no god. What I am is a failure."

"What? If your father is—"

"If you're anything like your brother, then you think you know it all," she remarked. "But, just like him, you don't know what is and isn't possible. You have no idea."

"Then tell me."

Millicent gave me another tight-lipped smile as she shook her head, sending a mist of cold water across my chest and face.

Frustration burned through me, nearly as potent as the encroaching bloodlust. "What the hell? How are you not a god?"

"Where would I even start if I answered your questions? And when would your questions stop? They wouldn't. Every answer I gave would lead to another, and before we knew it, I would have retold the entire history of the realms." Millicent blinked and then turned away, stepping over my legs. "The real history."

"I know the real history."

"No, you don't. Neither did Malik."

Air punched out of my lungs at the sound of my brother's name, momentarily stunning me. My brother... I hadn't seen him since he'd wrapped my hand. What he'd said about the Handmaiden surfaced:

"*She's had very little choice.*" "Malik knows," I bit out. "That son of a bitch knows who you are."

Millicent moved quickly, crouching by my legs. Close enough that if I kicked out, I'd take her down. She had to know that, but she remained where she was. "You have no idea what your brother has had to do. You have no—" She cut herself off with a sharp twist of her neck. "Everything the Queen does…she does for a reason. Why she took you the first time. Why she kept Malik. She needed someone from a strong Atlantian bloodline to help Penellaphe through her Ascension. To make sure she didn't fail. She lucked out when you came back into the picture, didn't she? The one she originally planned to use. And then *our* mother *waited* until Penellaphe was going through her Culling—that's happening now. And now she's waiting again for Penellaphe to complete the Culling."

"Poppy has Ascended to her godhood—"

"She hasn't completed the Culling," Millicent interrupted. "But when she does, my sister will give our mother what she's wanted since she learned that her son was dead."

"Revenge?"

"Revenge against *everyone.*" Millicent leaned in, placing a hand by my knee. Her voice dropped to a whisper. "And she doesn't want to remake the kingdoms. It's the *realms.* She wants to restore them to the way they were before the first Atlantian was created. When mortals were subservient to the gods and the Primals. And that—that will destroy not only the mortal realm but also Iliseeum."

Shock rippled through me. "And you think Poppy will help her do this?"

"She won't have a choice. My sister is destined to do just that. She is the Harbinger foretold."

"Bullshit," I snarled. "She—"

"Remember what I told you before? Our mother isn't strong enough to do such a thing. But she created *something* that was. Penellaphe."

Cold air poured into my chest. "No."

"It's the truth." Her features pinched, and I saw it for a moment before her eyes lowered. Sorrow. Deep, endless sorrow. "I wish it wasn't because I know that no matter what I do—what *anyone* does— the Queen will succeed. Because you will also fail."

I leaned as far as the chain allowed. "Fail at what?"

Millicent lifted her gaze to mine. "At killing my sister."

I jerked back against the wall, barely registering the burst of pain along my back.

"Penellaphe will complete her Culling soon." Millicent rose. "Then, her love for you will become one of the very, very few weaknesses she will have. You will be the only thing that can stop her then. If you don't, Penellaphe will help end the realms as we know them, causing millions to lose their lives, and subjecting those who survive to something far worse. Either way, my sister can't survive this. She will die in your arms, or she will drown the realms in blood."

Poppy

I paced the bedchamber the following afternoon, the meal one of the less-chatty Handmaidens had brought in devoured only because I couldn't afford to weaken.

Another white gown had been brought in with the food. Opting to wear what I had the day before, I'd destroyed the gown with a spark of eather. I shouldn't have used the essence for such a childish thing, but the momentary joy it had brought was hard to regret.

Every so often, I sent the double doors a glare. I hadn't seen or heard from the Blood Queen since they'd returned me to my chambers the evening before. I'd stayed in this damn room, only because I didn't want to risk Kieran's and Reaver's safety in addition to Casteel's.

I'd checked in with Kieran through the *notam*, letting him know that both Casteel and I were okay. He was relieved, but through the connection, I knew he had his doubts about Casteel.

I had doubts, as well.

My touch would've only brought him a few hours of relief—if that. Maybe not even that long. All I could do was pray that he'd been given blood and food. That healing those injuries had given him a longer reprieve.

I'd desperately tried to sleep. To reach Casteel. I hadn't been able to. The room was too quiet and too big. Too lonely and too familiar.

Too—

I stopped myself.

None of that would help. What would, was focusing on what came next, which was what I'd been turning over in my mind for hours. Our plan had been to get into the capital and free Casteel and my father. That was still the plan. Except we'd been technically captured, and I didn't know where my father was being kept if not here.

I would have to force Isbeth to tell me where he was when I came back for him.

I hated that—utterly *loathed* the idea of leaving Ires behind. But I had to get Casteel out, and soon.

Because he was not well.

I'd healed what injuries I could, but he was teetering on the edge of bloodlust and at risk of losing parts of himself. I couldn't allow that to happen.

Searching out Kieran's unique imprint, I found the cedar-rich sensation.

Liessa?

A wry grin tugged at my lips. *Don't call me that.*

My Queen, instead?

I sighed. *How about neither?*

His chuckle tickled its way through me. *What's going on?*

We need to get out of here.

There was a pause. *What are you thinking?*

We need to get to one of the Temples. Casteel has to be held somewhere near there. Underground. I paced by the window. *We have the spell. Once we find the entrance to the tunnels, we can use it. It's what we'd need to do next that I'm not so sure about.*

Several moments of silence passed where I felt the woodsy sensation surrounding me. *We can try the way we planned to get in.*

Through the mines?

Yes. We can try to access them. Or...

My heart thumped heavily. *They'll expect that. There must be a better way.*

Fight our way out.

I stopped at the window, staring across the capital. *I'm not sure that's a better option.*

Fighting will be our only option no matter what, Kieran reasoned. *Either through one of the gates or from inside the Rise and into the mines.*

We hashed it out, going back and forth until Kieran decided. *The quickest way is to go straight for the eastern gates. We have Reaver. We have you. We can fight.*

I worried my lower lip. *If we do that—if I do that—we risk people seeing me as a demis. We risk the people believing the worst about us and fearing what is to come.*

We do. There was another gulf of silence. *But right now, we can't worry about that. That's not our concern. Cas is. Getting the hell out of here is. And if that means taking down a part of the Rise, then we take it down, Poppy.*

I closed my eyes. The essence in my chest thrummed.

We can't save everyone, Kieran reminded me. *But we can save the ones we love.*

A jolt ran through me. I'd known when speaking with the generals that there was a chance our plans could crumble around us. That we'd need to take down the Rises. That there would be untold loss of life. That we'd become the monsters the people of Solis feared.

And that stood true now.

Kieran must've sensed my acceptance because his next words were: *We just need a distraction.*

A distraction. A big one that would give us time to make our way through Wayfair and to the Temples.

My eyes opened, and I focused on the black stone of the Rise, looming in the distance. *I have an idea.*

My patience was stretched to its limits as I sat on the thickly cushioned chair in the alcove of the main floor of the Great Hall. A dozen knights and Handmaidens lined the wall behind me.

The sun had just begun to set for the evening when the Blood Queen summoned my presence. And yet, here I sat as she *mingled.*

I scanned the packed floor, the faces of so many mortals blurring together as they chatted and vied for a few moments of *her* time. She moved among them, flanked by Millicent and another Handmaiden. Like a vibrant bird, ruby crown shining, she smiled graciously as the mortals bowed. She didn't wear white tonight. She, like Millicent, was draped in crimson.

I wasn't quite sure how the gown remained on her body. Or if the upper half was made of some sort of body paint. It was that tight and sleeveless, defying gravity. What neckline it had plunged to her navel, revealing far more than I ever wanted to see, considering—whether or not I wanted to admit it—she was my mother. The lower part of the gown was looser, but I didn't dare look too long at the gossamer fabric. I didn't need that trauma in my life.

"You look as if you're enjoying yourself."

At the sound of Malik's voice, I stiffened even more. "I'm having the time of my life."

There was a brief, rough chuckle as he brushed past my chair, sitting on one of the empty two that were on either side of me. "I'm sure you are."

I said nothing for a few moments. "I have no idea why she summoned me to the Great Hall."

"She wanted you to see how loved she is," Malik replied. "In case the display in the Great Hall wasn't sufficient."

Glancing over at him, I watched him lift a glass of red liquid to his lips. I couldn't be sure it was wine. He had spoken softly, but the knights and Handmaidens were close enough to have heard him. No one else was around. What I'd felt from him the day before preyed on my mind as I returned my attention to the floor. "Of course, they love her. They're the elite of Carsodonia. The wealthiest. As long as their lives are easy, they will love whoever sits on that throne."

"They're not the only ones. You saw that for yourself."

I had. "Only she gives Blessings with Atlantian blood." I looked at him again. He shrugged. "Something that cannot have any long-lasting effects."

He took another drink.

"And she has them afraid—"

"Of you," he spoke. "The Harbinger."

I forced a slow, even breath. "What she told the people yesterday was a lie. Those in Oak Ambler and the other cities haven't been abused. You, no matter what you think now, have to know that the Atlantians—your father—would never have done what she claimed."

Malik once more had no response.

"The people here will eventually learn the truth," I continued into the silence. "And I don't believe that every mortal in Carsodonia believes her to be a benevolent Queen. Nor do they support the Rite."

Malik lowered his glass. "You'd be right not to believe that."

I watched him closely, opening my senses to him as he stared out over the floor. The cracks were still in those shields. "I saw Casteel yesterday."

His face showed nothing, but I caught the sudden taste of sourness. Shame.

"He wasn't in good shape." I lowered my voice as I clasped the arms of the chair. "He was nearly lost to bloodlust. He'd been injured and—"

"I know." His jaw was hard, and when he spoke, his voice was barely above a whisper. "I cleaned him up the best I could after the Queen sent you such a lovely gift."

Malik had been to see him.

Casteel hadn't shared that, but there really hadn't been many opportunities for him to relay information. Someone *had* wrapped his hand. That had to mean something. That, and the raw agony I felt from Malik. What it meant exactly, I wasn't sure.

I leaned toward him, and the shoulders under the white shirt tensed. "You know how to find him, then," I whispered. "Tell me—"

"Careful, Queen of Flesh and Fire," Malik murmured with a brittle twist of his lips. "That is a very dangerous road you're embarking upon."

"I know."

His gaze slid to mine. "You don't know much if you think I will answer that question."

I tamped down the rising tide of anger. "I felt your pain. Tasted it."

A muscle began ticking in his jaw. "That was, by the way, very rude of you," he said after a moment. "And it hurt."

"You lived."

He gave a short huff of laughter. "Yeah, I lived." He took another drink. "That's what I do."

The sardonic twist of his words had me studying his features. "Why? Why are you here. With *her*? It's not because she opened your eyes to anything, let alone the truth. She's not that persuasive."

Malik said nothing as he stared ahead, but I saw his attention shift beyond the Blood Queen to the dark-haired Handmaiden. It was brief. I would've missed it if I hadn't been watching him so closely.

"It's her."

His gaze shot to mine, and then his expression slipped into a half-grin. "The Queen?"

"Millicent," I said quietly.

He laughed again, another short burst of dry sound.

I sat back. "Maybe I'll ask the Blood Queen if she thinks you're here for her or for her Handmaiden."

Slowly, Malik leaned across the small space between us. "Ask her that,"—that lone dimple appeared—"and I will wrap you in the bones of a deity and throw you into the godsdamn Stroud Sea."

"That's a bit of an excessive threat," I replied, as satisfaction surged through me. It *was* excessive. Which left very little reason as to why. He had to care. "It's the kind of reaction I'd have if you threatened Casteel."

Malik looked at me.

I smiled. "Except mine wouldn't involve deity bones or the sea. Nor would it be an empty threat."

He finished off his drink. "Noted." His gaze flicked to the floor. "She comes."

The Blood Queen approached. Malik rose. I didn't. Murmurs drifted from the floor as I stared up at her. Isbeth's features sharpened as she swept past me and lowered herself onto the chair on my other side. Only then did Malik sit. Dozens of eyes watched as Millicent remained in front of us, joined by the other Handmaidens. Their straight backs provided a rather impressive screen of privacy.

Someone handed the Blood Queen a glass of bubbling wine. She waited until the servant disappeared into the shadows before saying, "We're being watched, and they find your lack of respect toward a Queen—your behavior—to be disgraceful."

"And if they knew the truth about you? About the things you've done?" I asked, watching a young couple speak as they gazed up at the statue of what I had always assumed was Nyktos but apparently wasn't.

"I doubt that it would change much for most in this room," she noted. "But we know what they'd do if they learned who you are."

"A god and not a Harbinger."

"One and the same to many," she murmured.

I stiffened. "Perhaps, but I am willing to prove to them that they have nothing to fear from me."

"And how will you do that?"

"Well, I could start with not taking their children and using them as cattle," I replied.

"Was Tawny used as cattle?" She gestured at the crowd with a jeweled hand. "Or any number of the Lords and Ladies in Wait in attendance tonight?"

"No, they will just be turned into creatures who will then prey upon others with little remorse."

Her dark gaze slid to mine. "Or they will cull the weak from the masses."

My lip curled. "You really believe that?"

"I know that." She took a drink.

It took a lot to stop myself from knocking the crystal glass from her hand. "And the children taken during the last Rite? The ones that were hung beneath Redrock?"

"Serving the gods."

"Lies," I hissed. "And I cannot wait to see your face when all of those lies are exposed."

She grinned as she looked out over the floor. "Do you think that I will allow your armies to lay siege to the capital like I have the other cities? Cities I don't even consider a loss?" She turned her head to me. "Because they're not a loss. But what has happened in those cities will not occur here. If your armies arrive at the Rise, I will line those walls and gates with newborns. And whatever draken you have left, whatever armies still stand, will have to burn and cut through them."

I could only stare as I slowly realized that she was serious. My fingers dug into the arms of the chair as the Primal essence throbbed deeply within me. A faint tremor ran through me as I stared at the statue, but I only saw those mortals on Oak Ambler's gates and the ones beneath Redrock. Beside me, Malik stretched forward as Millicent turned slightly. The couple standing before the statue frowned as they looked down to where the freshly dropped night-blooming rose petals…vibrated.

That was me.

My anger.

I was doing that.

Briefly closing my eyes, I reined in my emotions, and it was a lot like all those times I'd worn the veil and had been brought before Duke Teerman. When I had to just stand there and take whatever he dealt. It was also a lot like closing off my senses to others. Instead, I closed myself off from *my* emotions. Only when the eather had calmed in my chest did I reopen my eyes. The petals had settled on the floor.

"Smart," the Blood Queen whispered as Malik relaxed. "I see you have learned to control that power to some extent."

I forced my grip to loosen on the chair arms. "Is that what you wanted to talk to me about? How you will slaughter more children and innocent people?"

"It will not be I who slaughters those mortals," she stated. "It will be the armies under your command who do." Her stare was intense. I felt it tracking over every inch of my face. "Or it will simply be you who does it. So, if you want to avoid that, you will make sure your armies stand down."

I cut my gaze in her direction. "Now we're going to discuss the future of the kingdoms? Do you think I will negotiate with you when this is how you plan to proceed?" The words came out of me in a rush. "I won't give you Atlantia. I won't order my armies to retreat. And I won't let you use innocent people as a shield."

Her attention shifted to the Prince. "Malik, if you don't mind, I need to speak with my daughter in private."

"Of course." Malik rose, bowing as his eyes briefly met mine. He walked down the short set of wide steps, passing Millicent as he strolled onto the floor and was immediately swamped by smiling Ladies and Lords.

"They are so very charmed by him," the Blood Queen said. "He'd have to beat them off with a stick if he wanted to."

The Handmaiden looked away from Malik, her attention traveling farther across the Great Hall.

"Do you know what has kept me alive?" she asked after a couple of moments. "Vengeance."

"That is…entirely cliché," I remarked.

Her laugh was soft and short. "Be that as it may, it is the truth. And I imagine the reason it's become so cliché is because vengeance has kept many alive during the darkest moments of their lives. Moments that last years and decades. I will have it."

"The vast majority of Atlantians had nothing to do with what was done to you or your son," I told her. "And yet, you think that controlling Atlantia will somehow give you that vengeance. It won't."

"I… I must admit something to you." The Blood Queen angled her body toward mine. The scent of roses reached me. "I never really had any intention of ruling Atlantia. I don't need the kingdom. I don't even want it. I just want to see it burn. Ended. I want to see every Atlantian dead."

Casteel

She will die in your arms…

Millicent's words kept cycling through my head. I hadn't slept since she'd been here. I couldn't stop thinking about who she was—what she'd shared. I couldn't deny that she was Poppy's sister. They looked too much alike. Hell, if the hair was the same color and Millicent had fewer freckles, they could *almost* pass as twins. And what she had said about Poppy? What she'd said I needed to do?

I growled low in my throat.

Fuck that.

Even if Poppy were powerful enough to wreak the kind of havoc Millicent had warned of, she would never do it. That kind of evil wasn't in her.

Millicent might be Poppy's sister, but I didn't trust her. And I didn't trust a damn thing that had come out of her mouth.

Footsteps echoed from in the hall, jerking my head up. Golden Boy entered. Alone. He carried no food or water with him.

"What in the hell do you want?" I snarled, my throat dry.

"I wanted to see how you were doing, Your Majesty."

"Bullshit."

He smiled, his facial paint and clothing so damn golden that he shone like a bulb of light. "You're starting to look…not so well again."

I didn't need this jackass pointing out what I already knew. Hunger gnawed at my insides, and I swore I saw his pulse thrumming in his neck.

But the Rev just stood there, staring.

"Unless you're here to tell me about the weather," I drawled, "you can show yourself the fuck out."

Callum chuckled. "Impressive."

"Me?" I smirked. "I know."

"Your arrogance," he said, and a low rumble radiated from my chest as he stepped forward. His smile widened. "You're chained to a wall, starved and filthy, unable to do anything to aid your woman, and yet you're still so arrogant."

Another growl clawed its way up my throat. "She doesn't need my aid."

"I suppose not." He touched his chest. "She stabbed me yesterday. With my own dagger."

A rough laugh left me. "That's my girl."

"You must be very proud of her." He knelt slowly. "We'll see how that changes."

"It'll never change," I swore, my jaw throbbing. "No matter what."

He studied me for a few moments. "Love. Such a strange emotion. I've seen it take the most powerful beings down," he said. Millicent's words knocked around in my head again. "I've seen it give others unbelievable strength. But out of all the many, many years I've lived, I've only seen love stop death once."

"Is that so?"

Callum nodded. "Nyktos and his Consort."

I stared at him. "You're that old?"

"I'm old enough to remember the way things used to be. Old enough to know when love is a strength or a weakness."

"Don't really care."

"You should. Because it's a weakness for you." Those pale, unblinking eyes were unsettling as hell. "You know how?"

My lips peeled back. "I bet you're going to tell me."

"You should've fed from her when you had the chance," he said. "You're going to regret not doing that."

"Wrong." I'd never regret not jeopardizing Poppy's safety. Never.

"We'll see about that, too." The Rev held my stare for a long moment and then moved.

He was quick. I jerked back at the sight of a glint of steel. There was nowhere to go. My reflexes were shit—

Pain exploded in my chest, taking with it the air in my lungs in a fiery wave. A metallic taste immediately filled my mouth. I looked down to see a dagger deep in the center of my chest and red everywhere, coursing down my stomach.

I lifted my head, biting out, "Missed my heart, dumbass."

"I know." The Rev smiled, yanking the dagger free. I grunted. "Tell me, Your Majesty. What happens to an Atlantian when there's no more blood coursing through their veins?"

The wound felt like it was on fire, but my insides were drenched in ice. My heart gave a sluggish lurch. Bloodlust. Complete and absolute. That's what happened.

"I hear it makes one as monstrous as a Craven." Rising, he lifted the dagger to his mouth and ran his tongue along the blood-soaked blade. "Good luck."

28

Poppy

I want to see every Atlantian dead.

A cold press of unease slid down my spine as I locked eyes with the Blood Queen. "Even Malik?"

"Even him." She sipped her champagne. "That doesn't mean I *will* see him dead. Or your beloved. I need you to work with me. Not against me. Killing either of them would only hinder what I want. He"—she pointed her glass toward the cluster surrounding Malik—"and his brother will survive my wrath. I have nothing against the wolven. They too may live on as they please, but the rest? They will die. Not because I blame them for what was done to me. I know they had no role in Malec's entombment or our son's death. I don't even truly blame Eloana."

"Really?" I said doubtfully.

"Don't get me wrong. I loathe that woman and have something very special planned for her, but she's not the one who allowed this to happen. I know who is truly responsible."

"Who is that?"

"Nyktos."

I drew back, stunned. "You...you blame *Nyktos*?"

"Who else would I blame? Malec wanted the heartmate trials. He called for his father. Even asleep, Nyktos would've heard him. He answered, and he refused," she told me, and another wave of disbelief crashed through me. "Because of that, Malec Ascended me. And you know what happened next. I don't just blame Eloana or Valyn. I blame Nyktos. He could've prevented all of this."

Nyktos. He really could have. But for him not to grant his son something like that after seeing what'd happened when he refused it before, and the god had died, didn't make sense. "Why would he refuse?"

"I don't know." She glanced down at her diamond ring. "If Malec knew, he never shared. But the why doesn't matter now, does it?" The skin at the corners of her mouth tensed. "Nyktos caused this."

Preventing what had happened and being the root cause were two very different things. Isbeth blamed others for everything she did. Her ability to avoid accountability was shockingly impressive.

"I don't see how you think you can actually achieve revenge against the Primal of Life," I said.

Her laugh was as light as chimes as she brushed a thick ringlet from her cheek. "Nyktos appreciates all manner of life, but he is particularly fond of the Atlantians. Their creation was a result of the heartmate trials—the product of *love*. Malec once told me his father even saw the Atlantians as his children. Their loss will deliver the kind of justice I seek."

I thought that, perhaps, she was far more out of her mind than I had previously believed. "And you think I will somehow help you kill hundreds of thousands of people? Is that what you want from me?"

"You already have."

"I have done no such thing—"

"You haven't?"

Clutching the arms of the chair, I leaned toward her. "What exactly do you think I've done or will do?"

"Your anger. Your passion. Your sense of right and wrong. Your love. Your power. All of it. At the end of the day, you are just like me. You will do what you were born to do, my dear daughter." She raised her glass to me. "You will bring death to my enemies."

All you will liberate is death.

Sucking in a sharp breath, I jerked back from her. She spoke as if I had no choice. As if this were preordained, and some words spoken eons ago outweighed my free will.

Energy pulsed in my chest, charging the air around us. Her smile didn't falter—not once as she flicked a long look around the Great Hall—a room packed with mortals. I knew then this was why she'd waited until now to tell me that she wanted to see Atlantia burn. She'd already begun to use the people as a shield.

Then again, when had she not?

But she was wrong. My anger. My sense of fairness. My love. My power. They were strengths. Not fatal flaws that would result in the deaths of untold innocents.

"You're wrong," I said, hands trembling as I grasped the arms of the chair again. "I'm not you."

"If that's what you need to tell yourself," she replied with a smile and a wink. "But if you had to cut down everyone in this room to save what you hold most dear, you would without hesitation. Just as I have."

My breath stopped. My heart stuttered. I wanted to deny what she claimed. I needed to.

But I couldn't.

And that struck every raw nerve in my body. "You may have given birth to me, but blood is the only thing we share. We're nothing alike. We never will be. You're not my mother, my friend, or my confidante," I said, watching that smile fade from her face. "All you are is a Queen whose reign is about to come to an end. That is it."

The faint glimmer of eather appeared in her eyes as her grip tightened on her glass. Her lips thinned. "I don't want to be at odds with you, daughter. Not now," she said, and the sudden bitter taste of grief pooled in my throat. "But force my hand, and I will force yours and prove just how much we are alike."

Casteel.

She was threatening Casteel.

My skin went as cold as that hollow, aching place inside me, and when I spoke again, my voice sounded like it had in Massene. Smoky. Shadowy. "I could kill you right now."

Her eyes met mine. "Then do it. Unleash that power, child. Use that rage." Eather glimmered in her eyes. "But before you do, remember that you're not sitting before an Ascended."

A short, shrill scream pierced the Great Hall, followed by the sound of shattering glass, and then silence. I twisted in the direction of the shout, stomach dropping when I saw the couple that had stood by the statues fall to their knees, blood raining from their eyes and ears— their mouths and noses. Louder, longer screams rang out as mortals scattered from the couple as they *shrank* into themselves, collapsing into nothing but skin and bones held together by silk and satin.

Malik and Millicent whipped toward us as people cried out,

moving farther away. But Isbeth…she hadn't taken her eyes off me. Not once. But she'd done that, and that kind of power was…

It was horrific.

I didn't know if I was capable of such a thing. I didn't ever want to find out.

The Blood Queen sat back, her head tilted as she studied me. "I believe you will benefit from some time alone. And then tomorrow, we will speak further." She motioned one of the knights forward. "Escort her to her chambers and make sure she remains there."

I rose as several of the knights left their stations to surround me.

There would be no tomorrow.

No more discussions.

Turning from her, I walked the edges of the alcove, my hands steadying. Instinct told me that we had run out of time. It didn't matter what she thought I'd do, nor did I believe that I could quell my temper enough to halt her hand—to stop her from senselessly harming others. Instinct also told me that Isbeth wouldn't go for Casteel immediately. She had two others to slaughter before resorting to that.

Kieran.

And Reaver.

She would do it to prove that I was as unstable and cruel as she was.

All you will liberate is death.

Though maybe she knew me better than I knew myself. Maybe the prophecy was exactly as she and others believed. Perhaps Willa was wrong, and Vikter had been sent to guard something evil. Perhaps I *was* the Harbinger.

Because if she did as she threatened, I would drown in the blood I spilled.

That meant *I* was out of time.

I searched for Kieran's imprint and sent him a quick message. *We need to make our move tonight.*

His response was immediate and full of resolve. At the entrance to the Great Hall, I looked over my shoulder, finding the Blood Queen standing beyond the alcove, the fine crystal glass still in hand as she watched me like the predator she thought she was.

I looked away, my will forming in my mind. The eather pulsed in my chest.

The glass the Blood Queen held shattered, reminding her that no afraid, submissive Maiden had sat next to her.

The moon had found its place in the sky over the city, its light drenching the rolling waters of the Stroud Sea. I stood at the window. Beyond the inner walls of Wayfair and the Temples of Nyktos and Perses, the Rise loomed.

It was the tallest Rise of them all, nearly as high as Wayfair Castle. Hundreds of torches lined the land just beyond the Rise, their flames vibrant and steady, serving as a beacon of safety and a promise of protection. They were all aflame.

A distraction.

A big one.

I thought of the mist—how it swirled around the Craven and blanketed the Skotos Mountains. It was Primal magic. An extension of their being and will. Which, I figured, meant it could be summoned.

I didn't know if this would work. I wasn't a Primal, but I was *the* Primal's descendant. His essence coursed through my veins. The draken answered my will. The Primal *notam* connected me to the wolven.

Placing my hands on the stone window's ledge, I closed my eyes and called the eather to the surface. The essence answered in an exhilarating rush as I pictured the mist in my mind, thick and cloud-like as it was in the Skotos. I saw it seeping out from the ground, growing and expanding. My skin warmed as I imagined it rolling across the hills and meadows outside the capital, thickening until it obscured everything in its path. I didn't stop there as I opened my eyes.

Silvery sparks crackled across my skin as I stared at the Rise and waited, reminded of a different night and city, a different *me* who believed in the protection of the Rise. That safety.

A flame beyond the Rise began to ripple wildly. The eather swirled through me, over me as I continued *calling* the mist forth. Summoning it. Creating it.

The flame beside the first began to dance, and then another and another until the whole mass rippled in a frenzy, spitting embers dozens of feet in every direction. The two torches at the end of the line were the first to go out, and then they all went out in quick succession, plunging the land beyond the Rise into utter darkness.

Flames sparked all along the wall. Burning arrows were lifted and fired. They arced through the night and then plummeted down, slamming into the trenches of tinder that traveled the entire length of the eastern wall. Fire erupted, casting an orange glow over the land...

And over the thick, swirling mist seeping toward the trenches. Mist that slipped under the tinder and over the flames, blanketing it until its thick weight choked the light from the fire.

Mist that any on the Rise or in the city would believe to be full of the twisted forms of the Craven.

Horns blew from the Rise, shattering the night, but I didn't stop there.

I continued calling the mist forward and I...I *felt* it answer, rushing to the foot of the Rise. It spread out along the massive structure. I heard shouts as I saw the mist climbing in my mind, billowing until it reached the battlements and towers along the Rise.

And then I saw it before me, becoming a cloudy, milky-white curtain against the night sky.

My breath caught at the sight of it. There would be no Craven in that mist. It wouldn't cause harm. That wasn't my *will*. It would only incite chaos and confusion.

It had already started as another horn blew.

The Primal mist crested the Rise in a great wave, spilling over and streaming down the sides. Distant, panicked screams rent the air as the fog poured into Carsodonia and filled the streets. The shouts of fear sounded closer and louder as the mist flooded the districts and bridges, swamping the hills and valleys until it swallowed the inner walls of Wayfair.

I stepped back from the window, lifting the hood as I turned. Sliding the strap of the satchel under my cloak and across my body, I unsheathed the wolven dagger.

It was time to fight our way out.

29

Stalking toward the door, I shut down my emotions—that sense of right and wrong. I had to do it if I had any hope of finding Casteel and escaping.

I curled my fingers around the gold handle. Eather flooded my veins and sparked from my fingers. Thin wisps of shadows streaked the silvery aura. It was slightly unnerving to see. The energy washed over the metal, *melting* the lock. Opening the door, I stepped out into the hall.

A Royal Knight turned, eyes widening in surprise above the black gaiter covering the lower half of his face. I snapped forward, thrusting the dagger above the plates of armor and through the vulnerable base of his throat. I wrenched my arm, severing the vampry's spinal column. The knight dropped as another reached for his sword.

My will formed in my mind and became reality. The black mantle draped over the knight's shoulders whipped forward and lifted, wrapping itself around his face. I dipped under his outstretched sword as he staggered back. His muffled shout ended abruptly as I shoved the dagger into his side, between the armored plates. The bloodstone chiseled through cartilage and sank deep into the vampry's heart.

The castle's walls started to tremble as the thick iron doors began lowering on the main floor. Two more knights stepped out from the hall's shallow alcoves, swords already drawn, and gaiters lowered to pool at their chins. "We have orders not to kill you," one said, stepping forward. "But that does not mean we won't hurt you."

I didn't even dignify that with a response as I prowled forward, vampry blood dripping from the tip of my dagger. My will stretched outside of me. Shadow-tinged aura spilled out. The knights lifted from the floor as if giant hands had grabbed them by their ankles, slamming them into the stone floor and then high above, against the ceiling. Stone and bone cracked, shattering beneath the armor.

Doors flung open at the end of the hall. A half-dozen knights rushed from the tower, halting as sharp screams of alarm echoed from distant parts of the castle. Some glanced behind them. Others bared their fangs, charging toward me.

All of them were in my way.

And time was precious.

I kept my emotions and thoughts locked down. I didn't think about what I must do—what I *would* do. There would be time later to dwell on the carnage I was about to unleash—and already had.

The shadowy, silvery webbing raced across the floor, climbing the walls and ceiling. It fell upon the knights, seeping inside them and finding the joints in their bones, the fibers in their muscles and organs, vital even to vamprys. There was no chance for them to do anything with the swords they'd drawn, to shout out a warning to others. Or to even scream.

I tore them apart from the inside, not allowing myself to think about how similar it was to what Isbeth had done. They collapsed into themselves, falling to the floor in piles of limp armor and empty skin.

All but one.

A Revenant was among them, standing beyond the ruined bodies. I started forward, pulling the eather back in.

His dark laugh was muffled. "Harbinger."

"Good evening."

He charged me, and I dipped low, grabbing a fallen sword from the ground. A hand grasped my shoulder through the cloak as I twisted. The Revenant jumped back, expecting me to kick, but that wasn't what I'd planned. I shot to my feet, spinning as I drew the sword through the air in a wide arc, bringing the blade across the Revenant's gaiter-covered neck, severing the spine and the head.

As the Revenant fell, I really wished there was time to see exactly how they regrew their heads, but there wasn't. I entered the stairway, leaving a hallway of death behind.

Racing down the wide, spiraling stairs of the turret, I started to count the seconds. Hopefully, my memory served me correctly, and this stairwell emptied near the kitchens and breezeways. If I were wrong, there would be a lot more space to travel…

And a lot more death.

On the third-floor landing, the door swung open, banging off the wall as Kieran walked through. Blood dotted his face and throat, but I picked up no sign of pain from him.

"You did that?" he demanded. "The mist?"

I nodded. "I didn't know if it would work."

He stared as I came down several more steps. "You summoned the mist, Poppy."

"I know."

"I know of only two things that can do that. The Craven," he said, his eyes wide, "and the Primals."

"Well, now you know of three things. Where's Reaver?" I asked, knowing that the draken would've answered my will.

"Wherever those screams were coming from," he answered, lifting the hood of his cloak.

Oh, dear.

"We need to talk about the whole mist thing later." Kieran started down the stairs. "How much time do you think we have before we're locked in?"

"Less than a minute."

"We'd better hurry then," Kieran said as a door flew open on the floor below, blown off its hinges.

My brows rose as Reaver entered the stairwell. His face and clothing weren't sprinkled with blood. They were *drenched* in it as he looked up at us from the floor below.

Kieran sighed. "Well, I'm glad that wasn't one of my shirts."

The draken smiled, revealing blood-smeared teeth. "Sorry," he replied as I sheathed the dagger. "I'm a messy eater."

I decided that was something else I would think about later as we joined him, and Kieran hastily filled him in on the plans.

"About damn time we're making a move," Reaver said. "I was beginning to wonder if we were going to move in."

I snorted at that.

"There's going to be a lot of guards," Kieran warned as we arrived at the main floor.

"I'll handle it," I said, not allowing myself to think about what that meant. If we didn't get out of the castle before it locked down, I would have to blow through walls and people—walls that protected the mortals that served within Wayfair. Maybe the knights would simply step aside. Stranger things had happened.

"And if there are Revenants?" Kieran questioned.

"Then I'll handle that," Reaver answered as I pushed open the double doors.

A wide hallway greeted us, filled with the lingering scent of tonight's supper. I turned to my left, relieved when I saw the darkness beyond the doors to the breezeways. The relief was short-lived. The heavy iron door had rocked into place, beginning to lower.

Kieran was right. Two-dozen or so knights packed the crimson-bannered hall. So did servants. They stood among the knights, clutching baskets and platters of empty dishes, their fear evident in their expressions and scratching against my shields. I wasn't sure if it was the mist at the walls of the Rise, the knights, or…Reaver's blood-drenched face. But there was no sign of any Revenants.

Where were they?

The knights knew immediately who we were, even with Kieran's and my faces hidden. Any hope I had that they might step aside was quickly squashed as one of the knights lurched forward, grabbing a young servant boy. Dishes toppled from the tray, shattering on the floor as the knight jerked the boy back, folding a curved blade across the boy's neck. Several other knights did the same, grabbing the no-longer-frozen servants. They hauled the panicked mortals forward, and it reminded me of yet another night—one that had taken place in New Haven.

My insides went cold.

"Take another step toward us—" a knight began, holding the trembling boy in place. Tears tracked the servant's cheeks, but he made no sound. "And we'll kill them. All of them. Then we'll kill the wolven and whatever the hell that other thing is with you."

"I'd be offended by that statement," Reaver remarked, "if what was left of your souls wasn't about to be ushered into the waiting Abyss."

I inhaled deeply, and the essence of the Primal god joined with my will. The shadow-tinged, silver webbing attacked the weapons first, crushing the blades on daggers, knives, and swords.

Still no Revenants among them.

"The shadows are back," Kieran noted under his breath.

"I know." I went after the knights next, breaking them apart until nothing remained of them but crumpled heaps. Within a few heartbeats, only the servants stood before us. They did not move nor speak a word as we moved past them, but their fear…it had amplified and grown, crashing through my shields, and settling heavily in my chest.

The knowledge that I had frightened them, that they stared at me, believing me to be exactly what Isbeth had warned the people of—the Harbinger—weighed on me. That terror followed me out onto the mist-blanketed breezeways, into the heavily floral-scented air. The rose gardens were near. Heart thumping, I turned as an iron door rattled into place, sealing up those inside the castle. I stared at the doors. Many of the Ascended were in there. *She* was in there with all the death we had left behind.

"This way," Kieran spoke, stepping out from the breezeway and into the thick mist.

My throat dried as the lights above went out, plunging the breezeway into darkness. I pulled my attention from Wayfair, and my thoughts from what I'd done inside.

Only Casteel mattered right now, and we still needed to get past the inner Rise and to one of the Temples.

We took off for the gate facing the city, running past the vine-covered walls of the garden—a place I'd spent many days in as a child. It beckoned like a nightmare now, but another haunt emerged before us. "I have no idea how long it will take for the mist to dissipate," I warned them.

"It's not windy, so I imagine it will linger for a bit," Kieran said. "Hopefully, long enough for us to find Cas and get to the gates."

"I don't think we'll get that lucky," Reaver said. "We would've if you'd used the mist for anything other than confusing people."

"I didn't want to harm anyone," I told him.

"And that is why we have to rely on luck," he replied.

Royal Knights stood at the gates between Wayfair Castle and the homes occupied by the wealthiest of Carsodonia. We slowed, knowing the mist only cloaked us momentarily.

We were free of the castle, but it would take the Blood Crown no amount of time to realize that we were missing, and that there was nothing in the unnatural mist. Then, the entire city would be full of knights and more.

I stepped ahead, but Kieran caught my hand. "If you keep using the essence, you're going to weaken," he reminded me. "And Cas will need to feed soon. You need to conserve your energy."

My muscles locked tight as I fought the urge to tap into the eather and make quick work of what lay ahead. "You're right."

"I know." He squeezed my hand. "But I appreciate you actually admitting it."

"Shut up," I muttered, slipping my dagger free. "Doesn't mean I can't fight."

"No." Kieran's grip tightened once more, and then he let go. "It doesn't."

Anticipation tightened my muscles as the Royal Knights sensed us seconds before we left the darkness and neared the torch-lit gates.

Reaver launched out of the night, a blur of crimson and sun as he streaked across the fire-lit ground. He grabbed the closest knight...

I quickly learned exactly how he'd gotten so bloody, and I sort of wished I hadn't.

He grabbed the front of the knight's gaiter, yanking it down as he opened his mouth—his wide and gaping mouth full of teeth that no longer remotely resembled a mortal's. His head snapped down, and he tore into the knight's throat—into tissue and muscle. Tore straight through bone. Blood geysered as Reaver bit through the knight's godsdamn spine. My mouth wanted to drop open, except I might've vomited if I had allowed it.

"Remind me to stop antagonizing him," Kieran murmured.

"Uh-huh."

Reaver tossed the knight aside and then sprang into the air, landing several feet ahead in a crouch as one of the knights stalked forward, face free of cloth and smirking. The scent of stale lilacs rose.

"Revenant," I warned.

"Fun times are over," the Revenant said, lifting a heavy broadsword.

"Wrong." Reaver rose. "Fun times have just begun." He exhaled.

I stumbled to the side, bumping into Kieran as a powerful stream of silver flames poured out of Reaver's mouth. It hit the Revenant, and then he turned, striking two knights. They went up in flames. Screaming, they flailed about, managing to catch another knight on fire in the process.

Laughing, Reaver turned and caught a knight's arm before he could make use of his sword. The draken twisted sharply, cracking bone. The knight's howl of pain stopped abruptly as Reaver went for his throat.

He yanked his head back and turned to us, spitting out a mouthful of blood. "Are you two just going to stand there?"

"Maybe," Kieran murmured as Reaver dropped the knight.

I came out of whatever stunned stupor I was in as several knights charged us. Everything was happening so fast, there was no time to determine who was and wasn't a Revenant. I shot forward, grasping a knight's sword arm. Twisting hard, I spun around, using his weight and momentum against him. The cloak whipped around my legs as I turned and flipped the knight onto his back.

Kieran was there suddenly, bringing a dagger down on the fallen knight's arm, piercing straight through. Dipping down, I picked up the fallen bloodstone sword. Sheathing my dagger, I rose as a knight swung his sword straight for my head.

I met the blow, the impact jarring. The knight's black cloth gaiter muffled his growl as I kicked out, catching him low—between the legs. He howled, losing his balance. I swung, bringing the sword across his throat. Blood sprayed my cheeks as Kieran let out a grunt of pain. Heart lurching, I whirled around.

A knight had pierced Kieran's shoulder with his sword. He caught the knight's arm, stopping him from thrusting the blade any deeper. I started toward them—

A stream of silvery flames rippled through the air, slamming into the knight. The man screamed, dropping the sword as he staggered away, swept up in the unnatural fire.

"Are you okay?" I asked, reaching for Kieran.

He caught my hand. "I'm fine. Barely a flesh wound."

I opened my senses to him, feeling the hot, stinging pain. It may be just a small wound, but it *was* hurting him. "I can heal it—"

"Later," he insisted. "We need to find Cas. That's the only thing that matters." He cocked his head toward Reaver. "Thanks, man."

"Whatever," the draken replied, stalking forward. "I don't want the *Liessa* to be upset."

The tension around Kieran's mouth loosened into a half-grin as he followed the draken, his hand still wrapped firmly around mine.

"Casteel isn't the only one that matters," I told him as we hurried along under the canopy of jacaranda trees. "So do you, Kieran."

The heavily blossomed branches and the mist were too thick for the moonlight to penetrate, but I felt his stare as I channeled energy into him. As the three of us passed the stately manors that had gone completely dark and quiet as tombs, I healed his wound. Only when I could no longer feel his pain did I pull my hand free. He held on for a moment and then let go.

We came upon the final interior wall and gate, the section guarded by Rise Guards. Only half a dozen were on the ground as most traveled the battlements on the outer Rise surrounding the city.

An arrow zinged through the mist, fired from ground level. Reaver's hand snapped out, catching the shaft of the projectile. He turned his head toward the guards, his blue eyes luminous as his pupils became thin, black slits.

"Seriously?" Reaver held the arrow before him and blew out a breath—a smoky breath that sparked and then quickly ignited. A narrow trail of silver flames parted the mist, obliterating the projectile. "Who's next?"

The guards scrambled into the fog, dropping their weapons and leaving their horses behind.

"Clever mortals," Reaver remarked.

"Now, why couldn't the knights have done that?" I asked.

"Because we don't threaten the mortals' food source." The draken prowled forward, eyeing the guards who had shrunk against the wall as if they were attempting to become one with it. "I'm watching you. All of you. Keep being clever and you'll survive this night."

None of them moved as Kieran eyed the horses. "We should stay on foot," I advised as we entered the road skirting the walled fort known as Eastfall. "Everyone will be heading inside. The horses will draw attention as the mist starts to fade."

"Good call." Kieran kept a watchful eye on the walled fort. "Where should we go?"

I scanned the mist-covered road ahead. "If Carsodonia is anything like Oak Ambler, there has to be an entrance to the tunnel system."

"Agreed," Kieran said. "Do you know which one is closest?"

"I think the Temple of Nyktos is. We should start there."

"The Shadow Temple," Reaver said, looking up.

I glanced at Reaver. "The what?"

"That's what the Temple was originally known as when this kingdom was called Lasania. The Sun represented the Primal of Life, and the Shadow represented the Primal of Death," he said.

I had no idea that those Temples were *that* old. Then again, I couldn't remember if my parents had ever taken Ian and me to them before we left Carsodonia. I hadn't been allowed to enter either place of worship when under the Blood Queen's guardianship.

I'd never been allowed to leave the castle grounds.

"The one you called the Shadow Temple," I asked, "is it in the area of the Garden District ne—?"

"Sits at the edge of a neighborhood known as the Luxe," Reaver finished for me.

I shot him a frown. "Yeah."

Reaver cleared a bit of the blood from his face with a swipe of his forearm. "I think I remember how to get there."

"How familiar are you with Carsodonia?" I'd lived here for years and a much shorter time ago than Reaver. When he spoke of Lasania and Iliseeum, he'd made it sound as if he hadn't been in either very long.

"Familiar enough to remember the way," he replied, and that was all he said, leaving just *how* familiar he was a mystery. We picked up our pace and steered clear of Eastfall. The dormitories were silent. Those training there had most likely been sent to the wall or beyond to deal with what they believed was a Craven attack.

I tossed the sword aside as we reached the outskirts of the Luxe— a neighborhood I remembered being known for its lavish rooftop gatherings and hidden dens I wasn't supposed to know about. Reaver led us straight into one of the vine-covered passageways that Ian used to talk about. He'd been allowed to leave Wayfair and explore them when we were younger, so I only ever heard of the trellised tunnels that snaked throughout the entirety of the Garden District, leading to anywhere you wanted to go.

The distant sound of a shrill scream shattered the eerie silence of the city. The kind only one creature could make.

A *Craven*.

"Gods," I whispered. "The mist. It must have beckoned the Craven from the Blood Forest. I didn't…"

I hadn't thought of that.

"Luck is on our side then," Kieran said from behind me as we followed Reaver through a tunnel heavy with sweet pea blossoms. "This will keep them occupied."

"Agreed," Reaver chimed in.

They were right. But where the Craven were, death awaited. I clamped my jaw shut. I hadn't wanted that, but death…

She was an old friend, as Casteel had once said.

"Don't think about it." Kieran's hand curved over my shoulder. "We're doing what we have to."

It was almost impossible not to think about the consequences. What if the Craven managed to get over the Rise here like they had tried before in Masadonia? The Rise had never failed, but as far as I knew, a Primal mist had never swamped Carsodonia before, either.

Reaver's steps slowed as we cleared the sweetly scented passageway, and I saw that not even the Primal mist dared to cloak Nyktos' Temple. It was the only thing visible.

The Temple sat in the foothills of the Cliffs of Sorrow and behind a thick stone wall that encircled the entire structure. The street was empty as we crossed it and passed through the open gate, trekking across a courtyard constructed of shadowstone. I couldn't suppress a shudder as I looked up at the twisting spires that stretched nearly as high as the cliffs, the slender turrets, and sleek, pitch-black walls. At night, the polished shadowstone seemed to lure the stars from the sky, capturing them in the obsidian stone. The entire Temple glittered as if a hundred candles had been lit and placed throughout.

We climbed the wide steps, crossing between two thick pillars. The doors were open wide, leading to a long, narrow corridor.

"If this Temple is anything like the one in Oak Ambler, the underground entrance would likely be behind the main chamber," Kieran said.

"There could be Priests and Priestesses," I reminded them as we strode forward.

"How should we handle them?" Kieran asked.

"Burn them?"

I shot Reaver a look. "If they don't stand in the way, then leave them be."

"Boring," he replied.

"They could warn others that we're here," Kieran pointed out. "We don't have to kill them, but we will need to keep them silent."

I nodded as we walked toward the cella—the main chamber of the Temple. Moonlight streamed in through the glass ceiling, streaking the jet floors in soft light. No Priests or Priestesses could be seen. Only a few dozen of the hundreds of candelabras staggered along the walls were lit. There were no pews or benches for worshipers to gather. There was just the dais and what sat upon the raised platform.

I'd never seen such a throne before.

Carved from shadowstone, it was larger than the thrones in both Evaemon and here. Massive. Moonlight caressed the chair, glinting off the back carved to resemble a crescent moon—just like the throne had been in Wayfair.

"Did Nyktos ever sit upon this throne?" I whispered.

"Only for a brief time." Reaver strode forward.

I crossed into the cella. "Why is there only one—?"

The unlit candles roared to life, casting bright, silvery-white light throughout the cella. Hair rose on the nape of my neck and under my hood as I looked around.

Kieran halted behind me. "That was...odd."

"It's her." Reaver continued on, heading for the right side of the dais.

"Me?"

"You carry the blood of the Primal in you," he said. "And you're in the Primal's Temple. It's reacting to your presence. The essence left here."

All of that sounded silly, except there *was* an energy to the cella, one that coated the very air I breathed and crackled over my skin. The eather in my chest hummed.

"You're so very special." Kieran gave me a half-grin as we edged around the dais.

"Very," Reaver said dryly.

I glared at the draken's back. "Neither of you sound like you think that at all."

"*So* special," Kieran added.

I rolled my eyes as we passed a colonnade. I saw several doors, all closed. Ten of them in all. Frustration burned through me as I scanned the area. "You wouldn't happen to know which door we should try, would you?"

"No." Reaver stopped. "That spell? You think it will work from here?"

I wasn't sure. I'd wanted to use it once we were underground, but Lord Sven had said that the spell would remain in place until the missing object—or person—was found. Plus, the last thing we needed was to start randomly opening doors and potentially coming face-to-face with the Priests and Priestesses that had to be here somewhere. We would have to try it and hope for the best.

"I can do it here." I reached for the satchel, hoping that I was right about there being access to the tunnels beneath the Temples. "I just need—"

Reaver spun suddenly, at the same moment Kieran did. They'd heard the silent steps before I did. I turned, reaching for the dagger as a hooded figure appeared in the shadows between the columns. He blended in so well, I almost didn't see him at first.

Kieran lifted his sword, and my heart kicked in my chest. That figure, the height and the shape and the voice.

"No need to use that sword," the hooded figure advised, the voice sending a jolt of recognition through me. *Malik.* But it was something else...

"We're going to have to agree to disagree on that," Kieran growled.

"I can't blame you for thinking that." Hands rose, lifting the hood back. Bright amber eyes flickered over the three of us. "I saw you all making a rather hasty exit from Wayfair and running into the mist—leaving quite the mess behind."

Kieran's chin had lowered, his hold on the sword steady. "Is that so?"

Malik nodded, keeping his hands visible and at his sides. "Thought I should give you all a follow. I'm the only one. For now. It won't be long before your absence is noted." He paused. "I know why you're here."

"Congratulations," Kieran snapped. "All that means is you're an inconvenience I'm only a little conflicted about handling."

The Prince's gaze shifted to mine. "You asked me earlier if I knew how to get to Cas. I do," he said, and my senses stretched out to him. There were no shields. Nutty resolve gathered in my throat. "That's why I'm here. I'll take you to him, and then you all need to get the hell out of the city."

"Yeah," Reaver drawled as Kieran glanced at me. "How convenient of you to show up and be so helpful."

"Not convenience. Just a huge-ass risk." Malik's gaze didn't leave me. "You can sense my emotions. You can tell I'm not here to trick you."

"What I can feel doesn't determine if you're lying. Especially if you're purposely hiding your emotions under the guise of another."

"I'm not." He stepped forward, stopping when Kieran lifted the sword higher, pointing it at Malik's chest. A muscle throbbed in his temple. "I aided Cas after she sent that *gift* to you. Did my best to get rid of the infection his body couldn't fight. Whether any of you want to believe it or not, I don't want my brother here. I don't want him anywhere near here. You need to trust me on that."

"Trust you?" Kieran's laugh was harsh.

"We don't have time for this," Reaver argued. "Either kill him or make sure he can't betray us."

Malik's eyes flared brightly. "It's her. You're right. I'm here because of her."

I tasted tangy, almost bitter anguish again. It was powerful, but what cut through it was sweet, reminding me of chocolate and berries.

I inhaled sharply. "Millicent."

Kieran frowned. "The Handmaiden?"

He nodded. "Nearly everything—" Malik's voice roughened. "Nearly everything I've done is for her. She's my heartmate."

My mouth dropped open. I hadn't been expecting *that*.

"What in the actual fuck?" Kieran muttered, his sword lowering an inch. "The Handmaiden? The *Revenant*? The really weird, possibly insane—"

"Careful." Malik's head cut sharply toward Kieran as anger pulsed through him. "Remember when I said you shouldn't get involved with Elashya? That doing so would end only in heartache?"

"Yeah, I remember." Kieran's skin seemed to thin. "I told you if you brought that up again, I'd rip your fucking throat out."

"Exactly." Malik's smile was loose, but the acidic burn I felt promised violence. "I still love you like a brother. You probably don't believe that, but make no mistake, if you say one more negative thing about Millicent, I'll rip *your* fucking throat out."

My brows rose.

"This is all heartwarming and shit," Reaver hissed, "but we seriously do not have time for this."

"You stayed because of her," I said.

Malik shuddered. "I've done many unimaginable things for her. Things she will *never* have any knowledge of."

Making up my mind, I stepped forward. "I believe you. That doesn't mean I trust you. Show us where Casteel is. But if you betray us, I will kill you myself."

30

Malik had led us past the row of doors and farther into the depths of the Temple. The entry point was a door we never would've thought to open—one that led to a pantry that hid a false wall.

The entrance to the underground chamber was narrow and appeared as old as the Temple, the steps crumbling under our weight. It dumped into a hall that fed into numerous pathways, and we didn't walk more than ten feet before taking a left or a right.

I had no idea how anyone could remember this path, but I knew one thing for sure—the spell may have worked down here, but we never would've found our way back out without blowing through the ceiling and into the gods only knew what. Because there was no way we were still under the Temple.

We all kept our eyes on Malik. Kieran's distrust of his former brethren was as strong as his reluctant need to believe that Malik hadn't forsaken his family and his kingdom for the Blood Crown. He was fighting it. I could taste and see that every time my attention shifted back to the Prince from wherever he was leading us. There was anger in the set of his jaw. Hope in how his chest rose sharply. Disappointment in the narrowing of his eyes. Uncertainty in the glances he sent me, ones that mirrored mine. Had we made a mistake? If we hadn't, did the reason Malik remained with the Blood Crown justify any and all of the things he'd done?

"Why didn't you help Casteel escape?" I asked. "You could've at any point."

"You've seen what kind of shape he's in. He wouldn't have made it far," Malik answered through clenched teeth. "His disappearance would've been noticed quickly, too. They would've caught him, and that wouldn't have ended well for Cas."

"You could've gotten him out of the city and to us," Kieran challenged.

"I won't leave her here," Malik said without hesitation. "Not even for Cas."

Kieran's conflict grew, but mine lessened. Because I could understand that. I'd chosen to save Casteel over my father before I even left for Carsodonia.

"How much longer?" Reaver demanded.

"Not very much," Malik assured. "But we need to hurry. I ran into Callum minutes before the horns blared, and he hightailed his ass to Isbeth. We got into it," he said, and I noticed his knuckles then. They were red, the skin angry and ripped but already healing. He'd definitely been in a fight. "Callum was…"

"He was what?" I asked.

Malik glanced at me. "He was just saying some shit about Cas. He's always saying shit. Still, I got a bad feeling. I was going to check on Cas myself when the mist hit the city, and I saw you all."

"Do you think he did something?" A cold wind of worry swept through me.

"Anything is possible with that fucker."

Dread built. Everything looked the same as ten steps back. I began to fear that we'd been played, and I would have to kill Malik in this underground maze.

We rounded a corner, and the scent of musty decay reached us. Damp, torch-lit walls came into view, as well as a long, straight hall with just one cell to the left. A deep, awful growl rumbled from within.

A frayed sort of sound left me. I picked up my pace and then broke into a run, passing Malik.

"Poppy," Kieran shouted as I rushed through the opening—

Jerking back, I choked on a scream as the *creature* chained to the wall lunged forward, its arms outstretched. Shock seized me. My feet slipped out from under me, and I went down hard on my ass, not even feeling the impact of the fall.

I barely recognized *him*.

His skin was ghastly pale, almost like a Craven's. The striking lines and planes of his face were contorted, lips peeled back, and fangs thicker and longer than I'd ever seen. His eyes... Good gods, they were pitch-black—not a hint of amber visible. And his chest...

A jagged hole mangled the center of his torso, just below his heart. Blood covered his stomach. The floor. I realized it was what had caused me to slip.

"Oh, gods," I gasped, my heart cracking open.

Casteel snapped at the air, the chains groaning as he pulled them taut. The shadowstone band cut into his throat, but it didn't stop him from swiping at me and snarling.

"No." Kieran grasped my shoulders, hauling me clear as his agony pummeled my senses. He stared at the man who was more than just a friend to him. "*No.*"

My senses opened, reaching out to Casteel as Kieran lifted me to my feet. I came into contact with no wall. No anger or pain. Not even a hint of anguish. There was nothing but a yawning, crimson void of insidious, unending hunger.

No sign of Casteel remained in the thick, red haze of bloodlust.

"He wasn't like this yesterday." I shuddered. "That wound—"

"Callum," Malik snarled, entering the cell. He stuck close to the wall as Casteel whipped to the side, tracking his brother's movements. His bloodied chest vibrated with sound. "He did this."

Fury exploded, stirring up the Primal essence. "I want him dead."

"Noted," Reaver said from the entrance.

"We need to get him calm." I started to move closer. "Then we—"

Kieran's arm came around my waist, pulling me tight to his chest. "There is no way you're getting close to him."

Casteel's attention snapped in our direction. His head tilted as he snarled.

"He's...he's too far gone," Kieran said, his voice hoarse.

My heart stuttered to a painful stop. "No. He's not. He can't be." I rubbed the blood off my palm. The golden swirl was dim in the fading candlelight. "He's still alive."

"But he's in bloodlust, Poppy." Kieran's voice was loaded with broken shards of pain. "He doesn't recognize you."

Casteel snapped forward again. The chain jerked him back sharply. I cried out as he staggered and went down on one knee.

"That is not Cas," Kieran whispered, shaking.

Those four words threatened to destroy me. "But we can get him back. He just needs to feed. I'll be fine. He can't kill me." I pulled at Kieran's arm. When he didn't let go, I twisted toward him, our faces inches apart. "Kieran—"

"I know." Kieran clasped the back of my neck, pulling my forehead to his. "He needs to feed, but he doesn't recognize you, Poppy," he repeated. "He will *hurt* you. I can't stand here and allow that. I don't want to see that happen to you. I don't want to see how it will fucking destroy him when he comes out of the bloodlust and realizes what he's done."

Another shudder hit me. "But I need to help him—"

"What my brother needs is to feed and have the time for that to pull him out of bloodlust. He may need multiple feedings. Something we don't have the time for here," Malik said, shoving shorter strands of hair back from his face. "We need to get him out of here. Someplace safe where we have time." A muscle throbbed in his temple as he stared at his brother. "I know of a place. If we can get him there, we'll be good for at least a day or two."

"Are you serious?" Kieran exploded as Casteel's head whipped around. "You expect us to trust you?"

Malik's lips thinned. "You don't have much choice, do you?"

"Literally walking out of here and into the arms of that bitch Queen is a better choice," Kieran spat.

"Come on, man. You know we can't feed him here. You know he needs time." Malik's eyes were as bright as citrine jewels as he faced off with Kieran. "If we try to do that here, we're going to get caught, and all of us—yes, *all* of us—are going to wish we were dead."

That couldn't happen. "How do we get him out of here?"

"You really want to risk this?" Kieran demanded. "With him?"

"How long does it take to recover from bloodlust?" I asked instead of answering. "How long before the person can become enough of themselves again?"

Kieran sucked in air, but no words came out. Looking away, he dragged his hand over his face.

"We don't have a choice," I said, softening my voice. "Malik knows that. I know that. You do, too. So, how do we get him out of here?"

Kieran's hand fell to his side. "We'll have to knock him out."

My throat dried. "We have to hurt him?"

"It's the only way." Kieran shook his head. "And then hope he stays unconscious long enough."

Heart hurting, I turned back to Casteel. He thrashed, reaching for me. I saw nothing of him in his face. His eyes. "I...I don't know if I can do it without hurting him more. I've never used the essence for something like that, and I—"

"I can do it," Malik said. "Kieran, I'm going to need you to distract him long enough for me to get behind him."

Kieran gave a sharp nod and then made his move, stepping around me. A second later, Malik rushed under the chain. Casteel whipped around, but Malik was already behind him. He folded an arm around Casteel's throat, clamping down on his windpipe with what I knew was likely one squeeze away from crushing that cartilage.

Casteel threw himself back, knocking Malik into the wall, but Malik held on, squeezing and squeezing as Casteel clawed at his arms, at the air—

I wanted to look away. I wanted to close my eyes and scream, but I forced myself to see this. To watch until Casteel's movement became sluggish and blurred and he finally went limp in Malik's arms.

It took minutes.

Minutes I knew would haunt me.

"Gods," Malik grunted, gently laying Casteel down. He looked over his shoulder at the wall. "The chains? They're in there pretty well."

"Reaver?" I rasped. "Can you break them?"

The draken strode forward, kneeling near the wall. He looked over at us. "I would suggest leaving the chains on him until we know he's calm."

"No." I stepped forward. "I want the chains off."

"I want them off, too," Kieran said. "But we'll probably need them when he wakes up."

"Yeah," Malik agreed. "The last thing we need is for him to get away from us."

I hated this. Hated all of it. "Can we get the shackles off his ankles and neck, at least?"

Malik nodded, looking down at his brother. "We can do that," he said, his voice thick.

Reaver leaned down, his mouth opening as Kieran turned me away.

"Good gods," I heard Malik rasp as silvery flames lit the dark walls. "You're a fucking draken." There was a beat of silence. "That's why those knights were smoldering."

Kieran's gaze met mine as I heard a heavy chain fall, clanging off the stone. Silently, he lifted his hands to my cheeks. Another chain hit the floor. I flinched. Kieran swept his thumbs across my cheeks, wiping away tears. A third chain clattered, and Kieran's eyes went beyond me. A few moments later, he nodded and let go. I turned to see Reaver carefully placing the bone chains still attached to the shackles on Casteel's wrists on his too-still chest.

I looked down at my palm. The golden imprint shimmered faintly in the shadowy cell. *He's alive.* I kept telling myself that. *He's alive.*

Kieran went to Casteel's side. "I'll carry him."

"No," Malik bit out. "He's my brother. And if you want him, you're going to have to pry him from my dead fingers. I'm carrying him."

Kieran looked as if he wished to do just that, but he relented. "Then where are we going?"

Malik strode forward. "To a friend's."

I followed him out of the cell, stopping long enough to place my hand on the stone. The essence roared through me as I brought the ceiling of the cell down.

No one would ever be kept there again.

We followed Malik through a winding maze of halls and tunnels until he turned into a narrow, cramped passageway that smelled of damp soil and sewage. I knew we were near ground level.

The opening ahead looked to be what remained of a brick wall. It had half collapsed, leaving an opening wide enough to squeeze through. I followed close behind Malik, my attention never straying far from Casteel. He hadn't stirred once under Kieran's cloak, which had been draped over him, hiding his body and the chains.

There was no time to stop and heal Casteel's wound, something that cut at me with each step we took. But that kind of wound wouldn't only take a few seconds to close, and we ran the risk of waking him during the process.

"What were you all planning to do when you found Cas?" Malik asked as I wiggled through the opening, the rough edges of the bricks snagging my cloak. "Fight your way out the main gates?"

Silence greeted him as I straightened, looking around. The mist was still heavy here but not nearly as thick.

"That's exactly what you all were going to do." Malik cursed under his breath. "Do you think you really would've made it out? Even if the Craven hadn't joined in the fun?"

"What do you think?" Kieran joined us outside, followed by Reaver.

"What I think is that you all would've been caught down there. And even if Cas weren't in the shape he was, Isbeth would've done exactly as she threatened to do once she realized that you were missing."

"She threatened to put children on the walls and the gates of the Rise," I answered, feeling Kieran's gaze on me as I turned around, looking up. Above, the mist muted the glow of the streetlamps, but I could see enough to realize where we were. "The Golden Bridge."

"Yes." Malik started up the slope of the embankment, his hooded figure nearly disappearing into the mist. The ground was muddy and full of a slop I didn't want to think about. "The tunnel entrance caved in there a few years ago. The Craven have been getting out from there, but no one's fixed it."

"Out?" Kieran questioned as several rounds of fiery arrows lit up the sky beyond the Rise. I tore my gaze from there.

"What do you think happens to the mortals the vamprys get a bit gluttonous with? Can't let them turn in their homes," Malik said as we cleared the embankment and continued on through the thick, still-swirling mist. "They're dumped underground where they turn. Sometimes, they get out, you know, when the gods are angry. Of course, a sizable tithe to the Temples helps assuage that anger enough for the Craven to be dealt with."

My eyes narrowed on Malik's back. "And you're okay with that? Innocent people being turned into monsters? Money being taken from people who can't afford it?"

"Never said I was okay with any of it," Malik replied.

"But you're here." Reaver scanned the mist and the empty street. "Accepting it all for a female?"

"Never said I accepted it either."

Nothing was said after that for a long time, but Kieran seemed to watch Malik even closer. We walked what I knew was the very outskirts of the cramped district of Croft's Cross, even though I couldn't see any of the buildings stacked on top of one another in staggering, clustered rows. It was the smell of the sea and the scent of too many people forced to live in a too-small place that tipped me off.

The mist was fading over the edges of the district near the sea. I saw more of the moonlight-kissed waters, but orders were still being shouted from the Rise, arrows still being lobbed. No horn had blown again, alerting the citizens that it was safe.

The mist was damper here, closer to the ocean, and a fine sheen of sweat dotted my brow beneath the hood. The slender streets of what seemed to be shops and homes appeared empty and silent through the mist. Not even our footsteps could be heard as we cut between two one-story buildings and began climbing the steep path—an earthen pass through birch trees.

"Who is this friend?" Kieran broke the silence. "And where in the hell are we walking? Atlantia?"

"Stonehill," I answered as Malik snorted. "Aren't we?"

"We are."

Stonehill was a district somewhere between Croft's Cross and the Stroud Sea, where those who had a little coin but not a lot called home. Usually, there was one family per home and little space between the normally one-story houses with terracotta roofs used for patios.

"And this friend?" Kieran persisted as we found our way onto another uneven sidewalk.

"Someone who can be trusted," Malik answered as we came upon a stucco home with no courtyard and a door leading right onto the sidewalk. I was able to see that it was dark beyond the two latticed windows on either side of the door. "His name is Blaz. Wife's name is Clariza."

"And how do you know them?" I asked as he hit the bottom of the door with his booted foot. "Why should we trust them?"

"I met Clariza one night in Lower Town when she and her friends were smuggling barrels from a ship that'd come in from the Vodina Isles. Barrels that smelled suspiciously of black powder," he answered, kicking the door again and stirring up the mist. "You should trust them because those barrels did, in fact, carry black powder that they plan to use to blow up the inner walls of Wayfair."

Reaver slowly looked at him. "What the fuck?"

Descenters. They had to be Descenters. But how was Malik involved?

"And you should also know," Malik continued, "that they do not believe you to be a Harbinger of doom."

Well, that was good. "And you? Do you believe that?"

Malik said nothing.

The door cracked open just then, revealing a sliver of a tan cheek and one brown eye. That eye lifted to the shadowy recesses of Malik's hood, dropped to the cloaked body in his arms, and then darted to where we stood. The eye narrowed. "Do I even want to know?"

"Probably not at first," Malik responded in a voice barely above a whisper. "But, yeah, you will once you know who I have in my arms and who stands with me."

Wariness radiated from Kieran, tasting of vinegar as he crowded Malik's back.

"Who's in your arms?" the man I could only assume was Blaz demanded in an equally low voice.

I didn't think Malik would answer.

He did.

"The King of Atlantia."

My mouth dropped open as Blaz uttered, "Bullshit."

"And I have his wife with me," Malik continued. I thought for a moment that Reaver might actually eat him. "You know, *the* Queen."

"Double bullshit," Blaz replied.

Sighing, Malik looked over his shoulder to where I stood. "Show him."

"Yeah." The eye narrowed even further. "Show me and then tell me what my good man here was smoking that got him showing up at my door on a night like this, telling wild stories."

The fact that the man hadn't shouted to the sky at the mention of Atlantia was somewhat reassuring.

Deciding that we were already knee-deep in whatever this was, I edged past Kieran and came to stand beside Malik. I lowered the hood of my cloak.

That eye swept over my face and then darted back to the scar on my brow, going wide. "Holy shit," he gasped as Kieran reached over, tugging my hood back into place. "It's you. It's really you. Holy shit."

"Are my scars that well known?" I asked.

"Scars?" Blaz mumbled as the door swept open wide. "Holy shit on a sardine sandwich. Yeah, come right in."

"I am slightly concerned about this mortal," Reaver muttered.

I was more than slightly concerned about all of this, but when

Malik walked in, I followed without hesitation since he carried Casteel. Kieran was right behind me, entering a small foyer. The space had no light, so all I could make out was the shape of what appeared to be low-to-the-floor chairs.

"It's not the scars," Kieran said, his voice low as Blaz closed the door behind Reaver. "It's your eyes. They're streaked with silver. Been that way since you entered the stairwell in Wayfair."

I blinked rapidly, even though I had no idea if that would help or if it did. Maybe the adrenaline was causing it?

"Blaz?" came a soft voice from the narrow hall, lit only by a wall sconce. "What's going on?"

"You should come in here." Blaz backed up slowly into the hall. The man's hair matched his name. Fiery strands brushed the skin at his temples that surely burned upon a few moments in the sun. A beard in a deeper red color covered his jaw. "We've got guests. Elian and special guests."

"Elian?" I repeated under my breath, thinking I recognized the name.

"That's his middle name." Kieran nodded at Malik's back. "Named after their ancestor."

Elian Da'Neer. The one who'd summoned the gods after the war with the deities to smooth over relations with the wolven. The very first bonding between wolven and Atlantian resulted from the meeting. Was that why Tawny hadn't known Malik when she'd been at Wayfair? Because she'd known him as Elian?

A moment later, a short figure stepped out from one of the chambers off the hall and into the lamplight. Shoulder-length dark hair framed cool, olive-beige cheeks and a rounded chin. The woman appeared to be about the same age as Blaz, somewhere in their third decade of life. She wore a dark sleeping robe, belted around the waist.

Her hands weren't empty.

Clariza held a slender iron dagger as she crept forward. "What kind of special guests did you bring us, Elian?" she asked, dark, intelligent eyes darting over the group and lingering on Reaver, whose face was the only one visible. His pupils were normal, but the mortal still swallowed.

"The King of Atlantia," Blaz answered, joining his wife. "And the Queen."

"Bullshit." Clariza echoed her husband's early sentiment. "Have you been indulging in the Red Ruin?"

Casteel was likely to awaken at any moment. I stepped forward to avoid any lengthy attempts to prove our identities when I could just show them. I lifted the hood, letting it drape from my shoulders.

Clariza's eyes went wide. "Holy shit."

"What he claims is true. My name is Penellaphe. You could've known of me as the Maiden at one time. He does hold my husband in his arms. He's been held by the Blood Crown," I told them, noting the tightening in Clariza's jaw. "He's been injured and is in need of shelter so I can provide him with aid. We were brought here because we were told that we could trust you."

Without taking her eyes off me, Clariza lowered herself to one knee. She placed one hand over her heart and the other, which held the dagger, she pressed to the floor. Her husband followed suit.

"From blood and ash," she said, bowing her head.

"We will rise," Blaz finished.

I shuddered. Those words echoed through me, the meaning so very different from when I'd first heard them.

"That's not necessary. I'm not your Queen," I said, glancing at Casteel's shrouded form. "We're just in need of space. A private place where I can help my husband."

Malik's head cut sharply in my direction but he said nothing.

"You may not be our Queen now," Clariza said, her head lifting, "but you are a god."

"I am." I swallowed thickly, worry pressing down on me. "But you still do not need to bow before me."

"Not what I expected to hear from an actual god," Blaz mumbled. "But I'm not going to complain." He reached over, taking his wife's hand so they rose together. "Whatever you need."

"A chamber?" Malik suggested. "With a sturdy door." He paused. "And walls. Just in case."

Clariza frowned.

"We have a bedchamber that Riza's mother once used." Blaz pivoted and started walking. "Not sure about how sturdy the walls or door are, but they're standing."

We followed, passing what appeared to be an entryway to a sitting chamber and then another closed door. Blaz opened the rounded door to the left on the opposite side of the hall.

"He's been starved, hasn't he?" Clariza asked as her husband hurried into the chamber, lighting a gas lamp on a small end table.

My gaze snapped to her as Malik carried Casteel to the narrow bed. The chains clanged together as he laid him down, drawing Blaz's attention.

"My great-great-grandmother was Atlantian," Clariza explained. "My grandmother used to tell me what happened when her mother couldn't easily find another Atlantian to feed from. From what I remember, it didn't sound like many walls or doors are strong enough."

I had a lot of questions about why her family had chosen to remain and not head for Atlantia, but those questions would have to wait as I went to the other side of the bed. Malik pulled the cloak off.

"Fucking gods." Blaz's gasp turned into a wheeze. "Sorry. That was probably offensive. I am deeply regretful."

"It's okay." My heart ached anew as I took in Casteel's too-pale skin and the grisly wound.

"Shit," Malik cursed, and my gaze flew to Casteel's face. The dark slash of brows had furrowed. I saw tension creeping into the stark lines of his features.

"You should all leave," Kieran advised, coming forward as Malik took hold of the chains. He lifted them from Casteel's chest. "He's about to wake."

31

Clariza grasped her husband's arm and had already begun backing toward the door. "I'll get some food ready and heat up some fresh water. He'll need both."

"Thank you." I forced a smile, flicking a glance at Reaver.

The draken sensed my will. He turned to the mortals. "I'll help."

In other words, he would keep an eye on them. They may be Descenters and currently planning to launch some sort of attack on Wayfair, but that didn't mean I trusted them with Casteel's life.

"Sure. You can tell us where you're from while helping," I heard Clariza say as she stepped into the hall. "Like exactly how far east you come from."

That would've normally been an odd thing to say, except for the fact that Reaver hailed from the farthest-east place one could get.

"You've got a lot of things you need to be sharing after you're done in here." Blaz pointed at Malik as he paused at the doorway. "A lot of things."

The door closed on that. I looked over at Malik. "Do they know who you are?"

"No," he said. "They don't."

Casteel's eyes opened then, the irises pitch-black. I wasn't prepared to see that again. My heart splintered even more, but there was no time to dwell on it.

He came off the bed, lashing out like a cornered pit viper. I jumped back, hitting the wall. His fingers grazed the front of my shirt as Malik curled the chains around his forearm, grunting as he hauled Casteel back. Cursing, Malik tried to get his brother back onto the bed, but Casteel was incredibly strong in this state.

"Malik can feed him," Kieran bit out as Casteel let out a low howl. "I'll take the chains."

"No." I pushed off the wall. Kieran's gaze shot to me. "I have a whole lot more eather in me. Wouldn't my blood bring him out of bloodlust much faster?"

Kieran didn't answer.

Malik did. "It's unlikely that my blood will do much for him at this point," he said, his jaw clenching as he dug in his heels. "We both know that. She's a god. Her blood is the best choice."

Kieran's worry filled my throat like too-thick cream—his concern for me and for Casteel. "I can heal him first. I just need to touch him. That should calm him."

Malik's eyebrows rose in doubt as Casteel turned on him, forcing Malik to jump onto the bed and move to the other side.

"I just need one of you to distract him." I clasped Kieran's cheeks. "I'll calm him first. Okay? I won't let him hurt me. None of us will."

A muscle thrummed against my palm as Kieran's eyes glowed a luminous blue. "Fuck. I hate this."

"Me, too." Stretching up, I pressed my lips against his forehead.

A fine tremor ran through him, and then he released me. "Please…"

Kieran didn't finish. He didn't need to as I faced Casteel. He was only a few feet from me now, snarling and snapping.

"I'll get behind him this time." Kieran looked at Malik. "I need you to get him close to you."

Malik nodded.

Kieran took a deep breath. "Once I get a good hold on him, you've got to do your thing. Understood?"

Casteel howled, the sound so eerily similar to that of a Craven that my insides turned cold.

But I wasn't afraid.

I was never scared of Casteel. Not even in this state.

"Ready?" Kieran said.

"Yes."

Malik yanked the chains toward him, attempting to wrap them around one of the bedposts. Casteel twisted toward his brother, taking his eyes off Kieran. The wolven darted behind Casteel, clamping one arm around Casteel's chest, pinning his arms to his side as he managed to get his hand under Casteel's jaw.

Casteel went *wild*, thrashing, growling, and spitting. He threw his weight back, slamming Kieran into the wall. Plaster cracked. The chain slipped away from the bedpost.

"*Now*," Kieran grunted.

Tapping into the eather, I began to conjure up happy thoughts—memories of him and me under the willow tree in Masadonia. Memories of him playing with my hair and teaching me how to control a horse. All of those and more filled my thoughts as my hand closed around his skin—his cold, *cold* skin. Silvery-white light sparked from my fingertips.

"Don't do this," Kieran rasped as Casteel bucked against him, straining toward me. The sheer intensity of Casteel's bloodlust pulled Kieran away from the wall. "Come on, man."

Casteel broke Kieran's hold around his neck.

"Shit," Kieran groaned, his boots skidding across the wood floor.

Malik was there, having dropped the chains to grab his brother by the chin. "I got him."

"Please, Cas," Kieran said—begged really. "You've got to let her help you find calm."

Casteel's answering growl raised the hairs all over my body as warmth rushed from me. I knew the moment the healing energy hit him because Casteel went rigid. The shimmering web swept over him, filling the chamber for the briefest second before fading into his skin. The ragged wound in his chest was awash with eather as Casteel staggered back, falling into Kieran. They both went down to the floor, and Malik and I followed.

"Gods," Malik uttered as he stared at his brother's rapidly healing chest. The glow had faded, revealing a bright pink patch of newly formed skin. His eyes shot to Casteel's face. "Cas?"

His lids were lowered, lips parted as he panted for breath. He trembled so badly he shook Kieran.

I slid my hand up his arm. His skin was still far too cold. "Casteel?" I whispered.

His eyes opened wide, and a thin strip of gold was visible as they locked with mine. He was there—a piece of him recovered, at least.

I lifted my wrist to his mouth. "You need to feed."

"I...I can't," Casteel forced out, words guttural as he twisted his head to the side.

"You have to." I cupped his cheek with my other hand.

"I'm...I'm barely *here*...right now." His gaze flew back to mine, and I saw it then, the red glint in the darkness there. "You need to get away from me."

"Cas—"

"Get away from me." The red glint brightened.

"You fucking idiot," his brother growled, grip tightening on Casteel's chin. "We don't have time for you to be all heroic and worry about taking too much blood from a godsdamn *god*."

Casteel's head jerked back, cracking into the side of Kieran's. Tendons stood out starkly in his throat as his lips peeled back over his fangs. "Get her away from me!"

The force of his words knocked me back.

Malik twisted toward me. "He's not going to do it without some real strong motivation. Like, for example, the scent of your blood."

"No," Casteel roared, his feet kicking against the floor as he pushed himself and Kieran back. Malik lost his grip on his brother's chin.

"Do it." The muscles of Kieran's arms bulged as he fought to hold Casteel in place. "Do it before the entire neighborhood hears him."

I moved quickly, unsheathing my wolven dagger. I pressed my lips together to silence the hiss of pain as I dragged the edge of the blade across my wrist.

The moment the scent of my blood hit the air, Casteel's head swung around. No longer fighting to pull away, his entire being appeared fixated on the blood welling up on my skin.

"Feed," I begged. "*Please*."

And then his head snapped down.

His fangs grazed my skin as his mouth closed over the wound. I could've shouted with joy as I felt his mouth pulling at my skin. He drank deeply.

"That's it," Kieran said, his voice low as he smoothed limp strands of hair back from Casteel's face. "That's good."

I scuttled closer, my leg tangling with his as I carefully touched his cheek. My senses brushed against the whirling, crimson-tainted darkness that seemed to fill every part of him. I searched the stark hunger there, finding wisps of tangy anguish as I smoothed my fingers over the rough bristle on his cheeks. I tasted the pain—icy and bone-deep as I kept touching his cheek. His jaw. The kind of mental hurt that cut so much deeper than any physical pain. I closed my eyes, channeling some relief into him as I'd done before—

Casteel moved without warning, tearing his mouth from my arm, faster than any of us thought him capable of. None of us had a chance to react. The chains clattered across the floor as he came at me. Grabbing hold of my hip, he dragged me under him as his body came over mine.

Kieran shouted. "Cas—"

The cold, uneven surface of the wood floor dug into my back. My heart gave a startled lurch as he gripped where the cloak was clasped. Buttons flew, pinging off the floor. His head streaked down. The fiery pain of his fangs piercing the skin of my throat was sharp and sudden, briefly robbing me of breath. I bit down on my lip as he fed hard and deep, his mouth moving fiercely against my throat.

"Nope." Kieran loomed over us, forcing his forearm under Casteel's chin. "That's a nope."

A violent growl rumbled through Casteel. His right hand sank into my hair, jerking my head back as he worked an arm under me. Trapping my arms between us, he pulled me as close to him as he could.

"I know you don't like it, but you're going to like it a lot less if you hurt her," Kieran warned, grasping a fistful of Casteel's hair.

The rippling snarl from Casteel came from the very depths of his being. I could taste the keening sense of rising desperation. It was so potent, I almost heard his words. *Not enough, not enough.* If we stopped him now...

We'd lose him again.

Searching for Kieran's eyes, I found them and forced a smile. "It's okay."

"Bullshit," Kieran growled.

"It is," I insisted. And it was. The sting of pain was more of a burn now, but it *was* fading. This wasn't a clean strike like the times before, but it was nothing like when an Ascended fed. I didn't feel as if I were being ripped apart from the inside, and that could only mean that more than just a fragmented piece of Casteel remained. There were several more. We just needed to give him time to piece them together. "He needs more. I can *feel* that."

I managed to work one of my arms free, and Casteel made a desperate sort of sound as the faint, bitter taste of fear reached me. Did he think I was going to push him away? Stop him?

Never.

Smoothing my hand across his bristly cheek, I felt the muscles in his jaw working as he swallowed. I threaded my fingers through his hair, curling them around the back of his head, holding him there.

"I don't like this," Kieran said.

"If Cas stops before he gets enough, it'll be worse," Malik warned from somewhere in the chamber. "You know that."

Kieran held my gaze and then cursed, his head bowing. He slid his arm out from under Casteel's neck, but he didn't go far. He crouched close.

Casteel didn't like any of that. His body twisted away from Kieran, tucking me almost completely under him and against the solid wood at the foot of the bed.

His mouth didn't leave my throat, didn't stop sucking, and I felt each dragging pull. Every swallow. The staggering tugs against my skin were almost too intense, causing my breath to catch repeatedly.

But the red haze of clouds inside him wasn't nearly as thick. It was scattering. The anguish and sense of desperation still whirled through him, but there was *more* now. He took harder pulls, deeper, wringing a gasp from my tightly pressed lips.

Kieran shifted closer, but Casteel's bite no longer hurt. It simply burned with a different kind of heat, one that was wholly inappropriate given the situation.

I squeezed my eyes shut, focusing on his emotions and what I tasted from him. There was a tang of sorrow, but the icy pain was fading. And under all of it, beneath the storm, was something sweet and warm…

Chocolate.

Berries.

Love.

The rumble Casteel made was softer, rougher. His mouth slowed, and the draws became languid but still deep. The hand in my hair loosened enough that the tension went out of my neck, but I didn't move. The smoky, spicy flavor filling my throat invaded my blood. He made that sound again, the thick, humming rumble, and my entire body shuddered. He twisted over me, his body heating against mine. I tried to ignore the storm building inside me, but those lips at my throat, the steady and deep pull of my blood flowing from me and into him, made it hard to focus on anything but how his body felt against mine. An aching pressure settled in my breasts and lower, between my thighs, where I felt him thickening and hardening.

"Well, fuck…" I heard Kieran mutter a moment before the hot, wet slide of Casteel's tongue against the side of my throat sent a tight, pulsing shudder through me.

My eyes flew open.

"Not sure if this is the right time for any of that." Kieran threaded his arm around Casteel's shoulders, pulling him back an inch.

A throaty growl came from Casteel, but it was nothing like the wild, primitive sounds he'd made before. This was from a different kind of hunger. One that my body responded to, answering with a wet rush of heat. But the relief…gods, the relief swirling through me, was just as powerful as the arousal.

I was able to free my other arm. Clasping his cheeks, I lifted Casteel's head. Gold. Brilliant, burnished gold eyes locked onto mine.

"Cas," I whispered.

Those beautiful eyes glimmered with dampness. *Tears.* "*My Queen,*" he said in a voice thick and raw.

A shudder took me as I gripped the sides of his face, finally seeing that the rich, golden-bronze hue had begun to return to his skin. I lifted my lips to his—

Casteel turned his head, pressing his cheek to mine. "I can't feel your mouth on mine." His words were a raw whisper in my ear. "If I do, I'm going to fuck you. I'm going to get so deep inside you that there will be no part of you I don't reach. Right here. Right now. It doesn't matter who is in this chamber. It's already taking everything in me not to be inside you."

Oh.

Oh, goodness.

Someone cleared their throat. It could've been his brother, and…well, I didn't really want to think about that.

Pulse thudding at the rich, smoky flavor swamping me, I parted suddenly dry lips as he lifted his head. "Okay. So, how are you feeling? Other than *that*?"

Thick lashes swept down, halfway shielding his eyes. "I'm…here." His throat worked on a swallow. "Together."

I shook again. That wasn't a lot of words, but I knew what he meant. So did Kieran. His relief was potent, rolling off him in refreshing, earthy waves.

Casteel eased his fingers from my hair, dragging the tips of them down my cheek. Somewhere on the floor, a chain clattered. He stilled, his attention shooting to them. "I need these off me. Now."

My eyes found Kieran. "Get Reaver."

Malik didn't hesitate, leaving the chamber. Slowly, Casteel's gaze left those chains, returning to mine.

"It's okay," I told him, brushing my fingers through his hair over and over. "We'll get them off."

Casteel said nothing, those diamond-bright eyes fixed on mine, his stare intense and all-consuming. The hollowness of his features was filling out, but I still saw stark shadows of need there.

Reaver skidded into the chamber, followed by Malik. A door clicked shut.

"The chains," I said. "Can you break them around his wrists?"

"I can do that." Reaver started forward.

"Thank the gods," Kieran muttered. "But I would take it—"

Casteel's head twisted in my grasp, his body vibrating as he growled deep and low at Reaver.

"Slowly," Kieran finished.

The draken turned his gaze on Casteel, the skin of his features thinning. Ridges appeared along his cheek, his neck. "Really?"

"Hey. Hey." I struggled to pull Casteel's attention back to me. "That's Reaver," I told him, and his nostrils flared. "Remember? I told you about him. He's a friend. He's also a draken. You're not going to win that battle."

"I think he wants to give it a go," Malik remarked.

The way Casteel tracked Reaver's movements told me that Malik wasn't far off the mark.

Reaver knelt by us. "I'm going to need you to lift one arm at a time," he instructed. "And I'm going to need you to do that without trying to bite me because I bite back."

Casteel was silent, but he lifted his hand from my cheek. He watched Reaver lower his head, eyeing how closely the draken got to me. His upper lip began to curl.

I turned his head to me, and the chill immediately went out of his golden eyes. There was nothing but heat when he looked at me. And hadn't it always been like that? From the first moment in the Red Pearl to now? It had. There was so much I wanted to say. So many things. But all that came out was, "I've missed you."

A flare of silvery-white washed over Casteel's profile. He didn't even flinch, but his jaw flexed when the shadowstone shackle hit the floor. "I never left you."

"I know." Tears crowded my throat.

"Other hand," Reaver ordered.

Casteel shifted his weight onto his left arm, and his lower body settled more fully against mine. There was no mistaking the thick, rigid length of him. Flecks of brighter gold churned in his eyes. "Are you safe here?"

"*We* are safe here." I kept combing back his hair as that stream of silvery fire lit the space between our bodies and the bed. "For now."

His gaze lowered to my mouth. There was wanton intent in his stare, sending a shivery wave of awareness through me. "Poppy," he whispered.

The shadowstone shackles hit the floor, and Kieran quickly grabbed them as Casteel's head lowered to mine. His breath danced over my lips. "I need all of you to leave. Now."

Footsteps moved away from us, but Kieran hesitated, remaining where he was on the floor beside us. Twinges of concern broke through his relief. "Cas..."

Only then did Casteel look away from me. He turned his head toward Kieran. He lifted his bandaged hand, clasping the wolven behind the neck. They leaned in, pressing their foreheads together. The rise of a sugary, sweet emotion crowded out the concern and even relief.

"Thank you," Casteel rasped, the two words choked.

"What the hell are you thanking me for?"

"Everything."

Kieran shuddered, and they stayed that way for a long moment before Kieran shifted away from Casteel. Unlike with Reaver, Casteel made no move to stop the wolven as he reached for me. Kieran's hand brushed strands of hair back from my face, and then he bent over, pressing his lips to my brow. Emotion clogged my throat, and I didn't know if it belonged to them, me, or if it was a combination of all of us.

Kieran said nothing as he pulled away, and the strangest urge to reach out and stop him swept through me. I didn't understand where that want had come from. Or if it was mine or Casteel's. And I didn't know why it felt wrong *not* to act on it.

But then Casteel and I were alone, and those beautiful, golden eyes, so full of fire and love, were locked onto mine. It was just us, and nothing *else—absolutely nothing—*mattered. Not the patches of dried dirt and blood that covered nearly every inch of his skin. Not the mist outside or the Craven I'd unintentionally called forth. Not what came after this—the Blood Queen or the war.

Nothing but *us* and our love and need for each other.

"Cas," I whispered.

He became so still, I didn't think he even breathed as he looked down at me. But what roared through him was a madness of movement. I felt *him* inside me—his desire and need churning with mine. The ache blossomed anew, throbbing and pulsing and heating my blood and skin.

His nostrils flared, and the gold of his eyes burned even brighter. Not a single part of me felt any shame over how acutely he sensed my arousal.

"*Poppy*," he repeated, and then his mouth was on mine.

The kiss...

There was nothing soft about it. We came together in a clash of teeth and lips and raw, overwhelming emotions. His hand dug into my hip as mine fisted his hair. The kiss was maddening. Feral. Possessive. It was the kind that one drowned in, and I'd never been happier to do so. His tongue swept inside my mouth, against mine, and I tasted my blood, rich and warm. There was something wild about that. Something uncharted.

His mouth moved over mine, his fangs nicking my lower lip. I started to curl my legs around his waist, but the hand at my hip stilled me. He lifted his head, his chest rising and falling raggedly. A bit of blood glistened on his lip.

I stretched my head up, catching that drop of blood and his lip between mine. He groaned, eyes closing briefly. When they reopened, they were twin fires of molten gold.

Casteel shifted onto his knees, lifting his body from mine. Before I could even guess what he was about, he gripped my hip once more. He flipped me onto my belly and then hauled me onto my knees.

"I need to feel your skin against mine," he bit out in a voice that was barely recognizable.

My loose braid fell forward as one hand went to the hem of my tunic, shoving the shirt up over my head. He tugged it down so it pooled at my wrists.

The roughness in the way he tugged the gauzy cloth down, where it caught beneath my breasts, sent a wicked thrill through my blood. His hand, though... The gentleness in how he trailed his palm down the center of my back, caused my heart to swell.

Sliding his hand down my ass and then between my thighs, he

curled his finger there, brushing against that heated part of me. I shuddered—

My entire body jerked as he tore through the breeches, bearing my ass and the most sensitive parts of me to him. My head swung to the side in surprise. I started to turn—

A rumbling sound of warning filled the chamber. Instinct stilled me—all my senses heightened. My eyes flew to his, but his were fixed on the tear he'd created in the breeches. He looked as hungry as he had before, but I knew it wasn't blood that he was starved for now.

He lifted my hips, and I barely saw him move. All I knew was that his mouth was on me. Air fled my lungs. His tongue delved inside my slick heat as his head twisted, dragging a cry of pleasure from me as one fang grazed my sensitive nub of flesh. The strokes of his tongue were firm and determined. He licked and sucked. He *feasted*, feeding from me as desperately as he had at my throat. I was lost. My body tried to follow, but the hands at my hips held me in place.

Casteel *devoured*.

I shook and trembled, the heat building in me fierce and intense—almost too intense. My fingers curled, pressing into the floor as he dragged a fang over the bundle of nerves once more. I jerked, crying out at a sharp prick of pain. His mouth closed around the throbbing flesh, and that sensation echoed in the bite mark on my throat. And that—*that*—was too much.

I choked on a scream as I shattered into thousands of silk-draped shards, barely able to hold myself up as tight spasms wracked me. I was still trembling when his mouth left me. I felt the press of his glossy lips against the center of my back.

"Honeydew," he growled. "You taste of honeydew, and your skin smells of jasmine. Fuck."

Head limp, I looked back at him. I watched his hand go to the flap of his breeches. He tore at them, sending little discs of metal scattering across the floor. My body flushed as he shoved the ruined, dirtied breeches down his lean hips, freeing the thick, hard length of his erection.

He stretched over me, his mouth grazing my jaw and then the line of my neck, sending a hot, tight shiver down my spine. The feel of his skin, now blazing hot against my back, shook me.

He brushed his lips over my skin, and then I felt his fangs on those ultra-sensitive bite marks as the head of his cock nudged my slick core. He didn't pierce the skin. His fangs were just there, holding me in place as one hand folded around my hip again and the other curled around my chin. He tilted my head farther back and to the side. Another illicit thrill rocked me, pushing all the air from my lungs. All those briefly relaxed muscles went taut once more. I panted as a sharp swirl of anticipation sliced its way through me.

"I'm not..." His body shook against mine, his fingers trembling against my cheeks, my throat and arms, as he dragged them down, following the curve of my waist. He gripped my hips, his fingers pressing into the flesh there, and when he spoke, his voice was thick and needy, a coarse and ragged whisper. "I'm not...I'm not in control."

A pounding pulse of desire followed those words, becoming a roar in my blood. It was such an intense wave of sensation, leaving the tips of my breasts tight, and the very core of me throbbing all over again. "Neither am I."

"Thank fuck," he grunted, and then his mouth closed over mine.

After ending the kiss, Casteel struck, sinking his fangs into my throat as he thrust deeply, all the way to the hilt. I cried out, my back arching. The twisting ache of pain-tinged pleasure tore its way through my body, sparking every nerve and igniting into a blaze of wild, raw sensation that became pure ecstasy. The feel of him filling me, stretching me, left no room for anything else. His presence dominated.

Casteel held me there, on my hands and knees, back arched with his fangs still deep in the side of my throat. There was no hesitation, no moment of reprieve. He moved behind me, fast and hard, and drank from me, deep and long. I felt each pull against my throat and every tug and push of his throbbing length throughout the entirety of my body. His weight—the force of how he lunged in and out—took me to the floor, trapping me there. The cold press of the wood against my breasts, and the heat of his body on my back as he kept my head lifted, neck exposed, was a sinful shock.

Suddenly, he lifted me onto my knees again, drawing me back so I was flush with his chest. The tunic finally slipped free of my wrists, but his arm snagged mine, pinning them below my breasts. His thrusts were a raging storm, and the sounds he made as he fed—the sounds *I* made as he took me—were *scandalous*. And I *reveled* in it.

He rose without warning, standing with one powerful surge. A ragged gasp of surprise parted my lips as my feet left the floor. Good gods, his strength...

Casteel turned sharply, pressing me against the bedpost. "Brace yourself, my Queen."

I almost came again, right there, at the sound of his raw demand. Gripping the beam, I had no way of preparing myself. Not as he drew me to the tips of my toes, his hips churning against my ass. His hand fisted in my hair as he tugged my head back.

The feel of his mouth closing over his bite mark sent a flood of pounding desire through me. He shifted, pulling me away from the beam and then pressing me down so my hips were against the hard board at the foot of the bed. His mouth was still fused to my neck, and he was still so deep, driving into me, over and over. My fingers dug into the blanket as I panted for breath. One of his arms hooked under my knee. He lifted my leg, changing the angle, deepening his thrusts, and intensifying the feel of him. And then he went *wild*.

There was nowhere to go, no escaping the fire the hard pound of his hips fanned, or the wild, rawness of how his mouth moved at my throat. And I didn't want to flee. I didn't know what that said about me, to know there was no control, no restraint. That this was a claiming, and I willingly went into those flames as the headboard banged against the wall in a fast, almost erratic thump. The sounds. The slick feel of him. The utter dominance—

My body stiffened, tightened. The release was sudden and sharp, exploding through me in pulsing waves. And still, he didn't stop. He plunged in and out, his hips rolling and grinding until I was spinning and falling—

Casteel tore his mouth from my neck and pulled out. He turned me onto my back and grabbed my hips, pulling me to the edge of the bed. And then he was thrusting into me again. My head kicked back as I gasped—

He froze, staring down at me…

I followed his gaze, trailing down the delicate golden chain to where his ring rested between my breasts. "I've worn it close to my heart ever since I received it."

Casteel shuddered, and his mouth came down over mine, silencing a shout as he ground his hips against me. He kissed and kissed, and then his mouth left mine, his head lifting. Those ruby-red lips parted.

"Never again," he snarled, his word punctuated by deep, stunning thrusts. "Never again are we taken from one another."

"Never," I whispered, shuddering at the taste of him—my blood and me—now lingering on my lips.

His head dipped, this time to my breast. The edges of his fangs drew across a peak and then sank into the skin. My entire body bowed as his mouth closed over the turgid flesh.

I swept my arms around him, cradling his head to me as I wrapped my legs around his plunging hips. He stoked the fire once more, enflamed me until muscles low and deep inside me clenched—tightening and coiling. Casteel grunted, groaned, his movements becoming jerky and frenzied. My senses snapped open wide, connecting me to him, and all I felt and tasted was his lust, his love. It matched mine, surrounding both me and him. Never had I felt anything like this—like *him*.

"I love you," I gasped as all that coiling tension started to unfurl.

His mouth left my breast and found mine. "Always," he breathed and thrust in deep and hard, stiffening. There was no stopping us from tumbling over the edge, shuddering, shaking, and falling into bliss.

Together.

Always.

And forever.

32

Casteel

I watched Poppy drag the washcloth down my arm, wiping away soapy residue, my attention rapt. Obsessed.

The shirt that had been given to her slipped down once more, baring a creamy shoulder. She'd battled that sleeve since she'd put the tunic on, and for once, I was glad she was losing a war.

There was a freckle on that shoulder. I'd never noticed it before. Just below the delicate bone. It played peekaboo through the strands of her hair, which were now free of the braid and falling in a riot of loose waves and half-formed curls.

Poppy had changed.

The sprinkling of freckles across the bridge of her nose and cheeks had darkened from her time spent in the sun. Her hair had grown, those still-damp ends from the quick bath she'd taken nearly reaching the curve of her ass. Her face had slimmed slightly. I didn't think anyone else would have noticed, but I did, and it made me think that she hadn't been eating well. And that…

I couldn't think about that without wanting to tear down the walls around us. The kind mortals who'd sheltered us didn't deserve that, so I focused on her eyes.

Every time the thick fringes of her lashes lifted, it felt like the whole damn house shifted.

Her eyes were like they'd been when we dreamed of each other—spring green pierced by wisps of luminous silver. And they had stayed like that since I'd found myself again.

But the change in her was more than physical. There was a *stillness* about her now that had never been there before. Not exactly a calmness since there was still some frenetic energy about her, as if her mere presence influenced the air around her. But something about her was deep and settled now. A confidence? An awakening? I didn't know. Whatever it was, she was the most beautiful being I'd ever seen.

I hadn't taken my eyes off her for longer than it took to blink. Bad shit came when I did. A sense of surrealness—or a panicked fear that this was some sort of hallucination. It had happened when I stepped into the adjoining bathing chamber to relieve myself and make use of the razor and cream that had been brought in with the water. It had been dark. No electricity. The dim light from the bedchamber did nothing to shatter the darkness. For a moment, I thought I was back there in that cell. I felt the shackles at my wrists and ankles. My throat. I'd locked up, one hand on the sink basin, and the other clutching the handle of the razor.

That was how Poppy had found me.

She'd brought the lamp inside, placing it by the vanity. Nothing was said. She'd just wrapped her arms around my waist, pressing herself against my back, and she'd remained that way until the panicked fear abated. Until I'd finished shaving away the itchy bristles of growth.

I couldn't believe that she was here.

I couldn't believe *I* was here. Pieced back together. Almost whole. My memories had gaps. Dark voids caused by the bloodlust. But I was sitting in a hip tub, nestled in the corner of a chamber, under what I could've sworn was a painting of the Skotos Mountains.

While Poppy had gently coaxed me into the warm, clean water, insisting on being the one to wash away the filth, she'd shared with me all that had occurred. The events in Massene. The old woman with the stolen Primal essence. What had gone down in Oak Ambler. Tawny's strange recovery and the truth to who Vikter was. What she'd borne witness to beneath Castle Redrock and at the Temple of Theon. What Isbeth had told her about her father. The reason Malik had remained. I knew some of it. Some, I didn't. Much of it left my damn chest aching, and anger simmering in my gut, ruining the thick, herb-laden stew that had been brought in.

I hated the guilt I saw skittering across her face. The lingering pain. I knew my Queen could stand on her own. I was here because of her strength. Her courage. But I should've been there to shoulder some of the weight I knew she bore.

She hadn't been alone, though.

I had to keep reminding myself of that. It was the only thing keeping me from descending into a different kind of bloodlust. She had support. Kieran had been with her. As well as others, but Kieran…yeah, knowing she had him was how I kept the building rage in check.

How proud I was of her—of all she had accomplished—also helped. Poppy was fucking extraordinary.

And I had been nothing but a monster chained to a wall when she came for me, unable to do a damn thing to help assist in our escape. Pressure settled on my chest. I'd been a liability. The dangerous, weak link.

Fuck. That was a hard truth to swallow.

"You know," Poppy said, drawing me from my thoughts as she lowered my right hand into the water. "Those breeches you destroyed?" Her startlingly strange and beautiful eyes lifted to mine as she picked up my left arm and set about wiping the suds away. "They were the only pair of pants I have."

Some of the tightness eased from my chest. No doubt she had sensed the tangled emotions behind where my thoughts had gone. "I would say I'm sorry, but I'd be lying."

A wry grin appeared as she drew the washcloth over my upper arm. "I appreciate the honesty."

I watched her head tilt. The wine-hued strands slipped to the side, revealing the puckered, red puncture wounds on her throat. The sight of them caused a dual reaction, which resulted in my head and dick being completely at odds with each other.

Something I wasn't entirely accustomed to since they were usually on the same page when it came to Poppy.

"Had you ever heard of *viktors* before?" she asked.

"No, but given the way Vikter was with you, it makes sense." The man had behaved as if he'd been Poppy's father and hadn't been all that impressed by me. Made me wonder exactly how much the *viktors* knew and saw.

"Tawny said that he was proud of me," she whispered.

I stilled. "Did you think he wasn't?"

"I don't know," she admitted, her voice hoarse. "I hoped so."

"He had to be, whether or not he knew what his purpose was as a *viktor* or not," I insisted quietly. "There's no way he couldn't have been."

She nodded.

I leaned over to press a kiss to the top of her forehead. "That man—or whatever he was—loved you as if you were his own flesh and blood. He was proud of you."

Poppy blinked rapidly, giving me a soft smile. "Sit back. I'm not done with you."

"Yes, my Queen." I did as she ordered, and she inched closer, her brow pinching with a quick wince. My stomach dropped. "Did I hurt you?"

Her eyes rose to mine again. "You've already asked me that question five times."

"Seven times, actually." I only had brief memories of feeding from her—at her wrist and then at her throat. I remembered enough to know I hadn't been gentle. The larger-than-normal wounds on her throat were proof of that. "Did I?"

Poppy saw what I stared at. "Your bite barely hurt."

She'd said that before, and I knew she lied. I also knew I hadn't exactly taken care with all that had come after. "You winced."

"It wasn't that. Just a bad pain in my temple or jaw. Nothing to do with you. It's already gone."

I wasn't sure I believed her. "I was rough with you. Then and after."

The washcloth stilled just above my wrist. "I enjoyed every moment of that and then some."

A rush of satisfaction hit me, but there was no ego-fueled smugness. Another burgeoning worry took shape as my mind continued putting itself together. Poppy had shared a lot with me, but there was one thing she hadn't mentioned. "Did you ever find out if you need to feed?"

Poppy sat back, still holding my arm as she nodded. "Apparently, all gods have to feed—supposedly not as much as Atlantians, and a god doesn't have to feed off another god or an Atlantian. Any blood works, as long as it's not a draken's." She paused, her brow pinching. "It's not really clear how often I need to feed. Using my abilities will speed up the need, as will injuries."

"Then you need to feed." I started to lift my wrist to my mouth—

Poppy stopped me, her grip on my arm warm. "You need every drop of blood you have. You need even more blood."

"I took a lot, Poppy."

"I feel fine right now," she said, tilting forward once more, her gaze steady on mine. "And I did have to feed a couple of days ago, right before we hit the road between Three Rivers and Whitebridge. I'd started to feel the need to feed. I...I had to."

"Kieran," I said, my eyes searching hers. "You fed from Kieran."

Her head cocked to the side. "Why am I not surprised that you somehow knew that?"

Knowing that Kieran had given her this aid brought nothing but relief. He would've made sure she was comfortable and safe, and that there wasn't even an ounce of shame to be felt. Gods, I owed him so much. "I couldn't see you going to anyone else. You're close to Delano and Vonetta—and the others—but Kieran is...it's different with him."

"It is," she whispered, bending and kissing the damp skin of my arm. "I also figured he was the one person you wouldn't mind feeding me."

"I wouldn't care who you used if you had that need."

She raised a brow. "Really?"

"Really."

"So, if I had decided to feed from Emil?" she suggested, and my jaw clenched. "Or Naill—"

"Okay. You're right," I admitted. No matter who she sought aid from, I never would've held it against her. The other person? Thoughts and prayers for their ass, though. "Kieran is the only one."

Poppy laughed softly. "I waited for as long as I could because I didn't want to do it with anyone but you."

"Because of my selfish-as-hell nature, I appreciate the sentiment. But, Poppy, I wouldn't want you to wait. You know that, right?" I searched out her gaze. "Your well-being trumps my illogical jealousy."

"I know. I really do." Her teeth dragged across her lower lip. "It was different than feeding from you. I mean, I could read Kieran's memories, but it wasn't like it is between us."

"It's not always like it is with us." I reached over with my right arm, tucking a stray piece of hair behind her ear. "It's not always so intense. We can control the emotions surrounding the feeding to a certain extent, just like we can make the bite something one should fear or crave."

"I was wondering about that," she admitted with a grin. "If you felt like that when you fed from others. You know, for...knowledge purposes."

"Yes, for knowledge." Smiling, I trailed my fingers down her cheek.

Her chin lifted. "Why else would I be asking, if not for educational purposes, Cas?"

I trembled. There was no stopping that reaction. "You shouldn't call me that."

Her nose wrinkled. "Why? You like it when I do."

"That's the problem. I like it too much," I told her, and she smiled, wide and bright. And, gods, I could live on those smiles. Thrive. "There's still a lot we need to talk about."

A whole hell of a lot.

Poppy's smile faded just a bit as I dropped my right hand back to the side of the tub. "I know. I figure we can talk about how we're going to get out of Carsodonia once Kieran and your brother return."

My brother.

I tightened my grip on the rim of the tub. He and Kieran were out there while the mist still blanketed the city, making sure no one nearby had alerted the Crown of any suspicious occurrences.

Poppy glanced at the door. "I hope they don't harm each other." Her brow creased. "Too badly."

"You worry for Malik?" I raised a brow. "You believe him?"

"I believe he spoke the truth about why he stayed. I tasted his emotions. He loves her. But there was also a lot of guilt and agony under that. I don't know if that's for what he's done by staying here or something else."

A little bit of empathy crept into me. Not a lot. I couldn't feel sorry for him or anything until I knew for sure that he wasn't playing us.

Until I knew if I'd have to kill him or not.

Beyond that, I didn't know what to think. I wanted to believe that love drove Malik's choices, but the knowledge that he'd chosen the Revenant over his family and kingdom didn't sit well with me.

Neither did the knowledge that I would've done the same for Poppy.

But this Revenant…

Poppy's *sister*.

How did she factor into all of this?

And how in the hell was I going to tell Poppy about her?

Poppy resumed trailing the cloth over my hand, along the golden marriage imprint. Her movements stilled once more. "Does it still hurt?" she whispered.

I looked down to see that she stared at what remained of my finger. The infection was gone. Thanks to Poppy's blood, new skin, now a glossy pink, stretched over the once exposed bone and tissue.

And maybe Malik's aid.

What the fuck ever.

"What hurts is knowing that you knew it was done."

Pressing her lips together, she shook her head as her eyes closed briefly. "I should've been the last thing you were worried about."

"You will always be the first thing I worry about."

A visible tremor shook her as she leaned forward, pressing a kiss to the knuckle. Placing my hand back into the water, she draped the cloth over the rim of the tub. She reached behind her neck, lifting the golden chain and the ring. "This is yours. It belongs with you." Her eyes lifted to mine, bright and mesmerizing. "Can you wear it on your right hand?"

I cleared my throat, but it was still scratchy. "I can wear it wherever you want me to."

"Wherever?" she teased, even while her fingers trembled as she worked the clasp on the chain.

"Wherever you want," I affirmed. "On any finger or toe of your choosing. I can have it pierced to my nipple. Or have it melted into a bolt and pierced in my cock—actually, you might enjoy that."

Poppy's gaze flew to mine. "In your...*cock*?"

Said cock hardened at the sound of her saying that, at how her lips parted around the word. I nodded.

Her cheeks pinkened as she tipped forward. "That's possible?"

"It is."

"Wouldn't that piercing hurt to have done?"

"Probably hurts like the fires of the Abyss."

She glanced down at the ring. A moment passed. "And...and why would I find that enjoyable?"

Gods.

I *loved* her curiosity. "I've heard that many find the rub of the ball that holds the bolt in place to be very pleasurable."

"Oh." She drew in a deep breath. "And does the wearer of such a piercing find it pleasurable?"

"Oh, yeah." I grinned as the color in her cheeks spread down her throat.

"Interesting," she murmured, her brow creasing once more. I would've given anything to know what she was thinking. But she lifted the ring. "I think your pointer finger on your right hand will do." A small grin appeared. "For now."

I chuckled roughly. "For now."

She rose onto her knees as I offered her my right hand. My chest seized. Never would've thought I could go from talking about cock piercings to being choked up in under a minute, but here I was. Throat clogged, I watched her slide the ring onto my right pointer finger, the gold warm from being so close to her body. A feeling of completeness surged in seeing the ring there.

A little bit of renewal.

Her beautiful eyes glimmered as they held mine. "You...you keep asking if I'm okay, but are you?"

My chest clenched again, but the feeling was colder and more brutal. In a second, I tasted the bitter panic of being trapped—chained and unable to do anything to fight back effectively.

To be of any aid to Poppy.

"Cas," she whispered.

A ragged breath left me as I threaded my fingers with hers. "I think I need to work on rebuilding those mental shields around you."

"I'm not trying to read your emotions." Poppy pursed her lips. "Okay. That's a lie. I am. I know I shouldn't. It's just that... I don't know what you went through, and I saw the marks on your body. The *cuts*. There were so many."

"They took my blood," I told her, gaze following hers to our joined hands. "Daily for a while. They put it in these vials. I assumed it was being used for the Revenants, but they stopped doing it a couple of days before you arrived."

"Isbeth might've been using it for the Revenants, but I think she could've been using it for the Royal Blessing." She, too, stared at our hands, and a long moment passed. "Did she...did they treat you like they had before?"

My chest burned as I lifted my gaze to her face. "No one touched me this time. Not like that."

A shuddering breath left her. "I'm relieved to hear that, but it doesn't make any of what was done better. Not when she kept you in that place. You had bite marks on your leg. You'd been starved—" Cutting herself off, she inhaled deeply. When her eyes lifted, I saw that the silver wisps of eather had become luminous. "I know you're going to tell me that you're okay. That you're fine. And I know you're strong. You're the strongest person I know, but they hurt you."

She bent, kissing the knuckle below the ring. The feeling of her lips beat back the threatening chill. "You once told me that I didn't always have to be strong when I was with you. That it was safe for me *not* to be okay," she said, and the muscles in my neck cramped. "You told me that it was your duty as my husband to make sure I knew that I didn't have to pretend. Well, it's my duty as your wife to make sure you know that, too. You're my shelter, Cas. My roof and my walls—my foundation. And I am yours."

A jagged knot filled my throat as I found myself staring at the painting of the mist-shrouded mountains. The inclination to tell her that I was fine was there. It's what I'd done the last time when my parents or anyone asked. Even Kieran. Even when lying to him was pointless. I didn't want any of them to worry. They'd already spent enough time doing that. And I didn't want to put that on Poppy. She already carried enough.

But I didn't have to pretend with her.

Not anymore.

I was safe with her.

"There was a time that I feared I would never hear you say my name outside of a dream." The words were hard and rough, but I forced them out. "It wasn't that I feared you wouldn't come for me. I knew you would. That knowledge also scared the hell out of me, but it was the darkness of the cell. The hunger. The knowledge that, eventually, it would get me, and I would break. Fracture again. I wouldn't even recognize my name to know that it was you who spoke it. So, yeah, I'm not..." I swallowed. "I'm not completely fine, but I will be."

"Yes," she whispered. "You will be."

Neither of us said anything for several long moments. Finally, I looked at her, and all I saw was *devotion* in her eyes.

To be on the receiving end of that? It made my fucking heart skip.

"I don't deserve you."

"Stop saying that. You do."

"I truly don't." I lifted our hands, pressing a kiss to the top. "But I'll make sure that I am worthy from now on."

"Then I'll make sure that you realize you already are."

A faint grin pulled at my lips. "I should probably get out of this tub. Kieran has to be back by now." And there were things I needed to tell her. Things I needed to remember.

"He is." Slipping her hand free, she reached for a towel that had been placed nearby. "He told me through the *notam*. Just a couple of minutes ago. I think they're giving us space."

"I have to admit,"—gripping the sides of the tub, I rose. Water ran off me, falling in drips—"I'm kind of jealous of that *notam* thing."

"Yeah, well, I have that, but you all have the fangs, the special hearing, seeing, and smelling." She rose, too, and my attention immediately got caught on the hem of that shirt and how it fluttered around those thighs, barely covering the thick curve of her ass. "So, I think it's only fair that I have this."

I dragged my gaze upward. "I bet you're still disappointed about not being able to shift into anything."

"I really am." She drew the towel over my arms and then down my chest.

"I can dry myself."

"I know," she said as she motioned for me to step out of the tub. "But I am feeling rather helpful right now."

"Uh-huh," I murmured, watching her drag the cloth along my hip and over my lower stomach, where the muscles stood out far more starkly than they should have.

I needed more of that stew and a lot of protein. Her blood would help fill me out, but some of the weight I would have to pack on the old-fashioned way.

The towel rasped over my back and then lower as Poppy walked around me. And then, I stopped thinking about all the calories I needed to consume.

Poppy was suddenly on her knees before me, moving the slightly rough towel down my left leg. Her head...fuck, it was *right there*. Inches from my dick, and there was no way I could ignore that. My throat dried. She guided the towel back up, along the inside of my leg, slowly. Up and up, she went. A tight tremor of anticipation shot through me. The back of her hand brushed my sac, and my entire body clenched.

She moved onto the other leg, her features utterly serene. *Innocent.* As if she had no idea what that touch had done. Bullshit. She knew. The small curve at the corner of her lips told me so as she started the slow, torturous climb back up my leg.

"Poppy," I warned, knowing damn well that if she continued, talking would be the last thing on my mind. Hell, it was already quickly becoming that.

"Hmm?" She drew the towel along the back of my thigh.

"I'm sure you're not unaware—" I clamped my jaw shut as her

hand brushed between my legs once more.

"Unaware of what?" she asked, her breath caressing the flesh of my thigh.

"Of what you're doing," I said hoarsely.

Dropping the towel, she placed her hands on the sides of both of my legs and looked up at me. Well, not all the way up. Poppy's gaze didn't go past my rigid length. Her stare. The way her lips parted. Her flushed cheeks. None of that helped keep my thoughts on track.

"I know exactly what I'm doing," she said, trailing her hands up the sides of my legs.

"And what exactly *are* you doing?"

"Showing you just how deserving you are."

I opened my mouth, but she stretched higher and pressed her lips to the old scar just inside my hip. The brand that never quite faded.

That kiss.

It wrecked me.

And she didn't stop there. Those soft lips trailed a path across my thigh. I was rock-hard, and she hadn't even touched me yet. Not really. The reaction had nothing to do with the absence of sex the last several weeks. I'd gone far, far longer than that. This punch-to-the-gut kind of lust had everything to do with her.

Poppy drew back just enough for me to see the blush on her nose and cheeks as she curled her fingers around the base of my dick. Choking on her name, I almost came right there.

Fractured green-and-silver eyes met mine as she drew her hand down my length. "I love you, Cas."

"Always?" I bit out.

"And forever." Her voice thickened as she slid her palm along me slowly. "Because you're worthy."

I trembled, my hands opening and closing at my sides. A faint sheen of sweat broke out over my forehead as she moved her palm down my length again. Her strokes were slow and tentative. And her mouth…godsdamn. Her hot little pants of breath teased the head of my cock. She hadn't even taken me in her mouth yet, but I could already feel the familiar coiling at the base of my spine, that deep tightening. "I'll believe anything you say right now."

Her laugh was light, teasing the head of my dick. "Believe it. Because if you weren't?" That hand kept moving, slow and steady and *hot*. "I wouldn't be on my knees before you."

"No. You wouldn't be," I gasped, unable to keep my hands at my sides. I touched her cheek. Threaded my fingers through her silky hair. "It's funny, though."

"What is?"

"I may be the one standing, but it's me who is still bowing to you."

Her smile was wide, crinkling the skin at the corners of her eyes. And, gods, those smiles…they were too rare. Too exquisite.

"Deserving," she whispered.

And then she took me into her mouth.

My shout was rough, echoing through the small chamber. Probably the whole damn building. I didn't care. The entire world centered on the feel of her mouth, the slide of her tongue as she kept moving her hand, working me with artful perfection.

But I kept myself still. I didn't tug on her hair. I didn't fuck her mouth. I didn't—

Poppy took me deep—deeper than I thought she would—and sucked. My hips jerked. My hand tightened in her hair. I nearly rose to the tips of my toes. "What godsdamn chapter in Miss Willa's diary was that in?"

Her laugh was a hum that nearly broke me, and I could sense the rapid increase in her pulse and breath. She enjoyed this, finding pleasure in pleasuring me. And that was its own powerful aphrodisiac. My hips moved then. I couldn't stop myself. My hand flattened on the back of her head. My head falling back, I shook. Nothing. Nothing in any realm compared to her. I was close, the tightening becoming taut. My thrusts were less shallow, less gentle.

Groaning, I pulled out of her mouth. Her hand on my hip firmed, but I gave her no choice. I hauled her onto her feet and brought my mouth to hers. She tasted of the fruity drink that had been served with the stew. I backed her up, lifting the borrowed tunic.

"You should be proud of me," I said when we parted long enough for me to pull the shirt over her head. "I didn't tear this off."

Her laugh was my personal sun. "Very proud."

I guided her to the bed, visions of settling between those plump thighs and sinking deep into her dancing in my head. But Poppy placed her hands on my shoulders and turned me.

Pushing me down to my ass and then onto my back, she climbed onto the bed, her knees on either side of my hips, straddling me.

"Fuck," I gasped, my heart pounding.

Her hair fell forward, sliding against my chest as she reached between us, palming my cock. I didn't even know what I said when I felt her wet heat against the head of my cock. Could've been a prayer. My hands went to her hips, steadying her as she began to lower herself, inch by sweet, hot inch. I feared this would be over before she even fully seated herself.

"Gods," she breathed, stiffening as our pelvises met. The fingers on my chest dug in. A soft, feminine sound left her as she withdrew slowly, to where only the tip was left, and then slid back down.

Poppy continued the breathtaking rise and fall, finding her rhythm and angle. Her back arched as she rocked above me.

I liked control. Had always been that way. But with Poppy...watching her find her way, watching her *live* and love without shame? Nothing was more powerful. More earth-shattering. I'd gladly give up control over and over for this—for her.

But then she began to really move.

Faster. Harder. I met her movements, fingers sinking into the flesh of her hips. The feel of her was slick and tight as she squeezed my dick. The sight of her—her full breasts, the curve of her waist, the creases at her thighs, and all that flushed flesh—was my undoing.

Poppy gripped my left wrist, drawing the hand that'd once had the ring from her hip to her breast—her heart. Her fingers threaded with mine.

She owned me.

Heart and soul.

As she rode me harder, I slid a hand to where we were joined. I found that bundle of nerves, pressing down with my thumb.

"Oh, gods," she cried out, and I felt her spasm around me as she jerked.

"I think you like that." I groaned as she ground against me.

"I do," she panted. "A lot."

Her breathy moans and my grunts filled the dimly lit chamber, joining the slick sounds of our bodies coming together. My fangs throbbed. I wanted her vein, but I'd already taken too much. So, I focused on how she fit as if I were made for her. How she moved over me with wild abandon and all the love and trust she gave to me. Was always giving me.

I wanted to stay deep inside her for hours—lose myself in her. But she was in me, under my skin, and wrapped around my heart as tightly as she was around my cock.

Bracing herself, she leaned forward, curling her hand under my head. She brought my mouth to her breast. To the hard nipple and the two puncture wounds I'd left behind earlier. I closed my mouth over the hardened nub.

"Feed," she whispered against the top of my head, her hips rolling. "Bite. Please."

I don't know which of her words snapped my restraint. It was probably the *please*. My lips peeled back, and I sank my fangs into the marks I'd already left behind. She jerked in my arms, crying out as her body contracted around mine. Her blood hit my tongue. Warm. Thick. Ancient. I swallowed greedily and drank deeply, taking her into me. Her blood was lightning in my veins. Pure power wrapped in jasmine and cashmere. The way she clamped around my dick was my undoing. The breathy "*Cas*" that left her lips. Her blood hitting my throat, my gut. All of it sent me over the edge.

The powerful release rolled down my spine. I folded my arms around her, pinning her to my chest as I thrust up, lifting both our bodies from the bed. I released my fangs from her flesh and found her mouth, kissing her as I came. The release fucking destroyed me in the best way. Wave after wave, it seemed never-ending, leaving me stunned by its intensity.

By everything I felt for her.

It took quite some time before my pulse slowed. I kept her where I wanted her—on top of me. In the quiet moments that followed, I realized something. My fingers stilled in her hair as my eyes opened. "Poppy?"

"Yeah?" she murmured, her cheek plastered to my chest.

"I haven't been on that herb," I told her, a real fucked-up mess of conflicting emotions firing off. "The one that prevents pregnancy."

"I figured," she said, yawning. "I started taking precautions."

My brows flew up. "Was that in the diary, too?"

Poppy laughed. "No. I asked Vonetta," she said, lifting her head. I decided I really needed to thank Netta. "She told me what to take since a baby Casteel would be the last thing we need—at least, at the moment."

Confusing-as-fuck emotions slammed into me, a mix of cold, hard terror and sweet anticipation. "What about a baby Poppy?" I brushed her hair back. "With deep red hair, freckles, and green-and-silver eyes?"

"My eyes are still like that?"

"Yep."

She sighed. "I don't know why they're like that, but your question? Are you being serious?"

"Always."

"You are not always serious."

"I am now."

"I don't know. I mean…yes?" Her nose scrunched. "One day, far, far, far, far from now. Yes."

"When we're not in the middle of a war, for example?" I smiled up at her. "And I'm ready to not be the center of your attention?"

"More like when I'm confident that I won't accidentally leave the child somewhere I shouldn't."

I chuckled, lifting my head and kissing her. "Later."

"Later," she agreed.

Lowering my head, I tucked her hair back. "I want you to feed."

"You probably need to feed again."

"Probably, but that's not why I want you to feed. I don't want you to grow weak," I told her. "Not ever, but especially not when we're in the middle of Carsodonia."

She nodded after a moment. "I'll see if Kieran is willing—"

"He'll be willing."

Poppy frowned. "You sound a little confident for it not being your blood."

"He'll be willing," I repeated, thinking she really had no idea when it came to Kieran and what he would or wouldn't willingly do for her.

"Whatever," she muttered, dropping her chin to my chest. "We should get up. We need to come up with a plan. Deal with Malik. Figure out how to get out of here. Hopefully, find out something about Tawny's current condition. Come back. Kill that bitch," she said, and my brows rose. "And then I need to free my father. I sort of promised Nektas I'd do that. You met him briefly in his draken form," she continued with another yawn, and my brows rose even higher. "My father's got to be in Carsodonia—"

"He's at Wayfair." The shadows surrounding one of the dark voids in my mind shattered. "Isbeth said he was."

Her eyes widened. "How did you…?"

"After you told me he was the cave cat, I goaded her into talking about him. Stabbed her in the chest, too." I grinned as I remembered. "Didn't kill her, but I bet it hurt."

Poppy blinked. "You stabbed her?"

"Yeah, with a Craven bone."

"I wish I'd seen that." Her eyes were wide once more. "I love you so very much."

I laughed at the utter wrongness of that. "Back to your father? She said the cave cat was where he was always kept."

"Where he was always kept," she murmured as I smoothed my thumb along her jaw. "The chambers under Wayfair, down the main hall." She dipped her head suddenly, kissing me. "She said he wasn't in Wayfair."

"She lied."

Poppy shivered. "Thank you."

"No need to thank me." I kissed her. "You think you can find him again?"

Lifting her head, she nodded. "I think so, but getting into Wayfair again…"

"We'll figure it out," I assured her. "And we will tackle that daunting list of things you spoke of. Together. Except for killing Isbeth. You want that? It's all yours," I said, and she smiled in a way that should've concerned me but only made me harden.

"By the way, my list wasn't even over," she told me. "There's more stuff. The Ascended. The people. The *kingdoms*. Your parents."

Anger sparked. She'd told me what my mother and father had said about everything. "I really don't want to think about them at the moment."

Her gaze lifted to mine. "I am still thoroughly angry with them, but they…they love you. They love both of you. And I think it was that love that became one of the reasons they never spoke the truth."

"They fucked up."

"Yeah, they did."

"Big time."

"I know, but there's nothing we can do about that."

"Don't be logical," I told her.

"Someone has to be."

Reaching down, I squeezed her plump ass and was immediately fascinated by how the silver wisps in her eyes brightened in response. "That was slightly rude."

"You'll get over it."

"Possibly," I said, loving the small smile that appeared as we teased one another—the normalcy of it. Gods, I would never take it for granted. I hated to ruin it. But I had to. "I need to tell you something."

"If it's about your *cock* being a changeling, I know," she said dryly. "I can feel it."

A surprised laugh left me. "Believe it or not, it's not that."

"I'm shocked." She yawned again, snuggling against my chest. "What is it?"

I opened my mouth, watching her. When she blinked, her eyes were slow to open and quick to close again. She was tired, and I doubted that she'd gotten much more sleep than I had over the last several weeks. Not only that, I had taken a lot of blood. She had to be exhausted.

I glanced at the small window. It was dark beyond the opening. Even if the mist was still thick, we wouldn't be going anywhere tonight. Not with the Craven at the Rise. There was time.

There had to be.

Poppy needed to sleep and then feed. Those were the two most important things. Even more important than telling her about Millicent. And that wasn't me avoiding telling her about the Handmaiden. I wouldn't keep secrets from her ever again, no matter how badly I wanted to. Because I knew this would mess her up and was why she needed to be rested and fed. Strong. No one needed to learn this kind of news half-asleep and weakened.

"What?" Poppy asked, her voice barely above a whisper. "What did you want to tell me?"

I dragged my hand up her back and over the thick strands of her hair. I cupped the back of her head, keeping her cheek pressed to my chest. "Only that I love you," I said, lifting enough to press a kiss to the top of her hair. "With my heart and my soul, today and tomorrow. I will never get enough of you."

"You say that now…"

"Not in a hundred years." I looked down at her, seeing a hint of a soft smile. A beautiful one. I could live on her smiles. They were that precious. Each one a godsdamn gift. I could exist on her laughter. The sound was that important. That life-altering. "Not in a thousand years. *Never. Enough.*"

She gave me a squeeze and then started to lift her head.

I stilled her. "I know. We need to get up, but just…let me hold you for a little bit. Okay? Just a few more moments."

Poppy immediately relaxed, just like I knew she would upon the request. And just like I'd suspected, when her eyes closed once more, they didn't reopen. She fell asleep, and I…I stared at the bridge of her nose, her parted lips, smoothing my hand through her hair as Millicent's words broke free from the void.

She'll die in your arms.

33

I couldn't sleep.

Not when Millicent's warning preyed on my mind. But I stayed with Poppy, running my fingers through her hair. Soaking in her warmth. Counting the steady, strong beats of her heart. Listening to each breath she took until footsteps neared the door and then stopped.

Only then did I lift her from me, carefully easing her onto her side. She didn't wake. Didn't make a sound as I drew the thin blanket over her body. That was how exhausted she was.

I rose, stopping to brush the strands of hair back from her face and kiss her cheek. As close as I was, I saw the faint gray shadows under her eyes. It took nearly every ounce of control I had to leave that bed, but I did. I deserved a fucking medal for it.

Stopping where a neat pile of clothing had been left on a small armchair, I pulled on a pair of black pants. Buttoning the flap, I looked over my shoulder at Poppy. She slept on her side, just as I'd left her, one shoulder bared above the blanket, and her hair a stream of flames spread across the bed behind her. A knot lodged in my chest, a bundle of memories. Of the first time I'd held her while she slept on the cold, hard ground of the Blood Forest. The last time before I was taken, in the ship on that gently rocking bed. She always looked so damn peaceful. Beautiful. Strong. Brave, even in rest.

And I was hers.

I turned away before climbing right back into the bed. My flesh already missed the feel of hers as I went to the door, opening it.

Kieran was leaning against the wall, his head tipped back. His eyes opened, locking on mine. He went completely still as I closed the door. His mouth moved, but I heard no words as he lurched forward. I met him halfway. One or both of us staggered a little as we collided. His hand trembled as he clasped the back of my neck. The knot of emotion in my chest grew as I held him as close as I had Poppy, and in that silence, I thanked the gods—sleeping, dead, or whatever as I dropped my forehead to his shoulder. For him being there for Poppy. For him just being here. For a bond thicker than blood or tradition.

"You whole?" Kieran asked in a voice that felt as rough as my throat.

I closed my eyes. "Going to be."

"Good." The hand at the nape of my neck firmed. "Missed you, man. Something fierce."

"Same."

"Also wanted to punch you in the dick for doing what you did," he said, and a thin laugh left me. "Still want to, to be honest."

"You know why I did it."

"I know." Kieran squeezed the back of my neck. "That's the only reason why I'm not punching you right now."

I laughed again, lifting my head. "That and the fact you're afraid Poppy would kick your ass for it."

He chuckled roughly. "True story."

Gripping his shoulder, I met his stare. "You do know why I gave myself up, right? I had to stop Isbeth. She was hurting Poppy."

"I know. I do. I wouldn't have expected anything less from you," he said. "Doesn't mean I had to like it. Doesn't mean Poppy had to either."

Nodding, I felt that tremor in his hand again. And knowing him for my whole life, I saw the shadows of dread in his eyes. The unasked questions. The evil he feared had preyed upon me, and the nightmares he worried would see a resurrection.

I clasped his cheek with my left hand and leaned my head into his. "It wasn't like last time. The only thing taken from me was my blood."

Some of the shadows cleared but not all of them. "Was that all, though? Truly?"

A muscle ticked in my jaw. The quiet of that cell. The coldness. The hours and days and weeks of that—the desperation and everything else. No, that wasn't all.

Kieran palmed my cheek. "You got me. You got Poppy. You aren't alone. We're both here. Always and forever."

Fuck.

The knot hit my throat and dampened my eyes. "Yeah," I said in a voice full of gravel. "I know."

His chest rose in a deep inhale, and then his gaze flicked to the closed door. He didn't ask. Didn't need to.

"She's asleep."

Visible relief hit him. His eyes closed briefly and then reopened, the irises glimmering. "She'll need to feed. It can't be you. I'll do it as soon as she wakes."

"Thank you."

"No need to thank me for that."

"But I do."

He shrugged. "Not like I minded feeding her."

"I'm sure you didn't," I replied dryly.

One side of his lips curled up as he dropped his hands. "Come. There's stew left on the hearth. You need to eat more."

"Yes, Mother."

Kieran snorted as he led me down the short, narrow hall, past two more closed doors. I looked behind me, hearing no movement. "What's it look like outside?" I asked.

"Mist is fading, here and at higher points in the city, but it's still thick in the lower areas." Kieran entered a candlelit kitchen, picking up a bowl from one of the shelves along the wall. "Sounded like they're still dealing with the Craven. If they've realized any of us are missing, they're not out in full force yet."

"That'll change soon enough," I said, scanning the wide chamber. Blinds covered a large window behind a table and chairs. Several daggers were scattered across the table's surface. "How long do you think we have?"

"Probably the rest of the night and maybe the day." He went to the pot at the hearth. "We've got to make our move before nightfall."

Made sense. We wouldn't have to deal with the knights then, but the Revenants? Another story. Isbeth may not be leashed to the moon like the Ascended, but she wouldn't dare to come out during the day and risk exposure.

I glanced at the entryway again. "Where is everyone?" Namely, where was my fucking brother?

"The mortals—Blaz and Clariza? They're asleep." Kieran ladled a small lake's worth of stew into a bowl. "Good people. Did Poppy tell you the woman's a descendant?"

"She mentioned it." I took the bowl and spoon, stomach rumbling at the herb-heavy scent. The bowl felt a little strange in the four-finger grip, but it was something I'd have to get used to.

Kieran went to the small table, taking a seat. I stood since I'd spent enough time on my ass. "The draken's snooping around outside, hopefully keeping himself unseen and not burning anything."

My brows rose as I chewed the chunks of vegetables and chicken. Something Poppy said came back to me. "Did he really try to bite you?"

"Fuck, yeah, he tried." Kieran's jaw hardened. "He isn't real keen on social skills. You'll probably find him amusing."

I grinned, swallowing the thick stew. The grin faded, though, as Kieran watched me. I didn't want to ask because if the answer was one I didn't want to hear—that my brother wasn't here—I'd lose my shit. But I had to know. "Malik?"

"Asleep in the front room, passed out on the settee."

I felt something. Didn't know if it was surprise or relief.

Kieran leaned forward. "He helped you when you were in that cell?"

"Saw him once. He got rid of the infection." I lifted the remaining fingers on my left hand.

"Only once?"

"He made it sound like it was a risk to me to do so," I told him between mouthfuls.

"You believe him?"

"Don't know," I admitted, my stomach souring. Still, I kept eating. "You?"

He rubbed his chin. "He says he can secure us a ship. That we can be smuggled on and make our escape that way."

"Is that so?" I went to the hearth, refilling my bowl only because the sooner I was back to normal, the sooner I could care for Poppy's needs. "And you trust him that much—trust him with Poppy's safety?"

"There are only a handful of people I trust with her safety, and he sure as fuck isn't one of them," Kieran replied. "But he helped us get you out. He hasn't tried to leave, and he could've alerted the guards we saw when we were scoping out shit. He didn't. He's risking a lot, and he knows what will happen if he's caught."

I thought it over. "I don't think he's going to betray us."

Kieran nodded.

"But he's a huge liability," I said, lifting the stew-heavy spoon to my mouth.

"The Handmaiden."

"If she really is his heartmate, she's leverage that can be used to control him. Probably already has been."

"Only if Isbeth knows," Kieran countered. "Do you really think she'd still be living and breathing if Isbeth did?"

"Yes."

He frowned. "Why do you think that?"

"I'm about to blow your mind." I finished off the remaining stew, setting the bowl beside me. "Millicent is Isbeth's daughter. Her father is Ires. She's Poppy's sister."

Kieran's lips parted, and a long moment passed. "What in the actual fuck?"

"Yeah." Folding an arm over my stomach, I dragged a hand down my face. "If I hadn't seen Millicent without the paint on her face, I wouldn't believe it. But it's true. She's damn near the spitting image of Poppy."

"The fuck?" Kieran whispered, straightening.

I would've laughed, except none of this was funny. "And there's no doubt in my mind that Malik knows that."

Kieran gave a slow shake of his head as his hand fell to the table beside the daggers. "But she's a Revenant," he said, and then gave me a brief rundown of how and why the third sons and daughters could become Revenants.

It all kind of made sense, considering how mortals had been created.

"She's something *like* a Revenant," I said, sharing what Millicent had told me. That did nothing to clear up any confusion because what the Handmaiden had said was about as clear as the soup in that pot.

"Gods," he uttered. "Have you told Poppy?"

"I didn't want to unload that on her when she was so exhausted. Once she wakes up and feeds…"

"Shit."

"Yeah."

"That's going to mess with her."

The muscles in my shoulders cramped. "It will."

He ran a hand over his head, where his hair had grown since the last time I saw him.

"Wait. Did Poppy tell you that there was more to that prophecy? What Tawny told her?"

"She told me bits of it—fuck. The first-and-second-daughter parts? Didn't even connect when Poppy said it. Fated for the once-promised King?" I looked toward the hall. "If Malik speaks the truth about her being his heartmate, it makes sense."

"And doesn't because Poppy isn't going to remake any realms."

I nodded. "You know, Millicent even called herself the first daughter. She also referred to herself as her mother's failure."

"Failure at what?"

"I don't know, but I'm thinking it's what Isbeth plans." I pushed away from the counter as more of what Millicent had shared with me cleared in my mind. "She told me she planned to remake the realms." I went to the window, pulling the blinds back a little to see thin wisps of mist-strewn night.

Kieran turned in his chair. "Yeah, we heard that. One of the Priests in Oak Ambler said it was Poppy's purpose."

Closing my eyes, I let the blinds fall back into place. I recalled jumbled words spoken by Millicent and the Blood Queen, some slipping past me before I could make sense of them. "Millicent said that to remake the realms, you had to destroy them first. And I think that's how Isbeth failed with Millicent. She would've had to go through the Culling—Ascend into her godhood. I don't think Millicent survived it."

"And you think Isbeth made her into one of those things as a way to save her?" Kieran sounded incredulous. "You think she cares that much?"

"I think she loves Poppy in her own twisted, fucked-up way. I think that's why she also didn't touch me this time around." I faced Kieran. "And I think she probably loves Millicent in that same demented way of hers. After all, the death of one child propelled all of this into motion, didn't it?"

"Shit." Kieran looked up at the exposed beams of the ceiling. "So, what? You think Millicent was her first, and Poppy was her second attempt at creating something she thinks will destroy the realms?"

"Yeah."

"Poppy will never do something like that. Never," Kieran said from between clenched teeth with a swipe of his hand. Gods, I couldn't love the wolven more. His loyalty to our Queen was everything. "Yeah, she's had her moments—ones you haven't seen, where she's…she's something else. Like when she saw what Isbeth had done to you."

I had to breathe through the rage. I had to resist picking up one of the daggers and slamming it into the wall of a mortal's home. Ones who'd done nothing but aid us. I had to get over the guilt.

"But it's still Poppy," Kieran said, and shadows crept across his face, quickly disappearing. "Isbeth may have succeeded in creating a powerful god, but she ultimately failed."

"Agreed." I went to the table, my movements stiff. "There's more. I know there is. But my head, man…it's got these patches of nothing. They're slow to fill out." Placing my hands on the table, I leaned over. "I know Millicent said that I needed to stop Poppy. That, soon, I would be the only one."

"Stop her as in…?" Kieran stiffened, and the change that swept through him was vast and quick. His skin thinned. His eyes turned luminous. "Kill her?"

"Not going to happen," I reminded him.

"Damn straight, it's not," he growled. "Because I'm going to go round up Reaver and let him burn that wannabe Revenant."

"You really think Poppy will allow that once she knows who Millicent is?" I asked, and Kieran snarled low. "I don't think Millicent wants Poppy dead. It's almost like she believes there's no other way."

"Because she thinks Poppy's the Harbinger?"

I nodded.

"She's not. And I don't give a fuck about the differences between wanting Poppy dead and thinking there's no other way," he fired back. "You telling me there is one?"

My stare met his. "You know damn well if she proves to be a threat to Poppy, I will hand-deliver her to Reaver. I'd rather have Poppy's hate than see her harmed."

Kieran sat back, his fingers tense on the table. "Poppy will never hate you."

I snorted. "You underestimate her capacity for feeling strong emotions."

"Actually, I don't." His eyes flicked to mine. "The only thing that drove her close to destroying Solis was her love for you."

Love.

Isbeth's taunting words resurfaced from the darkness. *I never wanted that weakness.*

I straightened.

Love can be weaponized, weakening a...

My heart started pounding.

"What?" Kieran demanded. "What is it?"

"Poppy told me the draken said she hadn't completed the Culling yet," I rasped. Millicent had said the same. It was why Isbeth had done all she had. Why she'd taken me in the first place. Why she waited.

"Yeah. So?"

"A god isn't powerful enough to destroy the realms, Kieran. Isbeth would know that."

And a god wasn't powerful enough to do as Millicent claimed, either, to hand Isbeth her revenge against Nyktos.

Kieran opened his mouth, but then his gaze cut to the shielded window. His eyes widened, and I knew that he'd realized the same thing I had. It was impossible, but...

Kieran's head swiveled back to me. "The mist. She didn't summon it, Cas. She *created* the Primal mist."

Hours later, as the sun crested over the city, I sat in bed beside Poppy, ankles crossed and back against the headboard. She hadn't woken when I joined her, but she *had* snuggled close, resting her cheek against my chest.

I hadn't slept more than an hour—if that. For totally different reasons now. I sat there, toying with the soft strands of Poppy's hair as she slept. Simply stunned by her. Marveled.

The door cracked open, and Kieran entered. His steps were quiet, careful as he approached the bed. "I hate to do this..."

"I know," I said, looking down at Poppy. He didn't want to wake her. Neither did I, but it was necessary. Time wasn't on our side.

Tucking strands back from her cheek, I bent over and kissed her brow. "Queen," I called softly, smoothing my thumb along her lower jaw. Poppy's brows pinched as she wiggled closer. I grinned as Kieran sat on her other side. "Open those beautiful eyes for me."

Her lashes fluttered and then swept up. Sleep clung to her gaze.

Those gray shadows under her eyes were still there, but the silver streaks were bright, piercing the spring green. "Cas."

A groan rumbled from my chest. "You're my favorite kind of torture," I told her, kissing her brow. "Kieran's here."

She turned her head slightly, looking over her shoulder. "Hi."

Kieran smiled at her as he leaned over her hip, bracing his weight with his hand on the bed. His features softened in a way I hadn't seen from him in a long time. "Morning."

"Morning?" she repeated, blinking. "I slept that long?"

"It's okay. You needed the rest, and we couldn't leave anyway," I told her, squeezing her shoulder.

"Did you rest?" She glanced back at Kieran. "Did either of you two rest?"

"Of course," Kieran lied so smoothly, I almost believed him.

Poppy watched Kieran for a moment and then looked up at me. "How are you feeling?"

"Divine," I told her, rubbing my thumb along the curve of her collarbone.

She studied me closely and then sat up, the thin blanket pooling at her hips, and the riot of waves and curls going in every direction. "Is Malik still here?"

I ignored the sudden lurch in my chest as I curled an arm around her waist, figuring she was mere seconds from climbing out of bed. "He is."

"Just saw him." Kieran's gaze flicked to me. "Still sleeping."

"And Reaver?" she asked as I pulled her between my legs so she was pressed to my chest. She allowed it, relaxing into me in a way that almost made it hard to believe she'd used to sit so stiffly near me. "Is he—?"

"He's fine," Kieran said. "Hasn't burned anyone alive." He paused. "Recently."

I arched a brow.

"Reaver," Poppy murmured with a sigh, resting a hand on my arm, "has this obsession with burning people. Guess it's a draken thing."

"I think it's just a Reaver thing," Kieran stated dryly.

"True." A small grin appeared as she lifted my left hand to her mouth, pressing a kiss to the top. "What about the mist? Did any Craven get into the city? How will we—?"

"So many questions—" Kieran laughed as he reached over, tucking that particularly rebellious strand of hair back from her face, the one that kept slipping forward. "That need to wait."

Her eyes narrowed on him. "I don't think any of them need to wait."

"They do," I said, and that glare flipped to me. I smiled.

"Don't smile at me," she snapped.

My smile grew. "So feisty."

Her stare warmed even as her chin jutted. "Stupid dimples," she muttered.

Laughing, I lowered my mouth to hers, kissing her. "You love my dimples," I told her, straightening. "And you need to feed."

She opened her mouth, then closed it.

"I volunteered without even being asked," Kieran assured her. "With all the eather you've used, and the blood you've given Cas, it's a necessity."

Poppy was quiet for a moment. "I know, but I…"

Curling my fingers under her chin, I tipped her gaze back to mine. "Your hesitation can't be because of me."

"It's not." She turned her head down, kissing the tip of my finger. Her eyes fixed on Kieran. "It's just that I don't like using you as a—as a snack."

His brows flew up. "Well, first off, I don't like to think of myself as a snack. More like a whole damn meal."

Dropping my face to the top of Poppy's head, it took everything in me not to laugh.

"Okay, Mr. Whole Damn Meal, I don't like using you in general, and you know that." Moving suddenly, she shoved her elbow into my stomach, causing me to grunt. "And you? It's not funny."

"Of course, not, my Queen," I replied, grinning into her hair.

She moved to jab me with her elbow again, but I curled my other arm around her, stopping her as I laughed. Tilting my head, I kissed her cheek. "You're not using him. It's a mutually beneficial act."

Poppy twisted her neck to look at me. "How is that a mutually beneficial act?"

Kieran opened his mouth and then wisely closed it when his gaze met mine. "Because," I said, loosening my hold on her, "it makes him feel useful."

She rolled her eyes.

"Poppy." Kieran leaned forward, placing his fingers under her chin and turning her attention to him. "You know I'm happy to be of aid to you in this way. You're not using me. You're allowing me to help you.

There's a world of difference between those two things."

Quietly, she stared at him, and I had a feeling she was reading him. Whatever she felt, I'd have to thank Kieran for later, because she nodded with a sigh. "Okay."

A bolt of relief shot through me. I gave her another quick kiss on the corner of her lips and then lifted a hand. I didn't need to say anything. Kieran offered his, and Poppy tensed against me as I lowered my mouth to his wrist. Her grip returned to my arm as she turned, giving me room. I hesitated over Kieran's skin, raising my eyes to hers. Tiny nails dug into the flesh of my arm as she watched me pierce Kieran's skin. An earthy taste touched my tongue. I didn't drink, and I didn't go too deeply. Kieran didn't even move, but Poppy's worried gaze shot to the wolven.

"I'm fine," he assured.

Lifting my head, my hand was still around Kieran's when he brought the welling blood to her mouth. There was a moment when Poppy didn't move, but then she lowered her head, closing her mouth around the marks.

Kieran moved then.

Just a small jerk. One I didn't think Poppy noticed as I gathered the strands of her hair that had fallen forward, brushing them over one shoulder.

My hand left Kieran's then, and I curled my arm around her waist, resting my hand on one hip. She gave a little jolt at the touch and then her leg curled under the blanket, pressing against mine as I drew my other hand up and down her back.

I watched her—the thick fringe of lashes fanning her cheeks, the way her throat worked on each swallow as I moved my fingers across her hip in slow, steady circles. I didn't take my eyes off her. I saw the moment the shadows under her eyes cleared. I inhaled, breathing in a familiar scent. The corners of my lips tipped up as I bent, kissing the top of her head and then her temple.

Those sharp, little nails dug into my flesh as a pink flush seeped across her cheeks. Her eyes flew open, narrowing on Kieran. The bastard was grinning, looking way too proud of himself, and I had a feeling she had stumbled into his memories, and he was showing her something she likely found highly inappropriate.

And intriguing.

Because that scent increased, joining another, and my blood thickened in response. Poppy gave a restless wiggle, causing her hip to brush against my entirely intrigued cock. I squeezed her hip, pulling her tighter to me.

Poppy swallowed one last time and then lifted her mouth. "Thank you," she whispered, folding both her hands around Kieran's forearm, just below my bite. A silvery glow radiated from her hands, and it didn't matter how many times I saw her do this. It was fucking awe-inspiring. The two puncture wounds faded within a few heartbeats. She let go of his arm. "You're still a jerk, though."

Kieran's laugh crinkled the skin at the corners of his eyes. "You take enough?"

Poppy reclined against my chest. "Yes."

"Good." He looked at me with bright eyes—eyes that pulsed with eather behind the pupils—as he clasped the back of Poppy's head and bent, kissing her forehead. He rose from the bed. "I'll be waiting."

The moment the door closed behind Kieran, I clasped her cheeks and turned her gaze to me. The pink flush in her skin had deepened.

"My Queen?"

The tip of her tongue wet her lips. "Yes?"

"I need you on my cock." Dipping my head, my tongue traced the flick of hers. "Now."

Poppy shuddered.

I slid my hands down her sides, lifting her hips and drawing her onto her knees. Her mouth found mine, and her kiss—fuck, it tasted of sweetness and something warm. Earthy. Her hands went to my shoulders, to the hair on the nape of my neck. We had a lot of important shit to talk about and get done, but I needed the same as she did. To be inside her. I reached for the buttons on my breeches, barely managing to unhook them without ripping them off. I gripped myself as I curled my arm around her waist, pulling her down.

The first touch of her, hot and slick, nearly undid me. As did the breathy sound she made against my lips as I drew her down until no space remained between us. Nothing. I threaded my fingers through her hair as I slid my hand under the hem of her shirt, cupping her ass.

"As I said before..." I rocked her against me. "You're my favorite kind of torture."

She moaned, trembling. "You're just my favorite." Her breath caught as I squeezed her ass, grinding her down on my dick. "You're my favorite everything."

I nipped at her lower lip. "I know."

"Arrogant."

"Just telling the truth." I took her mouth with mine, drawing in the unique flavor of her kiss. "I can taste his blood on your tongue."

Her hips gave a delicious little jerk, but she started to pull back. I stopped her. "It's not a bad thing," I told her, keeping her hips moving, working. "What does his blood taste like to you?"

"You didn't...taste it?" Her words came out in short pants.

"Tasted earthy to me."

"It...his blood tastes like a fall morning," she said.

"I'm a little envious of that." I slid my hand over the soft flesh of her ass, slipping a finger between the cheeks and into the tight flesh there. Her entire body stiffened as she sucked in a sharp breath. "Does that hurt?"

"No," she whispered, her chest rising and falling rapidly against mine. "It just feels different."

"But good?" I watched her closely, searching for any hint of discomfort as I remained still beneath her.

Poppy bit down on her lip. "Yes."

I smiled at her and then started moving her hips again. "You read about something like this in Miss Willa's diary?"

Her face was even pinker. "Maybe."

I chuckled roughly, taking the lip she'd bitten with mine. The hands at my shoulders trembled. "Were you curious about it when you read it? I bet you were."

"Maybe a little," she said.

"Gods." I nipped her neck, avoiding the nearly healed bite marks. "I love that fucking book."

"Not surprised to hear that..." She jerked, and she felt hotter, wetter. "I didn't think it would feel so—" Her moan was a full-body shudder as I pressed in deeper. "I didn't think it would feel like..."

"Like what?"

"Like this." Her forehead fell against mine. "Hot. Wicked. Full."

Her breath was on a loop, catching and releasing, and I didn't think she realized that I wasn't guiding her movements any longer. She rode me, her breath hot against my lips and her body moving in sinuous curls and plunges. She enjoyed the wickedness. Thoroughly. I heard it in those inhales. Felt it in how she tightened around my dick and my finger. When she came, she took me over the edge right with her. The release shook us both, leaving me feeling as if I'd lost control of all the muscles in my body.

It took a lot of willpower to ease myself out of her and leave her on the bed, curled on her side once more, looking thoroughly fucked in a most indecent way. I didn't linger long in the bathing chamber, cleaning up quickly before returning to her, sitting near her hip.

Poppy was awake, though her eyes were only half open. There was peace in her soft smile that I hated to disturb.

But I had to.

She was rested, fed, and fucked.

All I could hope was that those three things would help her process what I had to tell her.

"There is something I need to talk to you about. It's going to be hard to believe, and it'll be a shock."

The change in Poppy was immediate. The smile vanished, and she'd gone completely still as she stared up at me. "What?"

I drew in a deep breath as I tugged the hem of her shirt down. "The Handmaiden that you think my brother is in love with? The one he claims is his heartmate?"

Her brows snapped together. "Millicent?"

"Yeah. Her." I swallowed. "She came to my cell a few times. I know she told Malik the wound in my hand was infected. And then she came again, after I saw you. She showed me something. That's how I know that what she told me is true. I saw it. There's no denying it. She's…she's your sister, Poppy. Your full-blooded sister."

34

Poppy

"My sister?" There was no way I could've heard him right. I sat up as if that would somehow change what he'd said. "She can't be my sister, Casteel."

A warm vanilla taste gathered in my throat as he smoothed his thumb just under the scar on my left cheek. "She is, Poppy."

There was like some sort of barrier that flat-out repelled the whole idea. "And you think this, all because she told you so?"

"Because she *showed* me," he said gently. "Have you seen her without that mask painted on her face?"

I frowned. "No."

"I have." He trailed his thumb along the curve of my jaw. "I've seen what she looks like after she's washed away the paint and dye."

"Wait. Was she *bathing* in front of you?"

"Sort of." One side of his lips curved up, and there was a hint of a dimple in his right cheek. "She, with little warning, straight-up dunked her head in the bath that had been brought into my cell."

That sounded like an odd thing to do.

But then I remembered how she'd climbed into that chair and lay upside down for no reason whatsoever.

"Her hair isn't black," he continued, and I thought about the flatness of her hair color, how it had looked patchy in some areas. "It's a very pale blond, nearly white."

I jerked back as an image took hold—one of the woman I'd seen in those strange dreams or memories. The one I'd believed to be the Consort. She had hair so pale it reminded me of moonlight. My heart started pounding.

"And her face?" Casteel leaned in, sliding his hand to the nape of my neck. "She has your eyes, except the color is different. Her nose. The structure of her features. Even the tilt of her jaw." His gaze searched mine. "She has way more freckles than you do, but she could almost pass for your twin, Poppy."

I was staring at him again, caught in a storm of disbelief. Almost pass as my *twin*? If that were true, how could I *not* have seen it? But the mask—the facial paint—was thick and large, making it difficult to even tell what her bone structure was like.

But he couldn't be right. Somehow, he'd been misled. Tricked.

Leaning back, I shook my head. "This doesn't make any sense. Revenants are the third sons and daughters. And if she were my sister, then that means I have two *more* siblings. And she would be a goddess."

"I thought the same thing at first—that she had to be a goddess. But she said she wasn't. The only thing I can figure is that she didn't survive the Culling, and Isbeth used her knowledge of the Revenants to save her," he told me.

A ragged laugh left me, and Casteel's concern gathered in my throat, rich and thick like cream. "She can't—if she's my sister…" I trailed off, throat clogging as I remembered her desperation—the hopelessness that felt a lot like what I'd sensed from Ires as a child. I swallowed hard. "She said she saw me when I was a child. If what she says is true, why wouldn't she have said something?"

"Maybe she couldn't. I don't know." Casteel brushed a few strands of my hair back. "But she is your sister."

Could this really be true? Had Ian known? I remembered her shock when he was killed. Her sorrow. There'd been no other children in that castle other than Ian and me when we were younger, but she had also said that she was nearly as old as Casteel.

A sister?

Good gods, it just couldn't be true—

What Isbeth had said came back to me. *He was angry, but when we came together to make you, he was not forced. Neither time.*

Neither time.

I hadn't paid attention to those words then. Or maybe I'd just assumed she'd meant they'd only been together twice.

"If she is Isbeth's daughter, then how is she okay with her father being caged?" I asked, my heart still racing. I knew Cas didn't have the answer to that, but I couldn't stop myself. "She has to know Isbeth has him somewhere. Does she not care? Is she just like her mother?"

"I don't think she's like Isbeth. If she hadn't gone to Malik—"

"*Malik.*" I scrambled off the bed, turning to look for my clothing. "Malik would know."

"Possibly." Casteel stood, finding my shirt halfway under the bed. He seemed about to speak again but fell silent as he donned a black linen shirt that shouldn't have been as loose on him as it was. I had to stop my worry from growing into something bigger. He would regain the weight he'd lost, along with his strength—faster than I even probably expected.

The pants left for me were definitely breeches. They fit, if a bit snugly, but I really didn't want to walk about pantsless, so I wasn't complaining. Someone had also loaned me a vest, one that had seven hundred tiny hooks running up the front. I slipped it on over the shirt and started the tedious work of hooking the clasps without missing one.

"Let me help." Casteel came to me, his hands replacing my trembling fingers. It took him a moment to get used to not being able to use his pointer finger on his left hand, but he managed far more quickly than I.

The intimacy of his aid had a quieting effect on my mind. My thoughts stilled as I watched him work the tiny clasps into the hooks. There weren't seven hundred of them. Possibly thirty. I wished there were seven hundred. Because this moment felt so normal, despite everything. Something couples might do every day.

Something I'd missed desperately.

The backs of his fingers brushed the swell of my breast as he finished the last couple of clasps. "Have I told you how much I love this particular item of clothing on you?"

"I believe you have." I straightened the hem where it fit and flared slightly over my hips. "Anytime I wore a garment like this, I thought about how much you liked it."

That dimple appeared again, and I didn't think it was so stupid then. He trailed a finger along the curved-edge bodice of the vest. A tiny strip of lace had been stitched there, the same deep shade of gray as the vest. "I think I would love it even more without the shirt."

"I bet you would," I replied wryly. My breasts and stomach were already testing the limits of the clasps, doing very little to hide the deep cleavage peeking through the V-shaped neckline of the shirt. Without the shirt, the entire kingdom would get quite the eyeful.

His other dimple made an appearance as he gathered the sleeve that had come undone and began rolling it. "I know that what I just told you is a huge shock, and it's only one of many in recent months," he said, folding the sleeve around my elbow. "I know it's going to mess with your head once you accept it as truth."

It was already messing with my head.

"And that's not something you need right now." He moved on to the other sleeve, giving it the same treatment. "But I couldn't keep that from you."

I looked up at him. Dark, glossy waves had fallen over his forehead, nearly into his eyes. The smooth jawline was familiar, and the hollowness under his cheeks already less noticeable. For forty-five days, I'd dreamed of standing before him. I'd wanted nothing more than that, and he was here.

Once he was finished with the sleeve, I stretched up and kissed him softly. The striking lines of his face softened under my palm. "I don't know what to even think or what to believe, but telling me was the right thing. I would've done the same if you had a random brother or sister out there, roaming about."

He grinned. "I don't think my familial ancestry is nearly as interesting as yours."

I shot him an arch look as I stopped to pick up the sheathed dagger and strap it to my thigh.

Casteel waited at the door, his eyes a heated gold as he watched me. Slowly, his gaze lifted to mine. "I still find that dagger sheathed to your thigh wildly arousing."

I smiled, joining him. "I still find that to be slightly disturbing."

"Only slightly? I see my dysfunction is rubbing off on you."

"That's because you're a bad influence."

"Told you once before, my Queen." He touched his thumb to my chin and then moved the hand to my lower back as he opened the door, causing my heart to flutter about. Gods, how I'd missed these little touches. "Only the already enticingly wicked can be influenced."

I laughed as I stepped out into a coffee-scented hall and immediately came face-to-face with Kieran.

He'd been leaning against the wall and straightened upon seeing us. "I haven't been out here long," he said, his pale gaze flickering over both of us. "I was just coming to tell you guys that you needed to stop making out for five seconds."

"Liar," Casteel murmured with a grin. "You've probably been out here the whole time."

Kieran didn't respond, and Casteel went to him as my senses opened, stretching out to the wolven. The heaviness of worry had replaced the teasing amusement from when I had fed from him. He was still concerned about Casteel, but I didn't think that was the only reason he'd lingered outside the chamber. I thought that perhaps he just needed to be near Casteel.

And I also thought that Casteel possibly sensed that somehow because when he went to Kieran, he pulled him into a tight embrace.

Seeing the two of them together, holding each other so tightly, brought a wealth of warmth to me. There was no bond between Casteel and Kieran—I'd broken that when I Ascended into my godhood. But the love they felt for each other went beyond any type of bond. Still, there was also a bit of sorrow because I doubted that Casteel had shared any of those gestures with his brother.

Nothing was said, but as always, there seemed to be some kind of silent communication between them, one that must've come from knowing one another for so long.

Casteel extended his arm to me. I came forward, placing my hand in his. He tugged me into his side, and a heartbeat later, Kieran's other hand fisted in my hair. The air shuddered from me as I squeezed my eyes tight against the rush of tears—the rush of...sweet emotion. The simple gesture was a powerful reminder that this moment wasn't just about them. It was about us.

I breathed deeply, feeling as if it were the first real breath I'd taken in weeks. My eyes closed as Casteel's and Kieran's warmth surrounded me and reached inside. To the cold place in the center of my being that I forced myself not to think about. It had heated in those moments when it was just Casteel and me and nothing between our bodies. Nothing in my mind but the feel of his skin against mine. The chilly emptiness had returned while I bathed him, though. Abated for only a little bit when I fed and what had come after. But it had returned as I'd dressed.

But now there was only warmth as I stood between them.

Kieran shifted, pressing his forehead to mine. "Not feeling tired or anything?" he asked, his voice low. "You think you got enough blood?"

I nodded, stepping back, but I didn't make it very far. Casteel's arm had tightened around my waist. "I need to speak with Malik."

Casteel glanced down at me. "I told Kieran while you were sleeping."

"Do you believe it?" I asked him.

"I didn't at first, but I don't see why she'd lie or how she could look so much like you." Kieran turned. "Malik's in the kitchen."

"Still surprised he's here," Casteel said, and I tensed at the wariness in his tone.

Kieran nodded. "I can understand that."

Casteel's hand returned to the center of my back and remained there as we followed Kieran down the hall to the area of the kitchen. I'd only taken a few steps before one word entered my thoughts.

Sister.

I exhaled roughly as we passed through a rounded opening. The chamber was well lit, but the shades had been drawn on the windows lining the wall, blocking out the morning sun. Blaz and Clariza were at a well-worn table, the surface dull and full of many nicks of various sizes. Marks that must have come from the various daggers and blades laid out upon it.

Malik sat with them, staring at the cup of coffee between his hands. He didn't look up as we entered, but his shoulders tensed in the same way Casteel's did beside me. There was no warm, long-overdue embrace. There was no acknowledgment.

Chairs scraped against wood as Blaz and Clariza rose, and I suspected they were about to kneel. "Not necessary."

The two exchanged glances. Blaz gave me a toothy grin as he sat.

"Thank you for opening your home to us." Casteel addressed them as his hand moved up and down my back. "I know that this was of great risk to you both."

"It's our honor and worth whatever risk," Clariza said, her eyes wide as she clasped her hands together. "You look much better."

Casteel inclined his head. "I feel much better."

"Would you like a cup of coffee, Your Majesty?" Blaz asked.

"Coffee would be nice." Casteel glanced at me, and I nodded. "And you don't have to use any title. We are not your rulers."

Clariza gave a small smile as she rose. "I'll get you two some coffee. Blaz tends to make it more cream and sugar than actual coffee."

"I see nothing wrong with that," the mortal replied, leaning back.

Neither did I as Clariza hurried to the hearth. There was a lot we needed to be updated on, but Malik remained at the table, his head bowed and body rigid. I glanced at Casteel. He eyed Malik. Had been since we entered the kitchen. I looked around, my brows knitting. "Where's Reaver?"

"Cleaning up," Malik answered, taking a sip of coffee.

"Finally," Kieran muttered, and Casteel looked at him.

I opened my mouth and closed it, but then Malik finally lifted his gaze. The question burst out of me. "Is Millicent my sister?"

Several sets of eyes landed on me as the mortals' lemony curiosity gathered in my throat, but Malik... His eyes narrowed as he sat straight. "Blaz? Riza? I hate to ask, but can we have a moment?"

Blaz rolled his eyes. "I don't know. I would like to know the answer to this question. I'd also like to know who Millicent is."

"I bet you would," Malik replied acidly.

Clariza came to us, two cups in hand. "There are also some biscuits if you're hungry," she said as I took one of the cream-colored mugs. "Blaz and I will check on Reaver."

"Thank you," I whispered.

Her stare held mine for a moment, and then she nodded. She turned to her husband. "Up."

"Really?" Blaz exclaimed. "You know how nosy I am, and you're asking me to leave?"

"Really." She pinned him with a stern look that was rather impressive as I took a deep drink of the hot, rich coffee.

Blaz sighed, grumbling as he got to his feet. "I'm going to eavesdrop, just so you know."

"No, he won't." Clariza threaded her arm through his. "He'll just bitch and moan in our bedchamber."

"Could just be moaning instead of bitching, you know?" Blaz responded with a waggle of his brows.

"You keep talking," she said as they walked from the kitchen, "and that becomes even more unlikely."

Casteel's lips twitched around the rim of his mug. "I like them," he said as they disappeared down the hall.

"They're good people," Malik said, staring up at me. "Did Millicent tell you this?"

"She told me," Casteel answered. "And *showed* me."

"You don't believe him?" Malik asked of me.

"I believe that's what he was told, but I don't see how it's possible," I said. "Even if she looks like me—"

"She does," Malik interrupted, and my stomach dipped. A muscle ticked in his temple. "It's eerie how much you two look alike."

"Not just looks," Casteel commented, that hand still moving up and down my back—soothing, grounding. "Personality, too."

My head swung to him. "Excuse me? We really are talking about the same person, right?" I glanced at Kieran. "The one who flounced—literally *flounced*—out of the chamber and sat upside down in a chair for no reason at all?"

"There are similar mannerisms. The way both of you...move," Casteel said, and I *felt* the frown permanently etching onto my face because I didn't *flounce* anywhere. "She also has a tendency to..."

"Ramble?" Malik finished for him, a half-grin appearing.

My eyes narrowed. "I do not ramble."

Casteel coughed on his drink as Kieran silently hoisted himself onto the counter, his brows lifted.

"I do not," I insisted.

"Yes, you do," Reaver said, entering the kitchen. He glanced at Casteel. "Reaver. Nice to meet you. Glad you didn't bite me, and I didn't have to burn you alive."

I had nothing to say to that.

"Nice to meet you, too," Casteel drawled, eyes glimmering with a hint of bewildered amusement as he stared at the draken. "Thank you for your aid."

"Whatever." Reaver strolled past us, heading for the covered plate near the hearth.

"Anyway," I said, focusing on Malik while Casteel watched Reaver. I realized this was probably the first time he'd gotten to see a draken while *here*. "If she's my sister, how is she a Revenant and not a goddess? Is it what Casteel suspects? Did she have problems Ascending?"

Malik said nothing.

Casteel's hand stilled on my back as Reaver shoved half a biscuit into his mouth. "Brother, if I were you, I would start sharing whatever it is you know."

"Or what?" Malik inclined his head in an act that was so shockingly similar to Casteel's, I thought maybe there really was something about sibling mannerisms. "You're going to make me?"

Casteel's laugh was dry. "I don't think you have to worry about *me* making you do shit."

"True," Malik murmured, smirking as his gaze flicked to me. A moment passed. "Cas is right. Millie...she would've been a god if she'd survived the Culling. She didn't."

"Wait a second," Reaver said, wiping crumbs from his mouth with the back of his hand. "That Handmaiden is Poppy's sister?"

Kieran sighed. "Where have you been?"

"Not in the kitchen," Reaver snapped. "Obviously."

The wolven rolled his eyes.

Reaver focused on Malik. "Ires is the father?" When Malik nodded, the draken's brows flew up. "Oh, shit. *She's* going to be…" He shook his head, taking another bite. "If that is true, the Handmaiden would've needed blood—"

"She has a name," Malik interrupted, his tone flat. "It's Millicent."

Reaver cocked his head to the side, and for a moment, I feared there might be fire. "*Millicent* would've needed powerful blood to complete the Ascension into godhood. Meaning, she would've needed the blood of a god. Or a descendant of the gods." He gestured at Malik. "An Atlantian, for example. Elemental. The blood is stronger in them, but there's no guarantee it would've been enough. There's never a guarantee." He looked at me. "You could've even died."

Casteel stiffened.

"I didn't," I reminded him, which felt silly to do because, obviously, I hadn't.

"It wasn't enough for Millie," Malik confirmed. "*Your* blood wasn't strong enough."

My stomach hollowed as I turned to Casteel.

"What the fuck?" he whispered.

"Isbeth took your blood while she held you captive and gave it to Millie, hoping it would be enough. But you were too weak at that point. Isbeth hadn't taken your captivity and what it would do to you into consideration."

Casteel stared at Malik, his features sharpening and becoming starker. I stepped in closer to him. He was just as shocked as I was.

"But Isbeth has Ires," Kieran said. "Why couldn't she use his blood?"

"The cage Isbeth keeps him in nullifies the eather in his blood, rendering him powerless, and his blood useless," Malik explained. "Another thing she hadn't exactly considered. That's why she kept you alive when she had other Atlantians killed. She needed your blood."

I pressed my fingers to my temple as Casteel's hand started moving again up and down my back. "Then how did she become a Revenant?"

"Callum," Malik answered. "He showed Isbeth what to do."

"The golden fuck?" Casteel growled.

"How old is this…Callum?" Reaver's eyes narrowed.

"Old. Don't know exactly. Don't know where he even came from, but he's real old. Callum knew how to make Revenants. It's magic. Old, Primal stuff." Malik's jaw worked. "As fucked up as Isbeth is—and none of you truly knows how fucked that actually is—she loves her daughters. In her own twisted way."

My stomach gave another sinking twist.

"She couldn't let Millie die, so she used that old magic. And because Millie had eather in her blood, it worked," Malik said after a moment. "It saved her, and she became the first daughter, and Isbeth started plotting for another chance. A second daughter."

First daughter.

The full prophecy Tawny had shared with me had referenced the first daughter with blood full of fire and fated for the once-promised King. Good gods, we had even hypothesized that it had referred to Malik.

This Handmaiden was my sister, the first daughter spoken of in Penellaphe's prophecy, and we…

"We are truly the product of a madwoman's thirst for vengeance."

"No." Casteel turned to me, lowering his mug. "You are more than that. You always have been."

I was. I repeated that over and over until it felt true.

Malik smiled tightly. "Millie should've kept her mouth shut about who she truly is. Only a handful of people know, and most of them are dead now." His gaze shifted to his brother. "She knew what would happen if she told someone that little secret. That person would be killed, and Millie would bear the brunt of Isbeth's displeasure."

I stiffened.

"So, it's got me wondering, why would she tell you that? There had to be a reason for her to take such a risk." Malik stared at his brother, unflinching. "Wasn't there, Cas?"

Casteel had set his mug aside. "She said some shit."

His brother's lips thinned. "I bet she did."

The hand on my back slipped away as Casteel stepped forward. Kieran tensed where he sat, his eyes burning a pale, luminous blue.

"Let me clarify," Casteel said, his voice dropping low in that soft, deceptive way it did that was often a prelude to someone being relieved of a vital organ. "She said some stuff that may be true, and other stuff that's definitely bullshit."

Malik chuckled. "Sounds to me like she said what you didn't want to hear."

"You know what I want to hear?" Casteel's chin dipped. "Why you're here. Why you're helping us now."

"Maybe you should tell your wife why her sister would take such a risk," Malik countered.

"Are they going to fight?" Reaver murmured.

"Looks like it," Kieran answered, glancing at him. "It wouldn't be entirely abnormal if so."

My heart had started pounding again. "What did she say?"

"I was going to tell you," Casteel growled, his anger stroking my skin. "But it's nothing worth repeating."

Malik raised his brows. "Maybe it's you who's living in denial. Can't blame you for it. I wouldn't want to believe it either."

"Believe what?" I grabbed Casteel's arm, stopping him as he took another step forward. "What did she tell you?"

His eyes swung to me, but he said nothing. My senses stretched out, coming up against a wall. Air snagged in my throat. He was blocking me, and that could only mean—

"You were created for the same reason that Millie was. For one purpose," Malik said. "Your sister failed her Ascension. You didn't. And you already said what that purpose is. Except you're focusing just on Atlantia, and it's so much bigger than that. Your purpose is to—"

"Remake the kingdoms," I cut in. "The realms. I know. I've heard that."

Malik shook his head. "Your purpose is to *destroy* the realms. Mortal *and* Iliseeum. That's how she plans to remake them."

"That sounds a bit excessive," muttered Reaver.

I drew back. Isbeth had said that she wanted to see Atlantia burn. But this…this was not the same. It was entirely something else. It sounded a lot like…

Beware, for the end will come from the west to destroy the east and lay waste to all which lies between.

Stomach dipping, I inhaled sharply.

The prophecy—what had it said? That the first and second daughters would remake the realms and usher in the end. No. Just because it had been written didn't mean it would happen. What Isbeth wanted didn't matter for a slew of reasons. "First off, I'm not even powerful enough to do something like that."

Malik leaned forward, *"First off,* you aren't powerful enough *yet* to do that. You haven't completed your Culling. Then, you will be."

"Powerful enough to destroy the realms?" I laughed. "A god isn't that powerful."

"I don't think that's what you are," Casteel said.

Slowly, I turned to him. "Come again?"

"It's something I figured out a bit ago," he told me. "I don't fully understand or know how it's possible, but I don't think you're a god."

"Then what the hell am I?" I threw up my hands.

"A Primal," Malik announced.

I rolled my eyes. "Oh, come on."

"He speaks the truth," Reaver announced, and we all turned to him. "Both of them. You're a Primal—born of mortal flesh."

35

A dull roar filled my ears. My hand fell from Casteel's arm. *Born of mortal flesh, a great primal power...*

"At first, I thought you knew this," Reaver continued, drawing me from my thoughts. "You were able to summon us. You held the Primal *notam*, but then I realized you knew so very little about, well, anything."

I snapped my mouth shut.

"And you didn't think to tell her?" Casteel asked. "Once you realized she didn't know?"

The draken shrugged.

Casteel straightened to his full height. While my emotions were too all over the place, his anger was red-hot. "Did you just *shrug*?"

"Yes, he did." Kieran glared at the draken. "If you'd been around him longer, that wouldn't have surprised you."

"Look, I figured she was already dealing with enough," the draken reasoned. "Whether she knew or not, wouldn't have changed anything. She'd already survived the beginning of the Culling. There's no danger to her or risk to her completing the Ascension as this point."

"I don't even know what to say." I blinked rapidly. "You could've told me so that I was prepared. So I wouldn't learn this on the same day I learned I had a sister. Or when I—"

"Sounds like you know what to say," Reaver interrupted dryly.

"And you haven't finished your Culling. So, congratulations. You'll be prepared."

"You are the worst," I whispered, suddenly remembering something he'd said about the draken knowing what my will was. *It has always been that way with the Primals.* And when I'd said I wasn't a Primal, he hadn't agreed. Come to think of it, I didn't think he'd ever referred to me as a god, either.

"Wait a minute. Why would the *notam* have been an indicator that she was a Primal?" Kieran asked. "The gods have the *notam*."

"Why would you think that?" Reaver frowned. "It's a Primal *notam*. Not a god *notam*. Only a Primal can form any type of *notam*—a bond such as that."

"Because that's—" Kieran cursed. "I don't think anyone really knew. We just assumed it was connected to the gods."

"You assumed wrong," Reaver stated flatly.

Out of the chaos that was my mind, something suddenly made sense. "That's why Malec never had the *notam*." I turned to Casteel and then Kieran. "I thought it was because of his weakening powers, but he wasn't a Primal." My head swung back to Reaver. "That's why you said I would be more powerful than my father. Why I wouldn't have to feed as often. And the mist? I didn't summon it, did I?"

"Only a Primal can *create* the mist." Reaver's head tilted, and a curtain of blond hair fell across his cheek as he picked up another biscuit. "Which is a sign that you're probably close to completing the Culling. That, and your eyes."

"The streaks of eather?" I asked. "They're going to stay like that?"

"They may turn completely silver like Nyktos'," he answered. "*Or* they may stay like this."

Feeling dizzy, I started to take a step back. Casteel's hand came around the nape of my neck. He turned, stepping in close.

"A Primal?" A slow grin spread across his lips as he caught my gaze, holding it. "I don't know what I should call you. Queen? Highness? Neither seems fitting."

"Poppy," I whispered. "Call me Poppy."

He bent his head, brushing his lips over the bridge of my nose as his mouth neared my ear. "I'll call you whatever you like, as long as you call me yours."

I let out a short laugh and felt Casteel's smile against my cheek. He'd successfully pulled me back from the edge of a panic spiral.

Reaver made a gagging sound. "Did he seriously just say that?"

"Unfortunately," Kieran muttered.

Ignoring them, I fisted the front of Casteel's shirt. "You knew?"

"I only just figured it out. Some things that both Isbeth and Millicent said—they didn't make sense. Or I couldn't remember right away."

Drawing back, I stared up at him. "Like what?"

His gaze searched mine. "Like when both spoke of Isbeth's plans to remake the realms. And the time they gave me blood, and she said…" Shadows crept into his golden eyes. He briefly closed them and then looked at Reaver. "One thing I don't understand. How is she a Primal and not Malec or Ires?" he asked, sliding his hand under my hair and cupping the nape of my neck. "And how is she a Primal born of mortal flesh?"

Reaver was quiet as he set his half-eaten biscuit aside. "That is something I cannot answer."

"Cannot, or will not?" Casteel stated, his eyes hardening into golden jewels.

Reaver stared at Casteel and then his gaze flicked to me. "Cannot. You are the first Primal to be born since the Primal of Life. I do not know why. Only the Primal of Life can answer that."

Well, it was highly unlikely that we'd be able to make a trip to Iliseeum anytime soon to try and figure that out.

"But what's even more important is why the Blood Queen believes that she will destroy the realms." Reaver eyed Malik.

"She won't," Casteel stated without hesitation or doubt. "The Blood Queen is so consumed by vengeance that she's convinced herself that she can use Poppy."

"Yeah, that's what I thought, too. In the beginning," Malik added. "But then I learned that Isbeth wasn't the only one who believed that the last Chosen would awaken as the Harbinger and the Bringer of Death and Destruction."

"Bullshit," Casteel growled, even as the gentle sweep of his thumb continued. "The prophecy is bullshit."

"Not when spoken by a god," Reaver bit off. "Not when voiced by the goddess Penellaphe, who is tied closely to the Fates."

Malik looked at me. "Isbeth naming you after the goddess who warned of you was no coincidence. She did it thinking it would bring her good luck with the Arae."

For a moment, a brief second, a bolt of pure panic went through me, stirring the eather in my chest. If I were to fully become a Primal, I would be powerful enough to do just as the prophecy stated. My gaze snapped to Kieran, and he knew where my mind had gone. He too was thinking of what I'd asked of him. Kieran gave a curt shake of his head.

I started to take a step back—to go where, I didn't know. But I reminded myself that I was more than just a byproduct of Isbeth's vengeance.

I…I *wasn't* Isbeth's tool. Her weapon. I was mine.

My thoughts—my ideals, choices, and beliefs—were not preordained nor governed by anyone but me. The panic eased, breath by breath. "No matter what the prophecy says, I have free will. *I* control my actions. I wouldn't do something like that," I told him, and a whisper rose from that cold place deep in my chest. One I desperately ignored. "I won't take part in whatever Isbeth thinks I will do."

"But you already have," Malik countered, and a chill swept over my skin as those words echoed in Isbeth's voice. "You were born. Your blood was spilled, and you Ascended. Upon that Ascension, you were reborn—birthed from the flesh and fire of the Primals. You awakened." He shook his head. "Maybe you're right. Perhaps your choice—your free will—is greater than a prophecy. Than the Fates and what Isbeth believes. Hell, that's what Coralena believed. She was sure you would usher in change, but not in the way Isbeth wanted."

My body flashed hot and then cold. "You knew my mother?" As soon as I said it, I realized that, of course, he had known her. He would've been at Wayfair when she served as a Handmaiden.

"I did." His gaze lowered as tension bracketed his mouth. "She believed that, given a chance—if you were raised away from Isbeth and the Ascended—you wouldn't become the Harbinger who would destroy the realms."

A shudder ran through me as a memory of that night surged.

"It has to be done," the faceless man said. "You know what will happen."

"She's but a child—"

"And she will be the end of everything."

"Or she is just the end of them. A beginning—"

I stepped back, my heart thumping. "A beginning of a new era," I whispered, finishing what Coralena had said to…

Malik watched me, and my stomach twisted with nausea.

Casteel's arm encircled my waist as he pressed into me from behind. "Poppy?" He lowered his head to mine. "What is it?"

My skin kept flashing from hot to cold as I stared at Casteel's brother, but I didn't see him. I saw the man with shadows for a face.

The cloaked figure.

The Dark One.

"*Poppy.*" Casteel's concern radiated in waves as he shifted so he stood beside me.

The sourness of shame crowded the back of my throat as Malik said roughly, his voice pitched low, "You remember."

That voice.

His voice.

"No," I whispered, disbelief flooding me.

Malik said nothing.

"What the hell is going on?" Casteel demanded, his arm around me tightening as my stomach churned. I started to bend over, forcing myself to swallow down the bile that had risen.

"I was broken," Malik said to Casteel. "You were right. What they did to Preela broke me. But I was never loyal to that bitch. *Never.*"

Casteel tensed at the name.

"Preela?" I whispered.

"His bonded wolven," Kieran growled.

Oh, gods…

"Not after what she did to you. Not after what Jalara did to Preela. Not what she made me do to Mil—" He inhaled sharply, stiffening as raw, suffocating anguish lashed my skin. The kind of sorrow that went beyond the bone and hurt more than any wound could. And it was so potent I could barely feel Casteel and Kieran's surprise. It got lost in the icy agony. "I wanted to kill Isbeth. The gods know I tried before I realized what she was. I would've kept trying, Cas, but that prophecy." His nostrils flared as he shook his head. "It was no longer about her. You. Me. Millie. None of us mattered. Atlantia did. Solis did. All the people who would pay the price for something they had nothing to do with. I had to stop her."

Casteel's arm slipped away from my waist, and he turned to his brother.

Malik's eyes closed tightly. "I couldn't let Isbeth destroy Atlantia or the mortal realm. I couldn't let her destroy Millie in the process. And she *was* destroying her." Anger and guilt swirled through him, stirring the eather deep in my chest. Flat eyes opened, locking on mine. "I had to do something."

The floor felt as if it rippled under my feet. I couldn't feel my legs. A cup toppled behind me, rolling across the counter. Reaver caught it, his eyes narrowing as they cut to the trembling blinds over the window.

The rattling daggers on the table.

"You had to do what, exactly?" Kieran asked, but Casteel had gone silent because he…gods, he was processing everything. Fighting with himself to believe it.

Malik still stared at me. His voice hoarse, he said, "I was prepared to do anything to stop Isbeth, and Coralena knew that. Because Leopold did."

But she had—

He's her viktor.

Memories of that night in Lockswood slammed into me, clear and without the shadow of trauma. I leaned into the counter as they came, one after another after another. All of it in rapid succession and in seconds, stunning in its clarity.

Shocking in what the recollections revealed.

Anger surged through me, burning away the disbelief. But that wasn't the only emotion. There was a storm of them, but the sorrow was just as powerful because I remembered. *Finally.* And a part of me, something that was either not touched by that fury or stemmed from that same cold place in me, also *understood.*

"I remember everything," I said, and the room steadied. *I* steadied as I focused on Malik. "Why? Why didn't you do it, then? Finish it?"

Casteel's head turned to me, and I saw that his skin had paled, almost as bad as it had when he'd been in bloodlust. "I've done a lot of terrible things—committed deeds that will haunt me to my last breath and beyond—but I couldn't go through with it. Even believing what I did, I couldn't," he said with a dark, choked laugh. "Apparently, killing a child was a line I could not cross."

"Motherfucker," Kieran rasped.

"No," Cas said, and that one word was harsh. It brooked no room for argument. It was a proclamation. A plea. "Tell me it isn't so."

I wanted nothing more than to be able to do so.

"I had my chance, too. When I pulled you out from the cupboard? I was going to then—right then. I was going to end it. But I couldn't. And I tried again." Malik's head fell back as he looked up at the ceiling, and my hand fluttered to my throat where I felt the phantom press of a cold blade. "I tried again, but that time, I saw it—saw what Coralena did."

I see it. I see her staring back at me.

Those disjointed memories made sense now that they had been pieced back together. "What did you see? Who?"

Malik's eyes closed then, and all the while, Casteel hadn't moved. "*Her.* The Consort. I saw her in your eyes, looking back at me."

I inhaled sharply as Reaver cursed.

"I don't know how it's possible. She's asleep, right?" Malik said. "But I saw her."

"The Consort sleeps fitfully," Reaver said. "Sometimes, things happen that reach her even in sleep, partly waking her."

"You're the Dark One," Casteel said in that deceptively soft way of his. I swung to him, and I should've paid attention to him sooner. If I hadn't been caught up in my discoveries, I would've sensed the void of icy rage forming beside me. "You led the Craven to the inn in Lockswood. You went there to kill her."

"The Craven followed the trail of blood I left behind," he admitted. "It was the only way I knew I'd get past Coralena and Leo."

Kieran said something. It caused Malik to flinch, but Casteel was a throbbing mass of fury, and it stroked the essence in my chest. I had to shut my senses down. It was too much.

Casteel's eyes were a bright gold, and his voice—gods, his voice was smooth and laden with power. A whisper that was a boom had his words falling over my skin and filling the room. "Pick up a dagger, Malik."

And Malik, Casteel's brother, picked up a dagger with a shaking hand—a long, thick one with a wickedly sharp blade. The tendons in his neck stood out.

"On your knees," Casteel demanded.

Malik's entire body trembled as he obeyed, falling to his knees.

"Put it to your throat," the King coaxed, his voice velvet and iron.

A compulsion.

He was using compulsion.

Malik did just as he'd been forced to do.

"Just so everyone knows," Reaver said, "I'm not cleaning up this mess."

I was rather conflicted. On the one hand, I was glad to see that Casteel had gotten a lot of his strength back. On the other, he was going to force his brother to slit his own throat.

I didn't know how I felt about that—about the knowledge that it had been Malik. My brother-in-law. I didn't know how to feel about the fact that I actually understood why Malik felt he needed to do what he had.

But what I did know was that I couldn't let Casteel do this. It wouldn't kill Malik, but it would do some serious damage, and Casteel didn't need that weighing on him. That was a mark I would not let him bear.

I stepped forward, glancing at Kieran. He glared at Malik, his chest rising and falling rapidly, and his skin thinning. The wolven would be no help here. "Don't do it, Casteel."

"Stay out of this," he barked, his gaze having captured his brother's. Casteel's chin rose. A faint trickle of blood appeared, coursing down Malik's throat.

"Not going to happen. Malik didn't harm me," I reasoned. "He stopped before he could."

"He stopped before he could? Do you hear yourself?" Casteel fired back. "You *were* hurt because of him."

"She was," Malik whispered.

I shot a glare at the Prince. "You should just be quiet."

"He left you there to be torn apart by the Craven!" Casteel roared.

"He didn't, though. He got me out of there," I said. "I remember now."

"The Craven had already gotten to her," Malik told him. "Bit her. Clawed her—"

"Shut up," I hissed at Malik as a shudder ran through Casteel. Reaching out, I grabbed his arm. "He thought he was doing what was right. It was messed up. He was wrong. But he stopped. He didn't hurt me—"

"Stop saying that!" Casteel's head whipped toward me, his eyes swirling, golden spears. With his attention broken, his compulsion on Malik shattered. The dagger hit the floor as Malik's shoulder slumped. "He *did* hurt you, Poppy. Maybe not with his hands, but those Craven never would've been there if it weren't for him."

"You're right." I pressed my palm against his cheek, channeling—

"Don't." Casteel jerked his head back from my touch. "Don't you dare use your powers. I need to feel this."

"Okay. I won't," I promised, placing my hand on his cheek again. He didn't pull away this time, but I felt his muscles flexing under my palm. "You're right. The Craven never would've been there if it weren't for Malik, but he acted on what Isbeth believed. The fault lies with her."

"That changes nothing." He glared down at me as Malik rose to his feet. "He's not innocent in this. He wasn't manipulated. He made a choice—"

"To protect his kingdom. To protect *you*. The realms. That is why he made his choice. None of us have to like it or agree with it, but we *can* understand it."

"Understand it? Being ready to kill a child? To even consider it?" he exclaimed in disbelief. "To put you in harm's way. You? My fucking heartmate?"

"He didn't know that then." I fisted the front of his shirt.

"Even if I did, I still would've done it," Malik admitted. "I still would've—"

'Shut up!" I shouted.

Malik shook his head. "It's the truth."

Casteel moved so fast, I didn't think even Reaver could've stopped him—if he had wanted to. He shot across the kitchen, slamming his fist into his brother's jaw. The punch knocked Malik back into the chair. He had no chance to recover. Casteel took him to the floor, his arm swinging so fast that it was nothing but a blur. The fleshy smack of his fist making contact echoed through the kitchen.

"Casteel!" I yelled.

He grabbed Malik by the shirt, lifting him from the floor as he kept punching his brother.

I whipped toward Kieran. "Are you going to stop him?"

"Nope." Kieran crossed his arms. "The fucker deserves it."

Malik had apparently had enough. He caught Casteel's wrist and flipped him, then sat up, blood running from his nose and mouth. The brief reprieve lasted a whole second as Casteel sprang to his feet and slammed his knee into Malik's chin, knocking his head back.

And then down they went again, rolling into the legs of the table.

I turned to Reaver—

"Don't look at me." Reaver picked up his biscuit. "This is entertaining as fuck."

My eyes narrowed. "You guys are useless," I snapped, pivoting toward the brothers. I was *this close* to beating the snot out of both of them myself. Tapping into the eather, I lifted my hand. A silvery glow sparked across my fingers. "Knock it off," I said over the grunts. Either they didn't hear me or chose not to listen. "Oh, for godssake, I should be the furious one, and yet I have to be the rational, calm one."

In my mind, I willed them apart, and what I willed…well, it joined with the essence, and it worked. Perhaps a little too well since I wasn't all that worried about not harming either of them in the moment.

One second, they were rolling around like two overgrown

toddlers. The next, they were skidding across the floor in opposite directions. Malik slammed into the wall below the window with enough force that it shook the entire house. I winced as Kieran caught Casteel before he took out the wolven's leg.

Casteel's head snapped in my direction. Blood smeared his cut lip as he leaned into Kieran's legs. "What the fuck?"

"*Exactly.*" I pulled the eather back in.

"Shit." Malik pitched to the side, coughing as he braced his weight on one arm. "That hurt more than any of his punches did. I think you cracked a few ribs."

"I'm about to crack your face if you say one more word," I retorted.

"Crack his face?" Casteel repeated, his brows flying up.

"Yours, too," I warned.

A slow, bloody grin spread across his lips, and that stupid, godsforsaken dimple appeared. I just knew he was about to say something that would make me want to punch him.

"Uh, I hate to interrupt," Clariza said from the doorway, having entered without any of us noticing. I turned to her, my cheeks heating. Her eyes were wide. "But there's a small army of Rise Guards in the street, going from house to house."

In the time it took my stomach to drop, the shocking discoveries were swept aside. Casteel was on his feet, joining me as he dragged the back of his hand over his mouth. "How close are they?"

"Two homes down," Blaz answered, ducking past Clariza. He carried several cloaks, handing one to each of us as he went straight to the table, grabbing two daggers. He sheathed one inside his boot.

Malik cursed. "We need to get out of here. Now."

"I'll grab our weapons." Kieran hurried past us, entering the hall.

"You go out the back." Blaz tossed Clariza a slender dagger, which she slipped under her sleeve. "We'll keep them occupied for as long as we can."

Concern for them blossomed. "Can you not come with us?"

Hiding another dagger, Clariza sent me a brief smile. "I'd love nothing more than to see my ancestral home, and I plan to do that one day, but our place is here. There are people who depend on us."

"Descenters?" Casteel asked as Kieran returned, handing him a sword. I saw that he had my satchel.

Blaz nodded. "Elian can tell you that quite a few people stand in opposition to the Blood Crown. An entire network working from within to usurp the Ascended. You may hasten that when your armies arrive, but until then, we're needed here."

At the sound of his ancestor's name, Casteel shot Malik a look and then stepped forward, clasping Blaz's shoulder. "Thank you—thank you both for your aid."

Clariza bowed as I slipped the cloak on. "It's our honor."

A knock sounded from the front of the house, and Casteel turned, grasping my cheeks. His touch calmed my nerves. "My Queen?"

"Yes?"

"I think you'll be happy to know," he said, sliding his hands to the edges of the hood as he lifted it, "that you're about to crack some faces."

A rough, shaky laugh left me, and my heart calmed. I twisted toward Clariza and Blaz as Reaver and Malik moved to the back of the house. "Be safe."

"We need to be on our way," Malik said, lifting the hood of the cloak he'd donned as another knock came from the front.

Clariza lifted her chin as she placed her curled fist over her heart. "From blood and ash," she said as Blaz did the same.

"We will rise," Casteel finished, hand over his heart as he, the King, bowed to them.

I stepped behind Kieran, looking up at Malik as Blaz went down the hall. "Will they be safe when the guards come?"

"Possibly," he answered.

That wasn't exactly reassuring.

"You and I aren't done with our conversation either." Casteel stepped in front of me, his cloak hood shielding his face.

That also wasn't reassuring.

"That'll have to wait," Kieran said, his hand on my lower back.

"Where to?" Reaver reached for the back door.

"The harbor," Malik answered. "Lower Town."

Nodding, the draken opened—

Four Royal Guards stood there, their white mantles rippling in the wind.

"Where do you think you're all going?" an older guard asked.

Only Reaver was uncloaked, but the guard took one look at the rest of us, hooded with our identities hidden, and withdrew his sword. "Step back," he ordered.

I didn't have a chance to even summon the eather.

Reaver snapped forward, grasping the guard's sword arm as he stretched out his neck. His jaw loosened, and his mouth gaped wide. A low rumble came from his chest as a stream of silvery fire rippled out from his mouth.

My eyes went wide.

"Holy shit," Casteel murmured, stiffening in front of me as silvery flames rippled over the guard.

"Yeah," Kieran remarked.

Reaver shoved the screaming guard back into another, and the unnatural fire swept over the other man. Turning, Reaver let out another powerful stream of flames, quickly laying waste to the guards at the back door.

The scent of charred flesh rose on the wind, turning my stomach as Reaver straightened. "Path is clear."

Casteel turned to the draken. "Yeah, it sure is."

A sharp yelp of pain sounded from the house, spinning me around. Clariza cried out in alarm.

"We need to leave," Malik insisted, toeing aside burnt remains.

We needed to, but...

"They aided us," I said.

"And they knew the cost," Malik argued as rough shouts echoed from the front of the house.

"As did we when we came to their door." I stepped forward. Kieran's hand tightened briefly on my cloak and then relaxed.

"Agreed," Casteel said, his grip firming on the sword.

"For godssake," Malik muttered. "This isn't the time to be heroes. If you're caught—"

"We won't be." Casteel's cloaked head turned to me.

I nodded, letting the essence rush to the surface as heavy footsteps bounded down the hall. Several Royal Guards raced forward. The throbbing eather lit across my skin as my will merged with the essence. A faint, silvery webbing spilled out from me as it sparked across my hand, the shadows twining with the glow thicker now.

"That's new," Casteel commented.

"Started a couple of weeks back," Kieran told him as the guards jerked to a halt.

The swords dropped from the guards' hands, clattering off the floor as their necks twisted to the sides, cracking.

"You'll probably be concerned to hear this, but also not surprised," Casteel said, and the smoky, spicy flavor in my mouth crowded out the taste of death. "But I found that wildly...*hot.*"

"There's something wrong with him," Reaver muttered from behind us. "Isn't there?"

There most definitely was, but I loved him for it.

Kieran snorted as another Royal Guard entered. The essence stretched out from me as my chin lowered. The webbing pulsed and then recoiled—

"Revenant," I spat.

The bare-faced, unmasked guard smirked. It was then that I saw his eyes. Pale blue.

Casteel twisted sharply, grabbing a dagger from the table as he threw it in one smooth motion. The blade struck true, striking the Revenant between the eyes. "Let's see how long it takes for you to get up from that."

"As long as it takes for the blade to be removed," came a voice. The golden Revenant strolled out from the shadows of the hall. Callum.

"You," Casteel seethed.

"I imagine you're faring much better than the last time I saw you," Callum replied as fury whipped through me. He wasn't alone. A quick glance showed at least half of dozen guards with him. All pale-eyed.

"Reaver," I said. "There's something I would like you to do for me, and you'll be *really* happy about it."

The draken's smile was bloodthirsty as he walked between Casteel and me.

Callum glanced at Reaver, a painted wing rising on one side of his face. "I think I know what you are."

"And I think you're about to find out for sure." Smoke wafted from Reaver's nostrils.

"Maybe later." Callum held up a hand.

Clariza appeared in the hall, her nose bloodied and a blade at her throat. A guard shoved her in Callum's direction. He took hold of her as Blaz shuffled forward, held by another guard.

"Are you that much of a coward to use them as shields?" I demanded, furious.

"You say coward," Callum said as Clariza's anger gathered, hot and acidic, in my throat. "I say clever."

Kieran came to stand on my other side. "This fucker's got jokes."

"Endless ones." Callum eyed the wolven. "When this is all over, I shall like to keep you. I've always wanted a pet wolf."

"Fuck you," Kieran growled.

Anger wasn't the only thing I picked up from the couple as violence thickened the air. Salty resolve filled them, too. They were prepared to die.

But I couldn't allow that.

"Stand down," I said to Reaver.

The draken rumbled, but the smoke faded.

Callum smiled. "Some would say humanity is a weakness."

"Because it is," another voice intruded, and every muscle in my body tensed.

Callum and the other Revenant stepped aside as I immediately moved to stand in front of Casteel. A figure cloaked in crimson came forward, but I knew it was no Handmaiden.

Slender hands lifted, lowering the hood, revealing what I already knew.

Isbeth stood before us. The ruby crown was absent, as was the powder that lightened her skin. It struck me then that I had seen her like this in her private chambers, with warmer, pink skin. That time, just at dusk, when she'd shown me the Star jewel—a diamond coveted throughout the kingdom and known for its silver glow.

"*The most beautiful things in all the kingdom often have jagged and uneven lines, scars that intensify the beauty in intricate ways our eyes nor minds can detect or even begin to understand,*" she had said.

It was true. Just as those like her, with smooth and even lines, flawless skin, and endless beauty could be evil and ugly. And my mother was the most monstrous of them all. What of my sister? She may not want to see the realms destroyed, but what had she done to stop our mother?

"Your compassion for mortals is admirable, but it's not a strength," Isbeth said, glancing at Reaver before those dark eyes settled on me. "A true Queen knows when to sacrifice her pawns."

"A true Queen would do no such thing," I said, yanking down the hood since there was no point in wearing it now. "Only a tyrant would think of people as pawns to be sacrificed."

She smiled tightly. "We'll have to agree to disagree." Her head tilted toward Casteel. "One of you destroyed my cell. An apology would be welcomed."

"Do any of us look as if we're about to give you an apology?" Casteel shifted his stance so he blocked the hooded Malik. Kieran did the same.

"Stranger things have happened," she said. "Even stranger than a

Primal mist that was without Craven until it drew them from the Blood Forest to our walls. Now *that* was clever. Impressive, even."

"I don't care what you think," I bit out.

Isbeth arched a brow as she looked around the kitchen, her lip curling in distaste. "Did you really think you'd escape? That you'd walk right out of the capital, and with something that belongs to me, no less?"

I snarled as the eather throbbed in my chest.

"I wasn't speaking of you." Her gaze moved behind us, and her smile twisted coldly. "*Him.*"

Casteel stiffened as the Blood Queen stared at where Malik stood quietly. "He doesn't belong to you either."

"I was so proud of you," Isbeth said. "And yet, yet another Da'Neer betrayed me. Shocker."

"Betrayed?" Malik sounded as incredulous as I felt. "You kidnapped and tortured my brother. You held me captive and used me for whatever you desired. And you accuse *me* of betrayal?"

"Here we go again." Isbeth rolled her eyes. "Gods, let it go."

"Fuck you," Malik spat.

"Neither of us has been interested in that in many years," she retorted. "So, no thank you."

Nausea rose sharply as I stared at this woman—this beast—who was my mother.

Her gaze flicked back to me. "If you had stayed where you belonged, you could've avoided this. We would've spoken today, and I would've given you a choice. One that would've resulted in his freedom." She jerked her chin in Casteel's direction. "And far less mayhem. But this way? It's far more dramatic. I can appreciate that, as I too love to make a scene."

My hands squeezed into fists. "What are you talking about?"

"A choice," she repeated. "One that I'm still willing to offer because I'm that gracious and forgiving."

"You are delusional," I said, rattled by the realization that she truly believed those words.

Isbeth's eyes narrowed. "You know where Malec is. You said so yourself. If you expect to leave this city with your beloved, you will find him and bring him to me."

36

"What in the hell?" Malik exclaimed, his tart confusion echoing mine, but our confusion wasn't the only emotion I felt. A fainter trace came from…

Callum stared at the Blood Queen, his grip on Clariza still firm but his brows rising under the winged mask.

"What does he have to do with anything?" Casteel demanded.

"Everything," she replied, toying with the diamond ring. "Bring him to me, and he will give me what I want."

"You think he will help you destroy the realms? Punish Nyktos?" Casteel's brows lifted. "You know how long he's been entombed. He won't even be able to hold a conversation with you, let alone help you destroy anything."

Isbeth's gaze sharpened. "But he will."

"Your Majesty," Callum began. "This is not—"

"Silence," Isbeth ordered, her stare fixed on me.

The Revenant stiffened, his eyes narrowing. He was clearly unaware of whatever Isbeth planned or wanted.

And I was, well, utterly thunderstruck. *This* was how she believed I would aid her in destroying Atlantia and possibly the realms? By freeing Malec? Casteel was right. Malec wouldn't be in any state of mind to take part in whatever she thought she could accomplish. "Just to make sure I understand this correctly, you think I will leave, find Malec, and then return with him so that you can then use him to destroy my kingdom? The realms?"

"That's exactly what I think."

I glanced at Reaver, who had gone completely still and quiet as he watched the Blood Queen. "Why wouldn't you just ask that I tell you where he is?" I questioned.

"Because I wouldn't believe you."

"And yet you believe I will do as you request once I leave here?"

Her stare met mine. "As I said, I would've offered you his freedom in exchange. I still do."

"Do I look like I'm in chains?" Casteel snarled.

"They may not be around your neck, but those chains are still there. Except, now, they're around everyone's neck—just in different forms. Revenants surround this pitiful example of a home. The entire district is full of them. Too many for your interesting traveling companion to handle without harming those innocent people you all worry so much about. Should've known you'd bring a draken with you." She sent a quick, displeased look in Callum's direction. He'd handed off Clariza to another but remained half shielded by her. "Be that as it may, you have to know that your charming—albeit destructive—escapades have come to an end. And while you may believe the worst of me, I am a most generous Queen."

I almost choked.

"Find Malec and bring him to me, and I will let you leave. I will allow Casteel to go, too." She watched me closely, waiting. "Your answer should've been immediate, Penellaphe. I know you will do anything for him."

I *would* do anything for Casteel, but Malec was *a god*—one who had been entombed for hundreds of years. He was the son of the Primal of Death and his Consort. I couldn't even begin to fathom what releasing him would mean or do.

I quickly glanced at Reaver again. His expression was unreadable. What in the world would Nyktos and his Consort do if Malec were freed? Then again, as far as I knew, they hadn't intervened upon his entombment.

But this was it? How she sought to use me? This was what I was born to do? Then why had she waited until now to ask this of me? She could've made the request the first moment she'd spoken to me here. She could've sent her offer with her *gift*.

Something about this didn't make sense. Hell, a lot of things, actually. Starting with why she believed that Malec would be able to give her what she wanted, and ending with what she thought would happen afterward. "If I agree, then what? You and Malec destroy Atlantia, remake the realms, and call it a day? And if I refuse?"

Her eyes hardened. "If you refuse, I will make sure you regret it until the last breath you take."

The Primal essence roared to life, pressing against my skin. I knew immediately that she was referencing Casteel. "And what do you think will happen to you if you do that?"

"I know what you will do," she said, smiling. "But I also know you won't let it get to that point. You will, in the end, come to your senses and do as I bid. And I know this because whether or not you admit it, we are alike. You care for him more than you care for any kingdom."

"Shut up," snarled Casteel, stepping forward.

Several of the Revenants moved in closer as Isbeth said, "But it's true. She's the same as I. Where we differ is that I have the courage to admit that." Her gaze shifted back to me. "So, what will it be?"

My thoughts raced forward, beyond this moment. I was confident that I could kill the Queen. She was powerful, but I wouldn't hold back on her. At the very least, I would seriously injure her.

But if what she'd said was true, and Revenants did surround us? Reaver would only be able to take down so many. People *would* get hurt. Those I cared dearly about might be among them.

And that cold part in me…

The part that tasted of death…

It wasn't like my mother.

It was worse.

I glanced at Casteel. His gaze met mine, and he gave me a curt nod. I hated even entertaining the idea of complying with Isbeth, but she had to know there was no way that Malec could assist her in seeking revenge. I didn't think he had anything to do with her plans. Her offer stemmed from the desperation of being reunited with her heartmate, no matter what condition he may be in, and that he was her weakness.

One we could exploit. Starting with agreeing to her demands with no intention of fulfilling them.

"I will bring you Malec," I decided.

There was no rejoicing. Isbeth was quiet for a long moment. "You asked me how I could trust you to return. I had your King once to ensure your cooperation. Now, what do I have to do to ensure that you will not seek to betray me?"

"I guess you will just have to wait and see," I retorted.

Isbeth gave a close-lipped laugh as her eyes shifted to Callum. That was the only warning. The Revenant hesitated for only a moment, but he was quick, unsheathing a slender black dagger as he snapped forward. *Shadowstone.* Reaver turned to him as Casteel swung his sword.

But Revenants were incredibly fast.

Callum dragged the shadowstone down Kieran's arm as he whispered something—words in a language I couldn't understand but that the essence in my chest pulsed in response to. A shadowy, reddish-black smoke hovered over the shallow cut, much as it had swirled around the chamber in Massene when controlled by Vessa.

"What the fuck?" Kieran exploded as Malik grabbed him from behind, yanking him back. The shadow rippled over Kieran's entire body, throwing Malik back as Casteel drove the blade through Callum's chest.

A thin streak of blood appeared on Kieran's arm as he tried to shake off the shadow. I grabbed his arm as the shadowy smoke sank into his skin, disappearing. "What did you do?" I cried out as panic erupted, my head whipping toward Isbeth. All I saw was Tawny's prone body, unmoving after being struck by shadowstone.

Callum stumbled back, pulling himself free of the blade. "Gods." Blood frothed from his mouth as he fell onto the table. "That stung like a—" the Revenant said as he slid to the floor, dead for now.

Heart thumping, I closed my hand over Kieran's wound, conjuring healing warmth.

"No need to panic," Isbeth said softly. "He will be fine. The shadowstone will have little effect on a wolven. It's the curse Callum passed on that you should be concerned with."

"What?" Casteel's eyes were a storm of golden, swirling flecks.

"One with a time limit. One only I can lift," Isbeth answered. "Return with Malec, or your precious wolven dies."

Kieran's lips parted, and my rage swelled once more.

Casteel lunged at her, but Malik twisted, catching him as Kieran snapped forward—

"Let it go." Reaver threw out an arm, blocking Kieran. He stared down at the wolven. "Let it go."

Kieran growled, throwing off Reaver's arm. But he backed away, breathing heavily. The cut remained on his arm. With as shallow as it was, only the briefest touch should've healed it.

Isbeth remained unmoved, bored even. I hated her. Gods, I *hated* her.

"I need time," I managed. "Therefore, Kieran needs time."

Her eyes lit with that faint glow. "You have a week."

"I need longer than that. The kingdom is vast. Three weeks."

"Two. Your wolven will be fine for that length of time. No more."

"Fine," I clipped out, sensing Kieran's worry. Two weeks sounded like a lot of time, but not when we had no idea where to begin in the Blood Forest. If we could narrow down Malec's location... "I need something else. Something that belonged to Malec."

Her brow pinched. "Why?"

"Does it matter?" I asked.

"Depends. Will I get it back?"

"I don't know. Maybe? With it, I should be able to reach his tomb quicker."

Isbeth's gaze narrowed on Callum, already returning to life. Her lips pursed as she glanced down at the diamond ring she wore. "I have this. It belonged to him. He gave it to me."

"I knew it was Atlantian gold," Casteel murmured.

"It should work," I said. Just as my blood should also work, at least according to Lord Sven.

She started to remove the ring, hesitated, and then pulled it off as Callum rose slowly. "It's all I have of him." Her gaze lifted, eyes shining with unshed tears. "That's it."

I said nothing.

I felt nothing as I lifted my hand, palm up. "I need it if you want me to find Malec."

Pressing her lips together, she reached over and dropped the ring into my hand. I took it, slipping it into the pouch with the toy horse. A shudder went through her, and for a heartbeat, I tasted her bitter grief.

I didn't care.

"We shall meet at the Bone Temple, beyond the Rise, two weeks from now," Isbeth said, dragging her gaze from the pouch I'd placed the ring in. "You remember it."

"Of course." The ancient Temple was located between the most northern point of Carsodonia and Pensdurth, built before the walls around both cities had gone up. It was where the remains of the Priests and Priestesses were supposedly entombed.

"Then it's a deal." Isbeth took a step back and stopped. "I will allow Casteel, the draken, and the wolven to leave. But not Malik."

"As I already said,"—Casteel's eyes glowed a bright gold—"he does not belong to you any longer. He leaves with us."

"It's okay." Malik brushed past Kieran. "Go and find Malec."

"No." Casteel whipped around, and I knew in an instant that Malik *wanted* to return to Isbeth. Not for her, but for Millicent. And the eager, cruel light in Isbeth's eyes told me that Malik would pay greatly for his actions, likely with his life. Malik had to know that.

"You cannot have him," I told Isbeth. "You want Malec? You will let all of us go, including Malik—" I stopped myself before I said her name. My *sister*. Before I asked for her. She wasn't among the Revenants here. If I said her name, I would be putting her in danger.

"Let me pass," Malik growled, his panic rising and settling heavily on my chest.

"Not going to happen," Casteel warned.

"I wasn't asking."

Casteel pushed him back. "I know."

I grabbed Malik's arm. "You're no good to *anyone* dead."

He pulled his arm free, beyond reason, and I thought of Casteel while we'd been in Oak Ambler. How he'd handed himself over to Isbeth. Willingly. For me. No one could stop him. No one would stop Malik, either, and Casteel realized that. His gaze flicked to Kieran.

The wolven struck, slamming the hilt of his sword into the back of Malik's head. The resounding crack sickened me. I turned to Kieran.

"What?" With Casteel's aid, he caught Malik's dead weight. "He'll be fine."

"Huh," Callum murmured, wiping blood away from his mouth with the back of his hand. "That was unexpected."

"Agreed," Isbeth drawled, brows arched.

"Him or Malec," I said. "That's your choice."

Her eyes narrowed once more, and then she sighed. "Whatever. Take him. I've grown tired of him anyway. You're free to leave through the Rise like a civilized group of people. I trust that you will not make a scene on your way out." She turned, lifting her hood. Once more, she stopped. "Oh, and one more thing," she said. There was just a flick of her eyes.

That was all.

Clariza and Blaz went stiff in their captors' grasps, eyes so wide that nearly the entire whites were visible. Blood drained rapidly from their faces. Tiny fissures appeared across their cheeks, their throats, and in any visible skin. I stumbled back into Casteel as their skin shrank and collapsed as they fell—as they shriveled into themselves, becoming nothing more than dried-out husks.

A guard nudged them with his boot, and they—pieces of them—shattered.

"Don't even bother trying to restore life to them," Callum said. "No one comes back from that."

Shock seized me as I stared at the strips of dried, decayed skin drifting to the wood. My hands trembled as I lifted my gaze.

"You know what they say," Isbeth remarked, tugging the cowl of the crimson hood close to her throat. "The only good Descenter is a dead one."

The roar in my ears returned, hitting my chest, and the essence rose to the surface in a heartbeat. There was no stopping it. I didn't even try as that familiar taste gathered in my throat, shadowy and full of fire.

Death.

Ancient power throbbed in my bones, filled my muscles, and coursed through my veins, seeping into my skin. I screamed, giving death sound.

Silvery light laced with thick, churning shadows spilled from me. Someone shouted as I stepped forward, the floor *cracking,* the wood splitting under my steps. The temperature of the room dropped until ragged breaths formed misty clouds. Cold rage left me in a burst of energy—a shockwave of essence hitting the air. The table and chairs turned to dust as the rage slammed into the walls. They stretched under the weight. Plaster and stone groaned. The roof shuddered, and then the walls *shattered* as the dark, oily sensation spread inside of me. Old. Cold. A harbinger.

Some of the stone turned to ash in the sunlight. Large chunks flew through the air, mowing down the Revenants who had been outside, crashing into and *through* nearby buildings as the shadow and light spread out around me, forming thick, crackling tendrils. My skin flashed cold and then heated with a series of sharp tingles. There had been mortal guards among the Revenants. The churning mass of moonlight and midnight found them, stopping them as they rushed toward me, and I left nothing of them behind.

I was done with this.

Salty wind whipped in, along with shrill sounds. Screams that carried a bitter taste. Fear. The wind and the screams lifted my hair as I called on the essence. Clouds darkened overhead and over the sea, rolling in and thickening, a dark snarl joining the growl. The floorboards splintered as I stalked forward, toward the Revenants guarding *her*. She stood in the center of them, her face hidden, but I felt her smile. Her pleasure. *Excitement*. It bubbled in my throat, mixing with the death and terror as mortals spilled into the streets, scrambling from their nearby homes as the walls began cracking and shuddering. Roofs peeled off and whipped into the air as a bolt of lightning slammed into the cliffs.

"*Do it. Let all that rage out*," a voice called, coaxed. It sounded like the one that had whispered in the darkness so many years ago. "*Do it, Harbinger.*"

I wanted to.

My *will* began to grow beyond me, calling on—

An arm closed around my waist, piercing the churning and snapping mass around me. The contact startled me. A hand curled under my chin, pulling me back. "Stop," a different voice urged, one that warmed the cold spots inside me and cooled the heat of my skin. Casteel. So brave. So loyal. He pulled me back against his chest, unafraid of the power lapping at his skin, sparking off it. But he had no reason to be afraid. I wouldn't hurt him.

"You need to *stop*," he said.

"No," I argued, the word soft and full of shadow and fire. Another roof peeled off, flying out to sea. "I am done with this." I started to pull away.

Casteel held on. "Not like this. This is what she wants. The Revenants aren't attacking, Poppy," he said, his voice low and in my ear. "Look, Poppy. Look around you." He turned my head, and I saw the...

I saw the thick tendrils of eather spitting embers, and the ruined homes beyond the one we were in. The dark clouds, and the mortals on their knees, hands over their heads as they hid under trees and pressed themselves against the sides of trembling walls. I saw them in the streets of Stonehill, shielding children as limbs of trees snapped and fell to the ground. They were terrified, huddled and crying and *praying*.

But I wouldn't hurt them.

"You are not her," Casteel said, squeezing me. "That's what she wants, but you are not her."

I saw Kieran then, the tendons in his neck stark as if he were fighting the need to shift...

As if he fought the realization that he would have to do what I'd asked of him in Oak Ambler.

My entire body shuddered. I closed my eyes. I wasn't... I wasn't her. I wasn't death. I didn't want this. Scaring mortals. Hurting them. I wasn't her. *I wasn't. I wasn't. I wasn't.* Panicked, I shut down my senses and pulled the Primal essence back. The shadow-tinged eather retracted and recoiled, returning to me. The weight of unspent power settled in my chest and on my shoulders as I opened my eyes.

Dark clouds scattered and sunlight returned, glistening off the unfired shadowstone arrows held by the still-standing Revenants and pointed at us—at me. The mortals had risen but had all gone quiet and still, their fear scratching against my shields.

And then I heard their whispers.

My gaze shot to where the doorway to the kitchen had once been, to where the remains of Clariza and Blaz lay. Another tremor rocked me as I lifted my stare. I didn't see Isbeth at all in the crush of Revenants, but I saw Callum.

He stood only a few feet away, his golden shirt stained with blood, and his blond hair windblown. He *smiled.*

I jerked, pulling against Casteel's hold.

"Later," he whispered, smoothing his palm over my cheek. "Later, we will stand in what is left of his bones. That, I promise you."

Callum's head tilted—the only indication that he'd possibly heard Casteel. His smile grew, and I knew that none of them had been sure I would react in such a way, but they had hoped I would. Because those whispers...

I'd done what I had demanded the Atlantian generals *not* do upon seizing the cities. I'd destroyed homes. I'd possibly even hurt innocent mortals. And in my rage, I'd become what Isbeth had painted me as.

The Harbinger.

37

Casteel

Poppy went stiff against me as we rode the horses—provided to us at the edge of Stonehill—past grazing sheep. She'd been mostly quiet since we'd left what remained of the homes, but this was different.

The clusterfuck that was my mind since we'd left Carsodonia slowed as I glanced down at the top of her head, her hair a deep copper in the sunlight.

A smile spread across Poppy's upturned face—the first one I'd seen since we'd walked out of the rubble of that home. "*Padonia.*"

My heart actually *skipped* at the sight of the smile. "What?"

Eyes closed, she held up a hand. Then, I understood. Poppy had been using the Primal *notam* to reach the wolven for the last couple of hours—namely Delano.

The Primal *notam* took on a whole new meaning now.

Wonder swept through me once more, along with a lingering trace of disbelief as the pinch of concentration settled into her brow. My wife was a *Primal god.*

Man, if I didn't think I was worthy before…

I almost laughed, except the deaths of the mortal couple who'd aided us was a haunting presence.

As was the way the mortals had responded to Poppy, fleeing farther into Carsodonia in fear.

My gaze flipped to the rolling green hills. All I saw were sheep, nervous farmers, and Rise Guards. Couldn't really blame the anxious mortals. Our group drew attention, and it had nothing to do with us traveling outside the Rise without a guard or any Huntsmen.

It was partly because of Kieran. In his wolven form prowling beside us, he was larger than any wolf the farmers or guards had ever seen. And it was also Malik, bound by a portion of the chains that had been around my wrists and astride a horse guided by the draken. None of us trusted that he wouldn't run back to Carsodonia the very second he got a chance.

That beautiful curve of Poppy's lips faded as the thick fringes of her lashes swept up. "I reached Delano," she said, like it was nothing. As if she had spoken to him while he stood a few feet away. "They were supposed to wait for us in Three Rivers, but he said they had to go to Padonia first—it's near Lockswood."

My arm tightened around her waist. "I know where it is." I didn't know much about the mostly farming community. Had no idea what Ascended ruled or how many called the isolated town home. But I did know that Craven attacks were frequent due to its proximity to the Blood Forest. "Did he say why they went there?"

She shook her head. "Delano said he would explain once we got there but that we'd understand. The bulk of the armies are with them, except for a few battalions they left to secure the other cities we took." Her hand returned to my arm, and her fingers moved idly. "I don't know what could've drawn them there. We didn't plan on taking Padonia, instead focusing on the larger cities first. But I...I sensed it wasn't good."

Only the gods knew what level of fuckery had drawn them there. I shifted behind her, sliding my hand to her hip as I looked past the hills to the distant crimson glow on the horizon where the Blood Forest loomed. "Padonia is closer to the Blood Forest than Three Rivers. We'll meet with everyone, see what the hell is going on, and then travel to the Blood Forest from there."

Poppy turned her head to me, her voice low. "I let Delano know about Malik. I wasn't able to tell him a lot, other than it's complicated." She paused. "I thought your father should be given a heads-up."

While I wasn't sure my father deserved it, our friends did. I lowered my head, kissing her cheek. "Thank you."

A smile started to return, but she turned her head suddenly, inhaling sharply as she raised her hand to her other cheek, rubbing just below the bone.

"You okay?" I asked as quietly as possible. Still, the draken and Kieran turned their attention to us.

"Just an ache. I think I've been grinding my teeth," she said, glancing back at the mortals as she lowered her hand to my wrist. That simple touch...gods, I cherished it. Several long moments passed before she said, "I should've known she'd do something so terrible."

I knew exactly where her mind had not only gone but also stayed since we'd ridden out of the capital, passing homes here and there adorned with white banners above the doors. Banners that, according to Malik, signified that they were a haven for Descenters. "The fact that you didn't is why you're nothing like her." Dipping my head, I touched my lips to her temple once more. "Some things you can't prepare yourself for, even if you see them coming. She is one of them."

Poppy shifted her attention forward, to where the horizon shone as if it had been bathed in blood. "How long do you think it will take for us to reach Padonia?"

"About a day's ride, less if we push. But I don't think these horses can handle that."

"I don't either." She patted the mare. "They'll need the rest."

We traveled a few more hours. Along the way, Kieran snooped around the abandoned farmhouses, alerting us when he found something of use in those that appeared recently vacated. A few blankets here. Bundles of cured beef there. The draken spotted cherry bushes near the old road. It wasn't much, but we'd make do.

The sky was turning a shade of deep blue and violet when Poppy pulled herself from her thoughts. "After we find Malec and make sure the curse is lifted..." Poppy rested against me, but her body was slowly becoming taut with tension. "We need to end this."

End this.

I'd spent the better part of my life working toward destroying the Blood Crown. So long that it almost felt surreal now that we were on the cusp of doing it.

That we'd come to a point where the end was in sight.

"We do." I moved my thumb in a slow, steady circle on her hip, knowing she liked it as much as I did. The ancient Temple Isbeth had designated as a meeting place formed in my mind, a blurry memory from many years ago. "The Bone Temple is outside the Rises of both Carsodonia and Pensdurth, situated in the shadow of the capital. Our armies should be able to enter Carsodonia through their northern gates."

"It's not an ideal entry point," Poppy said. "We'd be coming in through Stonehill and Croft's Cross, and we wouldn't be able to give people any warning."

"No, we wouldn't be able to." That knowledge settled heavily in my gut. "But the gates there won't be as reinforced as the main ones."

She nodded, exhaling slowly. "Those white cloths on the doors of homes? Windows? In Masadonia, they meant that one was cursed—infected by a Craven. I had no idea they meant anything else, especially not that they designated a haven for Descenters."

Neither had I.

"How many?" Reaver asked of Malik, and I tensed. "Do you know how many?"

Malik lifted his head. "Thousands, if not more. All who would give aid the moment they realized that Atlantian armies were at the Rise."

"Thousands," Poppy murmured. "That's…that's a lot."

"But there are hundreds of thousands that believe you to be the Harbinger," Malik added. "And what happened in Stonehill won't do much to sway their minds or loyalties."

Poppy stiffened.

"Shut up," I warned.

"It's not personal," he said, looking at Poppy. "I'm just telling the truth."

"I know," she replied quietly. "What I did won't help our cause."

By sheer force of will, I managed to stop myself from launching from the horse and doing worse than bloodying my brother's nose again. There was a whole lot of shit between us. I could've eventually accepted why he'd chosen to remain under the Blood Queen's fist—fuck, I'd do the same if she had Poppy. I wasn't a big enough asshole not to admit that. But it was *him*. The Dark One who haunted Poppy's nightmares. And he was looking at her for far longer than he fucking deserved.

Poppy squeezed my wrist, and I unlocked my jaw, forcing my attention from him.

"I can't believe you are all actually planning to give her Malec." Malik faced forward, adding his two-fucking cents that none of us had asked for. "That you would do anything she wants."

"Perhaps I knocked your head around a little too hard since it appears you've forgotten that we don't have a choice." My eyes narrowed on him. "We will not let any harm come to Kieran."

Malik's gaze cut to the wolven, who eyeballed him as if he wanted to take a chunk out of his leg. He shuddered, stretching his fingers where they were bound at his back. "I don't want to see anything bad happen to you. It's not like I don't care."

"You know what I don't care about?" I smiled tightly. "Your opinion on this."

"Real mature," Malik spat.

"Go fuck yourself."

Poppy's hand tightened on my wrist once more. "She won't be able to keep him because she will be dead soon afterward," she told him. "And it's not like Malec is a risk. He can be in no condition to be a threat to us or anyone. At least, not in the short period of time he will be in her presence. But even if freeing Malec poses a risk, we're still taking it."

The draken frowned. "Are you all really that worried about the curse?" He asked what had to be the most idiotic question one could.

"Yes," Poppy stated flatly. "We're really that worried."

His head tilted. "The curse probably won't work on your wolven—" He stopped himself. "Well, then again, it *might* work. The essence the Revenant used carried Kolis's stench. That was a Primal curse. So, maybe you have a right to worry."

I stared at the draken. "Care to elaborate on this thought process?"

"I can't believe I have to explain this out loud," the draken muttered. "You're Joined, right? Both of your lives are tied to hers—to her very long, like nearly unending lifespan. Unless she goes down, neither of you two should."

I heard Poppy's sharp inhale.

"But again," the draken went on, "that was a Primal curse, so…"

The draken was still talking, but I wasn't listening. Poppy's nails dug into my wrist as she stared down at Kieran. He'd slowed, only because our horse had. Under the thick, fawn-colored fur, I saw that the muscles of his shoulders were tense.

"Hell," Malik muttered and then laughed roughly. The lines of his face relaxed. "I hadn't even thought of that."

I tightened my arm around Poppy's waist. Her grip on my wrist eased, and her fingers moved, mimicking the circles I made on her hip. She relaxed.

And so did I.

Poppy

My mind drifted from what I'd learned and all that had happened as we stopped for the night, eating our dinner of cured meat and cherries amid the black walnut trees.

Everything was hard to take in.

But Casteel was here.

He was free. So was his brother—whether he liked it or not. They were both free. That was almost all that mattered right now.

Almost.

Unfortunately, the curse that Callum had placed on Kieran ground all other thoughts to a halt. It also mattered now. My chest clenched as, in my mind, I saw that shadowy smoke seeping into his skin. Heard what Reaver had said—had suggested could be an answer in case we couldn't find Malec, or Isbeth sought to betray us just as we plotted to do the same to her.

It also wasn't the first time I'd thought of the Joining being—

A dull flare of pain spread across my upper jaw, causing me to inhale sharply. Wincing, I rubbed at my cheek. The ache sank into the very roots of my teeth and then faded as quickly as it had appeared.

"Your head hurting?" Kieran asked from where he sat beside me, having shifted into his mortal form a bit ago.

"Just a little, but not anymore." I glanced down at his arm. The shallow cut was still there. My touch had done nothing. "How are you feeling?"

"The same as the last time you asked. I feel fine." Kieran studied me closely. "You've been quiet today."

I lifted a shoulder. "There's a lot to think about."

"There is," he agreed. "But I know what one of those things is. What you did in Stonehill."

I opened my mouth then closed it. My mind kept getting stuck on a lot of things, but that...I couldn't stop thinking about that cold spot spreading through my body when Isbeth had ordered the mortal couple slaughtered. "I lost control," I whispered.

"But you didn't."

"Only because Casteel stopped me."

Kieran leaned in, his head low. "Is that what you really think? That Cas or any of us could really stop you?" When I said nothing, he curled his fingers around my chin, lifting my gaze to his. "*You* stopped yourself. Don't forget that."

I wanted that to be true. So did he. That didn't make it true. "And don't forget what you promised."

"I wish I could, Poppy." He dropped his hand. "But I can't."

My throat burned. "I'm sorry."

"I know." He lifted his chin. "Cas comes."

I turned as Casteel prowled out from the mass of trees. He'd been scouting the surrounding area to see if there were any signs of Craven nearby.

"Are we good here?" I asked.

"As good as we can be anywhere," he answered as Kieran rose, stopping long enough to tug gently on a strand of my hair. I didn't even want to think about the mess my hair had to be in. Casteel extended his hand. "Come. I want to show you something."

I arched a brow but took his hand. As I stood, I saw that Kieran had stopped by Malik, who was being watched over by Reaver.

"Careful," Casteel advised as he led me through the trees. "There was no sign of Craven activity, but there are a lot of unripe walnuts scattered about."

Looking down, I wondered exactly how I was supposed to avoid them since the floor of the woods was nothing but shadows of grass and rocks. "What are you showing me?"

"It's a surprise."

We walked deeper into the woods where the last rays of sun barely penetrated the heavy limbs. Cas lifted a low-hanging branch out of the way. "Here." He tugged me forward. "Look."

I eased past him and the tightly packed trees, dipping under a limb. What I saw left me speechless. I straightened, my eyes wide. Casteel had brought me to the edge of the walnut tree grove, to where the earth sloped sharply down into a valley full of stunning shades of blue and purple soaking up what remained of the sun. A river snaked among the vivid trees, its water so clear, I knew immediately that it was the River of Rhain.

"The Wisteria Woods," Casteel said, curling an arm around me from behind. "They follow the road to Padonia and all the way to the Blood Forest."

"I forgot about them." My gaze lifted to where I could see crimson staining the horizon. "It's beautiful."

"Magnificent," he murmured, and when I looked over my shoulder, I saw that his attention was fixed on me. He drew me close to his chest, and gods, I'd missed this. The feel of him—his body pressed so tightly to mine. The confidence in how his hand ran up the side of my body, and the ease in which I sank into his embrace. "I did think you'd like the view, but I also had an ulterior motive for leading you away from the group."

My mind immediately went to very, very inappropriate places when I thought about those ulterior motives. I imagined he needed to feed again to fully restore his strength. Something which my body immediately gave its approval for with a flush of heat. "Ulterior motives? You? Never."

His laugh touched my cheek. "I wanted to see how you were holding up. A lot of unexpected news was just dumped on you."

My brows lifted. "Your ulterior motive is that you wanted to *talk*?"

"Of course." His palm grazed the curve of my breast, causing me to gasp. "What else could it be?"

I bit my lip. "I'm okay."

His hand made another slow, sweeping pass down my side. "Remember what you said to me in Stonehill? I said that first, Poppy. It's okay not to be okay when you're with me."

"I haven't forgotten." My heart swelled as I watched a breeze stir the heavy stems of the wisterias below. "Secrets and new discoveries about myself don't really rattle me like they used to."

"I don't know if that is a good or a bad thing."

Neither did I. "It just is. But I'm...I'm processing it all." I turned my head to the side. "And you? How are you feeling?"

"I'm processing what all those tiny hooks in your vest are keeping hidden from me," he said, sliding his hand over my stomach. "And the fact that it was I who clasped them."

I laughed. "That is not what you're processing."

"Is, too." His breath teased my lips. "And I'm also processing my need to rip my brother's throat out. I can multitask like that."

My heart stuttered. "Cas—"

His mouth took mine as his chest rumbled against my back, and that hand...it slid up over my breast until those nimble fingers, his thumb and middle, found the hardened peak through the thin vest and blouse beneath. He pinched. Not hard, just enough to cause my hips to twitch as a bolt of wicked pleasure darted from my breasts. "I don't want to talk about him. Later, we can. Just not now."

I wanted to know what he was thinking, but I could taste the tart conflict and confusion he felt. So, I let it go—for now. I kissed him instead, and received another teasing tug on my tingling, sensitive flesh.

"I'm also thinking about how amazing you are," he said when our mouths parted. "You're a force to be reckoned with, Poppy."

The building heat cooled as that cold place inside me stirred, and the eather throbbed. I turned my head back to the valley. "I'm something, all right."

His fingers eased from my breast. "What is that supposed to mean?"

I opened my mouth but couldn't find the words to describe what it meant. It wasn't like I didn't have any words. I had too many. "I…I blew apart that house."

"You did." His hand at my hip moved then, sliding toward my navel.

"I damaged other homes." My eyes closed as those fingers started to move over my breast. "I could've killed innocent people."

"You could have."

My heart lurched.

"But you didn't," he said softly, slipping his right hand past my navel. "You know that."

All I knew was that I hadn't sensed any pain as we left Stonehill, but that didn't mean I hadn't ended the life of someone innocent. That was possible. "Are you sure?" I whispered.

"I am," he assured. "You didn't hurt anyone innocent, Poppy."

"Because you stopped me," I whispered, my lips parting as he quickly undid the clasps on my breeches. The flap parted, and the material loosened. "*Casteel.*"

"What?"

The breath I took hitched as his fingers slipped inside the thin scrap of undergarments I wore. "You know *what.*"

"I know I had nothing to do with you not harming anyone innocent," he countered, dipping those fingers between my thighs. My entire body jerked as my eyes fluttered open.

It was strange—the seriousness of the conversation and how my body responded nonetheless to the teasing touch. My stance widened, giving him more access. "How do you know that?"

"Because if that were what you wanted?" His finger dragged over the aching flesh. "If that was your will, you would've harmed those mortals before I could stop you." He sank a finger into my heat, wringing another gasp from me. "You made a conscious effort to stop. I know that because I know how the essence works, Poppy."

I stared at the wisteria trees as his finger moved, slowly in and out, never going too deep. My hips chased those shallow plunges. Heat flowed through my veins, easing the knot of coldness that pulsed near the essence. Maybe he was right. When I summoned the mist, my will had not been to cause harm. Nor had it been when the wave of rage left me.

But was that true when it came to the explosion of rage?

I hadn't really been thinking at all. I'd just been furious. Had I gotten lucky then?

"You understand that, right?" Casteel's breath was hot against my neck. "Your will, as you said, is yours."

My heart beat faster as his finger thrust deeper, and the pastel hues of the wisteria trees turned darker.

"Your will is not controlled by a prophecy," he continued, the sharp edge of his fangs grazing my throat and sending my pulse skittering. "Your will is not controlled by a Queen or anyone else but you." He worked another finger in, and my knees stiffened as I rose onto the tips of my toes. "You are not a harbinger of death and destruction, Poppy. You're a harbinger of change and new beginnings. Tell me you believe that."

"Yes," I panted. "I do."

Casteel's head tilted, and the pierce of his fangs in the wound he'd created before stunned me. My muscles tightened, and my thighs clamped around his hand as the fiery sting traveled through me, quickly followed by a roar of acute pleasure as his mouth closed over the reopened marks, and he drank.

Shuddering, my eyes fell shut as he drank from me—took my blood and took me with his fingers, as that insidious voice in the back of my mind scolded me. I wanted so badly to tell him that I believed what he'd said as strongly as both he and Kieran did. So, that was what I'd done. I'd lied. I lied to him, and I didn't like it. Didn't like how it made me feel. And I didn't like that I'd made Kieran promise what he could never share with Casteel. But his touch—those fingers and his mouth—chased away more than the coldness. It crowded out the guilt as I rode Cas's fingers, rocking against his palm and the hardness pressing against my lower back. With my senses open, the smoky flavor of his lust and the sweetness of his love drove me to a rippling, sudden release that he wisely silenced with his hand.

I was still trembling when his fingers eased from me, and he took one last, dragging pull from my throat. His arm loosened at my waist as he lifted his hand. I turned halfway, halting when heated, golden eyes met mine. My breath caught as his blood-tinged lips closed over his slick fingers.

"I don't know which part of you tastes better," he murmured.

My body flushed hot. "You are...you are so very bad."

He grinned down at me but it was lost in a stark pulse of need as I reached for his breeches. He said nothing, simply watched me intently as I undid the flap, tugging the breeches down his lean hips. His body jerked as I curled my fingers around his cock, and he groaned as I went to my knees.

"Who's the bad one?" he asked, his voice thick and wonderfully rough.

"You." I drew my hand up his length. "And you're a bad influence."

His hand curled around the back of my head as he drew me in until my lips brushed his tip. "I've told you before, Poppy. Only the bad can be influenced."

I grinned up at him, enjoying these stolen moments where nothing existed but us. "I read something in Willa's journal."

"I bet you read all kinds of things in her journal," he replied, fingers tangling in my hair. "But what are you thinking of now?"

"She wrote that the vein...this vein—" I said, dragging my thumb across it. He groaned. "Can be extraordinarily sensitive. Is that true?"

"Can be." His chest rose sharply.

"She also claimed that it was even more sensitive to the tongue," I said, my face warming.

"Why don't you assuage that curiosity of yours and find out?" He paused. "For research purposes."

I laughed and then found out as I dragged my tongue along that thick vein. Willa had been correct. It was a sensitive spot. Liquid had already begun beading on the head of his cock when I closed my mouth over him. I drew him in as deeply as I could and didn't worry about what I was doing because I knew he loved it. The way his hand tightened on the back of my head told me that. As did the thrusts of his hips and the spicy taste that joined the earthy flavor of his skin.

"You know, I think…" He shuddered as he gathered the strands of my hair away from my face with his other hand. "I think you really like my cock in your mouth," he said, and I sucked harder. He groaned. "I also think you like it when I say inappropriate things like that."

My face heated even more because I really did.

"My Queen is a very—" His curse was sharp, and the rhythm of his hips picked up. "Fuck."

Casteel didn't try to pull away. This time, he held me there as he came, his entire body shaking as the release took him. When his tremors subsided, I kissed the underside of his cock and then the faded brand on his hip before redoing his breeches. His hands slipped to my shoulders, but he didn't draw me to my feet. Instead, he joined me on the ground, pulling me into his lap and against his chest. We were both still breathing a little fast as he redid the clasp on my breeches.

"There is something else we need to talk about," he said as he straightened the edge of my vest.

My head was nestled under his chin as I watched the moon rise. We probably had a long list of things we needed to discuss, but I suspected I knew what was the most pressing. "The Joining?"

He folded his arms around me. "What are you thinking?"

A lot. In those quiet moments that followed, as the moon continued its nightly climb, I was thinking a lot. "I can't bring wolven back," I said finally, unsure if I had told him that when I'd bathed him at Stonehill. "Or draken. I can't bring back any being of two worlds."

Casteel said nothing.

"And Kieran…he was okay with that, even though it terrified me. Losing him." Shuddering, I closed my eyes and drew in a staggered, too-short breath. "I can barely even think it."

"Don't." Casteel's fingertips grazed my cheek as he tilted my chin up and back. I opened my eyes. "You're not going to lose Kieran."

"I want to believe that." I turned my head, kissing the palm of his injured hand. "I want to believe that we'll find Malec, and that Isbeth won't betray us. That we'll take Carsodonia and suffer no losses. That we will survive this, and everyone we care about will, too. But that's a fairy-tale ending. A perfect one that most likely won't become reality."

Casteel traced the lines of my face, and for a moment, I soaked up the feel of his touch, letting there be nothing but that. "We can make it the closest thing to reality."

"With the Joining," I whispered.

His gaze returned to mine as he nodded. "It won't protect everyone."

My chest ached. "If I could Join with all those I care about, as awkward as that would be," I said, and Casteel gave me a half-grin, "I would. But I don't think it works that way, does it?"

"I don't think so."

I sighed. "But it will offer Kieran and you a better level of protection. Right? It could supersede this curse."

"Right." He moved his thumb to my lower lip. "We would live as long as you. The way you age, however that will be, will also be the way we age." He lowered his head, kissing me. "But it's a big decision, Poppy. It will not just be your life that you bear the weight of. It will be mine and Kieran's."

"But as the Queen, don't I already bear the weight of the lives of all our people?" I asked. "Don't you?"

A faint smile appeared as the sweet and rich, clove-y taste of cinnamon reached me. Love. Pride. I kissed his thumb. "You do. We both do. But this is different." With his other hand, he tucked several strands of my hair back behind my ear. "The Joining can be intense."

Warmth crept up my throat. "I know."

"Even if it doesn't become something sexual, the sheer intimacy of the act goes beyond that."

I swallowed. "What does it actually entail?" I asked, unsure that what little Alastir had said was true.

"It has to be under the moon, among nature. I don't know why, but that's a part of the unknown when it comes to how it works. There's a...magical quality to it that goes beyond blood. There have been rumors of it not working in the past—like the intentions to do it were not genuine or something," he shared. "But other than that unknown part, there can be nothing between us. And, yes, by *nothing*, I mean clothing."

My face began to warm even more. "Oh."

"All of us would have to be bare and open to one another. To the elements and to the Fates," he explained, and I resisted the urge to roll my eyes at the mention of the Arae. "We must remain in contact with one another throughout the entire ritual."

"And we would drink from one another?"

"You would feed from us first." His fingers dropped to the skin below the sensitive bite on the side of my neck as he went into more detail. It was a lot, and my body already felt as if it were as red as the

Blood Forest. "You can see how things can…escalate into more."

Oh, did I ever. "I don't know how they couldn't," I admitted.

"They don't if you don't want them to," he told me. "And if it does become something you need, then it does. Nothing that you're not comfortable with would ever transpire. I wouldn't allow it. Neither would Kieran. It's as simple as that."

Was it really? I twisted in his lap, looking at him straight on. "And if it did…become more? What would happen afterward? Between us?"

His head tilted as his eyes searched mine. "You love me, right?"

"Yes."

"I love you," he said, flattening his palm against my cheek. "And you love Kieran."

I jolted, my stomach dipping. "I…" I didn't know how to answer that.

"I love him," Casteel said in the silence. "Though not in the same way. Not as I feel for you. Because what I feel for you…no one has ever owned that before. No one ever will."

My throat dried. He didn't have to tell me that. I already knew it. "Kieran…he means a lot to me."

"You mean a lot to him."

A burn filled my eyes for some silly reason as I stared at Casteel's throat. "I don't know how to explain what I feel. Because I don't understand it."

"I get it," he said, and I really thought he did. "There's more."

I blinked away tears and peeked up at him. "There's more to take into consideration. Really?"

He nodded. "We both have to be prepared that this may not be the only Joining. If Kieran were to find someone, he may want to join their life to yours. You'd have to go through the Joining again."

"So he wouldn't outlive them." I exhaled slowly. "I wouldn't want him to face that. I would do the Joining again if that was what he wanted."

"No. You wouldn't allow him to go through that." Casteel dragged his hand through my hair, pressing his lips to my temple.

"And what do you think Kieran wants?" I asked. "Would he want to do this?"

Casteel stared at me for what felt like a full minute. "Honestly?"

"Of course."

"Before you came into the picture, Kieran would've agreed simply because it would've been something I requested. Not because there was a bond, but because he would do anything for me. Just like I would do anything for him. But now? He would do it for you."

I frowned. "But we're doing it for him."

"And for me in a roundabout way, but he'd do it if that's what you wanted," he insisted.

My stomach and chest fluttered as if a dozen birds were taking flight all at once. "And if we decide to do this, when would it happen?"

"Knowing you, you'll probably want to do it as soon as possible." He kissed my forehead. "But I think we should wait until after we go into the Blood Forest and return to Padonia—"

"But—"

"This is a big choice to make, Poppy. One that can't be undone. You may not think you need the time to make sure, and maybe you don't, but I still want you to have that time."

"You don't need that time, though. You know what you want."

He brushed several strands of hair back from my face. "I do, but that's because I grew up knowing what the Joining is and everything it entails. This is something new to you."

I appreciated the thoughtfulness behind making sure that I didn't change my mind. This *was* a big deal, and there was also the chance that if we did the Joining, it wouldn't protect Kieran against the Primal curse. Even knowing that, the chance that it *would* was more important. The Joining could also protect Kieran and Casteel in the battles to come.

It also meant never having to say goodbye to either of them.

But it was also more than all that. It was also the knowledge that if Kieran ever had to honor the promise he'd made to me, and I misjudged what Casteel would do, he wouldn't be able to truly harm Kieran. Both would remain safe if I were entombed.

Meeting Casteel's gaze, I drew in a deep breath. "I will take the time, but I know my answer won't change. I want to do the Joining."

38

Casteel

I sat quietly beside Poppy as she slept under the walnut tree, having fallen asleep mere moments after placing her cheek on my rolled cloak. I didn't want to disturb her, but I also couldn't stop myself from touching her. It was as if I were under some sort of compulsion. I'd readjusted the cloak draped over her half a dozen times. I'd toyed with her hair, smoothing the wispy strands that had fallen on her cheek, and then waited hopefully for the breeze to undo my work so I had a good reason for touching her again.

It was all ridiculous. Perhaps even a bit obsessive, but the contact was grounding, especially in the dark and quiet. My hand shook slightly as I pulled the cloak up to her shoulder. The contact stopped the looming and panicked fear that drove my mind back to that cell.

Dragging my gaze from her, I looked over to where Malik was chained to one of the trees. His chin was down against his chest, but I knew he was awake.

And I was willing to bet that he was plotting his escape.

I didn't know what to think when it came to Malik, but one thing was clear. He wasn't loyal to Isbeth. It wasn't the Blood Queen he sought to return to.

It was his heartmate.

Still, I didn't think I could ever forgive him.

I wasn't even sure I could forgive my parents for their lies.

Kieran drifted out of the night, coming to my side. He crouched beside me, his voice low. "I'll watch over her."

The fist of emotion clenched. "I don't know if I want to speak to him."

Kieran eyed Malik, his jaw tense. "You don't want to, but you need to, and you should."

"Was that supposed to be wise advice?"

"Someone has to impart wisdom around here."

I smirked, letting my hand fall from my mouth. "Hopefully, we find a person to take on that role."

Kieran chuckled quietly as he glanced at Poppy. "You know, she never slept like this when you were gone. She hardly slept at all. And when she did, there wer almost always nightmares. I think that's why she sleeps so deeply now. Her body is trying to make up for the loss."

I closed my eyes.

Hearing all of that... Fuck, it was a kick to the heart. I reached over, my fingers grazing her cheek just so I could *feel* her. "If I could take back any pain she suffered, I would."

"But you wouldn't change a thing you did."

"No."

He let out a heavy sigh. "What Reaver said earlier..."

I turned my head to him, a faint sliver of moonlight cutting across his cheek and one eye. "The Joining?"

Kieran nodded. "Reaver wasn't even sure if it would block a Primal curse."

"It could, though."

A long moment passed as he stared down at Poppy. "I don't want either of you to feel like you have to do that for me. We'll find Malec, and then we'll kill that bitch."

I studied him. The line of his jaw was hard. Set. Determined. I'd seen that expression a thousand times. Like when we left for Solis to find the Maiden. He hadn't been on board with the idea, but he'd stood beside me the entire time. As resolved then as he was when I'd ordered him to remain in Atlantia while I went on my idiotic quest to kill the Blood Queen and King all those years ago. I knew the slight rise of his lips meant that he was reluctantly amused, something I'd seen a lot of when he was first around Poppy. I knew what he looked like when he was furious and when he'd been ripped apart by grief. I'd seen him go utterly cold. Empty. I knew his face well enough to know when he looked upon someone he cared deeply about. Those fine, barely noticeable lines of tension around his mouth disappeared. Kieran *softened*. He'd done that when he looked at Elashya—whenever he spoke of her. He softened in almost the same way now when he looked upon Poppy.

I reached over, clasping his shoulder. "We are not brothers of the same blood. We are not friends due to some bond," I told him, and his gaze met mine. "We are not loyal to each other because of courtesy or tradition or title. We have always been above all that. And, in a lot of ways, we're two halves of the same whole. Different than Poppy and me, but not *that* much different. You know that."

Kieran closed his eyes.

"Poppy and I have spoken about it."

"I figured that's what you were off doing." He paused. "Well, *one* of the things I figured you two were off doing."

I grinned as I watched him. "When it comes to the Joining, it's not because we feel as if we need to. It's because we want to," I told him. "It's for you as much as it will be for us."

Kieran swallowed again. "I just wanted you to know—wanted *her* to know—that I don't expect it."

"We both know that."

He cleared his throat. "So, you did talk about it?"

"We did." I squeezed his shoulder. "And you know what our answer is—what she decided."

"I do." Kieran's eyes opened. "And how do you feel about that?"

"You know how I feel about it."

A grin appeared. "Intrigued?"

"I'm always in a state of constant intrigue when it comes to her," I admitted.

"Yeah," he breathed, looking down at her. "I bet she had so many questions."

I grinned. "All valid ones you probably secretly wished she'd asked you so you could feel useful."

Kieran laughed under his breath. "Yeah, I do."

"I wanted her to take the time to make sure this is what she wants," I told him, and he nodded. "If she still wants to do the Joining, we'll do it when we return from the Blood Forest."

"That's good. I want her to be sure."

His gaze flicked to me. "Go talk to your brother. She'll be fine with me."

"I know." Giving his shoulder one last squeeze, I rose and left. When I looked back, Kieran had taken my place beside her, watchful and alert, and that warmed my chest.

I made my way across the small clearing. Malik showed no awareness of my approach, but he *was* aware. All those ugly emotions crowded my chest as I knelt in front of him. I said nothing. Neither did he for several moments. When he did speak, I fucking wished he hadn't.

"You hate me."

Jaw clenching, I twisted my neck from side to side. Did I? Yes. No.

"Wouldn't blame you if you did." He stretched out a leg. "I know you looked for me this whole time. I heard what the Descenters called you. The Dark One—"

"Except you were the only Dark One that ever mattered."

His shoulders tensed as he continued. "I didn't want you to look for me. I wanted you to give up on it. Prayed that you did. And I kept thinking you would hear about me—about a man called Elian, who was often seen at Wayfair. That you would know, would assume, that I'd betrayed you and would give up. You didn't. Should've known better. You were always a stubborn brat—"

"I don't give a fuck about any of that. You don't even want to know what I would do for Poppy, so I get it. You did it for your heartmate." The moment the words were spoken, I *breathed* how godsdamn true they were. "It's what I did to Poppy to free you. I lied to her. Betrayed her. And, yeah, that's on me. Something I've got to work out. But it's also what you did to her that I cannot fathom, no matter what you believed she would do as an adult. She was a child. And you—who abhorred violence of any kind—*never* would've even considered harming a child."

Malik said nothing.

That ugly fist of emotion clenched tighter. "It doesn't matter that you weren't able to follow through on it. She got hurt because of you, Malik. Bad."

"I know," he said in a ragged way as if it hurt him to admit it. *I* wanted to hurt him for even acknowledging it.

"Do you? Do you know the scars that none can see? How they run so damn deep in her? Your actions tormented her for years." I lowered myself onto one knee, planting a hand in the cool grass to stop myself from planting it in his face. "You left her there to die."

Malik's head lifted then. Identical eyes met mine. "I didn't. She tried to tell you that back in Stonehill. How do you think she survived that night? Primal god or not, she hadn't entered her Culling yet." He leaned forward as far as the chain would allow. "You know that means she would've died if left there. None of the others who survived the night would've been able to get her out of there. I did. I took her back to Carsodonia, and that fucking—" A tremor coursed through him, and his laugh was low. Harsh. "I didn't leave her there."

I stared at him. Poppy had said that he'd gotten her out of Lockswood. He'd spoken the truth. But did it matter? "Is that supposed to redeem you somehow?"

"Fuck, no. Because you're right. I was the cause of those scars—hidden or not." Malik slumped against the tree. "I saw Penellaphe. Not often. Isbeth kept her away from most, but I saw her before they placed her in that veil. I saw what my actions had done. And trust me when I say it should bring you a little peace to not have seen the aftermath when it was so new."

I rose swiftly and took a step toward him, stopping short when I saw Kieran do the same across the clearing. I turned away from my brother, dragging in the cool night air until it dampened some of the rage.

"Did Alastir ever tell anyone that he saw me?"

I turned to him.

"Because he did."

Holy fuck. "No."

Malik's eyes closed. "He saw and recognized me. I don't know if I should feel relieved or not that he kept that to himself."

But had he? Or was that something else our parents had lied about? Was that why they'd believed Malik gone to them? To Atlantia? Why they'd pushed so hard for me to take the throne?

"That night, when I looked into Penellaphe's eyes and saw the Consort, I believed Cora then. You know, that she was right," he said after a moment. "That Penellaphe would end the Blood Crown. But over the years, I realized that it didn't matter who Penellaphe was in her heart. All that mattered was whether Isbeth found a way to exploit her power." His eyes opened. "And you know she will. You saw it at Stonehill. In Oak Ambler. Isbeth stokes her anger, and Poppy responds with rage."

"Shut up."

"And when she completes her Culling, it won't be rage she

responds with. It will be death. It will be exactly what Isbeth is counting on. Something—"

I shot forward, closing my hand around Malik's throat. "Poppy will never destroy a kingdom, let alone a realm. No matter what Isbeth does," I told him, aware that Kieran had risen again but remained at Poppy's side. "She, unlike her mother *and* me, is able to control her anger."

"Do you know how badly I want to believe that?" His voice broke.

I went cold as I held his gaze. "If you even think of harming her now, I swear to the gods I will tear you apart, limb from limb."

"If I wanted to try something, I would've made a move when she was younger and returned to Wayfair," he bit out. "I haven't. Neither has Millicent."

"Yeah, that's right. Millicent said it had to be me once she finishes the Culling."

"And that wasn't easy for her to say to you."

"She didn't appear to struggle that much with the words."

"Millie doesn't know her sister, but she wouldn't choose that kind of end for her. She's just trying to protect the people." He held my stare. "And I hate that you even had to hear that. I do. To carry that kind of knowledge…that it will soon only be you who can stop her."

"Don't feel too badly for me, brother." I dug my fingers into his windpipe just enough to cause him to flinch. "For I won't lose one second of sleep to it because I would never do such a thing, nor would she give me a reason to."

"And if you're wrong?" he forced out.

"I'm not." I let go of his throat and backed off before I did something I might regret. "We're going to find Malec. We're going to bring him to Isbeth."

"But what the draken said about the Joining—"

"We haven't done it." I stared up at the sky, unsure of why I'd even admitted that.

"Fuck. For real? You're married to your heartmate and haven't Joined? You? Kieran? Hell…" A little of the old Malik I knew slipped in then. "I just assumed you had. Apparently, so did the draken." He paused. "Will you? It might not work against a Primal curse, but—"

"That's none of your fucking business. But, Joined or not, I won't risk it." I faced him. "Neither will Poppy."

Malik glanced over at Kieran. He had returned to Poppy's side, sitting in a way that had him bent over half her body as if he were shielding her. "You sure you aren't Joined?"

"Yes," I said wryly. "Positive."

"Huh," he murmured.

Several long moments passed as I stared down at him. "Why didn't you ever try to take her life again when she was young and vulnerable?" I asked, even though I wasn't sure I should know. Because as I'd said, Poppy was far better at controlling her anger than I was. "Why didn't Millicent if she too believed in the prophecy?"

Malik gave another shake of his head. "That's her sister. Millie couldn't do it. Didn't matter that Penellaphe was never supposed to know about her."

"And you? You stopped believing in what Cora said."

"I...I just couldn't do it. And by the time she was old enough that I no longer saw her as a child, they sent her to Masadonia," he said, his eyes thin slits. "And by the end, I'd heard of the Dark One. You. And I figured..."

I tensed. "You figured what?"

"That you would kill her to get back at the Blood Queen."

Cursing under my breath, I looked away. There was a brief time when I would've done just that. Before I met Poppy. When I knew her only as the Maiden. Those brief moments, though, fucked with my head, even now.

I dragged a hand over my face. I still didn't know if Malik having a change of heart mattered. Or if it ever would. I knelt once more. "Do you or do you not want to defeat Isbeth and the Blood Crown?"

Malik's eyes hardened into chips of amber. "I want to see them burn."

"What about Millicent?" I asked.

"She wants the same." His gaze fell to where Poppy slept and then returned to mine. "She wants to be free of her mother. To finally be able to live."

"If that's what you really want, you won't run back to the capital and get yourself killed. You'll fight beside us. You'll help us find Malec and then kill Isbeth. You will help us end this."

"I will help you," Malik said. "I won't try to escape."

I took that in, wanting to believe what he claimed as badly as he wanted to believe what I said about Poppy. Problem was, that faith wasn't gained by words. Faith was earned by actions. "There's something else I need to know about that night in Lockswood. What in the hell was up with that rhyme?"

"What?" He frowned. "What rhyme?"

"The pretty poppy one. Pick it and watch it bleed." I searched his features.

"If that's a rhyme, it sounds about five levels of fucked up," Malik said. "But I have no idea what you're talking about. I've never even heard anything like that."

The battlements of the Rise surrounding Padonia came into view as we crested the rocky hill the following morning. Anticipation and resolve rose swiftly, as did a bit of awe. The Wisteria Woods I'd seen the night before now crowded the earthen road and the city of Padonia itself, their trailing limbs of varying shades of blue and purple giving way to the deep crimson of the outer edges of the Blood Forest.

Poppy was clearly taken with the beauty, her gaze crawling over every inch of the landscape. I hoped it helped her forget that we'd passed the road to Lockswood no more than an hour ago. Her shoulders hadn't relaxed until the wisterias became more visible. Still, she'd been quiet most of the morning.

Shifting in the saddle, I glanced over at Malik. Between our conversation last night and the upcoming reunion with our father, I was caught up in my head and hoping to the gods that I wasn't making a huge-ass mistake by removing the bone chain from his wrists and allowing him to ride freely.

I just hadn't wanted our armies' first sight of their Prince to be one of him in chains.

Poppy folded a hand over the arm I'd encircled her waist with as she turned to the side, looking up. "Are you okay?"

"Not sure," I admitted, glancing down at her. "Been thinking about what I'm going to say to my father."

"What have you come up with?"

"Nothing that's suitable for repeating," I said with a dry laugh.

She glanced forward as the bridge over the River of Rhain became visible through the twining vines of bluish-purple. "We can delay this if you need more time."

"We don't need to do that." I kissed the top of her head. "It's best if I get this over with."

The tops of many of the tents became visible, and it looked as if the bulk of the armies had camped outside the Rise. A risky move, but one that had most likely been decided in favor of not destroying the fields inside.

From the town, a low, rumbling roar gained our attention. I slowed the horse as Kieran stopped alongside us, the sound of hooves and paws reaching our ears. "We're about to have company." I squeezed her hips and then dismounted. I reached for her, and she placed her hand in mine without question or hesitation. The horse we rode was only now getting used to Kieran in his wolven form, and I had a feeling we were about to be swamped by many more. I didn't want him throwing Poppy.

Her lips pursed. "I still cannot believe I don't have better hearing or vision. Ridiculous."

"Or shift into anything," I reminded her as the noise grew louder, closer.

"That, too."

"You're perfect as you are." I bent, kissing the corner of her mouth. "Average hearing and all."

"That was corny," she said, grinning as she peered at me through a fringe of lashes with those fractured green-and-silver eyes. "But cute."

A white wolf was the first to burst through the wisteria vines, racing straight toward us. There was no stopping my smile as Delano all but launched himself in my direction.

"Oh, dear," Poppy murmured, calming the nervous horse.

I caught the damn wolven, laughing as I stumbled back. Delano wasn't the largest wolven by any means, but he was still heavy as an ox and strong as one, too. I ended up on one knee and tried to—well, calm the furry, wiggling mass that was Delano as he pressed his head into mine.

"Missed you, my man." Clasping the sides of his head, I held him tightly until a fawn-colored wolven identical to Kieran but smaller in weight and height nudged him out of the way.

My chest warmed as I embraced Netta. She was a little less sedate in her eagerness, only nearly toppling me on my ass once. "Missed you, too."

"What about me?" came a drawl.

I smoothed a hand over the top of Netta's head as I said, "Didn't think about you once, Emil."

"Ouch," the Atlantian said with a laugh, and then in a softer voice, I heard him say, "I knew you would get him."

Looking up, I saw the auburn-haired bastard take Poppy's hand in his and hold it to the gold and steel armor adorning his chest. For once, I didn't want to punch his throat through his spine. Only because the adoration in his stare was that of respect.

And because he released her hand quickly.

Other wolven surrounded me, and I gave up, remaining on my knee as they each came to either brush against me or push their head against mine. I gladly waited. For a wolven to do such a thing was a sign of respect, and I was honored to be on the receiving end.

When I was finally able to rise, another emotion rocked me. It was seeing Poppy greeted in the same way—watching her turn to bury her face in the fur of Delano's neck and then hold Netta tightly to her. Hearing her laughter as the wolven pressed into her. Her acceptance of them—that shining love in her bright eyes—and their clear worship of her did something to my chest and my fucking eyes.

That was my *wife*.

My heartmate.

Godsdamn.

Clearing my throat, I looked at the tall Atlantian standing before me.

"Held back," Naill said thickly. "Didn't want to get trampled."

Laughing, I closed the distance between us, embracing him. "Good to see you."

"As it is to see you." His arm hung around my shoulders. "Hasn't been right without you."

I blew out a ragged breath. "But I'm back now."

"I know you are. Just don't leave us again."

"Don't plan on it."

Naill gave me one last squeeze before stepping back. He caught my left wrist. The glance was brief, but his amber eyes turned hard. "We're going to make them pay for this."

"We are." I clasped our hands with my other.

When Naill moved to the side, Perry quickly replaced him and pulled me in for a one-armed embrace. The armor he wore dug into my chest, but I didn't care. Neither of us spoke for a long moment, and then he said roughly, "You look good."

"Feeling that way," I told him. "You've been keeping an eye on Delano?"

"Always. It's like a twenty-four-hour assignment." Perry laughed, leaning back, his amber eyes shining. "Not once did any of us doubt that Kieran and our Queen would find you. Not for one damn second."

My throat thickened. "Neither did I."

Exhaling slowly, Perry stepped back and finally looked to where Malik stood. The arm around my shoulders tensed. "Gods, it's really him."

"Yeah." I watched Delano approach Malik. The other wolven watched closely, cautiously. Their uncertainty regarding the Prince hung heavy in the air.

"He looks..." Naill joined us, and I noticed a muscle flexing in Perry's jaw.

"He looks nothing like I expected," Emil finished.

In other words, he didn't look like the messy pile of flesh and bones I had when I returned from several decades of captivity.

Emil clasped my hand, and I pulled the fucker in for a close, tight embrace. "Delano said Malik didn't want to return?" he asked quietly.

Perry glanced at us. "And that Poppy told him it was complicated."

"It is." I turned, slipping an arm around Poppy as she came to stand beside me, but I didn't take my gaze off my brother.

Malik knelt in front of Delano as Kieran crept close, eyeing both of them. My brother spoke, but even I couldn't pick up on the words. Whatever he said, though, Delano responded with a slight nudge of his head against Malik's hand.

The act sent a small shudder through Malik and didn't go unnoticed by the other wolven. The tension thickening the air eased. Poppy pressed against my side, her palm resting just below my chest as Malik placed a trembling hand on the top of Delano's bowed head. Malik's eyes closed as Poppy's fingers curled into my shirt, his features pinching as he turned his head, dragging his shoulder along his cheek. I knew what Poppy had to be sensing. The emotion was clearly etched into Malik's face. Sorrow.

Preela, Malik's bonded wolven, had been Delano's sister.

39

We descended the hill to Padonia, flanked by the dozens of wolven who kept pace along the narrow road and had even branched out farther, into the Wisteria Woods. Netta and several others had already returned to town. Horns sounded as we cleared the thickest of the trees, and the valley that Padonia rested in opened before us.

A sea of white tents sat at the edge of the River of Rhain and at the foot of the Rise, where— My godsdamn breath snagged in my chest.

Banners.

Gold and white banners rippled from the battlements atop the Rise, each one bearing the Atlantian Crest—the one Poppy had chosen with the sword and arrow fixed in the center of the sun at equal lengths.

Gods.

She'd done it.

Changed the centuries-old crest. Showing the kingdom and the realm that there was a balance of power between the King and Queen, no matter the fact that she was so much more powerful than I.

Seeing it was a punch of unexpected emotion, straight to the chest. I tightened my hold on Poppy, dipping my head. "You're fucking perfect," I rasped in her ear.

She turned her head slightly, her brows puckering. "What for?"

"Everything," I told her, blinking back dampness. *"Everything."*

Poppy looked to the Rise. "The banners," she whispered. "You like them?"

"I cannot wait to show you how much I fucking love them." I nipped at her ear, drawing a soft gasp from her.

Her face flushed, but the sharp, sudden rise of her arousal told me she couldn't wait for me to show her either.

I straightened, refocusing on the Rise itself. Branches of the nearby wisteria trees had climbed the structure, pressing into the stone and smothering the Rise in the lavender-colored limbs.

"Well, that's a problem," I murmured. "The wisteria trees."

"They're beautiful," Poppy whispered. "It's the most beautiful Rise I've ever seen."

"It is, but you're not going to like what I'm about to say," I replied.

She sighed. "I think I know what you're going to say. The trees need to be cut back."

A faint grin appeared. "They need to be pulled out. Should've been done long before it got to this point. It's likely already weakened the Rise."

"It has," Emil confirmed from where he rode slightly ahead, Kieran trailing between us as Naill rode to our left. "The trees have breached the eastern walls in some areas."

"Well, the Ascended have never been known for their upkeep of infrastructure," Poppy murmured. "Speaking of the Ascended, what of the Royals who oversaw Padonia?"

"They'd abandoned the city before our arrival," Emil answered with a snort of disgust. "Just as they did in Whitebridge—"

"And Three Rivers," Malik spoke, breaking his self-imposed silence. "Most of the Royals had fled to Carsodonia. They have been arriving since Poppy relieved Jalara of his head."

Naill's gaze cut to him. "Yeah, well, the Ascended didn't simply flee Whitebridge and Padonia."

Dread took root. "What did they do?"

"It wasn't like Oak Ambler. They left a graveyard behind in Whitebridge." Naill looked away, his jaw working. "Like they did in the northern lands of Pompay."

"Oh, gods," Poppy uttered, stiffening. "Was there...?"

"No mortal—adult or child—was left alive in Whitebridge," Perry confirmed, swallowing thickly as the dread burned to the ground in a wave of fury. "Thousands were dead and had already turned. We lost some wolven and soldiers. There were just too many Craven."

Poppy's head lowered as she leaned into me. I wished there was something I could say, but for something like this, there was nothing. Absolutely nothing.

"They did the same in Padonia, but the people here fought back," Naill continued, and her head lifted. "A lot of mortals died, but it wasn't as bad as it was in Whitebridge. They took out a few of the Ascended in the process."

"What of Three Rivers?" I asked, pushing the rage down.

"The Ascended there fled but left the mortals alive," Emil said. "Not sure why. Maybe those ruling there were different than the others. I don't know."

"Do you?" I demanded of Malik.

He'd gone pale as he stared ahead. "I didn't know that'd happened in Whitebridge or here," he said hoarsely. "But I've seen Dravan at Court—he's the Duke of Three Rivers. Keeps to himself. Don't know much about him."

"But you do know him?" Naill asked, and when Malik nodded, his eyes narrowed. "Exactly how complicated have things been for you, *Prince* Malik?"

"That is a rather long story," I interrupted as a dark shadow crossed the road, stirring the tops of the wisteria trees as we rounded the bend. "That will have to wait."

The gates of the Rise came into full view, but it was what flew above us that had garnered my attention.

All I saw through the cloud cover was a flash of smoky gray before the shadow fell over the bridge and tents. My jaw loosened as a creature as large as Setti swooped, touching down on its hind legs upon the Rise, its curved horns glistening in the streaks of sun that had broken through the clouds.

The draken made a soft trilling sound that sent a wave of goosebumps over my flesh.

"*Meyaah Liessa?*" Reaver said, having slowed his horse. "If you have no more immediate need of me...?"

"No." Poppy smiled slightly. "You can do as you please."

The draken bowed his head and then dismounted, handing the reins to Perry. He quickly disappeared into the woods.

"That's Nithe," Poppy said, gesturing to the gray draken on the Rise.

All I could do was nod. Because, my gods, I couldn't believe I was actually looking upon a draken again.

Two more shadows fell overhead as we reached the bridge. A green one that was a little larger than Nithe, and a third slightly smaller one.

"The greenish one is Aurelia," Poppy added. "The brownish-black one is Thad."

I nodded again as wings the length of their bodies spread out wide, slowing their descent. They came down on either side of the gate. Thick claws dug into the top of the Rise, shaking the wisteria limbs as their long necks stretched out. Their heads lifted to the sky, the row of horns and the frills around their necks vibrating as their staggering call echoed through the valley.

The call was answered from the woods. Our gazes snapped up as an even larger shadow fell over us. My eyes widened upon the sight of a purplish-black draken crossing over the tents and the Rise.

"And that's Reaver," Poppy said.

"Yeah," I muttered, blinking slowly. Reaver was nearly twice the size of a warhorse, but he glided soundlessly.

The other three draken took flight, lifting from the Rise in a powerful surge of wings that sent the air rippling through the valley. They joined Reaver as they flew over Padonia. The sight of them was something I'd never thought to witness as I watched them disappear into the horizon while we crossed the bridge, joined by the wolven who'd entered the woods. They flooded the pathway to the gates as soldiers drifted out from among the tents.

I drew our horse closer to Malik's. He stared forward, as rigid as the dead. As Emil and the others rode past, the soldiers caught sight of Malik—of Poppy and me, and then the *sound* came.

Shouts erupted. Golden Atlantian swords were thrust into the air and banged off shields—shields engraved with the new Atlantian Crest. They lowered in a wave as we rode past, the soldiers dropping to their knees, thumping hands and hilts off the ground.

Poppy squirmed into me as the cheers continued, and the gates opened. She wasn't used to the response. Hell, I never really got used to it, but this was different.

This was how a Queen and King were greeted.

I found her hand, closing mine around it as we rode between the two branches of the River of Rhain and through the gates. The shouts continued inside the Rise, where soldiers were camped near the entrance.

And still, the sound followed even as we reached the fields of crops, and mortals came out from the stalks of corn, lifting their scythes and cheering. The mortals *cheered*.

I leaned into Poppy. "Was it like this in Oak Ambler or Massene?"

Poppy's hold was a death grip. "No." She took in a trembling breath. Her smile was just as shaky as Kieran drew closer to us, his ears perked. "This is…it's a lot."

My hold tightened on her as we rode down the road, past the cluster of homes and businesses where mortals streamed into the streets, and others stopped where they were on sidewalks, bowing with their hands over their hearts and palms to the ground.

Emil looked over his shoulder at Poppy. "Your plan worked, by the way. They heard about what we did in Massene and Oak Ambler before we even reached Three Rivers. They knew we didn't come to conquer. The same here."

The smile on Poppy's face was steadier now. "It was *our* plan," she said. "And everyone who followed. You. Vonetta. All of you."

Emil smiled, ducking his chin as he faced forward, the recognition warming his cheeks.

Pride lifted my chin even higher. She'd been so afraid of taking the Crown. Of not being a good Queen because she believed she wasn't ready, trained, or worldly enough. And yet, she knew that she had played a role in this—a major role—but not all of the roles.

Wisteria trees returned, lining the road, and the sound of rushing water followed us to the manor in the center of the town. The woods had even pressed in here, leaving the interior Rise barely visible.

Larger tents were positioned around the fortress wall and inside the courtyard. I looked ahead, my heart becoming a knot as several generals stood at the entrance to the manor.

A handful of younger Atlantians rushed us with wide eyes, bowing hastily as we dismounted. They began rounding up the horses as Netta returned, striding past the generals. She wasn't alone. A mortal I hadn't seen since Oak Ambler followed—one who looked vastly different with her white hair pulled back from her face. A strange sensation settled in my chest as I eyed Tawny.

Poppy stepped around me, going to Netta and Tawny. The mortal reached Poppy first, embracing her, and I tensed for no good reason other than…

Kieran's gaze caught mine. He raised his brows. He'd warned me that the mortal didn't feel right. It wasn't exactly something bad. Just different. A sensation I couldn't place.

"How have you been?" Poppy asked, clasping Tawny's hands. "You feel warmer."

"A little." Tawny smiled. "Probably because Vonetta has me being all active and stuff."

Poppy arched her brow at Netta, who grinned. "Gianna and I have been teaching her how to fight. She's a quick learner."

"Only because of what Poppy has taught me," Tawny said.

"I only taught you to stick the sharp end into something," Poppy amended.

Tawny grinned, letting go of Poppy's hand. "Hey, if that is more than half the knowledge required, I've learned."

I relaxed as Poppy turned to Netta. "I wish to have another hug, one where we're both on two legs."

Laughing, Netta obliged as Delano stayed close to Poppy. "I've missed you," Poppy said, pulling back. "You've been well? No injuries? Are you—?"

"I'm okay." Netta clasped her shoulders. "We're all okay."

"Because of you," Poppy insisted. "You've led the armies spectacularly."

"I had help."

"Namely, me." Emil rounded the horses.

Shaking my head, I handed the reins to a steward. "Setti? Is he here?"

"Yes, Your Majesty," the young male answered. "Given nothing but the freshest hay and feed as he's awaited your return."

"Thank you."

I turned to find Tawny standing not too far from me. Damn. Her eyes... They were leached of all color. "I'm glad to see you up and moving about."

She eyed me as bluntly as I had done with her. "And I'm glad to see that according to everyone I've asked, you love Poppy just as fiercely as she loves you, and I don't have to punch you for lying to her."

Poppy whipped around. "Tawny."

"And for kidnapping her," she tacked on.

"*Tawny.*" Poppy hurried over to us as Netta laughed.

"What?" The mortal who felt like *something else* crossed her arms. "I'm just pointing out that everyone—"

"And she did ask *everyone*," Emil chimed in.

"Said you were utterly devoted to Poppy," Tawny finished.

"That is not what you're pointing out," Poppy countered.

Fighting a grin, I inclined my head. "If you feel as if you still need to punch me, I won't stop you."

Poppy shot me a look.

Her friend simply studied me as if she were attempting to determine if I was worthy of such effort. "I'll keep that in mind for later."

"No, you will not," Poppy said. "You can't go around punching the King."

"Someone forgot to tell you that," Kieran replied, brushing past Poppy.

"You punch him?" Tawny asked, blinking.

"No. Not really." Poppy's cheeks turned red.

"She has stabbed me, though." I took Poppy's hand. "In the chest."

"Oh, my gods," Poppy snapped as Tawny's eyes went wide. "You really need to stop telling people that."

"But I deserved it," I added, my smile fading as I turned to the entrance and saw that Hisa had joined the generals. It was who walked with her that drew my attention, though. My father. Tension crept into my shoulders as I looked to see Malik dismounting several feet away. I turned to Naill and spoke, my voice low. "I want you and Emil to keep an eye on Malik."

Naill nodded. "Done."

Keeping Poppy's hand in mine and Kieran at my side with Netta with Delano at hers, I started toward my father. Aware that Malik had fallen in step behind me, I braced myself for several rounds of awkward reunions.

I recognized the generals before me. Lizeth Damron stood next to Perry's father, who sported a rather impressive beard. My stare fixed on Aylard, the general Poppy had warned me about, as they lowered to their knees.

"La'Sere remained at Three Rivers," Netta informed us. "Murin at Whitebridge."

"Have you had any issues with them?" Poppy asked as Tawny trailed behind Netta. "Aylard?"

"Nothing we haven't been able to handle," she shared as the generals rose and stepped aside.

My gaze locked with my father's, and just like that, I froze, unable to go any farther. He came down a step. He looked older than I remembered—the lines at the corners of his eyes deeper, the brackets around his mouth now grooves. His armor creaked as he lowered himself to one knee, bowing.

"You may rise." It was Poppy who gave the softly spoken order I'd once taught her since I, apparently, had forgotten how to fucking speak.

I still hadn't moved as my father rose, his golden eyes never straying from mine. "*Cas.*"

At once, I was a small boy, years away from his Culling, shaken with the need to run and take his outstretched hand. But I was rooted to where I stood.

Poppy squeezed my hand, reminding me that we were not alone. Eyes were on us, many belonging to those who had no idea that their former King and Queen had known who the Blood Queen really was.

A tremor ran through me as I released Poppy's hand and reached for my father's. He clasped my arm, his eyes bright as he pulled me in for a tight embrace. I felt my father, who had always been larger than life and stronger than anyone I knew, shake. My eyes closed, and I shook, too. Anger crashed into love, and all I knew in that moment was that this wasn't the time to demand answers from him. Accountability would come, but it was not the kind that required an audience. It was not the kind that needed to be owned when we were about to end this war with the Blood Crown.

"I didn't want her to go," my father said, his words muffled. "I demanded that she stay. She put me in my place really quick."

A thick laugh rattled me. "I bet she did."

"And I'm glad she did." His embrace tightened, and then he said, even lower, "I know there's a lot we need to discuss."

"There is." Swallowing, I stepped back, and Poppy's hand was there when I reached for it. "But it will have to wait."

He nodded, finally lifting his gaze to Poppy. He began to speak to her, but his attention strayed beyond us to his eldest. He paled as if he'd seen a wraith, and Malik…he wasn't looking at our father at all.

Our father swallowed hard and moved to step forward. "Malik," he said roughly, and that sound, it broke a little of the hardness that had built in my chest. Our father sounded like a man looking upon a child that had died.

Malik stared at the wisterias growing along the manor, his face impassive. "It's good to see you, Father," he said flatly. His voice empty. "You look well."

Our father stiffened for several seconds and then became a man on a battlefield, staring at the one who'd just struck him down. "As do you, son," he replied in a tone as vacant as Malik's had been. That muscle ticked in his temple, the only sign that he felt anything at all. The same moved in Malik's. Our father cleared his throat. "Food and drink are being prepared." He turned stiffly to us. "I imagine there is much to speak about."

"There is," I said, looking at our Queen as she curled herself into my arm. "There's a war to be ended."

My father stared at my left hand as we filled him and the generals in on what had occurred in Carsodonia and Isbeth's demands while we ate the roasted meat and drank the rich ale.

He tried to hide that he saw what had been done to my hand. So did the others. I thought that it might make things more comfortable for them if I kept it hidden, but the absent finger was a part of me now. They needed to get used to it. So, I kept my hand on the table, visible to all.

"What in the world could the Blood Queen want with Malec?" Sven asked.

Poppy wiggled a bit in my lap as she stared at the table, her finger stilling over the cut in the wood she'd been idly tracing. I'd snatched her when she returned from making use of a nearby privy, pulling her into my lap. Probably not the most appropriate seating arrangement for such a conversation, but I couldn't care less about what the others thought. I wanted her there. Needed her as close to me as possible. The feel of her kept me grounded and gave me strength.

And I just liked the curve of her ass in my lap.

Seated to my left, Kieran took a drink of his ale, his eyes widening slightly above the rim of his cup. My gaze briefly flickered to where Malik sat between Emil and Naill. Knowing that the generals present only knew the Blood Queen as Ileana, it really limited what we could say. Malik hadn't spoken at any point. Hadn't even glanced up from the tankard of ale he kept refilling. Not until Sven had asked his question. Now, he stared at our father.

Our father was also doing the table-stare thing as he picked up his tankard and took a hefty drink. He exhaled roughly, lifting his gaze to Malik and then me. "The Blood Queen's real name is Isbeth."

Surprise rippled through me as Poppy's head snapped up. The generals went silent in their shock. I hadn't expected him to admit that. One glance at my brother told me that he hadn't either. That same glance also told me that he was thoroughly enjoying our father's discomfort. Malik smirked.

Lord Sven was the first to recover, sitting back in his chair. "Surely, you're not referencing the Isbeth we all know."

"Yes, it's the Isbeth you are all familiar with," Father continued with a heavy breath. "Malec's mistress."

"And the first vampry," Aylard said.

"She wasn't that." Father looked at the Atlantian general. "She was never a vampry. Malec Ascended her, but a god cannot make a vampry. A god makes something else entirely."

"Isbeth is a demis," Poppy spoke, looking up. "A false god, but a god in all the ways that count. She has masqueraded as an Ascended this entire time, and not many of the Ascended even know what she truly is."

Aylard faced Poppy. "But you did this whole time? You knew and you didn't tell us?" Incredulity crept into his tone as Poppy nodded. The hollows of his cheeks flushed with anger. "How could you keep such information from us?"

Not a single part of me liked his tone. "That information wasn't necessary for you to know until it was," I said, before Poppy could. "But your shock and anger are misplaced. It is not *your Queen* you should be demanding answers from."

Aylard stiffened, the flush deepening.

"My son speaks the truth. It is I and Eloana who bear all responsibility. We kept the truth of her identity hidden from most," my father replied. "Our Queen could've revealed who the Blood Queen was at any time, but I believe she did not do so out of respect for us." His gaze met mine. "Respect that neither Eloana nor I believe we have earned."

I looked away, inhaling deeply.

Sven shook his head in disbelief. "You kept this a secret for years—*hundreds* of years."

Father nodded.

"This kind of information is imperative," Aylard continued after clearing his throat. "It changes what we know about the Blood Crown. It's not just power they want."

Sven nodded. "It's revenge."

Emil let out a low, muffled whistle from Kieran's other side. "This is awkward," he murmured.

I had to agree with him.

"And whether or not our Queen kept this information from us due to respect or not is irrelevant. No offense meant, Your Majesties," Aylard said. Slowly, my attention shifted back to him. My hand resting on Poppy's hip stilled. "You knew she was virtually a god and chose to keep us in the dark while you planned to send our armies to deal with her? That is something we needed to know."

Poppy straightened. "I will deal with Isbeth. None of our armies will."

"That's beside the point!" Aylard exclaimed. "You have no right—"

"Careful," I warned.

Kieran lowered his glass to the table as he fixed his stare on the Atlantian general. "I have a feeling that things are about to get more awkward," he said under his breath to Emil.

Emil snorted.

"I would suggest you think very long and hard about what you believe you have the right to say to my Queen." I held the Atlantian's gaze. "Before you speak again. Or you will discover fairly quickly how your King responds when you offend your Queen. Fair warning, it will likely be the last thing you do for quite some time."

Aylard's complexion became mottled as he looked away, his posture unnaturally stiff.

"All of you are right. And you're also wrong," I said, after I was sure that Aylard had gotten my message. "It does change what we know. It changes the history of our kingdom. But it doesn't change the future. The Blood Crown still needs to be destroyed, and the war ended. That is what we need to be focusing on now. That is all."

Across from us, the wolven general leaned into Hisa, whispering, and then looked at Father. "Agreed," Damron said. "So, I think we all know why she wants Malec."

"We do, and we don't," Poppy said as I gently squeezed her hip.

"Obviously, there are personal reasons. She still loves him, but she also believes that he will be able to give her what she wants."

"Atlantia?" Damron figured.

"The destruction of Atlantia," Poppy corrected softly. Low curses followed. "She believes that he will be able to remake the realms as one. That is her ultimate plan."

Father's brows shot up. "There's no way he would be of any assistance to her." He looked to Poppy. "We know that he cannot be in a good state."

"We do." Poppy tucked a stray piece of hair back from her face. "That's the part that doesn't make sense. But you remember what Framont said—the Priest in Oak Ambler? We were right about who he believed the True King to be. It's Malec. But what we don't know is how or why Isbeth thinks he will be able to do anything for her."

As Poppy spoke, I watched Malik for any hint that he would bring up the prophecy or any of the parts about Poppy being the Harbinger. He didn't. Yet.

"But he would be able to recover eventually," Vonetta said from where she sat, the chair Poppy had sat in empty between us. "Wouldn't he?"

Father nodded. "He would need to feed a lot, and I imagine it would take time. At that point, even once he recovered, there's no telling what mental state he'd be in or what he might do."

I sent Naill a curt nod, and he rose, along with Emil. They quietly nudged Malik from his seat, escorting him from the chamber. Malik may have agreed to aid us in defeating the Blood Crown, and he may already know what we planned when we returned with Malec, but he didn't need to know any of the details. I trusted him to a point, but I wasn't a fool.

"But we won't allow that time to transpire," I informed them once Malik was gone. Our father's jaw had hardened with Malik's departure, but he remained quiet. "We will do as she asks and bring her Malec, but only to lift the curse she placed on Kieran and to draw her out of Carsodonia. She will not get a chance to use Malec in any way. When we meet with her in two weeks, we will end this war, once and for all."

All the generals listened intently as Damron said, "I'm liking the sound of that."

The discussion of how we would take Carsodonia went rather smoothly, considering how it had begun, mainly because Aylard was practicing his shut-the-fuck-up rule of life. Plans were made to call

Murin and La'Sere in from the surrounding cities. Cyr was too far out in Oak Ambler. There was no time for us to reach him and for the general to join us, but word would be sent to him anyway. We talked over what we could of how we planned to lay siege to Carsodonia, doing so with the knowledge that we had to be fluid in those plans— plans we would also need to include the draken in on when they returned from their flight.

"Have you heard from Eloana?" Poppy asked of my father. "Was she able to tell you anything about where she entombed Malec?"

Father cleared his throat. "Yes. Just before we arrived in Padonia. Eloana was able to give some detail," he said as Poppy leaned forward, the length of her braid slipping over one shoulder. "Malec's entombment is in the northeastern-most portion of the Blood Forest."

"That would be…" Poppy picked up the edge of her braid.

"Near Masadonia," Delano told her as I dragged my thumb over the curve of her hip. "A few days' ride from here, if that."

Poppy began twisting her braid. "Anything else?"

"You've been in there," Father said, gesturing with his chin to a narrow window. "You know that a lot of it looks alike. But she did say that there were ruins in that portion of the Blood Forest. The remains of whatever existed there long before the Blood Forest grew. He would be close to that."

"There could've been any number of small towns there at one time." Sven scratched at his beard. "But there was nothing there but fields during the War of Two Kings."

So, whatever had once existed there had been old. Possibly even as old as when the gods were awake.

"That helps, though." Poppy glanced over her shoulder at me and then Kieran, who nodded. "I can use the spell you told me about," she said to Sven. "I have something that belonged to him. A ring."

Sven gave her a warm smile. "Clever."

A pink, rather adorable flush stained her cheeks. I leaned in, pressing a quick kiss to the nape of her neck. "When we find him," she began, "I don't think we should attempt to wake him. Do any of you know if that will be possible?"

My father shook his head, looking at Sven. "Well…" the Lord began, and Perry filled a glass with whiskey, sliding it in his direction. "It really depends. Was he entombed in any sort of casket?"

"He was," Father confirmed. "A casket covered in deity bones."

"That should be fun to transport," Kieran remarked.

"So, I imagine if you don't open it, he should remain as he is when you find him," Sven said.

"He's unconscious," Poppy said, and Sven's stare turned curious. "That was how my father knew that something had happened to him. When Malec lost consciousness, it woke Ires."

"Interesting," Sven murmured, back to scratching his beard. "So, he's the Primal of Life and the Consort's son," Sven began, "and his entombment had to have some effect on the environment."

"Besides the Blood Forest?" I said, and Poppy straightened. Hell. I couldn't believe it'd just occurred to me. "That's why the Blood Forest is there. The trees grew because he was entombed there."

"Just as the trees grow for you," Kieran said, looking at Poppy.

"I thought you all knew that," Sven remarked, his brows lifted.

"Apparently, they didn't," his son said, and Delano grinned because we hadn't.

Poppy's head tilted as she studied my father. "Who exactly helped Eloana with a Primal spell? Do we know whose Primal essence she used?"

"Wasn't me," Sven remarked.

"I believe Wilhelmina helped her," Father said, and none of us had been expecting that. "What essence she used…I don't know."

"But do we know what becomes of Malec once we defeat the Blood Crown?" Hisa asked. "Do we put him back into the ground?"

All eyes, including Aylard's, turned to us. I didn't answer, having enough sense to know that it wasn't my place to do so. It was Poppy's.

"No," she said, squaring her shoulders. "We make sure he returns home with his brother, to Nyktos and the Consort."

40

Poppy

It was early evening by the time we finished discussing our plans to leave for the Blood Forest, and I was able to spend some time with Tawny. I entered the chambers, relieved to find two deep tubs side by side, both filled with steaming water.

While Casteel had lingered behind—hopefully to speak with his father—I inspected the chambers as I undressed. The exposed beams of the ceiling and the white-washed stone walls reminded me of the bedchambers in New Haven. However, these were far grander, outfitted with sitting and dining areas separated by a standing screen. The wardrobe doors were open, and I found the clothing Vonetta had brought hanging there. But it was the items that hung next to it that brought a smile to my face.

Clothing for Casteel.

They truly hadn't doubted that we'd return. Together.

A crate sat at the bottom of the wardrobe—the one that held King Jalara's crown. Another would join it soon. I still didn't know what I would do with them.

I drifted to the table by the bed and placed my hand on the cigar box, knowing what lay inside.

Our crowns.

Inhaling deeply, I left the box closed and went to the tub. A faint ache returned to my jaw as I bathed and washed away what felt like a week's worth of grime before drying off and finding a robe, slipping it on. A knock sounded on the door just as I finished tying the sash.

"Come in," I called out, passing the standing screen.

Kieran entered, closing the door behind him. "You're alone? I figured Tawny would be with you."

"I was with her, but she grew tired."

He glanced around. "I just wanted to check in and see how you were holding up."

My brow rose. "I'm fine. And you?"

"Perfect."

I stared at him.

Kieran stared back.

"Are you also here because Casteel is speaking with his father?" I asked.

He laughed roughly. "That obvious?"

"A little." I padded over to one of the chairs by an unlit fireplace. A decanter of some kind of amber liquid sat on a small table beside a couple of glasses. "Want something to drink?"

"Sure," he answered as I poured two drinks. "I figured if I lingered, Cas would use me as an excuse to not talk with his father."

My chest tightened as I handed Kieran a glass. "I hope he's speaking with his father and with Malik, but…"

"But he's got to have a lot in his head." Kieran leaned against the mantel as I sat in the chair. "And he may not be in the right headspace to hear whatever his father wants to say."

I took a sip of the smoky whiskey, thinking of what Valyn had told me. "I don't think he'll like what his father has to say."

"Neither do I." Kieran took a drink, staring out the narrow window as my gaze dropped to the thin scar on his forearm.

Curling my legs up, I sank into the cushy chair as I watched Kieran. Casteel would've definitely found his way to me sooner rather than later if he believed I was alone. But Kieran could've visited with his sister or any of the friends he hadn't seen in weeks. He could be spending time with Malik. But he probably also wasn't ready to sit down and talk with him. Either way, Kieran was here because of other reasons, and I had a good idea what they were. "Did Casteel tell you that we spoke about the Joining?"

Kieran glanced over at me. "He did." A moment passed. "He said that you wanted to do it."

Telling myself not to turn a hundred shades of red, I took another small drink. "He wants me to take the next couple of days to think it over, but I know the answer. It's not going to change."

His wintry eyes held mine. "You should take those days, though, and really think it over."

"I will, but it's not going to change. Casteel went over everything. I know what it entails—what could and couldn't happen." I knew what the Joining entailed. Casteel had gone over it in detail as we sat above the Wisteria Woods. No matter what it did or didn't become as we joined their essences to mine, it would be intimate. Intense. Life-altering. None of us would be the same afterward in any way. "Are you sure this is what you want? Truly?"

"It should be me asking that question, Poppy."

I lowered the glass to my bent knee as I watched him go to the chair across from me and sit. "We wouldn't be having this conversation if I wasn't sure."

"True." He leaned forward, glass in hand. "The same goes for me, Poppy. I'm here because I want to be." The hue of his blue eyes was vivid, the glow behind the pupils brighter. "I don't think many wolven would turn down Joining with a King and a Primal."

My cheeks warmed. I still couldn't believe that was what I was, but that didn't matter at the moment. "You're not just any wolven. It would be no one else but you."

Kieran dipped his chin as a sweet taste gathered in my mouth, at odds with the bite of whiskey. "Don't make me feel emotional about this. If you do, you're going to make this weird."

I laughed. "Well, it's about time I'm the one who gets to make something weird."

He shook his head as he clasped the back of his neck with his free hand. Several long moments passed. "You know I love Cas, right?"

"I do," I whispered. "And I know he loves you."

"I would do anything for him. I would do anything for you," he said, echoing what Casteel had said. He looked up at me. "And knowing that you would do this for me means..." He swallowed. "There really aren't words other than that my reasons for agreeing to the Joining have very little to do with Cas being a King or you a Primal god and everything to do with the love I have for both of you."

My breath caught as a knot of emotion lodged itself in my chest. "Now you're making this all emotional."

"Sorry."

"No, you're not."

Kieran grinned, lowering his hand as I fought the urge to ask him what kind of love he felt for Casteel. For me. I knew it wasn't a familial one and that it went beyond what one felt for friends. I also thought that it wasn't the same as what he'd felt for Elashya or what Casteel and I felt for each other. But I also knew that what I felt for Kieran wasn't the same as what I felt for Delano or Vonetta or Tawny. It was...*more.*

He sat back, eyeing me as he rested his ankle on his knee. "You have that look."

"What look?"

"The one that says you have a question you're trying not to ask."

"No, I don't."

Kieran arched a brow.

I sighed, thinking it was rather annoying that he knew me so well. Needing courage to ask what I wanted to know, I took a longer drink. It did very little to aid me. "What...what kind of love do you feel?"

He studied me until I almost started squirming in the chair. "There are many kinds of love, but when it comes to you, it's the kind that allowed me to make that—" He inhaled sharply, his jaw hardening. "It's the kind of love that allowed me to make *that* promise to you, Poppy. It's the same kind of love that allowed you to ask that of me."

Casteel

The bedchamber was dimly lit when I entered. Kieran's scent lingered by the fireplace, where two empty glasses sat on a small table. Stripping off the weapons and straps that held them in place, I left all but one dagger on the chest by the standing screen.

My heart gave an unsteady leap when I looked at the bed and saw Poppy there, curled on her side, the blanket pooled at her waist and her robe loosened, baring one creamy shoulder. As I stripped off my clothing and made quick use of the cooled bathwater, I didn't think my heart would ever stop giving little jumps whenever I looked upon her. Didn't think I would ever get used to looking at her and knowing that I was hers and she was mine.

I made sure I was completely dry before stepping toward the bed. I didn't want to wake her—well, that was a lie. I wanted to see those beautiful eyes. Have her gift me with one of her smiles. Hear her voice. Her laugh. So, yeah, I wanted her awake, but the morning would come soon enough. We all needed our rest, for the journey into the Blood Forest wouldn't be an easy one. Carefully pulling back the blanket, I eased into bed and kept my godsdamn hands and arms to myself. If I touched her, then yeah, I would spend the night staring at the ceiling with a hard cock.

Forcing my eyes closed and my breathing to steady, by some kind of miracle, I fell asleep. I didn't know how long I rested before I found myself in that musty and dark cell, scratching Craven claws and the rattling of chains the only sounds. The band at my throat was almost too tight to swallow or breathe deeply, and the pain in my hand and in—

I woke with a jolt, my eyes flying open to see shadows swaying across the exposed beams of the ceiling. *I'm not there.* My heart thumped. *I'm here.* Air wheezed in and out of my lungs as I repeated those words like a fucking prayer.

The bed shifted slightly as I dragged my hands down my face, feeling the roughness of calluses—of what was absent there.

Poppy rolled toward me, pressing the length of her half-clothed body against mine. "I missed you," she murmured.

Fuck.

My heart.

Her voice.

It calmed me.

Lowering my hands, I curled an arm around her back, soaking in her warmth and softness. "I missed you."

She wiggled in closer, sliding a leg between mine. "Did you talk with your father?"

"Long enough to tell him that whatever he felt he needed to say, it had to wait." I tangled my fingers in her hair. "He wasn't happy to hear that, but he backed off."

"So, you didn't really talk to him at all."

"I don't want whatever he has to say in my head right now," I admitted. Nothing he could say at the moment would make me understand why he and my mother had kept the Blood Queen's identity from us. "Not when there's everything else—finding Malec. Meeting with Isbeth. Ending the war."

Her hand slid over my chest. "I can understand that." She yawned softly. "It's why I didn't ask Malik any more questions about that night in Lockswood or about Coralena and Leo."

I glanced down at the top of her head. She wasn't ready for whatever Malik had to share. Just as I wasn't when it came to my brother and our father. "You should go back to sleep."

"I will." But that hand of hers drifted down my stomach.

"That doesn't feel like you're going back to sleep."

Poppy didn't say anything for a few moments. "Are you okay?"

Had my nightmare reached her? Or had she woken and simply sensed the lingering mess of emotions? Closing my eyes, I took a deep breath. When I didn't answer, when I couldn't, she turned her head, pressing a kiss to my chest.

"You will be," she whispered.

"Yeah, I will be."

"I know." Her hand slid under the blanket.

My entire body jerked as her fingers grazed the tip of my already hardening cock and she rose halfway.

She didn't give me a chance to say another word. Not that I was complaining. Her lips found mine, and her kiss was a sweet sweep. My arm around her tightened as she parted my lips with her tongue. The kiss went on until I throbbed for her.

Gods, I *always* ached for her.

"Cas," she whispered, closing her fingers around my dick. "I need you."

I shuddered at her words—at the truth. It was I who needed her, and she knew that—knew that her touch, her closeness, was grounding. A reminder that I was *here*.

"Now," she demanded.

Her bold order brought forth a chuckle as I cupped her cheek. "What is it you want?"

"You know," she whispered against my lips.

"Maybe." I slid my hand down her throat, past those sensitive, healing bite marks, and over her breast where her nipple pebbled beneath the cotton of the robe. I kept going, over the soft swell of her belly and then between her legs. "But you should tell me." I brushed the backs of my fingers over her damp heat, smiling when she moaned.

"Just in case."

Her grip on my dick tightened. "I want you to touch me." She rested her forehead against mine. "Please."

"You never have to say please." I drew my finger along the very center of her. "But it does sound so pretty on your lips."

Poppy's breath caught as I slipped a finger inside her. She nipped at my chin, causing my entire body to jerk once more. I thrust my finger deeper. "Like this?"

"Yes."

I kissed her, easing my finger in and out. "And like this?" My voice was rough, heavy.

Her back arched as her hand began moving in time with my shallow thrusts. Her hips began to move. "Mm-hmm."

Smoothing my thumb over her clit, I marveled at the way her entire body tensed—how her hand stopped moving. I grinned. "And what about that?"

She moaned, and it was a sound I could listen to for an eternity. "I really like that," she said, but her hand left my cock and folded around my wrist, pulling my touch from her. "But I want more."

Poppy moved then, letting go of my hand and easing onto her elbows. The robe, half-untied, slipped down her arms. Never in my life had I been more grateful for the enhanced eyesight she was so envious of.

Rosy breasts thrust up, their tips puckered. Her cheeks were flushed, legs spread wide, open and inviting. My godsdamn mouth watered at the sight of her. I rose halfway. "You're beautiful." I took in every inch of exposed flesh. "You know what I don't understand?"

"What?"

"How you don't spend all day with those pretty fingers between those pretty thighs." I slid a hand under the robe, gripping her hip. "That's what I would do if I were you."

She laughed. "You'd get very little else done then."

"It would be worth it." My gaze landed on where her hand rested on her lower belly, mere inches from that wonderful heat of hers. "I just realized something." My throat dried. "Have you ever touched yourself?"

A blush swept across her cheeks, and after a moment, she nodded. And damn if that didn't send an almost painful bolt of lust through me. "I would love nothing more"—picking up her hand, I lifted it to my mouth. I closed my lips around the finger bearing our ring—"than for you to show me exactly how you touch yourself."

Her inhale was an audible one as I lowered her hand to the shadowy space between her thighs. I let go, and for a moment, I didn't think she would do it.

But I never should've doubted her.

My Queen backed down from nothing.

The delicate tendons along the top of her hand moved like piano keys as she slipped that finger inside herself, moving it in tiny plunges.

"Fuck," I groaned. "Don't stop."

Her breaths came in short little pants as she continued playing with herself, and the scent of her arousal filled every single one of my senses. I was obsessed, watching her. Didn't even blink. Not once as her breathing continued picking up speed, as her hips moved to meet the thrusts of her finger.

"Cas," she moaned.

I could come just watching this. There was a good chance I would. "I want to worship you."

Poppy shuddered.

And then I did, starting with her toes and working my way up her calves to her thighs. Her finger moved faster as I neared, and I stopped long enough to flick my tongue through the wetness there. She cried out, her back arching as I began paying homage to her once more, trailing a path across her stomach and the curves of her hips. I took my time as if we wouldn't be on the road once more in a few hours. I paid extra attention to those breasts, licking and sucking until she trembled—until every part of me was hard, heavy, and swollen. Only then did I reach between us, pulling her hand away to my mouth, where I sipped at her taste.

"I think I will need to see you do that daily."

"Gods," she rasped. "You are so bad."

"Yeah, I am." Closing my hand around hers, I pressed it into the mattress beside her head as I eased a leg between those soft, plump thighs. I gave her my weight, sinking into all that warm softness, and she took it all with a soft smile. "But I can be good. I can even be more bad. I can be whatever you want."

"I just want you." She pressed her palm to my cheek. "As you are."

Hell.

I shook like a fragile sapling in a windstorm at the touch of her heat against the head of my dick. I sank into her slick heat, lashed by shards of pleasure. "I love you. I'm so very much in love with you."

Her arms wrapped around me, holding me tightly as she lifted her legs, curling them around my hips and urging me forward. "I love you always and forever."

I ignored the throbbing in my fangs. I wouldn't feed. I wouldn't take anything from her tonight. I would just give.

My heart hammered as I began moving, intending to go slow and steady, to make this last. But the soft sounds she made, the startling friction of our bodies, and all that came before this made it impossible. Nothing felt like her. Absolutely nothing compared to how she made me feel and how her very presence invaded every cell of my body. There was no me. There was no her. There was only us, our mouths clinging to each other's, our hands and hips sealing together. We were so close, so tight as I ground against her, that I felt it when Poppy broke. The spasms obliterated my control. My release blew through me, coming and coming in tight waves that left my body jerking for several moments.

Poppy's mouth sought mine, and she kissed me softly. She was, gods, she was everything. I loathed separating us, but I knew I was seconds away from collapsing on her. Letting out a ragged groan, I eased out of her and onto my side. Gathering her in my arms, I held her close, and she held me tighter. When my eyes closed this time, I knew that no bad dreams would find me.

My Queen simply would not allow it.

41

Poppy

The Craven stumbled through the thick mist, its coal-red eyes mindless with hunger, and its sallow, patchy, gray skin clung to its skull for dear life.

"That..." Casteel twisted sharply, his movements as graceful as any dancer's at the balls once held in Masadonia. His bloodstone sword sliced through the air with a hiss, cutting through a Craven's neck. "Is an old one."

Old was an understatement.

I had no idea when this Craven had been turned. Its skin was as bad as its clothing. Its mouth dropped open, baring jagged sets of fangs. Howling, the Craven raced toward me. I firmed my grip on my wolven-bone dagger—

A sleek, russet-hued wolven exploded from the mist, landing on the Craven's back and taking it down.

"Oh, come on," I grumbled. "I had that one."

A cedar and vanilla imprint reached me through the *notam*. Vonetta's laugh drifted through my thoughts.

My eyes narrowed on her. *You're not even supposed to be here, Regent.*

Her laugh got louder, stronger as she tore into the Craven's chest with her claws, going straight for its heart.

My lips curled. "That's gross."

"There's definitely more for you to stab." Emil caught a Craven, shoving it back into the damp, grayish bark of a blood tree. "Because they're like...everywhere. Take your pick."

I spun as a shriek blasted the air. I made out the shapes of at least a dozen more Craven in the mist.

Three days in the northeastern region of the Blood Forest, and this was the first time we'd come across a horde this size. We'd seen a few Craven here and there—at most, half a dozen. But today—or was it tonight? It was hard to tell this deep in the forest, where the sun couldn't penetrate, and snow flurries were a constant companion—it was like we had come upon a nest of them.

I jumped to the side as Naill struck down one that seemed to rise from the ground. "I can't be the only one who thinks this many Craven is odd," I said, bracing myself as the ones in the mist flowed forward, their low-pitched whines rapidly increasing in sound—and annoyance.

"You're not," Casteel agreed, unsheathing his second bloodstone short sword as he joined me.

Kieran, in his mortal form, threw a dagger, impaling a Craven to a nearby tree as we, along with Naill and Perry and half a dozen wolven, formed a circle. "Maybe we're getting close to the ruins or even where Malec is entombed."

That was what I had been thinking as I kicked out, knocking a Craven back into Delano's path. He shoved his blade through the Craven's chest as I turned, jabbing my dagger into another's heart. I hadn't wanted to use the locater spell until we reached the ruins, so I hoped this meant that we were nearing that location.

Stepping forward, I narrowly avoided Sage and another wolven as they loped past me, corralling the Craven into a tighter circle. I caught one who was more skeleton than flesh, holding my breath as I thrust the dagger into its chest.

"You know, I could help," Malik drawled from the center of our circle, where he leaned against a wagon, holding our horses' reins. We hadn't given him much choice when it came to accompanying us into the Blood Forest. While I trusted that he would not return to Carsodonia, that trust only went so far. He needed to remain with us.

Casteel darted, spinning as he lashed out with both shortswords, slicing through two Craven's necks. Flashing golden eyes met mine. "Did you hear something?"

"Nope." I followed, catching one of the shortswords that Casteel tossed in my direction.

Sage forced another group of Craven forward. I spun, cutting through the neck of one and jabbing my dagger through the other's chest. Kieran brushed past me, striking down another.

"I would just need a weapon," Malik continued as I whirled, catching sight of Perry cleaving a Craven in half with a bloodstone axe—an actual *axe*—as I leapt over a cluster of rocks. "Any weapon. I'd even take a sharpened stick at this point."

"Funny how I keep hearing something." Casteel leapt over Rune, a large black and brown wolven who'd joined us. The wolven snagged one of the Craven as Casteel landed, thrusting his sword forward. "And the nagging-as-hell voice keeps repeating the same thing."

"*Can I have a sword?*" Kieran tossed a limp Craven aside. "*Can I have a dagger? A stick—?*"

"Real fucking mature," Malik snarled.

"You're not getting a weapon." Casteel kicked off a moss-covered boulder, catching a Craven in the back as I shot forward, bringing the sword down on another's neck—a small one. Too small. "You're not getting a weapon. Not even a blunt object such as a rock."

I *felt* Malik's eyes roll. "Thought you believed me when I said I wanted to fight the Blood Crown?"

I arched a brow at Casteel as Vonetta dragged a Craven forward by its ankle.

"Believing you want to destroy the Blood Crown is one thing," Casteel said as I dispatched the Craven Vonetta had by the ankle.

"How am I supposed to help you fight the Blood Crown with no weapon?" Malik demanded.

"Use your charming personality?" Naill quipped.

The edges of my heavy cloak spun as I turned, dipping low as Casteel's sword hissed above my head. "We'll cross that bridge when we get to it," Casteel said, grabbing my arm as I rose. He pulled me in for a quick kiss. My stomach dipped in a most pleasant way as he then twisted, thrusting his sword through a Craven's chest. Letting go, he looked over his shoulder to where his brother stood. "So, until then, let's try shutting the fuck up."

Kieran shot me a grin as I knocked back a strand of hair that had fallen into my face. "Doubt that's going to happen," he said.

"Nope." I jumped forward as a Craven grabbed hold of Sage's tail, jabbing the wolven dagger into the base of the poor soul's skull, severing its spinal column.

"What in the actual hell?" Emil started, glancing down at his hand.

"Are these blood trees leaking? What is this?"

"I'll give you one guess." Perry shoved Malik back as a Craven broke rank, charging them. "It's in the name."

"Fucking disgusting," Emil muttered, wiping the rust-colored substance from his palm on his thigh.

I wasn't sure if the trees were really oozing blood, but it definitely wasn't normal sap, and I decided I wouldn't dwell on that.

"Heads up," Naill yelled. "To our right."

Casteel and I turned at the same time. Through the thick mist, I saw several more shadowy forms. "There has to be dozens more," Casteel said as the wolven growled low in their throats.

Blowing out an aggravated breath, I looked at Casteel. "I know we're talking about me holding off on using the eather, but this is getting really—"

The leaves above us rattled as a fierce wind whipped through the small clearing, scattering the mist and kicking up the scent of rot and decay. I tipped my head back as Kieran snapped forward, grabbing the front of a Craven's tunic and slamming his blade into its chest. An even darker shadow fell over us, blotting out what little light made it through the trees.

"About damn time," Kieran muttered, dipping to tap his sister's back, who was a second away from rushing the new group of Craven.

Reaching out through the *notam*, I called the wolven back. Several howls responded as they leapt out of the mist, rushing past us into the circle. Casteel wrapped an arm around my waist, hauling me clear off my feet and against his chest.

"Careful," he murmured in my ear.

Several branches sheared off and fell like arrows around as Reaver descended among the blood trees, his wings spread out wide before snapping back.

Kieran stumbled to the side. "Fucking *gods*, every time." Wintry-blue eyes flashed. "Tell me he doesn't do that on purpose."

Since telling him that would be a lie, I said nothing as Reaver extended his long neck and roared. Silvery fire streamed forward, momentarily blinding as the flames cut through the mist and rolled over the Craven. The fire took them out at once, dozens gone in a matter of seconds, leaving nothing but ash and fading mist behind.

"Nice of him to finally join us," Emil remarked, earning a smirk from Kieran and a narrow-eyed glare from Reaver as his horned head snapped in Emil's direction. The Atlantian held up his hands. "I meant

I'm happy to see you."

"You think he found anything?" Casteel asked as he brushed a wayward strand of hair back from his face.

"I hope so," I said, sheathing the dagger as Casteel took his sword back. Reaver had taken to the air the day before, scouting for any sign of the ruins Eloana had sent word of. "We're already at three days. That means at least three more to get out of here. Another day to reach Padonia."

"We'll be fine," Casteel assured me, hooking the two clasps that had come undone on my cloak. "We'll get out of here and to the Bone Temple in time."

I nodded, but it would take close to three days to reach the Bone Temple. I nibbled on my lower lip as a flare of dull pain shot through my jaw. We needed to find Malec and get back to Padonia with some time to rest. To prepare.

"Don't worry." Kieran stepped in close to us, his gaze catching mine as he picked up my braid, tossing it over my shoulder. "I know that's easier said than done," he continued as a shimmery light swept across Reaver's body. "But we're good. We got this."

Casteel pressed a kiss to my temple as he looked to where a mortal stood where the draken had crouched seconds ago. "Naked Reaver time," he murmured.

Everyone was pretty much used to that. While most of us studiously avoided looking below the face, Sage practically sat front row and made no qualms about sizing him up, no matter what form she was in.

"About a day's ride north," Reaver announced as Naill tossed him his clothing. "There are some ruins of what appeared to be a small town."

It took a little less than a day for us to reach the ruins. How Reaver had seen them from the sky was beyond me. Nothing but stone foundations and crumbling, half-standing walls were left.

"This has to be it, right?" Vonetta asked as Casteel gripped my waist, helping me down from Setti. His act was sweet, considering I no longer needed the assistance.

"It has to be." I turned to Reaver. "You saw nothing else?"

"I traveled to the shores," he answered, hopping up onto a wall and crouching. "There was nothing but this. The ruins are large. The forest thickens from here, but this was no small village."

"Thickens more than this?" Emil gestured at the tightly clustered trees.

Reaver nodded as a flurry of snow swirled across the decaying structures.

Kieran unhooked the satchel, bringing it over to me as Delano, now in his wolven form, and the others spread out through the ruins, keeping watch. "You think this is a good spot?"

"Honest?" I placed the satchel on a wall, opening it. "I hope so."

He chuckled as Perry came closer, and Malik slowly dismounted— under Naill's constant watch. "I wonder what used to be here."

"No idea." Casteel's brows furrowed as he scanned the ruins. "It could have fallen while he slept and became lost to time."

A shiver danced over my skin as I pulled out the parchment and a slender piece of charcoal. To think that a town full of people—possibly hundreds if not more—could have been wiped completely from history was unsettling.

Casteel picked up a small rock, placing it on the parchment to hold it in place. "Thanks," I murmured, writing Malec's name when something occurred to me. "What was Malec's last name?"

"O'Meer," Casteel answered.

I eyed Reaver. "That can't be his real last name, is it?"

Reaver slowly turned his head toward me. A long moment passed. "No, it is not."

"Does he even have a last name?"

"Nyktos did not, but…" The wind lifted the pale strands of his hair. "If he were to be recognized by a surname, it would be Mierel."

"Mierel," I repeated, the press of charcoal against parchment leaving a smudge. "Is that the Consort's last name?"

A pause. "It once was."

Casteel's gaze met mine, and then I wrote it out. Malec Mierel. The eather hummed in my chest.

"What next?" Casteel asked, his chest brushing my arm.

I reached into the pouch at my hip, bypassing the toy horse I really needed to return to Casteel. I pulled out the diamond ring, placing it on the name. "I just need my blood now."

"That reminds me," Casteel murmured, unsheathing his dagger. "I owe you a very large diamond."

I grinned as I reached for the dagger. "You do."

Casteel held the dagger. "I don't want to watch you cut yourself."

"You'd rather be the one to draw blood, then?" I asked.

"Not in this fashion." He gave me a heated look that caused my face to warm. "But I would rather do it than watch you inflict pain upon yourself."

"That is strangely sweet."

"Key emphasis on *strange*," Kieran said as he leaned back, crossing his arms. Vonetta and Emil crept closer.

"Ready?" Casteel asked. When I held up my hand and nodded, he bent his head and kissed me. He nipped my lip as the quick prick of pain traveled across my finger. "There you go."

Feeling myself flush even hotter, I held my finger over the ring and parchment, squeezing until blood beaded and dropped, splashing first the ring and then staining the paper.

"I really hope there's more to it than that," Vonetta murmured.

"There always is," Emil told her.

"You remember what my father told you?" Perry asked.

Nodding, I cleared my throat. "I call upon the essence of the goddess Bele—the great huntress and finder of all things needed. I ask that you guide me to what I seek to find, connected by blood, name, and belonging."

No one spoke. I didn't think anyone even dared to breathe too deeply as my blood seeped into Malec's name. And just when I thought I might've misspoken a word or something, the parchment where my blood had soaked through *ignited*.

Vonetta gasped, stepping back into Emil as a lone flame shot into the air, nearly as tall as the trees, and that flame was cold. *Icy*. The essence in my blood stirred as the flame rippled violently and then shrank to where the parchment was scorched and charred, beginning to burn away until nothing but the ring Malec had given Isbeth was left on the stone wall.

Casteel's hand fell to the center of my back as Kieran unfolded his arms. A gust of wind came from above and behind us, catching the ashes and lifting them into the air. Panic exploded for a moment, but the ashes joined with the flurries, and thousands of tiny specks brightened until they shimmered like fireflies.

"Whoa," Naill murmured as the glittering funnel of ash whirled and spun forward, forming a churning cyclone that shot between him and Malik and cut through the trees.

"It's going too fast." Kieran jerked back from the wall as Reaver hopped down. Shimmery, silvery light zigzagged through the trees, stretching. "That's way too fast."

All of us started forward, the wolven leaping over the ruins to chase the glittering lights—

The sparkling ash dropped suddenly, falling to the ground like luminous snow. The wolven drew up short as the light remained, forming a sparkling path through the Blood Forest. My lips slowly parted.

"It's kind of beautiful," Vonetta whispered. Emil's gaze slid to her as he shook his head.

"Well," Malik drawled, stepping forward. "I think it worked, in case anyone was wondering."

Casteel grinned, but the curve of his lips froze as he caught himself. His expression smoothed out, and his jaw hardened again.

Gods, that made me sad.

I reached over, touching his arm. Casteel smiled for me, but it didn't reach his eyes. "We should follow and do it quickly," he said. "We have no idea how long this will last."

Picking up the ring, I placed it in the pouch as Casteel went to Setti.

"Time," Kieran said quietly to me. "Give him time. Both of them."

"I know." And I did, but as we started following the glittering, weaving trail, an odd unease settled in the cold, hollow part of me. A sense of dread I couldn't place rose, but it felt like a warning. A reminder.

That there wasn't always time.

The winding path blanketed the area, shimmering over the ground as it wove in and out of the trees. Casteel rode Setti while I walked with Delano close to my right, feeling too antsy to sit. I wasn't the only one. Reaver walked ahead, and the wolven were even farther out. Kieran rode beside Casteel, but somehow, Malik ended up walking beside me.

Which was probably why Delano was so close he occasionally brushed against my legs.

"I'm beginning to think this trail will lead us straight to the Stroud Sea," he remarked, his words leaving misty clouds behind.

"I'm beginning to think the same thing." We'd been walking for at least an hour, the sparkling trail disappearing behind Emil and Vonetta, who rode at the back.

Several moments of silence passed between us, and I knew without looking that Malik kept glancing at me. I also knew without checking that the quick looks were really starting to anger Casteel.

We'd made our way around several low-hanging branches when Malik asked, "Why haven't you asked me about that night?"

Acid gathered in my throat, and I had no idea if that was coming from Casteel, Kieran, or both.

"You must have questions," Malik continued quietly, staring straight ahead. "You likely have things you want to say."

I laughed, but the sound was dry. "I have a lot of things I want to say, but none of them will change the past." And what answers he could have for whatever questions I may ask probably wouldn't do much for my state of mental well-being or Casteel's. There was one thing, though. I swallowed. "How did Coralena die?"

"You sure you want to know that?" Malik exhaled heavily as he held a limb back. "She was forced to drink the blood of a draken."

Horror and grief collided as Reaver stiffened ahead, and I immediately regretted asking the question.

"It was quick," Malik added quietly as Delano crowded me, his head brushing my gloved fingers. "I do not say that to lessen what was done. It's the truth. Cora was—Isbeth favored her. It was one of the few times she didn't drag out punishment or death."

Pressing my lips together, I shook my head. I didn't know what to say to that. I didn't know how to feel about it.

"Cas, he…" Malik looked over his shoulder and then focused on me as flurries drifted from the sky. "He mentioned some kind of rhyme you said you heard that night. That wasn't me."

My gaze shot to him, my throat drying. Somehow, in the aftermath of everything, I'd forgotten. "I know," I whispered, my skin chilling even further as the essence pulsed in my chest. "That came after. It wasn't your voice. It was like…"

It was like the voice I heard in Stonehill, urging me to unleash my fury. To bring death. That hadn't been Isbeth.

"Poppy?" Concern radiated from Casteel.

I'd stopped walking. Delano pressed against my legs as my heart thumped—

An imprint brushed against my thoughts, one that reminded me of fresh rain. *Sage?*

We found the end of the trail, her response came. *There's definitely something here. It has a bad feel to it.*

My brows rose, and I looked up as Casteel drew Setti to my side. "The wolven found the end of the trail. Sage says where they're at has a bad feel to it."

Casteel's features were hard as he nodded. It only took a handful of minutes for us to join the wolven, where they paced restlessly through broken pillars, in front of a wall of rock that traveled as high as a Rise and was covered in blood trees, nearly stacked one on top of the other. Their unease was a tangible entity, coating my skin.

The trail ended right at the edge of the trees before a rocky hill that was more of a mountain than anything else. I looked down, seeing that the trail was already beginning to fade.

"What the hell?" Casteel murmured as he swung off his horse. "It's a damn mountain of rock and blood trees."

"I didn't see this from the sky at all," Reaver said, looking up. "This has to be where the forest was the thickest."

Casteel strode past me, entering the crowded rows of trees. "There's an entrance in there—in the rock."

Delano followed as I went to Casteel and peered around him, into…vast nothingness. "Can you see anything?"

"A little. Looks like a tunnel," he answered, squinting. "Kieran or Vonetta? What do you see?"

Kieran was the first to join us, leaning around me to look inside. "Definitely a tunnel. A natural one, kind of like what's in the mountains back home. Wide enough for a group to walk through single file."

I took a deep breath. "We are really going to have to walk in there, aren't we?"

Sage nudged my hand, her words reaching my thoughts. *We go first.*

"No," I said out loud in case anyone else got the same idea. "We have no idea what's down there."

That's why we go first. Delano's springy imprint reached me.

"Poppy," Casteel began.

"I don't want them going into the gods only know what."

He stepped in close. "Neither do I."

"But we have way better senses than any of the Atlantians here. Or even you," Vonetta said.

Kieran nodded. "She's right. We will know if something's down there that we need to be careful of before anyone else will."

"You can all argue all you want," Malik said. "But it's pointless. Because something is coming."

All our heads snapped toward the rock. I saw nothing but darkness—

A sudden gust of wind hit the trees, rattling the branches. The air smelled strange and emitted a low howl, raising the hairs all over my body.

"I really would like a weapon," Malik announced.

Reaver's head lifted. The leafy branches stilled above and all around, but that sound…it still came. A moan from inside the tunnel reached us from the darkness.

"What in the gods' name is that?" Kieran asked, bloodstone sword in hand. "Craven?"

In the darkness, thicker, more solid shadows took form. Shapes that drifted forward.

Definitely not Craven.

They glided out from the trees, draped in black. Their very thin layer of skin had the ghastly, waxy pallor of death. Although these *things* had some semblance of a face—dark eyes, two holes for a nose, and a mouth—it was all kinds of wrong, stretched so far into the cheeks it was as if a permanent smile had been carved into their faces and then *stitched* closed. The entire mouth. But they were more skeleton than flesh.

"Aw, hell," Casteel muttered.

I knew what they were. So did he.

Gyrms.

42

"Great," Emil muttered as Vonetta groaned. "These fuckers again."

But their stitched mouths…

I would definitely have nightmares about this later.

"Don't," Reaver warned Rune, who prowled toward the mouth of the tunnel. "Don't bite them. What's in them is not blood. It's poison."

Casteel's gaze cut to the draken. "They've attacked Gyrms before."

"Not this kind." Reaver lifted his sword. "These are Sentries. They're like Hunters. Neither type you would've encountered before."

The corners of Casteel's lips turned down. "I'm going to have to take your word for it."

"You'd better," Reaver replied. "Or the junk that's in them will eat the insides out of the wolven."

My eyes widened. "Don't engage with them," I ordered the wolven. "Guard Malik."

None of them looked happy about that, especially Delano, but they backed off, circling an even-less-thrilled Atlantian Prince.

"Maybe you should use your fire then," Kieran suggested. "Especially since you're all about burning shit."

"The fire will not work on them," Reaver said. "They are already dead."

"*What?*" Casteel mouthed, and I had so many questions—all that would have to wait. Eather pulsed in my chest as I gripped the wolven dagger. These looked like a creepy combination of the ones the Unseen had conjured in Saion's Cove and what had been guarding Iliseeum. I shuddered. The Primal essence had worked on the Gyrms and the skeletons before, but did that mean it would work on this type?

"We do this the old-fashioned way." Casteel shifted his sword to his other hand.

The Gyrms had exited the tunnel and stopped moving, their arms at their sides. All of them. Well over a dozen.

"Do you think they have hands?" Casteel asked.

My gaze flicked down. The sleeves of the robes were too long to tell. "I can't believe that's what you're looking at."

Kieran glanced at me. "What are *you* looking at?"

"Did you see their mouths?"

"Of course," Casteel murmured.

"I can't stop staring at them."

Kieran sent me a sharp look. "Really?"

"Their mouths are stitched closed. It's creepy, but I guess it's a good thing," I said.

Casteel looked over at me. "And why do you think that's a good thing?"

"Because that means there can't be—" I quieted as one of the Gyrms cocked its head to the side. A low, breathy moan came from its sealed mouth.

"That's…well, disturbing," Emil noted.

Vonetta shook her head as she palmed her blades. "You are the king—"

"Of good looks and charm?" he suggested.

"Of understatements."

My grin froze as the Gyrms moved in unison—and they were fast. Long, slender blades descended from both sleeves—blades that glinted like polished onyx in the slivers of sunlight. "Shadowstone," I muttered as Naill inched around a blood tree.

One of the Gyrms' heads snapped in his direction. Its hairless head tilted. The creature moved, its robe billowing out from behind it like a stream of shadow. Perry spun, his blade meeting the Gyrm's, a clash of crimson and night.

The remaining Gyrms streamed forward, moving in a precise vee. I shot forward as Casteel's sword arced through the air, cleaving the creature's head from its shoulders as the Gyrm grabbed for me.

"All right, these aren't like the skeletons in Iliseeum," Casteel announced. "Head or heart seems to do the trick."

"Thank the gods." Emil spun, slicing off a Gyrm's head.

I moved under another's outstretched arm. In the back of my mind, I noticed that the Gyrm hadn't swung on me, which was notably odd. I popped up behind the creature as it turned, slamming the dagger into its chest. The Gyrm shuddered and then *collapsed* into itself, reminding me of what happened to Ascended when struck down by bloodstone. But this creature didn't crack. Instead, it shriveled as if all moisture had been drained from its body in one breath and then shattered into nothing. All of it, including the shadowstone sword, leaving only the smell of lilacs behind—stale lilacs.

A hand clamped down on my shoulder, bony fingers pressing through my cloak, jerking me back. I twisted at the waist, bringing my arm down on the Gyrm's with a hard enough blow to knock the grip loose. Casteel leapt through the air, slamming into the Gyrm, spinning it around. I whirled, thrusting the dagger into its chest as Casteel shot me a wild grin before turning to meet another.

Delano's thoughts brushed against mine in a wave of springy-fresh air as I stepped back. *These Gyrms aren't attacking you.*

I followed his imprint back to him as one of the Gyrms swung its sword on Perry. *I noticed.*

Maybe they recognize you.

Maybe they did, but that wasn't stopping them from attacking the others...or coming at me. Two Gyrms started toward me, blades at their sides. The eather vibrated, pressing against my skin. I opened my senses, but like with the other Gyrms, I felt nothing but emptiness—cold hollowness.

Kieran shoved a Gyrm back against a tree. "More are coming." He thrust his blade through a creature's chest with a snarl. "About another dozen."

"Of course." I stalked forward.

"At least, they're not coming out of the ground this time," Vonetta pointed out as she thrust her blade through a chest.

"There is that," Naill agreed, swinging his sword through the air.

A Gyrm to the left made a move as if he sought to get behind me. "I don't think so."

Turning sharply, I kicked the creature in the chest. It stumbled back. I twisted, swinging the wolven dagger down on another Gyrm's forearm. The bloodstone, ever so sharp, sliced through the papery-thin skin and hollow bone, severing the arm. The pale fingers spasmed open, releasing the shadowstone sword it clutched. Catching it by the handle, I swung the sword high and wide, cutting through the other

Gyrm's neck, meeting utterly no resistance. The shadowstone sword collapsed in my hand, disappearing as Casteel struck down the one it belonged to.

I pouted. "I kind of liked that sword."

Kieran shot me a look as he pushed another Gyrm back. "Too bad."

"You're no fun." I firmed my grip on the dagger. "You know that, right? No fun—"

"Holy shit," Emil exclaimed, stumbling back. "Their mouths. Holy shit. Their mouths."

"Is he just now realizing they're stitched closed?" Casteel shoved his sword through the back and into the heart of a Gyrm.

"Told you it was disturbing." I knocked a Gyrm's hand aside. "Touching without permission is not okay."

The Gyrm's head tilted, and then it smiled. Or tried to. The stitches stretched and then popped, tearing free. The mouth dropped open as something black and shiny wiggled out—

"Why does it have to be snakes?" I jumped back, stomach churning with horror as the serpent slithered forward, quickly blending in with the dark ground. "Snakes. I hate snakes."

"I warned you all." Emil slammed his sword into the ground and the sound the serpent made when he struck it was not right. It was so wrong. It was an ear-piercing shriek.

"What the fuck?" Malik hopped onto a low wall.

"You did not give details!" Vonetta shouted, dancing back as Sage pawed at the ground, sending a snake flying through the air. "Once again, you failed to give details!"

"All you said was 'their mouths.'" I gasped, scanning the ground, having lost sight of the little wiggling bastard. "Why? Why are there snakes?"

"Most Gyrms have them inside," Reaver said, slamming his sword into a serpent.

I couldn't even process that utter...*fuckery*. A Gyrm prowled forward, another disgusting creature spilling from its mouth. I backed into a boulder. Scrambling off the ground, I rose to my knees on the rock. "Nope. Nope. Nope. Will eather work on these things?" I asked Reaver.

"From you?" His lip curled in disgust as he stabbed a serpent. "Yes, only because you're a Primal about to finish the Culling."

Casteel spun toward me as a grin tugged at his lips. "Are you hiding on a boulder?"

"Yep."

"You're adorable."

"Shut up." The eather pulsed violently in my chest as Casteel chuckled. I let the energy come to the surface. A silvery glow washed across the ground—oh, gods, there was more than one serpent. Three. Seven—

Kieran snapped forward, slamming his boot down on one. The sound. The stain. Bile clogged my throat.

Six. I saw six snakes. There were probably more, and I was *so* not going to sleep for the next ten years. The Primal essence answered my will as it spread out from me as a network of shimmering, silvery-white light laced with churning shadows. It washed over the ground, sparking when it hit a snake and then igniting. The ropey nightmares screamed, blistering my ears as they went up in smoke.

The remaining Gyrms spun toward me. Like with those skeleton soldiers in Iliseeum, the essence drew them like a Craven to spilled blood. Stitches tore, mouths opened, and serpents spilled onto the ground, racing toward the boulder.

"Maybe it's time for you to go all Primal on these creeps," Malik called from his wall.

My skin and hands tingled, warming as the corners of my vision turned silvery-white. Power rushed through my veins. Essence erupted from my hands in silver flames from where I knelt.

The eather crackled and spat, darting between Perry and Delano and striking the Gyrm behind them as the fiery essence licked and rolled across the ground, burning through the newest batch of snakes. I turned, eyes narrowing as I saw the remaining Grym stalking the wolven. It was gone in a flash of silver.

And then the blood trees were empty of anything that could spew serpents from its mouth. "Any more coming?"

Kieran had edged closer to the mouth of the tunnel. "I don't think so."

"Stand back," I said, getting an idea. Using the eather, I twisted toward the opening in the rock and sent a thin stream of energy forward. Light splashed against the walls as it traveled deep into what was clearly a cave.

When it revealed no more Gyrms, I pulled the eather back. The silvery glow faded.

"Did any of those serpents bite anyone?" Reaver demanded.

"Answer now. Their bite is toxic."

Everyone answered in the negative as Delano planted his paws on the boulder and stretched up, nudging my arm. I reached over, sinking my fingers into his fur as I sheathed the dagger.

Breathing heavily, I looked over to where Reaver stood in the wagon. "I just need to know," I said, willing my heart to slow, "why do they have snakes inside them?"

"They have no insides. No organs," Reaver answered. "The serpents are all that fills them."

All of us turned to Reaver. Perry swallowed as if he were one second from vomiting. I dropped my hand from Delano's neck. "Well, that...that is even more disturbing. I wish I hadn't asked."

Casteel stopped in front of me, extending his hand.

"I'm fine." I sat. "Just going to stay right here."

"For how long?" he asked as Delano hopped onto the boulder, settling onto his belly beside me.

"Not sure."

His lips twitched.

"Don't you dare smile," I warned.

"I'm not," he swore, and that was definitely a lie. "There are no more serpents, Poppy."

"Don't care."

Casteel wiggled his fingers. "You can't stay up there, my Queen. We need to get Malec, and we may need your extra-special Primal badassery to do it."

My eyes narrowed on him. "It irritates me when you're right."

"Then you must be irritated often," Casteel replied.

Kieran snorted. "Please, get down from there before my sister joins you, and we have to talk three of you off a boulder."

"I am *this* close to joining you," Vonetta admitted as she kept looking at the ground.

Delano nudged my arm again, and I sighed, taking Casteel's hand as I scooted off the boulder. When Delano hopped down beside me, I tipped my head back. "If I see a snake, it's your fault."

Laughing under his breath, Cas pressed his lips to the top of my head. "Adorable."

"So, I couldn't be the only one who noticed that they weren't attacking her," Perry pointed out as Malik lowered himself to the ground.

"Oh, yeah." I turned to Reaver. "Did they recognize me as

his…niece or something?"

"They probably recognized the Primal essence," Reaver said.

"But the Gyrms conjured by the Unseen *did* go after her," Casteel bit out.

"I don't know what these Unseen are, or how or why they'd be summoning Gyrms," Reaver said. "Tell me."

I gave him a brief rundown. "I guess the whole Unseen thing came into creation while you all were sleeping."

"Sounds about right," Kieran muttered.

"Three things." Reaver held up three fingers. "First off, I need my rest. If I don't get my rest, I get cranky."

"Who sounds like the sensitive one now?" Kieran fired back.

"And when I get cranky, I like to set things on fire and then eat them," Reaver continued, and I briefly closed my eyes. "Secondly, those weren't just some random Gyrms that can be conjured to do one's bidding. As I said, they were Sentries."

I opened my eyes. "What is the difference between them?"

Reaver still held up one finger. "Most of them were once mortal—those who summoned a god and pledged servitude to them upon death in exchange for whatever favor the god granted them. Hunters hunt things. Sentries—you guessed it—guard things. Items. Usually, people. But Sentries, like Hunters and Seekers, can sense whatever they're searching for. They either find said thing and bring it back, or they die in the process of defending it."

My gaze flicked back to the ground. Those things had once been mortal? Good gods…

Now, I felt a little bad about killing them.

Casteel slid his arm around my waist, squeezing. "So, these Gyrms were down there for hundreds of years?"

Reaver nodded.

"That must've been really boring," Emil said.

"Again." Vonetta looked at him. "Understatement."

"And it wasn't whatever your mother did that sent the Sentries here," Reaver said.

"What do you mean?" Casteel's eyes narrowed. "And can you please stop giving Kieran the middle finger?"

"I was actually giving it to everyone, but whatever." Slowly, Reaver lowered his middle finger. "I have a feeling this mountain formed as a way to guard Malec's tomb, but these types of Gyrms can't be summoned by Primal magic. They can only be *sent* by a Primal."

Slowly, I turned to the mouth of the cave. "You think Nyktos sent them? That he and the Consort knew where their son was?"

Reaver was quiet for a long moment. "When Malec left Iliseeum, he did so right before the others went to sleep. He didn't leave on good terms, but the...Primal of Life, even in sleep, would've sensed his vulnerability. The deity bones would've likely blocked their ability to know where he was," he said, and I realized that whatever Isbeth kept Ires in likely had to be the same. "While sleeping, the Primal of Life must've summoned the Sentries to protect him."

My Primal badassery wasn't exactly needed from there. No more Gyrms appeared as we entered the cave, coming upon the bone-smothered casket at the end, resting halfway under the earth in the center of a chamber that was barely large enough for all of the Gyrms to have waited in.

I didn't want to think about that. About how Nyktos had sought to protect his son. Reaver destroyed the roots of the blood trees that had wound their way around the chains. I didn't want to imagine how his inability to find Ires and do the same for him must plague him every second, both awake and asleep. It had to be why the Consort slept so restlessly.

We left the bone chains on the casket in case the movement stirred the one inside. All of us were quiet, listening for any signs of life as the wooden, unmarked casket was carefully carried out from the cave and placed in the wagon. Reaver stayed with it as we began our trek back to Padonia.

At first, I thought it was out of worry that Malec would wake and attempt to escape, but I saw Reaver a few times, sitting beside the casket with his hand resting on top of it and his eyes closed. And that...that left me with a messy knot of emotion in my chest.

As we neared the edge of the Blood Forest, and Casteel and I rode beside the casket, I finally asked Reaver what preyed on my mind. "Were you friends with Malec?"

He stared at the casket for quite some time before answering. "We were when we were younger, before he began to visit the mortal realm."

"It changed after that?" Casteel asked as he guided Setti around several piles of rocks.

Reaver nodded. "He lost interest in Iliseeum, and that loss of interest became a…a loss of affection for all who resided there."

"I'm sorry to hear that," Casteel said, his gaze flicking over my head to where Malik rode beside Naill.

Reaver's stare followed his. "It is strange, is it not, that he was named so closely to Malec?"

I didn't say a word.

Casteel did. "My mother loved Malec. I think a part of her always will. Naming Malik was a way to…"

"To honor what could have been?"

"Yeah." Casteel was silent for a moment. "I was thinking about what you said. If Nyktos could send Sentries to watch over Malec, wouldn't he have known when Malec was entombed? Couldn't he have prevented that?"

Reaver was quiet for a moment. "The Primal of Life could have. Malec must have been weakened greatly to be entombed. Hurt. Both Nyktos and the Consort would've felt that. Neither intervened."

I stared at the casket, a general sense of unease returning. They sought to protect him but not free him.

"Do you know why they didn't?" Casteel asked.

Reaver shook his head. "I don't, but I imagine they had their reasons."

None of us slept all that well when we stopped to rest the following nights. I thought that we were more than a little unnerved about *who* was in that casket more than the creatures that called the Blood Forest home. That feeling didn't ease until we finally rode out from beneath the crimson leaves on the ninth day.

"You think we'll reach Padonia by nightfall?" I asked as we rode farther ahead.

"I do," Kieran said from the horse that kept pace beside ours.

"We'll have a day of rest before we have to leave for the Bone Temple," Casteel tacked on.

"I wish we had longer—ouch." I leaned back, pressing my palm against my suddenly aching jaw.

Casteel frowned as he glanced down. "What is it?"

"I don't know." A taste gathered in my mouth, iron-rich. "My mouth hurts." I prodded at my upper jaw—

"If it hurts," Casteel said, curling his fingers around my wrist, "then maybe you shouldn't poke at it."

"That would make too much sense," Kieran remarked as Casteel drew my hand away from my mouth.

"I don't recall asking for your opinion," I shot back.

Kieran grinned. It faded quickly, though.

"Poppy." Concern radiated from Casteel as his gaze flicked up from my hand. "Your mouth is bleeding."

"What?" I ran my tongue along my gums. "Well, I guess that explains the taste of blood in my mouth. That's kind of gross."

"Cas…" Kieran eyed him.

I frowned, opening my senses to them. The concern had disappeared. "What?"

"Is it your mouth or your jaw that's been hurting?" Casteel asked, still holding my wrist as if he expected me to keep poking myself.

Which was possible.

"It's more like my jaw—the upper. And the pain sometimes radiates to my temple," I said.

"And it comes and goes?" Casteel changed his grip on the reins.

I nodded. "Yeah. It doesn't even hurt anymore. And I think it stopped bleeding." I glanced back at him. "Why are you asking?"

One side of his lips curled. "Because I think I know why it's been hurting." The grin deepened until the dimple appeared. "Or, at least, I'm hoping so."

Smiling, Kieran shook his head as Casteel urged Setti to the side of the road, slowing him so that Emil and Vonetta rode past us. The wolven following at our side did the same as Casteel drew up to where Reaver remained in the back of the wagon. Malik and Naill rode on the other side.

"What?" Reaver asked.

"I have no idea," I said.

"Got a question for you," Casteel started, letting go of my wrist.

"Great," Reaver muttered.

Casteel was unfazed by the less-than-eager response. "Do Primals have fangs?"

My eyes went wide.

Reaver scowled. "To answer that random-as-hell question, yes. How do you think they feed?"

The other dimple graced us with an appearance as Casteel tilted his chin down. "That's why I think your jaw's been hurting."

I couldn't say anything for a full minute. "You...you think I'm getting fangs?" I asked.

Casteel nodded. "We don't get ours until we're about to complete the Culling. Our mouths will hurt on and off and bleed. It's like teething."

"Why am I not surprised you haven't realized that yet?" Reaver muttered, giving us his back.

I was going to have...fangs?

Holy shit.

Immediately, I lifted my hand, and Casteel caught my wrist once more with a chuckle. "Don't mess with your mouth, Poppy."

How could I not? I was growing fangs! I ran my tongue over my gums, feeling nothing strange there. Sugary amusement filtered through from Casteel, but that wasn't the only thing I felt as he rejoined Kieran. A spicy, smoky flavor gathered in my throat, too.

My neck craned back as my eyes snapped to his. "You're *excited* about this, aren't you?"

"Hell, yes, I am." He lowered his head to mine, his voice low when he said, "I cannot wait to feel your fangs on my skin."

Warmth crept into my face. "Cas—"

"On lots of places," he added.

"Fucking gods," Kieran muttered.

Casteel laughed as he brushed his lips over mine. He then explained what he thought I could expect, changing the subject to something a bit more appropriate. The fangs would come in, pushing out the other teeth, which was really gross to think about. But he said they descended once they broke through. None of that sounded like fun.

"It really isn't," Kieran said when I voiced exactly that. "Cas was a fucking whiny baby that day."

"Yeah, well, when you have two teeth being pushed out, let me know how that feels," Casteel shot back.

Thoughts of my teeth occupied my mind for the remainder of the journey, and there was a good chance those thoughts would also haunt my dreams. It wasn't that I was disturbed by the idea of having fangs. They would actually make feeding easier, but it would be different.

Further proof of how much I'd changed.

And was still changing.

43

Upon returning to Padonia, Malec was placed in the stables, which was, well, it seemed wrong somehow, but where else would we be able to place him? No one would want a casket containing a god in the Great Hall.

I'd placed Isbeth's ring back in the pouch, along with the wooden horse. I really needed to give that back to Casteel, but as I sat on the edge of the bed after bathing, wearing nothing more than a gauzy, knee-length chemise I'd found in the wardrobe, I wasn't thinking about Malec, the ring or the horse. I'd decided there was no point in dressing any further since… Well, since I would only have to *un*dress.

My stomach tumbled a bit. The faint ache had returned to my jaw and temple while I spent time with Tawny, but it had mostly disappeared while bathing. I didn't know if the headache had to do with the Culling and me getting fangs as Reaver had said or what was to come.

The Joining.

I couldn't let my mind wander too far down that path. Not because I was uncertain or afraid. But because I knew if I *did* think too much about it, I would only work myself into an anxious mess.

No one needed that.

I'd managed to doze off while Casteel bathed, and it had been strange to wake without Kieran there, curled against my hip.

Casteel came out of the bathing chamber, dressed in his breeches.

"You and those silly straps again," he said, a dimple appearing as he tugged on one of the thin straps. "How are you feeling?"

"Good."

He arched a brow.

I laughed softly. "I'm feeling okay. Only because I'm trying not to think about the fact that we have an entombed god in our stables."

"Yeah, I think everyone is trying not to think about that." He sat beside me.

The breath I took was shallow. "Where is Kieran?"

A slight grin reappeared. "He's waiting for us."

My stomach took another tumble. "Okay."

Thick lashes lifted, and golden eyes met mine. "Are you sure you want to go through with this?"

"Yes," I said without hesitation. "I do. You?"

"Of course." He drew the strap up my shoulder.

"And Kieran?" I asked. "He still wants to do this?"

"Yes." The smile played over his lips. "That's why he's waiting for us."

My stomach spun again. "Then what are we waiting for?"

Casteel chuckled. "For you."

I started to stand, but he clasped my cheek. "What?"

"Nothing." His left palm found mine, pressing our imprints together. "Nothing except that I'm in love with you. That I will always be in love with you, from now until our last breaths."

My heart swelled as I leaned into him, filling with emotion so powerful and deep that words couldn't even capture what I felt. "I love you."

Casteel kissed me, taking my mouth softly with his. It was one of his sweet kisses. The gentle kind that left every part of me warm—even the cold, hollow parts. "Ready, my Queen?" he whispered against my lips.

"Ready."

Wearing cloaks and what little clothing we had on underneath, Casteel led me out from the chamber and down a back hall. We left the manor unseen through a set of doors that led to an overgrown garden that Kirha would have enjoyed.

It made me think of Jasper. "Where is Jasper?"

"With my father and Hisa."

"Not Vonetta?"

"I think she's with Emil." He arched a brow as he led me down the walkway. "Something's going on between them, isn't there?"

"You're just now realizing that?"

He snorted. "Better question is, has Kieran figured that out?"

"I think he was just beginning to when we left Oak Ambler."

His grin kicked up a notch. "Thoughts and prayers for Emil."

"More like thoughts and prayers for Kieran if he tries to intervene. Vonetta likes Emil. I don't think she'll take all that kindly to Kieran not minding his business."

"True."

With Cas's hand firmly wrapped around mine, we entered the Wisteria Woods and went beyond the inner fortress wall, deeper into the forest. The sound of rushing water grew closer as we wandered through the twining vines, appearing a silvery purple in the moonlight. As we walked, Casteel talked about how Kieran and he had made sure they wouldn't get lost in the tunnels they had explored when younger. They used to mark the stone walls with their initials, and I wondered if that was what they'd done now. If Kieran had carved his name into the trunks, allowing Casteel to know exactly where to find him in the maze of heavily clustered trees.

Casteel's words, his voice—all of him—had eased my nerves by the time he parted another heavy curtain of limbs. Beyond him, I saw that we'd reached the bank of the River of Rhain. And then I saw Kieran.

Sitting by the edge of the river, he rose and faced us as we walked out into the narrow clearing. He wore only breeches like Casteel had on under his cloak. I'd seen him shirtless hundreds of times, sometimes without even a stitch of clothing, but it seemed different now. "I was beginning to wonder if you were going to sleep the night away."

"I have a feeling she'd stab me if I allowed that," Casteel commented as the wisteria limbs fell back into place behind us.

I shot him an arch look. "I didn't mean to fall asleep."

"It's okay." Kieran grinned and looked up at the star-drenched sky as we stopped in front of him. "I didn't mind waiting. It's beautiful here. Peaceful."

It was, with the water of the river so clear it looked like rushing pools of silver, the chirping birds in the trees, and the heavy, sweet scent of the wisteria. When Kieran's gaze returned to me, I felt my heart skip. There was no room to think about anything but what was happening here. I cracked open my senses. What I felt from Kieran was the salty nuttiness of resolve. There was also something sweet and soft, a little bubbly and smoky. I didn't sense any uncertainty. I felt the same from Casteel—well, *almost* the same. There was sugary amusement, and he felt hot with a different, heavier softness—spicy and sweet. I looked around. "Are we alone out here?"

Kieran nodded. "No one will get close to us."

He said that with such certainty, I had a feeling I knew why. I turned to Casteel. "We're being guarded?"

"By the wolven," he confirmed. "They're not close. They won't hear or see anything, but they will make sure no one gets too near us."

I nodded. "Do they...do they know what we're doing?"

"Would it bother you if they did?" Kieran asked.

I thought about that and realized that it didn't. Well, if Vonetta wasn't with Emil and was among them, I truly felt sorry for her. Because that would be so awkward for her. "It doesn't."

Kieran's approval was a ripple of buttery cake. "They see it as a great honor to protect such a tradition."

"Oh," I whispered, blushing. "I'm glad they approve."

Casteel's lips curved into a smile as he pressed them to my forehead. I drew in a shallow breath, the decadent scent of pine and lush spice surrounding me. His breath danced over my lips and then the curve of my cheek as he dipped his head to speak softly in my ear. "I thought you'd like it here, with the river and the wisterias."

"I do."

"Good." He kissed the space below my ear. "Going to ask you again. Going to ask you a lot. You want to do this?"

Throat dry, I nodded.

His lips grazed the shell of my ear, sending a shiver through me. "We need to hear you speak the words, my Queen."

"Yes," I said, clearing my throat. "I'm sure."

He pressed a kiss to the sensitive spot below my ear as his fingers brushed the skin at my throat. He unclasped the hooks, and the weight of the cloak fell away. "We can stop this at any time."

"I know." The touch of his fingers against my bare shoulders and sliding under the thin straps of the slip sent a jolt through my body.

He curled his fingers around the straps. "Nothing will happen—absolutely *nothing*—that you don't want to take part in," he said, kissing the underside of my jaw. "No matter what you think we may want or what you feel from us."

"We expect nothing," Kieran said, his voice close.

"I know." My heart beat so fast, it was like the fluttering wings of a wild bird taking flight. "I'm safe with both of you."

"Always," Kieran confirmed.

Casteel's lip brushed my chin. "And forever."

A ridiculous surge of emotion swelled in my throat, and with my senses locked down, I knew the sweet rush was all mine. Tears crowded my eyes. I loved them. Both of them. In different ways and for different reasons that I didn't understand, but I really did. And that knowledge left me a little unsteady.

Casteel's hands lowered, and cool air followed the slip, sluicing over my chest and stomach and farther still until only moonlight dressed my skin. I shivered, but I didn't think it had anything to do with the cool air. Casteel's mouth touched mine, and it was another sweet and soft kiss.

When his mouth left mine, he whispered, "You can open your eyes whenever you're ready."

He stepped back, and that wild flutter in my chest moved to my stomach. The urge to cover myself was there, but I resisted. With there being a quality of unknown to how the Joining worked, some magic that wasn't about blood or words, I didn't want to do anything that might risk it not working.

I felt their stares almost as if they were a physical caress, soft and warm and...*worshipping*.

In those moments, I heard nothing but the bubbling of the nearby river and then the nightbirds calling to one another from the trees above in a chorus that felt ancient—primal—a little magical and wholly tempestuous.

My eyes opened.

I saw Casteel first bathed in the silvery moonlight. He truly looked as I had always believed a god to appear. A raging storm of flesh and bone, all exquisite angles and lines. His eyes were pools of honeyed gold as they locked onto mine, and I felt it slip past my shields. A sweet taste gathered in my throat, reminding me of chocolate-covered berries with a hint of cinnamon. His love and his pride filled me, and a wealth of emotions swelled once more.

Then I saw Kieran standing beside Casteel, shoulder to shoulder. Like they had been before I entered their lives. Like they always would be. I took in the proud, untamed planes of his face and the strong curve of his broad jaw. His skin was a mesmerizing silvery brown in the moonlight, and he reminded me of some otherworldly being I'd conjured from my imagination. Captivating and impressive in both forms, his eyes were the blue of winter, and the glow of eather behind his pupils was vibrant. My shields slipped again, and what I felt from him was the same as I'd felt before—sweet and soft. Not as intense as what came from Casteel, but no less meaningful. Nothing about Kieran was less.

Both had discarded their clothing in those silent moments while my eyes had been closed. Their bodies showed years of training and fighting in the lines of muscle and the marks upon their skin. Casteel carried more reminders in the countless scars that always tugged at my heart upon seeing them, but Kieran bore his fair share. I hadn't noticed them before, the faded claw marks across his chest, the long-ago healed punctures near his waist. Kieran was leaner, the cut of his body more formed even with Casteel only beginning to put his weight back on. I wondered if it had to do with all the running he did in his wolven form. I almost asked but stopped myself before I opened my mouth.

Kieran would probably appreciate my self-restraint.

Then I looked lower. In the back of my mind, I knew that it probably wasn't a wise choice. Not because they wouldn't want me to, and obviously not because I didn't want to, but because I *was* looking. It wasn't like I hadn't seen either of them naked, but I tried to be appropriate about it when it came to Kieran.

I was currently being highly inappropriate as my gaze drifted down their hips, to where both were…well, no less scandalous than I.

I knew that Casteel was pleased with every inch of my body—the hips that some might find too full, the thighs that might be too thick, the belly too soft, and the scars that marked me. But it was clear that neither found what they saw displeasing. Or maybe it had nothing to do with what they saw or how I looked. Perhaps it only had to do with what they felt. What we shared. Either way, they were…

Good gods.

"Always so curious," Casteel murmured.

My gaze flew up, my face heating.

One side of Casteel's lips curled upward, and I saw the hint of a dimple appearing in his right cheek.

"Shut up," I rasped.

He chuckled, but when his eyes touched mine again, they asked an unspoken question.

I swallowed, hoping it would calm my heart as a breeze rippled through the glen. It didn't, but my voice was there. "I'm ready."

Both seemed to draw in the same breath and then, together, they came to me.

44

My legs felt a little loose as a cyclone of sensations whipped through me, so fast and so ever-changing I could only make sense of a few of them. Nervousness crashed into curiosity and gave way to uncertainty, which a sharp wave of anticipation that had nothing and everything to do with what might or might not happen then swept aside. It was the entire ritual. The whole act of joining our essences together. Would we feel different afterwards? Would things change, no matter if we ended at blood being exchanged or went beyond that?

With blade in hand, Casteel stopped a hairsbreadth in front of me as Kieran came to stand behind me. Neither of them touched me, but their proximity already warmed my night-kissed skin.

As I stood there, I was reminded of New Haven, when Kieran had been there when Casteel needed to feed. This was a lot like then.

Except we were all naked as the day we were born.

If I had thought it would be easier to ignore our nudity when I wasn't able to see all the naughty bits, I'd been wrong. I seemed all the more aware of it now.

Casteel's gaze flicked up and behind me. He nodded, and then Kieran's chest touched mine. My breath caught at the feel of him, the skin that always ran hot—of the sudden feel of *him* against my lower back as he adjusted his stance.

"Sorry," Kieran said in a voice rough and thick that tickled the back of my shoulder. "It's just that you're beautiful, and I'm, well…"

He trailed off, and I'd never heard him so thoroughly rattled. "I'm trying to behave…appropriately."

"It's okay," I told him, swallowing to ease the dryness in my throat as I made sure my senses were locked down. The last thing I needed was to connect with whatever Kieran may be feeling. That wouldn't aid in anyone behaving. "Your…er, physical response is only natural," I added, my face flaming.

Just as the shivery awareness of Kieran that centered on every part of our bodies that touched was just a natural reaction.

Casteel's grin spread until that infuriating dimple in his left cheek became visible, and his stare turned downright wicked.

Kieran and I were attempting to behave appropriately. Apparently, Casteel wasn't. He bit his lower lip, revealing a hint of fang.

His lack of behaving appropriately didn't come as a shock.

At all.

Kieran sighed heavily. "No help whatsoever, man."

Laughing under his breath, Casteel's stare found and held mine. "You'll drink first," he reminded me in a soft voice. His stare held mine. "From my chest first, and then from Kieran's throat. We'll each drink from each other after you. Then, we will both drink from *your* throat. We will need to be in constant contact with each other once you start drinking and then through the whole thing."

Feeling my cheeks heat even more, I nodded as I stopped my imagination from running wild. He'd explained all of this. Because a wolven could not take in blood like an Atlantian, a blade was used to draw the essence from the Atlantian, and the mark was made near the heart at the center of the chest, roughly where I felt the eather throbbing restlessly in mine. Blood was taken from the wolven's throat because they were a conduit of sorts, the bridge designed to link the lifespan of the Atlantian to their mate. But in our case, to link his with ours—theirs with mine. Blood was then drawn at the same time from the strongest one—the one who would hold both life forces.

Me.

Casteel's gaze still fastened on to mine, he brushed his fingers over the curve of my cheek. "You need to speak the words I told you," he instructed softly.

I took a shallow breath, recalling them and what to do. "Do you, Casteel Da'Neer, enter this Joining freely and with will of your own, only your own?" I asked as I lifted my left hand. It trembled slightly.

"I enter this Joining freely and with will of only my own," he said, taking my left hand in his.

The nightbirds fell silent.

I lifted my right hand. "Do you, Kieran Contou, enter this Joining freely and with will of your own, only your own?"

"I enter this Joining freely and with will of only my own." Kieran's warm right hand enveloped mine, and he brought our joined hands to the center of my chest where Casteel's ring had once rested between my breasts.

The air stilled around us.

And with the last words needing to be spoken—it was only a handful, but the realm seemed to hear them—the Primal essence stirred even more as if it were waking up and listening.

"I love you, Penellaphe Da'Neer," Casteel whispered, dipping his head to drag his lips over mine. "From this moment to your last moment."

I shuddered at what he'd said. Those words had nothing to do with the Joining. They were just a reminder. "I love you, Casteel Da'Neer," I whispered thickly. "From this moment to *our* last moment."

The same shudder ran through his body as he brought the blade up. Without looking away, without flinching, he drew the sharp edge across his chest, slicing open his skin. Blood immediately welled, beading. Casteel tossed the blade aside and then stepped into me. The contact of his body against mine, with Kieran planted so firmly behind me, and the feel of Casteel rigid against my belly, was another stunning, sharp jolt to my system.

My heart started racing again, beating so fast I wondered how it could sustain such a speed as Casteel placed his right hand on Kieran. Could Kieran feel it beneath our hands? Could Casteel hear it pounding away?

Kieran's left hand went around the nape of Casteel's neck, and then all three of us were connected.

They waited for me, and they didn't have to wait too long. I stretched up, my pulse skittering as their bodies seemed to conform to mine in a way that almost felt as if they were bracing me, becoming two pillars of support. Something I found ironic when I would become the one who would support them.

My mouth brushed Casteel's chest, and he gave a little jerk that I felt throughout my entire body. My lips tingled at the first touch. I closed my mouth over the wound, drawing his blood into me.

It felt like forever since I'd tasted him. My memories did him no justice. His blood tasted like citrus in snow. I drank, sucking at his skin, drawing his essence into me.

Casteel's groan rumbled through him, vibrating against my breasts and moving to Kieran. I felt his head fall back. The taste of him—his essence—was an awakening, a freefall rush without compare. His blood was warm and thick, heating my already inflamed skin. In the recesses of my mind, I realized I hadn't even considered the effect of Casteel's blood. It was probably for the best that I hadn't considered it until now, until his blood was lighting up every cell in my body, and the eather in my chest started to throb.

"Poppy," Casteel moaned, his chin grazing the top of my head. "That's enough."

I heard him, but I took and took until that hidden-away place in me, the cold part, began to warm—

"If you don't stop," Casteel said, his body taut against mine, "this will stop right here and end in a very different kind of joining."

Those words reached me. Flushing at the sensual warning, I forced my mouth from his chest and lifted my gaze to his.

Looking at him then, stark need etched into every line of his face, didn't help keep my thoughts focused on the goal at hand. Lowering my gaze, I flicked my tongue over my lower lip, catching the last drop of blood that had gathered there.

Casteel groaned again as his hand tightened around mine. "*Behave*," he ordered roughly. "Or you're going to make Kieran blush."

"Yeah," came that not-so-dry response. "That's exactly what's going to happen."

I had a feeling I was the only one blushing as I moved just a little out of the way, enough for Kieran to reach Casteel. The position caused *areas* of him to come into contact with *areas* of me, and I desperately tried to ignore it as his mouth replaced mine.

Casteel jerked again as his burning, golden eyes locked onto mine. I could barely breathe as Kieran drank from him, and Casteel watched me, his chest beginning to rise and fall more rapidly. At first, I was concerned that he wasn't ready to part with so much blood, but when I cracked my senses open just enough, I immediately knew that wasn't the case.

His lust was like a whirlwind, and even a little bit of it was a fierce weight to bear. His lip curled back, revealing more of his fangs as Kieran drank from him. An aching pulse went through my breasts and centered between my thighs. Casteel's nostrils flared, and he growled, low and heated.

I felt a little dizzy when Kieran stopped, and they carefully turned me so Casteel was at my back. My lips still tingled, so did my throat, and I felt that sensation starting to spread through me as I slowly lifted my gaze to Kieran's.

Kieran's stare captured mine. My heart leapt unsteadily at the sight of the streaks of eather in his eyes. He turned his head to the side, exposing his throat. Casteel bent over me, leaning so he could reach Kieran, leaving absolutely no space between us. Every nerve ending seemed to spark all at once at the feel of them pressed so *inappropriately* close. They had to feel my heart when it skipped as Casteel struck, sinking his fangs into Kieran's throat. They had to feel the rather indecent tremor rocking me at the sight of Casteel biting Kieran.

At taking his blood.

I couldn't even blink.

I could barely breathe as I watched Casteel's throat work on each dragging swallow. As the tautness went out of Kieran's face, and his lips parted. As the thick, hard length of Casteel throbbed against my lower back.

Dimly, I wondered how anyone could possibly remain unaffected by this.

Casteel lifted his head, and the scent of Kieran's blood reached out to me. The essence swirled madly in my chest as Casteel's grip remained firm on me. I stretched up once more, Kieran's and my joined hands lodged firmly between our bodies, and the fine dusting of soft hair on his chest that I would've sworn wasn't there before scattered my thoughts. His skin...it felt even hotter, harder. Maybe even a little thinner. I swayed. I wasn't sure why. I didn't feel weak, but I *was* unsteady, as if I were an arrow fired without thought or aim.

I trembled as my mouth closed over Kieran's throat. His blood, the wild and woodsy taste, was surprisingly complementary to Casteel's, and that thought drew a muffled giggle from me. Both of their hands tightened on mine. They probably thought I was losing it, but it wasn't my mind I was failing to control.

It was my body as I drank from Kieran. The feel of his chest moving in deep, rapid breaths against my breasts. The rumbling weight of him as I drew his essence into me. The hot, hard press of Casteel at my back, his breath on my shoulder. His mouth there. His *fangs* were there as I drank—not piercing my skin, just there. I shuddered. My hold on my abilities slipped. The rich taste of blood, earthy and decadent, got lost in the swell of smoky spice gathering in my throat. I had no idea which one it'd come from or if it was both of them. Or mine.

The night still seemed to be listening as Casteel managed to stop me with a tug of his fangs. No cold parts remained inside me, even though I trembled as someone turned me back to Casteel once more.

Casteel dropped his forehead to mine. "You okay?" he asked, his voice ragged and breathless.

I nodded, catching the scent of Kieran's blood on his breath.

"Need to hear you say it," Kieran said, and he sounded just as raw as Casteel.

"Yes," I whispered, my skin tingling with the heat of Casteel's and Kieran's blood, my body throbbing from the warmth of theirs. "I'm okay."

"I'll have to bite you twice," Casteel said, and I remembered. My toes began to curl against the damp, cool grass. "It'll…be intense."

Kieran's hand, still held around mine and against my chest, tightened.

Casteel kissed me quickly and then waited for me to give him permission as if he didn't already have it. Eyes closed, I pressed my head back against Kieran's chest, exposing my throat to Casteel.

For a moment, none of us moved, and the waiting was almost too much.

And then Casteel struck fast. I jerked at the pierce of his fangs, caught off guard no matter how much I expected it. *Wanted* it. It wasn't something one could prepare for. The mix of all-consuming pleasure and biting pain was startling. He didn't drink, though. His head lifted, and he bit again, sinking his fangs into the other side of my throat. My entire body arched, pressing into both of them, my eyes flying open wide as Casteel latched on to the left side of my throat.

As Kieran did the same, closing his mouth over the right side.

I cried out this time, not from pain but from the dual intensity of their mouths moving at my throat. It was too much. My arms jerked against my will, but they held my hands, keeping us joined. A riot of sensations hit me like a drenching downpour. Every part of my body tightened to almost painful points. The roar of blood in my ears abated, and the only thing I heard was them—their rough, needful sounds as they drank.

My eyes remained wide, fixed on the sky and the stars that seemed to cartwheel through the night, growing brighter and brighter.

And so did I.

The eather rose to the surface, shadow-laced silver rippling from the center of my chest and wrapping around Casteel and Kieran, forming crackling ropes of light that twisted and twined their way around our bodies.

Only their mouths, their tongues, moved at my throat, and I wasn't sure if they could see what I did, the combining of our essences. I didn't think they were even aware as they took and took, and the silvery cords burned brighter. There was so much heat pressed against my front and back, burning inside me, filling my throat, my chest, and pooling in my core. My hold on my abilities slipped and fell away, and what they felt joined the downpour, sweeping me up with it.

Their mouths weren't the only things moving. I was. My hips. My body. I twisted between them, softer sounds joining their muffled ones as the tips of my breasts dragged across Casteel's chest, and the curve of my rear against Kieran's thighs. My feet slipped on the grass, and a rough, hard thigh wedged between mine. The change of position was startling. I felt Kieran now nestled against me, where Casteel had shockingly, wickedly touched days before. I shook at the feel of him, and the feel of the strong thigh pressed against the aching, swollen flesh between mine.

No thought guided my actions. No hint of shame. Only instinct as the cords continued to weave their way around the three of us. I rode the thigh as I squeezed their hands, tighter and tighter. Everything was too much and yet not enough. I moaned as their lips moved on the skin of my throat. Pressure curled and curled, and I clamped my thighs around the one between my legs—

I gasped as one or both of them lifted me until my toes barely touched the ground. Suddenly, it wasn't just the thigh I rocked on but the hot length of a cock that I slid and rubbed against. Slowly, I became aware of the lips stilling at my throat and their mouths no longer being there, even though I still felt their dragging pulls both there and in my core.

Blinking open my eyes, I saw that the crackling cords of essence still vibrated around us.

Casteel's and Kieran's chests moved in shallow pants. Other than that, they were still, even though I felt their need. Heavy spice cloaked my skin, my blood peppered with it. It was almost painful, the combination of it all, and yet neither moved. They were still, even as I rocked against the thigh, against the cock, growing wetter, knowing that they could see the silvery cocoon that had formed around us— knowing that they watched me, my breasts, my hips, my face as Kieran's chest cradled my head, and my eyes locked onto golden ones. They watched as eagerly as I had when they fed from each other, and a new hidden part of me, one I'd recently discovered, reveled in it—in the sensuality, the freedom, and the primitive power.

They simply held me, their hands firmly in mine as I rode the now-damp thigh and erection. They made no moves because we…we came to it. The blade-sharp point. A line. The edge. We were there, and I was dancing along it. They stayed there with me, hearts pounding in tandem, and I knew it would be easy to back away from it, to put a stop to this. I knew that they would remain as they were, allowing me to shamelessly seek the pleasure I was so close to feeling. I knew they would follow my lead wherever it took them.

They waited.

The humming cords of essence snapping and crackling around us waited, and golden eyes held mine. My ceaseless churning stilled, and I knew we were wildly dancing sparks, alive and on the verge of igniting until we were nothing but flesh and fire.

And I *wanted* to be the fire.

I wanted to burn.

"*Yes*," I whispered, and the cords throbbed.

Casteel trembled. Both of them did. And neither moved for a long moment. Then, Cas drew our joined hands to his mouth, kissing the top. My right hand was also lifted, Kieran doing the same. I trembled.

"Fucking unworthy of you," Casteel growled, and before I could tell him any differently, his mouth was on mine.

Oh, gods.

That kiss was unlike anything I'd ever experienced before. I tasted my blood on his lips. I tasted Kieran's as his tongue swept inside my mouth. He drank from me as he had from my neck as a rough palm skimmed the curve of my hip and then my waist. My hands were still in theirs, and I had no idea whose hand touched me, but the cords were still there. I heard them hissing and spinning as that palm traveled up my stomach, closing over an aching breast. I moaned into Casteel's mouth. His lips captured my cry as fingers found the tingling peak of my other breast. Casteel's mouth left mine only when I thought I'd surely pass out, and that mouth of his blazed a trail down my throat, past the bite marks and lower still. His tongue lapped at my breast, over the fingers there. My moan got lost in the groan that I felt along my back.

Their hands eased from mine, and the cords remained, shimmering in the space around us, between us, and in us. I curled a hand around the nape of Casteel's neck. I threaded my arm around Kieran's, pressing my fingers into the skin of his biceps. Casteel drew the sensitive nub of peaked flesh and that finger that had been tormenting the same skin into his mouth. He sucked deeply and hard, dragging a ragged gasp from me.

"*Fucker*," Kieran grunted.

Casteel's laugh gave way to a growl as my body arched once more. As a hand landed on my hip, urging me to move. I gasped at the hair teasing the heightened flesh there—at the wicked slide along the heated erection. Fingers grazed my stomach, dancing below my navel and lower. My breath kept catching as a rough pad of a finger rolled over the bundle of nerves at the apex of my thighs. The finger toyed as Casteel's mouth moved to my other breast.

"Wouldn't want this one to get lonely," he said, palming the flesh and lifting it to his mouth.

Kieran's hand remained on the other, damp from Casteel's treatment, and I didn't know whose hand was on my hip, whose finger was teasing, whose—

I cried out as the finger slid through the gathering heat and then inside me. My body burned as the finger moved in unison with the mouth at my breast, and with each draw, the finger sank into me. My fingers tightened around Casteel's hand. My nails dug into Kieran's arm.

"Oh, gods," I panted.

"You're going to start praying?" Kieran asked, his breath hot against the bite marks on my neck, sending a pulse through me.

"Maybe," I admitted, and the finger plunged faster, deeper.

Casteel laughed as his head rose. His tongue moved over my lips.

"What would you pray for?" Kieran asked, his cheek pressed to mine.

"What—?" Casteel stole my words as he kissed me. "What?"

"He asked what you would pray for," Casteel said, and that finger inside me was joined by another. "I think I know."

Kieran's chuckle was dark and sensual. Teeth tugged on my ear. "I bet you do, but I want to hear her say it."

"I-I can't believe you're asking questions." I groaned as fingers tugged at my nipple, as fingers plunged deeper. "You of all people."

"This is the only time anyone else gets a chance to ask a question," Kieran replied, and I felt a surprisingly sharp nip at my shoulder that I strongly believed was him. "What would you pray for?"

"For something that could bring you more pleasure than a finger?" Casteel's mouth tugged on mine. "Or two? Or do you want a tongue between those pretty thighs of yours?"

My blood was burning now.

A hot lick soothed the sting on my shoulder. Maybe that was Kieran at my shoulder. Perhaps it had been him at my mouth. When I opened my eyes, neither was at my shoulder or mouth. I started to look down, but then Casteel was there, his fingers curled around my chin, lifting my mouth to his.

Fingers cupped my rear, guiding me farther back on that thigh, on that cock. Both of them shuddered.

"Or would you pray to come?" a sultry voice whispered in my ear.

"I think that's definitely it."

"I don't think I like either of you all that much at the moment," I said.

"You're a terrible liar, *meyaah Liessa*," Kieran teased. "I know that's not true. I can almost taste just how much you like us at the moment."

"That's your overinflated ego," I responded. Before I could say any more, someone tilted my head back, and my mouth was taken in another deep kiss.

"I think he just wants to hear you say an inappropriate word," Casteel advised, and it was definitely his mouth on mine at that point. "Cock. Aroused. Come. You'll make his night."

"I think that's you who wants to hear it," I said, dragging in deep breaths when his lips left mine.

"That would not be a lie," he confirmed, chuckling. "Tell us what you want, my Queen."

Everything had stopped. The fingers. The kisses. The hands. My hips. I gave a very mature grunt of frustration.

"What do you want?" Kieran asked.

My nails dug even harder into his skin, earning a laugh. "I...I want to come," I snapped. "There. Are you happy?"

"Fucking thrilled," Casteel said.

"And then some," Kieran added.

My head was tilted again, and a tongue swept inside my mouth. I didn't even realize I was being lowered until my knees hit the damp grass. My eyes opened as my mouth was released, and the cords...they were still around us, so blinding in their intensity now that we were nothing more than shadows.

And everything was *greedy*. Hands. Mouths. Tongues. Teeth. *Fangs.* We were so greedy, and that burn in my blood finally ignited. I was a fire that had spread to them and caught.

I truly had no idea whose hands gripped my hips or whose mouth came down on mine, I only knew that I was being guided onto a chest, that another pressed against my back. Only knew that a mouth was on mine, capturing my near scream of relief when I felt the thick, hard heat piercing me as quickly as Cas's fangs had earlier. Only knew that my palm was led to another rigid length, joining the hand already there. What I had asked for found me quickly, hitting me in shockwave after shockwave. The harsh grunt against my neck, the way those hands grabbed on to me, holding me in place, told me I hadn't found release alone. Nor was I alone when I was stretched onto my side, my mouth claimed by the one who held me from behind, keeping my leg draped over his hip as the one against my chest took me steadily, relentlessly, and I fell over that edge again. I could've had both of them inside me tonight, not at once but at different times. It could've only been one of them who'd moved inside me, but I knew who rolled me onto my back, whose lap I was held in when a dark head and a wicked mouth found its way between my thighs, licking and tormenting, tasting and teasing until I shattered apart. Until I felt a hot splash against my lower back, a release driven by my frenzied motions as I was devoured.

"Honeydew," Casteel murmured, lifting his head as I went utterly boneless.

I didn't even remember being taken into Casteel's arms or how the three of us ended up tangled, limp, and exhausted under the shimmering cords. But we stayed there until those cords faded around us and into our flesh, joined by our essences, our breaths, and our bodies—from now until our last breaths.

Our skin was slow to cool as we lay on the grassy riverbank, our bodies bathed in moonlight. We were still tangled up in one another, legs and arms entwined, and I was drawn to Casteel like always. My cheek rested on his chest, and Kieran's lay on his shoulder.

I knew in my heart and in my chest, where the eather hummed softly, that the Joining had worked. That was what all those silvery, glittering cords were, connecting us together from now until the *end*.

None of us spoke as the birds trilled softly to one another, high above us in the wisteria trees. It wasn't an awkward silence but rather a comfortable, content one as Casteel's heart thumped steadily beneath my cheek, and Kieran's against my upper back.

And as I lay there surrounded by their warmth, with each breath carrying their earthy and lush scents, I searched for any hint of shame—or regret for being the one who'd led the three of us to that line and then danced right over it, allowing for the Joining to become something infinitely *more*. In those calm, quiet moments where I began to realize that our hearts beat in tandem, and our breaths matched in pace, there was no shame. Nor was there a taste of regret or confusion from either of them. All I tasted were soft and airy things.

Peace.

I felt their peace.

I felt mine.

And I didn't know if I should feel conflicted about what we'd shared—actually, I did. It struck me then that there wasn't anything I was *supposed* to feel. It didn't matter what I would've thought or felt a year ago. All that counted was what I felt now. What we felt. And that was something good. *Right*. Peaceful.

Beautiful.

Casteel moved slightly, turning his head toward mine. A smile tugged at my lips as I felt his mouth brush the crown of my head. His one hand was threaded with mine, resting just below his chest. A silly little part of me even wished we could stay here on the bank of the river, beneath the wisterias, remaining in this slice of the realm that we had somehow carved out for ourselves that now belonged to us.

But we couldn't. The world waited just a few feet away, and all the things I wouldn't allow myself to think about earlier awaited.

Kieran moved, easing his arm out from under Casteel and me, and then I remembered. I twisted at the waist. "The mark on your arm?"

Pausing, Kieran lifted his left arm. "It's gone," he whispered, turning his arm over as bubbly, sugary wonder gathered in the back of my throat.

Relief was a tentative feeling washing through me as I stared at his unmarred skin. "Do you think that means the Joining usurped the curse?"

"I don't know," Casteel said, his voice thick. "I don't think we'll know unless Isbeth attempts to renege on the deal and refuses to lift it."

"Which means we still need to bring her Malec." My gaze lifted to Kieran's.

He nodded. "I know you don't want to wait and see," he said, and he was correct. "But I think it means we have to continue as planned."

"Just to be sure." I bit down on my lower lip as I laid my head back on Casteel's chest. I knew the Joining had worked. We'd all seen the silver cords. The mark was gone on Kieran's skin, but no one knew if a Joining could counteract the power of a Primal curse. "Do either of you feel different?"

Casteel cleared his throat. "I did feel...tingly."

My brows knitted. "I'm not sure if that's a serious answer or you just being indecent."

"When am I *not* being indecent?" Casteel asked with a chuckle.

"That's a good point," Kieran said, resting his hand on my shoulder. "But I think this is a rare time when he was only being slightly indecent. Because I know what he's talking about. I felt...tingly, too. All over."

"When the cords were wrapped around us," Casteel added, turning his head toward mine. "I felt it inside me. Warm." He paused. "*Tingly.*"

I grinned. "And how about now?"

"Normal," Kieran answered.

Casteel's thumb swept over the top of my hand. "Indecent."

"So, no different?" I surmised.

"Nope."

Kieran's hand slipped from my shoulder as he sat up farther, stopping to drop a kiss where his hand had been before rising. The sweetness of the act tugged at my heart. I lifted my cheek just enough to see him walking toward the river. "What's he doing?"

Casteel's arm lifted, curling around my shoulders, replacing the lack of heat I felt due to Kieran's absence. "I think he's going for a swim."

My eyes widened as Kieran did just that. Walked straight out into the rushing water and dove under, resurfacing a few seconds later. "That water has to be so cold."

"It's not that bad." Kieran looked over his shoulder at us as glistening water coursed down his neck and spine. "You two should try it."

I shook my head.

"Thanks, but I really don't need all my fun bits freezing off," Casteel replied as he trailed little circles over my shoulder and upper arm.

"Cowards," Kieran taunted as he waded out farther.

Casteel chuckled. "Poppy will get upset if her favorite part of me becomes damaged."

I rolled my eyes as Kieran laughed. "You're ridiculous," I muttered.

"But you love me." Casteel rolled, shifting me onto my back as half his body came down over mine. "And especially all my ridiculousness."

I placed my hand on the center of his chest. "I do."

The dimple on his right cheek appeared as he caught a lock of my hair and tucked it back from my face. "How are *you* feeling? And I'm not asking if you're tingly inside."

"I feel...normal." I reached up, curling my fingers into the soft strands of his hair.

"Could use a little more detail, my Queen. What does *normal* mean for you?"

"It means I feel okay. Not regretful." I trailed my fingers across his face to the small indent in his right cheek. "I don't feel ashamed. I'm relieved we did the Joining. I pray that it worked, and I…I enjoyed all of it."

Casteel's eyes searched mine intently. "I'm so fucking glad to hear that."

"Did you think I'd regret it?"

"I didn't think you would—or at least I hoped not," he told me, his voice quiet as he traced the line of my jaw. "Thinking about something, and then doing it, and then *feeling* it afterward are three very different things."

He was right. "And you?"

"How do I feel about it all?" Lowering his head, he kissed the bridge of my nose. "You're asking when you already know?"

I mushed my lips together.

Casteel chuckled. "I feel honored, *meyaah Liessa*. Humbled." His lips brushed the corner of mine. "Awed. Relieved. Chosen. Yes, I feel chosen. Loved." He nipped at my lower lip, sending a bolt of heat through me. "*Intrigued.*" Lifting his head, I saw that the other dimple had taken form. "But back to that tingly part." He drew his hand down my arm, grazing the curve of my breast with the tips of his fingers. "Are you feeling that?"

"I'm always feeling that when it comes to you."

"Knew it," he murmured, kissing me once more. This one was longer, deeper, and languid. "I'm thinking about tempting fate with freezing my interesting bits and joining Kieran. Come with?"

I shook my head. "I think I'll stay right here."

"You sure?"

"Yes." When he hesitated, I gave him a little shove. "Go."

Dipping his head, I opened for him and got lost enough in his parting kiss that taking a dip in the frigid waters didn't sound like a bad idea. Casteel rose, stopping to pick up one of the discarded cloaks. He knelt, motioning for me to sit up. As I did, he draped it over my shoulders, pulling the halves closed around me.

"By the way," he said, tucking his fingers under my chin, "you're beautiful when you're like this, wrapped in nothing more than a cloak. As beautiful as you are when you're draped in fine silks and dressed in breeches and a tunic. And tonight, when you moved between us? When you opened yourself to us?" he said, and my breath caught, "and your essence spilled out from you, surrounding us? Entering us? Entering *me*? I felt *worthy* of such a beautiful gift as you."

Tears filled my eyes as he kissed me softly. I couldn't speak as he straightened, and I watched him walk into the river, joining Kieran. Blinking back the dampness, I curled my fingers around the edges of the cloak and brought it to my chin. I watched Casteel and Kieran, standing waist-deep in the water, and hoped both knew just how worthy they were.

How lucky I was.

And as I pulled the cloak tighter, desperately ignoring the hollowness slowly returning like an unwanted visitor, I prayed to gods that slept that I was worthy of them.

I woke at dawn the following day, wrapped tightly in Casteel's arms. It wasn't long before he eased me onto my back and we came together slowly, kissing and exploring as if we had all the time in the world.

We didn't.

A clock was counting down, ticking away minutes and seconds, but as the cool, gray rays of dawn seeped into the chamber, we cherished each of those heartbeats deeply.

"When will you speak to your father?" I asked as I sat on the bed, eyes closed as Casteel dragged the brush through my hair.

"Soon," he answered.

I arched a brow. "We leave for the Bone Temple in a few hours, so I hope *soon* is actually soon."

"It will be." He gently worked the brush through a tangle. "How in the world did your hair get so knotted from walking a handful of feet?"

I snorted. "That is a question I have asked a thousand times."

His laugh was soft and sweet, and I smiled, loving the sound as much as I loved him. He was quiet as he managed to untangle the hair and then moved on to another section. "My father is not going to be happy with what we have decided."

No, he would not be.

After returning from the banks of the River of Rhain, we'd spent the better part of yesterday morning in bed, sleeping...and definitely *not* sleeping. Then we finally managed to do the responsible thing and meet with the generals to discuss our plans in more detail. Casteel and I had decided on some things that had needed to be shared.

None of us knew what Isbeth truly planned or what she was capable of as a demis, and since I was days or possibly weeks away from completing the Culling, I was—as much as it ate away at Casteel to acknowledge—not infallible. I could be gravely wounded...or worse. Which also meant that Casteel and Kieran...

The mere thought of that made me want to hurl, but it was a reality. And because of that, it also meant leadership needed to be in place. Thankfully, there already was.

Vonetta *was* the Crown Regent.

In the event that neither Casteel nor I could rule, Vonetta would ascend the throne. She needed to be healthy and whole for that to occur. So, Casteel and I had...asserted our authority and ordered Vonetta to remain at Padonia with a decent force of about fifty thousand soldiers. Of course, she had not been at all pleased to hear that, but when the reality of what it meant hit her, she had appeared as if she'd needed to sit down.

It wasn't the shock of realizing that she would rule Atlantia that had her taking several short breaths. It was the realization of what would have to occur to cause that.

And Casteel would, as Kieran had put it when we'd spoken to him about what we'd decided, pull rank again when it came to his father.

"Finished." Casteel laid the heavy length of hair over my shoulder as he bent, kissing the nape of my neck.

"Thank you."

"My pleasure." He climbed off the bed with a level of grace I would never master, probably not even as a Primal.

My gaze roamed the defined lines of his chest and stomach as he pulled on the black tunic that would be worn under armor, relieved to see that he had filled out even more. In a day or so, I imagined he would be back to his normal weight. What my blood could do for him was really a miracle.

He returned to where I sat to put on his boots. "I'm going to talk to him now."

"Do you want me with you?" I asked.

Casteel shook his head. "Probably best if you're not." He glanced at me as he tightened the buckles on his boots. "He'll probably want to bring up the shit he and my mother should've said ages ago. Then I'll look at you and think about how differently things could've gone for us if we had known the truth, and then I'll want to punch him."

"Don't punch your father, Casteel."

A faint grin appeared as he moved on to his other boot. "Is that an order, my Queen?"

"It really shouldn't have to be one."

"But?"

"Yes."

He leaned over, stealing a quick kiss. "Kieran will be with me. He won't let me punch him."

Thinking of how Kieran had let Casteel repeatedly punch his brother, I wasn't so sure about that.

"Meet you in the receiving hall?" Casteel touched my cheek. I nodded, and this kiss…it was long enough to leave me wishing we had more time.

After Casteel had left, I braided my hair and rose, putting on similar attire as he had dressed in. The leggings were almost as thick as breeches, and I tucked the black shirt into them, opting for a vest brocaded in gold to wear over it. Strapping the wolven-bone dagger to my thigh, I smiled as I thought about how ill-fitting Isbeth would believe the clothing to be for a Queen. I didn't don any armor or remove the crowns from their box. That would come later. Leaving the chamber, I made a quick stop in the kitchens, grabbing a muffin, and then roamed outside, giving Casteel ample time to speak to his father.

I caught sight of Thad perched on the Rise that overlooked the stables, his wings tucked close to his narrow, brownish-black body. I followed his watchful stare, my heart skipping.

Finishing off the muffin, I crossed the overgrown courtyard and entered the stables. Only a few horses remained inside, as most were with the soldiers, being outfitted with armor. I stopped to give Setti a sugar cube and shower him with affection before walking to the back of the structure. Straw crunched under my feet as I reached out, holding the pole as I turned the corner.

Malec's wooden casket remained in the wagon, ready to be led out the closed stable doors behind it. Several lengths of dull, whitish-gray bones lay across the top, and I realized that several bone spurs had embedded themselves in the wood.

Folding an arm over my waist, I suppressed a shiver. The casket. Malec's presence. It had an impact that was hard not to notice, chilling the air. Tiny goosebumps rose all over my skin. I inched closer, holding my breath like a silly child as I reached out, pressing my palm against the casket.

The wood was *warm*.

I pulled my hand back, pressing it against my chest where the eather hummed, and the cold place inside me ached.

Would the wood that entombed me be cold?

I sucked in a sharp breath, unsettled by my dark thoughts. Malec's fate wasn't mine—

Unsheathing the dagger at the soft crunch of straw, I whipped around.

Malik stood in the hall outside the stall, his eyes wide behind a lock of sandy brown hair that had fallen in front of them. "Jumpy?"

"I'd rather call it careful," I said, lowering the dagger but not putting it away. No one else was with him. "You're out here alone?"

"Not supposed to be." A half-grin appeared, one so similar to Casteel's it was a little bizarre. "But I'm really good at being where I'm not supposed to be."

"Uh-huh."

"I'm sure Naill will realize soon enough that I'm not in my cell—er, I mean my *chambers*," he amended.

I watched him draw closer. "Why are you out here?"

"Saw you heading this way from the window." He stopped at the back of the wagon and did the same as I did, placing his hand on the casket. He showed no reaction to the temperature, which made me wonder.

"Does the wood feel warm to you?"

He shook his head. "Does it to you?"

I started to answer but shrugged. "I hope you aren't out here trying to do something to him in an attempt to stop us."

Malik laughed roughly. "Can't say it hasn't crossed my mind."

"You'd risk Kieran like that?" I demanded, my stomach toppling because I hated—absolutely *hated*—the whole wait-and-see thing surrounding whether or not the Joining had usurped the curse, or if Isbeth would lift it.

"All manner of things have crossed my mind," he answered. "But I prefer to not be burned alive by a draken."

"That shouldn't be the only thing that stops you."

"No, it shouldn't be. And it wouldn't have been before," he said, and I knew he meant before the Blood Queen captured him. "But I'm not the same person I was then," he said, and the faint tang of sadness gathered in my throat.

"You're a person who would sacrifice those who care about you now?"

His lips twisted into a mockery of a smile. "Who would you have sacrificed to free Casteel?"

"I sacrificed none," I told him.

Malik looked at me. "You didn't?"

I stiffened. "I will free my father."

A long moment passed. "But you and I both know that if you had to choose, there would be no choice." His gaze flicked to the casket. "To be honest, I'm relieved to hear that. Casteel deserves someone who will burn the realm for him."

"And you don't?"

He let out a dry laugh. "Is that a serious question?"

I studied his coolly handsome features. "You subjected yourself to decades of the gods only know what for Millicent. Would she not do the same for you?"

Malik laughed again, and this time, it was real. "No. She's more likely to set me afire than a realm."

My brows flew open. "You said you were heartmates—"

"We are." He angled his body toward me. "But she doesn't know that."

Confusion rose, and then I remembered him saying that he'd done unimaginable things that she would never know about. "How doesn't she know?"

"She just doesn't."

"Then how do *you* know?"

His head inclined. "You ask a lot of questions."

"So I've been told."

"Has anyone ever told you that asking questions is a sign of intelligence?"

"I haven't needed to be told that," I said. "Because I already know."

Malik smiled then. "I just know."

Sensing that I wouldn't get much more out of him about that subject, I moved on to things I was more curious about. "Do you think Millicent will be there with Isbeth when we meet with her?"

His shoulders tightened. "Gods, I hope not. But she probably will be. Isbeth will likely demand her presence."

I nibbled on my lower lip as I stared at the bone chains. "Why hasn't Millicent tried to stop her?"

"What makes you think she hasn't?" Malik countered. "You've seen what Isbeth can do. Millie is strong, she's fierce, but she is not a demis."

He had a point, but... "Then why didn't she try to kill me? She believes I'm the Harbinger, right? She had an opportunity, as did you— especially when I was younger."

"Millie has never tried to convince herself that she could kill a child or her *sister*." Malik's stare bore through me. "She is not evil just because she's Isbeth's daughter."

But they apparently thought *I* was. "And what about you? You were evil enough to think you could do it."

"I was desperate enough." Malik paused. "And broken enough that I latched onto any purpose."

I remembered what Casteel had said to him. "Your bonded wolven? Preela? How did that break you?"

"Jalara killed her in front of me," he answered so flatly that I almost thought the swirl of grief was mine. "It wasn't quick or honorable what he and the others did to her." He faced me. "And you don't have to ask what that was. You carry a part of her with you. You hold it in your hand even now."

Slowly, I looked down at the bloodstone dagger I held—the *wolven*-bone grip that never warmed to my touch. "No."

Malik said nothing.

My gaze flew to his. "How would you even know?"

"I saw each one made of her bones. I will never forget what they look like."

A tremor ran through my hand.

"And it was gifted to Coralena, who in turn, gave it to Leopold," he continued, a muscle ticking under his temple. "How you came into possession of it afterward, I am curious to know."

"Vikter gave it to me," I whispered. "He was a *viktor*, too."

Malik smiled tightly. "Well, it sounds like *fate* to me, doesn't it?"

46

Casteel

From the window of the receiving hall, I watched several soldiers riding toward the Rise to join the rest of the armies outside Padonia's gates.

Two hundred thousand men and women prepared to end this war. Ready to fight. Ready to die. The weight of their loyalty and determination sat heavier on my shoulders and chest than the armor I now wore.

Kieran silently joined me at the window, his shoulder brushing mine. I glanced at him. He was dressed in black trimmed in gold but without the armor. He'd trimmed his hair at some point since I'd last seen him. My gaze dropped to his arm, where the cut had been. The Joining had worked. As close as Kieran and I had always been, our hearts had never shared the same beat, not even with the bond. But had it usurped the curse?

The kick in my heart echoed in his. He looked at me. "Do I want to know what's on your mind?"

He didn't need to know, as I was sure it already preyed on his mind enough.

I turned back to the window. "I was thinking about how I want to see every single one of these soldiers live to see the realm at peace." That wasn't a lie. "But I know not all will."

He nodded. "I'd tell you the same thing I've told Poppy, but you already know what that is since you were the one who told me when we first left Atlantia."

I knew what he spoke of. "You cannot save everyone, but you can save the ones you love," I said. "And how did Poppy respond to that?"

One side of his lips rose. "You're here, aren't you?"

"As are you."

"Exactly." There was a pause. "I summoned your father as you asked. He comes now. You still plan to pull rank?"

I nodded.

"He's not going to like it."

"I know, but he will have to deal with it." Taking a deep breath, I turned as my father entered the receiving hall along with Lord Sven, his helmet he wouldn't need tucked under his arm.

"You called for me?" my father asked, and the lines at the corners of his eyes seemed deeper than they had been even the day before.

It was a surreal feeling to be the one summoning my father.

Kieran turned to stand shoulder to shoulder with me as I said, "There's something that I didn't discuss with you yesterday."

My father inclined his head, but the sudden narrowing of Sven's eyes told me the damn man had a good idea what I was about to say. His jaw tightened, but he gave a quick, curt nod that my father didn't see.

"The Queen and I..." I started, and my father immediately tensed at the formal use of our titles. Being King for so long, he knew that what I was about to say brooked little room for argument. "Have decided that with Netta remaining in Padonia as regent, she will need strong leadership to stand beside her."

Two red splotches appeared on his cheeks. "Cas—"

"Someone the remaining armies and the people of Atlantia trust," I continued, my voice hardening as I held his stare. "And that the regent can lean on for support if neither the Queen nor I is able to rule."

My father sucked in a sharp breath, those splotches rapidly disappearing.

"You know that's possible," I said. Something I hated to even acknowledge, but it was a harsh reality, nonetheless. Poppy hadn't completed her Culling. Technically, she was still a god, and gods were easier to kill than Primals. If she were struck down, Kieran and I would go down with her.

Hell, I would go down, even if we weren't Joined.

"Of course, it is a possibility," my father stated. "But there's Jasper."

"Jasper has never led any of the armies," Sven intervened. "Yes, he has the trust of the people of Atlantia, but he's not in a position to lead any armies that remain."

A muscle ticked in my father's temple. "And you think I'm worthy of that trust?" he asked me.

I stiffened. "I believe you would guide the regent toward what is best for the kingdom and wouldn't be foolish enough to repeat your mistakes."

He glanced at Kieran. "Your advisor should remain—"

"If our failure on the field occurs, Kieran won't be able to support the regent," I cut him off.

Understanding flared in his eyes, as did a bit of relief. He knew what I'd meant, and he also knew that I, along with Kieran, would be afforded more protection than anyone on that battlefield. "I am to remain while both my sons ride into battle?"

"Yes," I said. "As it should be."

He was quiet for a long moment, and then he exhaled a ragged breath. "If this is an order, then I will obey."

My head tilted. "You don't really have a choice."

His shoulders tensed. "Answer one thing, as a son to his father. Is it only the trust of the people and my experience that has guided this decision?"

My father and I needed to discuss a lot of things once we saw this war to the end. And even though we planned for the possibility that we wouldn't succeed, we did so only because that was what a responsible Queen and King did. However, no part of me didn't believe there would be an after. Still, I said what I needed to say anyway. "You're the one who taught me that I cannot save everyone," I began. "But I can save those I love."

Poppy entered with Tawny and Vonetta not long after the meeting with my father, but I only became aware of her because my heart stuttered. I wasn't sure if that came from Kieran or me. Because he too stared as I did.

Her thick braid, the color of wine, lay over the armor fitted from the shoulders to the hips. Greaves protected her thighs and shins. The hilt of a sword was visible, resting above her left hip. Nothing was different about her armor or the white mantle draped across her back. No special embellishments or marks outside of the golden Atlantian Crest painted upon the breastplate of all our armor. But no one looked as regal as she did—or as strong.

Poppy looked like a Goddess of War—no, a *Primal* of War.

A dart of pure, unadulterated, and red-hot lust clenched my stomach at the sight of her crossing before the windows lining the hall. The feeling was almost as powerful as the wave of respect. Every step she took was steeped not in the confidence of a Queen but that of a soldier, one who, like *her* soldiers, was prepared to fight to the death.

The corners of her lips curved up just a little as her eyes locked on mine, and a faint blush crept across the scar on her cheek. I didn't even try to hide what I felt. I wanted her to know just how fucking magnificent I knew her to be as I crossed the remaining distance between us.

Taking her hands in mine, I bent so my mouth was at her ear as I whispered, "I want to fuck you in this armor. Can we make that possible?"

The catch of her breath brought a smile to my face. "That may be uncomfortable for you."

"Worth it." I kissed the scar along her temple and straightened. "I spoke to my father."

The pink began to fade from her cheeks, but her heart still pounded. As did mine. As did Kieran's. "How did he take it?"

"About as well as you'd expect," I told her, glancing at the cigar box Netta held.

"Better than I thought," Kieran said, coming to our side. He reached over, tugging on the tail of Poppy's braid. She sent him a grin.

"I hope that's true," Netta said. "Because I'm the one who's going to be stuck with him for the foreseeable future."

"What do you have in that box?" I asked.

Tawny arched a brow. "I was wondering the same thing."

"The crowns," Netta answered, holding the box for me. "Poppy left without them. I'm not sure if she actually forgot or if it was intentional."

Poppy lifted a shoulder.

"Oh." Tawny's eyes widened, and I noticed that a bit of color had begun to fill them. "I haven't even seen them."

I lifted the lid, and Tawny's soft inhale followed. The golden bones sat side by side, gleaming in the sunlight streaming in through the window.

"They're beautiful." Tawny looked up at Poppy. "I would wear that every day and night. Even to bed."

My brow rose as I realized that I hadn't made love to Poppy yet with the crown upon her head. A slow smile began to creep across my face. Poppy's gaze shot to mine.

Kieran sighed. "You have, likely unintentionally, given Cas ideas."

"I'm curious about these ideas," Tawny remarked as I took out one crown.

"No, you're not," Poppy quickly said.

"Hold still," I murmured to Poppy as I placed the crown upon her head. "Perfect."

Tawny watched Poppy lift the remaining crown. "Are they made of actual bones?"

"They are," I answered.

"For real?" Tawny didn't appear as enamored with the crowns as she had a few moments before.

Poppy cringed as I lowered my head. "I try not to think about that."

"Whose bones are they?" she asked.

"I don't think anyone knows the answer to that," Kieran said. "All we know is that they're not deity bones. Some believe they're the bones of a god."

"Or a Primal," Netta added. "But they only reveal their true appearance when a deity or god sits upon the throne." She paused. "Or a Primal."

Poppy placed the crown on my head. "There," she whispered, her eyes glimmering as her hands lingered for a moment. Our eyes met, and the whole damn realm fell away. "Now, it's perfect."

Emotion clogged my throat and seized my chest. It wasn't the crown upon my head that worked me over but the hands that had placed it there.

A horn blew from outside the Rise. I touched Poppy's cheek and then stepped back, giving her a few moments with Netta and Tawny before it was time to part ways. My father reappeared, joining Netta and Tawny as we walked outside where our horses had been readied for us, and Naill and Emil waited with the wolven. The gray steed next to Setti was of his bloodline. Phobas had been named after the Goddess of Peace and Vengeance's warhorse. I'd been surprised to see him here, but he would make a fine horse for Poppy.

Another horn blew, and white-and-gold banners lifted all along the road leading to the gates of Padonia and beyond. The three of us stopped at the top of the stairs. The wolven bowed their heads as a low rumble echoed from the wisteria trees. Unable to stop myself, I looked up. Four shadows fell over the lines of soldiers as Poppy reached between us, taking Kieran's and my hands in hers.

"From blood and ash," I shouted, lifting the hand joined with Poppy's. People echoed the words through the town and the valley.

Poppy looked up at me and then faced the crowd as she lifted the hand that held Kieran's. "We have risen!"

Poppy

The two-day ride to the Bone Temple, which took us through a narrow section of the Blood Forest, was mostly without incident. There were Craven attacks, but they had been dealt with quickly as General Murin and his forces rejoined us, along with La'Sere's division, having ridden from Whitebridge and Three Rivers.

Our armies had camped just outside the Blood Forest for the night, and as the moonlight lit up the ceiling of the tent, Casteel drank from the vein at my neck, and I, upon his reassurance that he had recovered enough, took blood from the cut he made on his chest. The intimate act had become as natural as breathing, and there'd been no hesitation as he guided my lips to where his blood welled.

And his taste…

Like always, it was bright, like citrus in the snow, and it heated my veins along with that hollow place inside as he moved over me and then inside me, his blood on my tongue, and my name a whisper on his lips. I fell asleep wrapped in his arms and woke in the middle of the night, disorientated from the dream I'd had. I only remembered bits and pieces of it. The back of a woman wearing a crown of black diamonds on her silvery hair, sitting on a throne much like the one I'd seen at the Temple of Nyktos. She had been *weeping*. There was also a man with sandy-blond hair standing to her left. Something about him was so familiar. He had begun to turn and spoke just a word. But I woke before I could see his face.

Still, the sadness of the dream gathered like tart ale in my throat. The woman... It had been the Consort. I knew it. And the man...

He had *felt* like Vikter.

But even if he were a *viktor*, why would I have seen him with the Consort? That didn't make sense. Slowly, I became aware of the rolled blankets under half my body, and the toasty heat pressed to my front and back. All thoughts of the strange dream vanished.

My cheek was nestled in the crook of Casteel's shoulder, and I was tangled up with him as if I were some kind of tree bear, my leg tossed over his, and his arm curled around my waist. He held me tightly, as if even in sleep, he was afraid I would somehow slip away from him.

But he wasn't the only source of heat.

I dragged in a deep, heady breath that carried the scent of spice, lush pine, and earthy cedar and was immediately reminded of the mist-heavy night in the Skotos Mountains.

Kieran slept behind me.

I didn't know when he'd joined us, but his leg was tucked between mine, his arm just below Casteel's on my hip. My eyes fluttered open. In the faint moonlight seeping through the canvas of the tent, I saw my hand and Kieran's, his resting below mine on Casteel's stomach.

There was no space between the three of us. Not even an inch. I felt each of their breaths, steady and deep, and was sure if I concentrated hard enough, I would learn that like our hearts, our breaths were set to the same pattern.

I knew then, like the night in the mountains, that I had turned to Casteel, and so had Kieran. Casteel had his own gravitational pull that we both responded to in sleep. Also, like that night, nothing felt sinful about how we were...snuggled together. The only thing different now was that it felt natural. Well, that and the fact that we were Joined.

I waited for embarrassment to creep in. Soldiers and wolven were all around us. Many had to know that Kieran had entered the tent, but there was no shame. Instead, it felt as if it were meant to be this way. And thinking that was a sure sign that I should probably make myself go back to sleep.

Or punch myself.

Because it sounded silly.

Could I knock myself out?

Gods, I was almost willing to find out.

I closed my eyes, but sleep didn't come, no matter how warm I was. Or how safe I felt nestled between them. It was easy to forget what awaited.

Kieran moved behind me, and my breath snagged in my chest. The furs Casteel had tucked around me were between Kieran and me, but the slight shift of his body caused his leg to slide farther between mine. His movement stirred Casteel enough that his arm tightened around me, his fingers pushing into my hip for a few brief seconds. I bit down on my lip as my pulse skittered at the press of Kieran's thigh and the feel of Casteel's body against mine. A rush of shivery awareness swept through me. I kept my eyes closed as I…

I didn't know what I was doing, but my mind had shamefully skipped its way back to the night on the banks of the River of Rhain as my fingers curled against Casteel's stomach. Kieran settled after a few seconds, his chest rising and falling steadily as I lay there, completely still.

Seconds ticked into minutes, and my mind began to wander with the sound of rustling leaves and the muffled snores of those lucky enough to sleep. Something occurred to me then. Of all the times that Kieran had slept beside me while Casteel was gone, he'd only been in his mortal form once, and that was the night I'd asked him to put me in the ground if I became something to fear. I didn't know what it meant or if it said anything at all. But nothing and everything had changed between the three of us since the Joining. Our relationship remained as it had been, but there was an intimacy now that hadn't been there before. A closeness. A bond we were reminded of every time I felt our hearts beating in tandem. I really wished I was asleep and not thinking—

Fingers touched my chin, startling me. My eyes flew open as my head was tilted back. The faint burn of gold pierced the shadows of the night. My heart sped up as Casteel drew his thumb along my lower lip. I started to apologize for waking him, but he lowered his head, brushing his lips across mine. The kiss was soft and so very sweet. I could never pick a favorite kiss of his, but these...*these* were special, tasting of love and devotion.

But so were the deeper kisses, the dark ones full of need and yearning. And that was what this kiss became. His tongue slipped between my lips and moved against mine, silencing any sound I would've made. His arm tightened around my waist, his fingers at my hip pressing in harder, drawing me even closer and sending a wholly ill-advisable dart of wanton pleasure through me.

Casteel's lips left mine, but they didn't go far. "Sleep, my Queen."

"Both of you need to go to sleep." Kieran's low voice rumbled against my back.

My eyes went wide, even as I felt Casteel's lips curve into a grin against mine. "Sleep," he repeated, kissing me once more before guiding my cheek back to his shoulder. His hand left my chin and slid down his chest to my hand. To Kieran's beneath mine. To both of ours. Casteel hadn't used compulsion, but my eyes shut, and I drifted back to sleep with our three hands joined.

47

We crested the last of the Niel Valley just as the sun began to set, turning the sky a deep, violet-blue. Kieran rode to Casteel's right, and Delano and the wolven traveled alongside me as the northern portion of the Rise surrounding Carsodonia came into view. The area of the Bone Temple and Pensdurth sat at a much higher elevation than Carsodonia, much like Masadonia, and the air was a little cooler and less humid. With my hands steady on Phobas's reins, I looked at Sage.

The wolven cut away from the pack, followed by General Sven's and Murin's divisions, heading for the front gates of Carsodonia as planned. The draken remained in the heavily forested area at our backs, since we weren't sure if the Blood Crown had learned how many draken had survived the attack. In case they hadn't, we wanted that detail to remain unknown. With the draken's speed in the air, it would only take minutes for them to reach us once needed.

I glanced behind me to where Hisa and several Crown Guards rode beside the wagon. I'd kept checking on the wagon, almost as if I expected the casket containing Malec to disappear somehow.

Which was as silly as most of the thoughts I'd had in the middle of the night.

Our hearts were calm as we continued forward, carefully watched by the guards along the Rise. Their bows were readied, but none had fired upon us as we rode on, our Atlantian banners rippling in the faintly sea-salted breeze. The silence was unnerving, shattered by the horns blaring from the corners of the Rise. The same ones that blew when they spotted the mist. I wondered if the people were seeking shelter in their homes, hiding this time from who they'd been led to believe was the Harbinger of Death and Destruction instead of the Craven.

My gaze lifted to the archers on the Rise, and my senses swept out. Bitter fear gathered in my throat, stroking the restlessly stirring eather. "They're afraid."

"As they should be," Casteel commented, and I dragged my attention from them, focusing on my King. He also eyed them. "Atlantian armies have never traveled this far west."

"Not even in the War of Two Kings," Kieran added. "Most of those guards up there have probably never even *seen* an Atlantian or a wolven—or were aware that they had."

"They'll probably be shocked that we look like them," Emil said from behind us, where he rode with Naill and Malik. "And not like the Craven."

"All that is likely true," I said. "And it means that when this is over, after we've ended the Blood Crown, we need to prove to the people of Carsodonia and the rest of Solis that we are not the monsters they have been warned about. It won't be as easy as it was in Padonia or any of the cities farther east," I reasoned, though I wouldn't say any but Padonia had been particularly *easy*.

"We will." Casteel's gaze found mine. "It will take time, but time is what we will have on our side."

I nodded. We had time, but so did all the Ascended who'd fled their cities, either abandoning them or leaving nothing but death behind. They were behind those walls now. They too would need to be dealt with.

But it was what waited before us that needed all of our attention now.

The Bone Temple lined the horizon, a sprawling structure built upon thousands of heavy blocks of stone which held the bodies of the entombed Priests and Priestesses. The Temple was as tall as the Rise itself, with marble and limestone pillars that stretched even higher, and steep steps that climbed the north and south sides. Vines smothered the ones to the east and west and had even begun to climb the pillars.

"Well," Naill drawled as the grounds beyond the Temple came into view. "It looks like the Blood Queen brought a few friends along with her."

"She most definitely did," Casteel murmured. "Not unexpected."

And it wasn't. There was no way Isbeth would meet us in the open like this without substantial forces. Just as we hadn't.

In the rising moonlight, the ground looked red beyond the Temple, blocking the northern gates and spreading as far as the eye could see. Soldiers in black and crimson armor stood shield to shield, their faces covered by helmets or gaiters.

"What are we looking at?" Casteel asked as we drew closer.

I let my senses sweep out. A mixture of varying degrees of emotion came back to me. Salty resolve. Vast nothingness. Fear. A shallower emptiness from those shielding their emotions. "Mortals, knights, and Revenants," I told them.

"How incredibly diverse of the Blood Queen," Kieran murmured.

My gaze swept to the floor of the Temple. I couldn't see who was there. Was Millicent with our mother? Would she intervene on her behalf once it became clear what we planned? Or would she aid us?

Casteel gave the signal, and the horses slowed before stopping as we neared the foot of the Temple. He looked over at me, and I took a shallow breath, nodding.

Loosening my grip on the reins, I dismounted as Casteel did the same. The others who would join us at the Temple followed as Casteel went to where the generals waited. "Remember the plan," he said. "The wolven will alert you when it's time."

General Aylard and Sven nodded as Naill and Emil carefully unloaded Malec's casket from the wagon.

"Be careful," Sven called to us.

Remembering what I'd heard before, I replied with, "But be brave."

Hisa caught my eye and grinned as she helped Naill and Emil. I smiled as Casteel caught Malik by the arm. The curve of my lips faded.

"Stay close to me," Casteel spoke, his voice low as he met his brother's stare. "Don't do anything that could jeopardize what we're doing here or your life."

Malik's expression was stoic, but he nodded.

"You could at least smile," Kieran said to Malik as Casteel let go of his arm. "At least you have a sword this time."

"Gee, thanks," Malik muttered as Casteel shot him a look a wise person would've shut up upon receiving. "You know, for allowing me to have the bare minimum protection."

"How about you stop bitching and help us?" Naill grunted. "For a sleeping god, the fucker sure is heavy."

Cursing under his breath, Malik went to the front of the casket. "Maybe it's not that he's heavy. It's just that you are all weak."

"Say that again," Hisa warned, her eyes flashing a sharp amber from above the face guard of her helmet, "and I will kick your ass."

Malik said nothing as he helped lower the casket to the ground, but his lips twitched as a sugary taste gathered in my mouth.

"What is it with the Da'Neer men and being amused when women threaten them?" I asked.

Kieran snorted, taking my hand and turning me to face him. "It probably has a complicated answer," he said, carefully taking hold of my crown and lifting it so it didn't snag in my hair. Neither Casteel nor I would wear our crowns. We would already be targets on the field, and we didn't need anything making it easier to pinpoint us. "Buried in deeply rooted issues that span many generations."

"I find that *deeply* offensive," Casteel remarked, coming to us as I smiled.

"Sure, you do." Kieran took my crown, placing it in the box that a Crown Guard held—a much more ornate, wooden, engraved thing with the Atlantian Crest. I supposed people had gotten tired of seeing the crowns in a cigar box. He then turned to Casteel and removed his crown with the same gentleness, placing it beside mine. He looked between us as the guard mounted his horse and rode off to keep the crowns safe. "Are we ready?"

Casteel looked down at me. "My Queen?"

My pulse increased slightly, and a flutter of nervous anticipation bloomed in my chest. The essence thrummed. "Yes."

"Then it's time." Casteel's mouth brushed mine. His lips tasted of the salty breeze as he took my left hand. His thumb ran over the dazzling, golden swirl. "We will end this tonight, one way or another. And then, I'm going to find that diamond I told you about." He kissed me again. "But before that, I'm going to get what I want. You. In the armor."

"Gods," Kieran half sighed, half laughed.

Casteel's lips curved into a smile against mine. "It's not like you aren't thinking it."

My eyes went wide as Kieran sounded as if he choked on his breath. What I suddenly felt from him while Casteel chuckled wasn't embarrassment. It was sharp and heavy, too fleeting for me to latch onto. My eyes narrowed on Kieran as Casteel took my hand. "Are you shielding your emotions?"

"I would never do such a thing," Kieran replied, his expression one of pure innocence."

"Uh-huh," I muttered as Casteel led us around the wagon and toward the Temple.

The moment we began our climb of the steep steps, followed by Delano and the other wolven, whatever Kieran was or wasn't feeling slipped to the background. What was about to happen was bigger than me—than Casteel *and* me. Even bigger than Kieran. The future of the kingdoms rested on what happened tonight. There was no way to mentally prepare for this. Not when I'd been in the veil not so long ago and only known as the Maiden. My heart beat as fast as it had when we rode up to the Rise of Oak Ambler and a fine tremor ran through me.

As we neared the top of the steps, and just about when my legs felt as if they would turn to liquid, Casteel halted. He turned to me and squeezed my hand. "Remember what we told you in Evaemon?"

I shook my head, my thoughts racing far too much to even begin to recall what he could possibly be referencing.

His eyes caught mine, the gold glimmering in the starlight. "You have faced Craven and vampprys, men wearing masks of mortal flesh. Stared down Atlantians who've wanted to harm you, seized cities, and freed me," he said, touching my cheek. "You're more than a Queen. More than a goddess on the verge of becoming a Primal. You're Penellaphe Da'Neer, and you're fearless."

My breath snagged in my chest.

Kieran touched the other side of my cheek, turning my gaze to his. He smiled. "And you run from no one and nothing."

Emotion clogged my throat, and as it had in Evaemon, their words were as powerful as the eather thrumming in my chest.

They were right.

I was brave.

Strong.

And I wasn't afraid.

Nodding, I faced forward as Delano brushed my legs, and several of the wolven prowled past us. I lifted my chin and straightened my shoulders, my heart steady as we crested the top of the steps.

Delano stayed at my side as the wolven spread out, their bodies sleek under the moonlight as they wove between the pale stone statues of the kneeling gods lining the pathway to *her*.

Draped in a tight-fitting, crimson half-coat and gown, the Blood

Queen stood before an altar once used to display the bodies of the deceased Priests and Priestesses. The ruby and diamond crown upon her head glittered like the stars blanketing the sky, as did the ruby piercing her nose, and the wide, jeweled belt at her waist, visible beneath the halves of her coat. Her lips were as red as her clothing, and as she stood there, she was equally as beautiful as she was horrifying.

My mother.

My enemy.

She wasn't alone. Callum stood to her right, as golden as the sun itself. Dozens of Royal Guards and knights flanked her, and a line of Handmaidens stood behind the altar, but it was one who caught my eye.

Millicent was dressed as the other Handmaidens in a sleeveless crimson tunic fitted to her hips. Slits on either side revealed pants of the same color with daggers sheathed to both thighs. The painted markings were back, swirling up and down her arms, and the deep, reddish-black mask painted upon her face obscured what Casteel had seen. Our shared features. The sides of her hair were braided like mine and swept back to fall down her back, the color a flat, dull black.

One look at her, and I knew she wasn't shielding her emotions. Millicent's unease was strong and tart, mixing with the heaviness of her concern as her attention drifted over the three of us and beyond, to where I suspected she looked for Malik. I had no idea what was going on between them—how or why she disliked him like Malik claimed and yet obviously worried about him. I didn't know where her true loyalties lay, but neither of those things mattered.

Only our mother did.

"You brought an army with you, and you're dressed for battle," the Blood Queen spoke. "Should I be concerned?"

My gaze locked with hers, and I didn't allow myself to search for any sort of feeling toward her. "You should always be concerned."

Isbeth smiled tightly as she stepped forward, her hands clasped at her waist. "I hope you didn't come all this way just to be clever. Where is Malec?"

"We have him, but you need to lift the curse first," I said.

"Or what?" Callum answered.

Delano's head lowered as his lip curled back, and a low growl rumbled from him. I reached for the *notam*, calming him—soothing the others as they prowled across the Temple floor, their instincts riled by so many vamprys and Revenants.

"Or we set his casket on fire," Casteel responded coolly. "And then kill you."

"You keep saying that," the Revenant replied, "yet here I remain."

Casteel turned his head to Callum, and his lips curled in a shadow of a smile. "And here I stand."

"The curse will be lifted once I see that you have Malec with you and he still lives," Isbeth interjected before Callum could. "I need proof that you have fulfilled your end of the bargain before I complete mine."

I glanced at Casteel. He gave me a curt nod, and through the *notam*, I reached out to Rune, who waited with the others. The wolven's response was swift. "He comes."

Isbeth's stare left mine, traveling to the steps as Casteel said, "He remains asleep."

"Of course," she responded with a quick glance. My head cut to my left as Millicent quietly moved forward. "He will until given blood."

I watched Millicent move forward even more, tensing.

"He will sleep deeply until then," Isbeth continued. "Nothing in either realm could wake him at this point."

"And yet, you believe that he will wake upon being fed and then give you what you seek?" Casteel queried as I inched forward, partially blocking him and Kieran.

"I know he will," Isbeth said.

I saw the moment Malik and the others arrived at the top of the Temple steps. Isbeth's hands unlocked. One fluttered to her chest as they traveled between the kneeling, faceless gods. Millicent's steps faltered, and her concern rose, pressing down on my shoulders.

They placed the casket before where we stood, and then Malik and the others stepped back. I moved forward, reaching into the pouch at my hip. My fingers slid over the horse as I withdrew the ring. I placed it on top of the flat surface of the casket, beside the bone chains. Isbeth lifted a hand. Several knights moved forward, their dark, soulless eyes the only parts of them visible as they retrieved the casket, carrying it to the altar as Millicent approached me.

Delano eyed her warily as her pale eyes flicked briefly to Malik and then to me. "Where is the blond?" she questioned quietly. "The one called Reaver. Your draken."

"You worried about where he may be lurking?" Casteel countered as Isbeth turned her back on us.

Millicent didn't look at him. "No." Her eyes remained on me, and as close as we were, it was hard not to notice that we were the same height. "But you should be."

My brows rose while the knights began pulling the bone chains from the casket. "And why is that?"

She looked over her shoulder at the clatter of bones hitting the Temple floor. "Because *she* didn't ask about where he is," she answered, and Kieran's head snapped in her direction. "One would think she'd be concerned about the one thing that could take out a large portion of those on the Temple grounds."

I glanced at the altar. Isbeth was sliding the Atlantian diamond back onto her finger—I wasn't even sure why I'd bothered to return it—as a knight jammed the tip of his sword into the seam of the casket. Wood groaned. It was unlikely that Isbeth was currently aware of where Millicent was at the moment. She was solely focused on the casket, having moved to the other side of the altar. Callum watched, though.

"Nor did she mention the fact that you're about fifty thousand less than you were when you crossed the Niel Valley," Millicent went on, her gaze lowered. Another knight worked at the center of the lid, and I heard another cracking, popping sound. "She is fully aware that they are no longer with you, which could only mean that they have been sent somewhere else."

Focusing on Millicent, a hundred different things rose to the tip of my tongue. There was so much I wanted to know, but all I said was, "I know."

Millicent's gaze flew to mine, and I knew she understood what I meant. That I knew who she was.

One side of her lips twitched and rose and then flattened. "Then you should also know that there is something very wrong about all of this."

Tiny bumps spread out along my arms as the knights freed the top of the casket and lifted the lid. Millicent turned back as they placed it on the floor. The knights all stepped back. Only Isbeth moved forward, and she did so slowly, almost fearfully.

Malik had made his way to Kieran's side. He didn't look at Millicent, but I knew he spoke to her when he whispered, "Are you well?"

I didn't know how Millicent answered. I was completely focused on Isbeth as she clutched the rim of the casket and stared inside. An arrow of raw, pounding agony pierced straight through me, surprising me. The emotion belonged to Isbeth. The Blood Queen shuddered.

What I could see of Malec was...it wasn't good. Strands of dull, reddish-brown hair lay against sunken cheeks. Too-dry lips were parted, peeled back over fangs as if he had lost consciousness while screaming. He was skeletal, and more weathered flesh than man. A husk of whoever he may have once been. And the sight of him, no matter what his actions might have caused, was a pitiful sight.

"Oh, my love," Isbeth whispered and then slipped into a hoarsely spoken language I didn't understand.

"Old Atlantian," Kieran explained.

I may not understand what she said, but I understood the agony mingled with the sweetness of love. The sorrow. There was no relief. No joy or anticipation. Only the bone-deep, icy anguish that hurt more than any physical pain.

"As you can see, we have held up our end of the deal," Casteel said, silencing Isbeth. "Lift the curse."

Isbeth didn't move or respond for what felt like an eternity. My heart seized. If she didn't do as she'd promised and the Joining hadn't usurped the curse...

I reached down, grabbing Kieran's hand. He was stoic, his emotions shielded, while Casteel was a rapidly building storm of rage.

Then Isbeth nodded.

Callum came forward, driving Millicent back and away. Her reaction to him was unsettling. I'd seen her handle Delano in his mortal form as if he were nothing more than a child. But this Revenant was supposedly old—really old. The essence stirred as he drew close. Through the *notam*, I nudged Delano back.

"Lift the wounded arm," Callum requested with a pleasant smile. The Revenant was utterly unfazed by the wolven's and Elementals' glares.

I let go of Kieran's hand, and he did as Callum requested. The Revenant cocked his head to the side. "The mark of the curse?" One wing rose as he looked down at me. The smile spread. "It's gone."

"It is," Casteel answered.

"It shouldn't be."

"And?" Casteel's voice was soft, in the way that was always a warning.

"Nothing. It's just interesting." Callum closed his fingers around Kieran's arm as he withdrew a dagger, one made of some sort of milky-white stone I'd never seen before. "This may sting."

"You harm him, and you will regret it," I warned.

"I only need to make a shallow cut as before," Callum said. "But I suspect there is not much I could do that would seriously harm him." His hand was quick, making a shallow cut on the same area of Kieran's forearm as before. "Now is there?"

I didn't even bother responding as a faint black shadow lifted from the shallow slice. My heart tripped. Did that mean the Joining wouldn't have overpowered the curse? I didn't know, and I wasn't sure if we would ever know. What I did know was that it didn't matter.

"Gods," Naill muttered as the inky mist flowed out from Kieran's blood and rose to where it disappeared into the night.

"There you go." Callum dropped Kieran's arm, sheathing the strange dagger as he smiled brightly.

"That's it?" Casteel asked.

The Revenant nodded.

Kieran's arm flew out in a flash. I saw a glint of bloodstone, and then the hilt of the dagger was flush with Callum's chest. "Thank you," he growled, jerking the dagger up and out. "Fucker."

Callum staggered back. Blood trickled from his mouth. "Godsdamn it…"

A rough laugh came from Millicent as Callum hit the floor. "Never gets old," she said, stepping over his body. "He recovers fast, though. Go for his stupid head next time."

"Advice taken and accepted," Kieran muttered, glancing at me as I folded my hand over his arm. "I'm fine—" He sighed as the healing warmth hit him. His eyes flicked to Casteel.

"Let her do her thing," Casteel replied, his focus now on Isbeth. "It makes her feel good."

Kieran quieted then, and when I lifted my hand, there was no mark. "You do feel fine?" I asked, not trusting the Revenant at all.

He nodded.

"He's fine," Millicent snapped. "Unlike the Queen, who appears seconds from climbing into the casket."

"Would that be a bad thing?" Emil asked.

A choked laugh left me, the sound quickly fading as I saw that Isbeth leaned over Malec's body.

"He's my heartmate—a part of me. My heart. My soul. He's my everything. If Nyktos had granted us the trials, we would be together."

"And ruling over Atlantia?" Casteel surmised.

"I don't think so. He was done with that godsforsaken kingdom," she said. "We would've traveled the realm, found a place that we were at peace with. There, we would've stayed. Together. With our son. Our children."

Who knew if what she spoke was true to anyone but her, but it was painful to witness, nonetheless.

Isbeth smoothed a palm over Malec's cheek, her hand trembling as she bent over him more, her mouth inches from his dry, pale lips. "I love you now as much as I loved you then when our eyes first met in the rose gardens. I will always love you, Malec. Always."

I shifted under the weight of the raw tide of emotion that Isbeth did nothing to shield. Tears rolled down her cheeks, leaving faint tracks in the pale powder she wore.

"You know that, right?" Her voice had lowered as she reached for the jeweled belt at her waist. "You have to, even now, as you sleep so deeply. You have to know how much I love you." Isbeth's fingers trailed down the side of his neck as she pressed a kiss to his still lips.

"That's really disgusting," muttered Emil.

It was.

And it was also sad. As terrible and evil to the core as Isbeth was, she still loved deeply and painfully. It would hurt even more when she realized that we had no intention of allowing her to keep him.

"Fuckboy is awake," Kieran muttered as Callum slowly climbed to his feet. "Heads up."

Casteel reached between us, folding his hand around mine. He winked at me, and other than proving that he could pull that off without looking ridiculous, it was a sign. It was time. Looking away from the sad scene playing out before us, I narrowed my senses until I could only feel the *notam* and searched out Sage's fresh rain imprint—

"And that's why... That's why you have to understand," Isbeth said to Malec's sleeping form. "You know how much I loved our son. You understand why it must be like this. That it cannot be any other way."

Concentration broken, my head jerked toward Isbeth at the same moment as Millicent's. Isbeth jerked her arm up. Casteel pulled me to his side at the first glint of shadowstone. The jeweled belt at her waist had hidden a shadowstone dagger. I tapped into the eather, worried that she would turn that dagger on any number of people standing near—

Isbeth screamed—and, gods, that was the sound of pure anguish. She brought the dagger down—into Malec's chest. His heart.

My mouth dropped open.

Isbeth had…

She'd stabbed Malec in the heart with shadowstone.

Shadowstone could kill a god. I remembered Reaver saying as much.

What we'd just witnessed didn't make sense. Not in any realm. But she had…she had killed Malec. Her heartmate.

"What in the actual *fuck*?" exclaimed Casteel, dropping my hand as Millicent staggered back, her eyes going wide.

Kieran cursed as Isbeth jerked her hands free of the dagger. Her body folded over Malec's. "I'm sorry. I'm so sorry," she wept. "I'm so sorry."

My arms fell to my sides. The shock of seeing the glimmering, ruby-encrusted hilt jutting from Malec's chest rooted me to where I stood. And that astonishment rolled, coming in waves from all who witnessed it—all except one.

The golden, now-bloody Revenant.

Callum *smiled*.

A nearly overwhelming sense of dread exploded in my chest as Callum slowly turned his head toward me. He clasped his hands together, bowing. "Thank you."

The essence stirred violently. I reached out, clasping Casteel's arm.

"Thank you for doing what you were prophesied to do long ago. Thank you for fulfilling your purpose, Harbinger." Callum's pale eyes brightened behind the golden mask, and the eather, it thrummed through my veins. "It wasn't exactly as foretold or how many of us understood, but prophecies…well, the details aren't always exact, and interpretations do vary."

"I don't understand," Millicent said, her wide-eyed gaze darting between Callum and our mother.

"What is it that you don't understand?"

"Everything," she seethed. "Everything about what just happened."

"You mean what could've happened to you if you hadn't been a failure?" Callum countered, and Malik shot forward, blocked only by Casteel, who was simply faster. "You would've bled for him, and he would've rewarded you greatly for it."

Millicent drew back, her skin paling under the mask. Her stare hit mine, and suddenly, I understood. Mouth dry, my gaze fell to Malec. "That was supposed to be me, wasn't it?"

"You succeeded where she didn't," Callum said. "And I've been waiting a long time for you. *He's* been waiting for the sacrifice. The balance the Arae always insist upon. Waiting for the one born of mortal flesh, on the verge of becoming a great Primal power. You arrived as promised, but..." He extended his arm. "But you weren't the only one. As long as both shared the blood of the Primal of Life and were loved, it would restore *him*. She just needed you—someone of his bloodline—to find Malec. We all know that Ires surely wouldn't have done that. We'd have had to free him. And, well, he's kind of...pissy, to say the least."

"What in the hell?" demanded Naill.

Callum cocked his head. "I just didn't think she'd do *that*. Not until she asked for him. And even then, I truly didn't think she would go through with it, to be honest." He laughed. "I thought it would be a fifty-fifty shot on who she chose. You. Or Malec."

Heart pounding, I pressed my hand to my chest as clouds appeared over the sea, darkening the night sky. I was on the verge of becoming a Primal, and it struck me, finally, the *why now* of it all. Why Isbeth had waited until *this* time to exact her centuries-old plans. She'd had to wait until I entered the Culling so she could... I stared at the altar. So she could *kill me*. But she had...

But it wasn't me on that altar.

Malec wasn't the True King of the Realms as we believed. This really had nothing to do with him or even me. We were just pawns.

Suddenly, I thought about the prophecy. "'*The Bringer of Death and Destruction*,'" I murmured, and Casteel's gaze flew to mine. "Not Death and Destruction, but the *bringer* of it." My hand lifted to my mouth. That godsdamn prophecy... "And I did just that."

"Fuck," Malik growled.

"This is not the right time," Casteel said under his breath, "but I just want to point out that I always said you were not death and destruction."

Kieran shot him a look because it really, really wasn't the time, and because while Malik's reluctance to give Malec to Isbeth may not have been rooted in knowledge of what was to come, if we had listened to him...

No. If we had known, we wouldn't have stopped. We wouldn't have risked Kieran. Right or wrong, it was as simple as that.

"Then what is this?" Millicent demanded. "Who is the Harbinger?"

"She is the Harbinger." Callum's head swung to her. "The warning." His eyes widened. "What did you think, dear? That *she* was the one who would destroy the realms?" He glanced at me. "A Primal born of mortal flesh? Her?" His laugh echoed through the valley. "Seriously?"

I stiffened. "At any other time, I would find that kind of rude."

"No offense meant, Your Highness," he said with a mockery of a bow. "It's just that it would take eons for you to become *that* powerful, and that was if the power didn't drive you mad first."

The limp, flat hair flew about Millicent's face as she shook her head, while Isbeth continued sobbing—as the dread grew and grew. The last part of Callum's comment was something we'd have to worry about later. "*No.*"

"Yes." Callum tipped his head back as he eyed me. "It should've been you on the altar. That *was* the plan. That is what all of this has been about. You." He pointed to Millicent and then to me. "And *you.* Yeah, we'll have to deal with *you* later." Callum winked. "But now, it's time."

"Time for what, you silly fuck?" Kieran snarled, grasping the hilt of his sword.

The Revenant's eyes closed. "Time to bow to the one True King of the Realms."

Casteel stepped toward him. "And who is that supposed to be?"

Pressure settled on my shoulders. An awareness that brought a chill to the nape of my neck. That heavy, oppressive feeling—the same as I'd felt the night that Vessa had struck down the draken, and in the woods outside of Three Rivers—cloaked my skin. I'd felt it before when we were in Stonehill and I'd heard *that* voice urging me to lose control.

The same one I'd heard that night in Lockswood when I'd been floating in the nothingness.

"He's been waiting." Callum ignored Kieran, his chin dipped, eyes eager and voice soft, full of worship—so very much like the Priests and Priestesses in Oak Ambler. "This whole time, he too has slept fitfully. Kept well fed under the Temple of Theon."

Kieran's skin blanched as a shudder rocked me. "The children," I gasped. "The extra Rite."

"He had to be strong enough to awaken, and he was." Callum dragged his teeth along his lower lip. "When you shed the mortal flesh and began your Ascension, it freed him. And soon, when Malec takes his final breath, he will be at his full strength. All these years—all these centuries and centuries—he's been waiting. Sleeping even more restlessly after your birth. Sensing you, *feeling* you. He's been waiting and waiting for the proverbial key to his lock, for his...pretty poppy to pick and watch bleed."

Red-hot rage swirled through Casteel, gathering in my throat like a pool of acid. He moved so fast, I didn't see his hand until it was tearing through Callum's chest, and the Revenant's heart was in his palm, dripping blood and thick tissue.

Malik and Millicent turned to him. "What?" Casteel snarled, throwing the heart aside. "I couldn't listen to another word. Not even going to say I'm sorry. Fuck him."

Delano's imprint brushed against my thoughts. *Something's coming...*

No, someone was already here.

Death.

Destruction.

Stale lilacs.

Oh, my gods.

The dread exploded into panic as I jerked to the side. *"Kolis."*

48

A blast of energy rippled out from Malec, unseen but felt. Dark. Oily.
Suffocating as it slammed into us. There was no warning—no time to
prepare. The statues of the kneeling gods exploded, all down the
Temple. Casteel and I skidded back several feet into Kieran. He caught
both of us while Malik lost his balance and went down on one knee.
Millicent was knocked against the pillars. Twisting at the waist, I saw
Delano and several of the wolven hunched low to the ground, their
ears flattened, and their teeth bared. And that lingering energy, it made
my skin crawl and smelled of stale lilacs.

Grasping my arm, Casteel righted himself as he turned to Kieran.
"You okay?"

Kieran nodded as small pebbles rattled across the ground. I looked
down as sound followed, a low rumble of thunder that came from
below and grew louder and louder until the earth shook, and the Bone
Temple trembled. The foundation of the altar Malec had been placed
on shattered, sinking about a foot. Deep cracks raced out from the
slab, forcing the wolven back. A gray mist seeped out of the fissures
and carried the scent of stale lilacs.

Of death.

"This can be stopped!" Millicent shouted. "If it requires
sacrifice—death—Malec hasn't passed yet. He still breathes. We
can't—"

The cracks exploded, sending chunks of stone flying. I shouted as a large chunk hit Millicent in the side of the head, snapping her chin back. She staggered, her legs going out, but Malik twisted, catching her before she hit the floor. Blood coursed down the side of her face as Malik pressed his palm to the back of her head.

"She'll be okay," he said, his voice ragged. "She'll be okay. She just needs to wake up."

I hoped that was soon. The shaking made it difficult to stand, and the fractures spread, widening as they traveled the length of the floor, one heading straight for Casteel. He jumped, nimbly avoiding the gap, but several of the Royal Guards weren't nearly as lucky. They disappeared into the fissures, their screams echoing until they passed beyond where no sound could travel. Pillars trembled as the cracks spread down the steps of both sides of the Bone Temple, where the Atlantian armies waited at our backs, and the Revenants stood to our front. Both sides scattered to avoid the widening cracks.

The shaking ceased, but the gray mist continued rising. The wolven crept forward, sniffing at the mist as a guard yelled, "Help! Help!"

Naill turned to where the guard held the edge of a crevice, the man's fingers bleached white. "Godsdamn it," he grunted, starting forward—

"Wait," Casteel ordered, holding up a hand. Naill halted. "You hear that?"

"Please. Gods, help me!" the guard shouted.

"I don't…" I trailed off as the sound reached me. The sound of something…*scraping* against stone.

All around, soldiers looked down as Delano and Rune crept forward, followed by several of the other wolven. They sniffed at the mist, at the deep cracks now wide enough to disappear into.

Naill bent, reaching for the guard when the man screamed. A burst of hot pain lanced my senses as the Atlantian jerked back and the guard disappeared. "What the…?" Naill rose, his hand still suspended in air.

Bitter fear stretched suddenly and coated the inside of my mouth. I spun to where the wolven on the ground below the Temple started slinking back from the cracks. They turned sharply and *bolted*, sliding sideways, their paws skating on the damp grass as they scrambled overtop of one another.

"I've never seen wolven run." Emil unsheathed his sword. "Not from anything."

"Nor have I." Casteel pulled his sword free.

An Atlantian soldier's terrified scream pierced the air as he was *pulled* into the crack.

"Something's in the ground," Emil announced.

"Not something." Callum rolled onto his side, the wound...dear gods, the ragged hole in his chest still there, though no longer oozing blood. "The True King's guards. The dakkai."

"The what?" Kieran held his swords.

"It doesn't matter what they are," I said, closing my hands into fists as I tapped into the essence. "They won't be anything for long."

Callum smirked.

"And neither will you," I warned, letting my will stretch out to summon the draken.

"Whatever they are, they're coming," Casteel yelled, the sound that reminded me of barrats scurrying over stone intensifying. His gaze swung to mine. "Take care of our men and women. We'll handle this up here."

The corners of my vision turned silvery-white as I nodded.

One dimple appeared before he braced himself. A heartbeat later, creatures erupted out of the fissure, nearly Setti's size, their hard-shell skin slick and the color of midnight. They were shaped like the wolven but larger, and they...they were featureless except for two slits where the nose should be, and wide mouths full of jagged, sharp teeth.

Well, that was a whole bucket full of nightmares right there.

One of the dakkais leapt toward Emil, but his reflexes were fast. He plunged his sword into the creature's chest. Silvery eather swirled down my arms as Casteel spun, cleaving the head off one as Delano leapt over a fissure, colliding with a dakkai that had gone for Malik as he helped Millicent sit up.

I turned to the soldiers below, relieved to see that Setti and many of the horses had been untethered and had made their escape as more of the creatures spilled out of the ground below. A burst of essence left me, hitting a line of dakkais. My stomach churned at the sound of breaking bones. They hit the ground but more quickly took their place. I walked toward the steps as the eather ramped up in my chest. Another pulse, this one stronger, swallowed the creatures.

"Incoming!" Naill shouted, grabbing Rune's scruff and dragging him back as a shadow broke through the clouds overhead, falling over us.

A stream of silvery fire cut across the Temple floor, turning the realm silver as Aurelia swooped down, striking the creatures. Twin funnels of luminous flame pummeled the ground as Nithe and Thad arrived.

"Protect your King!" Isbeth shouted from the altar, head lifted, and cheeks streaked with black liner.

A shout rose from where the army of Revenants waited. They charged, a sea of crimson flooding the sides of the Temple. Nithe landed near the soldiers and then Thad as I caught sight of Malik fighting Callum.

"Shit!" Casteel spun, kicking a dakkai back. He leapt over the crack, grabbing me by the waist as he pulled me behind the pillar.

Casteel's body pressed mine into the pillar as a volley of arrows rained down on the Temple floor and the grounds. For the briefest second, there was only him and his scent, and then that second ended. I flinched as burning pain scalded my senses, followed by screams.

"From the Rise." Casteel's breath hit my cheek. "Can you take them out?"

I peered around the pillar, getting an idea of how many were there as another barrage of arrows came. I jerked—

"Shut it down." He palmed my cheek. "Shut it down, my Queen."

Sucking in a sharp breath, I nodded. I shut it down as best I could.

"You got this?"

I met his stare. "Yes."

Casteel stepped back, turning to plunge his sword into a dakkai, and I stepped out from behind the pillar. I focused on the Rise, and the essence responded at once. The archers' bows slipped from their hands as their necks cracked. They fell, and while I knew more would arrive, we had a reprieve.

Turning, I cursed as a horde of dakkais rushed the Temple. The eather arced out from me in a wave of fire, turning them to ash. Across from me, several dakkais spun, howling as they abandoned their attack on Naill and Emil. Their heads rose, and then they charged as Kieran joined Casteel. The essence whirled through me as I lifted my hands to those racing up the steps and the others leaping across the Temple. Fire not too different than what came from the draken manifested, erupting from my palms and slamming into the creatures. They went down, twitching and smoldering. We didn't have time to mess with them. "Get to Malec," I told Kieran and Casteel. "And get that dagger out."

"On it." Casteel caught my chin in his palm and kissed my cheek before rushing forward.

In my mind, I saw the essence traveling out around me, around the

Temple, where it recoiled from the Revenants but flowed over the dakkais. My entire vision turned silver as that *taste* gathered in the back of my throat. The cold place in me throbbed. I breathed through it as dozens and dozens of streams of light arced out from me, racing across the Temple and the ground below.

When I pulled the eather back, I saw no living, faceless creature among those battling at the foot of the Temple. Smiling tightly, I reached out to Sage through the *notam* as I turned, and…

I felt *nothing*.

My breath caught as my eyes locked on Isbeth's. Her hands were flat on Malec's chest, moving up and down in shallow breaths.

"There's more!" Emil shouted.

I whipped around, my heart lodging in my throat as I saw the dakkais. They came from the fissures, but this time, there were *hundreds* of them, climbing over one another, their blade-like claws scoring soil and stone. And they—

Good gods, they swarmed the armies and the wolven in a wave of screams and yelps. Blood sprayed the air. Aurelia took flight but not quickly enough. The creatures launched onto her back and wings, clawing and biting.

"No!" I shouted, summoning the eather as I willed the draken to take flight. Thad lifted, shaking the dakkais from him as several Atlantian soldiers fired arrows at the ones climbing Aurelia. The essence stretched out from me as dakkais flooded the steps, growling and snapping.

A dark shadow fell over me with a gust of wind that blew the braid across my face. Reaver landed, shaking the entire Temple as he swept his wings back and stretched out his neck, sending a stream of fire at the dakkais on the Temple and then to those on the steps. The flames were so bright, they blinded me momentarily, so I didn't see Reaver until he shifted into his mortal form.

"Do not use the essence. It's drawing the dakkais to you. You won't be able to fight all of them off," Reaver told me from where he crouched, nude, beside me. "You must stop whatever it is they did to unleash them. That is all you must do."

My breath caught as my gaze flew to Callum. That damn smirk. He knew.

"Fine," I bit out, withdrawing my swords. There wasn't enough time to explain everything. "It's Malec. He's dying. That's what's causing this. He dies, and Kolis will be at full strength."

"If that happens, we will all pray for death. Get to him. *Now,*" Reaver said, and then he rose. A shimmery, silvery light erupted all over his body as he lengthened and grew. Scales replaced flesh, and wings sprouted from his back.

Reaver lifted into the air, roaring a stream of fire that cut through the space above my head as I struck a dakkai rushing me. My heart lodged in my throat as I glanced over my shoulder to the Temple grounds as Reaver lit it up, and I…I knew I could do nothing to aid the soldiers down below. Malec couldn't die. That was the priority. I turned, withdrawing the wolven dagger as I thrust my sword into a dakkai's stomach and spun, coming face-to-face with a Royal Guard. I didn't let myself think or feel as I drew the dagger across his throat.

I jerked back as bright silver flames erupted inches from my face and Nithe flew overhead. I jumped to where the cracks in the Temple weren't so wide. Gods, it was mayhem—the snarls and grunts coming from the fire, the mist and smoke, the twisting, falling bodies. I caught sight of Hisa, her helmet gone and blood dotting her face as she shoved her sword through a dakkai. She spun, her eyes meeting mine. "We can—"

I jerked as her words cut off, ending in a gurgle. We both looked down at her chest, where a shadowstone blade protruded.

The soldier yanked the blade free, and Hisa folded, her body hitting the ground, limp, and her eyes open. I knew that if a shadowstone dagger to the heart could kill a god, it surely killed an Atlantian quicker. I locked eyes with the Revenant who'd killed her and launched forward, my swords slicing through leather and bone. I cut through the Revenant's shoulders, severing the arms as the back of my throat burned, and eather pressed against my skin. I leaned back, kicking the Revenant into the path of Reaver's fire, and then spun back to Hisa. I started toward her—

"The dagger!" Millicent thrust her sword into a Revenant's chest. "We need to get the dagger out!"

My attention snapped to Isbeth, to where her hand was on the hilt, her eyes closed. *Hisa.* Oh, gods, there wasn't time. Fury poured into me as I cursed, forcing myself away from Hisa.

I caught a dakkai as it leapt, bringing my sword down on the back of its neck as its claws grazed my arm. The pain was fiery hot, but I ignored it as I whirled, slamming the wolven dagger into a guard's chest. Through the chaos of death, smoke, and mist, I saw Casteel spinning as he struck dakkais and guards alike. He had blood on his throat. His arm. I saw Kieran closer, his body not faring much better as he kicked a dakkai off a soldier. A high-pitched yelp spun me around. Dakkais swarmed the black-and-brown wolven, taking Rune down. I started forward, my path cut off as a Revenant came through the mist and smoke.

"Shit." I blocked her swing with my forearm as I searched for Rune with the *notam*, my throat burning more and more when I felt nothing. The eather pulsed violently in my chest as I twisted, kicking and catching the Revenant in the chest. Ignoring the call to use the essence, I spun and dragged the sword across her throat, severing her head—

A blur of white leaped out of the smoke. I sucked in thick, blood-heavy air as Delano's paws landed on my chest, knocking me back, out of the path of a stream of fire.

"Thank you," I gasped, briefly clasping the back of his neck as I kissed his forehead. "We need to get to Malec."

I'm with you, came his answer.

We rose, fighting our way across the Temple. Delano leapt, taking down a guard racing along the lower walls of the structure. I shot forward, thrusting my sword into another just as a dakkai took down a guard, its jagged teeth tearing into the man's throat. It became really clear that while the dakkais avoided the Revenants, they did not make an exception for the mortal guards.

"Naill!" Emil shouted, shoving the body of a dakkai off him as he rose, the chest of his armor ripped open. Crimson streaked his stomach. "Fuck!" He grunted, jabbing his sword back as another dakkai leapt toward him.

And Naill...he was down, on his back, his hands open, his armor torn apart. My heart cracked.

"*No.*" Casteel spun, golden eyes flashing as a beast launched off the wall, knocking a wolven aside. Picking up speed, he slid under the creature, dragging his sword across its belly. He popped up to his feet and took off for Naill.

"Get to her!" Millicent shouted as she grabbed Malik's arm, thrusting him to the side. His armor had been splayed open by dakkai claws, as well. My breath caught as Millicent went flying backwards, a dakkai on top of her. There was no time.

Shutting down my senses, I whirled back to the altar. Isbeth had retrieved a sword.

Shouts went up from behind us. I skidded to a stop, looking over my shoulder to see the guards along the Carsodonia Rise rushing the battlements, arrows lit with fire as they aimed. Instead of at us, they fired upon the dakkais climbing the Rise. My heart stuttered. If the dakkais got into the city...

Letting my will stretch out to the draken, I saw Nithe's midnight wings turn sharply as he aimed at the Rise. I didn't look for Aurelia. I couldn't. I couldn't let myself do that as I started running, leaping over a body. My grip tightened on my dagger. Every part of my being focused on Isbeth as she lifted the sword, her hands and arms trembling as the blade hovered above Malec's throat. My heart lurched as I realized what she had planned. I cocked back my arm and let the dagger go.

I held my breath as the blade flew through the air, headed straight for Isbeth. Her head jerked up, and the dagger spun backward.

"Shit." I skidded, slipping as Delano crashed into me, knocking me aside.

Air punched out of my lungs as I hit the floor—hard. Delano landed half on top of me, and I groaned, planting my hands on his shoulders as I lifted my head to meet his bright blue eyes. "That was unnecessary. I would—" Something hot and wet dripped against my hand. I looked down at the streaks of red in his fur. With dawning horror, I saw *my* dagger protruding from his chest. The sword slipped from my hand. "*No.*"

Delano shuddered.

I tapped into the eather, channeling all the healing energy I could. I didn't care about the dakkais. I didn't care about Malec or Kolis because I couldn't lose Delano. I wouldn't. I wouldn't lose—

The fur thinned under my hands, replaced by skin. Pale blond hair appeared, flopping into eyes that didn't blink. Didn't focus. Didn't see.

"No!" I carefully rolled Delano onto his side, grasping his shoulders, shaking him. There was nothing. I reached for the dagger but halted. "Please. Please don't do this. Get up, Delano. Please. *Please.*"

There was nothing.

Tears blinded me as silvery fire erupted over my head, rippling over the dakkais racing toward us. Sorrow rose sharply, crowding out everything else. Grabbing Delano, I pulled him away from the edge as someone screamed. Emil stumbled back, his swords slipping from his hands as he went down on one knee in front of the Revenant who had speared him through the chest. Kieran was suddenly there, his mouth open in a roar as he swung his sword through the Revenant's neck.

Casteel spun then, his fangs bared as he skewered a Revenant. Blood drenched his face, his armor, and beneath my hands, Delano's skin was already beginning to cool.

"I told you, my daughter." Isbeth's voice was soft but clear through the madness. "I said you would give me what I want."

That fissure inside me that had broken open upon Vikter's death tore wide now, coming from that hollow place inside me. My entire body jolted as grief-laced fury poured out of me, icy and endless. The sword fell from my hand as my other slid away from Delano. Rage joined the essence of the Primals, pressing at my skin as I rose and slowly turned.

I looked at Isbeth as she raised the sword above Malec once more, and I screamed.

Energy pulsed out from me, crackling and spitting as it spilled across the floor and slammed into Isbeth, knocking her back. She lost the sword as she caught herself. The Temple shuddered as eather pulsed from me, smacking into the dakkais drawn to me.

Isbeth rose, backing up. Bracing herself, she lifted her hand. "Don't make me do this, Penellaphe."

"I'm going to kill you," I said as I stalked forward, and it was *that* voice, the one full of smoke and shadow. "I'm going to rip you apart."

Her eyes flared wide as she skidded back several feet. A burst of eather left her.

And I *laughed*.

The energy hit me, and I took it in—the fiery pain, the burn of it—letting it seep into my skin and become a part of me. And then I sent it back.

Isbeth flew backward into the pillar. The impact cracked the marble as she fell forward onto her knees. "Ouch," she snarled, lifting her head.

I smiled even as blood dripped from me—from the hits she'd landed—and hit the stone. Roots spilled out from new fissures in the stone as I walked, my eyes narrowing on her.

Her skin split open at the hairline as I stalked forward, another blood tree taking root, then another and another behind me. Blood beaded along the slice curving toward her temple, narrowly missing her left eye. Another deep cut formed across her forehead and ran through her brow.

Another pulse of eather hit me as she staggered to her feet. I drew that into myself as my throat burned. As an ache settled deep in the center of my back, and my jaw throbbed. I lifted my hands, and all the fallen weapons rose from the Temple floor and flew forward.

Isbeth waved her arm, sending them scattering. "Cute parlor trick."

Closing the distance between us, I cocked my head to the side as a chunk of stone slammed into the side of her head. Blood gushed from her nose, her mouth. "How's that for a cute parlor trick, *Mother*?"

Isbeth stumbled, catching herself. Her head whipped toward me. "You want to kill me? It won't bring any of them back. It won't stop what is coming—"

A wave of eather rolled from me, striking Isbeth. She fell back, laughing.

The air charged around me as lightning cracked overhead. I sucked in that energy as I saw Millicent fighting to get to Malec. Isbeth lashed out. A pulse of light struck my leg and splintered off, striking Millicent as she grasped the dagger protruding from Malec's chest. She spun back, landing in a pool of blood near a toppled pillar, the blade limp in her hand.

"Betrayed by both of my daughters." Isbeth wiped the blood from her face. "I'm so very proud."

Snapping forward, I grabbed the crown. She howled as the jewels snagged, tearing clumps of her hair free as I yanked it from her head. Rage fueled me as I drew back my hand and backhanded her with the crown, knocking her to the floor.

"Gods," she grunted, spitting out a mouthful of blood and teeth. "That was uncalled for."

The energy ramped up, and I shattered the crown, bits of rubies and diamonds falling to the floor. I knelt, grasping the back of her hair. Shadow and light swirled under my skin as she met my stare. "Your reign has come to an end."

"I chose Malec," Isbeth said, gripping my arm, her touch burning. "It had to be him because I couldn't kill you. I *wouldn't* because I love you," she whispered, slamming her hand into my chest.

The eather burned straight through me, overwhelming my control as it lifted me from my feet and sent me flying backward. Every single nerve ending screamed out in pain as the eather shot through me. It was like being struck by lightning, robbing my breath and stealing muscle control. I knew I was falling, but I could do nothing to soften the impact.

"Poppy!" Casteel shouted.

Every bone in my body shook as I hit the floor. Bright lights flashed behind my eyes as I rolled to my side. The breath I took scorched my lungs. My ribs protested the movement as I tried to sit up. The ache in my back spread into my shoulders, and all the while, those lights kept flashing, allowing me only glimpses of the chaos around me. Reaver was down, shimmery lights sparking from him as he attempted to shake off the dakkais. Malik lay with one arm over Millicent as if he sought to shield her with his last breath. Not a single inch of their bodies wasn't scorched or torn up. No more draken flew, and Kieran, he yelled my name, too as the lights flashed—

Suddenly, there was no light. No color or sound.

Then, a speck of silver throbbed and expanded, growing brighter, and in that light was *her*. Hair, the color of moonlight, fell over shoulders in a cascading mass of tangled curls and waves. A luminous sheen nearly masked the freckles across the nose and cheek and gave the skin a silvery, pearlescent glow. But I recognized her from the dreams that weren't dreams. Her eyes opened, and I saw they were the color of spring grass—green laced with bright, luminous eather.

"It wasn't supposed to be this way," she whispered, but there were no blood tears now. Acidic, icy-hot anger fell upon me. An endless fury I had never felt before, *could* never experience because it had grown for decades. Centuries.

My entire body spasmed as I remembered what Reaver had said— what Vikter had told Tawny. The beginning verse of the prophecy. *Born of mortal flesh, a great primal power rises as the heir to the lands and seas, to the skies and all the realms. A shadow in the ember, a light in the flame, to become a fire in the flesh...*

To speak her name is to bring the stars from the skies and topple the mountains into the sea...

Her name was power, but only when spoken by the one born as she, and of a great primal power.

"He told me you already knew her name," Tawny had said.

She stared back at me, and I saw us when I'd been floating in that nothingness, drifting until she had appeared to me. Until she'd said, *"It wasn't supposed to be this way."* When she told me that I'd always had the power in me.

But those weren't the only words she'd spoken to me. I now remembered. She had told me her name. She had begged me to wake her.

How could the Consort be so powerful?

Because she was no Consort.

She held my stare and smiled, and I...I *understood*. She, too, had been waiting.

I opened my eyes, and through the smoke and mist, I saw Casteel and Kieran surrounded by dakkais. By Revenants. They closed in on them as I planted my palms against the stone, and my hands *sank* into the rock as I threw my head back and screamed the name. Not that of the King of Gods, but the Queen of Gods.

The *true* Primal of Life.

49

Isbeth's dark eyes went wide as they locked onto mine. Her lips moved, but I couldn't hear what she said. Casteel whipped around, blood spraying into the air as a bolt of lightning struck the Temple—struck *me*.

Casteel's pain and Kieran's fear slammed into me as my armor and boots exploded from me. My clothing ripped as every cell in my body lit up, and the pain—it was all-consuming. It would kill me. It would kill them.

My lungs seized.

My heart stuttered.

Blood pooled in my mouth. Teeth loosened, and two fell from my open mouth. The Temple didn't tremble. It was the *realm* that shook violently. Weight settled in my shoulder blades, entrenching itself deeply, burrowing all the way to where the eather throbbed and swirled. My blood cooled and then heated. A hum hit my bones and spread to my muscles. My skin vibrated. A crack of deafening thunder rolled overhead. The air charged, and my body…*changed*. It started with a rumble inside me and then became a roar, like the sound of thousands of horses racing toward me, but no horse or soldier stood. It grew and grew as I pushed myself onto my now-bare feet. All over my hands and arms, splotches of shadow and light churned inside my skin.

I lifted my eyes, seeing a strange shadow before me—the outline of my head and my shoulders and two...*wings*. Just like the statues guarding the city of Dalos that had once protected the Primals within. Except these were made of eather, a swirling mass of light and darkness. My entire form was suddenly nothing more than crackling, flaming silver light and endless shadows.

Vaguely, I became aware of Casteel and Kieran, their eyes wide and their awe bubbling in my throat and against my skin.

Thick, shadow-filled clouds appeared. Wind whipped, blowing my hair back and tugging at my torn clothing. And the wind, it smelled of *fresh* lilacs.

And then the very air itself split open, spitting crackling light as a thick, white mist seeped out of the tear, spilling over me, over the ruined ground to blanket the bodies.

A great, black-and-gray shape several times larger than Setti flew out of the chasm in the air, its wings so massive that they momentarily blocked the rising moon. Another deafening roar tore through the air as the draken glided over the Temple, opening its powerful jaws. A stream of intense, silvery fire erupted, spinning into a funnel that slammed into the creatures climbing the Rise.

"*Nektas,*" Casteel rasped.

My entire being focused on Isbeth. She stood behind the altar, almost transfixed. And the endless fury I felt from *her* joined mine.

Her.

Seraphena.

The true Primal of Life.

The one I'd gotten the gift of life and healing from. Not Nyktos. His gift was the shadows in my skin, the death in my touch, and the coldness in my chest.

My *will* swept out from me, rushing over the Bone Temple and the grounds below and beyond. I took a step, and I did so as something infinite. Something *Primal.*

Power drenched the air as the aura receded just enough for me to see that the luminous sheen had settled and turned to a pearlescent, silvery, and shadowy glow. With each footstep, the stone trembled and cracked, and the mist followed me, settling over the bodies and cradling them.

I walked forward, feet bare to the blood, the shattered shields, and the broken swords. And then I *glided*, lifting from the ground. The battered bodies of soldiers, wolven, and draken—of my friends and those I cared for—rose along with me. Delano. Naill. Emil. Hisa—

"It's too soon," Isbeth shrieked, and her fear—her *terror*—was just as strong as her grief had been, raining bitter ice upon me. She stumbled over the body of a dakkai and pressed against the altar Malec lay upon. "What did you do?"

I felt myself rise as Reaver's and Malik's bodies drifted from the pools of blood, my head kicking back. And then, everything *stopped*. The wind. The moans. My heart. The only movement was that of Nektas as he flew down the length of the Rise, leaving a wave of essence-fueled fire in his wake. My fingers splayed out at my sides.

I gave sound to my rage. To *hers*. The scream that ripped from my throat wasn't just mine. It was *ours*.

The sound hit the air like a shockwave, shattering stone and toppling the newly rooted blood trees. Casteel turned, attempting to shield Kieran, but there was no need. They wouldn't be harmed as my fury rippled above us, tearing the sky open. The rain came, blood-red and drenching.

And final.

Millicent slowly sat up, her pale eyes going wide as a dakkai raced from the smoke—two and then four and five, their claws kicking up chunks of stone. My head snapped in their direction, and that was it. The dakkais simply *disappeared* mid-run or leap, obliterated with just a look. Nothing was left of them. Not even ash as the wave of energy spread out, catching the remaining dakkais and the Revenants, turning them to dust.

The blood rain stopped, and not a single drop touched me as I turned my attention back to Isbeth.

"You." The one word dripped so much power, so much barely leashed violence, that a cold shiver even ran down my spine. Because that was me...and it was also Seraphena. Her essence—her consciousness—moved inside me.

"It's too late," Isbeth said. And I *sensed* that it both was and wasn't. She dragged her arm over her bloodied face. "It has already been done."

"*She* knew what you plotted," I told her. "*She* saw it in her sleep. Saw it *all*."

Isbeth's terror choked me as she shook her head. "Then she has to know I did it for Malec. It was all for her son and her grandson that they took from me!"

"It was all for *nothing*." I lifted my hand, and Isbeth's body went rigid, her mouth open but issuing no sound. No words. Nothing. The clouds thickened even more as she rose, suspended several feet above the ground. "It was love that made you. She would've forgiven Malec for what he did by making you. But your hatred? Your grief? Your thirst for vengeance? It has rotted your mind more than the blood of a god could have ever done. What you have become—what you have brought upon the realms—will not save you."

Isbeth's right arm jerked backward. The crack of bone was loud, and the flare of pain I felt was red-hot.

"What you have wrought and brought upon these realms will not heal you or steal away your pain," I said, and her other arm snapped. "It will not bring you glory, peace, or love."

Isbeth's left and right legs broke at the knee, and I took in the pain, let it become a part of me.

"And for what you have done to those of her blood, you will be erased," I proclaimed. Blood seeped from Isbeth's eyes. Her nose. Her mouth. "Nothing of you will be recorded in the histories that are yet to be written. You will not be known, neither for the deeds you've done as a mortal nor for your infamy as a Queen. You are not worthy of remembrance."

Isbeth's spine *cracked*. Her upper body wilted backward, and the pain...it was absolute.

A sudden awareness pressed upon me. An awakening. One that echoed not through this realm, but in Iliseeum and deep within the City of the Gods as Nektas landed behind me. A presence filled me, and when I spoke, it was the voice of the true Primal of Life. "I was once taught that all beings are worthy of an honorable, quick death. I no longer believe in that. For your death will be dishonorable and endless. Nyktos awaits the start of your eternity in the Abyss."

The presence eased from me as Nektas's wings spread out, scattering the ashes of those who had been destroyed. In the following seconds, all I felt were *opposites*. Apathy and sorrow. Loathing and love. Relief and dread. I pitied the shattered woman before me, one who had been broken long ago. I hated what she'd allowed herself to become.

Isbeth had never been a mother, but I...I'd once loved her, and she'd loved me in her own, twisted way. That meant something.

But something wasn't enough.

I lowered my hand, and dots of blood appeared all over Isbeth's skin. Her pores bled. I trembled as her flesh cracked and peeled, as muscle and ligaments tore, as bones splintered and hair fell, no longer rooted to skin.

"Don't look," I heard Casteel saying as he tried to reach me. "Close your eyes. *Don't*—"

But I looked.

I made myself watch as my mother, the Blood Queen, took her last breath. I made myself look until Isbeth was no more—until the realm fell away from me.

50

Slowly, I became aware of a soft touch against my cheek. A brush of fingers along the curve of my jaw and below my lips. A hand smoothing my hair. A voice. Voices. Two stood out the strongest.

"Poppy," one called.

"Open your eyes, My Queen," another said—pleaded, really—and I could never deny him.

My eyes fluttered open, locking with ones the color of honey and framed by a thick fringe of lashes. *Him.* My husband and King. My heartmate. My everything. Blood streaked his face, matted his hair, but his skin was unmarked beneath it, rich and warm. His fingers were warm against the skin below my lips. "Cas."

Casteel made a rough sound that seemed like a cross between a laugh and a groan, and it came from somewhere deep within him. He lowered his lips to my forehead. "*Queen.*"

I reached up, touching the side of his jaw. He shuddered as he pressed his lips against my forehead. Slowly, I became aware that my head was cradled in his lap, but it was not his arm that braced my neck, or his hand on my cheek. Casteel's head lifted, and my gaze drifted to eyes the shade of winter.

Kieran smiled down at me as he dragged his thumb down the side of my cheek. "Nice of you to decide to rejoin us."

"I don't…" I swallowed. My mouth felt weird. I reached up—

Kieran caught my wrist. "Before you even ask, *yes.*"

My breath snagged as I gingerly ran my tongue along the line of my upper teeth. They felt normal until I hit a small, sharp point, drawing blood. I winced.

"Careful," Casteel murmured. "They'll take a little bit to get used to."

Oh, my gods. "I have fangs."

Kieran nodded. "Cas is going to have to walk you through getting used to them. Not my wheelhouse."

My gaze swung to Casteel. "What do they look like?"

His lips twitched. "Like…fangs."

"That tells me nothing."

"They're adorable."

"How can fangs be adorable—*wait.*" Fangs weren't the most pressing issue here, nor even the fact that I had finished the Culling. I sat up so quickly, both Casteel and Kieran jerked back so I didn't collide with them. My gaze swung over the cracked pillars, and Naill—

Naill sat with his back against one, his head tipped up, his eyes closed, but his chest was moving up and down—a chest that had been ripped open. His deep brown skin had lost the ghastly gray pallor of death.

I stared at him, knowing that I'd seen him fall. I'd watched him die. "I…I don't—"

A cool nose brushed my arm, and my head whipped to the side. Vibrant blue eyes set in white fur streaked with red met mine. A shudder shook my entire body. "Delano…?"

His springy imprint brushed against my thoughts. *Poppy.*

Crying out, I threw my arms around the wolven. Casteel let out a rough laugh as I buried my face in Delano's neck. I didn't know how he was here, and I couldn't stop shaking as I held him, soaking in the feel of his soft fur between my fingers and against my cheek. Kieran's hand moved up and down my back, and I realized then that I was crying—sobbing really—as I held Delano in a near chokehold. He allowed it, though, wiggling his body as close to mine as he could get. He was *alive.*

"Poppy," Casteel whispered, gently tugging on my shoulders. "The man's got to breathe."

Reluctantly, I let go, but Delano didn't go very far as Casteel folded his arms around my waist from behind. I felt his head rest on my shoulder as Kieran swept away the tears on my cheeks with featherlight touches. I looked—

My heart stopped again when I saw Emil standing, the destroyed armor gone and the ragged tear in his shirt made by the spear I'd seen go into his chest all the more visible. He was…he stood next to Hisa, who sat on a low wall, her hands hanging limply between her knees as she stared at me.

"How?" I asked, my voice ragged. "How are they alive?"

"You," Kieran said.

My brows pinched. "What?"

"You," Casteel repeated, pressing his lips to my cheek. "You brought them back. All of them."

"Look." Kieran touched my chin, turning my head to the ground below the Temple.

What I saw floored me.

Soldiers milled about, avoiding the cracks in the ground. Some sat like Naill and Hisa. But all bore leftover traces of battle. Shredded armor. Torn clothing. Dried blood.

"You passed out," Casteel said, his forehead pressed to my temple. "And that's when they came back. All of them. Even the damn guards."

"It was both the craziest and,"—Kieran's voice caught—"and the most beautiful thing I've ever seen."

"All these little…I don't know what," Casteel said, his laugh thick with emotion. "Orbs? Thousands—hundreds of thousands—of them came from the sky. It looked like the stars were falling."

To speak her name is to bring the stars from the skies…

I stiffened, my head jerking to the Rise where I saw Aurelia and Nithe perched beside Thad. I didn't see— "Reaver?"

"He took Malec to Iliseeum."

My heart lurched at the voice I'd heard once before, in Iliseeum. Kieran rocked back, and then I saw Nektas crouched before the altar, his long, black-and-silver-streaked hair falling across bare shoulders and over the distinct pattern of scales in his warm, copper skin.

"How are you wearing pants?" I blurted out.

A silent laugh went through Casteel as he held me tighter. "How, out of everything, is *that* what you question?"

"If you'd seen Reaver naked as many times as we have," Kieran muttered, "you'd think that was a valid question, too."

Nektas's eyes, with their thin, vertical pupils, fixed on me. "I can manifest clothing if I choose to do so. Reaver is not nearly old enough for that."

My brows lifted. "He's not?"

"He may be older than everything you know, but he is still a youngling," Nektas explained, and my heart twisted, because I thought of *his* youngling. Jadis. "And to many, he is still Reaver-Butt."

Reaver-Butt? Casteel stiffened behind me.

"Wait." Kieran blinked. "What?"

"It was a nickname he liked when he was very young." Nektas shrugged. "The point is, he's not powerful enough to manifest clothing."

I had to let that nickname go for the time being. "I'm sorry about Jadis. I…" I fell silent, wishing there was more to say but knowing there was nothing.

Nektas's eyes briefly slammed shut, the skin around them tightening. "She has not passed."

I glanced between Kieran and Casteel. "What? Reaver believed that she had been—" I didn't want to say *killed*. "How do you know?"

"I can feel her. She is here, in this realm." Nektas's eyes opened to the sky. "I am her father. Reaver would not be able to sense her as I can. She lives."

Shocked by the revelation, I told myself that this was good news. And it was. It was just…where was she? And why hadn't Isbeth used her? "We'll find her."

Nektas nodded. "We will."

"Reaver took Malec to Iliseeum?" I asked, glancing at where the casket lay in pieces upon the altar. "That means Malec lives?"

"For now," Nektas said.

Well, that wasn't exactly reassuring, but relief washed over me anyway. I leaned into Casteel. "Thank the gods," I murmured, looking back at Hisa and Emil as Delano lowered to his haunches, pressing against my legs. Wait. I twisted, searching for… "Where's Malik?" My heart skipped. "Millicent?"

"Millicent ran off," Casteel explained. "Malik went after her."

The knowledge that both were alive brought me some comfort. But had Millicent run off because she had witnessed the death of our mother? At my hands? I didn't think that it was only me who had done that, but did she fear the same would happen to her? Was she upset? Angry?

Swallowing, I shut those thoughts down until I had time to figure them out. "How did I bring everyone…?" It had been my *will*. I remembered. I'd let my *will* sweep out from me as the mist cradled their bodies, but I wasn't the Primal of Life.

"It wasn't just you who brought them back. You're not that powerful yet. You had help," Nektas said, and my gaze shot back to him. "The Primal of Life aided you, and Nyktos captured their souls before they could enter the Vale or the Abyss and then released them."

"Probably could do without the guards and all of *them* coming back," Kieran muttered.

The draken eyed him. "Balance. There must always be balance," he said. "Especially when the Primal of Life granted such an act as this."

A shiver rolled through me. "Seraphena—the Consort. She's the true Primal of Life."

"She is the heir to the lands and seas, skies and realms," Nektas said, speaking softly. But the words...they were full of respect, and they reverberated like thunder in my chest. "The fire in the flesh, the Primal of Life, and the Queen of Gods. The most powerful Primal." He paused. "For now."

For now?

"How is that possible?" Casteel asked.

"It is a complicated journey to how the Consort became the Primal," Nektas said, looking at me. "But it started with your great-grandfather, Eythos, when he was the Primal of Life. And his brother, Kolis, the true Primal of Death."

"Kolis is my great-uncle?" I exclaimed, forgetting the whole for-now part.

Nektas nodded as Emil and Naill drew closer, giving the ancient draken a wide berth as they listened.

"Your family ancestry is even more interesting than I originally believed," Casteel murmured, and Kieran snorted. "What does he have to do with this?"

"To make a long story short, Kolis fell in love with a mortal. Scared her while she was picking flowers for a wedding. When she ran from him, she fell from—"

"The Cliffs of Sorrow." My eyes went wide. "Her name was Sotoria, right? That was real? Ian..." I glanced back at Casteel. "Ian told me that story after he Ascended. I thought it was just something he made up."

"Interesting," Nektas murmured. "It's real. Kolis went to Eythos, asking that he bring her back to life. Eythos refused, knowing that restoring life to the dead wasn't something that should be done often." His gaze centered on me, and I sort of wanted to crawl into the ground to avoid his knowing stare. "It started a bitter animosity between the brothers, which resulted in Kolis using some sort of magic to steal his brother's essence—allowing Kolis to become the Primal of Life, and

Eythos the Primal of Death. But neither were meant to rule over such things. Kolis couldn't take all of Eythos's essence, nor could he erase all of his. An ember of life remained in Eythos, and another ember had been passed onto Nyktos. But Eythos feared that Kolis would discover the ember within Nyktos, so he took it."

"And placed it in a mortal," I finished. "In the Consort. That's why she was only partially mortal."

Kieran leaned forward. "Then what is Nyktos? I thought he was the Primal of Life and Death."

"He's *a* Primal of Death," Nektas answered. "But he's not the *true* Primal of Death, nor was there ever a Primal of Life *and* Death. That was a title given to him long after he went to sleep, and not one he would've ever answered to."

"I feel like I need to sit down, except I'm already sitting," I murmured, and Casteel gently squeezed the back of my neck. So many things that Reaver had and *hadn't* said now made sense. "So that's why her name cannot be spoken? Because she's the Primal of Life? That's...*bullshit*."

Several pairs of eyes landed on me.

"It is! Everyone is like *oh, Nyktos this* and *Nyktos that*, and the whole time, it should have been *Seraphena this* and *Seraphena that*. Did Nyktos even make the wolven? Was it even him who met with Elian to calm things after the deities were killed?"

"Nyktos did meet with the Atlantian and the kiyou wolves," Nektas shared. "But it was the Consort's essence that gave the wolven life."

I stared at him for what felt like an eternity. "That's some sexist, patriarchal bullshit!"

Casteel's body shook against mine again. "She has a point."

"She does." Nektas lifted his chin. "And doesn't. The Consort is the one who chose it to be this way. For her to remain unknown. Nyktos only honors it because it is as she wishes."

"But why?" I demanded.

"You know..." Kieran said. "For once, I would also like to know the answer to a question she's asking."

I shot him a glare.

"Because of this." Nektas spread his arms. "Everything Nyktos and the Consort have done. Everything they have sacrificed was to prevent this."

Alarm bells began ringing inside my head.

Casteel's amusement quickly faded. "What part of all that just went down is the *this* you're referencing?"

The draken zeroed in on Casteel's tone as his head tilted. "What Kolis did when he stole Eythos's essence had catastrophic consequences. It prevented any other Primal from being born. The Consort's Ascension was like a...cosmic restart," he explained. "But only if a female descendant was born and Ascended would that restart begin anew. And it begins with you and your children if you choose to have them. They will be the first to be born Primal since Nyktos."

"I..." I started, my head feeling as if it might spin right off my shoulders. "That is a lot."

"It is." Casteel's thumb moved along the curve of my neck. "Why only a female?"

"Because it follows whoever the current Primal of Life is."

"So if Kolis hadn't taken Eythos's essence, and Nyktos had eventually become the Primal of Life as he should have, then Malec and Ires would've been Primals?" Casteel reasoned. "But they weren't because it took a female descendant to be born first?"

Nektas nodded, and I was glad that Casteel understood that because I wasn't sure I did.

"But what does that have to do with preventing this?" Kieran asked.

Nektas's gaze shifted to me. "Because what Nyktos and the Consort did to stop Kolis—what balance the Fates demanded—meant there could be no more Primals born. The *why* behind that, well, there's not enough time in the realms to go into that," Nektas said. "But Nyktos was supposed to be the last born Primal, and the Consort would be the last Primal born of mortal flesh. You," he said quietly, "were never supposed to be."

"Sorry?" I whispered.

The draken cracked a small grin. It was brief, but I saw it. "The plotting that brought about your creation is not something you should apologize for," he said, his voice softening. "Malec and Ires were already well on their way to being born by that point. But what was done to stop Kolis meant that Malec and Ires could never risk children. Malec did anyway, but that...that is Malec," he said with a sigh. "We all got lucky before."

"Because it meant risking having a daughter." My skin chilled. "That's why they stayed in Iliseeum."

"Until they didn't." Nektas's gaze flicked to the night sky. "They were not forbidden to come here. They were born in this realm. But they were strongly advised against it. The risk was too great. Creating that cosmic restart allowed for what Nyktos and the Consort did to stop Kolis to be undone."

But we'd stopped it. Malec lived. For now. "Why were they born in the mortal realm?"

"Nyktos and the Consort felt that it was safer that way."

His answer left me with more questions, but there were far more important ones to ask. "So, I'm what? A loophole?" I said, and Kieran scowled. "One that Isbeth learned about and exploited?" It could've been Malec who told her of this or... "Callum. Where is he?"

A growl rumbled through Casteel's body. "I think he peaced out the moment you called out the Consort's name."

"That's because he knew what it meant." Nektas's features had sharpened. "He must be found and dealt with."

"That is at the top of my list of things to do," Kieran said.

"Good." Nektas's gaze settled back on me. "You are not just a loophole. You're many things. The Primal of Blood and Bone—the true Primal of Life *and* Death." He spoke in the way he had when he'd spoken of the Consort, and the essence hummed through me. "Those two essences have never existed in one. Not in the Consort. Not in Nyktos."

"Is that a good or a bad thing?" I whispered.

"That is yet to be known."

Casteel's arms tightened around me. "We already know that it means something good."

Nektas eyed him as tiny kernels of unease took root. "Then make sure of it." He rose with a fluid grace at odds with his size. "Ires? Have you found him?"

Setting the worries aside for another time to stress over, I cleared my throat and ended up dragging my tongue across my fangs again. I winced as I figured it was well past the point I should stand. Rising to my feet, I held back a smile as both Casteel and Kieran held me as if they worried I'd topple over again. "I know where he is."

"Then take me to him," Nektas said.

I started to turn when I halted, looking down. Something strange caught my eye. "What is that?"

Kieran toed aside a fallen sword that had fallen on the vines that had grown over the steps. But where most of the vines were dark green in the starlight, this section was the color of ash. Not charred. Just gray.

And it had spread from there in thin, dull veins, turning the moss underneath the same lifeless color.

I bent, reaching for a vine, but Casteel caught my hand. "*Why,*" he asked, golden eyes tired but dancing with amusement, "must you touch everything?"

"I don't know. Maybe I'm a tactile person?" I said, and one side of his lips tipped up, hinting at a dimple. My fingers curled around empty air. "What do you think this is?"

"Kolis," Nektas said from behind us. "As I said, what was done to stop him has been undone."

The three of us faced him, our hearts lurching at the same moment. Casteel's eyes narrowed. "Malec lives. We stopped what Isbeth planned."

Nektas's head cocked. "You stopped nothing."

My stomach twisted as I suddenly understood what both Callum and Isbeth had meant—why I had sensed that we hadn't stopped them and were too late. "Kolis was already awake."

Nektas nodded. "And what was done here tonight freed him."

"Son of a bitch," Kieran growled as Casteel's lips parted.

"You only slowed what was done, preventing Kolis from returning to full, flesh-and-bone power. But he will if left unchecked." Nektas stared at the ashy vine, his lip curling. "His corruption is already here, tainting the lands. *This* is why the Primal of Life aided you in restoring life to so many. You will need every one of them if you have any hope of stopping him."

"Entomb him again?" I asked.

"Kill him."

My mouth dropped open.

"And exactly how do we do that?" Anger and frustration burned through Casteel. "When it appears that the Primal of Life and Nyktos were unable to do so?"

"If I knew the answer to that, do you think I'd be standing here?" Nektas questioned, and I snapped my mouth shut. Those vertical pupils constricted and then expanded. "Take me to Ires. We must find Jadis. And then, I will need to return to Iliseeum, and you—all of you—must prepare. Kolis is not the only one who has awakened. The Consort and Nyktos no longer sleep. That means the gods will be awakening all across the many Courts of Iliseeum and in the mortal realm, and many of their loyalties do not lie with the Primal of Life. The war you fought hasn't ended. It has only just begun."

Discover A Shadow in the Ember
by Jennifer L. Armentrout

Flesh and Fire
Book One
Available in hardcover, e-book, and trade paperback.

#1 New York Times bestselling author Jennifer L. Armentrout returns with book one of the all-new, compelling Flesh and Fire series—set in the beloved Blood and Ash world.

Born shrouded in the veil of the Primals, a Maiden as the Fates promised, Seraphena Mierel's future has never been hers. *Chosen* before birth to uphold the desperate deal her ancestor struck to save his people, Sera must leave behind her life and offer herself to the Primal of Death as his Consort.

However, Sera's real destiny is the most closely guarded secret in all of Lasania—she's not the well protected Maiden but an assassin with one mission—one target. Make the Primal of Death fall in love, become his weakness, and then…end him. If she fails, she dooms her kingdom to a slow demise at the hands of the Rot.

Sera has always known what she is. Chosen. Consort. Assassin. Weapon. A specter never fully formed yet drenched in blood. A *monster*. Until *him*. Until the Primal of Death's unexpected words and deeds chase away the darkness gathering inside her. And his seductive touch ignites a passion she's never allowed herself to feel and cannot feel for him. But Sera has never had a choice. Either way, her life is forfeit—it always has been, as she has been forever touched by Life and Death.

Also From Jennifer L. Armentrout

Writing as J. Lynn
Wait for You
Trust in Me
Be With Me
Stay With Me

Writing as Jennifer L. Armentrout

Fall With Me
Dream of You (a 1001 Dark Nights Novel)
Forever With You
Fire In You

The Blood and Ash Series
From Blood and Ash
A Kingdom of Flesh and Fire
The Crown of Gilded Bones
The War of Two Queens

The Flesh and Fire Series
A Shadow in the Ember

The Covenant Series
Half-Blood
Pure
Deity
Elixer
Apollyon
Sentinel

The Lux Series
Shadows
Obsidian
Onyx
Opal

Origin
Opposition
Oblivion

The Origin Series
The Darkest Star
The Burning Shadow
The Brightest Night

The Dark Elements
Bitter Sweet Love
White Hot Kiss
Stone Cold Touch
Every Last Breath

The Harbinger Series
Storm and Fury
Rage and Ruin
Grace and Glory

The Titan Series
The Return
The Power
The Struggle
The Prophecy

The Wicked Series
Wicked
Torn
Brave
The Prince (a 1001 Dark Nights Novella)
The King (a 1001 Dark Nights Novella)
The Queen (a 1001 Dark Nights Novella)

Gamble Brothers Series
Tempting The Best Man
Tempting The Player
Tempting The Bodyguard

On Behalf of Blue Box Press,

Liz Berry, M.J. Rose, and Jillian Stein would like to thank ~

Steve Berry
Doug Scofield
Benjamin Stein
Kim Guidroz
Social Butterfly PR
Ashley Wells
Chelle Olson
Hang Le
Kasi Alexander
Malissa Coy
Chris Graham
Jessica Saunders
Dylan Stockton
Kate Boggs
Dina Williams
Deon McAdoo
Stacey Tardif
Laura Helseth
Jen Fisher
Richard Blake
and Simon Lipskar